You will feel like you're immersed in a totally foreign world where values of valor, honesty and courage really mean something. **Saving Big Ben** *took me back to my time on flaming decks on the USS Franklin, CV 13. A real page-turner that anyone with a taste for heroism, valor and adventure will not be able to put down.*

Robert E. St. Peters, EM2C,
President of the *USS Franklin* Museum Association
and crew member of the *USS Franklin* on March 19, 1945.

Fiction can be truer than life. If you want to know what it felt like to have your life hanging by a thread, trying to fight a war in the Sea of Japan, while a huge aircraft carrier is sinking under your feet and rockets are zooming over your head, read Saving Big Ben. I was there and I still find it hard to believe!

Ray C. Bailey,
Gunner/Retired Naval Photographer
and crew member of the *USS Franklin* on March 19, 1945.

I watched the daring efforts to save the Franklin while manning a fire hose on the fantail of the USS Santa Fe. Saving Big Ben enables the modern reader to experience those frightening yet courage-filled times. An outstanding book. Congratulation to Peter Prato for returning those valorous memories.

Tom Paulovich, S1C,
Crew member of the *USS Santa Fe* on March 19, 1945.

Very best!
Peter Prato 10/4/01

SAVING BIG BEN

A Historical Novel

The Saga of the *USS Franklin*
The Most Decorated Ship in Naval History

by Peter J. Prato, Ph.D.
Gunner's Mate 3rd Class, *USS Altamaha, CVE 18*
1945-1946

Direct from the *USS Franklin's* Declassified Deck and Action Logs

Copyright © 2000 Peter J. Prato, PhD, LLC

No part of this work may be reproduced in any form or by any means, without the written permission of the publisher. Exceptions are made for brief excerpts in published reviews. This book was published by:

Stress Resource Publishing Company, LLC
8400 East Prentice Ave
Penthouse
Greenwood Village, CO 80111
Phone: (303) 409-7607
Fax: (303) 758-1435
E-mail: prato@worldnet.att.net
       and
Stress Resource Publishing Company, LLC
699 Peters Avenue, Suite A
Pleasanton, CA 94567
Phone: (925) 484-2330
Fax: (925) 484-3112
Toll Free Phone: 1-866-484-2330
Website: www.stressresource.com
You may order on-line. Discounts for bulk purchases.

Library of Congress Cataloging
Prato, Peter J., PhD
    Saving Big Ben: a historical novel: the saga of the U.S.S. Franklin, the most decorated ship in Naval History / by Peter Prato, Ph.D – 1st ed.
    p. cm.
    " Direct from the Franklin's declassified deck and action logs."
    Includes bibliographical references and index.
    ISBN: 0-9676695-1-0

    1. Franklin (Aircraft carrier)--Historical Fiction. 2. World War, 1939-1945--Naval operations, American--Fiction. I. Title.

PS3566.R275S28 2000 813.6
                QBI00-500073

"Abandon her? Hell, we're still afloat!" Leslie Gehres, Captain, *USS Franklin, CV 13*, March 19, 1945

DEDICATION

This novel is dedicated to the brave men in the crews of the *USS Franklin* and *USS Santa Fe*, who saved the *Franklin* and brought her home after she was nearly destroyed in the Sea of Japan on March 19th 1945 by Japanese bombs. It is further dedicated to the 832 valiant men who lost their lives on the Franklin that historic day and to all of the courageous men and women who served in the Armed Forces during World War II. Your gallantry and valor, in the greatest war in American History, were unparalleled. May your heroic actions live in the minds of grateful Americans forever.

SECOND DEDICATION

A second dedication is made to Sensei Hideki Iwakabe and Sensei Hiroshi Umemoto, respected instructors, dear friends and comrades in the Martial Arts. Your patience and empathy carried me past the cultural prejudices of the period that I have just written about and lived through. For this understanding I shall always be grateful. This book is also dedicated to the memory of Father Daniel B. McNamara, S.J., (1895-1986), esteemed mentor and spiritual guide, whose influence and direction will always be a significant part of my life path.

ACKNOWLEDGMENTS

The author wishes to acknowledge and express his gratitude and thanks to the following individuals and institutions for their splendid help in the preparation of this book. First, our thanks to Mr. Robert St. Peters, President of the Franklin Museum in Alton, IL. His guidance and advice were of enormous value. The author also wishes to thank Mr. Ray Bailey of San Diego, CA. Both men were part of the brave crew who brought the *Franklin* home in 1945. With Mr. St. Peters' recommendations and assistance and with photos from Mr. Bailey's authentic collection of action photos, many of the dramatic pictures included in this novel were obtained.

We wish to acknowledge the efforts of Mr. Jack Green, Photographic Section, United States Naval Historical Center, for his assistance in obtaining some of the additional action photographs contained herein. Further, we wish to thank the employees in the United States Historical Foundation and in the National Archives for providing the actual photographs and the *USS Franklin's* Deck and Action Logs. Our thanks are extended to Mr. Robert Jackson of Time Life Syndication for assisting with the articles from *Time* and *Life* magazines that are included and to Mr. Steve Russ of Medals of America Press for the use of the citations featured on the cover of *Saving Big Ben*. All provided a special assistance in the completion of this novel.

Our additional gratitude and thanks are extended to Bill Gunston, author of *Combat Aircraft of World War II,* and to *Jane's War at Sea 1897-1997 Centennial Edition* (London 1997) for the drawings of the American and Japanese aircraft and to Mr. Emmanuel Gustin and Mr. Carl Pettypiece for their efforts in creating and maintaining the web site from which they came. Finally, the author wishes to acknowledge the creative efforts of his editors, Mr. Jeff Burdick and Ms. Ann Kempner Fisher for their extensive and valued assistance in creating the fictional parts of this novel, and the technical support of Mr. Andy Cleary and Deborah and Dan Angeloni of Orbit Design in Denver, CO and Mr. Steve Winkel of 1st Book Library in Bloomington, IN, for their exceptional creativity and excellent contributions to the structure of the on-line novel and its cover.

©Peter J. Prato, Ph D., LLC. (2000) All rights reserved including the right to use the contents of this book in any form, including motion pictures, television productions, Internet publications, plays, dramas and/or narratives of any kind.

INVOCATION

The Hymn of the United States Navy

Eternal Father, strong to save,
Whose arm doth bind the restless wave,
Who bidd'st the mighty ocean deep
Its own appointed limits keep,
O, hear us when we cry to Thee
For those in peril on the sea!

                James Whiting, (1825-1878)

ABOUT THE AUTHOR

Peter J. Prato, Ph.D.

Dr. Prato received his Bachelor of Arts degree from the University of Denver and his Master of Science and Doctorate in Stress Psychology from California Coast University. He served in Admiral Spruance's Fifth Fleet as Gunners Mate 3rd Class aboard the *U.S.S. Altamaha, CVE 18*, a "Jeep" carrier during the later part of World War II. After the war ended he was privileged to board the *U.S.S. Santa Fe* and met some of the crewmen who participated in the daring rescue of the *U.S.S. Franklin* in the Sea of Japan less than fifty miles from Shikoku. From these meetings came the inspiration to write this book.

Dr. Prato is the Chairman of the Board of the Gibraltar Capital Corporation and Gibraltar Realty and Acceptance Corporation. He is a director of the Stress Resource Network located in Pleasanton, California. He belongs to the National Honorary Society in Psychology, the Colorado Speakers Association, and is a past member of the Board of Directors of the Kempe Children's Foundation. Dr. Prato has trained in Japanese Shotokan Karate for seventeen years. He has attained the rank of 2nd Degree Black Belt and is currently training for a 3rd Degree Black Belt ranking. He is the author of three other books, *Reflections of a Soul's Journey,* a book of poetry, *Certainty from Uncertainty*, a text for spiritual enhancement, and *Financial Freedom for Women,* a book of financial resources exclusively for women.

His poetry has been published in the National Library of Poetry anthology *The Garden Of Life*. He lives in Denver, Colorado.

TABLE OF CONTENTS

CHAPTER	DESCRIPTION	PAGE
1	Boarding A Troop Train	1
2	Aboard *USS Franklin, CV 13*	9
3	Crew Problems	20
4	Shake Down	29
5	Aboard the Carrier *Enterprise*, Fifth Fleet	42
6	Destination: Eniwetok	55
7	Intermediate Destination: Harbor Island	61
8	Berth F, North Island, San Diego	68
9	Navy Discipline	75
10	Combat Maneuvers	90
11	*Franklin* Joins the Fifth Fleet	99
12	Temporary Headquarters, Fifth Fleet	121
13	North Pacific Ocean	132
14	The Invasion of Tinian	144
15	Attack Okinawa	148
16	The Battle of Leyte Gulf	166
17	Aboard the *USS New Jersey*	181
18	An Assessment of Damage	196
19	A Change of Command	199
20	Alameda Naval Air Station	211
21	A Wedding	229
22	Ulithi Lagoon, Caroline Islands	235
23	The *Franklin* Jinx	246
24	Bremerton, Washington	261
25	Rejoining the Fifth Fleet	289
26	Task Force 58.2 Forms	299
27	Tragedy Strikes	311
28	A Ray of Hope	334
29	Clearing the Wreckage—Burying the Dead	353
30	Slipping Out of the Sea of Japan	363
31	A New Ship's Motto	368
32	Caroline Islands	371
33	Was the *Franklin* Jinxed?	376
	EPILOGUE	390
	THE *USS SANTA FE*	394
	SHIPMATE ACKNOWLEDGMENT	395
	APPENDIX	396

CHAPTER ONE

4 January, 1944
Chicago, Illinois
Boarding a Troop Train
Destination: Norfolk, Virginia

Troop trains were all old, tacky and miserable—not a good place for Second Class Gunner's Mate John Oxler to shake off a heavy hangover. As the train left Chicago and gained speed, it jerked sharply from side to side jolting his head until he thought it was going to explode. His stomach felt like he'd guzzled bilge water. He shuffled his feet, trying to decide whether it was worth the effort to stumble to the head. If he was going to be sick, he might as well throw up here, right in the car. It wouldn't make much difference in this crappy pigpen.

John knew when he started drinking the night before that the alcohol would only briefly ease the intense anger and hurt that seared through his brain and into his heart, but he didn't care—he was willing to try anything. Now the clacking of the wheels on the tracks pounded in his head like hammers. He slid down into his seat and swung one leg of his six-foot, two-inch frame into an empty seat next to him.

"Ahhh, hell," he moaned, rubbing his temples. He wondered if he'd survive his hangover, let alone the war. At this point, he really didn't give a damn if he survived either. "Diane. Damn," he said under his breath. "Why do I have to be thinking of her again?" He pressed his hands over his eyes, trying to shut out every image of her—trying to erase the memory of the pages and pages of mushy letters she'd written, letters always sealed with love-hearts and lipstick marks. "Lies," he muttered, "every last one of them." His thoughts of her wouldn't go away—thoughts of her beauty, her velvet brown eyes, her dark, glistening hair that flowed down over her shoulders. He could feel her breasts. He remembered how they'd firmed when he touched them, how she quivered when he kissed them.

He squirmed in the uncomfortable seat and put his hands over his tanned, handsome face. He was angry with her, but his anger was only a camouflage for deeper feelings of remorse. Three weeks ago he had been shocked by the news that Diane, the woman he loved, was sleeping with another man. A shiver ran down his back at the thought of somebody else making love to her. It made him sicker than he already was.

He'd been a fool to trust her. Stupid to believe her. He was angry with her and with himself. He felt betrayed, duped and vulnerable. "Damn," he muttered angrily, "let it go. Be a man. Goddamn it. Be a man."

At twenty-three, he'd seen more of life—and death—than men twice his age. He was on the *Lexington* when she was torpedoed and sunk in the Coral Sea. Hell, he'd been one of the last to leave the ship and one of the very last to be picked up. The faces of good friends, burned to death in the huge gasoline explosions that ripped down the *Lexington's* hangar deck, were still vivid in his mind and added to his misery. The destroyer *Heermann* fished him out of the water. Less than two weeks later he was reassigned to the *Saratoga*. Twice he'd come under heavy enemy fire in the battle of Salvo Island and five more times in the following seven months. His closest call came on the cruiser *Vincennes* when she was nearly sunk by a Japanese battleship's gunfire. No matter how hard he tried, he couldn't push these memories out of his mind. On the *Vincennes* he was almost killed. A Japanese battleship's shell ripped the number one gun turret right off the deck. He remembered how the blast threw him violently against a bulkhead and knocked him unconscious. Somehow both he and the *Vincennes* survived, but five good friends in the gun turret and three more that were handling ammunition, didn't. The horror of these memories, the loss of all those good friends, was more immediate now—they were compounded by his losing Diane—Diane, his candle of strength and hope, the one person who could help him get through the war, was gone forever. He pressed the heels of his hands into his eyes again, pushing harder than before.

The train slowed down. The conductor walked through the car and bellowed, "Muncie! Muncie, Indiana!"

When the train stopped, a group of marines and sailors climbed aboard and made their way to the vacant seats. Last to come aboard was a marine staff sergeant who stopped in the aisle next to John. He gently tapped John's knee and said, "Sorry, Gunner. It looks like this is the last seat left."

John moved his leg and the sergeant slid into the seat next to him. After a few minutes, the train creaked into motion again. The two men sat in silence as the train rattled and gained speed. Out of the corner of his eye John glanced at the rugged marine's face and the three lines of battle ribbons with four battle stars on his coat. Tough-looking customer, but for some reason he reminded him of one of his football coaches back home in Pueblo, Colorado. He looked over and extended his hand. "I'm John Oxler, Sarge," he said.

The marine sergeant twisted in his seat and shook John's hand. "Jim Grantler," he replied. Then he turned back and they rode for a long while in silence.

"Boy, have I got a hangover," John finally said.

Grantler turned toward him, a big smile on his face. "Spend some time down on State Street?" he asked.

"Yeah. Too much time on State Street," John replied, "trying to drown my sorrows in whiskey."

"What are you sorry about?"

"I went home and found out my girl was sleeping with somebody else."

Grantler looked at him carefully. "Did you talk with a chaplain?"

John nodded. "I went to see one at Great Lakes Naval Station."

"What did he say?"

"He said it was all my fault."

Grantler looked puzzled. "Why?"

"Because I was sleeping with her," John replied with disbelief in his voice. "He said I committed a mortal sin and was being punished for it."

"Holy shit," Grantler said. "Everybody sleeps with his girlfriend these days. If that's a mortal sin, hell's going to be full of guys from the Marine Corps!"

"Well, he sure as hell didn't do me any good," John said. "I needed some help and understanding. All I got from that chaplain was a lecture."

"Do you want to talk about it with me?" Grantler asked.

John grimaced. "Yeah. Would you mind, Sarge? This thing's eating me alive."

"Sure, I don't mind. I've heard so many of these goddamned sad stories I've lost count."

John took a deep breath and leaned toward Grantler. "I found out about it the day after I got home, from a shoeshine boy in a barbershop," he said in a hushed voice. "Isn't that a bitch? What a screwy, fucking way to find out about a girl you love."

"Yeah, it is," Grantler replied. "But it's a hell of a lot better than the way some guys find out. I know guys who went home trying to surprise their wives and found them in bed screwing some other guy. In some cases, their kids were asleep in the next room."

"Goddamn, something like that would really rip me apart," John said.

"Yeah. It goes all the way from falling apart to beating the hell out of one or both of 'em."

"Ever happen to you, Sarge?"

"Yeah. I lost a girlfriend. Got a 'Dear John' letter complete with perfume."

"How'd you handle it?"

"Awww, it tore me up just like it did you. I was lucky though. We weren't married. It's guys with kids that are really torn apart. I tried drinking a lot. Finally found out it didn't work. It's a bitch. You have to get it out of your system somehow—struggle through it."

John was silent for a long moment then let out a sigh. "Yeah. I guess you're right, Sarge."

Grantler looked over at the two lines of battle ribbons and three battle stars on John's uniform.

"Looks like you've seen some stuff that's a hell of a lot worse than this, Gunner. You'll be okay. Just find a way to tough it out." Then he wiggled down into his seat. "Well, I think I'll try to get some shuteye." He closed his eyes. In a few minutes he was asleep.

John sank back in his seat, alone again. Memories of Diane washed over him again. It was early in 1942, just a few months after the Japanese attack on Pearl Harbor. He was home on leave after boot camp in San Diego. It was a wonderful, exciting time for him, filled with the attention and admiration of his friends. The real dangers of the war were in the distant future. Diane was with him all day his first day back, clinging to him, stealing hugs and kisses, pressing herself against him, letting her lips linger on his, across his cheeks, his ears. Her passionate behavior left no questions about her desire. He loved this and everything else about her.

"She must really love you, John," Ted Brady, a good friend, whispered, nodding toward Diane when she stood talking to some of her girl friends at a party he had given John.

John glanced at Diane. The moment he caught her eye, she started to walk back to his side.

"Yeah. I think she really does, Ted," John said, grinning.

"Here," Ted said, stuffing something into his hand.

"What's this?" John asked.

"The key to my apartment," Ted said.

John looked down at the key, then at Ted. "I owe you for this, Buddy," he said.

Ted nodded.

When Diane walked into his arms, John told her Ted had given him his apartment for the evening. "Can we go there soon?" he asked.

Diane's smile answered him. When she put her arms around him and pressed against him, he knew she wanted to leave as much as he did. He led her the short two blocks to Ted's apartment. The minute they opened the door they began groping their way to the bedroom, kissing and undressing each other as they went. She helped him pull off his tight uniform top; he took off her dress, bra and panties. He remembered sinking into the friendly, firm, bed, kissing her as they did. She drew in a ragged breath when he moved his lips slowly down to her breasts. He could feel the warmth of her body pressing harder against his. She'd trembled beneath him in anticipation. John's whole body filled with intense desire. He never wanted any woman as much as he did Diane. He couldn't get enough of her. He remembered how she groaned in ecstasy when they started to make love. "Oh, God, don't stop. Don't stop!" she'd cried out. She put her hands on the back of his head and used her legs to pull him closer.

Her orgasm was lustful and intense. "Yes, again! Again!" she demanded as she ran her fingers through his hair and then her hands across his chest. "You're wonderful, Darling," she whispered, then she pushed herself against him, demanding more and more. He gave her all the passion that was in him with every muscle in his powerful body and from the depths of his being.

They made love every day, every time they could, for the whole week of his leave. In the lulls between their lovemaking, they talked of their future, of marriage, of raising a family, of being together forever. He loved Diane desperately, passionately and believed she loved him the same way. She had become his whole life. Her letters had lifted his spirit in boot camp. Her love was his inspiration. Because of her love, he'd make it through the war. He'd make it back to her, and he'd spend the rest of his life with her.

The days of his leave flew by. "I just got home and now it's time to go back," he'd told Diane the last night they were together. Tears had appeared in her eyes as he made love to her.

The next day when he climbed aboard the train, Diane called out to him, "I'll write to you! I'll wait for you! I'll always love you!"

John waved to her as the train pulled out of the station and mouthed the words "I love you." He didn't take his eyes off her until she was out of sight.

Her letters came, written nearly every day at first, filled with the same urgency and passion as their lovemaking. "I love you. I miss you terribly. I can't wait to be with you again." She always sealed her letters with an imprint of her lips and scrolled little hearts around her beautiful lip prints. But within a few months Diane's letters came less regularly. It was very hard to admit this, but they did. In the month before the *Vincennes* came under fire, he'd received only a scattered few.

"Goddamned wartime mail," he'd complained every time he came away from mail call empty-handed.

When the *Vincennes* returned to Pearl Harbor for repairs, he stood in the phone line on the dock for over three hours to call her.

"Diane?"

"John? John, is that you?" her mother asked.

"Is Diane home?" he asked his heart pounding.

"John, I'm afraid she's not."

"How is she?"

"She's fine. I'm sure she'll be anxious to see you...."

"Is everything all right?"

"I think so, John."

Then there was a long pause. John noticed there were impatient men standing behind him waiting for their turn on the phone.

"I'll tell Diane you called," her mother said.

He remembered muttering "thanks" and hanging up. "Yeah, yeah," he'd said to the sailor who had anxiously grabbed the phone as he turned away.

The conversation with Diane's mother had left him depressed. His mood was sullen until later that day when he learned he was being transferred and had been granted a twenty-day leave with ten days travel time. "Twenty days! That's almost a lifetime," he'd muttered when he got the great news.

During the four days it took the troop ship to sail from Pearl Harbor to San Francisco, John thought of Diane constantly. Her naked body and their lovemaking were at the multi-colored center of his thoughts. He'd closed his eyes and called up every little detail of that last fantastic week of passion and love. She was so real. He couldn't wait to see her again, to reaffirm their love.

He'd arrived in Pueblo after midnight. When he got home his parents were waiting up for him. They were overjoyed to have him home again. The next morning he got up early and went out for a walk. He felt so happy and alive. It was hard to believe he was really home. He basked in fresh morning sun, felt the freedom of being alive and breathed the brisk air loaded with anticipation. Although he knew these streets like the back of his hand, they now were new and exciting under his feet. It was like seeing everything for the very first time. There was peace and safety here, and his heart jumped at the thought of holding Diane in his arms again.

His steps carried him past Jim Desmond's barbershop. He didn't expect to see anybody there this early, but Al, the shoeshine boy, was there getting ready to open the shop.

"Johnnie! Johnnie!" Al cried out, as he walked through the door. "You look great!"

"How you been, Al?" he asked, wrapping his arms around the smaller man.

"Good, man. Real good."

John looked around the shop. It looked the same, but something was strange, different.

"What's been going on, Al?"

Al looked at him closely, nervously. "How long you been home, Johnnie?"

"Just got home last night," John replied.

"Then you don't know?" Al asked.

"Don't know what?"

Al's eyes widened. "It's Diane," he stammered.

"What about Diane? Al!"

"She's sleeping with Harold Stapp," Al stammered. "He's really putting it to her. Everybody in town knows about them."

John was stunned. The thought of Diane with someone else made him nauseous. His knees weakened. He reached out and grabbed the door handle for support.

"Hey, you okay, Johnnie?" Al asked.

"Yeah, yeah. I'm okay. I'm fine." He staggered away from the shop, unable to get his jumbled thoughts organized. He was filled with confusion and disbelief. Diane? Harold Stapp? It couldn't be. It just couldn't be! He didn't remember his walk home. He did remember slumping into a chair, confused and heartsick.

"Why didn't you tell me?" he asked when his mother tried to comfort him.

"We were going to, this morning," she said, her face filled with worry and concern. "But you left before we got up."

Minutes passed. Then he announced, "I'm going to see her. I want to hear it from her. Then I'll believe it."

He remembered his mother shaking her head gently but not trying to stop him.

He walked to Diane's house in a confused, emotional blur. He didn't notice a thing—not streets, houses, bushes or trees. When he arrived he hesitated, then knocked sharply several times.

Diane answered. When she saw him, her eyes widened in shock. "What are you doing here?"

He stepped past her and entered the house.

"Is it true?" he demanded.

She didn't say a word. She just lowered her eyes. Her silence spoke volumes.

A long, hurt-filled moment of silence filled the space between them.

"I want my picture back," he said, surprised at his request and the steady tone of his voice.

Without a word, she turned and walked to a cabinet. She took out his picture, wrapped in a small face towel, and handed it to him. He remembered staring directly into her eyes. "Thanks for 'waiting' for me, Diane," he'd said sarcastically as he turned to leave.

She raised her eyes to his for just an instant, and then she looked away. "Good-bye," she said softly without looking back.

As John walked slowly home the urge to cry came over him, but he just couldn't and wouldn't, despite his world having just been shattered.

A sudden loud blast of the train's whistle startled him. The train rattled through a noisy crossing. He shook himself fully awake. The clamoring sounds of the train hammered at his head. The dingy smell of the car made him shudder. He had been in his reverie a long time. It had grown dark, and now almost everybody on the train was asleep. His pain and sadness grew worse. They were now almost unbearable. He thought about what Grantler said earlier, "You gotta tough it out—get it out of your system somehow."

He slipped quietly out of his seat and made his way back to the deserted area at the end of the train. There he fell against a stack of sea bags and hammocks, piled one upon another all the way to the ceiling. He cried, thankful that the noises of the train muffled his sobbing. He forgot where he was. It didn't matter. His body shook with sobs—deep, pitiful sobs that left him choking and gasping for breath. He cried and cried. Anger and helplessness flowed out with his tears. Finally, after what seemed forever, his tears slowed and then stopped. It was well after midnight. He was drained and exhausted but he felt more alive than he had for days.

When he returned to his seat Grantler was asleep and snoring loudly. John climbed gently over the marine's outstretched legs and sank into his seat. He tried to go to sleep. He squirmed and tossed. Thoughts of Diane dogged him. He was dejected, horny and lonely. All he had to look forward to now was the war and the repugnant prospect of life in the Navy.

The clacking of the train's wheels on the rails finally made him drowsy, and he fell into a troubled sleep. When he awoke, Grantler's seat was vacant. He looked at his watch. It was 07:00. His hangover was gone, and he felt strangely at peace. He looked out the window and watched the scenery rush by. The hurt was still there, but somehow he felt better.

After awhile Grantler reappeared. He was fresh shaven and smiling. "You better get some chow, Gunner," he said. "It's pretty good today. Eggs are powdered, but the bacon and spuds are fresh."

"Thanks, Sarge," John replied. "I'm really not very hungry."

"You feeling better, Buddy?"

"Yeah. I am. I appreciate what you told me. It helped me a lot. Thanks."

"No thanks necessary. Just pass it on when you can."

Grantler sat down, and they rode along silently watching the blue-green hills of Virginia roll by.

Finally Grantler asked, "What did you decide?"

"I'm going to show her," John replied.

"How you gonna do that?" Grantler asked.

"I'm going to work my ass off. I'm going to be the best goddamn gunner in the navy. That's how—and that's how I'll forget her, too."

Grantler nodded but said nothing.

The troop train arrived in Richmond, Virginia just after 09:00. When it stopped, Grantler pulled himself up out of his seat and grabbed his bag. As he straightened his tie and put on his coat he said, "Good luck, Gunner. This is where I get off."

"Do you know where you're headed?"

"I'm picking up with a new unit here. We're probably headed back to the Pacific."

"Well, good luck to you, Sarge and thanks again," John said.

Grantler flipped John a little salute, walked down the aisle and off the train.

Because more men got off at Richmond than got on, John had the luxury of the extra seat again. He stretched into it and rode this way for the remainder of the trip. As the train eased into Norfolk's depot, John could see a fleet of buses waiting. As soon as the train jerked to a stop, he grabbed his gear and headed for the nearest bus.

"This bus get me to the *Franklin*?" he asked the driver.

The driver nodded and jerked his head toward the truck behind the bus. "Stow your gear on the truck, sailor. It'll follow right behind us."

John walked to the back of the truck and hoisted his heavy sea bag and hammock roll onto the truck's high flatbed. As he turned the corner to return to the bus, another sailor, grappling with his gear, tripped on a rough spot in the asphalt. His bulky sea bag flew right into John's arms. John caught the heavy outfit and held it at shoulder's height. The sailor wound up on his hands and knees.

"You okay, Buddy?" John asked.

"Yeah. I think so," the sailor replied. He stood and looked back at the spot where he tripped. "Somebody ought to have that thing removed," he wisecracked as he dusted off his trousers.

John laughed. "Yeah, they should," he said. He deposited the sea bag and hammock on the truck and walked back.

The medium built, blond sailor, who was at least three inches shorter than John, smiled and extended his hand. "Gunner's Mate Third Class Stanislau Kwatkowski," he said. "My friends just call me Ski."

"John Oxler." When he shook Ski's hand he was a little amazed at the strength of Ski's grip. "Pretty good grip for a guy who can't hold on to his own gear," John said.

"Awww, hell, Gunner, cut it out. I tripped. Those things are so goddamned bulky."

John laughed. "It's okay, Ski. I won't tell anybody."

Ski chuckled and shook his head. "You assigned to the *Franklin*?" he asked.

"Yeah."

"You ever been to Norfolk? I heard it was pretty good liberty town."

"So they say."

"Maybe we can do some liberty together," Ski ventured. "A big handsome guy like you ought to really know how to pick up chicks."

John shook his head slowly and smiled. "My problem is I don't know how to keep them."

"What?" Ski asked.

"Never mind. Come on, it's cold as hell. Let's get on the bus."

CHAPTER TWO

6 January, 1944
Aboard *USS Franklin, CV 13*
United States Navy Yard
Norfolk, Virginia

Chief Petty Officer Richard Beckley walked onto the open bridge of the USS Franklin. Despite his foul-weather jacket, a cold, damp wind caused an involuntary shiver. He scanned the flight deck. He wondered where Chief Gunner Sullivan was. They planned to have coffee this morning. "Damn, it's cold," he whispered, then blew warm breath into his hands. He scanned the flight deck again, from the fantail past the powerful canvas-capped 20- and 40-mm guns on the port side. Massive. Nearly four football fields long and over one wide. His eyes came to rest on the Franklin's identification number, painted on the flight deck just aft of the bow. Thirteen—a number that was considered bad luck where he came from in Kansas. A feeling of dread unsettled him. As he had since the day he came aboard a couple of weeks ago, he forced it out of his mind.

Just then, Chief Gunner's Mate Peter Sullivan called up to him, "You all set for a cup of 'joe,' Chief?"

"Yeah. I was looking for you. How did you get up here?"

"I just slipped out through the hatch in the island," Sullivan said, nodding toward the ship's superstructure.

"I'll be right down," Beckley said.

They went down the ladders to the chiefs' mess hall and got two cups of coffee.

Beckley slipped into a chair, and Sullivan eased into the one next to him.

"It's always nice and warm down here," Beckley said.

"It always smells good, too," Sullivan replied. He paused and had a sip of coffee. Then he asked, "What'd you think about the commissioning ceremonies yesterday, Beck?"

"They were impressive. There was a lot of brass there."

"More than I've ever seen on one ship," Sullivan said. "Admirals—a bunch of them. Hell we even had Artemus Gates."

Beckley nodded. "Yeah, the Assistant Secretary of the Navy. You can't get much brassier than that."

"For me, the most impressive part of the whole ceremony was when they awarded those medals," Sullivan said, his voice revealing the emotion he felt. "A Distinguished Flying Cross, Navy Air Medals to those two young pilots and the Navy and Marine Corps Medal to that young enlisted man."

He paused. "Hell, they're just boys," he continued, slowly shaking his head. "I've got a son who'll be that younger guy's age in three or four years."

"The guy who got the Distinguished Flying Cross was a little older though," Beckley said. "All of twenty-five or twenty-six." He smiled at the irony of what he said. "Old at twenty-six just doesn't seem to fit."

Sullivan shook his head slowly. "No, it doesn't. But it's a young man's war...."

"Yeah, that's how we'll win it, too, with courageous young guys like that, risking their lives and proving themselves all over the fleet," Beckley said.

"What was the name of the lieutenant commander who got the Distinguished Flying Cross?" Sullivan asked.

"Zimler, I think," Beckley said.

"The word is that he slammed a couple of thousand-pound bombs into a Jap carrier at Midway," Sullivan replied.

"Yeah, that's what the admiral said. I was in that battle at Midway. I wonder what carrier he was aboard?"

"I heard it was the *Enterprise*—what were you aboard?"

"The *Yorktown*."

"Didn't she get sunk there?"

"Yeah," Beckley replied, slowly rubbing his chin. "It's the *strange way* she was sunk that's always troubled me," he said.

"What do you mean, strange way?" Sullivan asked.

"Well we went through most of that battle as slick as a whistle. We sank the *Soryu* just as she was ready to launch planes to attack us. We hit her with three five-hundred pound bombs—smack dab in the middle of her flight deck," Beckley said, excitement creeping into his voice.

"Wasn't the *Soryu* in the attack on Pearl Harbor?" Sullivan asked.

"Yeah, she was. So was the *Hiryu*," Beckley replied. "Our pilots, and planes from the *Enterprise*, attacked and sank her, too. Two of the four carriers that attacked Pearl Harbor blasted to the bottom within a few hours of each other."

"Jesus, that must have given everybody a big lift," Sullivan said.

"Yeah, we were having a field day. We went after a light Jap cruiser and got her. Then things changed just like that," Beckley replied, snapping his finger.

"What happened?"

"Nip bombers found us. They just seemed to slip through our screen. They hit us with three bombs and did some damage, but we still had all of our power and speed. I thought we'd make it out of there. A Jap submarine commander thought differently. He was submerged there through the whole battle, waiting for an opening. When it came, he hit us with three torpedoes. Two torpedoes slipped right under a destroyer—missed her by inches."

"So what's unusual about that?" Sullivan asked. "Everybody knows the Japs make sneak attacks."

"That's not the point," Beckley replied.

"Well, what the hell *is* the point?"

"In a matter of seconds, for us, things changed 180 degrees. It was freaky. Hell, come to think of it, that whole damned battle was freaky."

"What do you mean *freaky*? That was one of the greatest victories in our history."

"Yeah, it was. But as far as I'm concerned, it was still freaky," Beckley said.

"A victory like that? Where're you coming from?"

"Well, let's look at the facts. First, by anybody's standards, we were hopelessly outclassed."

"Outclassed? How the hell do you figure that? We won, didn't we?"

"Yes, we did, but look at the facts."

"Facts? What goddamned facts?"

"Consider this. The Japs had four battleships, one of them was the Yamato, the fastest, most powerful battleship in the world. We had *none—zero*. We had eight cruisers, they had twenty-three. We had three carriers—well, really less than three, because *Yorktown* was damaged in the Coral Sea and they just patched her up in Pearl and sent us right out again. The Japs had seven of their finest fleet carriers. Four of them were in the fleet that bombed Pearl Harbor."

"Strange. I didn't realize it was that one-sided," Sullivan said.

"Hell, it gets worse. None of the pilots on our third carrier, the *Hornet,* had ever been in combat. In their Marine Air Wing, seventeen of the twenty-one new pilots were just out of flight school," Beckley said.

Beckley shifted in his chair. "If that wasn't enough, we also had major equipment problems. Most of our equipment was old. Some of the dive-bombers couldn't dive—the fabric came off their wings. Our torpedoes were slow and unreliable, and our torpedo planes even worse. We had to go against the Jap Zero, at that time the finest fighter ever developed and flown by the most experienced combat pilots in the world."

Sullivan nodded. "Yeah, I guess that makes a pretty good case for getting clobbered," he said. "Yet we won, and top brass now says it changed the course of the war. How do you account for that?"

"Who knows? Admiral Spruance is a great commander and a great tactician. But almost always, when you're that heavily outmatched, you lose."

"So what do *you* think happened?"

"I think there was 'something' there beyond equipment—beyond skill and experience," Beckley said slowly.

"Yeah, but what?"

"I don't know, but there was *something,*" Beckley emphasized. "One of those strange things that make people uncomfortable when they talk about them."

Sullivan studied what Beckley said. "Well, that doesn't make me uncomfortable," he said after he had a long sip of coffee." "I've seen strange things happen, too."

"Where?"

"At Pearl Harbor."

"When?"

"On December 7, 1941."

"Was it in the attack?" Beckley asked.

"No, just before. We had a warning that a Japanese carrier fleet was approaching Oahu."

"Really? What the hell did they do with it?"

"It was disregarded," Sullivan said.

A quizzical look came into Beckley's face that wrinkled his forehead. "Disregarded? Come on. You gotta be kidding. You mean somebody knew the attack on Pearl was coming?"

"I'm not kidding," Sullivan said adamantly. "I was there, on the *Nevada*. A forward lookout by the name of Lockhart picked up the Japanese fleet on radar an hour before the attack."

Beckley was shocked. "For God's sake, then what happened?"

Sullivan drained his mug of coffee. "He reported it to an inexperienced lieutenant."

"When?"

"When they were still about a hundred and thirty miles away from Oahu."

"So what the hell did the lieutenant do?" Beckley asked, his voice still filled with disbelief.

"Without checking, he decided the planes were ours and told that to Lockhart."

"And what the hell did Lockhart do?"

Sullivan shook his head in dismay. "He accepted what the lieutenant said. He ignored what was on his screen and went off duty."

"You're telling me that we knew the attack on Pearl was coming and didn't do a damn thing about it?" Beckley asked.

"Exactly. It got hushed up, but that's the goddamned truth."

"Hard to believe, Chief, but if it's true, that's *exactly* what I'm talking about." Beckley paused and slowly shook his head. "Think about it, Chief," he said cautiously. "Doesn't it make you wonder what the hell was going on there?"

"Going on there? What the hell do you mean *'going on'* there? It was just plain bad luck."

There was silence, both men preoccupied with what they had said.

Then Beckley broke the silence. "I think it's more than just luck, Chief," he said. "It seems to me that a lot of times, there's *something* more—some kind of *'unseen hand'* pulling the strings...."

"Ooooh, come on," Sullivan said. "That's weird."

"Okay, maybe it is," Beckley said, "but take my case on the *Yorktown*. Suppose that Jap sub commander had decided to go north with the rest of the Jap fleet. Hell, by the time we got hit most of their fleet was running away with their tails between their legs."

"So you're saying *Yorktown* was sunk by something more than bad luck?" Sullivan chided, slowly rubbing the bottom of his chin.

"Well, there sure as hell was 'something' on that Jap skipper's side," Beckley insisted.

"Yeah, and it still sounds weird as hell," Sullivan countered. He paused and thought a minute. "Hell, if you want to talk about things like that, I've got an example for you."

"Yeah, what's that?"

"In a way, we were very lucky at Pearl Harbor." Sullivan said.

"How do you figure that? Remember, we lost over half of our fleet that day," Beckley reminded him.

"Strange things happened that kept two fleet carriers from being in Pearl Harbor during the Japanese attack."

"Which carriers?" Beckley asked.

"The *Enterprise* and *Saratoga*. On the third of December the *Enterprise* was sent to deliver marine fighter planes to Wake Island, and on the sixth of December the *Saratoga* was ordered to the West Coast for upkeep and repairs."

"I know you're right about that, Chief," Beckley said with a tiny smile, "but you have to change the number of carriers to three. The *Lexington* was there, too, and I was aboard her."

"You were there? Hell, I didn't know the *Lexington* was there."

"Yep. We left two days before the attack. On Friday, the fifth of December, we were sent to deliver bombers to Guam."

"I've always wondered how that all happened," Sullivan said, nodding slowly. "I could never understand how they just seemed to slip out of Pearl. It was almost like something strange was going on…."

"Exactly. That's what the hell I'm trying to say!" Beckley replied with certainty in his voice. "It's like something wanted those carriers out of harm's way. If the carriers stayed in Pearl Harbor they'd probably get sunk, too."

"Yeah, maybe so, but maybe not," Sullivan said.

"They sank five battleships and a bunch of cruisers and destroyers," Beckley pointed out. "I rest my case."

"Well, I guess in hindsight, the loss of those three carriers would have been a hell of a lot worse than losing five battleships."

"Right," Beckley said. "Despite all the damage, I guess 'something' smiled on us that day, too."

"Naaaa. I don't think so. It was just plain bad luck," Sullivan decided.

Beckley paused and toyed with the zipper on his jacket. "Okay," he persisted. "Let's talk about what you said happened before the attack on Pearl. Suppose that lookout had reached an experienced lieutenant—one who knew the danger of making a wild guess about those ships and planes. How would the history of that attack read today if our pilots and gunners had an hour's advance notice that morning? How many of the over twenty-two hundred people who died would still be alive?"

"How the hell can we even speculate on that?" Sullivan asked.

"What would have happened if our ships and planes were alerted and waiting for the Japanese that morning?" Beckley challenged.

"Again, who the hell knows? It probably would have changed the whole course of the war," Sullivan said as he looked past Beckley to the mess cooks preparing for the midday meal. "But, for me, it's still luck, some good, some bad."

Beckley rubbed his chin thoughtfully. "You call it luck. I call it something else; something beyond luck or chance, something like *fate*," he said. "What's scary for me is that nobody knows *what* it is or *who* causes it. Nobody knows...."

Sullivan looked at Beckley suspiciously. "I don't even want to touch that, Chief," he said "It still sounds weird as hell to me."

"Yeah," Beckley replied. "But I think Shakespeare was right when he said, 'It's in the stars, the stars above us, govern our conditions.'"

"The stars? Come on, that's even a fucking weirder idea," Sullivan said with a frown. "What the hell do the stars have to do with it? That makes the whole thing sound spooky as hell."

Beckley thought awhile. "Christ, I don't know how we got on to this," he said. "Maybe we should talk about something else. I was reared to be a little superstitious, and when I start talking about uncertainties like this, it bothers me."

"Why the hell do you let it bother you?" Sullivan asked skeptically.

"Because I hate uncertainty. When I can't figure out what's coming next—it bothers me."

"Well, I guess that bothers me, too. Why don't we talk about things that are certain," Sullivan said. "One thing that *is* certain is how the Navy has changed since the war began. Remember the old days when people pretty much served on the same ship through an entire career?"

"Yeah," Beckley replied with a hint of nostalgia in his voice.

"Well, look at the Navy today," Sullivan said with a touch of anger. "Hell, there aren't any more long tours of duty. Today they move us around like we were pawns in a chess game."

"That's for sure," Beckley said. "People get bounced around a lot."

"I was on the *Nevada* for twelve years before she got shot up," Sullivan responded. "Since then I've been transferred three times in two years. Every time a ship needs new gun crews trained, swish, there's this big sucking noise and I find myself on a goddamned new ship." He paused. "But maybe it's better this way."

"What do you mean better?" Beckley asked.

"The way we get transferred around now. You don't get too attached to people, so it doesn't hurt so bad when you lose them."

Beckley nodded slowly. "Yeah, I think you might be right there," he said slowly. "I was aboard *Lexington* for thirteen years. Went aboard right after boot camp. When she went down in the Coral Sea I lost some buddies that were like brothers to me." Beckley frowned, fighting to hold back painful memories. "When that first torpedo hit, the shock blasted a dozen men right off the flight deck," he said, sadness creeping into his voice. "Three more hits and three more big explosions—gasoline explosions. They're terrible! A hell of a lot worse than torpedoes."

"Which explosions took her down?"

"Both and neither. When we got hit she went into a twenty-degree list. Flames spread everywhere. The fire-fighting units couldn't keep up. We fought the fires for hours but couldn't contain them. Our skipper finally ordered her abandoned. Then she was sunk by torpedoes from one of our own destroyers."

"Was there any panic?" Sullivan asked.

"Hell, yes there was panic! Especially when the word came to abandon ship. Guys were rushing around like crazy. Some guys screamed, some prayed, some swore. Other guys were bleeding and burning. We lost two hundred and eighty men." Beckley looked down at the deck and shook his head as if trying to rid himself of memories he knew would be with him as long as he lived.

"It was almost that bad on the *Nevada*," Sullivan said sadly.

"Yeah, but you guys were in port. You could swim to shore."

"Well, maybe you're right," Sullivan said, "but when you lose a friend, *you lose a friend*. It's tougher than hell, I don't care how close you are to a dock."

"Yeah, I guess you're right on that, Chief. It doesn't matter where or how you lose them, they're still dead forever. When the *Yorktown* went down, I had only been aboard for three weeks. Those guys dying were somehow a little easier to take. I guess it was because I didn't have time to make any deep friendships." Beckley frowned and ran his hand over his wind-toughened face. "But even then," he said, "I don't know if you ever get over seeing guys die. For me, the worse thing about it is you never know how or when it might happen again."

About that time an officer walked down the ladder into the mess hall.

Both Beckley and Sullivan stood. The young officer walked directly to them. Beckley recognized him as the man who received the Distinguished Flying Cross at the commissioning ceremonies.

"I'm looking for Chief Beckley," he said.

"I'm Chief Beckley, sir."

"I'm Lieutenant Commander Zimler," the young officer said, extending his hand.

Beckley took it. "Yes, I know, sir. I was at the commissioning ceremonies. It's an honor to meet you."

Beckley paused. He was uncomfortable about what he should do next. "This is Chief Gunner Sullivan," he said.

Sullivan extended his hand and said, "Congratulations, sir. It's a great pleasure." Then he turned to Beckley. "I have to go back to the armory now," he said. "We're taking some new men aboard this afternoon, and they'll be looking for me. I'll see you soon."

After Sullivan left Beckley asked, "Is there something I can do for you, sir?"

"You from Kansas, Chief?" Zimler asked, smiling.

For a moment, Beckley was too taken back to reply. Then he answered, "Why, yes, I am, sir. How...how did you know that?"

Still smiling, Zimler said, "I was looking through the ship's log a couple of days ago and ran into your name, along with the name of your wife as your next-of-kin."

"Really? Was there anyone else from Kansas?" Beckley asked.

"Just you and me. I didn't see another one," Zimler said. "I'm from Wichita." He grinned and raised his eyebrows. "This big ocean came as a hell of a shock to a prairie boy like me."

Beckley matched the Commander's grin. "Me too. The first time I saw all that water, I couldn't believe it."

"Do you still live in Pratt?"

Beckley grinned back. "Yes, sir, I do, with my wife Mary and three kids. I sure miss them."

Zimler nodded understandingly.

Beckley felt honored and pleased by the warmth and friendliness of the young officer from his home state. The two reminisced for a few minutes about their hometowns, then Beckley said, "Well, I should be going now, sir. There are a few things on the bridge I need to attend to."

Zimler nodded. "I understand," he said. He extended his hand and as Beckley shook it Zimler asked him a question. "What do you think of the number thirteen, Chief?"

"What do you mean, sir?"

"Back home most folks think the number thirteen brings bad luck," Zimler replied.

Beckley nodded thoughtfully. "Yes, sir, I was raised to believe that too," he said. "I've thought about it some since I first came aboard. To be honest with you, sir, the number thirteen does bother me a little, but I tell myself it's just superstition." He struggled with Zimler's question. "I don't know. Maybe it is, maybe it isn't. Maybe only time will tell."

Zimler looked at him intently. Then he said, "Yeah, Chief, I guess you're right. I guess only time will tell."

An uncomfortable pause followed. Neither man said a word. Then Zimler turned to leave. "Stay in touch, Chief," he said as he walked toward the ladder.

The bus pulled up to the dock at 13:40. John and Ski saw the *Franklin* for the first time. "She's huge," John said. "Nearly twice as big as the old *Lexington*. Sleek lines—powerful guns, the world's best radar devices—and brand spanking new."

Ski seemed awe-struck. He sat down on his sea bag and pushed his hat back on his head. "This is the biggest ship I've ever seen," he said. "I hear they're already calling her 'Big Ben.'"

"Where the hell did you hear that?" John asked.

"One of the guys mentioned it on the train," Ski replied. "It sure is a good nickname. You know—Franklin—and she's big!"

"Yeah, it's a good nickname, and she sure as hell *is* big," John said, squaring his hat to go aboard.

"Hell, they could put a half a dozen destroyers on her flight deck and still have a little room to spare," Ski added.

The aura of the massive new carrier lifted John's spirits. He hefted his sea bag and hammock onto his shoulder. "Let's get aboard," he said. "You sure you can carry your gear up that gangway?"

"I tripped back there," Ski protested. "I can make it easy."

"Gunner's Mate Second Class John Oxler reporting for duty, sir," he said to the Officer of the Deck. "Request permission to come aboard, sir."

"Permission granted," the OD said.

Ski went through the same stiff ceremony, and they both stepped onto the hangar deck.

There was activity everywhere. Seamen moving and storing boxes of canned meat and vegetables; others stacking sacks filled with flour, onions and potatoes. Men were operating cranes, hoisting spare parts for guns and planes aboard. Still others were working with crates of antiaircraft ammunition that were stacked nearly to the overhead.

Ski stared at the intense activity. "What a fucking mess," he said after watching for a few moments.

"Yeah. It looks screwy," John replied, "but there's a system at work. Navy's got outfitting and supplying a carrier down to a science."

"Hell, I hope so. That's a lot of stuff to keep track of."

After a few minutes a chief boatswain's mate appeared. I'm Boatswain Frisbee," he said. "You new men! Muster around here."

John and Ski joined the rest of the men who had come aboard in a circle around Frisbee. As soon as they were gathered, he read each man's name from a list given to him by the OD and directed each to a meeting with his immediate superior. John and Ski reported to Chief Gunner Peter Sullivan.

"Down in the armory," Chief Frisbee told John as he handed them a diagram of the *Franklin*. "Two decks below, amidships. You can't miss it."

"Aye, Chief. Thanks."

They worked their way through the horde of men and crates toward a ladder that led below decks. Chief Frisbee was right; finding the armory was easy. Once they got there they greeted Sullivan.

"Gunner's Mate Second Class John Oxler reporting for duty, Chief," John said.

"Gunner's Mate Third Class Stanislau Kwatkowski, too."

They handed Sullivan their orders.

"Welcome aboard," Sullivan said. As he reached for their orders, John noticed a beautiful identification bracelet on his wrist.

"Nice bracelet. Is the anchor gold?"

Sullivan smiled. "Yeah, it is. It was a gift from my eldest daughter," he said proudly. Sullivan gestured to a couple of stools. "Have a seat," he said with a smile. Then he carefully studied their orders.

"You've seen a lot of action," he said, glancing up at John. "*Lexington, Saratoga, Vincennes*. Good. We need men with combat experience. Putting together efficient gun crews is never easy—especially on a new ship with a bunch of new men."

John nodded agreement.

Sullivan smiled. John liked him right away. Although there was a toughness about him that indicated he could maintain discipline, there was also an openness that made you feel you had known him a long time.

"Where you from?" Sullivan asked.

"Pueblo, Colorado. You've probably never heard of it."

"Yeah, I have. I've been in that area," he said. "I once flew into Peterson Field and spent a couple of nights in Colorado Springs. Place was full of soldiers. Great liberty town for sailors! I had a hell of a time there."

He looked at Ski's orders. "What do they call you?" "Stan?"

"No, Ski, Chief. Just Ski."

"Where are you from?" Sullivan asked.

"Muncie, Indiana."

"Don't know much about Muncie, don't even know where it is."

"Its about twelve hundred miles from here. Great town. Wonderful people. The train from Chicago runs right through it…"

"Hummm. Yeah, well okay," Sullivan interrupted. "You spent a year on a destroyer? It says you've been on 40-millimeter guns. The whole time?"

"Most of it, Chief," Ski replied. "I spent the first two months on 20-mms."

Sullivan nodded. "See any action?" he asked.

"A little. We chased some German subs around in the Atlantic off the East Coast. We had two confirmed kills, one probable. There were a bunch of subs out there when we first started, but the last three or four months most of them left because of our increased aircraft attacks."

Sullivan nodded.

"Where you from, Chief?" John asked.

"Boston."

"Up the coast quite a ways," Ski said.

"Yep. But, I got home for couple of days last week when I had a long weekend." Sullivan checked his wristwatch. "I'd like to spend more time talking with you guys but I've got to meet our gunnery officer. Get your gear squared away. I'll see you about your assignment right after muster in the morning."

"Thanks, Chief," John said.

They left the armory in search of Compartment D, living quarters for the gunnery division. They found it easily. They walked down the ladder into the cramped compartment filled with lockers and bunks, hung one atop the other, all the way up to the overhead.

"Well it sure as hell isn't home," John said as he hoisted his gear up onto a top bunk.

"Yeah," Ski replied, as he took the bunk just below John, "but it's a hell of a lot better than sleeping in a fucking foxhole."

"You can say that again."

That night after chow, Sullivan sought Beckley out. "What the hell was that all about with Commander Zimler?" he asked.

"He's from Kansas. That's where I come from too," Beckley replied as they headed aft, toward the fantail.

They reached the fantail, leaned on the railing and looked out over the harbor. The cold Atlantic wind blew into their faces, and the oily, salty smells of the harbor drifted into their nostrils. Darkness was falling, but Beckley could still identify the silhouettes of several of the ships present. The new *Hornet*, an *Essex* Class carrier like the *Franklin*, was there. The unmistakable lines of the battleship *Wyoming* and the silhouette of the cruiser *Memphis* could be easily identified. But there were other ships, obscured by the increasing darkness, he couldn't recognize. Their ghostly shadows moved back and forth with the action of the tide, their macabre movements added to the strange sensations Beckley felt about his meeting with Zimler. "Commander Zimler asked me if I thought the *Franklin's* number might be unlucky," he said cautiously to Sullivan.

"Oh, Lord, don't give me that shit again," Sullivan replied. "That's a bunch of superstitious crap."

"Well, they really believe it back in my home state," Beckley said, his face reflecting the honesty of his reply.

"But you don't believe that, do you?" Sullivan asked, his face filled with disbelief.

Beckley thought a while, then answered, "I don't think so—but when he asked me about it—it kind of got to me. Isn't it strange that an officer would ask an enlisted man a personal question like that—even if they did both come from the same state?"

"Hell, no! Not if he's really that superstitious it wouldn't be," Sullivan retorted. "It must have been *really* getting to him," he added as he turned away and headed for chief's quarters. "I'll see you tomorrow. Forget about that number thirteen bullshit. Thirteen's not any more unlucky than eleven or twelve."

When Sullivan was gone, Beckley looked out over the night-darkened waters. He didn't care what Sullivan said about superstition; the implications of bad luck from the number thirteen were troubling. "It's been bugging me, too," he said half aloud. "A lot more than I want to admit." Then he snapped at himself, "For God's sake, stop being such a damned fool." But despite this self-admonition, the strange feelings remained. As Beckley often did when he was troubled, he looked to the words of great poets to find an explanation. Some lines from Shakespeare drifted into his thoughts:

Oh. Pity God this miserable age,
What strategems. How fell. How butcherly,
Erroneous, mutinous and unnatural,
What way but death to stay these rueful deeds?
Oh, God. That one might read the book of fate.

The quotation startled him. It *did* make a statement, and he *didn't* like what it implied one goddamned bit!

CHAPTER THREE

United States Naval Yard
Norfolk, Virginia
Crew Problems

After muster the next morning, Beckley watched Captain James Shoemaker rush up the steps to the bridge. He seemed upset. When he stormed onto the bridge it was obvious. "Half this goddamned ship is AWOL," Shoemaker said in disgust as he looked directly at Beckley. "Get me the log will you, Chief?"

"Aye, sir." Beckley handed him the ship's log.

"Damn it," Shoemaker seethed. "I thought there might be problems here. Men thrown together from all over the fleet. When you displace sailors that means trouble."

"Aye, Captain. Sometimes it sure does," Beckley agreed.

"Nearly *all* of the time, Chief."

"Aye, sir."

"Sailors form deep alliances with ships and shipmates. When you transfer men into new surroundings they become distressed and tough to discipline."

"Yes, sir."

"We've got a bunch of recruits that are just boys, too," Shoemaker said. "Only a few months out of high school. This is going to be their first test at sea." Shoemaker seemed as worried as he was angry. "I've got a lot of concerns about whether boys of eighteen and nineteen can handle the rigors of sea duty, let alone those in combat." He reviewed the log again, then said, "This crew has to be shaped up fast. Beginning today."

Beckley watched as Shoemaker stormed to the after part of the bridge. When there, he looked out over the water, apparently still troubled by the report.

Beckley was somewhat dismayed by the captain's angry reaction. The *Franklin* had only been in commission three days. Why was he making such a problem? Beckley knew these issues would have to be addressed and addressed quickly or they could get out of hand. But why couldn't the Captain be just a little patient?

In a few minutes Shoemaker returned. "Chief, get Commander Day and ask him to come to the bridge as soon as possible."

"Aye, aye, sir."

When Commander David Day, the ship's Executive Officer arrived, Shoemaker was waiting.

"Chief, get me that log again and stand by here."

Shoemaker confronted Day with the ship's log. "Commander, have you tracked all the crap that's going on? AWOLs, drunkenness, thefts, misconduct, charges of insubordination. Good Lord, even one of the buglers is absent over leave! What the hell's going on?"

"Most of the crew's only been aboard for a week or two," Day replied with a trace of a smile. "*Franklin* wasn't in commission until a few days ago. I think they might have thought they weren't in the Navy any more."

Shoemaker glared at his Executive Officer. "That's bullshit, Dave, and it's not funny. We have to do something about this right away—today."

"Captain," Day said, now very serious, "a big part of the problem is these men were pulled together from all over the fleet. They just haven't had time to develop pride in themselves and in this ship."

"I know that, Dave," Shoemaker snapped, "but these guys are sailors. They should be proud and disciplined no matter what the circumstances."

"It's the transfers, too, Captain," Day said. "Transfers turn peoples' lives upside down. Men get pushed into new surroundings with shipmates they don't know or trust."

"Yeah. I know that, too, Dave, but we have to get this mess under control. Now! We can't take a ship into combat with an undisciplined crew. Both of us understand the possible costs of that. It could cost us our lives, the lives of everyone on this ship and maybe the ship, too," Shoemaker fumed.

"But Captain, we've only been in commission three days," Day protested weakly.

Shoemaker turned to Beckley who was standing by as ordered.

"Chief, would you please close that door?"

As soon as the door was closed Shoemaker said, "Commander, we've known each other less than two weeks. Because of this, there are things you don't know about me."

"Yes, sir," Day said somewhat dazed by Shoemaker's anger.

Shoemaker glared. "I was the navigator on the *Houston* in the Java Sea just after the war began. Japanese aircraft sank us. Eight hundred and thirty-one men were killed. I came out with this." He unbuttoned and rolled up his sleeve.

Beckley winced when he saw the Captain's arm. The skin nearly up to the shoulder was horribly scarred from burns.

"I've got more just like this on my chest and right leg. Do you know why we lost the *Houston*?" Shoemaker asked.

"Sorry, sir, I don't," Day replied almost sheepishly.

"It was because our crew was badly disciplined and the Japanese pilots were highly trained. Some of the gunners on the 20- and 40-millimeter guns actually bolted. They left their posts because they didn't have the discipline to stay there. Oh, we had our excuses. The war had just begun. This was their first time under fire. The Jap pilots were veterans." Shoemaker's voice trembled for an instant, then he quickly regained his composure. "Excuses," he continued, "they didn't bring back one damned life. I vowed then that I would never sail with an undisciplined crew again, and I mean to keep that vow. Understood?"

"Understood. What do you want me to do, Captain?" Day asked.

"We have to get these men trained. We have to train them so long and hard they'll feel like they're under attack. Train them night and day if necessary. Hopefully, discipline and an *esprit de corps* will emerge. That's the only way I know of getting them ready. You're the Executive Officer. Call a meeting of the division heads and get started. I'll be around to back you and lend any muscle that's needed."

"Aye, sir."

Day turned to Beckley and said, "Chief, have the boatswain pass the word to all division heads that there will be a special meeting in the wardroom at 09:30 hours, and Chief, get a chief petty officer from each division there, too." He smiled a weary smile. "You guys really run the Navy anyhow, so I want you all to hear the Captain's message to the crew."

"You want chief petty officers, too, sir?" Beckley asked somewhat taken aback by the Commanders request.

"Yeah, Chief, chief petty officers, too."

"Aye, sir."

At 09:00, the division heads and petty officers were assembled in the wardroom. Division heads were seated around the wardroom table. The chief petty officers sat on folding chairs behind them.

From the podium at the front of the wardroom, Day looked intently at the men who would command the *Franklin* in combat.

"Gentlemen," he began, "the Captain asked me to call you here to discuss a matter of grave importance concerning the crew and the future of this ship." With this said, he went on to outline the concerns that he and the Captain had discussed earlier.

"So it's urgent that we get this crew trained and disciplined. We have no time to waste. This is the Captain's message. It's very simple. They have to become trim, disciplined and prepared to fight, and he wants this done posthaste. Now! Is this understood?"

Every man in the room nodded.

"Okay. Now does anyone have any comments or suggestions?" Day asked.

At first there was only silence. Then Commander La Favor rose and said, "Sir, in Damage and Fire Control we've already begun. Today we have fifty-six men in fire-fighting school at the receiving station in Norfolk. We've been rotating them on a three-day basis ever since Lieutenant Caldwell and I came aboard two weeks ago. We've already lost three carriers because of poor fire and damage control. I hope this'll assure that never happens to the *Franklin*."

Day nodded. "That's great Commander. That's exactly what we want," he said, "and we need this from everybody." He paused and looked about the room. "I don't want to make a huge problem out of this," he continued. "I recognize we've only been commissioned a few days, and our crew was only fully assembled this morning. I also understand the problems caused by men being transferred around, away from shipmates and in most cases from wives and sweethearts. I know every ship in the Navy has the added problem of inexperience and youth. While these are real problems, they can't be an excuse for anything less than a fully combat-trained and disciplined crew. Captain wants this crew trained and he wants to begin today. Am I understood?"

Silence.

"One final thing, and the Captain wants me to make this very clear. The disciplinary problems that now exist on this ship will not be tolerated. I want each and every man in the crew to clearly understand that the penalties for even the smallest breach in regulations will be severe, and I mean *severe*." He looked about the room again. "Are there any further questions?"

No one answered.

"All rise."

Day left the wardroom. As he climbed the ladder to the bridge, he felt a surge of determination. "This crew will be disciplined and trained," he said under his breath. "They're not going to fuck up, not on my watch they're not."

After muster, John and Ski tried to see Chief Sullivan, as planned. They waited for over an hour and a half. He finally came topside in a big rush.

"I was just in an emergency meeting," he said. "Captain's upset about the crew. That was one of the reasons for the meeting."

"Upset. Why?" John asked.

"There's a lot of problems with the crew right now," Sullivan replied. "The discipline has been pretty lax the last few weeks. You know what happens sometimes when officers are just coming aboard and getting settled. A lot of guys were AWOL, shacking up in Norfolk, trying to forget for a while that there's a war on. Others reported late, there's been some insubordination, some petty theft, stuff like that. Chief Beckley told me after the meeting, there were even cases of guys pissing on the deck!"

"Beckley?" John asked. "Richard Beckley? About five-eleven, husky, dark brown hair, from Kansas?"

"Yeah," Sullivan said. "Why?"

"We were on the *Lexington* together. Great guy. One of the best."

"Small world," Sullivan said. "I'll tell him you're aboard. Anyhow, the Old Man's upset about the crew's discipline and the ship's combat training."

"Hell, Chief," Ski said. "A lot of us just came aboard yesterday."

"I know," Sullivan replied, "but this skipper is a real stickler for discipline and combat training."

"Combat training before a ship's been commissioned?" Ski complained. "Isn't that asking a hell of a lot?"

Sullivan shook his head. "Not with this skipper, it's not."

"But, Chief, we haven't even met our gun crew yet," John said.

"Look, you guys have been in the Navy awhile. You know what we're facing. When you put a new crew together for a ship this size there are a lot of personnel problems, and to be honest with you, I think maybe we got a few more fuck-ups than usual."

"What do you mean, Chief?" John asked.

"I guess it's just human nature," Sullivan said. "Commanders have a natural tendency to protect their best men. When you move men in from other ships, a lot of the time you get some of the dregs from the bottom of the barrel. Maybe this time we got more than our share. But what we got, we got," he continued. "Fuck ups or not, the skipper wants strict discipline and intense combat training and he wants it to start today. Now!"

"Lord, he must really be *tough*," Ski said.

Sullivan eyed Ski almost fiercely. "Hell, yes, he's tough. He has to be tough. There's a war going on, remember?"

Sullivan turned toward the bow. "Walk with me," he said. "I'll show you your stations. You guys seem to get along well. I'll put you both in the same gun crew."

As they walked forward on the flight deck along the starboard side Sullivan said, "I think with time, this crew will get squared away, too. Of course, it can't take too long or there could be some big problems."

"Yeah. There could be some damned big problems," John said, fully aware of what Sullivan meant.

They reached the forward sponson, an extension of the *Franklin's* side, eight feet below the flight deck, which housed the ship's antiaircraft guns. It was constructed of three-quarters of an inch armor plate, about enough to stop a Jap 13-millimeter machine gun shell, but not much more.

Sullivan pointed down to a 40-millimeter antiaircraft mount, 'a quad' with four gun barrels in each mount.

"From your resumes you've both had experience with quads."

John and Ski nodded.

Sullivan kept his eyes on the men working on the antiaircraft guns in the sponson below. "Find them a little sensitive?"

"A little?" Ski said with a chuckle. "I'd say more than a little. If you don't keep them really clean and well oiled they'll jam on you."

Sullivan nodded.

"And gun crews on 40-millimeters really need to be trained," John added, "especially the loaders. They've got to have perfect timing and an accurate drop into the chamber. But if the loaders know their stuff and if they're well kept, they'll work like a dream."

Sullivan was pleased. "You both seem to know your stuff about 40s," he said with a smile.

Sullivan looked directly into John's eyes. "These are your guns, and these are your men," he said. "It's your responsibility to turn them into combat-efficient gun crews and you're going to have to do it flank speed. Remember one little weakness in a link can affect the whole chain. Each man in your crew has to believe that to some extent the fate of this ship is in his hands. Come on. I'll take you down and introduce you."

Sullivan climbed down the ladder into the sponson and John and Ski followed. When they reached the deck Sullivan faced the men in the gun crew, who had suddenly become aware of their presence.

"Okay, gather around," Sullivan said.

Everybody stopped what they were doing and gathered into a semicircle facing them.

Sullivan glanced at John. "I want you to meet the man who is now in charge of these guns—Gunner's Mate Second Class John Oxler. And this is Gunner's Mate Third Class Stanislau Kwatkowski."

Each man in the gun crew acknowledged them while wiping oil and sweat from his hands and brow.

Sullivan continued, "They've both seen action and have a lot of experience on 40-mms." He grinned. "They're the guys who're gonna make a real gun crew out of you mutts."

Sullivan's characterization brought smiles to most of their faces.

"Now, front and center, introduce yourselves," Sullivan said.

One by one, each man stepped forward and introduced himself, giving his name, rate and an informal "hello."

As the introductions went on, John sadly realized that all of these guys were very young and that he might have to face danger and even death with them. He studied each man's face and voice, probing their eyes to see if he could see courage there. He gripped their hands tightly when he shook them and tried to remember anything and everything he felt.

Last to come forward was Gunner's Mate Third Class Paul Lowe. He shook hands with both John and Ski. "Gee, am I glad to see you guys. Keeping these guys busy has been driving me crazy."

With the introductions over Sullivan announced, "I'll leave you now. Check back with me before lunch, John."

"Aye, Chief," John replied.

As soon as Sullivan climbed the short ladder from the sponson to the flight deck, John took charge. He turned to the men in the crew. "How long you guys been aboard?" he asked.

Lowe was the "old man" of the bunch. He'd been on board three weeks. Seamen First Class Garcia, Bonin, Colson and Belasco had been there two, as had Seamen Second Class Michael Feinstein and Ralph Barker. Seven others were just out of boot camp. They'd come aboard with John and Ski the previous afternoon.

"Anyone have any experience on 40s?" John asked.

Kwatkowski, Lowe, Garcia, Belasco and Bonin raised their hands.

"How many of you have been in the Navy less than six months?"

Six hands went up.

Holy Mother of God! John said to himself, these guys are greener than grass. "Okay," he announced. "We'll start from the beginning. I've had a lot of experience with 40-millimeter quads, almost all of it in combat."

Every man's eyes were now riveted on John . He gestured at the 40-mm guns. "These are the finest antiaircraft guns in the world if they're handled right." He walked over and put his hand on the quad's tubular railing. "Firing a 40-mm gun effectively in combat is all a matter of practice and dedication," he said, "and I can assure you that you're going to get plenty of practice." He paused and looked carefully at each man. "Everybody understand that?"

Silence.

"I've got a question, Gunner," Ski said. "Where are the battle helmets?"

"They're back in the ready-service locker," Lowe replied.

"Has everyone been assigned one?" John asked.

"Not yet, Gunner," Lowe answered.

"That will be job number two," John said in a commanding voice. "Assign everybody a helmet. I want every man in this gun crew to wear a helmet, even when training."

"Awww," Belasco said, "those thing are heavy and hot."

"Yeah, they are," John said, "but they also protect the most vital part of your body."

"Not for me, they don't," Belasco said with a broad grin.

John smiled. He'd suddenly taken a liking to this outspoken young man. "So your brain's between your legs?" John asked.

Belasco smiled but said nothing.

"Okay, maybe your brain is the second most important part of you body," John said. "So you wear your helmet while drilling, no matter what part of your body it protects!"

"Yes, sir, Mister John; yes, sir, Mister John," Belasco replied. He nodded obsequiously. A big grin spread across his face. It revealed beautiful white teeth that contrasted strikingly with his black skin.

John studied Belasco. He was still smiling from ear to ear. "Okay, Belasco, you're a comic," John said, "but you wear the helmet at all times while training and that's an *order*. You got my message?"

"Yes, Gunner, I got it loud and clear now," Belasco replied, the smile gone from his face.

"We're going to make a gun crew out of you guys," John said. "By gun crew, I mean one that functions fluidly and efficiently under *any* circumstances. We're going to train you guys and we're going to train you hard and long."

Bonin groaned.

"You can groan if you want, sailor," John said. "You won't be groaning when you're eye to eye with a Jap pilot firing every gun he's got at you. I don't know about you guys but the last thing I want is for somebody to screw up when a fucking Jap Zero, Zeke, Judy or Betty is bearing down on me."

"You had those Jap planes bear down on you, Gunner?" Bonin asked.

"Wait a minute," Ski said. "I don't think I like that question. If you're wondering if John's had battle experience, both Chief Sullivan and I know his combat record. He has seen a lot of combat action, and I mean a lot of it."

"Where?" Bonin asked.

"He was aboard the *Lexington* when she was torpedoed in the Coral Sea. Let me tell you something, sailor. The Japs weren't shooting spit-balls there—they sank her with real bombs and torpedoes."

"Was anybody killed?" Garcia asked tentatively.

"Hell yes! Over two hundred men," Ski said. "Check with Chief Sullivan if you don't believe me. John was there. He can tell you how goddamned scary combat is. He was on the *Saratoga* when she came under fire, not once but five times in seven months, and he was nearly killed on the *Vincennes* by a direct hit from a Jap fourteen-inch gun. Three of his best friends were killed in that explosion. He missed death by an eyelash."

Ski paused. "If you guys want to talk about combat, you've come to the right place with the right guy."

There was silence. "Dios! That's scary," Garcia finally said.

"We have to be prepared, not scared," John said. "It's a real war out there. Gun crews that are *trained* survive. Gun crews that *aren't, don't*. You guys want to survive, you learn to operate these guns and you learn to operate them well. It's as simple as that." He paused. "Are there any other questions or comments?" He looked directly at Belasco, then at Bonin.

There was silence. Nearly every man in the gun crew was now looking down at the deck.

"Okay," John said. "Where are the 40-mm maintenance manuals?"

"I think there are some back in the ammo ready-service compartment," Seaman Second Class James Jardin, who was just four weeks out of boot camp, ventured.

"That's the wrong place for them, sailor," John said. "Break them out and start studying them, now. I mean studying them, not just reading them. I want everybody here to know these weapons inside out and upside down, and I want you to know them fast. At 14:00 we begin to learn how to really use these guns."

"I'll see you all right after chow," John said as he headed toward the ladder that led up to the flight deck.

On the way up, he looked back at the group. "Ski, Lowe, make sure they get into those manuals. What they learn from now on might be the difference between life and death, and not just theirs, yours and mine, too. I don't know about you guys, but I plan on living to see the end of this goddamned war!"

John walked briskly across the flight deck, his steps measured and quick. Taking charge of his gun crew was helping put Diane behind him. He felt better with each step. He'd show her. He'd make this gun crew the best goddamned gun crew in the Navy. His thoughts were interrupted by activity astern. Two huge cranes on the dock lowered brand new, still wrapped F6F Hellcat fighters, SB2C Helldiver bombers and TBF Avenger torpedo bombers onto the flight deck just behind the after elevator. As soon as they came to rest, dozens of men descended on them. They methodically stripped away their wrappings and lowered them onto the hangar deck on the elevator. When there, aircrews began the exacting process of getting each plane ready for air combat training and combat later on. John had seen this kind of activity before. *Franklin* would soon be going to sea. He turned away from watching the loading and headed back to the hatch in the ship's island. Ahead of him a chief with a familiar walk was going the same direction.

"Beck? Beck!" John called.

Beckley looked around. "Well, I'll be damned, John Oxler."

"Chief Sullivan just told me you were aboard, Beck."

The two shook hands.

"Gee, it's great to see you," Beckley said.

"I was going to look you up as soon as I had time," John responded in a joyous voice.

"We just came aboard yesterday, and there's a lot of pressure on us to get this crew battle trained."

"I know. The captain asked about progress with the crew this morning. You look great, John. Put on a couple of pounds. The weight looks good on you."

John smiled widened. "Wonderful to see you, too, Beck. It's been a long time."

"And a couple of stripes, too," Beckley said. He put his hand on John's shoulder. "Last time I saw you, you were a 'skinny-ass' seaman and we were getting ready to abandon 'Lady Lex.'"

"Over two years," John said. "I never got the chance to tell you how much I owed you, Beck. When the *Lexington* sank, your leadership stopped a lot of panic. You helped save a lot of lives. One might just have been mine."

They talked as long as time permitted. Then John said, "Beck, I have to go below and see if I can find Sullivan, then get some chow. It's great to be aboard with you. I'll see you soon."

As John began to walk away Beckley called to him. "John, drop by chief's quarters some night," he said with a grin. "We've got a friendly game of hearts going nearly every night. We won't be too tough on you."

"That'll be the day," John replied happily.

John went below deck to the armory. Sullivan was there, working on his daily report.

"Hi, John, how'd it go this morning?"

"As well as can be expected, I guess," John said. "They're really green. I went back to basics. I've got them reading the manuals. We'll start the intense training right after lunch."

"John," Sullivan said, "remember what I said this morning about this crew coming around with enough time?"

"Yeah, Chief, I remember."

"Well, forget everything I said."

"What do you mean?" John asked nervously.

"Forget what I said about time. This skipper's really tough. There's no tomorrow for him. It's now! He wants these gun crews trained and trained fast."

John nodded. "I'll give it everything I've got, Chief."

"I'm counting on that, John," Sullivan said crisply.

As John headed for the mess hall, he felt a knot start to tighten in his stomach. Suddenly he realized he didn't have much of an appetite either.

CHAPTER FOUR

Shake Down
***Franklin* on Trial**
Mid-Atlantic Ocean

At dawn one week later, the *Franklin* cast off all lines. With Captain Shoemaker at the conn, Beckley at the helm and Commander Day and Commander Moore, the ship's navigator, on the bridge, she steamed East Southeast at fifteen knots under cloudy, wind-blown skies toward York Split Channel. At 07:00 harbor pilot Commander E. G. Edwards came aboard, and the *USS Baldwin* took a position three thousand yards ahead as a submarine screen. At 07:45 Commander Edwards left the ship, and *Franklin* moved slowly toward the waters of the mid-Atlantic for sea trials.

"I think the tables are finally starting to turn," Shoemaker said after he reviewed a message rushed up from the radio room. "The Marines have just landed on Kwajalein."

"This is the second island we've gone after in the last sixty days, sir," Beckley said. "We're taking one island after another. Last month Tarawa, now Kwajalein. Where do you think we're going from there, sir?"

"After Tarawa and Kwajalein, I've got a sneaking hunch Admiral Nimitz will go after Eniwetok on the outer edge of the Marshall Islands. I think he's setting things up for an attack on the Marianas."

Beckley looked puzzled. "The Marianas, sir?"

"Yes. If we can capture the Marianas, we're in position to attack the Japanese mainland with B-29s," Shoemaker replied.

"Do we know many lives were lost on Kwajalein?"

"Not yet, Chief, it's too early, but that's a very small atoll. There shouldn't be many," Shoemaker replied in a dismissive tone.

"Begging the Captain's pardon, sir, but Tarawa was an even smaller island and our losses there were huge," Beckley challenged.

"But the Japs had two years to fortify Tarawa. They were really dug in there," Commander Day said, joining the conversation.

Shoemaker looked like he was studying what Day said. "It probably depends more on the kind of troops the marines find on Kwajalein," he said. "Tarawa, although tiny, was defended by more than five thousand seasoned Jap marines—all veterans of the Manchurian campaign—tough as mountain goats. They were trained to fight to the very last man, and they did."

"What I heard about Tarawa was that somebody miscalculated the depth of the tides there," Beckley said. "Amtraks got hung up on the reefs and the whole first wave was massacred."

"Where did you hear that, Chief?" Shoemaker asked.

"Heard it in Kansas just before I came off leave and reported here, sir. A friend of mine who lost a son in that action told me."

"That's hard to believe, but it might explain the fact that over two thousand marines were killed and double that number wounded," Shoemaker replied.

"But I agree with you, sir, things are really starting to change," Beckley said. "I remember those tough weeks and months after the attack on Pearl Harbor. The Japs seemed invincible. They seemed to go wherever and whenever they wanted."

"Yes, and we weren't able to do a damned thing about it, not even slow them down," Day added.

Shoemaker shook his head. "Well, it wasn't exactly a cakewalk for them, Dave," he said in a slightly irritated tone. "We fought them hard in Guam, and the British put up a powerful defense of Hong Kong."

"I was aboard the *Lexington* in the Coral Sea when they invaded the Philippines," Beckley said. "It looked awfully easy from there, sir. They took Leyte in a day. Then Vigan, Legaspi, Lingayen and Lamon Bay all toppled like dominos. They fell in less than a week."

Shoemaker nodded. "Yes, that's true, Chief," he said.

"To the average swab-jockey in the fleet, the Japs looked like nobody could stop them," Beckley insisted.

"Yeah, we all remember those early losses, Chief," Shoemaker responded. "The Japs dominated the whole Pacific all the way down to Australia, but all that started to change when we broke their code."

Beckley seemed surprised. "Broke their code, sir?" he asked. "I didn't know we got information from a Japanese code."

"Yeah, Chief, JN-25, the Jap's top-secret military code," Shoemaker said. "Naval Intelligence figured it out. They decoded a series of top-secret messages that outlined a major battle plan to destroy what was left of our Navy after Pearl Harbor."

"Wow! How much did we find out?" Beckley asked.

"Nearly everything, Chief. Nimitz knew about the Japs' plan to trap and destroy our ships in the Coral Sea and he knew about their plan to attack Midway."

"Do you mean he knew where and when the Japs planned to attack us?" Beckley asked.

"Yes. Where and when, within hours of their actual timetable," Shoemaker replied.

He paused and looked through his binoculars. "Well, we're through the channel, Chief. All engines ahead standard speed, come to course 145 degrees. As soon we're in open water we'll test the engines, then the antiaircraft batteries."

"Aye, sir," Beckley said as he responded to the captain's change in course and speed.

The *Franklin* eased to the southeast. Her speed accelerated to sixteen knots.

"We should be in position in about an hour, sir," Beckley said.

There was a long period of silence as the *Franklin's* bow cut through the cold, white-capped waters of the wintry Atlantic.

"I was in both of those battles, sir," Beckley finally said. "I had no idea we broke their code."

"Well, in the Coral Sea, as you know, it didn't help us too much, but it sure as hell did at Midway," Shoemaker said. "I was aboard the *Enterprise* with Admiral Spruance at Midway. Spruance knew *when* they were coming and the *size* of their fleet. His genius was to position the *Enterprise* and the *Hornet* northeast of Midway. Japs never expected an attack to come from that direction."

"I always wondered why the Japs attacked that God-forsaken little speck in the ocean in the first place," Beckley said.

"In the Coral Sea the Jap's plan was to lure the American and Australian Fleets into a trap and destroy them. As you know, that failed. Even though we lost the *Lexington*, we gained more than just fighting them to a standstill."

"Do you think we came out more than even there, sir?" Beckley asked skeptically.

Shoemaker rubbed his chin and nodded slowly. "Yeah. I do," he said. "We stopped their advance. When you compare it to the kind of butt kicking we were taking before that, someday it might even be considered a victory, Chief."

"With all due respect, sir, it sure didn't feel like a victory when we abandoned the *Lex*," Beckley said.

"No, I'm sure it didn't, but I think you'll find it was a bigger victory than most people thought, Chief," Shoemaker replied. "In the North Pacific, the Japs planned a carrier attack and an invasion of Midway, along with the three western-most islands in the Aleutians. They figured these attacks would draw out the remainder of our fleet and they could destroy us there."

"I think they could have, too," Day interjected. "They outnumbered us five ships to one."

"Maybe, and maybe not," Shoemaker replied. "Admiral Spruance is a hell of a tactician. He may have whipped them without the decoded information. The point is we *did* know the Japanese battle plan and the size of their fleet, so speculating about what might have happened is academic."

"I guess you're right, sir." Day said.

"The most important thing," Shoemaker said, "was we destroyed their plan to form a defense-ribbon anchored by bases in the Aleutians, Midway and Hawaii. At Midway, that plan wound up at the bottom of the ocean. Four of their top-line fleet carriers were blasted down with it, and maybe their plans to dominate the Pacific went down there, too."

Shoemaker focused binoculars on the heavy storm clouds that covered the eastern horizon. "Winter in the Atlantic," he said shaking his head. "This weather's rooted in. Let's get on with the sea trials and get ready to go to war. For the next half hour we'll test the ship's engines."

He lowered his binoculars and looked at Beckley. "All ahead flank speed, Chief. Steady on course 145 degrees."

"Aye, sir." Beckley cranked the ship's telegraph to Flank Speed.

The *Franklin's* powerful engines roared. The entire ship vibrated as she cut through the choppy waters of the Atlantic.

In a few minutes Commander Day announced, "Twenty-seven knots, sir."

"As soon as we top twenty-nine knots, Dave, we'll level off and maintain that speed for awhile."

"Aye, sir. We're passing through twenty-eight knots now, sir."

After a full twenty minutes at nearly twenty-nine knots, Shoemaker said, "They're as slick as a whistle—with lots of power. Now let's test the antiaircraft batteries."

The ship's siren wailed through the loudspeaker system. The klaxon bonged: "General Quarters! General Quarters! All hands, man your battle stations!" came the brisk announcements.

"Let's go!" John Oxler shouted as the call to arms blared through the loudspeaker system. "Be alive! Move! We fire live ammo for the first time."

There was a frenzied rush for foul-weather gear, helmets and Mae West life preservers, then an even more frenzied rush up the ladders to the gun pits.

John's gun crew strapped on their helmets. They ripped off the 40s metal breech caps, tugged off the canvas muzzle covers and took their battle stations.

A brisk command pealed through the ship's loudspeakers: "Starboard antiaircraft guns, commence firing."

"Do it just like we practiced," John shouted. "Forget these are live shells. Just like we practiced. Garcia, Bonin, Colson, Belasco, take your time. Make those drops accurate."

"Don't worry about speed," Ski added. "We're not testing you guys now, just the guns."

"That's easy for you guys to say," Garcia said, "but these goddamned shell casings are cold, slippery and heavy."

"Why can't we wear gloves?" Colson asked as the 40-mm's started to fire.

"No gloves!" John shouted. "They make the casings slipperier."

Noise from four 40-mm guns blazing away at imaginary aircraft filled the sponson. It was deafening and unnerving, and it unsettled John's inexperienced crew.

"Be alert!" John shouted. "Goddamn it, stay with it. Stay with it! Don't let the noise bother you."

A clip of shells slipped from a seaman's hands as he tried to pass it to Belasco. Belasco braced the clip with his knee and prevented it from smashing into the deck. He recovered the clip and dropped it into the muzzle.

"Belasco. That was great! Great concentration," John bellowed. "Concentrate guys. See what can happen? If those shells had hit the deck we might all be in big trouble."

The firing went on. Tension mounted. Another clip slipped and hit the deck. It sent four 40-mm shells scattering toward the gun pit's bulkhead. Two shells impacted heavily on the bulkhead, but neither exploded.

"Let's get these hot bastards thrown over the side!" John shouted. He picked up the first errant 40-mm shell and heaved it into the ocean.

"Grab one and heave it, goddamn it!" John shouted at Ski.

Ski seemed frozen in his tracks.

John pushed him toward one of the hot shells. "Grab the goddamned thing and heave it!"

Ski reacted to John's frantic command. He grabbed the hot shell and jettisoned it.

John heaved another over the side, and Lowe got the last one.

"Goddamn. That was close," John said curtly. "For God's sake, guys, concentrate. Slow it down and concentrate!"

He paused a moment, then shouted to Ski, "Who the hell dropped the clip?"

"I did," Jardin said.

"You trying to kill us all, Jardin? You drop another one and I'll kick your butt all the way up to your neck."

"Sorry, Gunner, it slipped."

"I know it slipped, but you guys *have* to concentrate," John said. "These shells aren't going to bite you. The goddamned noise is just noise—that's all. Be alert! Grab firmly and pass carefully—so the man next to you can get a good grip. Don't worry about speed. Just grab them firmly and pass them carefully."

What John said seemed to settle the gun crew down. Slowly they began to develop a rhythm—securely grabbing and passing each clip. Soon their firing speed began to increase.

"Way to go, guys. Way to go! That's the way it should be done!" John shouted.

After an hour of continuous fire without another mishap, a command came through the ship's loudspeakers: "Cease fire. All guns cease fire."

"Son-of-a-bitch," Garcia said, his shirt dripping with sweat despite the chilly February weather. "I'm beat. This drill was tougher than hell."

There was a chorus of agreement.

John nodded. "It was tough, because it was your first time," he said, "but you better get used to it. There'll be a day when you have to go for two, three, sometimes four hours with some son-of-a-bitch shooting back at you. Think about that the next time you feel tired with drills." John paused. "The smoking lamp is lit," he said. "Just stay away from the ammunition locker."

Then he turned toward the hatch to the ready-service locker and said to Ski and Lowe, "Let's get in out of the wind. I want to talk to you guys."

Once inside the locker, he said, "God, that drop was close. I've seen how much damage one of those drops can cause. Just one dropped shell exploding can rip up a lot of men. More than one and the whole fucking gun crew is ripped to pieces."

"Well, Gunner, it was their first time," Lowe reasoned.

"First time can become the last time when you're fooling with live ammunition," John replied. He paused again and stared out at the ocean. "Jardin admitting he dropped that clip tells me something about that kid," he said slowly. "For as young as he is, he's got guts."

"Yeah. And he's eager to do everything he can to help the gun crew," Lowe replied.

John nodded and looked at his watch, then out at the wind-chilled gun pit. "Nearly noon. Let's get some chow, then we're going to get back here and work with dummy clips the whole afternoon."

"Hell, John, it's colder than piss out there. The guys aren't going to like that," Ski warned.

"I can't care what they like or don't like, Ski. Cold or not, they have to get used to the feel of 40-mm ammo under cold and pressure, and it has to be *before* we handle live shells again."

"Okay, Gunner, we'll pass the word. Drills this afternoon at 14:00."

"After screwing up twice, nobody should bitch about drilling this afternoon," John said.

"I'll bet they are going to bitch," Ski contended.

"Not if they know their lives depend on it. I'll tell them how important these drills are this afternoon before we get started," John responded.

"It's sure goddamned cold," Lowe said again.

"So is a corpse," John snapped as he blew warm breath into his hands. "I'll see you in the chow line."

After they filled their trays with beans, boiled beef, cabbage and some canned fruit, they found a place at the table. When they were seated, John asked, "Did the guys do a lot of bitching, Ski?"

"Hardly any at all. It surprised the hell out of me. Belasco was actually happy to have the additional work."

"That tells me there's some bright guys in our gun crew. One exception might be a Gunner Third Class I know."

"So I blew one this morning," Ski said. "Have a heart, John. Anybody can make a mistake."

"You've had yours for the month, Ski," John said with a smile.

They ate their lunch in silence, each man alone with his own thoughts. Finally, when they were nearly finished, Ski said, "John, I'd like to ask you something. When we first met, you said that women were easy to get but hard to keep. I've been thinking about that ever since you said it. What the hell did you mean by it?"

"Why did you remember that? How many things have I told you since then that you didn't remember?"

"A big bunch, Gunner, but you know that had to do with pussy, and pussy is more important to me than anything about the war."

John shook his head and laughed. "Get your mind out of the gutter, Ski. It's not a story about pussy," he said. "It's a story about being dumped."

"You were in love with somebody and she dumped you?"

"Yeah."

"Did she write you a 'Dear John' letter, John?" Ski asked with a tiny grin.

"Naww. I found out about it when I was home on leave. It was a tough time but I'm getting over it."

"How you doing that?" Ski asked.

"Well, I'm taking it one step at a time. The first thing I'm going to do is train you guys to be the best gun crew in the fleet."

"What the hell does that do for you, John?"

"It makes me sure that we all survive the war, that's what. And the next time I tell you something *really* important, remember it. In the meantime, don't be so goddamned curious."

"Do you think you'll find another gal?"

"Who the hell knows? Come on, we got work to do. Let's get back to the gun pit."

30 January, 1944
210 Miles ESE of Norfolk
Fighter Wing Evaluation

The day dawned sunny and bright. The storm was gone, but the Atlantic continued to be cold and whitecapped. There was a fifteen-knot wind blowing in from the west. At 07:55 Beckley arrived on the bridge to stand the eight-to-twelve watch.

Captain Shoemaker and Commander Day were on the bridge when he got there. As he took the helm, Shoemaker gave him a course change.

"Come left to course 130 degrees, Chief."

"Aye, sir, 130 degrees," Beckley said as he spun the helm to the course change.

Beckley watched the *Franklin's* huge flight deck move steadily toward the new course and as he did *Franklin's* huge identification number thirteen, painted right in the middle of the deck just behind the bow, loomed up at him. He looked away to the ocean, but his eyes involuntarily came back to the huge number. His thoughts went back to his conversation with Lieutenant Zimler. He hoped that damn number didn't mean bad luck. Goddamn, any number but thirteen. The biggest, newest ship in the fleet and she might be carrying an unlucky number. Not just on her flight deck, but on the port side of the bridge, too....

"Helmsman. Mind your helm," echoed the stringent voice of the Officer of the Deck.

"Aye, sir," Beckley replied. His thoughts about the *Franklin's* number caused him to stray off course. He quickly made the correction. "Goddamned number. It makes trouble everywhere it goes," he muttered.

"Today we test the Air Wing," Shoemaker announced. "First flights are scheduled for 09:30." He turned to Beckley. "This wind's a problem today, Chief. We'll be going in and out of it with a lot of course changes when the Air Wing drills get underway. Stay with me on that, will you, Chief?"

"Yes, I will, sir." Beckley said briskly.

Shoemaker looked at the message handed him by the Chief Radioman.

"Marines captured Eniwetok," he announced. "Just took them four days and there was almost no loss of life."

"I don't understand our strategy, sir," Beckley said. "Sometimes it looks like we're fighting island to island, then other times it looks like we pass some islands up. How the hell do we know which islands to attack?"

"What you're seeing is a strategy developed by MacArthur and Nimitz because the Japs are such tough soldiers. They wanted to avoid fighting on one island after another. That would have been so goddamn difficult it would have been almost self-defeating."

"How could that be self-defeating, sir?"

"Why fight one battle after another and suffer losses in men and material that are so heavy they might put us out of the war?"

"Do you think there could be losses *that* heavy, sir?" Beckley asked, disturbed by Shoemaker's remark. "Strange, I always thought Top Brass looked at casualties and losses kind of like pawns in a chess game."

"In a sense they do, Chief," Shoemaker said. "They have to. But in a larger sense, I think losses hurt them just as they hurt you and me. I know they do with Spruance, and I'd bet they do with Admiral Nimitz, too."

Beckley persisted. "Maybe they do, sir, but enough to quit the war? Do they hurt that much?"

"Well, that's not their call, but I think I know one thing for certain. President Roosevelt wouldn't accept huge death tolls. Congress probably wouldn't either and the American public sure as hell wouldn't. That's how we could get off the path to victory."

Shoemaker cleared his throat and studied the waters ahead of him, then went on, "So MacArthur and Nimitz decided a way to minimize losses was to attack only those islands necessary to cut Japanese defense lines. MacArthur calls it 'leapfrogging,' Chief. When we capture the strategic island we need, we decide on our next move forward. All the islands in between are simply bypassed."

"But how do they decide which island, sir? There's a lot of them in the Pacific."

"Remember Rabaul?"

"Yes, sir, I remember Rabaul," Beckley said. "I was down in that area, sir. Scuttlebutt was that it would cost fifty to seventy-five thousand lives to take Rabaul."

"That's the whole point, Chief," Shoemaker explained. "It could have been more men than that, too, and only God knows how many ships and planes. It was a heavily defended fortress. The Japs considered it a symbol of their power in the South Pacific and they had that big Japanese Fourth Fleet to protect it. They'd sworn to defend it to the last man."

"So we circled around it?" Beckley asked.

"Roger. We bypassed it. We took Guadalcanal, Bougainville and Manus and put a ring around it," Shoemaker said.

"Then we sealed it off with air and naval power and left it there to wither on the vine," Commander Day, who was listening to the conversation, added.

"Exactly, and it's still down there withering away," Shoemaker said. "I think we took Tarawa and Kwajalein for much the same reason. I'd bet Nimitz wants to leapfrog past Truk, that big Jap base in the Caroline Islands. That's why I think we'll go after Eniwetok in the Marshall Islands. Take a look at a map. You'll see how capturing Eniwetok draws a tighter ring around Truk."

"Those are great guesses, sir," Beckley said. "Where would we go if you guessed again?"

"I'd guess we'd go after the Marianas, and my goal is to get this ship into some of that action as soon as possible. So let's get this goddamned shake-down over with and get on with what the *Franklin* was really built for."

About that time the first group of F6F Hellcats were lifted to the flight deck by the ship's huge after elevator.

"Looks like they're getting set up now, sir," Beckley said.

"Yeah. Let's come around into the wind. Change course to 270 degrees."

"Aye, sir. 270 degrees."

As Beckley watched the *Franklin's* bow move swiftly toward the northwest, the number thirteen came into view again. "Goddamned number. What a pain in the ass! I'm going to have to learn to ignore it," he said half under his breath.

As soon as the elevator was up and secure, air crewmen swarmed around the sleek fighters.

"Pilots man your planes. Pilots man your planes!" blared the ship's loudspeakers.

Pilots and gunners rushed across the flight deck and climbed into their planes. Tow motors moved them into position behind the ship's powerful catapult.

"Start the drills," Shoemaker commanded.

In less than two minutes the first Hellcat, its fuselage marked by a white star in a black circle, catapulted into the air. Then every twenty seconds after it was airborne, another Hellcat zoomed into the sky until all thirty-six were up and flying in formation. They circled the *Franklin* and each squadron of four made a modified pass at the flight deck. Then they turned, regrouped and landed without incident.

"Everything's going great so far, sir," Beckley announced.

"Yeah. Let's see what the bombers and torpedo bombers do."

As soon as the fighters were lowered to the hangar deck the SB2C Helldivers emerged. The TBF Avenger torpedo bombers would come up last.

"They're readying the bombers," Beckley said, as aircrews maneuvered the sleek, new Helldivers into take-off positions.

"Let's hope they do as well as the fighters."

"Aye, sir."

In a matter of a few minutes, the first Helldiver thundered into the cold, blue Atlantic sky. Then Helldiver after Helldiver powered off the flight deck until all thirty bombers were airborne. TBF Avengers were moved into the "park." They would go next.

Beckley watched the fluid movements on the flight deck. Slick as a whistle. Maybe that number thirteen on the flight deck *is* just a goddamn number, he thought. Japs will give us all the trouble we need. We don't need a bunch of bad luck to help them.

The SB2Cs circled the *Franklin* much as the fighters did earlier.

Without warning, the wind increased dramatically. Its added energy forced the *Franklin* to pitch and roll.

Beckley looked at Shoemaker with concern. "This wind might cause trouble in landings," he said.

"Yeah," Shoemaker replied. "Where the hell is it coming from? There's not a cloud in the goddamn sky."

After the Helldivers flew out about forty miles, they circled and headed back toward the *Franklin*.

A voice that Beckley identified as Commander Zimler's crackled through the ship's loudspeakers.

"Bald Eagle to Emerald base. Preparing to land bombers."

Commander Joe Taylor, the ship's air officer replied. "Roger, come on in but be careful. The ship's pitching around."

"Aye, sir."

The Helldivers formed their landing pattern and began their descent. One bomber after another landed without incident. As the last SB2C came in, the *Franklin* pitched heavily. The pilot's tail hook missed the arresting cable and slammed into the deck. Both wheels collapsed. It caromed crazily down the flight deck, its propeller churning up chunks of the wooden deck, then screeched to a stop right in the middle of the number thirteen.

Beckley stared at the smoking plane. "What a crazy accident!" he muttered, "and it ended right in the middle of that damn number."

Rescue crews were at the plane in seconds. Some helped the pilot and gunner out of the cockpit. Others sprayed the plane with foam.

"Looks like the crew's okay," Beckley observed.

"Yeah, but that plane's had it," Joe Taylor replied. "Spare parts is all it's good for now."

"What rotten luck," Beckley said.

"Yeah," Taylor said. "But it could've been worse."

The rest of the Air Wing's drills went as planned. The TBF Avengers took off and landed on schedule and without incident.

5 February, 1944
265 Miles ESE of Norfolk
Explosion

Although the sun could be seen pushing through mist on the eastern horizon, the ocean was a cold, steel gray. A twenty-knot wind ripped across the *Franklin's* flight deck. Tarps flapped loose and the wind blew a biting, icy spray through open areas in the ship.

Beckley huddled in his foul-weather jacket and pushed through the biting wind toward the hatch in the ship's island that led to the bridge. *Franklin's* huge identification number appeared through the spray. That goddamned thirteen again. Every time he turned around he had to look at that number. As he climbed the ladder to the bridge, he tried to shake off these unsettling thoughts. Just as he entered the bridge, an explosion thundered up from below. Fragments of steel and brass peppered the front of the bridge. A front window shattered.

"What the hell was that?" he yelled as he rushed to a front window that escaped damage.

"What was it, Chief?" Shoemaker shouted.

"It looks like a 20-mm gun just exploded, sir. The explosion sheared off a hunk of its barrel."

Shoemaker and Day rushed to Beckley's side.

"It looks like there's wounded, Dave. Go down and see what happened. Chief, you go with him."

When they reached the scene, a group of men from the adjacent gun pits, including Chief Sullivan and John Oxler, were already working with the wounded, their heads, shirts and dungarees splattered with blood.

"What happened?" Day shouted.

"A gun barrel exploded, sir," John shouted back.

"Any dead?"

"Yes, two, sir. The two men on the deck are dead."

"How many injured?"

"Three, sir," he replied.

"You guys okay?" Day asked.

"Yeah, thanks, we're both okay," John answered. "But, these two guys are really messed up bad. Face wounds."

Beckley edged closer to the gun pit. He glanced down and quickly turned away. What he saw shocked him. Two dead seamen, their faces a mass of shredded flesh, lay on the deck below. Their bodies were uncovered and still bleeding. What was left of them was so grotesque they seemed inhuman. It was hard to imagine they were healthy and alive a few minutes earlier. God, they were just boys. Their mothers were probably sitting at home reading their last letters or telling their neighbors how proud they were of them. Deep sorrow radiated through Beckley's body. "Poor guys. They didn't have a chance," he said, sadness pervading his voice.

Day shook his head. "No, they didn't. It's a terrible tragedy."

A few seconds later, a group of corpsmen rushed into the gun pit from the short ladder to the flight deck. They quickly took charge of the wounded.

Chief Sullivan and John Oxler stood and moved out of the way. They wiped their blood-spattered hands on a towel provided by a corpsman. Then they climbed up the ladder to the flight deck.

Despite the tragedy, John managed a smile. "How's it going, Beck?" he asked as he continued to wipe blood from his hands and arms.

"I'm okay, John," Beckley said. He looked into the gun pit. "Terrible tragedy. It makes you feel helpless to stand up here, not able to do a damn thing."

"Yeah, I know exactly what you mean. I felt better down there. At least I could do something."

"How can a gun barrel explode like that, John?" Beckley asked.

"I don't know, Beck. It's the first time I ever saw one do that. In fact I've never even heard of one exploding."

"What do you think caused it?" Beckley asked.

John shrugged his shoulders. "Who knows, Beck. Just some kind of goddamned bad luck, I guess."

"Do you think any of the three guys that lived will ever see again?"

"From what I saw, I doubt it. Their eyes were ripped out of their heads."

Beckley grimaced. "God bless them," he said sadly. "It was *very* bad luck."

The two fell into a depressed silence as they watched corpsmen jostle stretchers holding the wounded up the ladder to the flight deck and then down a ladder to the sickbay.

Then John finally said, "I have to get myself together and get back to my gun crew, Beck. The pressure to get my guys trained is really on, and damn, some of them are still almost civilians. Six just out of boot camp."

"That's tough, John," Beckley said, shaking his head sadly as John turned to leave, "but don't let it get to you. You'll get 'em trained. Just stay with it."

2 March, 1944
Sea Trials Completed
Heading Back to Norfolk

Beckley walked onto the bridge to stand the eight-to-twelve watch. Shoemaker and Day were there, locked in discussions about the *Franklin's* sea trials.

"Poor. That's all I can say about them," Shoemaker said.

"I know, Captain," Day replied, equally disappointed. "We used every safety precaution we knew—nothing seemed to work."

"But God, Dave, I've never seen so many goddamned freaky things happen," Shoemaker complained. "We lost five planes in landing accidents. One pilot killed and two injured, and three men wounded so badly they'll never see again. All this on sea trials?"

Day sounded genuinely puzzled. "I wish it had gone better, sir. Everything seemed to happen just when it wasn't expected."

"*Franklin* even failed the radar range and bearing tests, Dave."

"That got corrected, sir. There were just a couple of glitches in the radar system."

"How about that damage in the forward five-inch gun sight?"

"We got that fixed, too, sir."

"Did you find the cause?"

"No, sir. It just seemed to go haywire."

"Haywire?" Shoemaker asked, disbelief in his voice.

"I guess so, Captain. I can't explain it."

"With this kind of report you wonder if they'll let us go to sea," Shoemaker said.

"There were a lot of positives, sir. The engines ran smoothly. The catapult worked perfectly. With the exception of that one gun barrel accident, the antiaircraft gun crews performed well. They even seemed to be getting better. Some of them were picking up speed."

"What about that gun barrel explosion? What did you find out about that?" Shoemaker asked.

"Can't find a thing, sir. Nobody can explain it. Chief Sullivan, with nearly fourteen years in the Navy, said he'd never seen a gun barrel explode like that before."

"Oh?"

"No one else I talked to in the gunnery division could either," Day said. "We're going to have the barrel examined in Norfolk. Maybe there was a manufacturing defect, sir."

"That's another first I don't want linked to the *Franklin*, Dave," Shoemaker replied. "These accidents are just too many and too frequent. I hope your explanations get by the examining board."

Day took a deep breath and exhaled. "So do I, sir."

Beckley listened to the Captain and Exec in silence. There sure were a lot of glitches. Three of the five planes that crashed on landing were on his watch. What the hell did this all mean? Was there *really* some kind of jinx on the *Franklin*?

CHAPTER FIVE

13 March, 1944
Aboard the Carrier *Enterprise*
Fifth Fleet

On the bridge of the fleet carrier *Enterprise*, Admiral Raymond Spruance studied a top-secret message from Fleet Admiral Chester Nimitz, Commander in Chief of the Pacific Fleet. "Admiral Nimitz is flying in from Pearl Harbor," he announced to Lieutenant Tom Todesco, the Officer of the Day. "He should arrive sometime early tomorrow morning. Let's get cabins shipshape for him and his staff. They're going to spend some time here. I think something big is brewing."

"Aye, sir," Todesco replied.

Spruance moved into the small conference room behind the bridge and motioned Admiral Marc Mitscher to follow.

"Maybe Nimitz has something from the Joint Chiefs of Staff that tells us where we strike next," Spruance said as he closed the door.

"I hope so," Mitscher replied. "Since we captured Tarawa and Kwajalein, there seems to be a lull in the war. I'd like to know where we're going next and get the hell after it."

"Well, don't get impatient, Marc," Spruance said with a smile. "The Japanese will still be out there. They aren't going away."

"I'm not impatient, Ray, but hell, I'd like to get on with it."

"We'll know something as soon as Nimitz gets here, I'm sure."

"What do you think *is* happening?"

Spruance rubbed his chin and the side of his face. "If I had to make a guess, I'd guess that the reason for the lull is Nimitz has had to struggle with General MacArthur to see how the rest of the war is going to be fought."

"Really?" Mitscher asked.

"Yeah. I'll bet that's what's causing the delay."

"Isn't that a damned fool thing to be struggling over, Ray?"

"You'd think they'd have better things to do with their time," Spruance replied. "From what I heard, MacArthur's the cause of the problem. I hear he wants the whole war to be fought up the coast of New Guinea, then through the Philippines. He's obsessed with taking the Philippines back, and stubborn as hell about it. That gets in the way of his good judgment sometimes."

Mitscher smiled. "You'd better not let him hear you say that, Ray."

Spruance laughed. "Yeah, I guess you're right. He'd be all over my ass if he did. Anyhow, I'm sure we'll know more soon."

"You mean about who won the little war between them?"

"Maybe. But my guess is we'll also find out where we attack next."

"You mean you'd like to get on with it, too?" Mitscher asked with a smile.

"Hell, yes," Spruance replied. "I want to get this over with like everybody else, Marc, but I'm not obsessed with it. If you want me to be fully honest with you, and you never tell anybody I said it, I don't live for this war. I could find things to do without it."

"Like?"

"I've got a wife and family back in the States that I've never been able to spend enough time with. I want to spend *a lot of time* with them when this thing is over."

"Yeah. I understand what you mean. Well, let's hope what Nimitz is bringing will get us going again." Mitscher said.

#

At 10:00 the next morning, Admiral Nimitz was piped aboard the *Enterprise* and ushered to the ship's wardroom where Spruance and Mitscher were waiting.

"Admiral, how are you?" Spruance asked. He shook Nimitz's hand. Then Nimitz turned to Mitscher.

"Admiral, it good to see you," Mitscher said.

Then he extended his hand to Mitscher's Executive Officer, Admiral Arleigh Burke, who had joined them. Burke, who a few months before had won the nickname "31-knot Burke" for his high-speed, heroic attacks as commander of Destroyer Squadron 23 in the dangerous waters north of the Solomon Islands, smiled and shook hands.

"Arleigh, how are you?" Nimitz asked.

"Fine, and you, sir?"

"I feel good, thanks, and I'm happy to say that I have good news," Nimitz replied.

Spruance offered Nimitz a chair, then joined Mitscher and Burke on the other side of the conference table. "What's the good word, sir?" he asked.

"The Joint Chiefs bought Admiral King's and my argument that there should be two prongs of attack to force the surrender of Japan."

Spruance, Mitscher and Burke edged closer to the table. "Did you have to take on MacArthur to get them, sir?" Spruance asked.

"What do you think? Hell, yes! He wanted the full thrust of the war to go through the Philippines."

Spruance nodded. "I thought that might be what was going on."

"I'll bet he put up a big fight," Mitscher said.

"It was a battle, but not a big one. Believe it or not, he can be reasonable at times. When Admiral King demonstrated that a two-pronged attack would be more effective and save a lot of lives, he was willing to accept that. Then King told him that the Joint Chiefs of Staff wanted a two-pronged attack."

"I'll bet that helped," Spruance said as he lit a cigarette.

Nimitz grinned. "That's what helped us most."

"Sounds like it was easy, Admiral." Spruance said with a smile.

Nimitz chuckled and shook his head. "Nothing with General MacArthur is *easy*, Ray."

"Was there anything that finally convinced him, sir?"

"Yes, there really was. It was the big leaps we could make with amphibious forces in an ocean where the Japanese had only a limited number of bases. We used the example of the thousand miles of ocean between Eniwetok and the Marianas. There are limited numbers of Japanese soldiers and marines in this area when compared to the large number of men jungle fighting in New Guinea, and the great strength of the Japanese in the Philippines and on Formosa."

"Yes, sir, but what about those two Japanese fleets?" Mitscher asked.

"We convinced him that we could handle them, and I'm confident we can. We're getting stronger by the day. Do you realize that we have five fleet carriers coming on line in the next ninety days? *Wasp, Hancock, Lexington, Intrepid* and *Franklin* are all due to join the fleet in that time."

"Four new light carriers, *Monterey, Langley, Cabot* and *Bataan,* are coming, too," Spruance said.

"That's right, and there are four new battleships coming on line, too," Nimitz added. "We should be able to handle both Ozawa's First and Second Fleets with that added firepower, shouldn't we?"

"Those Jap fleets are big and tough, Admiral," Spruance replied, "and Ozawa's a damned good Admiral. He can cause us some real trouble."

"That's not what I asked you, Ray. Can we handle them with the added firepower coming on line?"

"The answer's yes, when we get that added firepower," Spruance replied.

"Don't you think you'd be able to whip Ozawa with the firepower you have in the Fifth Fleet now?"

"It'd be a hell of a battle, sir. One that could go either way," Spruance replied.

"Right now *both* Japanese fleets outnumber us in both carriers and aircraft," Mitscher said.

"And the *Musashi* and *Yamato* are somewhere in those fleets," Spruance added. "Those battleships are the biggest and fastest in the world. They can out-gun any battleship in our fleet today—or any we have on the production lines, for that matter. Some of our older battleships are out-gunned by three or four miles. Either the *Musashi* or the *Yamato* could stand out of their range and pick them off like cherries."

"Yeah, those big bastards worry the Joint Chiefs of Staff, too," Nimitz said. "In fact, JCS told me at our last meeting they wanted you to figure a way to take them out."

Concern spread over Spruance's face. "I'd be damned wary of trying to do that with the battleships we have now, Admiral," he said hesitantly. "Nothing we have can stand up to their 18-inch guns or their speed and armor."

"Sounds like a direct showdown with them now should certainly be avoided," Nimitz said slowly.

"Right now, avoided in every way possible, sir." Spruance responded with caution. "This is one battle we could easily lose if the breaks went against us."

"Well, that job has to be done sometime, Ray."

"Aye, sir." Spruance ground his cigarette vigorously into an ashtray. "But it'd be a hell of a battle right now."

Nimitz nodded. "With that discussed, gentlemen," he said, "let's look at our first step in *Operation Victorious*." He pointed to a chart of the Pacific that an aide had hung on the wardroom wall.

"Eniwetok," he said. "We capture Eniwetok, then we move west toward the Marianas. We capture Saipan, then Iwo Jima, Tinian and Guam. When we have these bases, we try to force their unconditional surrender, possibly with air bombardment alone."

"Do you think that's a *real* possibility, sir?" Spruance asked.

"Probably not, but it's nice to think about. Repeated air strikes on Japan's industrial cities and an invasion of the Jap mainland is the *real* possibility. The Marianas provide bases for the air attacks. From there, we can hammer them with B-29 Superforts. We…"

Nimitz was interrupted by a knock at the wardroom door.

"See who that is, will you, Chief?" Spruance asked the chief master-at-arms.

When the Chief returned he was carrying a message. "Message from your office in Pearl Harbor, Admiral."

Nimitz took the message and carefully read it over. Then he looked up and said, "Boy, those bright young men in Naval Intelligence—most of them walk around like they're on another planet. They probably will *never* know how much we owe them."

"What's happened now?" Spruance asked.

"They intercepted and decoded a top-secret message from Japanese Naval Headquarters in Tokyo."

"Lord, I don't know how those guys do it," Spruance said. "Reading that crazy Jap writing with all those funny little characters is tough enough, but making something of them in code—that seems impossible."

Nimitz handed him the message.

"I'm sure glad it's in English, Admiral," Spruance said with a grin, as he read the message. When he finished reading, he said to Mitscher and Burke, "This is a message from Admiral Soemu Toyoda, Commander in Chief of the Jap Navy, to Admiral Ozawa and the commanders of the First and Second Japanese fleets."

"Really? What does it say?" Mitscher asked.

"Toyoda's intelligence has somehow been able to find out about the new ships coming into our fleet," Spruance replied.

"How the hell do you suppose they found that out?" Mitscher asked.

"They got spies, too, Marc. The Japs even identify *Franklin* and *Hancock* by name. They have the type of ship, size, tonnage, plane capacity, firepower—the whole nine yards. They know almost everything about the carriers and the battleships that are coming."

Spruance handed the message to Mitscher.

Mitscher studied it and said, "Goddamn. They even have some dates of arrival and they're pretty damned close," he said. "And they know the timetable for many of the rest of the carriers and battleships still being built."

"Yeah, but it's the directive at the end that's the blockbuster," Spruance said. "The direct order to locate and annihilate the American Fifth Fleet."

"Yeah, and with all deliberate speed," Mitscher added. "It sounds like they'd like to force a major showdown before our reinforcements arrive."

"It sounds like Toyoda knows now what Admiral Yamamoto is rumored to have feared most," Spruance said. "The increasing strength of our fleet will one day put the entire Japanese Navy in jeopardy."

"You're damned right," replied Mitscher, "and he's going to have to do what that memo says—try to knock us out *before* this parade of strength arrives. I wonder how the hell he knew that our next major offensive was on the Marianas?"

"That information might not come from spies," Nimitz observed. "It might be an excellent, logical calculation," Nimitz said. "The Japanese know the Marianas are located at their back door. If I were sitting in Toyoda's chair, I'd reason the same thing."

"It couldn't have slipped out from our side?" Spruance asked.

"I don't think so," Nimitz replied. "The final decision on that part of *Victorious* was only made two weeks ago and was known to fewer than a handful of very trusted people."

"Do you think they can ignore MacArthur's offensives in New Guinea, sir?" Mitscher asked.

"No, I don't, but I know they can't ignore our capturing Bougainville, Makin, Tarawa and Kwajalein either," Nimitz replied. "One thing that concerned JCS was the Japanese High Command concluding that we'd mount a two-pronged attack."

"I guess that's something we don't have to worry about anymore," Spruance said.

"Yeah, now we've got bigger worries, Ray," Mitscher responded.

Spruance turned to Burke. "Arleigh, pass the word to all units in the fleet. We're going to double the lookouts on every ship. I want twenty-four-hour surveillance. Put all radar units on intense alert. Triple the combat air patrols. I don't want another Jap surprise attack—not from anywhere."

As Burke started to leave the wardroom, Nimitz extended him a small parting salute, then asked an aide for a glass of water. "It'd be nice if this was something a lot stronger," he joked as he took the glass.

Spruance and Mitscher both smiled.

"Well, maybe they know we're becoming more powerful," Nimitz said, "but they don't know *how* we'll strike next and with what kind of an attack."

"What do you mean, Admiral?" Mitscher asked.

"Knowing the Japanese, I think they'll expect a traditional head-on naval engagement. They're linear in their thinking. For them, there's one way to do something and only one way."

"You mean you have *another* way, Admiral?" Mitscher asked.

"Yes, at least I've got a different tactic," Nimitz replied.

"You mean you know a new way to fight them, sir?" Spruance asked.

"I think so, and it involves you, Marc."

"Me, Admiral?"

Nimitz smiled. "Yes, you Marc."

"I'm sorry for the stupid question," Mitscher said with a grin. "I was just surprised that out of all the Admirals in the fleet you singled me out."

"You're the best air wing commander we've got, Marc. Admiral King selected you to implement this new tactic, and he had my full agreement." Nimitz said.

"Do you mind telling me what the tactic is, sir?"

"Do you remember how we grouped our carriers in those battles with the Jap Fourth Fleet around Bougainville?"

"I do, but I don't understand where you're going with that, Admiral." Mitscher said.

"Well, what we did was form the biggest air wing ever assembled there," Nimitz said, looking directly into Mitscher's eyes.

"I hadn't thought about that, Admiral," Mitscher replied, seeming a little uncomfortable with the stare. "I guess it was. Come to think of it, I can't remember ever using an attack wing with that many planes in it."

"In fighting off the Jap Fourth Fleet in those waters, I think we discovered a new carrier attack strategy," Nimitz said.

"What's new about what we did there, sir?" Spruance asked.

"We grouped our carriers, Ray. We hit the Japs hard and fast with a lot of air and sea power and then we disappeared. I think it drove the bastards crazy. I don't think they ever figured out where all the planes and ships came from and where they went after we kicked their asses."

"How do you know that, sir?" Spruance asked.

"I had a hunch this was what happened, so I asked the commanders in the forces we sent to stop the Jap Fourth Fleet's attempts to reinforce Bougainville. We stopped them because of those grouped attacks. The air wing commanders confirmed it. They said the Japs never expected an attack by a task force that included four or five fleet carriers and large numbers of battleships and cruisers. When they focused on one plane or one ship, there were four or five others coming from different directions. Commander Levin, the guy that led the air wing attack, said it was 'like Joe Lewis fighting a fly-weight.'"

"But isn't there a danger in using this approach all the time, Admiral?" Spruance asked, "You know, constantly exposing three or four fleet carriers at one time?"

"Yes, of course, there's danger," Nimitz said, "but Admiral King and I decided the added firepower is worth the risk. We think our successes at Bougainville are proof of that."

Spruance shook his head. "I guess sometimes you can get so busy with a battle you miss the war," he said.

"Well that's how we whipped them down there, Ray," Nimitz reaffirmed. "We've designated this strategy a 'fast carrier attack' and the group of carriers that deliver it a 'Fast Carrier Fleet.' From here on, we'll use a fast carrier attack in every operation possible, and Marc, you'll command these forces."

Nimitz shifted in his chair. "So, Ray will command of the Fifth Fleet, Marc, and you'll command the new Fast Carrier Fleet. It took a long time to get to this, but it's one of the important new things I came to tell you."

"Where does the new tactic fit into our strategy in *Victorious*, Admiral?" Spruance asked.

Nimitz paused and thought a moment. "It changes the tempo of our attacks. It keeps the Japs guessing where they're going to be hit and the strength of the attack. It changes the fact that we're outnumbered and that changes the pace of the war."

"When do we begin?" Mitscher asked.

"Right away. I want you to make a fast carrier attack on the Japanese Fourth Fleet in Truk."

"I agree with that, sir," Spruance said. "Especially if they find out we're going after Eniwetok. They could attack our flanks from Truk. That could be a big bunch of trouble."

"Roger," Nimitz replied. "We attack Truk and proceed with the invasion of Eniwetok. Actually the decoded message gives us a huge advantage. We now know they're coming after us, and we know the size of their fleets. We're outnumbered, so we have to search them out—outsmart the bastards when we find them—like you and Marc did at Midway."

"Let's talk about the make-up of Marc's fast carrier force," Spruance said.

"You have the *Enterprise,* Marc. You can group her with *Yorktown* and *Essex*. That provides the air power. Then take three battleships, the *Iowa, Alabama* and *South Dakota* and the heavy cruisers *San Francisco, Wichita* and *Pittsburgh*. Pull out the light cruisers you need, but leave me the *Santa Fe*. The *Santa Fe's* skipper is one of the best seamen in the fleet. He can maneuver that light cruiser almost right up to a beach. I watched him work at Bougainville and Tarawa. He's the best I've ever seen in close-in shore bombardment."

Mitscher nodded. "Roger, we'll do that," he said. "This sounds good, Ray. It'll give us a lot of firepower, and it still leaves you with enough strength to get the bombardment of Eniwetok done."

Spruance turned toward Nimitz. "With the Admiral's permission, I'll transfer your flag and mine to the *New Jersey* for the bombardment."

"Good. I'd like to watch this operation unfold for a few days, then I'll head back to fleet headquarters in Pearl."

"We'll execute this plan tomorrow, Marc," Spruance said. "If we can whip their ass at Truk, it will secure our flanks and shorten the day we can have a martini in Tokyo."

Nimitz raised his glass of water. "I'll drink to that," he said.

15 March, 1944
The Fast Carrier Fleet Forms
255 Miles South of Eniwetok Atoll

The day dawned cloudy, cold and wet. A March winter storm had moved in overnight and followed the Fifth Fleet northward as it steamed to the invasion of Eniwetok. A thirty-five-knot wind swept across the flight deck of the *Enterprise*. Nimitz, Spruance and Mitscher pushed their way through it to the officer's wardroom for breakfast. After a chief steward's mate seated them and they ordered, Nimitz said, "Goddamn, it's cold up there. What's the forecast for the next couple of days?"

"More of the same, Admiral," Mitscher replied.

"I got word this morning that the *Intrepid* and the new *Lexington* will be joining the Fifth Fleet tomorrow, sir," Spruance said. "This makes me more comfortable for the air bombardment of Eniwetok. All we'd have to work with, after Marc's fast fleet is formed, are five light carriers."

"It's hard to believe," Nimitz said, shaking his head slowly, "that within a few months we'll have one-to-one carrier strength with the Japanese. When we fought the battle of Midway, not so long ago, *Saratoga, Yorktown, Hornet* and *Enterprise* were the only carriers in the entire Pacific."

"How well I remember," Spruance said. "And we lost *Yorktown* there, so we were outnumbered seven-to-one."

"Yamamoto knew what he was talking about," Nimitz said. "He was always afraid of what he called the American 'sleeping giant.'"

"I've heard that too, Admiral. Is that the truth or just scuttlebutt? Do we really know he said that?" Mitscher asked.

"Well, we can't be absolutely sure, Marc, but if I had to guess, I'd guess he did," Nimitz said. "Yamamoto knew the United States well."

"Wasn't he attached to the Japanese Embassy in Washington for a long time?" Spruance asked.

"Yes, and more than that, he studied at an American university. I think it was Harvard."

Mitscher looked surprised. "Harvard? You got to be joking," he said.

"No, it was Harvard. That's how he knew so much about our industrial capacity and our wealth of raw materials," Nimitz replied.

"What came over the news wires was Army P-38s shot him and his staff down. Didn't the Navy have anything to do with it, Admiral?" Spruance asked.

Nimitz ran his forefinger slowly under his lower lip. "Yes, we did. When we got word he was going to be in Rabaul, we encouraged Naval Intelligence to try to find out where he was going and what he was up to."

"How'd we know he was headed for Rabaul, sir?"

"Decryption. All the information came from decoded Jap messages."

"We broke their code *again*?" Spruance asked, with an incredulous look on his face.

"Hell, they didn't change it. By that time the guys in Intelligence were deciphering Japanese code like they were reading the newspaper."

"And the Japs didn't get wise?" Spruance questioned steadfastly.

"No, they didn't, and from the message we got yesterday, it seems they *still* haven't."

Nimitz paused and adjusted himself in his chair. "Anyhow, they sent out a message that revealed a complete timetable for Yamamoto's inspection of the southern battle areas by air. We decoded it."

"Did Admiral King give the order to trap and shoot him down?" Spruance asked.

"Nope. I did. It may make me seem ruthless, but what I saw was a tremendous opportunity. I felt if we could get Yamamoto, we'd damage the hell out of their whole war effort."

"That must have been a tough decision, Admiral," Mitscher said. "Yamamoto was a kind of tradition, like a fellow gladiator."

"Not for me," Nimitz said. "It's a part of war. Both Admiral King and I agreed to go after him with whatever it took."

"Do you mind if I ask how Army P-38s got the job and the glory, sir?" Spruance asked.

"The P-38s were the closest planes to Yamamoto, but they weren't the only planes in action that day. We sent up the 214th Marine Fighter Squadron from Vella Lavella. We were sure Yamamoto would have heavy fighter protection and we were right."

"VMF-214, Admiral?" Mitscher asked. "Isn't that Greg 'Pappy' Boyington's 'Black Sheep' Squadron?'"

"It sure as hell is," Nimitz replied.

"But they're a bunch of misfits…" Mitscher protested.

Nimitz laughed. "Yeah, I guess you could call them that, because they *are*." He rubbed the back of his neck. "Even Greg Boyington will admit that, but they were also the best damned pilots we had, Navy or Marine. Hell, they'd already shot down more than a hundred and twenty-five Jap planes."

"Then why didn't we hear a word about what they did?" Spruance asked.

"Because they attacked Yamamoto's *advanced* protection, a huge squadron of Zeros commanded by the Japanese ace, Yosh Harashi. They shot down eleven Zeros in a rugged, moving dogfight. That action left only four Zeros to protect the two Mitsubishi G4M bombers carrying Yamamoto and his staff."

"And that created a hell of a mismatch," Mitscher said with admiration.

"That it did, Marc," Nimitz replied with a knowing smile. "Then the sixteen P-38s from the Army's 339th Fighter Squadron did the rest of the job, and did it well. They shot down both bombers. They also got the four Zeros protecting them. They killed everybody in Yamamoto's retinue."

"That's incredible, Admiral," Mitscher said, "and the 'Black Sheep' Squadron didn't get *any* credit?"

"We tried to keep the whole thing hush-hush as long as possible for security reasons," Nimitz replied. "When the story was finally released, the report only covered the *immediate* action but none of the details of the great support provided by Boyington's squadron."

"I hope history corrects that someday," Spruance said.

"So do I, Ray. The 'Black Sheep' did a hell of a job on that advance guard."

"Well, anyhow, we got some vengeance for Pearl Harbor, sir," Spruance said.

"*Vengeance* was the operation's code name," Nimitz retorted.

"How do you think it affected the Japs, Admiral?"

"I think it was a terrible blow, Ray. Yamamoto was the ablest and most creative mind in the Japanese Navy—he engineered the victory at Pearl Harbor. I think his death was a major loss to the Japanese war effort."

"It's hard to believe that one man could be that important," Mitscher said with a trace of doubt.

"Look at the facts. Since his death the war's momentum has started to shift toward our side, and the Japanese are without their greatest military mind to counter that shift."

"Do you think the shift is *that* dramatic, sir?" Spruance asked.

"Absolutely. The only thing that's held us back is the lack of carriers and capital ships, and as you know, that's being rectified as we speak."

Nimitz gathered his napkin and laid it on his empty plate. "Let's get up to the bridge and arrange to transfer our flags to the *New Jersey*, Ray," he said. "I guess I don't have to say that most of the stuff we discussed the last two days is sensitive. You can let it out to our fleet commanders. I think that'll be a great boost for morale, but emphasize it's *top-secret*. I sure as hell don't want it to get beyond those who absolutely need to know."

At 11:15 the lookout in the crow's nest sent an alert to the bridge: "Two *Essex* Class carriers off the starboard beam. Range, twenty miles." The new carriers *Hancock* and *Lexington* were joining the Fifth Fleet.

At 14:00 Nimitz and Spruance left the *Enterprise* and went aboard the *New Jersey*. Two hours later Marc Mitscher's powerful Fast Carrier Fleet turned West Southwest to attack the Japanese fortress of Truk.

17 March, 1944
Aboard the Battleship *New Jersey*
25 Miles South of Eniwetok

A radiant sun pushed up over the eastern horizon. Its rays formed a glittering pathway across the quiet Pacific. The storm had passed, and the attack on Eniwetok, code named *Catchpole*, was about to begin.

At 06:30 one hundred thirty-five Hellcats, Helldivers and TBF Avenger torpedo bombers thundered into the air from six aircraft carriers. They quickly grouped into attack formations and sped toward the invasion point on the southeast coast of the atoll.

On the bridge of the *New Jersey*, Nimitz and Spruance watched the precise, orderly functions of their air wings.

Nimitz looked at his watch. "Six-fifty-five," he said. "Surface units will begin their bombardment in a few minutes."

"Intelligence tells us that Eniwetok is lightly defended," Spruance said. "But I've ordered a three-day bombardment just in case." He focused his binoculars on the sandy beach. "It doesn't look like there's much there, but it's better to be safe than sorry."

"Yeah," Nimitz said. "We didn't think there was much at Tarawa and it cost us two thousand dead marines—and nearly twice that many wounded."

"We badly miscalculated the softening up needed there," Spruance said with a frown. "I thought we could do it in two days, but I sure was wrong."

"We were both wrong, Ray. Don't take all that on your shoulders."

"I'm sorry, Admiral, but I disagree," Spruance said. "It was my final decision, sir, and I stand responsible for it, but I promise you, I will never let anything like that happen again."

At 07:00 the bombardment began. The sixteen-inch guns on the *New Jersey* exploded into action with a deafening broadside volley. Broadsides from the rest of the battleships followed. Heavy cruisers hammered the landing site from closer in. The pungent smell of burnt powder filled the air. At the same time, the air wings began bombing and strafing the fortifications on the highlands behind the beach. Huge mounds of earth and debris exploded into the sky. Japanese installations erupted into blazing death traps.

Closer to the beach the light cruisers began their attacks. Spruance focused his glasses on a light cruiser steaming deftly through the treacherous coral shoals. "Admiral, look at that cruiser out there, the one closest to the beach," he said as he lowered his binoculars and pointed. "That's the *Santa Fe*—the one cruiser I wanted to keep for shore bombardment."

Nimitz moved his binoculars in the direction Spruance indicated.

"Yeah, I see her now. She can't be much more than seven hundred yards from those Jap fortifications," Nimitz said. "She's in there close. Sticks out like a sore thumb."

"She was that close in at Bougainville and Tarawa, too."

"Who's the skipper?"

"Fitz. Harold Fitz."

They watched as the *Santa Fe* navigated through Eniwetok's tricky reefs. She turned broadside, targeted a 6-inch gun emplacement on the beach, and fired one shell after another into its concrete bunker. The bunker finally exploded and fire consumed it. When the smoke cleared, the gun barrel pointed in the air at an awkward angle, blasted out of commission.

"That *is* good seamanship," Nimitz said. "It takes skill and guts to do what they just did."

20 March, 1944
Engebi Island
Eniwetok Atoll

Three days later under a still cloudless sky, Nimitz and Spruance trained their binoculars on the battered, smoldering beach. A dense cloud of dirty smoke and floating debris made viewing difficult.

"We sure blasted hell out of them," Spruance said as he scanned the battered beach on Engebi Island.

"Land the landing forces!" the loudspeakers blared.

"There they go," Nimitz said. "May God go with them."

Marines from the Twenty-Second Marine Regiment, under the command of General Thomas Watson, hunkered down in their Amtraks. They moved swiftly through the heavy surf to attack the debris-covered beach. Young Americans from Idaho, Georgia, New York and nearly every other state in the nation prepared to root out the Japanese no matter what it took. They landed with ease. There was little resistance. They moved quickly inland.

"This bothers me," Spruance said. "It's too damned easy. See if you can get General Watson on the wire."

"Aye, sir," replied the chief radioman on watch.

"That was a hell of a bombardment," Nimitz said, seeming impressed. "Maybe we've scared them all off."

"If we did, it'll be the first time. The Japs don't scare that easily," Spruance responded.

"Let's see what General Watson says," Nimitz said.

In a few minutes, the radioman said, "I've got him on the wire, sir."

"General Watson, Admiral Spruance here," Spruance said. "Things look pretty easy. What's going on?"

"Some of the beach defenders were in shock from the bombardment," came the reply. "We've captured over a hundred of them. We found out from one that the main force, the First Amphibious Brigade, under the command of a General named Nishida, retreated to the caves on Parry Island north of here. They're a veteran unit of about twenty-one hundred men. We're moving up there to dig them out."

"Do you need reinforcements?" Nimitz asked.

"Negative. We've already called for an amphibious attack from two battalions from the One Hundred and Sixth Infantry Regiment."

"Do you see any problems?"

"Negative, sir. We'll dig them out. We've got tanks with flame-throwers and artillery. It's just a matter of time."

"What are your losses so far?" Nimitz asked hesitantly.

"Twenty-five marines dead and about fifty wounded."

Nimitz paused. "Roger," he said. "We'll move north to bombard Parry Island ahead of your attack. Good luck."

"Thank you, Admiral. Roger and out."

"Let's take a minute and have some chow, Ray," Nimitz said.

As they were eating egg sandwiches brought up to them, the chief radioman on watch said, "I've got Admiral Mitscher on the wire, from Truk, sir."

Nimitz and Spruance crowded around the bridge's microphone.

"Marc," Spruance said, "How is it out there? How'd it go?"

"It's wonderful. We kicked their ass," Mitscher replied, his voice somewhat altered by the static and distance.

"So the fast carrier concept works," Nimitz said.

"Even better than I expected, Admiral," Mitscher answered.

"How much of the Jap Second Fleet was there, Marc?" Spruance asked.

"What we attacked looked like only a small part of it, Ray," Mitscher replied. "We hit what was there with everything we had. You can scratch one light carrier, three cruisers and seven destroyers. We also got eleven transports, some of them filled with Jap marines."

"Jap marines? Where do you think they were headed?"

"Lord knows, Ray. Maybe to reinforce Eniwetok. I know where they were yesterday afternoon. They were in the water struggling to get to shore."

"Give me a rundown on how the tactics worked," Nimitz said.

"Well, Admiral," Mitscher said, his voice still flushed with victory, "they worked well, sir. Just like you outlined them the other day. In fact," he continued with a touch of humor, "they worked so well it was as though we'd used the tactics before, sir."

Nimitz chuckled and shook his head. He enjoyed Mitscher's attitude and confidence. "You have, Marc," he said with a broad smile. "You just didn't know it."

"Now all you have to do is cook up a scheme to sink the *Yamato* and *Musashi*, sir," Mitscher said with a chuckle.

Nimitz smile faded. "Well, that's another problem, Marc," he said. "I'll leave that to you and Ray. There's got to be a way to get those two big bastards. You guys just have to figure out what it is."

They finished their conversation with Mitscher and signed off. Then Spruance said, "Most of the Jap Second Fleet was missing. That bothers me, sir. I wonder where the hell they went?"

"From the sound of it, they could be anywhere, Ray. We have to be wary. Ozawa's a skilled tactician," Nimitz said.

"Yeah, and cunning, too. We have to stay constantly on the alert," Spruance said with concern.

"Well I'm sure when you locate them you'll find a way to handle them, Ray," Nimitz said. "I think I'll head back to Pearl Harbor in the morning. Would you have someone call Tarawa for a PBY? And, Ray," he continued with a grin, "be sure the request is in code."

"Aye, aye, Admiral," Spruance replied, with a smile of his own.

CHAPTER SIX

23 March, 1944
On Board the *USS Franklin*
Destination: Eniwetok

The *Franklin*, accompanied by the destroyers *USS Davis* and *USS Wainwright* steamed toward the Panama Canal, making eighteen knots on course 176° in Condition of Readiness III, on zigzag Plan 6. Her ultimate destination: Eniwetok and Admiral Spruance's Fifth Fleet.

She had completed her sea trials, was loaded with eighty-six aircraft and a crew of thirty-eight hundred and fifty-three officers and men.

When Beckley arrived on the bridge to stand the eight-to-twelve watch, Shoemaker and Day hovered over copies of a memo. Beckley walked the few steps to his post, and as he did, he heard Shoemaker say, "Oh, no, Dave. Admiral Spruance is the winner on that, hands-down. There's no doubt in my mind. He proved it at Midway and he's proved it ever since."

Beckley listened to the conversation intently. Sounded like the Captain was trying to convince the Exec about something.

"I guess what impresses me most about Spruance is his humility," Shoemaker said. "After his big victory at Midway, he scarcely said anything about it. When he did, he gave all the credit to his staff and men. To me that shows a lot of class."

Day studied what Shoemaker said, then nodded. "I can agree with that, Captain. He sounds like a man who knows what it takes to win, but I think Admiral Halsey is the best fleet commander in the Navy. You know there was some scuttlebutt about a screw-up in Spruance's bombardment of Tarawa."

"Screw-up or not, in the end, he crushed the Japs there."

Out of the corner of his eye, Beckley saw Shoemaker turn in his chair and look right at him. "Come over here, Chief. You were on the *Yorktown* at Midway, weren't you?" Shoemaker asked.

Beckley walked over, surprised by Shoemaker's question.

"Aye, sir, I was."

"What's an enlisted man's opinion of Admiral Spruance?"

"I think he one of the finest, if not the finest commander in the fleet, sir." Beckley answered. Then he hesitated, "If I may, sir, Admiral Spruance knows what it takes to turn tough battles into big victories, especially when the odds are against him. In my opinion, that's what he proved at Midway, and maybe at Tarawa, too."

"Okay. So you served under him at Midway," Commander Day said. "Does he have the kind of respect from his men that 'Bull' Halsey has?"

"I think so, sir. I think he has their respect and admiration as well. At least he has mine."

"You see what I mean, Dave?" Shoemaker said. "Admiral Nimitz made a great choice to put him in command of the Fifth Fleet. In my opinion, he's the best commander we've got to implement *Operation Victorious*."

"*Operation Victorious*, sir?" Beckley asked.

"Yes, *Victorious*, Chief. It's the overall plan to end the war," Shoemaker said. "It's top-secret. I can't say much more about it except, as you've probably guessed from our conversation, Admiral Spruance will be one of the men who masterminds it."

Beckley shifted his weight slightly. He was troubled about the conversation between the Captain and the Executive Officer and didn't want to wind up in the middle of it.

"The fact that we've got a plan to end the war is not top-secret, Chief," Day said. "I'm sure the Japs expect that King and Nimitz would have one, and after Midway, they probably expect Spruance to command it."

"Don't the Japs have a plan, too?" Beckley asked.

"Yes, they have, and the guys in Intelligence are decoding it like they're reading a novel," Shoemaker added. "That's why the details of our plan are so highly classified. I can tell you, however, our plan forecasts the final victory over the Japs by the end of 1946 or early 1947."

"Gee, that's great, sir. We could sure use some good news right about now."

"You talking about the Conduct Report, Chief?"

"Yes, sir. I read it last night. There're one hundred twelve men on it, for everything from 'taking alcoholic beverages aboard a naval vessel' to 'disobeying a direct order.'"

"Yeah, I read it, too," Shoemaker said. He looked directly at Day. "Commander, are we doing everything we can about this crew's discipline?"

"Aye, Captain, we are, but with this crew it's taking more time than usual," Day replied.

"Yeah, but one of these days we're going to run out of time, Dave. I thought you were going to come down on them hard."

"We have, Captain, very hard," Day said firmly. "But when do we reach the point where we're pushing them too hard?"

"Maybe never. From the looks of this report, I don't think we can ever push them to that point."

Just as Shoemaker finished his sentence, flight operations began on the flight deck. Crewmen maneuvered twenty-four F6F Hellcats into position behind the ship's catapult. They routinely hooked the first plane up and in less than ten seconds it was jettisoned into the air. The rest of the fighters were catapulted off, and in a few minutes had formed into attack units of six planes.

Beckley watched the air operations closely. Since they left Norfolk, there had been more accidents in the Air Wing. These accidents, coupled with his uneasiness about the crew, bothered him. He could tell from what Shoemaker just said that that the Captain was troubled, too.

"It seems like we're still having a lot of problems, sir," Beckley said.

"Yes, it does, Chief. I've never had a command like this," Shoemaker said uneasily as he scanned the activities on the flight deck. "There's just not enough time for everything. In the past, I've always had time to develop a new crew. I'm sure some of the accidents are a result of everyone pressing too hard."

"Is there anything that can be done, sir?"

"I don't know. Today's Navy wants instant results. I guess that's what I'm demanding from Commander Day," Shoemaker said.

"We're going as hard and as fast as we can, sir," Day reaffirmed, "but I don't think instant results are possible, Captain, especially with this crew."

While the Captain and Commander talked, Beckley watched Commander Zimler's Avenger go airborne. He was pleased to see him have a good takeoff. He and Zimler had become friends over the past few weeks, and he had begun to watch Zimler's takeoffs with extra concern.

A second Avenger, propellers whirring, was maneuvered in from the park and was hurriedly attached to the catapult. In a few seconds it was being powered into the air. Air crewmen moved in a third. It was attached and quickly hurled into the sky.

"Things are going well with the Air Wing today," Beckley said as he looked out the port bridge window to the flight deck. "Operations on the flight deck seem to get smoother and smoother."

Beckley studied his wristwatch. "Air crewmen are getting planes airborne in less than twenty seconds," he said, pleased with what was going on.

Suddenly, a horror-filled scream pierced the air. It was so shrill it could be heard on the bridge, over the ship's noise and wind.

"What the hell's that?" Shoemaker asked.

Beckley looked again. "I don't know sir. It looks like something happened to someone back in the park. There's a cluster of guys down there. They've red-flagged flight operations."

"Go down and see what it is," Shoemaker said.

"Aye, sir." Beckley hurried down the ladders to the flight deck. When he got to the flight deck, he ran into John and Chief Sullivan who had rushed up from the starboard gun pits.

"What the hell happened?" he asked.

"We don't know," John replied. "We just heard that wild scream."

"Let's get aft and see," Beckley said.

The three made their way aft through the waiting planes toward the cluster of air crewmen. "Watch these goddamned props," Beckley warned.

When they reached the cluster, Beckley jerked at an air crewman's jacket. "What happened?" he demanded.

"Aviation Ordinance Man Second Class Paul Marino, Chief," the crewman said. "He stumbled into a propeller."

"Is he dead?" Beckley asked, already knowing the answer.

"Yeah, I think so, Chief. It's hard to stumble into a prop and survive."

John edged his way into the cluster of men. When he came out, he was grimacing. "It cut off half of his head and right arm. There's blood all over. It's ugly."

Beckley and Sullivan edged in as corpsmen with a stretcher arrived and pushed their way through.

As they did, Beckley said, "Ugly is right, John. Those fucking propellers! You warn guys again and again about how dangerous they are, and *still* there are these kinds of accidents."

"It's tragic. It makes me want to throw up," Sullivan said.

The corpsmen edged their way out of the cluster carrying the stretcher with the air crewman's body covered by a blanket. Blood soaked through the blanket and was dripping on the deck as they went.

Beckley shook his head. "Aviation Ordinance Man Paul Marino is now a part of history," he said sadly.

They carefully made their way through the parked planes across the flight deck toward the bridge. By the time they reached the hatch, air operations had resumed. The ship's aft elevator came up with the first two SB2C Helldivers. They would go up after the Avengers. Pilots who would fly the Helldivers streamed up from the ready room onto the flight deck.

Just as Beckley turned to return to the bridge, Lieutenant Commander Ralph Durren, a talented pilot who served with Beckley on the *Yorktown*, called out. "Hey Beck," he said. He trudged over in full flight gear, apparently unaware of what just happened. "My wife's pregnant. I got the good news this morning. Our first kid."

"That's wonderful, sir," Beckley said with a forced smile.

John and Sullivan also offered their congratulations.

"Is she still in Idaho, sir?" Beckley asked.

"She's there now. She was in Norfolk until we shipped out." He shook the letter to and fro between his thumb and index finger. "It's the first letter since she went back home."

"That's sure great news, sir."

"Yeah, it is. I was glad she could come down to Norfolk for a couple of months. Lord knows when I'll get to see her again," Durren said. "Well, I better get to my plane. We're next in line for takeoff. Thanks, Beck. I just needed to tell someone about it."

"Have a safe flight, Commander," Beckley said.

When Durren was gone, Beckley turned to John and Sullivan. "Thanks for not ruining his day, guys. Right now he's got a bunch of happiness inside of him. He can find out about the accident later."

They watched as one plane after another zoomed into the sky. In a few minutes air crewmen positioned Durren's Helldiver behind the catapult. He waved and gave Beckley a "thumbs up" as his Helldiver was locked to the catapult. In a few seconds it was thundered into the air.

"Look out! He's not going to make it," John shouted his voice filled with horror.

They watched Durren's SB2C vault into the air, then crash nose-down into the choppy water.

"Plane down! Plane down!" blared the frantic command over the ship's loudspeaker system. "Air-sea rescue detail! Air-sea rescue detail!"

Franklin decelerated and came to a stop. A crash boat rushed out. A seaman standing nearby offered Beckley his binoculars. Beckley focused on the crash site. "That plane's really smashed up. Durren's not moving," he said. "He's slumped over, face down. Jesus, I hope he's not hurt."

"The crash boat will be there in a couple of seconds," Sullivan said. They watched as Durren's body was pulled from the cockpit.

"His head is just flopping back and forth," Sullivan said. "He's either out cold or he died from a broken neck."

"Good God, two in one day? I hope he's not dead. Not an exceptional young man like that," Beckley said in an almost prayerful tone.

Minutes later they learned that the impact of the crash had snapped Darren's neck.

A chaplain waited at the edge of the flight deck as the body was lifted on board. Beckley watched as the chaplain read from a small prayer book. He thought of Durren's wife and the child who would never know its father. He was filled with a mountain of sadness. When was all this goddamned stuff going to stop? When he found out John was aboard, he thought that might be a good omen. Maybe, just maybe, some of the crazy things happening on the *Franklin* might start to change. Without thinking, he looked toward the *Franklin's* superstructure. The huge number thirteen painted there alarmed him. Some words from Shakespeare came into mind…

Nothing is more certain than uncertainty;
Fortune is full of fresh variety,
Constant is nothing but inconstancy…

Beckley turned his head away. *What a shitty message! Was this a warning? he asked himself.* "Well, I have to go," he said aloud. "What crappy luck. Now I have to give the Captain this damned report."

That afternoon Beckley was summoned back to the bridge. As he climbed the ladder, he wondered why he'd been called since he'd pulled his watch earlier. When he got to the bridge the boatswain's mate on watch said, "Lieutenant Zimler wants to see you in the ready room."

As he came through the door to the ready room, Zimler was waiting. "These goddamned accidents are starting to get to me," he said.

"Begging your pardon, sir," Beckley said. "It seems a little strange when we talk about these things."

"What do you mean, Chief?"

"Well, you fly Avengers and Helldivers and land them on a deck that pitches and rolls and looks like a postage stamp from the air. That's one of the most dangerous and terror-filled jobs on earth. Sometimes I wonder how you could be bothered by…"

"I've got control in an airplane," Zimler interrupted. "I can understand and evaluate the risks but this…."

"Yeah. I understand," Beckley said. "And it seems like things keep happening. More in the last few weeks than I can remember in a year aboard the *Lexington*."

Zimler hesitated for a moment, then asked, "This sounds asinine, but could this ship be jinxed? We've had two horrible accidents in one day, one right after the other."

"I try hard to believe there's *no* such thing as a jinx, sir," Beckley replied.

"I know, I do too. But explain what's happening some other way. When was the last time you heard of a gun barrel exploding? Those barrels are examined with precision instruments when they leave the factory. That gun was brand new. The report I saw said the barrel was examined and cleaned the day before it exploded. Then that aviation ordinance man stumbles into a prop and gets his head cut apart, and we lose Durren, one of the best pilots in the air wing. His plane just got a thorough going-over yesterday. I checked on it myself. It was in perfect condition." He paused to think about what he just said. Then he shook his head. "Do you think we're making too much out of this, Chief?" he asked.

"I don't know, sir, maybe we are. But it's goddamned hard to shake things like this. That accident in the gun pit really got to me. What a tough way to die."

"I want to believe it's just a bunch of bad coincidences," Zimler said.

"So do I, sir. But things like this can give you the creeps," Beckley replied. "They just seem to be happening and happening. Those two, this morning, were just too close. One right after the other."

"Well, maybe things will settle down soon," Zimler said.

"They sure as hell have to, sir. It's tough to look down the road and think about fighting a jinx along with the Japanese Navy."

Zimler nodded. "We've just got to keep going until they stop," he said.

"Yeah. But what if they never stop, sir?"

Zimler shook his head but said nothing.

CHAPTER SEVEN

26 April, 1944
Intermediate Destination: Harbor Island
San Diego, California

Commander Day kept pressure on the crew as the *Franklin* steamed through the Caribbean toward the Panama Canal. Every day, day in and day out, it was one drill after another. The call to arms blared through the loudspeaker—morning, afternoon and sometimes late at night:

"General Quarters! General Quarters!"

"All hands man your battle stations!"

The drills were exhausting and pressure filled, but one of the healthy things that developed from these pressures was a friendly competition. When general quarters sounded, everybody rushed to see who could get to his station first. John's gun crew bought into the competition and, because John felt it was good for morale, he joined in too. He was trying to show by example that, although these were just drills, one day they would be the real thing.

This morning, Ski was last. He was pissed off when he arrived. "Those sons of bitches from the mess hall held me up," he complained.

Now everyone was at his station. The long wait began.

"Fuck, here we go again; hurry up and wait," Feinstein groused. "Goddamned Navy. Wait for everything—food, mail, pussy."

"Yeah, goddamn, it makes an hour ten times longer than it should be," Bonin lamented.

"Knock it off," John said. "We don't need any bitching or moaning."

John looked at Feinstein, then at Bonin. "This is general quarters—it's not a damned Sunday social," he said. "In case you knuckleheads haven't heard, there's a war on. Quit your bitching and attend to business. Someday some Jap is going to bear down on us with all his guns firing. We fucking well better be ready!" John was driving his men hard and he knew it. He also knew from painful experience that lives were riding on this—his crew's lives and his, too. "Let's try to make everything go perfect today, guys," he said. "No drops, screw-ups or accidents. Remember, we're firing at drones. They're *planes*, you know, like the things the Japs fly, so don't miss any of them."

"Today we're going to have a chance to show how good we are with these guns," Ski added. "Let's blow everything that comes in right out of the sky."

"Roger," Lowe said. "Today we're the best goddamned gun crew in the fleet!"

The *Davis* released the first drone. It streaked right toward the *Franklin's* starboard bow. John's gun crew brought it under heavy fire. Streams of 40-mm projectiles, every fourth a tracer, reached out and ripped into the speeding drone. It exploded in mid-air.

"Way to go! Way to go!" John shouted.

The *Wainwright's* drone headed right for the middle of the ship.

John's gunners swung their 40s aft and picked it up when it was still two thousand yards away.

"Great! Great!" John shouted. "We're out-shooting every gun crew on the ship." John was filled with joy and excitement. "Okay, Diane," he said under his breath, "this is my answer to you. You let a goddamned good man go!"

The drills lasted an hour and fifteen minutes. The *Franklin's* gunners shot down fifteen drones. John's gun crew had five of them.

John looked at his watch. It was 10:30. "There's going to be a twenty-minute break in the action," he announced. "Garcia, Bonin, Colson, Belasco. All you loaders go to the end of the ammunition line."

"What's wrong John? We're doing a good job, aren't we?" Garcia asked as he jumped to the deck from his loader's station.

"You're doing great," John replied, "but today I'm going to give every man in the ammo line a chance to load."

"Hell, I thought loader was my job," Colson said.

"It is," John reassured him, "but when the shooting starts, sometimes men go down—and the loader is whoever is healthy and closest to the breach. All second men in line, take the loader's stations," he continued in a rapid voice. "You guys have watched the loaders so this part of the drill should be easy."

"Just relax and get a good clean drop," Ski instructed. "Don't worry about speed. That'll come later."

"What if we let a drone get through?" Jardin asked.

"Don't worry about it. These drones aren't Japanese. They don't kill anybody." John replied.

With the gun crew realigned, the action began again. Each man took turns at loading the 40s and did surprisingly well. Not one of the drones got past the *Franklin's* guns.

John was pleased. "Great," he said in a loud voice. "You guys might make it as gunners yet."

The boatswain's pipe screeched through the loudspeaker:

"Attention all gun crews. Attention all gun crews. This is the last drone pass."

Davis and *Wainwright* each released a drone. One was directed at the *Franklin's* bow on the starboard side and one toward the stern to port. The drone coming John's way malfunctioned. It didn't rise. It sped toward the ship's side, scarcely forty feet over the water.

"Get that son-of-a-bitch before she gets here!" John screamed.

"It's coming in low! It's tough to draw a bead on it!" Ski yelled back.

The drone flew through the hail of fire and hit the starboard side just above the waterline, like a flea hitting a giant horse. It exploded and fell into the ocean. *Franklin* cut through the water as though it hadn't been touched.

"Do you suppose those bastards on that destroyer launched that drone low on purpose?" Ski asked.

"Naw. That was a mechanical failure—but it's a lesson." John raised his voice so everyone in the gun crew could hear him. "Jap planes could dive at you like that, so you have to be very accurate, even when they're that low," he said sternly, not realizing that he was making an ominous forecast of things that were soon to come.

"Secure from General Quarters," echoed through the loudspeaker.

John waited until the gun pit was cleared of empty shell casings. Then he went below. When he got to the gunnery compartment Ski was already there, sitting in his bunk washing the stripes on his dress blues with soapy water and a toothbrush.

John pulled himself up to the top bunk just above Ski. When he was settled, he leaned over and said, "Did the ship's dry cleaners close?"

"Naw. I just decided to clean my blues myself. The stripes just need a little touching up."

"Thinking about going on liberty when we hit Panama?" John asked.

"Nope. San Diego," Ski said with a lecherous grin. "There's a lot of pretty girls in 'Diego' and in a week or so we'll be there. I had some time before chow, so I thought I'd get these stripes clean."

John lay back on his bunk and closed his eyes. The gun crew is doing a hell of a lot better, he thought. The three weeks of intensive drills, mostly with life ammunition, seemed to bring them around. A clip hasn't dropped in two weeks and the guys are getting up some speed. He looked at his watch. It was nearly noon. "Let's go down and get in the chow line before it gets too long," he said to Ski.

John waited in the passageway until Ski hung his blues in his locker, then Ski joined him and the two made their way toward the mess hall. They went through one compartment after another filled with bunks full of sailors resting before the call to chow. "Smelly down here," Ski said. "You can sure tell when a ship gets into hot weather."

"Maybe you'd like it better in the infantry," John said with a grin. "Those infantry guys are out in the fresh air *all* the time."

"You sure know how to bring a guy around quick, Gunner," Ski said with a twisted smile. "Well, maybe the smell of sweat isn't so bad after all."

They reached the mess hall. There was almost no one in line yet. A mess cook pushed past them carrying a container filled with freshly washed tablewear. He dropped it heavily on a table at the beginning of the chow line. Ski grabbed tableware and a tray and John followed.

"Pork chops," John said.

"Yeah. They look pretty good," Ski responded.

They filled their trays and sat down at one of the tables.

"Why do dehydrated potatoes always look so gray?" Ski complained.

"If you put gravy over them they don't look so bad," John said with a grin.

"What if I don't like gravy?"

"Then butter them, or just eat them gray," John said. "For me, this beats hell out of cornbread and beans."

"Okay, I tried. I guess I can't rile you today, Gunner," Ski griped. "I'll eat the pork chops and the potatoes, even if they are a crappy gray."

"Let's finish and get back to the gun pits," John said as he sliced into a pork chop. "The crew is getting a hell of a lot better. I want to work with duds this afternoon. Let's see if we can increase their overall speed."

"Goddamned, John, drills with duds again?"

"We need the practice, Buddy."

When are you going to get us a day off?" Ski groused.

"When we get to San Diego," John said with a smile.

"I'm all set for that," Ski said, perked up by the thought. "I get excited just thinking about all those gorgeous girls there."

29 April, 1944
Pacific Ocean
Combat Preparations Fail

Beckley, along with Shoemaker and Day, looked over the edge of the bridge as *Franklin* cleared the last lock in the Panama Canal.

"Well, finally the Pacific," Beckley said. "For me, things always look brighter on the Pacific side."

Shoemaker set a course northwest, past San Salvador and Costa Rica, toward San Diego. Then he asked Beckley to get him the daily conduct report.

"This is disgusting," Shoemaker said as he studied the report. "We have to get more discipline into this crew. If we don't, there might be hell to pay. We could lose a lot of lives."

"Yes, sir," Beckley said. "It's dangerous. We had some difficulties in the crew on the *Lexington*, and we thought that crew was well trained."

"What happened, Chief?" Day asked.

"A lot of guys panicked when they came under fire, sir."

"I've seen the same thing, too," Shoemaker said. "I'm going to do something to try to stop this from ever happening to us." Then he became silent.

Beckley thought he was weighing options.

Finally Shoemaker said, "I'm going to transfer every man who has been disciplined by court martial in the last five months. They're now considered 'undesirables.' When we reach San Diego, I'm getting rid of all of them."

"Things might be changing, sir," Beckley said. "We've had some good reports, especially from the gun crews lately. They seem to be shaping up."

Shoemaker trained his binoculars on the tropical western side of Mexico. "I think I'm going to wait to comment on the gun crews until after this mock attack is over," Shoemaker said in a still skeptical tone.

"Yes, sir. A mock air attack should tell us a lot," Beckley responded.

"This will be our first exposure to combat conditions," Shoemaker said. "After it's over we should know a lot more about how extensive the problems really are."

Beckley looked into the northern horizon. Somewhere up there, Boeing B-25s were bearing down from bases in Southern California to "attack" the *Franklin*.

At 13:30 *Franklin's* radar spotted bogeys.

"Prepare to defend against hostile aircraft!" Shoemaker shouted.

The ship's klaxon clanged. Sirens blared.

"General Quarters! General Quarters!"

"Gun crews! Gun crews! Man your battle stations."

"Pilots! Man your planes. Pilots! Man your planes."

Fighter Squadron Able's engines rumbled to life.

"Show time, gentlemen," Commander Jim Crowley, a seasoned combat pilot, called out as he climbed into his Hellcat. As Flight Leader of Able Squadron, his was the first plane to streak into the sky. The take-offs went smoothly. In less than fifteen minutes twenty-six Hellcats were airborne and raced northwest to engage the enemy. They climbed to twenty-two thousand feet and leveled off there. Crowley was positioning them to surprise the B-25s, hoping to "shoot" them all down before any got through their screen.

#

Back on the *Franklin*, tension mounted. Lookouts squinted toward the horizon through high-powered binoculars, determined to spot planes yet too far away to be sighted. Gunners anxiously awaited the attack, 20-mm and 40-mm loaded with blank shells, ready to fire.

John's 40s were manned and in Condition I—Maximum Readiness—muzzle and breach covers off. Helmets strapped in place. Life jackets tautly secured. Each man in the gun crew was alert and ready. They all knew this was a drill, but despite this, they nervously awaited the test real planes would bring.

John felt his heart pounding in his chest. He was sweating from more than just the warm sunshine. This would be his first chance to see his gun crew perform under what could be considered battle conditions. "In about ten more minutes," he said softly to himself, "we'll find out."

#

"Bogeys! Bogeys!" Crowley screamed. Crowley, a veteran of air battles at Midway and Guadalcanal, had his fighters in excellent positions. They were higher than the bombers and had the sun at their back. The Hellcats attacked when the bombers were almost directly below them.

"Scratch one!"

"Scratch another one!"

"I got one, too!"

"Fly tight. Stay on target!"

The battle went on for twenty minutes. In the end, the Hellcats had nine kills, but six got through the screen.

"Group leader to base," Crowley radioed the *Franklin*. "Nine bogeys scratched. Six got through the screen. Repeat. Six through the screen."

Then he shook his head in disgust. "Goddamn it. We let too many get through."

\#

The B-25s approached for their first bombing run. They came in low and headed right toward the *Franklin's* starboard side, directly toward John's guns.

As they zoomed toward the bow, John shouted, "Commence firing! Commence firing!" His voice was nearly drowned out by the roar of the bombers' engines. The noise was deafening and the blanks fired from the B-25s' 50-caliber guns sounded very real. The bedlam seemed to unsettle John's inexperienced crew.

"Be alert, goddamn it! Stay with 'em! Stay with 'em! Don't let the noise bother you," John shouted.

A clip slipped through Bonin's hands.

John was furious. "Goddamn it, Bonin! Can't you hold anything? You knucklehead. Concentrate! Concentrate!"

"They're coming back!" Belasco shouted.

Another pass over John's 40-mms. Another dropped clip!

"Who the hell dropped it?" John demanded.

"I did!" Jardin shouted.

"Lord, Jardin, concentrate!" John screamed. "These planes are not Japs, sailor. They're *our* planes, goddamn it!"

The B-25s thundered in for a final run. This time John's gun crew worked smoothly. They fired round after round at the B-25s as they roared overhead. There were no dropped clips. Their performance was better, but John knew what would have happened in a real attack. "Not good," he said. "In fact it was poor. If those were Jap bombers, this ship would be burning. Not that it would matter to any of you knuckleheads because you'd have been blown up from the get-go."

John was frustrated. "We need more work. If we don't clean up our act, guys, we're going to get our asses creamed when the planes are Japanese and then bombs are real."

"Okay," he said as he walked toward the ladder to the bridge. "Let's get this gun pit policed up. Get rid of those empty shell casings and clean up the deck. We drill with duds again this afternoon. Take some time to think about what went wrong."

When John was out of sight, Ski said, "Okay, everybody gather around."

Everyone stopped what he was doing and formed around Ski and Lowe, who had joined him.

"You saw the look on John's face when he left the gun pit. He's pissed," Ski said. "Why do you think he's pissed?"

For a moment there was silence. Then Bonin said, "Because we screwed up. What the hell else could it be?"

"Maybe he's worried about his own ass," Garcia said.

"Hell yes, he is," Ski retorted with anger in his voice. "With this fuck-up crew he'd be a damned fool not to be. But let me tell you something—he's worried about you guys, too. He's seen a lot of action—seen a lot of people die. I've come to know John Oxler. He's one of the finest guys I've ever met. He wants to survive this war, but I want you knuckleheads to know that he wants each and every one of us to survive it, too. That's why he gets so damned upset when we screw up like we did today."

"I second that. That's the damned truth," Lowe said.

"I'm going to make a suggestion," Ski said. "I know you guys don't have to follow it. I think we should forget about chow and start training right now."

"Hell, no!" Garcia said. "Bullshit! I'm hungry."

"You're bullshitting yourself, Garcia," Ski retorted. "We can all miss a meal. Let's train right now like we've never trained before, and not because John Oxler wants us to. Let's train because *we* want to. Let's really make this gun crew the best in the fleet, not because we like to *say* we are, but because we *really* are."

"But Ski, I'm hungry as hell," Garcia said.

"Ski stared at Garcia for a long moment. "Would you give up a navy meal and a few hours to have a thousand of your mother's meals and live the rest of your life because you got through the war alive? Is that a good trade?"

Garcia thought for a moment. "Yeah. When you put it that way, Ski, it's a hell of a good trade." He looked at the rest of the gun crew. "You know, guys," he said, "this is the first time we're mustered here because *we* want to be here. For me it's a ticket home. Let's get after it."

"Yeah," Colson chimed in. "Hell, I'm the one that's responsible for my life, not John Oxler. I'm going to train like a son-of-a-bitch. I sure as hell want to get through this goddamned war!"

There was a chorus of agreement. Suddenly John's gun crew came alive. They went into their drills in earnest. They worked on everything John taught them, this time with an energy and urgency that they'd never had before. By the time John returned, their confidence had grown by leaps and bounds. They were going to become a topnotch gun crew, not because John Oxler wanted them to, but because they wanted to come out of the war alive.

CHAPTER EIGHT

1 May, 1944
Berth F, North Island
San Diego, California

Two days later, the *Franklin* steamed into San Diego harbor and docked in Berth F at the Naval Air Station. Soon after the ship secured, the ship's loudspeaker hailed John Oxler: "Gunners Mate John Oxler! Gunners Mate John Oxler! Report to Chief Sullivan in the armory."

When John got to the armory, Sullivan was waiting. "I want you to form a contingent to stand Shore Patrol duty tonight," he said.

"Gee, Chief," John said with a relieved grin, "you scared the hell out of me. I thought it was something important."

"This *is* important," Sullivan said. "The Captain wants the *Franklin* represented ashore by our best people. I'm selecting you to head this contingent. Take Kwatkowski and Lowe and anybody else you want from our division. Get the rest from the First Division if necessary. We need thirty men. You're in charge."

"Sure, Chief," John said, smiling. He was pleased with the compliment and pleased with this assignment. "There's no better place to find out where the girls are than on Shore Patrol duty," he said.

"You're there to keep order," Sullivan snapped. "No girl chasing or anything like that. Just keep sailors in line, especially those from this ship. Captain's very tired of fuck-up behavior. He wants to make a statement with our SPs."

John's smile faded. "Aye, aye, Chief," he said. "I was just kidding about the girls. We'll do a good job."

Early that evening, John and Ski, now both in full Shore Patrol attire, leggings, gunbelt, armband and nightstick, paired up to walk a beat along Third Street. The street was quiet. They patrolled for over an hour without incident.

Then Ski said, pointing to the USO they were about to pass, "Hey, John, how about a cup of 'joe' or something? Man, my dogs are tired."

John laughed. "Ski, do you ever think of anything but your feet or your stomach?"

"Yeah, women. Beautiful, naked women," Ski said with a lecherous grin.

"Anything else?"

"Not if I can help it." Ski's grin broadened. "How about it?"

John shrugged. "A little break sounds good to me, too."

Once inside, John got a Coke, Ski a cup of coffee and the two wandered through the huge room and wound up at the edge of the dance floor. A tall, dark sailor and an attractive, tiny blonde sat at a corner table, kissing when they thought no one was looking. A handful of couples danced dreamily to the recorded music of the Les Brown orchestra, with Doris Day as the vocalist singing, *"I'll see you in my dreams, hold you in my arms..."*

While Ski found a pretty brunette to talk to, John watched the couples on the floor. They were dancing so close they seemed melted together. As they glided by, an image of Diane came into his mind. He remembered how wonderful her body felt when they danced together, how she would put both her arms around the back of his neck and pull herself close to him. He realized he still had some feelings for her. It was easier to put her out of his mind when he was busy, but on a night like this…. He had a swallow of Coke and chewed on the ice. Then he looked away from the dancers to the people standing on the edge of the floor. Sailors were crowded there, trying to pick up local girls. A sailor who looked like he'd had one drink too many tried to hit on a classy blonde who was dressed like a dream. She gave him an icy look and moved away.

"You're not going to make out that way, mate," John muttered.

The people around the floor and the beautiful music diminished his thoughts of Diane. He glanced toward the dance floor again and nearly choked on his coke. There, not ten yards away, was the most beautiful girl he'd ever seen. Wow! What a beauty! His heart began to beat faster. His mouth felt hot and dry despite the ice melting in it.

The girl turned and looked around. Her eyes stopped when they came in contact with John's. She allowed her eyes to focus on him for just a moment, then a smile as elusive as Mona Lisa's began to form and she turned back to the girl standing next to her.

"Sweet Mother of God," John whispered. Had she really looked at him? Was the look what he thought it was? Was it real? His whole body flooded with joy and desire. He couldn't take his eyes off her. Suddenly he realized how foolish he must look, standing there with his mouth open, gaping like a schoolboy. He stopped staring at her and turned away. Come on Buddy, she's out of your league, he thought. Boy, she's gorgeous. I'd give anything to spend an hour with her, just looking into her eyes and dancing in the moonlight. He began staring at her again, hoping she would turn toward him. He longed to talk to her, take her in his arms and dance with her. He knew he looked silly, but he didn't care. All he could think about was for her to turn around again, for just a second. That's all. Just once more. *"Please,"* he begged silently.

She continued in her conversation with the girl beside her, seemingly oblivious to anyone else.

John lowered his head. He picked at his colorful SP armband. *This is what she was probably looking at, he said to himself.* He felt empty inside and scuffed the floor in disgust.

 As John readied to leave, he glanced over at her again, and at that very instant she turned and looked at him. Their eyes met again and locked for a moment. Then slowly she looked away and started to move her slender fingers through her long, dark brown hair. She brushed it back over her shoulder and began to stroke her neck gently. After a brief pause, she let her eyes drift back to John.

He felt a flood of confused emotion. He didn't know whether to acknowledge her or not. He wanted to do something, but what?

She smiled at him again. He felt a surge of passion that he hadn't felt since Diane.

He returned the smile, certain that he looked like a goofy kid.

Just then Ski tugged gently on his arm. "Hey, come on, John," he said. "We better get back on the street."

John looked at him like he'd been awakened from a dream. "What? Huh?"

Ski grinned as he glanced over at the girl. "Very pretty," he said off-handedly. "Come on, we gotta get out of here."

"In a couple of minutes," John pleaded. "I'll meet you at the door in two minutes." His eyes turned back to the beautiful girl.

Her back was to him; she had resumed her conversation with the girl standing next to her. Then she stopped talking, stepped away and walked to the other end of the group of girls she was with. She moved her eyes slowly back to John.

"Okay, John," Ski said, "Come on. You can ogle the girls another time."

"Just give me a couple more minutes, Buddy."

"If you're that taken by her, why don't you go over and introduce yourself? Ask her for her phone number or something," Ski said.

"I can't do that. You don't walk up to a beautiful girl and ask for her name and phone number, just like that," John retorted, as he snapped his finger for emphasis.

"You'll be sorry tomorrow," Ski said, "Faint heart never won fair damsel."

John made a move toward the brunette beauty.

Ski stopped him. "Wait a minute! I goofed. That wasn't good advice. Come on, we've got a job to do. We have to get back on the street—now!"

"For the last two minutes I've been thinking about saying to hell with it and staying right here," John said.

"That's what I thought. You can't do that. That's brig time, partner."

John sighed and nodded his head slowly. "Ski, sometimes you're a pain in the ass, but this time you're right."

John looked back again, then reluctantly followed Ski to the door, wishing all the while that he could come up with an excuse to stay that wouldn't get him into trouble. None came.

When they reached the street, John squared his hat and looked back. "She was the most beautiful girl I've ever seen," he said.

Ski grinned. "Partner, they all look wonderful this time of night. Let's get going before we both get into trouble."

John again looked longingly back in the direction of the USO. "It's not just the time of night, Ski. No way. It was real for both of us. I'm coming back tomorrow night," he said, "and I'm going to find her. Yeah, no matter what, I'm going to find her."

That night he slept better than he had in months. There were no images of Diane in his dreams. There were only images of the mysterious girl at the USO.

John was aroused from his dreams by someone tugging on his arm.

"One more dance," he mumbled, still half asleep. "One more dance…."

Ski laughed. "Not with me, mate."

John opened his eyes. "Damn you, Ski, you just ruined one great dream."

"Sounded like it. Come on, we've got to relieve the watch." He placed a sympathetic hand on John's shoulder. "Hate to drag you away from your dreaming, but duty calls."

"I'll be with you in five minutes," John said, a little irritated.

"You'd better take enough time to let that boner go down," Ski said with a smile. "Lowe and Feinstein might wonder what the hell's going on."

John ignored him. He was reluctant to leave his warm bunk and just as reluctant to admit that the dream was over. Slowly he pulled himself over the edge of his bunk. He tugged on his dungarees and finished dressing, all the while seeing the "girl of his dreams" clearly in his mind.

"Hey, dreamer," Ski said when John joined him, "I didn't think you were going to make it."

John waved him off. "Ski, you better let up a little," he said.

Realizing he might have gone too far, Ski changed the subject. "I heard that Harvey Bundson ran into trouble again last night," he said.

"Bundson? That asshole. He's always in some kind of trouble. What did you hear?" John asked.

"Boatswain in the First Division, Guy Marks, had two hundred bucks stolen right out of his wallet," Ski replied.

"What makes you think Bundson had anything to do with it?"

"He's the only guy I know who's dumb enough to steal from a shipmate, let alone a guy in the First Division," Ski said. "Some of the toughest guys on the ship are up there. What a screwy guy. He's either sick or getting beat up or cheating at cards or trying to swipe something."

"That'll catch up with him. Just wait and see," John said. "That's a lesson right out of my catechism, but it's true."

"Hasn't caught up with him so far. It bothers me to have a revolting guy like that in the crew," Ski said with a look of disgust on his face.

"Why? What the hell do you care?"

"Everything he does or touches turns to shit, John. What's to say that it won't spill all over on us?"

John thought for a moment. "Do you know what my dad would say about a guy like Bundson?"

"What?"

"He'd say, 'That poor son-of-a-bitch is walking under a very black cloud. Some day lightning will flash out of it and strike him.'"

"It sure as hell will if he keeps fucking around with guys in the First Division. You screw with those guys and some dark night when you're not looking, you'll get the deep six. Zip! Over the side you go. Shark food!"

"Naw. Nobody up there's going to do that," John replied. "I don't care how much of a fuck-up he is."

"Why not, John? That tattooed bastard is hostile, foul-mouthed and ugly. You fall down and he tries to pick you up by your wallet. I think he'd steal from his mother if he had a chance. He hasn't got a friend on this ship and he's got a lot of enemies. I'm telling you, I wouldn't want be in his shoes unless I was a strong swimmer."

"No way, Ski. I think you're way out in left field," John said. "Nobody's going to pitch him overboard. When he gets his, he'll cause it himself. It'll be something that drops on him or that he staggers into—he trips and falls into a open hatch or something like that."

"Well, maybe, but I think he'd still better be a real strong swimmer."

They reached the ladder that led down to Able Sponson. John went down the ladder. Ski followed. As he climbed down he said, "Bundson's like a character out of a bad novel. A real loner and those goddamned tattoos he's got make him look even more repulsive. His whole body looks like a walking ad for a whorehouse."

"Well, I can't hold that against him," John said. "Guys in the Navy get tattoos. I almost did once or twice."

"Okay, one or two tattoos," Ski said, "but John, nobody's tattooed like that son-of-a-bitch. Hell, his whole body's *covered* with them! Red hearts with women's names in them. Snakes, tigers, leopards, devils, and ropes tied in square knots around his ankles and wrists. You name it, he's got one."

John chuckled. "Yeah, but what do you care if the guy wants to look like a freak?"

Ski couldn't let go. "I don't, but he's such a shit head. He's even got a flag tattooed on the cheek of his ass."

"On his ass? Now how the hell do you know that?" John asked with a teasing grin.

"Oh, come on, Gunner, " Ski said. "Get off that shit. I was behind him in the shower line a couple of weeks ago."

"Oh, okay," John said, still grinning.

"He acted like he was actually proud of all that crap," Ski said. "Told me he was gonna put 'nother one on'…and 'nother one'…and 'nother one.' He said he that might end up with even ten or twenty more before he was done." Ski paused a moment.

"You're kidding." John said.

"No, I'm not. The problem is, I couldn't see where he would put 'em except on his pecker, and it's only big enough for a very tiny one," Ski said with a huge grin.

John started laughing, a deep belly laugh.

Ski looked at John and began to laugh, too.

"Don't worry, it'll catch up with him someday," John said, after he caught his breath.

"You really think it will?" Ski asked with a touch of doubt in his voice.

"Hell, yes," John said. "Just look at the guy. Nobody can be that screwed up and not come to a tragic end."

John adjusted the breach cover on one of the 40s. "Let's knock this talk off, Ski," he said. "I'm tired of it."

"Yeah, so am I," Ski replied. "But he still bothers the shit out of me. Well, maybe I'll be right—maybe he'll wind up as shark bait and we'll be rid of him."

"Well, I guess stranger things have happened," John said as he began to polish the flash-cap on one of the 40s.

The two young men worked silently for a while.

Finally John said, "A lot of strange things happen, Ski. I think about the war, the Coral Sea, the *Lex* sinking and the *Vincennes* getting shot up—the way my girlfriend dumped me. I never dreamed she'd do that."

John's thoughts went to Diane. He was prepared for her image to come back and bother him, but his mystery girl came into his thoughts instead. There she was before him, just as real as life. She turned her head and looked at him. She brushed the hair from her shoulder. She smiled that beautiful smile….

A smile came over his face….

"Hey, John. You with me, pal?" Ski asked.

"What?" John looked at Ski and smiled sheepishly.

Ski laughed aloud. "Where were you, sailor?"

John smiled broadly. "Awww, I was just thinking."

"About what?" Ski asked.

"Hmmm, everything. Life, the war, girls."

"You mean the gal from the USO, don't you?"

John nodded.

"Ooooh. She put the whammy on you, didn't she?"

"Yeah, she did. I have to find her. I have to see her again, Ski."

"Small chance now," Ski said. "You only saw her for five minutes. You don't know her name. You didn't go over and try to meet her."

"You stopped me, remember?"

"Yeah, because I was worried you'd never come back."

"Oh, come on, goddamn. I'm not an idiot. I would've just spent a few minutes with her."

"Partner, the way you were looking at her I wasn't so sure. I could see you taking her off to Mexico or someplace."BERTH F, NORTH ISLAND, SAN DIEGO

"So now, after you stopped me from getting her name, you're trying to convince me that you saved my ass?" John said with a grin.

"No, Gunner, I'd never try that. You're too smart, but the fact is that you *don't* have her phone number or her address. Nothing."

"I'm going to find her, Ski," John said, the grin now gone. "She and I were meant to be together."

"Oh, come on, Buddy. Get a grip. Do you know what the chances of that are?"

"Hell, yes, Ski. I *know* what the goddamned chances are," John said, with anger in his tone, "but I also know I'm going to find her. You just wait and see."

Ski studied John for a moment. "Okay, I won't screw up your dream. What the hell, there's always a chance. It's a very, very slim chance, but I hope she pops back into your life, you marry her and have five kids and you name the handsome one after me."

"That's a deal, Buddy." John said, shaking Ski's hand and smiling. "Now you just have to help me find her."

CHAPTER NINE

Naval Air Station
San Diego, California
Navy Discipline

It was Tuesday, the third day after the *Franklin* docked. On the bridge, Beckley was in the middle of the four-to-eight watch. The OD had just left to go to the head, and he was almost alone. There were just a few seamen milling around.

Captain Shoemaker appeared in the doorway.

"Captain on the bridge!" Beckley said tersely.

"As you were," Shoemaker ordered.

"Good morning, Chief," Shoemaker said. "You the only rated man up here?"

"Yes, sir."

"Where's the OD?"

"He went down to the head, sir."

"Chief, you've been in the Navy a long time," Shoemaker said slowly. "Sometimes the advice of a chief petty officer is better than that of an admiral. You guys are closer to the crew." He paused and motioned Beckley closer. "What the hell can we do to increase discipline and instill confidence in this crew?"

"I think you're doing everything you can, Captain," Beckley replied.

"But we both know that what we've done so far isn't enough. You saw how they responded to that mock attack. It wasn't very pretty."

"I think most of the crew was upset by that, Captain. I really believe they want to be combat trained, sir. I just don't think they've had enough time together."

"I've heard this business about time a hundred times, Chief, and I haven't accepted it once. But coming from a man who has been in the Navy as long as you have, well maybe I am asking too much."

"If I may, sir, maybe in certain things."

Shoemaker nodded slowly. "Well, you might be right. I guess I can't expect them to become trained overnight. One thing I can do is something I've been considering since we left Norfolk. We've got about one hundred and ninety misfits and malcontents on our log. I'm going to transfer every damned one of them."

Beckley nodded but remained silent.

"Some of these guys are poison," Shoemaker continued. "Let them screw up someplace else—not on the deck of a fleet carrier. We'll get as many of them replaced as we can from the personnel pool here, and we'll pick up the rest in Pearl. Maybe when they're gone we'll have a crew that we can really get into shape. What do you think, Chief?"

"Well, sir, we're going to be shooting at the Japanese soon, and they're going to be shooting back. We'd better be ready. If not, we'll be sliding a lot of men into the ocean in body bags."

Shoemaker looked more determined than ever. "I'll order the paperwork." He looked at Beckley. "I've got another idea, too, Chief," he said. "We can't drill for combat while we're docked, so I'm going to turn *everything* this crew does into a drill."

Beckley glanced at Shoemaker, but didn't comment.

"What do you think, Chief?" Shoemaker asked.

"I really don't know, sir. I've never thought about anything like that."

"It might help us with the discipline problem," Shoemaker said.

"It may, sir, but it sounds a lot like boot camp to me, sir," Beckley ventured.

"Yeah, it does. Where'd you first learn discipline, Chief?"

"From my old man, sir, but boot camp was sure next in line."

Shoemaker rubbed his hand across his chin. "You think the crew might resent the idea?"

"Hard to say, sir. It just might work, but I guess it could boomerang, too."

"I'll take the chance. I'm going to try it, " Shoemaker said.

That morning, word of Shoemaker's in-dock drills went out to the crew.

"Move along smartly."

"Carry yourself erect, sailor."

"Dress it up."

"Be alert."

"Take pride in what you do."

"Swab that deck clean."

"Make that brass shine."

"Do it over and over."

"Combat's coming."

"We'd better be ready."

Beckley watched the goings-on. To his surprise, the crew did look like they were shaping up a little. Maybe the Captain knew what he was doing after all. That's why he's a captain and I'm a chief, he thought.

After he told his crew what he thought Captain Shoemaker was trying to do, John followed orders to the letter. Under the hot California sun, guns were cleaned, assembled and then disassembled. Then they were torn down and put back together again. Men polished parts until they reflected the bright sunlight. Ammunition lockers were cleaned until they were spotless. Everything was put in its place.

"Clean 'em."

"Oil 'em."

"Check everything."

"Do it again."

"Until you can load 'em in your sleep."

"John, this is crazy," Bonin complained. "I've polished this goddamned breach three times today. Look at it sparkle. Nothing can make it shine more."

"Bonin," John said as he pulled himself onto the gun platform, "the Captain knows these goddamned guns are clean. This is not about cleaning guns and gun pits. This is discipline. The Captain's trying to get the crew disciplined."

"Why does he have to discipline me? I'm not a fuck-up. I've never been on report, not anything like that."

"Yeah, John, neither have I," Belasco added.

"I know," John replied, "none of you guys have, but that's not the point. There are some fuck-ups in this crew, and I think the captain is using this to teach them discipline. It has nothing to do with you guys personally."

"Then why in the hell do *we* have to keep cleaning and polishing something that's already cleaned and polished?" Bonin asked.

"Because you're part of the crew," John answered. "What would the screw-ups think if they found out that we were down in the 'gedunk' bar drinking Cokes and eating cookies while they were working their butts off?"

"Okay, I understand, but this is still a pain in the ass," Bonin replied.

"Think about it this way," John said. "Would you want a bunch of fuck-ups protecting your flanks when this ship comes under fire?"

Silence.

"Hang with it, guys," John said, "we'll all have a beer and laugh about this one day soon."

"Maybe we will," Bonin said, "but for now it's still a pain in the ass."

"Yeah, I know it is now, but it could become a hell of a lot bigger pain when all the chips are on the table later on," John emphasized.

Even while John was implementing the Captain's orders, his thoughts drifted back to his mystery girl. "I'm telling you, Ski, it's my destiny," he said as he stopped to wipe oil from his hands. I was meant to be with her and I'm going to find her."

Ski shook his head. "Well, I'll tell you again that it's crazy. I have to say it's one chance in a million."

"I'm going to find her, Ski."

"Man, you got it bad," Ski said. "You want my advice, go out and get laid. A good piece of ass will solve your whole problem."

"No way. I'm going to find her." He paused. "You coming with me?"

"Sure, I'm with you, Buddy."

That night, as dusk began to settle on San Diego, John and Ski stood on the corner of Third Street. The air was warm. The sun, sinking into the Pacific horizon, tinged everything with a golden glow. Sailors were milling around everywhere, pushing here, moving there, all desperate to enjoy a few hours away from the rigors of Navy life.

They watched the sunset for a while, then headed to the USO. It was early and the place was still nearly deserted except for a handful of sailors standing around in the lounge.

John looked around quickly and said, "She isn't here yet, Ski. Let's go out and get a burger."

They walked along to Bombay Joe's, a well-known sailor's hangout. Just as they got to the swinging doors, two Shore Patrolmen forged through the doors dragging a sailor. He was bleeding from a large cut over his eye and only half-conscious.

"It's our friend Bundson," Ski said, not seeming surprised.

"What happened to him?" John asked one of the SPs.

"Ahh, he pissed some guy off twice his size. The guy let him have it."

"Is he under arrest?" Ski asked hopefully.

"Naw, he's not drunk, just woozy," the SP replied. "We're going to take him back to his ship. Do you guys know him?"

"Yeah. He's off the *Franklin*, Berth F, North Island," John said.

"Thanks," the SPs said as they shoved Bundson into the paddy wagon.

John hurried his steps to get away from the ugly scene. "Maybe the Shore Patrol will catch him again for something more than getting his ass kicked," he said.

"Yeah, and maybe they'll throw him in the brig and toss away the key," Ski said as he and John walked into Bombay Joe's.

An hour later they were back on the street heading to the USO. They pushed through a sea of white-hatted sailors as they went. There were a few girls sprinkled in, too, some who were very pretty.

Ski spotted an attractive redhead walking toward them. He let out a loud wolf whistle. "Boy, what a lay she'd be," he said. "She's got no idea of the wonderful things I could do for her."

As she approached, Ski said, "Hi, Honey."

The beautiful girl tossed her head and hurried past, without so much as a look.

"Looks like she's not interested in the wonderful things you can do for her," John said with a grin. "At least not tonight she isn't!"

"Damn," Ski said. "I'm so horny I could honk, and I'm out here looking for a girl for you."

"Maybe we'll find one for you, too."

"Yeah. And maybe the war's going to end tomorrow and I'm going to be the first guy discharged. I'd sure like to have that redhead in bed for an hour or two."

When they reached the USO the music had started. There were a number of couples on the dance floor, moving slowly to the mellow notes of *Stardust*, with Hoagy Carmichael singing "*Sometimes I wonder why I spend the lonely night dreaming of a song....*"

John and Ski searched through the crowd, trying to find John's mystery girl. They separated and moved along the edges of the dance floor, looking carefully at each girl there.

A flash of brown hair. A slender neck. A beautiful figure. No, not her.

After they looked for a while, they realized that she just wasn't there.

"Let's go out for some air," John suggested. "Maybe she'll be here when we come back."

They left the USO and as they walked down Third Street John looked idly into the windows of the bars and restaurants they passed.

"She's here somewhere. I feel it in my bones."

Later they went back to check the USO again. They looked and looked. The girl was nowhere to be seen.

The next morning John got up, put his soap and shaving gear into his bucket and went down to the head to shower. When he got there, Ski was already shaving.

"How you doing?" he asked Ski.

"Fine. How are you?"

John shrugged. "I've felt better."

"We could've had some fun last night, Buddy," Ski said. "We both wasted our liberty. We didn't even dance once."

"I know Ski," John said. "I'm sorry, but thanks a lot for going with me. I just wasn't interested in dancing with anyone else."

Ski smacked his forehead with his open palm. "You mean with all those beautiful girls there, you didn't so much as want to hold one of them in your arms? You didn't want to breathe in one's perfume? Try to get in one's panties? I saw at least three great-looking chicks I wanted to make a move on."

"Why didn't you?"

"Hell, Buddy, I made a promise to you."

"Look, Ski, I just didn't want to look for anybody else. I don't care how crazy this makes me sound."

"I'm not going to comment on that, Gunner." Ski said.

"Why the hell not?"

"I might get in a peck of trouble."

From his post on the bridge Beckley, watched Shoemaker as he huddled with Commander Day and the rest of his staff.

"Gentlemen, we have got to keep pushing hard," Shoemaker said. "I think we're making some progress."

"With all due respect, sir," Day said, "these men need a little relief. I think we're pushing them too hard."

Shoemaker frowned. He paused, apparently thinking about what Day just said.

"Well, maybe you're right, Dave," he said, his voice registering both frustration and resignation. "Okay. We're between a rock and a hard place. If we push too hard we might burn them out. Is that what you're saying?"

"Sir," Day said, "I think the men are working hard and we're making progress. Not as much or as fast as we'd like," he continued as he glanced at the other officers in the room and got some supporting nods, "but we're making progress. Why don't we reward men who *do* perform consistently with some additional time ashore?"

Shoemaker looked at Day curiously. For a moment, he was doubtful. "The Navy says work 'em and then work 'em harder," he said. "But maybe I have to look at your idea." He rubbed his chin and stared out over the bay. After awhile he said, "Okay. Maybe incentives will help. Let's try them once, today, to see if they work. I'll try anything once. We have to get these problems solved, flank speed. The Japs are getting brutal—tougher than hell—the closer we get to Tokyo."

News about Shoemaker's extra incentives spread like wildfire. Everybody in the crew knew they could earn an extra night of liberty for more efficient efforts. Men moved quicker, performed sharper, volunteered for additional duties. No one reacted to this news with greater enthusiasm than John Oxler. "Boy, I'll do anything to get more time to look," he said to Ski. "I'll do a backflip off the flight deck for more liberty if that's what's necessary."

John, Ski and the rest of John's gun crew worked hard all day long. They cleaned, oiled, sanded, wire brushed and polished what they had already cleaned, oiled, sanded, wire brushed and polished. By 16:00 their guns and their gun pit were spotless.

Sullivan was impressed. He congratulated John and his crew. Then he took John aside and said, "I heard the scuttlebutt about your 'mystery' girl." He paused, lit a cigarette and nodded. "You and your guys earned the extra liberty," he said with a grin. "Good luck. I hope you all find what you're looking for."

That evening, as soon as they could get off the ship, John and Ski went ashore. On the bus headed for the downtown area, John started to feel desperate. "My time's running out," he said, "I've got to find her soon, Ski."

Ski nodded. "Yeah, I know the pressure you're feeling. I feel a little of it, too." Ski paused and adjusted his hat. "I hate to say this again, John, but could this whole thing be a dream?"

"No, absolutely not!" John said, his voice firm and determined.

"But let's face it, Buddy. How real is it? You got a casual glance. She gave you a little smile or two. That's not much to go on, Buddy. What happens if we don't find her tonight? What happens when we ship out of here?"

John felt doubt gnaw at him. His stomach tensed but his belief remained strong.

"It's real, Ski," he said. "I'll find her before we ship out."

When they got downtown they looked everywhere. They checked the USO. They checked people walking down the street. They wandered through the department stores, looked into shops and restaurant windows. They didn't find her. It got dark and they decided to check the USO again.

"If I'm ever going to find her, it will probably be there," John said.

When they got back to the USO, people were lined up, waiting to go inside. John and Ski fell into line. As they inched slowly forward, John looked carefully at every girl around. He didn't see her, anywhere. They neared the front door, pushed along by people who had crowded in behind them. When they reached the door, John looked into the vestibule. He searched the corners, peeked toward the dance floor. She wasn't there. "I'm tired and I feel bad," he said as they moved through the doorway.

"I know what you mean," Ski replied. "My dogs are barking, too. All I want is a cold drink and a soft chair."

They walked toward the hatcheck counter. "Another goddamned line," John said as he shuffled behind Ski and they edged closer to the counter. When they got there, Ski checked his hat. Then John handed his hat to the hatcheck girl. When he turned around, there was his mystery girl, standing right in the line behind. The hatcheck girl tried to hand John his check. She couldn't get his attention.

John tried to say something but nothing came out. "I...I've been looking for you for two days," he finally managed to stammer. He took a step forward. He could see from her expression that she was just as startled and happy as he was. She smiled that beautiful smile.

"Your check, sailor," the girl insisted.

Ski took the check and handed it to John. "Here's your check, Gunner," he said with a huge grin.

"Oh, thanks, Ski," John said as he took the ticket. "I'll hook up with you later, Buddy." He turned back to his "mystery" girl. "Can I get you a Coke?"

She shook her head. "You can ask me to dance though," she said.

John was ecstatic. Her voice was the voice of an angel. Wonderful! He'd found her! He was about to dance with her! Feelings of affection and passion resonated through his whole body.

They moved to the dance floor just as the haunting strains of *Bewitched, Bothered and Bewildered* floated through the room. The beautiful music sent feelings of happiness and delight cascading through his body. He could scarcely believe what was happening. He realized he'd never had these kinds of feelings before. He looked over her shoulder toward the edge of the floor and caught Ski's eyes for a moment. Ski's grin was jubilant. His arms were extended above his head, his hands clasped in a victory signal.

John smiled and nodded. Then he pressed his cheek more firmly against the lovely girl's cheek. Her perfume was delicate and enticing. The scent filled his nostrils and sent a wave of desire through him. He pressed her even closer. She responded by moving her hand from his shoulder to the back of his neck. They danced effortlessly together, as if they'd been dancing for years.

The music ended.

"Now I'd like that Coke," she said, holding onto his arm.

John got them each a Coke and they walked toward the terrace, sipping their drinks as they went.

When they reached the door, John put the Cokes on a table and took both of her hands. He looked at her. Her eyes were brown, very deep and soft. He drew her to him. "You're beautiful," he said.

Her eyes sparkled and she smiled.

"You know, ever since we first met, I had the feeling I knew you." John smiled sheepishly. "But I don't even know your name."

She laughed softly. "I guess you don't. And I don't know yours. It hasn't seemed to matter," she said.

"I'm John."

"I'm Sandra."

"It's wonderful to meet you, Sandra," John said. He extended his hand and she took it. The warmth from her hand sent waves of passion through him.

"Call me, Sandy."

"It's good to finally meet you. You can't imagine how hard I've been looking for you."

He ushered her through the terrace doors. The pungent smell from a rose bush at the edge of the railing filled the air—a sweet fragrance on a night that was even sweeter.

The terrace was nearly deserted. There were only a couple of sailors playing ping-pong. John steered Sandy to the terrace railing. They looked out over the lights of San Diego toward the ocean. Stars were glistening and there wasn't a cloud in the sky. They stood together for a few moments, saying nothing. The warm spring air, the scent of rose blossoms, with Sandy standing next to him—it was too perfect to risk spoiling with words.

John found what was happening to him hard to believe. He'd fallen in love with Sandy from across a room. Now, having danced with her, he was even more in love with her.

"I just...I just can't believe it's true," he finally said.

"What?" she asked

"That I've found you."

"I know, for me, too," Sandy said.

Just then, *Some Enchanted Evening* came drifting through the open French doors. John raised his arms toward Sandy. She smiled and moved close to him. The feel of her slender body pressing against his sent a shiver through him and there, behind the fragrant rose bush, they waltzed to the beautiful melody, as John softly sang snatches of the lyrics in Sandy's ear…"*once you have found her, never let her go….*"

When the USO closed, John and Sandy walked along the edge of the harbor. They held hands. The tide brushed against the breakers. A balmy breeze drifted in from the Pacific. The moon cast a golden glaze across the water….

"So which one of those is yours?" Sandy asked, gesturing toward the silhouettes of ships docked at North Island.

"The *Franklin*," John said. "It's the big carrier in the sixth dock. The one next to the crane."

She counted with her finger and nodded. "Have you been on other ships?" she asked, hesitantly pointing to the battle ribbons and gold battle stars attached to John's uniform above his breast pocket.

"Yeah," he replied. "Three."

"Can you tell me about them?"

"I was on the carrier *Lexington* when she was sunk in the battle of the Coral Sea. Then I was on another carrier, the *Saratoga*, for eight months. After that I was on a cruiser, the *Vincennes* for a while. A Jap battleship shot her up north of Rabaul. Then I was assigned to the *Franklin*."

Sandy nodded sadly. "I thought that might be the case," she said.

"Let's not talk about any of that tonight," John said quickly. He drew her toward him. "I just want to talk about you, about us."

He tilted her head up and kissed her. She responded to his kiss. Passion consumed

John. He moved his hand gently over her breast. He felt her tremble.

"Umm," she moaned softly. Their kisses grew more urgent. Still, when he tried to go further, she stopped him.

"It's too soon," she said, as she gently lifted his hand from her breast to her lips and kissed each fingertip.

They held each other closely. Time slipped by. Finally John turned and looked toward the *Franklin*. "I have to go now," he said.

She nodded. "I know. I feel like Cinderella," she whispered. "I don't want you to go. I want to see you again."

"I want to see you, too," John said. "Tomorrow night?"

"Can you get ashore?"

"Yes, I can. I earned a pass tonight, but I've got liberty tomorrow night."

"I'll be at the USO waiting," she said.

"Tomorrow night," he promised.

They parted with one of the most passionate, lingering kisses John had ever experienced.

5 May, 1944
Ready Room
USS Franklin

At dawn, the sun came up through a layer of thin clouds, casting radiant golden rays across San Diego Harbor. The morning air was filled with the soothing warmth that blessed southern coastal cities in California. At 06:30, Beckley and Lieutenant Zimler met for coffee in the ready room. They'd set aside the traditional barrier that existed between officers and enlisted men and were now close friends. When they had conversations about the *Franklin*'s problems, they had always been open and honest with each other. They continued to be troubled about many of the things that were happening.

"The aircrews aren't efficient enough yet," Zimler said, as he stirred powdered cream into his coffee. "I can't imagine how we're going to react when the Japs are shooting real bullets. In a couple of days we're going out for air combat exercises. I wonder if we're even ready for that."

"Yeah. There are still some glitches," Beckley agreed.

"This isn't the Navy I'm used to," Zimler said. "On this ship, for some reason, I'm always wondering what the hell is going to happen next."

"The captain thinks it's just a lack of training and discipline," Beckley replied, "but I'm not so sure. That stuff about a jinx or something like that, keeps popping into my mind."

"I don't want to even think about a jinx," Zimler said.

"But how else can you explain it, sir?"

"I can't, Chief. It's beyond me," Zimler said. "Maybe things will change."

"I hope so, sir."

Beckley left the ready room troubled by his conversation with Zimler. He climbed up to the flight deck and was headed for the bridge when he heard his name called.

It was John Oxler.

"John, how'd it go with the girl ashore?" he asked as John caught up to him.

John looked at him in amazement. "You know about that?"

A hint of a smile crossed Beckley's face. "I'm a chief, remember? I'm paid to know everything about everything."

John told Beckley that he'd found his girl. "It was…it was like out of a dream, Beck. Perfect."

"That's great, John," Beckley responded, but John could see he was upset about something.

John looked at him closely. "Something bothering you, Beck?" he asked.

"Aw, I just wish things were working out better with the crew," Beckley replied. "How do you think your crew will do, John?"

John hesitated. "I think we're going to be okay, Beck," he said. "We're coming around—getting better—but you know how hard it is to guess what guys will do in combat. You just can't be sure. At least I've never been able to."

"That's a fact," Beckley said. "Sometimes the biggest, strongest guys—guys you think will handle everything—crumble and hide. Then there's the little guy you never hear from. He stands tall and surprises the hell out of you."

John chuckled ironically. "Yeah, and sometimes even the little guys run and hide," he said.

Beckley shook his head as though he was trying to dispel his pessimism. "So tell me about finding your girl, John."

"Ski and I found her in the USO. I checked my hat, turned around and there she was right behind me."

"Just standing behind you in line?" Beckley asked getting interested in John's story.

"Yeah, I couldn't believe it. After we met, we danced until the USO closed. Then we took a walk along the bay. I've found her, Beck. She's the one."

"John, you only met her last night. Isn't that rushing things?"

"No, it's not. If you only knew what I went through to find her."

"Okay, you had a tough time finding her, but how much can you know about a girl in a few hours?"

"It's hard to explain, Beck. There's a part of me that says this couldn't be happening but there's a bigger part that says it's real and wonderful."

"John, we're only going to be here for a few more days—four or five at the most," Beckley said. "A couple of those days are going to be spent in drills off the coast. Then we're headed for combat and we may be out there a long time. Think about that. What girl is going to wait for a guy for two or three years, wondering when he's coming home or *if* he's coming home at all?"

"Yeah," John said. "I know. I know. But Sandy's different. I feel it deep inside. I think she'd wait for me."

"John, you're my oldest friend on this ship. I hate to say this, but do you know how many times I've heard that song?"

John thought for a minute. "Probably a lot of times, but this is different. You wait and see."

"I hope so, for your sake. But I remember the stacks of letters you used to get from that girl back home. Then you told me she jilted you. You don't want that to happen again. That's tough to take twice in a row."

"This girl's different, Beck."

"That's what they all say. Anyhow, be careful. Remember, when things seem too good to be true, it's usually because they *are*."

John thought about Beckley's cautious words the rest of the afternoon. Sometimes they made him angry, but most of the time he realized Beck was just trying to be a good friend. But he was wrong this time, damn it!

John slapped Ski on the shoulder as he walked past him, headed for the ladder topside. "I'll see you later, Buddy," he said, "I'm going ashore."

"Boy, are you lucky, John," Ski said with a wistful grin. "You must have a guardian angel or something."

John grinned. "I don't know about the guardian angel but I've got an angel waiting for me out there tonight."

"Man, what happened last night is hard to believe," Ski said. "I thought you were dreaming."

"I was. My dream just came true, that's all," John said, his grin widening with happiness.

When John arrived at the USO, Sandy was waiting for him out front. She was even prettier than the night before. She was wearing a simple, blue summer dress, her long hair shining in the setting sun, her smile inviting.

"Shall we go in and dance?" John asked, as he hurried to her.

"I have a better idea," she said with an impish smile.

"A better idea?"

"Come with me," she said, leading him by the hand. She led him down Third Street. "Close your eyes," she said when she stopped.

"What?"

"Close your eyes," she insisted.

"Okay," he said, closing his eyes.

She led him several more steps and then stopped. "Ta-daaa."

He opened his eyes. "A car? Where in the world did you get it?"

She was holding the keys up. Then she put them in his hand. He opened the passenger door for her and she eased into the front seat. Then he closed the door and slipped into the driver's seat. As he began to pull away from the curb, she slid across the seat and rested her hand on his shoulder. "It's my uncle's car. I'm spending a couple of weeks with him and my aunt," she explained.

Sandy suddenly realized that John was driving with a definite destination in mind. "Where are we going?"

"Oh, just to a nice spot up the coast," he said.

"Really? How do you know what's on the coast?"

"I was in boot camp here," he said.

"Gosh, it's beautiful," Sandy said as they drove into a wooded cove near La Jolla.

John eased the car into a secluded area and parked. Tall spruce trees, silhouetted against a nearly full moon created a mysterious, romantic ambience. The soothing sound of the surf cascading against the shore added to the enchantment. It was dark and still. The only sounds were the surf, the wind and the occasional screeching of seagulls. Through the trees they could see the deep, black void of the Pacific.

John turned off the engine, but left the key on so the radio would continue to play— the soft, romantic sounds of Glenn Miller's band. He looked at Sandy. "You're lovely," he said as he leaned forward and kissed her.

She responded to his kiss.

He kissed her more passionately, then softly kissed her closed eyelids, and the tip of her nose. He held her close. He felt her firm breasts pressing against his chest. They sat quietly in each other's arms for a long while. Then John moved back and looked into her eyes. "Sandy," he said. "I...I'm still afraid this is a dream."

She smiled. "I know," she said softly. "Me, too."

John gently touched Sandy's cheek. He was surprised to find moisture there. "You're crying," he said. "You're sad. What did I do?"

She smiled. "I'm not sad. I'm happy."

"And *that's* why you're crying?"

"Yes," she said after a moment. "Being this happy makes me sad," she said. "I don't want this to end."

"I don't either," John whispered.

There was a pause. Both were lost in their thoughts. The only sound was the muffled roar of waves breaking onto the shore. John looked out the window. The huge trees rustled in the wind. The stars sparkled above. He rolled down the window slightly. A breeze carrying the smell of spruce and pine filtered in.

"What's going to happen, John?" Sandy finally asked. "What you told me last night about the action you've been in...it frightened me. What if something should happen to you, John?"

John took her into his arms and held her tightly. "Don't worry, Sandy. I'm going to be all right. Now that I've found you, nothing can happen to me."

"How can you be so sure of that?"

"I'm just sure, that's all."

Sandy lifted her finger to his lips. "I know *you* feel sure," she said, "but for me, everything about the war is uncertain and frightening. My brother Robert's in the infantry, fighting somewhere in Europe. Sometimes we don't hear from him for weeks." Tears came into her eyes again. "We worry about him all the time. Where he is? Is he okay? What's he's doing? When will we see him again? It's all so scary." She paused and touched John's cheek. "Don't you see? I'm afraid to fall in love with you, John," she said. "I don't think I can take the worry and uncertainty we have for Robert twice...."

"But Sandy, I'm not leaving yet," John said, desperate to reassure her. "Except for a couple of days of combat maneuvers, I'll be around at least another three or four days."

"And then?"

John shook his head. "No one knows the answer to that," he said sadly. "When we leave San Diego, we go to the Pacific and the Fifth Fleet."

"And then?"

"We'll be in combat. But I've been in combat before. A lot of it, and I came out all right. With a girl like you waiting for me, I just *know* I'll be okay."

"John, that doesn't sound reasonable. How could I possibly keep you safe?"

"Love protects people, Sandy. A guy has to have someone to live for, to fight for, and to come home to. That's what keeps guys safe." John kissed the top of Sandy's head. "Don't be afraid. Your brother will come back safe, and I'll come back safe, too," he promised.

Her eyes glistened with tears. She looked at him. "Will you?"

"You bet I will."

Then Sandy kissed him, tenderly at first, then more passionately.

John responded to her kiss. They held each other tightly, like two people trying to blot out everything but each other. John covered Sandy's cheeks and neck with kisses. She kissed John that way too. Sheltered by the shadows of the trees and sounds of the surf, they both became lost in their deep affection. Concern for the war drifted away. Their only thoughts were of the love they were feeling for each other. Nothing else mattered.

Clouds slowly rolled in from the ocean and shaded the moon. The darkness deepened. They both knew the evening would have to end soon.

"Sandy," John said.

Sandy nodded and gripped his hand. "I know," she said sadly. "It's time to go."

John kissed her gently on the cheek. "Gee, I thought it would be easier tonight. It was hard to say goodbye last night, but I feel so much closer to you now. How do I say good-bye? I...I don't want to leave here." He hugged her. She hugged him back.

"Neither do I," she whispered. John pushed himself up in the seat. He looked through the windshield at the glitter of the moon on the water. "I'm wondering why this night can't go on," he said. "This damned war screws up peoples' lives." He kissed Sandy again with a greater depth and complexity than any kiss that came before it. It was filled with a deepening commitment and an even deeper disquietude.

They drew apart.

John turned on the ignition and touched the starter. The engine jumped to life and, a moment later, the beautiful cove receded into the night.

The next day, Sandy came to North Island to see John off. He'd given her the time of the *Franklin's* departure and knew she was coming. Sullivan gave him a half an hour to go down on the dock and say goodbye.

Beckley watched John go down the gangway and then saw John and Sandy embrace. The sight filled him with happiness. She's beautiful, he thought. I don't care what I said to John yesterday, that's a beautiful scene. I hope she turns out to be exactly the girl he thinks she is—in love with him as much as he is with her.

"Time to get back aboard, sailor," one of the *Franklin's* SPs on the dock cautioned.

John nodded to the SP and gave Sandy one last kiss. Then, without taking his eyes off her, John moved up the gangway. Sandy waved until he disappeared into the hangar deck. She turned to leave, and as she did, she took a handkerchief from her purse and wiped away tears.

"John," Ski called out when John appeared in their compartment. "Where were you? I was beginning to be concerned."

"Ski. Believe me, I'm not going to jump ship. Besides, we'll be back in a couple of days," John said.

"I'm happy I was wrong about finding your mystery girl," Ski said. "What I thought would be a nightmare turned into a beautiful dream."

John put his hands on Ski's shoulders. "Even more than that, Ski. She's wonderful. I think I want to spend the rest of my life with her."

Ski fanned his hand in front of his face. "Whoa, that's a little too much for me," he said. He paused. "Chief Sullivan was here looking for you a few minutes ago. Asked me to tell you he wanted to see you as soon as possible."

"Oh? Did he say why?"

"No. Just that it was important."

"Hey, Chief, what's the word?" John asked as he entered the armory.

"We've got some work to do, John," Sullivan said. "Captain transferred a bunch of men a couple of days ago and we took on a bunch of replacements."

"Did I lose any?"

"None from your regular crew. In fact you gained one man, a veteran Seaman First Class, Leon Arnold. Some of the other gun crews lost front-line men. You just lost three men from your back-up pool."

"Did I get them replaced?"

"Yeah. You got a mess cook and two guys from the supply division."

"These guys got any experience on 40s?"

"From his record, Arnold has. The back-ups don't."

"Well, it's important to get them all trained, especially the back-ups," John said. "You always hope you never have to use them but they better be ready if they're needed."

"Exactly, John. The Captain wants all new men trained, pronto," Sullivan said. "I suggest you, Ski and Lowe work with them on an individual basis for as long as it takes."

"Roger, Chief, we'll get to it this afternoon," John replied.

"Time's getting very short, John," Sullivan said. "Be damned sure these new men take their training seriously. We need to be fully prepared—we're going to be in the war before we know it."

John swallowed hard. "They'll all be ready when the time comes, Chief."

CHAPTER TEN

13 May, 1944
Combat Maneuvers
300 Miles WSW of California

Franklin was steaming in open waters, three hundred miles southwest of San Diego. It was a warm, cloudless morning. The ocean was calm. It stretched for miles like a giant blue piece of porcelain.

On the bridge, Beckley was at the helm and Shoemaker and Day were standing beside him, binoculars in hand. It was five minutes before the beginning of combat exercises. The entire air wing would participate. The drills would be as close to the real thing as an exercise could get.

"Steady on course, Chief, the maneuvers are set to start any minute," Shoemaker said.

"Aye, sir."

Shoemaker trained his glasses out into the distance. "The crew's a little bit shorthanded now," he said to Day as he scanned the horizon. "We'll train the men we got in San Diego and get the rest of our replacements when we get to Pearl Harbor. They promised me the men that come aboard in Pearl Harbor would be veteran seamen who will require very little training to fit in."

Just as Shoemaker finished his sentence, the klaxon sounded and the crew was called to battle stations:

"General Quarters! General Quarters!"

"All hands, man your battle stations!"

"Pilots, man your planes!"

Planes wheeled into takeoff positions on the flight deck. Wings were folded down and locked into place. Engines roared. Propellers whirred. Gun crews rushed to their battle stations. Fire-fighting stations were manned and ready. Emergency crews were standing by. A state of excited expectation hovered over the *Franklin*.

Beckley felt it. For the first time since he'd been aboard, he felt good about what was going on. He could see cohesion, cooperation and discipline. Everything was going smoothly. The ship's radar scanned the distant skies. Flight operations were underway. Gun crews were in place. Antiaircraft guns pointed up and ready.

On the flight deck, planes zoomed into the sky. Hellcats first, Helldivers and Avengers followed. They climbed sharply, circled and locked into tight formations. Fighters maneuvered for positions to attack each other. Bombers and torpedo bombers readied to launch attacks using the ship as a target. There was a maze of activity in the air above the *Franklin*.

"Everything's looking great, Captain," Beckley said with confidence. "Looks like we're ready for this."

Suddenly a huge explosion jolted the *Franklin*. Concussions from the blast vibrated through the bridge. Beckley was shaken, but recovered quickly and looked astern.

"What the hell was that?" Shoemaker said, steadying himself against the handle of the ship's telegraph.

"Two Hellcats collided in mid-air just off the fantail, sir." Beckley said.

Shoemaker rushed to the port side of the bridge and looked aft. Day, who had been in the navigator's shack, rushed in. They watched the twisted fireball that a few seconds earlier had been two sleek fighters. It careened down toward the sea.

Beckley scoured the sky. "I don't see any chutes, sir."

The flaming wreckage crashed into the ocean less than a hundred yards from the ship's starboard side. The ugly smell of burning oil and gasoline filtered onto the bridge.

"God," Beckley said in shock and dismay. "Nobody got out of that, Captain."

Shoemaker seemed stunned. Then he shouted, "Goddamn it! Halt the maneuvers! Order planes to return to base."

He turned to Beckley. "Come to course 270," Chief. We've got to get those planes down."

"Aye, sir, 270." Beckley replied as he spun the ship's helm hard to the right.

As the ship came about, Joe Taylor, the Air Officer, rushed onto the bridge. "I can't figure out what the hell happened," Taylor said. "We've practiced takeoff procedures nearly every day for the last three months."

"Well, something got screwed up," Shoemaker barked, his fists clenched. "Somebody obviously forgot where he was in the pattern."

"How in the hell can you forget where you are in pattern?" Taylor asked. "Maybe it was something else."

"Goddamned rotten luck, maybe," Shoemaker said. "Just when we thought things were smoothing out."

Zimler landed his Avenger and pulled himself out of the cockpit. He was distressed and angry. "How the hell did that happen?" he asked an air crewman when he dropped to the flight deck.

"I don't know, sir, I didn't see it," the crewman replied.

Lieutenant Chamberlain, the Protestant chaplain, approached to try to comfort him. Zimler waved him away. "Not now, Chaplain. Please."

The chaplain stepped back and lowered his eyes.

After Zimler moved past, he had a change of heart and stepped back.

"Chaplain."

"Yes, Lieutenant?"

"Did you know Lieutenant Weil?"

"Yes," Chamberlain replied, "I did. I met him at the commissioning ceremonies. He was often at Sunday services."

"He had a very strong belief in God. We talked about religion sometimes. I…I think it would be important to him if you could contact his family. He was a great pilot. Dedicated, smart, and very brave."

"Of course. I'll make special contact with the families of both men, Commander," Chamberlain said. "Are you okay?"

"Yeah, at least I think so."

"If I can help you, please come and see me. Anytime."

Seeing two close friends die such horrible deaths had shaken Zimler, but he wasn't ready for a chaplain. What he really needed was a friend. Someone who had been there before, someone who'd felt the devastation of a shipmate's death, who could understand the sadness he felt. He summoned Beckley.

"Chief Petty Officer Beckley," the loudspeaker blared. "Lay down to the officer's wardroom."

Beckley was startled. He glanced at the boatswain's mate on watch.

"Who is it?" he asked.

"Lieutenant Zimler, Chief."

Beckley looked at the captain.

Shoemaker nodded.

When Beckley got to the wardroom, he found Zimler sitting in a chair staring straight ahead.

"Sir," Beckley said, as he slipped into a seat across the table.

Zimler jerked his head as though he had been off somewhere. "What crappy, goddamned luck," he said. "What a hell of a way to die. Off the coast of California in a fucking collision."

Beckley was silent.

"I was in formation behind the collision, Beck," Zimler said sadly. "I saw it coming. I tried to warn them but I was too late." He paused and took a deep breath. "It breaks your heart to be so helpless—you see a collision like that and you can't do a goddamned thing about it. I knew both men well. One was Lieutenant Weil."

"Yes, sir. I remember him from the Air Medal he got at the commissioning."

"He was a close friend. I knew him as well as I do you, Beck."

Zimler shook his head and pushed himself up straighter in his chair. "We were trained to fight an enemy. That's our job and our duty. Good Lord! Why did they have to die like this?"

Beckley listened; he knew that was what Zimler needed right then.

"Weil and I made a pact just last night, " Zimler said angrily. "We promised each other we'd get together and celebrate when the war ended. Goddamn. I wish there was something I could have done."

"It was an accident, sir. I don't think there was anything anyone could do," Beckley said.

"There's been too many fucking accidents," Zimler growled. "Too many goddamned mistakes."

Beckley wanted to say something that would help Zimler with his anger and grief. "They didn't die in combat, sir," he said. "But I don't think they died in vain. They were doing their duty. They died bravely, valiantly." He paused. "Maybe Shakespeare said it best when he said…

> *Cowards die many times before their deaths;*
> *The valiant never taste of death but once.*
> *Of all the wonders that I yet have heard,*
> *It seems to me most strange that men should fear;*
> *Seeing that death, a necessary end, will come when it will come.*

"Shakespeare, huh?" Zimler asked.

"Yes, sir, *Julius Caesar*."

"It's also a lot of bullshit, Beck. Sorry, but those men were fighter pilots. They were trained to fight and kill Japs. Dying in an accident *is* dying in vain. I don't give a damn what Shakespeare had to say. It's wasteful and disgusting. There's nothing brave or valiant about it."

"Yes, sir."

Silence settled on the two men again.

After awhile Zimler said, "Sorry, Beck. I know you said that to help me. I didn't mean to be so sharp."

"I understand, sir. It was a piece of very bad luck—a shock to everybody."

Zimler slammed his fist down hard on the table. "Goddamn it! Goddamn it! Now I have to go see what the hell screwed up the takeoff plan."

When Beckley returned to the bridge, Shoemaker was talking to Joe Taylor. "Is this going to cause problems in the air wing, Joe?" he asked.

"I don't think so, Captain. Some of the men are upset, but we have to treat it as an accident and go on."

"Okay. Start maneuvers again. I don't want them to have a lot of time to think. Get 'em back into the air!"

"Aye, Captain."

"Attention all hands. Resume maneuvers! Resume maneuvers!" the loudspeakers boomed.

Pilots, who seemed wary before Shoemaker's order came, climbed back into their cockpits. Within minutes they were streaking back into the sky. They gained altitude and formed into squadrons almost as if nothing had happened. They fought mock air battles. They made bombing runs on the *Franklin*. The entire crew's performance was excellent.

John stood in the sponson watching his crew perform. They fired accurately and efficiently, protecting the *Franklin* against the mock attacks. He was proud of his gun crew. They were becoming a team worthy of defending a fleet carrier like the *Franklin*.

Beckley watched the action from the bridge.

"How do things look to you, Chief?" Taylor asked, as the last squadron of Avengers landed.

"I'm very sorry to say this, sir, but that crash might have helped the crew." Beckley replied. "They saw two men die right before their eyes. They saw what can happen in a war. I think everybody's going to be even more determined now."

"I hope you're right, Chief."

At 16:00 hours, just as Beckley was being relieved, Shoemaker received a message from Fleet Headquarters. He read it, then said, "We return to San Diego immediately. We're joining the Fifth Fleet in Eniwetok. We'll leave for Pearl Harbor tomorrow at 16:00 hours. No further liberty will be granted. All shore leaves are canceled. We're now under combat security. Where and when we're going is top-secret. No one leaves this ship without clearance—without a damned good reason."

That night John pulled off his dungarees and crawled into his bunk. He hadn't slept for more than a few hours in the last two days. Sullivan had ordered one drill after another. The drills earlier that afternoon were exhausting. Adrenaline kept him sharp and alert while he was in the gun pit. Now, he just wanted to rest and think about Sandy. The *Franklin* was returning to San Diego. In the morning he'd find a way to get ashore.

The next morning, as the *Franklin* docked, John approached Sullivan.

"I know what you're looking for, John," Sullivan said. "The answer is no. All liberties are cancelled. No one's leaving this ship." His voice softened. "Sorry, John."

John looked closely at Sullivan. "We're shipping out?"

"It sure looks like it," Sullivan said.

"When?"

"Probably this afternoon."

"At least let me phone her." John pleaded.

Sullivan considered the request for a moment. "Okay, I'll arrange for that, but don't forget security. You can't say anything about when we leave or where we're going."

"Thanks, Chief."

"Sorry I can't do more, John."

Once on the dock, John found a phone and dialed Sandy's number.

"Hello?"

John felt his spirits lift at the sound of her voice.

"Sandy? It's John," he said, feeling happiness that he wondered if he could contain. "How are you?"

"I'm fine. I miss you."

"I miss you, too," John said. "Sandy, we're…I think we're shipping out. All liberties have been canceled—no exceptions."

There was a long pause on the other end of the line.

"Sandy? Sandy, are you all right?"

"I'm…yes, I'm okay," she said, obviously struggling with her emotions.

"Sandy, these past few days, I can't tell you how much you've come to mean to me," John said. "The night by the cove, the beautiful trees and moonlight, the sounds of the surf, holding you in my arms…."

"John, I've thought about you the whole time you've been gone, too. When will I see you again?"

"I don't know. I'm sorry, but I just don't know," John said sadly.

"Can I come see you off?"

"I'm not sure when we're leaving. Even if I knew, I couldn't tell you."

"I think I'll try to come over this afternoon," she said. "At least, maybe I can see your ship one more time."

"Sandy?"

"Yes?"

"I love you."

He heard her gasp. "Sandy?" He knew she was struggling with her emotions again. Finally, she said, "I love you, too, John. And I'll wait for you."

"Write to me," John said, his voice filled with emotion.

"I will," Sandy said sadly. "As often as I can."

From his station in the gun pit, John watched Sandy arrive on the dock just as the *Franklin* began to move away. He waved to her and blew her a kiss. She saw him and waved a kiss back.

"I love you, Sandy," he yelled, but the noisy tugboats and crisp wind drowned out his words.

The *Franklin* moved away from the dock. He waved at her again. She waved back. Hopelessness and despair swept through every fiber of his body.

30 May, 1944
Pearl Harbor
Joining the Fifth Fleet

The *Franklin's* tugboats guided her past the rusted wrecks of the battleships *Arizona* and *Oklahoma* toward Battleship Row on the southeast shore of Ford Island in Pearl Harbor. It was an emotional experience for the whole crew. The great naval anchorage still showed the scars from December 7, 1941. Wreckage of the battleships *Arizona* and *Oklahoma* were rusting there, despite earlier valiant but futile efforts of salvage crews to right them. The Japanese surprise attack had sunk both ships. On the *Oklahoma,* four hundred fifteen officers and men were killed. The *Arizona* was dealt a worse blow. Over eleven hundred men died when she sank. Most were still entombed and decaying in her rusting, saltwater-filled hull. "A treacherous attack—a day that will live in infamy," President Roosevelt called it in his speech declaring war on the Japanese.

A Catholic chaplain, Father Joseph O'Callahan, stood on the crowded dock as the *Franklin* moved slowly toward Berth 4. He looked up at the *Franklin* in awe. She was a powerful fighting vessel—another image of America's growing naval strength. He ran his eyes over her massive frame from bow to stern—her sleek bow and forecastle—her 20- and 40-mm guns, canvas-capped, pointing ominously into the sky—her mountainous bridge, halyards filled with multi-colored flags, and her huge radar antenna—a symbol of America's increasing technological might. The *USS Ranger*, the carrier he'd first served on, seemed very small and outdated when compared to the gigantic *Franklin*. He took off his spectacles and wiped them with his handkerchief. Although he was a mathematics professor at Holy Cross College before the war, he had grown to love the sea and yearned to be back aboard a ship. As he watched the *Franklin* move slowly into her berth, he glanced into the sky. Silently, he blessed her and prayed that she would conduct herself with valor in battle. Then he realized what he was saying. Imagine, blessing a fighting vessel and praying that its actions would kill other men. What's become of Christian tolerance? What happened to love thy neighbor? What about thou shalt not kill? Dear Lord, what can I do with this? For O'Callahan, the war had called many things like this into question. Not the least of these was trust in what was truly right and just. In his quiet, contemplative times he'd often pondered these questions. Now, standing on the dock at Pearl Harbor, he was asking them again.

A sailor surged up to him and almost knocked him backward.

"Oh, I'm sorry, sir! Sir, do you know where I can find a telephone?" he asked, breathing heavily.

"What? Why yes, yes of course, Gunner," he replied, realigning his glasses. "Down two streets and turn left. There is a phone right there. It's a little bit hidden, just keep bearing left."

"Thank you sir…Chaplain…sir."

"Don't run over anybody else getting there," O'Callahan called after him with a grin.

"I won't, sir. Thanks again."

John got the operator. After the long routine of forwarding Sandy's number from one operator to another, there were two long rings. Sandy answered.

"John!" she exclaimed with joy in her voice, "We were just finishing lunch."

"I'm sorry," he apologized, "It's the time change."

"No, don't be silly," she replied.

"I'm fine. I miss you very much, Sandy."

"Oh, John, it's so good to hear your voice."

"It's wonderful to hear yours, too. I can't say much because of security, Sandy. Tell me what's happening there?" John asked.

"How about if I tell you I love you instead?" she asked.

"Sandy, those would be the most wonderful words I could hear."

They spoke guardedly but they talked as though they had just been together, as though no time had passed since he'd held her in his arms. That made the pain of saying goodbye even greater than it was before.

Over the next two days *Franklin* replenished her ammunition and supplies and took on fuel. One hundred and twelve veteran seamen came aboard to fill out *Franklin's* crew. By the end of the second afternoon, *Franklin* was ready to go to war.

That afternoon, John called Sandy again. When the operator finally got through, nobody answered. Her phone just rang and rang.

The next morning, *Franklin*, making eighteen knots through calm waters as Task Group 12.1, with the cruiser *Denver* and the destroyers *Cushing, Twigs* and *Rowe* in her screen, steamed West Southwest in Condition of Readiness III, for Eniwetok and a rendezvous with the Fifth Fleet.

John stood on the fantail watching the huge wake churned up by the ship's giant propellers. He gazed back in the direction of San Diego and blew Sandy a kiss. "I'll be back," he whispered. "I swear with all my soul." But doubt surfaced. An apprehension gnawed at him. She wasn't at home. Where was she? What was she doing? Could she be another Diane?

4 June, 1944
730 Miles SW of Pearl Harbor
Attacks on the Marianas

Three days out of Pearl Harbor, and now a part of the Fifth Fleet, *Franklin's* Combat Information Center received a message from Fleet Headquarters in Eniwetok. It was labeled "Top Secret."

"Get this right up to the skipper," the chief radioman said.

After Shoemaker read the message, he said, "Message from Admiral Spruance. We're going after Saipan in the Marianas. They're bombarding it by air and sea right now."

"Well, sir, you sure called that one right," Beckley said. "You told me you had a hunch we'd go after bases there."

"Yeah, it was a pretty good guess. My hunch now says we're going into the toughest part of the war."

"We've been hammering hell out of them lately," Beckley said. "Maybe that'll take some of the fight out of them, sir."

Shoemaker smiled at Beckley. "That's a beautiful dream, Chief, and I think you know it."

Beckley smiled back. "Yeah. I guess it is wishful thinking, sir. But who knows? Stranger things have happened before."

"Not this time and not in this war," Shoemaker said. "We'll be invading their back yard. Those Jap bastards are going to fight like they're possessed by the devil. From here on in, it'll be a life-and-death struggle for every inch of their ground."

"Well, sir, maybe this will make the war shorter," Beckley said.

"It will, if we're successful. But remember, despite the losses they took at Midway, they've still got two huge fleets out there."

"Well, there's one consolation, sir. We're adding ships to the fleet every day," Beckley said.

"That's right. And it's a consolation. But remember, Chief, this war can still go either way. We can lose it as well as win it."

"Let's hope things go the way they did for us at Midway," Beckley said.

"Let's hope they do. But you mark my words, in the battles to come, the cost in ships, sailors and marines on both sides is going to be huge."

Beckley nodded in sober agreement.

CHAPTER ELEVEN

7 June, 1944
Eniwetok Atoll
Franklin Joins the Fifth Fleet

The morning was beautiful; clear as a bell, not a cloud in the sky. The *Franklin* and her screen steamed north, at reduced speed, through the entrance to Eniwetok harbor. Major units of the Fifth Fleet were riding at anchor there.

On the bridge, Shoemaker and Commanders Day, Moore and Taylor looked over the powerful ships in the harbor. Present were the fleet carriers *Lexington*, *Enterprise*, *Hornet*, *Wasp*, *Bunker Hill*, and *Yorktown*, and the light carriers *Princeton*, *Cabot*, *Monterey* and *San Jacinto*. Closer to shore the battleships *Iowa*, *Indiana*, *Washington*, *Alabama* and *South Dakota* were docked. There were at least forty heavy and light cruisers and twice that many destroyers. The submarines *Bonefish*, *Puffer*, *Albacore* and *Cavalla,* attached to the Fifth Feet, were also present.

"We anchor at anchorage M 413," Commander Moore said, repeating the message that was coming through his headphones. "As soon as we drop anchor they want us to be prepared to take on supplies, ammunition and aviation gasoline. Supply and ammunition barges will be here at noon today. Oilers and gasoline lighters will come alongside tomorrow morning."

"Sounds like something big is coming up," Shoemaker said.

As the *Franklin* steamed toward her assigned anchorage, John, Beckley and Sullivan looked over the huge concentration of warships in the harbor. When they began to pass the cruisers, John came alive with excitement. "Hey, there's the *Santa Fe*. I'll be goddamned. I got a buddy from my hometown on that ship. I haven't seen him in three years."

Sullivan looked at Beckley who was also smiling and somehow sharing in John's happiness. "Why don't we go down and ask one of the radiomen to contact him," Sullivan said. "We can let him know you're here."

"I'll call down and tell them why you guys are coming," Beckley said.

By the time John and Sullivan got to the radio shack, a message had already been prepared. "All we need to know is the guy's name and rate."

"Rashinski, Thomas D, Signalman Second Class," John said.

The reply came back almost immediately. "Affirmative. He's here. He wants to know if you can meet him on the beach at the NCO beer station tomorrow tonight about 18:00?"

John looked at Sullivan.

"Better tell him you're not sure," Sullivan said. "I've got a feeling we're going to be very busy for the next few days." He turned to the radioman on watch. "Tell him we're going do everything we can to get them together."

When the *Franklin* dropped anchor, Beckley went up to his station on the bridge. As soon as he got there, a message came over the teletype from Task Group Command. Beckley handed Shoemaker the message. He read it and said, "We're part of the invasion of Saipan. We depart the day after tomorrow at 07:00. We have to be completely loaded and ready by then. In addition to our regular ordinance, we're going to battle-test a new weapon."

"A new weapon, sir?" Beckley asked.

"Yeah. A missile called the Tiny Tim. It's supposed to have the power of an 8-inch naval rifle."

"I thought we'd have more than three days, Captain," Day said, his voice sounding concerned.

"Yes, so did I. This really puts pressure on, Dave," Shoemaker said. "We'll have to work all hands as long as it takes, day and night if necessary. Pass the word. Let's get this ship ready to go to war."

Activity on the *Franklin* accelerated. As soon as she dropped anchor, barges loaded with food, ammunition, bombs and spare parts of all kinds surrounded her. In what seemed an endless stream, one crate after another moved up conveyor belts to the hangar deck. Loading and storing this mass of supplies took a much more serious tone now. Trial runs and air-combat drills were over. In the next few days the *Franklin* would be in the real war.

Gunnery was charged with assisting Aviation Ordinance in loading five hundred and one-thousand-pound bombs. John and the rest of the Gunnery Division worked until late that night. When they stopped, John was exhausted. He hadn't seen it so busy since they left Norfolk. On the way down to his bunk, he realized he hadn't thought of Sandy in several hours. It was a relief, but as he entered his compartment, his sadness came back. "I hope I get a letter tomorrow," he murmured. "I wonder *why* I haven't heard from her. She promised me she'd write, and I've already written to her four times."

8 June, 1944
Eniwetok Atoll
Preparations for Invasion

As John and Ski climbed topside to the flight deck for muster, they could see a line of barges headed for the *Franklin*. They were piled high with more ammunition and scores of five-hundred and one-thousand-pound bombs. One barge was loaded with hundreds of wooden cases.

"The new missiles have to be in those cases," John said. "The Navy must think they're great."

"Why do you say that?" Ski asked.

"Hell, it looks like we're taking them aboard by the hundreds."

"I hear they're experimental," Ski said.

"Yeah, they are," John replied, " but if they work like they're supposed to, they'll sure put a wallop into a plane's strafing run."

"They got a lot of power?" Ski asked.

"They're supposed to be very powerful," John replied.

"In those skinny cases? No way," Ski said.

"Well, we'll see. We're taking enough of them aboard to give them a damned good test, and the Ordinance Department seldom screws up when they design a new weapon."

After muster, the dreary work of loading bombs and ammunition began. Ski and John were in a detail that was assisting with the Tiny Tim missiles. The crates that contained them moved slowly up to the hangar deck on a conveyor.

After two full hours of heavy work, Ski said, "These things are going to come up forever. We must have taken on five hundred by now."

"One hundred and eighty-three out of a thousand we're taking aboard," John said, as he looked over an inventory sheet.

"Shit, we'll be here all day and tonight, too," Ski complained.

John, Ski, and two other seamen lifted a crate from the conveyor and added it to the stack on the hangar deck. After they eased the crate to the top of the stack, John said, "Yeah. I'm probably not going to get ashore to see my buddy, Tom."

"Your who?"

"We've been so busy I guess I didn't tell you. I spotted the cruiser *Santa Fe* as we came in yesterday," John said. "A good friend from my hometown is aboard her. I was in high school with him."

"Think he's still aboard?" Ski asked.

"Yeah. Sullivan and I checked by radio."

"Gee, that's really neat," Ski said. "Why don't I ever run into anyone from my home town?"

John adjusted his gloves. As they seized another rough missile crate, he said with a grin, "Maybe all your friends in Muncie are 4-F."

"Bullshit, Gunner," Ski said. "There are a lot of guys in the service from Muncie. I just don't have any luck running into them."

By noon they had taken on three hundred and twenty-seven missile crates.

"Okay," John said to the work detail. "Let's break for chow. Be back here at 13:15 sharp."

"At this rate we're going to be working late tonight," Ski said dejectedly as they headed down the ladder to the mess hall.

At 13:15 ammunition loading resumed. At 14:05 the destroyer *Patterson* came alongside to fuel and deliver mail, and a short time later an announcement came across the loudspeaker: "There will be a mail call in twenty minutes."

Work continued until the mailman appeared on the hangar deck and made his way detail by detail. When he reached their detail, John said, "Okay, let's take fifteen minutes."

John was praying for a letter from Sandy, but there was no mail for him and very little for anyone else. Although disappointed, he reasoned that the mail had not yet caught up with the ship.

The tedious job of supplying the *Franklin* for combat continued. When the destroyer *Hunt* came alongside later that afternoon, she brought more mail. John got two letters. One from his father and the other from his sister, but the letter he desperately hoped for didn't come. His doubt swelled. Were all the things she said on that last night just a bunch of bullshit? Why hadn't she written as she promised? He was beginning to doubt he could ever trust a woman again. It was disheartening as hell. "Damn, it's tough to go back to that weary, goddamned job," he murmured to no one in particular as he turned toward the conveyors.

The loading continued. By the end of the second day the *Franklin* was ready for combat. John realized that he wasn't going to get the letter he desperately wanted, and he wasn't going to get to see Tom, either. Well, there was something he could do about one of these two things. He showered and had chow, then went to the radio shack. When he arrived, all was quiet. The two radiomen on watch were having a cigarette and a cup of joe. John asked them to notify Tom that he wasn't going to be able to see him.

"Sure, Gunner, we'll get your message out right away."

"Tell him we'll get together as soon as possible," John said.

"Roger, Gunner," the radioman replied.

"There's a few people in the world I can count on," he said half aloud as he made his way to his bunk. "Tom's one of them. I wonder if Sandy is another?"

11 June, 1944
Central Pacific Ocean
Invade Saipan

The capture of Eniwetok and Ulithi in the Caroline Islands gave Admiral Nimitz the bases he needed to take the next step in *Operation Victorious*—the invasion of the Marianas. The code name for the Marianas operation, the most important operation to date, was *Forager*. Its objective: to secure and control bases for future attacks on the Japanese Empire. A huge American task force steamed through the calm waters of the central Pacific. In it were eight *Essex* Class carriers. They included the *Enterprise*, with Admiral Ray Spruance in flag; *Lexington*, Admiral Mitscher's flagship; *Hornet, Bunker Hill, Wasp, Intrepid, Yorktown* and the brand new *Franklin*. Protecting the Task Force was a screen that included the battleships *Iowa, New Jersey* and *Alabama*, and the new battleships *Washington* and *South Dakota*. The battle cruisers *Alaska* and *Guam* and the heavy cruisers *San Francisco, Indianapolis, Pittsburgh, Helena* and *Boston* flanked them. A score of light cruisers, which included the *Santa Fe*, and over thirty destroyers made up the screen's outer circle. This formidable fleet contained thirty-seven transports carrying twenty-eight thousand marines from the First Marine division and thirty thousand infantrymen from the Seventh and Ninety-Sixth Infantry Divisions.

On the bridge of the *Enterprise,* Ray Spruance was in secret talks with Admiral Nimitz, who was now back at Fleet Headquarters in Pearl Harbor.

"Saipan is first, then we go after Tinian and Guam," Nimitz said in a voice that crackled over the three thousand miles of air space. "This is the most important action of the war, Ray. The Japanese know what will happen if these islands fall. They're going to fight like hell to defend them."

"We're set to give Saipan a real heavy going over," Spruance responded, "It'll be heavier bombardment than we've ever delivered before."

"Right," Nimitz echoed. "We did a good job at Eniwetok and Kwajalein, Ray, but we have to be vigilant, especially here. This will be the toughest action since Tarawa, and remember, Ray, Ozawa's still out there with those two goddamned big fleets."

"Yes, sir," Spruance said. "Well, we've got six battleships in the bombardment group along with dozens of cruisers and destroyers. They'll blast away from dawn to dusk until we're sure their defenses are crushed. I've got our submarines out looking everywhere for those fleets."

"Excellent," Nimitz said, sounding genuinely pleased.

"We can call in heavy bombers from Tarawa if we need them," Spruance ventured.

"Hell, call them in," Nimitz replied. "Better to be safe than sorry."

"Aye, sir."

Spruance looked at his watch. "The bombardment should begin about now."

"Good luck. Good hunting, Ray," Nimitz said.

"Thanks, sir. Maybe we can bring you back Ozawa's scalp."

Almost as soon as Spruance finished his conversation with Nimitz, bombers and fighters from Mark Mitscher's Fast Carrier Forces attacked Saipan's airfields. At about the same time the battleships opened fire. From their positions east of the island, they hurled two-thousand-pound high-impact shells at the heavily fortified beaches. Minutes later, cruisers and destroyers began their bombardment.

#

Aboard the *Santa Fe,* Tom Rashinski got a semaphore message from the *Enterprise* and rushed it to the bridge.

When he got there, Captain Fitz and his Executive Officer, Commander Ed Wassern, were having a guarded discussion.

"Important message, sir," Tom said.

Fitz read the message and then said, "They want us in close again, Ed."

In a few minutes Fitz maneuvered the *Santa Fe* through the coral reefs to within eight hundred yards of the beach. She was so close that Japanese small arms fire could be heard whining off the ship's side and superstructure.

"Bearing 239," said a voice from the gun turrets.

"Range nine hundred yards."

"Coming on target."

"Request permission to fire, sir."

"Fire when ready!"

The *Santa Fe* blazed away at the heavy beach fortifications with her five- and six-inch guns. After the initial salvo, her 20- and 40-mm antiaircraft guns opened up, strafing anything that looked like a beach fortification or a cover for troops.

The bombardment was merciless. It continued hour after relentless hour through the rest of the day, until night fell and darkness obscured the island.

At dawn the next morning, the pounding started again. That afternoon at 14:00, B-24s from airfields on Tarawa joined the attack, dropping one-thousand-pound high-demolition bombs. Upon impact, they created a huge fire cloud. Smoke and debris scattered everywhere. It was hard to believe that anyone could live through this kind of intensive bombardment.

The shelling and bombing went on for four days. At 09:30 on the fifth day, Admiral Conolly signaled:

"Halt the bombardment. Land the Landing Forces."

LCVs, landing craft designed to carry vehicles, loaded with tanks, artillery and Amtraks broke out of their approach patterns and surged forward. The invasion was underway.

Wave after wave of marines from the First Marine Division, hunkered down in their Amtraks, approached the hostile Japanese beach. When they jumped onto the ugly, debris-laden shore, intense mortar and machine gun fire met them.

Tom Rashinski and Signalman Third Class Carl Corini, who had just come to the bridge, watched the marine attack.

"Man, I thought those Jap fortifications were beat to shit," Tom said. "Hell, the way it's going, it doesn't seem like we damaged them at all."

"Yeah. They're drawing fire from pillboxes hidden in all those palm trees behind the beach," Corini said. "It's not just the machine guns that are ripping them up, they're getting blasted by mortar fire, too."

"Mortars can be moved around. It's hard to take mortars out with ship-to-shore bombardment," Tom observed. "Man, have those fucking guys got guts! One goes down and another guy replaces him. I wonder if I could do what they're doing."

"Just be glad that you don't have that opportunity, sailor," Corini replied. "For me, I'm happy to be protected by six inches of armor plate."

"I still think I could do it if I had to, goddamn it."

"That's easy to say when you're a thousand yards away," Corini countered.

"I could do it if I had to!" Tom insisted.

"When you look at that beach, what the hell do you see?" Corini asked.

"What the fuck do you mean? It's an invasion force storming a beach."

"Yeah. But think about this. A lot of those guys are only eighteen and nineteen years old. They're too goddamned young and dumb to be afraid."

"Bullshit. Those guys are *fearless,* not stupid."

"Fearless hell, I'll tell you what they really are. They're gung-ho shit-heads. A lot of 'em ain't gonna see twenty," Corini said. "That's why I never joined the marines."

"Marines probably wouldn't have taken you anyhow, fuck-head," Tom shot back.

"Maybe not. But I'll tell you one more thing. I never even thought about joining.

There's going to be some very sad families back in the States tomorrow, and if I keep my head down, mine won't be one of them."

About that time a semaphore message flashed from the *Enterprise*: *"Cruisers withdraw from in-close positions. Return to stations in the bombardment group."*

Tom rushed the message to the Captain.

Fitz read it and commanded: "Helmsman, come left to 155 degrees."

"Aye, Captain."

"I guess they're going to give us a little relief," Fitz said.

The *Santa Fe*'s engines whined. She responded to the course change and moved swiftly back to assume her station in the middle of the bombardment group's defense ring.

With this pause in the action and his watch completed, Tom went below to catch up on some of the things he'd neglected for the past two weeks. He had to write to his parents and his sister, Jo Ann. He hastily scribbled letters to each of them. When he took them to the post office only the mail clerk was at there. "When do we get some mail, George?" he asked.

"I don't know. Everybody asks about the goddamned mail," the mail clerk replied.

"Goddamn, George, it's been twenty-three days."

"But what the hell do you guys think I can do about it?"

"Yeah, you're right," Tom said. "I guess out in this godforsaken area we're lucky to get any mail at all."

"Well, you're in luck today. There's a delivery scheduled at 14:00."

That afternoon Tom got two letters from his mother, one from his father and two from Jo Ann. He took his letters to his bunk to read in private.

Jo Ann's letter was nearly two months old. Tom ripped open the envelope and skimmed the letter. The beginning was the usual, worry about his health, prayers for his safe return. Shortages and rationing. Then came the bombshell. Diane had dumped John Oxler for Harold Stapp. He pictured Diane in his mind and felt himself growing angry. He put the letter down and closed his eyes. Goddamn, what a hell of a trick. She doesn't deserve a guy like John was all he could think. As far as he was concerned John was better without her.

He finished reading the rest of his letters and stowed them in his locker. Then he decided to take a shower and change his clothes. It had been two days since he'd been able to do either, and he smelled of sweat and battle smoke. He made his way to the head, still pissed about what Diane had done. The head was nearly deserted. He turned on the shower and savored the warm water. Even thought it was salt water, it felt great. Just as he began to dry off, the klaxon sounded: "General quarters! General quarters! All hands man your battle stations!"

"Shit. I wanted to get some sleep," he muttered as he threw on his skivvies and dungarees. When he reached the bridge, Corini was busy taking down a semaphore message. "We're headed back in," he said. "They located a big bunch of Jap snipers in those trees behind the beach. They want us to go in and strafe them."

He handed the message to Tom. Tom rushed it to the Captain.

Captain Fitz read the message and ordered a course change. The *Santa Fe* came about sharply and headed back to the hostile beach. Within a few minutes Fitz maneuvered through the jagged coral reefs to a close-in position. "Same goddamned battered beach," he said. "Dirty sand and junk and crap everywhere."

"It looks like those trees are loaded with snipers, sir," Tom reported. "Look at those poor damned marines. They're trying to take cover behind anything they can."

"Yeah, and a lot of them aren't finding cover. Look at the dead bodies. Goddamn those snipers," Fitz said with anger in his voice.

"Get our gunners on the horn," he shouted to his Executive Officer. "Tell them to strafe everything! Trees, bushes, bunkers, huts—anything that moves. But tell them, for God's sake, to watch out for the marines. They've got a tough enough action going there already."

"Aye, sir," Wassern replied.

Tom watched the *Santa Fe*'s antiaircraft guns swing into action and open fire. They ripped apart sections of the sniper-laden trees like a huge mowing machine. Fifteen LCIs, infantry landing craft refitted with missile racks, moved in ahead of the cruisers and attacked with missiles at very close ranges. Each volley tore up more of the trees and the beach.

"Savage," Tom said to Corini after he returned to his station. "Those new racks of missiles are really something. When they're fired, they sound like the loud crack of a whip. Just one volley can deliver a hell of a wallop. Maybe they'll put us out of business."

"Small chance of that," Corini said sarcastically

"Why the fuck not?" Tom retorted.

"Because you're dreaming, sailor, that's why not."

The concentrated attack continued. Palm trees, which were once only partly damaged, were now blasted to shreds. Bunkers hidden by the trees were brought under fire and destroyed.

"There's a mess of Japs getting blasted," Tom said. "Look at all those poor bastards hanging down in those coconut trees."

"They're the only kind of Japs I like—dead Japs," Corini said.

"Yeah, me, too," Tom replied. But somewhere inside he knew the corpses in the trees belonged to human beings, with mothers and fathers and sisters, not much different from himself. "I wish this goddamned day was over," he said. "I'm getting tired as hell with all this."

When the *Santa Fe*'s attack ended, Tom made his way below decks and into his bunk. He closed his eyes. As always, images danced through his mind. He thought of his parents and his sister and how much he missed them. He thought of John and the crappy thing Diane did to him. Finally, he switched to girls, lots of them, all nude and beautiful, all the girls he was going to have when he got home and this shitty war was over….

16 June, 1944
Aboard the Fleet Carrier Lexington
30 Miles South of Saipan

At dawn the next morning, Spruance boarded a patrol craft and went over to Mitscher's flagship. What Nimitz said earlier about Admiral Ozawa and the First and Second Imperial Fleets troubled him. He wanted to talk to Mitscher and his Chief of Staff, Admiral Arleigh Burke, who was one of the most perceptive strategists in the Pacific Fleet.

When Spruance got to the *Lexington*'s bridge, Mitscher and Burke were focused on the fierce battle being waged on the beach.

"They're bogged down, Ray," Mitscher said as he trained his binoculars back and forth on the fighting. "They're not moving inland—not at all."

Spruance grabbed a pair of binoculars and trained them along the beaches.

"They're drawing a lot of fire," Spruance said. "That's not a good sign. Goddamn. We hit 'em with everything we had, bombers, battleships, cruisers, missiles." He shook his head. "I'd like to know what the hell it takes to grub those little bastards out of their holes."

Both men strained at their glasses.

"That's violent fighting," Spruance said to Arleigh Burke who was standing by watching.

"Aye, sir, it sure is," Burke replied.

"Well, there's not much we can do from here," Spruance said. "That job's in the hands of marines now." He trained his binoculars on the beach again. "Poor bastards. It looks like they're going to have to do it the hard way again—with guns, bayonets, mortars and grenades."

Spruance took off his binoculars and laid them on the map cabinet. "I came over to talk to you about Ozawa and his two fleets." He looked around the bridge. "I think we'd better have this talk in private," he said.

The three admirals made their way to a conference compartment behind the bridge. When they were inside, Spruance got right to the point. "I'm worried about Ozawa," he said awkwardly. "I hear he's got a kind of inborn sense for what can be accomplished with ships." He paused and looked at Burke who was nodding his head. "You've heard that too, Arleigh?"

"Aye, sir, I have. I've heard he's a smart son-of-a-bitch."

"That troubles me, and he's so goddamned cagey," Spruance said. "I can't figure out where he's going and what the hell he's going to do next."

Mitscher and Burke nodded uneasily.

"What's that little son-of-a-bitch going to do with those fleets?" Spruance asked as he took off his hat and ran a handkerchief over his eyes and face. "Even with the ships we've added, each of those Jap fleets is as big and strong as we are right now." Spruance paused. He looked like he was uncomfortable with what he was going to say. "I think the Japs still have Yamamoto's idea of taking us out with a single major attack in their plans," he said slowly. "They tried it at Midway and we stopped them there. I think they'll try it again."

"Well, there's good reason for another attempt," Mitscher replied. "We've been kicking their asses lately. They're probably starting to get desperate."

"Yeah, we have been hitting them pretty hard," Spruance said. "We're starting to rattle the gate that leads to their homeland."

Mitscher looked at Burke and both men nodded in agreement.

"And we know they're coming after us, Ray," Mitscher said. "We better be damned wary of their movements."

"Exactly," Spruance said. "A big defeat for the Fifth Fleet could set the war back five years. That's why it's so damned important to know what Ozawa's got up his sleeve."

"Do we have any idea where those fleets are, Admiral?" Burke asked.

"We've got some information on them," Spruance replied. "A couple of days ago, I got messages from three of our submarines. *Bonefish* and *Puffer* both reported a large fleet of Jap warships assembled at Tawi Tawi in the Sulu Archipelago southwest of the Philippines. Then, not an hour later, *Seahorse* contacted us and reported a second Japanese fleet steaming south from Okinawa, headed in our direction."

"Goddamn, that's a lot of sea power moving around," Mitscher said.

"And you can bet they're not on a pleasure cruise," Burke added. "Sounds like they're getting ready for something—maybe something big."

Mitscher looked at Spruance, then at Burke. "Yeah. The big question is what, how, where and when?"

"If they combine those fleets," Spruance said, "they'll form the most powerful fleet in the world. Intelligence tells me that there are at least ten carriers and seven battleships out there, and two of them are the super battleships *Yamato* and *Musashi*."

"Think Ozawa might try to outflank our invasion forces?" Mitscher asked.

"Sneaky bastard just might," Spruance replied. "Our big problem is our responsibility for the marines on Saipan. This limits the hell out of us. We're not as flexible as we need to be to fight a battle with either Jap fleet—let alone *both* of them."

He paused. "It's still too early to know for sure," Spruance continued, "but the Jap fortifications on Saipan seem to be strong. I don't think our bombardment was as effective as we'd hoped. We need to stay close to Saipan. It could get very rough on those beaches before this operation is over."

He paused and rubbed his chin. "Give me your ideas on how we can locate Ozawa," Spruance said.

Mitscher thought a moment, then he replied, "Well, for openers I'd call in B-24s to sniff him out. B-24s have an eleven-hundred-mile range. They ought to be able to locate big fleets like that."

"Of course, we'll go with that for sure," Spruance agreed.

Burke squinted and slowly rubbed his chin. "I can't tell you where Ozawa's two fleets are or what he's going to do, Admiral, but I know what *I'd* do if I were in his shoes."

"Let's hear," Spruance said.

"They know where we are. Our invasion pinpoints our location. If I were Ozawa, I'd pick a place and time to fight. I'd position my fleet out about three hundred and twenty-five miles away from us. That's out of the range of our planes. He knows better than we do that his planes can fly at least twenty-five percent farther than ours because their limited armor makes them lighter."

"You think he'll try a massive air attack?" Spruance asked.

"Yes, I do, sir."

"With all that surface power including battleships like the *Yamato* and *Musashi* out there?" Spruance questioned. "Aircraft have never sunk a battleship or won a major naval battle alone, Arleigh. How'd you come up with that?"

"Well, first of all, I agree they're getting desperate—they need a big victory," Burke replied. "So if I were Ozawa, I'd send every plane I had to do as much damage to our fleet as possible. As soon as they did their damage, I'd fly them down to Guam to be refueled and rearmed. Once refueled and rearmed, I'd do the whole procedure in reverse. I'd fly back and attack us again. Then I'd turn my planes back to my carriers and start the whole process all over."

"Meanwhile his entire fleet, especially his carriers and battleships, are protected from counterattack by distance," Spruance murmured, mulling over what Burke just said.

"Exactly, sir."

"So you think this is going to be a battle of *planes* rather than *ships*?" Spruance asked.

"Yes, I do, Admiral," Burke replied. "I think he'll bring in his battleships *after* his planes inflict as much damage on us as possible."

"A fleet action without battleships shooting at each other?" Spruance asked.

"Yes, sir," Burke replied with certainty in his voice. "And if I were on our side, and I am," he continued with a grin, "I'd start bombing and strafing hell out of Guam right now. I'd take that base and those planes there away from him."

Spruance looked intently at Mitscher, then back to Burke. "I think you might have hit it right on the nose, Arleigh," he said.

Mitscher nodded in agreement. "I think he's got it right, too, Ray," he said. "Let's take Guam away from them."

"Agreed," Spruance said. "Alert all carriers. Blast hell out of Guam. See if you can get some B-24s from Manus to help. Those two-thousand-pound bombs make a big hole in an airfield."

The Fifth Fleet's Fast Carrier Forces became a beehive of activity. Up from hangar decks came squadrons of fully armed Helldivers, Avengers, Hellcats and Corsairs armed with bombs and missiles, ready to go after the airfield and planes on Orote Field.

#

On the *Franklin*, Joe Taylor addressed the pilots in the ready room. "*Franklin*," he said, "is about to make her first air strike of the war. We're going to attack the air facilities on Guam. We want to deprive the Japanese of the use of that island if they try to attack us. The word is that there are about forty-five Jap planes there. Our job is to take them out and damage the airfield so badly that it can't be used by the Japs in a crossfire action." Taylor paused and looked over the Air Wing. "Lieutenant Commander Bill Zimler will now discuss squadron composition and flight plan."

Zimler, in full flight gear, rose and walked to the podium. He looked carefully over the fighter pilots who were seated in a group beside Lieutenant Commander Joe Crowley on his right.

"Fighters will go off first to fly cover for the bomber group," Zimler began. "We don't think they know we're coming, but you can expect them to put up as many planes as they can if they find out. If they come, it's your job to take them on and clear them out. Remember, when they attack, try to get their formation leaders. Those of you who have been in combat know when the Japs lose a leader it throws them into a state of confusion. Shoot for the wing roots—the area where the wings attach to the fuselage. That's where their gas tanks are located. Hit 'em there and they'll explode like firecrackers. Understood?" he asked.

Silence.

"Bomber pilots—defer from attacks on Jap fighters. Fight only if you're attacked. Your job is on Guam. Each squadron has an experienced section leader and wingman. Those of you who have never been in combat have been put in formation behind them. Follow their lead. This will get you through the first phase of the attack."

Zimler paused briefly. "I want to caution you. Don't be a lone wolf. If you're tempted to go off on your own, *don't do it*. Lone wolves don't last long in these situations. Fly in tight formations. As much as possible provide cover for each other. If something unavoidable or extreme comes up, follow your instincts. Finally, be alert. The Japs have a way of slipping up on people. Don't let them bite you in the ass. Any questions?"

Silence.

Taylor walked back to the podium. "Well, this is our first action. If we want to distinguish *Franklin* as a fighting ship, this is our chance. Good luck. Good hunting."

Bill Zimler, and the rest of the squadron, made their way up to the flight deck.

Rear gunners were assembled there awaiting the arrival of their pilots. When Zimler arrived, Gunner's Mate Third Class Dino Antonelli moved in beside him.

"Got your long johns on, Dino?" Zimler asked. "It's going to be very cold up there. We're going in at twenty thousand feet."

"Yes sir, I've got 'em on, but I don't get cold. Remember, I'm from Wyoming where we skinny dip in those kinds of temperatures, sir."

"Are you ready to go?" Zimler asked.

"Yes sir," came Antonelli's instant reply. "Just like I'm back on the ranch—where I can shoot the left whisker off a field mouse at a thousand feet, sir."

Despite the gravity of the coming events, the hint of a smile creased Zimler's lips. Antonelli's confident attitude always made him feel good. As the two stood waiting for their TBF Avenger to come up from the hangar deck, the memory of his first meeting with Antonelli flashed through his mind. "Dino Antonelli, sir, Gunner's Mate Third Class from the great State of Wyoming," he remembered him saying, by way of an introduction.

"Antonelli? Antonelli? Is that Irish?" Zimler had teased.

"Smoked Irish," Antonelli responded with a grin.

Zimler remembered having a good laugh over Antonelli's response.

"Italian, sir." Antonelli then said, a broad smile stretching across his dark, handsome face. "My father's a cattle rancher. I understand you're from Kansas, sir?"

"Yeah, Wichita."

"That makes us neighbors, sir. After the war you'll have to come up and do some moose hunting with us—best moose hunting in the world in the great state of Wyoming."

Over the past few months Zimler had developed great confidence in his gunner. He was one of the thousands of dungaree flyers—young enlisted men who served as navigators and gunners—men who took as many risks as pilots but got a lot less credit. Antonelli didn't seem to mind this. He was confident in his role as a gunner and poised under pressure, despite the fact that he'd been shot down once in action over Tarawa.

"I'm a lucky Italian, sir. I came through without a scratch," he'd said when he told Zimler about being shot down.

"I hope some of your luck rubs off on us, Dino." Zimler had responded.

"It will, sir. Just you watch."

Their plane came up and was moved to the "park" behind the fighters. They made their way to the sleek Avenger and climbed into the crowded torpedo bomber's cockpits.

"Prepare to launch aircraft!" came the command from the bridge.

With that, the *Franklin* began her first air strike of the war. A squadron of Hellcats was launched into a clear blue sky. Then thirty-six TBF Avengers and SB2C Helldivers, armed with five-hundred-pound bombs and Tiny Tim missiles, followed.

Once airborne, Zimler established exact course and altitude. "Air Strike Able listen up. Course 205 degrees. Altitude twenty thousand feet. Remember, tight formations. Be alert. If my hunch is right, we won't get to them without a fight." Then he called back to Antonelli over the intercom.

"Dino!"

"Aye, sir."

"Keep your eyes peeled. They're sneaky."

"Aye, sir. Just like hunting moose in Wyoming. I'm ready for 'em."

The gun crews on the *Franklin* were in Condition I—Maximum Readiness. John, Ski and the rest of the Able 1 gun crew watched as the last Avenger climbed into formation.

"There's always something exciting about watching them take off," John said as he shielded his eyes with his hand and followed the flight of the last Avenger. "Somehow this attack seems more powerful than any I've seen before."

"Why?" Ski asked.

"Maybe it's because they're carrying those missiles," John replied. "After all that work of hauling them aboard, it'd be great to know that they were as powerful and accurate as they're supposed to be."

"Well, if they are, I'm going to be thankful that they're *ours* and not the Japs," Ski said. "After lugging those bastards around for three days, I decided I didn't want even one of them zooming down on me."

"You questioned if they'd work, remember?"

"Yeah, but even if they didn't, I wouldn't want it. Those are heavy fucking missiles. The longer I carried them, the more I respected them."

John looked over the gun crew. Everyone was focused on the air activity.

"Okay, guys," he said, "the show's over. Now let's concentrate on looking for Nip planes. Concentrate on the horizon, both forward and abeam."

"I don't see a goddamned thing, Gunner," Bonin said after staring into the distance for a few minutes.

"No, and you probably won't, but there's always a chance a Jap plane can sneak in under our radar," John cautioned.

"You mean my eyes are better than radar?" Bonin asked.

"They are if a plane slips through, goddamn it, so keep looking," John said sharply.

The combined attack group flew southeast at maximum speed. At 14:30 they were within twenty-five miles of their target, maintaining complete radio silence.

As they approached Orote field, attack group commander Dawson Martin, flying a Hellcat off the *Lexington*, broke the silence: "Attention Attack Group, this is Cobra-leader. There are at least forty-five Zeros and Zekes on Orote's runways," he said through the intercom. "I think we took them by surprise. There's nothing in the air and no exhaust smoke or props turning down there. It doesn't look like they're prepared for an attack."

"Hellcats from *Franklin*," he continued, "go in first with those special new missiles. Get as many as you can. Let's see how they work."

"Roger," Joe Crowley, commanding *Franklin's* fighters replied.

"Second wave will be F4U Corsairs flying off *Enterprise*, then fighters from *Lexington*, *Hancock* and *Wasp* will follow."

"*Franklin* squadron! Let's go!" Joe Crowley shouted. "Remember, use your missiles first!"

Twenty-four Hellcats peeled out of formation and streaked down on the Japanese airfield.

When the parked Japanese planes came into their crosshairs, *Franklin's* fighter pilots triggered their missiles. The missiles streaked toward their targets, blazing fire from their tails.

"I got a direct hit!" Crowley shouted. "Wow!" he screamed. "That Jap Zero just disintegrated into small pieces!"

Martin's voice crackled in over the intercom. "Wow is right! Those missiles are great," he said.

"They're better than great," Crowley shouted. "I've never seen a plane blasted into so many pieces before."

When *Franklin's* first run was completed, sixteen Zeros and Zekes were flaming masses of rubble. By the end of the combined fighter attack, all forty-seven Zeros and Zekes were destroyed or so badly damaged they'd never be used again.

"Avengers and Helldivers next," Dawson commanded. "Bombers from *Franklin* first. Go after the pillboxes. Get those gasoline storage tanks. Get everything you can with missiles—they're dynamite! Then get everything else—runways, hangars, machine shops, everything that's standing."

"Okay, Dino, let's go!" Zimler shouted through the intercom.

"Roger, sir, I'm ready."

Zimler put his Avenger into a steep dive and streaked toward the field. Antiaircraft fire, missing twenty minutes earlier, streamed up from fortifications around the field.

Zimler pulled a pillbox into his crosshairs and triggered a missile. The Avenger wrenched as the missile released, and a Tiny Tim trailed a stream of fire down to the pillbox. When it hit, there was a huge explosion and debris scattered everywhere.

"Wow!" Dino shouted. "A direct hit. There's nothing left there! Just like shooting a pumpkin with a shotgun, sir."

One bomber after another raged down on the airfield. Storage tanks were set aflame. Hangars were destroyed. Machine shops were burning. Just as the bombers began to concentrate on the runways, B-24s from Manus arrived. Two-thousand-pound bombs, aimed with deadly accuracy through top-secret Norden bombs sights, tore huge holes in Orote's runways. Together with the air strike's bombers, the B-24s pounded the runways until they were pockmarked with huge craters. When the two-hour attack was over there was almost nothing left that could be used for aircraft operations. The B-24s headed back to Manus and the air strike turned back to their carriers.

"Well, Dino, what did you think of the missiles?" Zimler asked as the attack group sped home.

"They're powerful as hell, sir!" Dino replied triumphantly. They sure helped tear up that airfield. It's going to take a lot of time and work to fly planes off those runways again.

19 June, 1944
Aboard the *USS Lexington*
76 Miles South of Saipan

At a little past six o'clock, the sun rose through some thin cirrus clouds and turned a long strip of the Pacific a shimmering gold. Night clouds had dissolved. They left a clear sky; one that would provide no cover for stealthy enemy aviators.

On the bridge of the *Lexington*, Spruance scanned the western horizon through binoculars.

"There's not a sign of anything out there, Marc. At least not that I can see," he said. "Three days of intensive searching by dozens of B-24s and not a damned word on either of the Japanese fleets."

"Well, Ozawa's not at Tawi Tawi anymore, if he really ever was there," Mitscher said after reviewing the message from General Blanchard just handed to him. "B-24s searched the entire operational area and parts of the Philippine Sea. No fleets there, anywhere."

"Yeah, the Pacific is so goddamn big even huge fleets the size of Ozawa's can disappear in it." Then, as though he had been mulling it over for some time, Spruance said, "I think I should go back to the *Enterprise*, Marc. I think I've done what I needed to do here."

Later, before he left the *Lexington*, Spruance said, "Stay in touch on strategy, Marc. I think Arleigh's got it right. We're going to plan for his type of air battle."

When Spruance returned to the *Enterprise* there was a message waiting. Spruance read it hurriedly. "Yes!" he exclaimed. "The submarine *Cavalla* has located a big Japanese fleet headed in our direction. It's big! It's got eleven carriers in it. They got positive identification on the carriers *Taiho* and *Shokaku*. There are five battleships and ten heavy cruisers."

"Does it include the *Yamato* or *Musashi*?" Admiral Lindel Hart, his executive officer asked.

"It doesn't say," Spruance replied, "but the sub's commander said they sank a destroyer and damaged a light cruiser."

Spruance paused and thought a moment. "Get Mitscher and Burke on the wire," he said to the chief radioman.

When they were in contact and he'd explained the situation, Spruance said, "I think we should rendezvous about a hundred and fifty miles southwest of Saipan. We'll be close enough to get back to support the marines if they run into trouble, but far enough South and West to prevent Ozawa from doing an 'end run' on us."

Mitscher's voice came through the speaker loud and clear. "Roger, Ray, that sounds like a good plan."

"This might be a big opportunity for us, Marc," Spruance said. "We know they're coming. We're ready. Maybe we can level one more of the playing fields."

Later Spruance sent a simple battle plan to Mitscher and Admiral Willis Lee who commanded the Battleship Line:

>*Prepare for a predominantly air war. Our aircraft will first knock out attacking enemy planes by assuming high-altitude positions in ambush, then go after enemy carriers and attack enemy battleships and cruisers to slow or disable them. Battle line will destroy the enemy by fleet action and sink any crippled ships if the enemy retreats. Pursue them vigorously to ensure as much destruction as possible.*
>
>*Desire you proceed at your discretion. Select tactics best calculated to meet the enemy under most advantageous conditions. I will issue general directives and leave the details to you. Remember, we must take every precaution to avoid being outflanked. We must be ready to cover Saipan at all times.*

As Spruance's message was being sent, *Enterprise's* radar spotted a large battle group in the Northwest quadrant of their screen. Spruance sent an urgent message to all commanders in the Fifth Fleet:

Huge Japanese fleet sighted bearing North Northwest. Range approximately 350 miles. Ozawa's making his move. All units prepare to attack. Good Luck. Good Hunting.

#

On the *Santa Fe* Rashinski decoded the message and rushed it to Captain Fitz.

"Sound General Quarters," Fitz said after he read it.

The klaxon pounded through the ship's loudspeaker system: "General Quarters! General Quarters!"

Within minutes every gun on the *Santa Fe* and every other ship in the Fifth Fleet pointed westward and waited in Condition I.

When the Japanese Fleet had closed to about three hundred and ten miles, an excited message crackled in from the *Lexington*. "Bogeys! Bogeys! A big bunch of 'em—bearing West Northwest—distance two hundred and ninety miles."

The Japanese air attack had begun.

#

On the bridge of the *Lexington*, Mitscher, Burke and Commander Dawson Martin, who would again command the Fifth Fleet's combined fighter wings, hurriedly reviewed their strategies:

Bombers off first. If not needed in the air defense, they would circle and attack Guam again. Fighters next, to conserve fuel. They would assume positions northwest of the fleet at twenty-five thousand feet out about sixty miles.

"Let's try to surprise the bastards if possible," Mitscher said.

"Aye, aye, sir," Martin replied, as he turned and hurried back to the ready room.

When they were alone, Mitscher said, "Arleigh, you were right-on with this call! The way the goddamn thing is unwinding, you could have written the battle plan."

#

On the *Franklin*, John and Ski watched as Hellcats, Helldivers and Avengers thundered off the flight deck. When airborne, they formed into squadrons and joined the massive attack group. Seventy-six fighters peeled off and headed northwest, engines straining to get as high as they could as fast as they could.

John focused his binoculars and watched the massive fighter squadron gain altitude and speed to its assigned position.

"They're circling at about twenty-five thousand feet," John said, as he peered intently through his binoculars. "Looks like we're going to try to ambush them."

Ski grabbed his glasses and focused them on the circling fighters. "Who the hell do they think they're trying to kid? The Japs will spot them, too. You have to have someplace to hide to pull off an ambush!"

"The Japs don't know we're waiting there," John countered. "That's how the ambush is going to come off."

"Bullshit! You think the Japs don't know we've spotted them?"

"That's right. They don't. If Mitscher thought they did, he'd be attacking them head-on."

Ski shook his head. "No way! As far as I'm concerned, Gunner, the idea of an ambush is a big dream."

"Well, we'll see. I sure hope it works. I'd hate to live with the thought that you were smarter than both Admiral Mitscher and Admiral Spruance," John retorted with a grin.

On *Franklin's* bridge there was a high state of tension. All eyes were focused on the western horizon. From this vantage point Shoemaker, Day, Taylor and Beckley could clearly watch the circling Hellcats and Corsairs through binoculars.

"Chief," Shoemaker said, "see if you can get some of the action on the squawk box."

Beckley gave the Captain's command to the chief radioman. After receiving only static for a few minutes, a voice burst through the loudspeaker: "Flight leaders. Be alert. We should be able to spot them in the next five to ten minutes. From now till we spot them, maintain maximum radio silence."

Beckley looked over at the Captain.

Shoemaker nodded and flashed a thumbs-up.

"Lot of pressure on those pilots," Beckley said. "It's the real war for them now, life or death. Some of those guys flying fighters won't be around tomorrow."

"If those Jap planes get through, maybe some of us will be missing, too," Shoemaker added.

The squawk box on the bridge erupted into life: "Bogeys! Bogeys! Lots of 'em, at two o'clock. About six miles South and West of us!" an excited voice from the Attack Wing shouted.

"Steady. Steady. Stay in formation!" Zimler's voice commanded.

Beckley and Shoemaker focused their binoculars on the gigantic battle as it began to unfold. The Japanese attackers flew directly toward the circling Hellcats and Corsairs. Sixty Hellcats and Corsairs ripped into at least that many Jap fighters and bombers.

"Jap Zero! High starboard at two o'clock!"

"I got one on my first pass!"

"I overshot the son-of-a-bitch!"

"I just burned one!"

"There's one down on the water!"

"Got him. Splashed him into the drink!"

"Get that son-of-a-bitch! He's diving on a destroyer."

"You've got one on your tail, Dick!"

"Scratch one fucking Zero!"

"Scratch another one!"

"I told you they couldn't ambush them," Ski said as he watched the furious dogfight.

"Maybe not, but it looks like we're winning," John replied. "So far I've counted five Zeros shot down and none from our side!"

The vicious air battle went on for about an hour. Then the Japanese planes suddenly broke away and headed directly for the ships in the Task Group.

"All hands be alert!" John shouted to his gun crew. "If they get through the outer screen, blast them."

As the Japanese fighters and bombers approached the Task Group, guns from the destroyers and cruisers in the outer screen blazed away. Battleships brought their powerful fourteen- and sixteen-inch naval rifles into the fight. Fighters from the carriers *Bunker Hill* and *Princeton*, held in reserve for just such an emergency, attacked.

"Hey, Gunner!" Garcia shouted. "Not a single plane is getting through!"

John focused his binoculars on the huge battle in the skies above him. "Keep your eyes open. In the gray of that horizon, they can be on you before you know it."

John's gun crew watched the enormous battle with excited apprehension. The action was now very close. They cheered loudly every time a Zero or Zeke went down in flames.

"A bomber just got through to a battleship!" Ski shouted. "I saw it score a direct hit on the *South Dakota*."

John trained his glasses toward the *South Dakota*. "Yeah, it hit her, but she's not badly damaged. She's still firing away with all her guns."

"Look! A Zeke's attacking the *Bunker Hill*," Colson shouted.

"Yes, and a Hellcat's right on his ass, blazing away with all his guns," Ski yelled back. "Look at those shells tear into its fuselage—that Zeke is getting ripped to pieces."

The Zeke exploded into a mass of flaming debris.

"They got the son-of-a-bitch," John said, as debris from the Zeke drifted down toward the water.

"Goddamn, those fly-boys are having all the fun," Colson said. "It might sound crazy, but right now I'd like to get a little of that glory."

"Your turn to be a hero will come, Colson," John cautioned. "Remember there are two kinds of heroes, one that's walking around in glory and the other that's buried under those little white crosses in military cemeteries. When a Jap plane comes zooming in on you, Buddy, you can never be sure which one you're going to be, so don't be so anxious to get your glory."

"That looks like about the last of them," Ski said. "The rest are turning tail and running home."

"How many do you think we got?" John asked.

"I didn't count but I'll bet it's over forty," Ski replied.

"At least that many, maybe more, and I don't think we lost more than two or three of ours," John said, pride filling his voice. "Now that's a goddamned victory, Ski, even if it wasn't an ambush!"

"For once, I have to agree with you, Gunner. It was a great victory," Ski said as he placed his hand on John's shoulder and grinned. "But you have to admit, I was smarter than Spruance and Mitscher on the ambush part."

John laughed. "Yeah, I have to admit you were, and my guess is you'll never let me live it down."

Dusk was falling and the skies were now completely clear of enemy planes. Only a few survived the heated action and some of them were badly damaged. There were fifty-four confirmed kills and six were "probable." News of the victory filled the intercommunication centers of the Fifth Fleet.

#

On the bridge of the *Lexington*, Mitscher's voice exuded excitement. "We kicked their yellow asses," he said.

Burke was equally delighted. "We sure did, Admiral. It was a hell of an action and this time there's no question about who the winner was." As he turned to congratulate Mitscher, a breathless radioman rushed onto the bridge.

"Admiral," he said, "two reports just in from the submarine fleet."

Mitscher grabbed the reports and anxiously read them. "Christ, wonderful!" he shouted as he turned to Burke and waved the messages vigorously. "Submarines, God, I love 'em today! *Albacore* torpedoed the *Taiho*, Ozawa's largest carrier. She went down with most of her crew. And *Cavalla* torpedoed the *Shokaku*. She went down, too. Am I grateful for our submarines? What would we have done with out 'em today?"

"So they got the *Shokaku*," Burke said. "That's the last surviving carrier from the Pearl Harbor attack. She's where she belongs now, down at the bottom of the Philippine Sea."

That night, in one debriefing after another, a central fact emerged. The Japanese pilots in this action were not the skilled pilots who fought American airmen to a standstill around Tulagi and Guadalcanal two years earlier. These pilots fought tentatively and seemed badly trained.

When Mitscher realized this glaring weakness, his entire strategy changed. "Put the word out, Arleigh," he said. "No more trying to trap them. If they come at us again tomorrow, we go after the bastards head-on."

The next day, Ozawa attacked with an even larger force. Radar on the *Lexington* located an attack group of over ninety planes coming from the Japanese fleet. *Franklin's* radar picked up at least forty bombers coming from airfields on Tinian and Rota. The Japanese were attacking again with over one hundred thirty planes."

Commander Dawson Martin and his fighter squadrons went back into action. They met the Japanese head on a hundred miles west of the Fifth Fleet. Their attack seemed to come sooner than the inexperienced Japanese pilots expected. At first, they were tentative and unsure. Then furious dogfights erupted all over the sky.

"Scratch one!"

"That's my third!"

"Scratch another one!"

"I just flamed another one!"

"It's my second!"

"I've got another one!"

"His engine's throwing oil!"

"Get out! You're on fire!"

"I ripped off his belly tank. He just blew up!"

"I got number four. He's goin' down!"

Always in the thick of the action, Joe Crowley bracketed his crosshairs on a Zeke fighter-bomber. He pressed his trigger button firmly. A burst of fifty-caliber shells lashed out at the Zeke and tore out pieces of its fuselage and wing. The Zeke exploded in a mass of flames.

"I got my third," he shouted over the intercom. "It just went up in flames. I'm flying through the smoke now."

"My wingman, 'Wattie' Neff, flamed another one," Crowley shouted. "This is a goddamn turkey shoot! The Great Marianas Turkey Shoot!"

The Japanese were hopelessly out-maneuvered and out-smarted. The damage to their fleet was severe: over two hundred forty planes were destroyed and another fifty-two badly damaged in the two-day battle. Two major carriers, five destroyers and twenty-one transport vessels were sunk or extensively damaged. American losses: thirty planes shot down and one battlewagon damaged.

The American victory had major consequences. It left the powerful Japanese First Fleet defeated, dispirited and virtually without aircraft, limping slowly back toward the safety of Okinawa.

Within hours, news of the American victories in the Philippine Sea flashed throughout the Pacific Fleet, and then around the world. Crowley's name for the battle stuck. In official Navy bulletins, on radios, on everybody's lips and in newspapers throughout the free world, it was the "Great Marianas Turkey Shoot," one of the greatest victories in the history of the United States Navy.

As all the news of the victories in the Philippine Sea came into the *Franklin's* Combat Information Center, there was tremendous jubilation.

"They got their yellow asses kicked!" men shouted. "Teach the bastards to screw with the Fifth Fleet!"

Shoemaker looked over a final message from Spruance and Mitscher:

19 JUNE, 1944. *ATTENTION ALL UNITS FIFTH FLEET:*

Units of the Fifth Fleet scored a decisive victory over the Japanese Imperial Navy. Confirmed kills: 245 aircraft—over 50 aircraft damaged. Submarine action sank the carriers Taiho and Shokaku and two other light carriers yet to be identified. Some damage to other minor surface units. It was a "turkey shoot." The Great Marianas Turkey Shoot. A word of extreme caution—there was no damage to major surface units. Neither Yamato nor Musashi were in this fight. The Japanese Fleet has withdrawn toward Okinawa. Most Fifth Fleet units returning to Eniwetok for supplies, a few repairs and a little rest. We kicked their asses!

Spruance and Mitscher

"This is great news," a smiling Beckley said as he read the message Shoemaker passed around.

"Yes, Chief, it is," Shoemaker agreed, "but we have to avoid overconfidence. Don't forget the communiqué also said that *all* the major Japanese surface ships escaped damage, and the Japs haven't stopped making planes and training pilots. It's sad to say, but this war is far from over."

Beckley's smile faded. "You're right there, sir," he said, slowly nodding his head.

CHAPTER TWELVE

25 June, 1944
Eniwetok Atoll
Temporary Headquarters, Fifth Fleet

At dawn, the *Franklin*, together with other units of the victorious Fifth Fleet, entered Eniwetok harbor and steamed slowly to their assigned berths.

On the bridge of the *Franklin*, Beckley looked over the warships that fashioned the momentous victory over the powerful Japanese First Fleet. Huge fleet carriers and mighty battleships steamed slowly to their anchorages. *South Dakota* was already there. Workmen were busy repairing the damage to her superstructure caused by the Japanese bomb.

Nearly every vessel there had a sign that proclaimed the words of Spruance and Mitscher's last communiqué:

"WE KICKED THEIR ASSES."

The submarines, which returned a day earlier, had a huge sign that extended entirely over their four masts: *"WE KICKED ASS TOO—FOUR CARRIERS WORTH!"*

As the *Franklin* steamed slowly past the light cruisers, Beckley focused a pair of binoculars on their sterns. About halfway through the tightly docked cruisers, Beckley spotted the *Santa Fe*. "Boatswain, pass the word for Gunner's Mate John Oxler and Chief Gunner Peter Sullivan to come to the bridge," he said.

When John and Sullivan reached the bridge, Beckley was waiting with a grin.

"I've got a surprise for you, John," he said.

"Yeah, and I'll bet I know what it is," Sullivan said, also grinning broadly. "You spotted the *Santa Fe*."

"We spotted her, too, Beck," John said, "but thanks a lot for thinking about me."

"John's in tonight's liberty section, Chief," Sullivan said. "He can finally get ashore to see his buddy from home."

"Yeah. We already made contact. We're going to meet at the beer station at 19:00."

Early that evening, John climbed into a motor wale boat and headed to the beach where the NCO beer station was located. As soon as the boat docked, John jumped ashore. Standing on the edge of the dock not thirty yards away was Tom Rashinski.

"Hey Tom!" John shouted. Tom returned the call with a wave.

When John reached Tom, the two shook hands, then they gave each other an awkward hug.

"It's been nearly three years," Tom said.

"Yeah. A long time," John replied. "Goddamn I'm glad to see you."

"Me, too, Buddy; there's been a lot of water under the bridge," Tom said.

They picked up their ration of beer and headed for a vacant table at the edge of the enclosure.

They talked of things back home and about their families. They shared some of their battle experiences. John told Tom about being on the *Lexington* when she went down and how close he'd come to death on the *Vincennes*.

Tom talked about Bougainville and Tarawa and his great respect for the *Santa Fe*'s skipper. Finally, he broached the subject of Diane. "Jo Ann wrote me about Diane," he said. He shook his head, "I can't believe she could do a thing like that to you, Buddy."

"Yeah, it's really tough to take," John replied. "I'm still not sure how I'm doing with it—some days great—some days bad, but I'm getting through it I guess."

He paused for a moment, unsure of where to go next. Then remembering that he was talking to an old and trusted friend, he told Tom the whole story about meeting Sandy. "I thought I found her, Tom—the girl of my dreams. When I left she said she loved me. She promised she'd write. That was over seven weeks ago. We've had a lot of mail calls and there was not one letter." He paused. "What the hell is it with women?" he asked as he looked down into the sand. "Can you trust any of them?"

"I don't know," Tom replied. "I don't know what goes on in their heads."

"I thought this was the real thing," John said, "I love you. I'll write to you—then nothing."

"Well, a couple of nights of necking is easy for a gal to forget, especially if you didn't get into her panties," Tom said absently.

There was another long pause. "My philosophy is lay 'em, leave 'em and forget 'em. That way you don't gel hurt."

Although it wasn't intended, what Tom said was depressing. John's spirits returned to the low ebb that haunted him after every mail call.

John looked at Tom. Tom seemed to be struggling for words again.

"What?" John asked.

"Why didn't you write to her?"

"I did. I wrote her *four* letters. I didn't get an answer to *any* of them."

"So why didn't you keep writing?"

"After what Diane did, I guess I'm afraid to trust women. Maybe none of them can be trusted."

"I'm not sure about that, Buddy," Tom said. "Why don't you cheer up until you have another mail call or two. You know how screwed-up the goddamned mail is, and let's face it, we've been kind of out of touch for the last few weeks."

"Yeah. Thanks, Tom, that's good advice," John said. "You're right. That makes me feel better."

The return-to-ship call rang out. They had talked nearly three hours.

"It's good to see you, Buddy," John said. "Remember me to your mom and dad and especially to Jo Anne when you write. Your sister is a sweetheart. She tried to help me after Diane."

"I'm glad you came into the Fifth Fleet, John," Tom said. "It's great to know there's somebody from home out here with me. Sometimes it can be one helluva messy fucking war."

27 June, 1944
Return to Action
Target: Iwo Jima

The next morning, a message came over the wire from Task Group Command:

ATTENTION U.S.S. FRANKLIN, TASK FORCE 58.2:

Prepare for departure at 08:00, 28 June. Load all aviation ordinance and take on all necessary supplies immediately. In addition to regular ordinance, you will continue to utilize missiles. Task Force 58.2 to be comprised of carriers: Wasp, Franklin, Saratoga, and Cabot. Cruisers: Boston, Canberra, Santa Fe and Pittsburgh and nine destroyers. Group battle plan is to seek out and destroy Japanese surface and air units on and around the island of Iwo Jima, Bonin Islands.
Raymond Spruance

The level of activity on the *Franklin* increased. It was late that night before all the ammunition was loaded. For John it was like a rerun of a bad dream. The *Franklin* had two mail calls. There was mail from home but nothing from Sandy. He was exhausted. "I give up," he muttered as he dropped into his bunk. "She's not going to write."

#

At 08:00 the *Franklin* hoisted anchor and Task Force 58.2 got underway. On the bridge of the *Lexington*, Ray Spruance and Marc Mitscher watched TF 58.2 steam by. "*Franklin's* a beautiful ship," Spruance said as he gazed at her through his binoculars. "She's the thirteenth carrier to come into the fleet in fourteen months, Marc. I can understand why Nimitz is dividing the Fifth Fleet. It's too big for a single chain of command."

Mitscher lowered his binoculars and turned to Spruance. "I'm sure much of the rest of the fleet is pretty weary, too. Some of the cruiser and destroyer crews have been out here for nine to ten months. Frankly," he concluded, "although I wouldn't admit it to anyone else, I could use a break in the action, too."

"Well, Bill Halsey will be here in about an hour," Spruance said, "and we'll get full details of what's going on from him. By the way," he added as he rubbed his chin thoughtfully, "Halsey was at the Honolulu Conference. Scuttlebutt is that Roosevelt, Nimitz and MacArthur decided on goals for *Operation Victorious* for the next six to twelve months. He's bringing us word on this, too."

"If we get the right message, maybe, in another year, we can get this goddamned mess wrapped up, Ray," Mitscher said. "At least I hope so, but whatever the word is, we'll get 'er done. It'll be interesting to find out what our top brass decided on," he added.

At 08:30 Admiral William Halsey was piped aboard the *Lexington*. Halsey was known throughout the Pacific Fleet as "Bull" for his swashbuckling combat style and as the architect of Jimmy Doolittle's astonishing B-25 raid on Tokyo in April, 1942.

He and Admiral John "Slew" McCain, who would relieve Mitscher, were immediately escorted to the wardroom. Ray Spruance, Marc Mitscher and their staffs were waiting.

After they had exchanged greetings, Halsey said, "Ray, I want to congratulate you and Marc on the victory in the Philippine Sea. That's the second time you guys stole my thunder." He laughed, but there was competitiveness in his voice. "Ever since you guys whipped the Japs at Midway, you've had the hot hand."

Spruance knew Halsey was sensitive about being replaced at Midway. "I replaced you at Midway because you had a skin infection, Admiral," Spruance said in an even tone. "If it hadn't been for that, you'd have been in command. You'd have probably done a hell of a lot better job than we did there."

Halsey frowned slightly. "I'm not so sure about that. You two make a pretty good team. That job you just did on the Japs in the Philippine Sea was a dandy."

"By the way," Slew McCain asked, "which one of you had the idea to call it a 'turkey shoot?'"

Spruance and Mitscher looked at each other and laughed.

"One of the pilots came up with the name after he got his third kill, Admiral," Spruance replied. "We didn't have anything to do with it."

McCain shook his head. "Incredible. What a great name for a battle."

Halsey chuckled and agreed. Then he said in a serious tone, "Here's where we are, gentlemen. As many of you already know, Nimitz has reorganized the Fifth Fleet into two task forces. He believes this realignment provides us greater flexibility. One task group will train and plan while the other fights. Nimitz believes this will reduce the time between operations and allow for more continuous and effective attacks. It will also get you guys some rest. He understands you've all been out here a long time, and that time away from combat is something everybody needs."

He paused. "When I'm in command, the Task Group will be identified as TF 38, and when Ray is in command, it will continue to be TF 58. As Admiral Nimitz put it, 'the team remains about the same but the drivers change occasionally.'"

After listening to more of the broad details of the reorganization plan, Spruance and Mitscher both agreed that they liked it.

Halsey ordered an aide to distribute mimeographed packets that contained full details of the reorganization. "Those are all the nuts and bolts of the change," he said.

After allowing time for Spruance and Mitscher to look them over, he asked, "Are there any questions?"

"What's the timetable for implementation, Admiral?" Spruance asked.

"As soon as we're sure that everybody understands what's happening, Ray. My guess is in about two to three weeks."

"Who decides what ships are where, Admiral?" Mitscher asked.

"We do, Marc. I can assure you Nimitz wants your and Ray's complete involvement."

Discussions then turned to the conference held in Honolulu between President Roosevelt, General MacArthur and Admiral Nimitz.

"I had hoped I could bring you more news about the future of *Victorious*," Halsey said. "But while the conference in Honolulu got a lot of press, unfortunately it developed only a limited number of directives. *Victorious* still calls for MacArthur to invade the Philippines, but there's not a specific time set yet. MacArthur wanted the invasion to come sooner, and Nimitz wanted it delayed."

He paused and looked intently around the room. Everyone seemed to perk up at the suggestion of a confrontation between these two powerful commanders. "Nimitz wanted to go after bases in the Bonin Islands first," Halsey continued as he looked carefully around the wardroom. "We don't know yet who won out, but believe it or not, Nimitz had the support of the Army Air Corps. Superforts have a range just less than three thousand miles. The round trip from Saipan to Tokyo and back is slightly more than that. The Air Force has found they have to squeeze out every ounce of fuel to make the trip both ways. They need a halfway base that their Superforts can divert to, in case they're disabled or run short of fuel. This explains the recent directives to attack Iwo Jima and Chi Chi Jima. They're primary targets now. Nimitz sees one of these two islands as that base."

"Do you have any idea which one it'll be?" Spruance asked.

"It'll probably be Iwo Jima," Halsey replied. "It has a longer airfield. But before we go after either, we need to take Morotai Island and capture Ulithi and Peleliu. MacArthur's infantry and Kinkaid's Seventh Fleet will handle Morotai. We'll get Ulithi and Peleliu with the Marines. Meanwhile, the Fast Carrier Forces will soften up Iwo and Chi Chi Jima. I understand, Ray, that you got word from Nimitz on that part of the plan late last week."

Spruance nodded. "Affirmative, Admiral. A task force left for the Bonin Islands just before you arrived this morning."

"You'll all be happy to know," Halsey concluded, "that Formosa has been bypassed. It's just too heavily fortified and too easily supplied from Jap bases on the Chinese coast. So the Philippines will become the great staging area for the future invasion of Japan. MacArthur got his way about this."

There were a series of questions on the implementation of *Victorious*. When Halsey finished answering these, he adjourned the meeting.

The master-at-arms rose and read the standard prepared statement: "To all in attendance: be informed the information in these proceedings is classified as top-secret. This information and discussions in this room are now fully secured."

"All rise," he said to end the meeting.

After Halsey and McCain left the *Lexington*, Spruance and Mitscher sat in the wardroom sipping coffee.

"Well, the grand plan we hoped for didn't materialize," Spruance said. "No overall plan to end the war."

"We didn't get it all, Ray," Mitscher said. "But what we got points us in the right direction. We're gaining ground every day, and it's just a matter of time until we're sitting outside of Tokyo, blasting hell out of them from there."

"And we did get a little time to rest," Spruance said with a smile.

"Yes, that's true," Mitscher replied. "I'll be certain the men who have been out there longest get rotated back first. I know it's not home or even Pearl Harbor, but it sure as hell beats being on the wrong end of a Jap artillery shell."

"Of course, Marc," Spruance said. "That's a number one priority for both of us."

2 July, 1944.
Steaming toward Iwo Jima
Bonin Islands

Task Force 58.2 steamed North Northwest on course 325° with a speed of twenty knots, toward the Bonin Islands. They were in Condition of Readiness III, zigzagging in Plan 6. The *Wasp* was the task force leader at the formation's center. *Franklin* and *Saratoga* each flanked her at distances of twenty-two hundred yards. *Cabot* followed at twenty-one hundred yards. The cruisers *Santa Fe*, *Pittsburgh*, *Canberra* and *Boston* formed the inner screen spaced forty-two hundred yards from center. Nine destroyers formed the outer screen.

At 12:26, Mitscher ordered a simulated surprise attack on the Task Group. Over a hundred planes towing practice sleeves buzzed the Task Group from every point on the compass.

Aboard the *Franklin*, a frantic call to arms roared through the loudspeakers.

"General Quarters! General Quarters!"

"Gun crews. Man your battle stations!"

Adrenaline flowed. John and Ski rushed up to their battle stations.

Guns from the destroyers in the outer screen filled the sky with glowing tracers and high-demolition shells. Cruisers added to the Task Group's defense with fire from their six- and eight-inch guns.

John's crew began firing as soon as the sleeves came into range. Ski and Lowe urged their men on. Synchronized bursts from John's 40-mm guns powered strings of tracers into the sleeves as they went by. One was ripped into tatters by the accuracy of their fire.

John was delighted. "Yes!" he screamed. "Yes! Get another one!"

They did. They shot up a second sleeve into more tattered pieces than the first. Then they did the same thing to a third.

When the attack ended John was filled with pride. "Good show," he said jubilantly. "Not one screwed up!"

Then he turned to Ski and Lowe and said, "A great job. I couldn't ask for a better one. Nice goin' guys."

Lowe laughed. "Gee, John," he said. "Is that all it takes to satisfy you? We can do that anytime."

"Yeah," the rest of the crew agreed. Ski just stood there grinning.

"You guys are shaping up. We're going to be ready," John said as he climbed the ladder to the flight deck.

By the time he got to his compartment some of the elation had worn off, and his thoughts drifted to Sandy. It was easy to forget her when he was busy, but the tough times came when he was alone with nothing to do and before going to sleep. "She *is* tough to forget," he muttered.

On the bridge everyone was in high spirits. Early reports far exceeded Shoemaker's expectations—especially the performances of gunnery and damage control.

"The new men are veterans—dedicated seaman," he said to Dave Day and Ben Moore. "They've really helped improve the efficiency of this ship. I'm sure happy to have them aboard."

"I agree, sir," Day replied. "I'll be honest with you, Captain. I didn't think they would make this much difference."

"Neither did I," Moore added.

"Well, that doesn't matter now," Shoemaker said. "What does matter is we've finally got a crew. I was very pleased by the reports from gunnery and damage control. A-1. Not a single screw-up in either division."

"Couldn't come at a better time," Day responded.

"I agree," Shoemaker said. Then he paused and shook his head slightly. "That whole business with the crew…I wondered whether we'd ever get it straightened out."

Joe Taylor rushed onto the bridge. "Captain," he said, "we just got a report from *Wasp*. Weather Control on Eniwetok is reporting a huge storm directly ahead. It's about one hundred thirty miles away."

"What does our radar say?" Shoemaker asked.

"Our radar confirms it, sir," Taylor replied.

"They say it's a big and slow-moving storm. It spreads all the way across their screens. It's too big to sail around. *Wasp* directs we rig for extreme foul weather."

Shoemaker instinctively raised his binoculars and scanned the distant horizon. "I don't see anything yet," he murmured, "but we're still pretty far away."

"At our speed we should be in it in about five hours, Captain," Moore said.

"Not much time," Shoemaker replied. "If it turns out to be a typhoon or even a storm that's as big as they suspect, we have to get everything lashed down on the double." He looked out over the horizon again. "This is typhoon season in this part of the world. We always have to prepare as though it might be a big one."

"Aye, aye, Captain," Taylor said. "I've canceled air operations for the rest of the day. This won't set us back. I was planning a general meeting with the Air Group for later today anyhow."

"Pass the word to rig for foul weather," Shoemaker said to the chief boatswain on watch.

The loudspeaker blared the command: "Attention all hands! Attention all hands! Rig for foul weather! On the double!"

In a matter of minutes, life jackets and foul-weather gear were on and the flight and hangar decks were filled with men rushing to tie down anything that was unrestrained. Planes were lowered from the flight deck by both elevators. They were lashed to the hangar deck with heavy cables. Covers and caps were put on guns. Watertight doors were closed and secured. Everything on the flight deck and in the gun sponsons was rapidly tied down. Bombs, missiles and torpedoes were removed from their wing racks and returned to the safety of ordinance compartments.

About 13:30 that afternoon winds began to increase, kicking up whitecaps all over the ocean. John, Ski and Lowe and the rest of the gun crew finished capping and covering their 40s. From their position in Able Sponson at the bow end of the ship, they stared at the huge storm lying directly in their path. The sky was a threatening mass of monstrous black clouds. Bolts of lightning struck through the clouds. They sent jagged electrical power ripping down to the surface of the ocean. As TF 58.2 moved into the storm, the bolts of lightning increased. With the lightning came the crack of thunder, which seemed to be just overhead. The strength of the wind increased dramatically and huge waves began to batter the task force. Every ship strained to force its way through the storm's vast power. A torrential rain mixed with hail pelted down.

The *Franklin* started to pitch and roll violently. One minute the bow seemed to be high on the horizon, the next it seemed to be crashing into the sea. *Franklin's* bow dipped so deep into the trough of the gigantic waves that her huge propellers lifted right out of the water. They screeched as though they were angry for being pulled from their natural depths. Huge waves cascaded onto the fantail. Rain and hail followed. Water began to drain into the hangar deck.

"Let's get below," John shouted, struggling to be heard over the noise of the savage wind and rain.

Ski and Lowe took up the command. "All hands below decks! On the double! We've done all we can up here."

The violent winds whipped a mass of salty spray across the *Franklin's* flight deck. Rain and hail cascaded down. Eighty-foot waves engulfed her, causing her to shudder under the impact. Sailors strained against guidelines to keep themselves from being swept overboard.

"John, this is crazy! What a storm! Look at those waves!" Carlson screamed.

John was fearful, too. In his nearly three years in the Navy, he'd never been in a storm like this. He'd do his best not to show his fear. He had to, because everyone else seemed so terrorized.

"Have you ever been bounced around like this before, John?" Carlson asked as they rushed down the ladder to the hangar deck.

"No, but don't worry. This ship is seaworthy. We'll be okay," John replied, surprised at the confidence in his voice.

A huge wave forced *Franklin* into a dangerous list to starboard. It jolted John's gun crew into the hangar deck bulkhead. Almost everyone wound up on his knees.

"Can this ship take this kinda pounding?" Garcia asked as he picked himself up and tried to brush off the water that soaked his dungarees.

"Hell, yes! This is a strong ship. She'll come through," John said.

Another huge wave jolted the *Franklin* to port. John, along with everybody else, lost his balance and skidded along the water-soaked deck toward the port side. They regained their balance. Their clothes were now soaked, grease-stained and filthy.

"Fuck!" Bonin howled. "How in the hell long is this goddamned thing going to last?"

"How in the hell do I know?" John replied. "Let's get to that hatch and go below."

The *Franklin's* bow pitched violently upward. Everyone skidded back toward the fantail.

"Is this goddamned thing going to capsize?" Garcia asked, his eyes wide with fear.

"This is the worst thing I've ever been in!" Bonin shouted, his voice filled with frustration.

"Don't worry about it," John shouted back. "There might come a time, when the Japs are blasting away at you, that you'd wish you were back in this storm."

"I hope that fucking day never comes," Bonin said.

John and his gun crew struggled to the hatch that led below. "Let's go to the mess hall," John said when they got down to the second deck. "The lower you go, the less you feel the ship's pitching and rolling."

When they got to the mess hall, there was already a large group of men there. Most were sitting at crowded tables with their heads buried in their arms. Others sat on the deck against the bulkheads, many with their heads between their knees.

"Find a place to sit and take one of those positions," John said. "They'll make it easier to ride this bastard out."

The *Franklin* creaked, rattled and groaned. The huge storm pitched her around like a cork. Fearful thuds echoed through the mess hall when something tore loose and banged against a deck or bulkhead. Despite the chaos, the mellow notes of the Benny Goodman Band drifted from the mess hall's loudspeakers.

John found a place along the forward bulkhead and sat down. He put his head between his knees and took a deep breath. He was wet, cold and tired. The fearful concerns of his gun crew troubled him. What the hell would they do in an attack—in a time of real crisis? A piercing yelp suddenly got his attention. He looked up and saw Bonin rushing for the head covering his mouth with his hat. He didn't make it. Half way to the hatch he threw up. Everything he had for breakfast spewed out into his hat and onto his shirt and dungarees.

The *Franklin* continued to pitch and roll violently. Huge waves pounded her bow mercilessly. Water drained below decks. The mess hall deck was now covered by at least an inch of dirty, murky water. It sloshed from port to starboard, then fore to aft and back. It seemed to have no sense of direction. Everyone was drenched, dirty and cold. Most just sat where they were, aware that there was probably no place on the ship that was any better.

John put his head back between his knees. His stomach started to feel queasy, but he resisted the urge to vomit. He was wet, cold, heartsick and miserable. He searched his thoughts for something to distract him from his distress. Sandy's image came. He tried to push it out of his thoughts by praying the *Our Father*. It didn't work. Her image came back again. The creaking, rattling and banging sounds faded, the chill from the annoying deck water and from his soggy, squalid clothes drifted away. His fear and misery left him. The music gradually died away…there she was as beautiful as ever. He felt her in his arms. Memories of her firm breasts touching his chest came rushing back. A flow of love and passionate desire rushed through him. He tilted her chin and kissed her. She yielded her body to him and murmured, "I love you…."

A foldaway table stored in an overhead rack crashed to the filthy deck! Another followed. A seaman rushed toward the hatch, vomiting his guts out.

The chaos brought John out of his reverie. "Damn," he said aloud. "She once asked me how she could help me. This is how. She could help me survive this crazy, goddamned war." He felt more miserable than ever.

Late that afternoon, the pilots in Air Group Thirteen fought their way to the ready room. The violent storm continued unabated. When Joe Taylor pushed his way in, a barrage of questions greeted him.

"Was it a full-blown typhoon?"

"How strong were the winds?"

"Was everything lashed down?"

Taylor answered as best he could with the limited knowledge he had. "If it's not a typhoon, it's damned close. The winds ripped away our wind gauge. The bridge estimated the wind to be between 95 and 105 miles per hour," Taylor said.

"How long will the goddamned thing last?" Jim Crowley asked.

"We should be through the worst of it in the next twenty-four hours."

"How will it affect flight operations?" Zimler wondered.

"Flight operations will resume as soon as possible after the storm, Bill," Taylor said. "We think that might be tomorrow afternoon. If not, then the first thing Thursday morning." Taylor paused and steadied himself on the ready room podium. "Let's get to the business at hand, he said. "I know this storm's a pain in the ass, but it'll end soon. The war will still be waiting. It's not going to go away."

A huge wave rolled the *Franklin* to port, causing the table and the podium to slide away from Taylor. He and Joe Crowley, who was sitting in the front row of seats, stopped it and moved it back.

"Worse goddamned storm I've ever been in," Taylor said.

He realigned the notebook he'd placed on the podium. "When we last got into action we did a damned fine job. I want to commend Commander Crowley. He got three kills and in the process became a bit of a celebrity. He named that action the 'Great Marianas Turkey Shoot' and the name stuck."

Crowley stared uncomfortably at the deck.

"However, for the most part in that action we were just 'dancing in the chorus,'"

Taylor said. "This week we're the 'main event.'"

"What's our first assignment?" Zimler asked.

"We're going to hit Iwo Jima. Nimitz wants it pulverized. Captain Shoemaker says they're going to make it a halfway station for B-29s. When it happens, it'll become another step in the ladder to the Japanese mainland."

"Is it heavily fortified?" Zimler asked.

"Aren't they all, Bill?" replied Taylor. "Yes. You can count on that. There are heavy fortifications and a large number of aircraft defending it. Zeros and Zekes for sure and I think we can expect some attack-bombers, Judys and Kates. There may be land-based aircraft, too—G4M heavy bombers—Bettys."

"The whole works? All of them?" Zimler asked.

"We can't be certain, so be prepared to see them all," Taylor replied. "One thing is certain. We'll be using Tiny Tims again. It's hard to believe, but from what you guys reported, those goddamned missiles carry a hell of a wallop. Spruance, Mitscher, all the top brass were impressed with their accuracy and power. They want us to keep evaluating their effectiveness." He paused and looked about the room. "All the same rules apply," he said. "Fly in formation, don't be a lone wolf, protect your tail and watch out for your buddies."

"What about naval units?" someone called out.

"They've got a small fleet there—a few cruisers, but mostly destroyers. Naval Intelligence says about fifteen to twenty in all."

"Any carriers?"

"According to Intelligence, the answer is no. If we find any ships, Nimitz wants us to go after them first, even before we attack the island. Get as many as we can—the more we sink—the shorter the war. So if we find any, let's pound the hell out of them."

Silence.

"Let me remind you of a couple of final things. Remember, if you get shot up and have to abandon your plane, don't panic. Give us a good read on your position. The Fifth Fleet's got a hell of a safety net out there. Nine out of ten downed flyers are picked up by destroyers or submarines, most within twenty-four hours."

"Finally, there may be casualties. Deaths in combat are inevitable. If there are, and you lose someone close, get some help. Don't hold your feelings inside. This could put your life at risk, too. I'm always available, so are both chaplains and the rest of the officers in the air group." Taylor paused. "Questions?"

Silence.

"In the meantime, get some rest if you can. We'll reconvene as soon as the weather let's us get planes in the air."

As Taylor and Zimler left the ready room, another monstrous wave engulfed *Franklin*. She rolled violently to port.

"Goddamn, Commander, this storm is violent," Zimler said. "I think I'd rather take my chances with the Japs."

CHAPTER THIRTEEN

**5 July, 1944
North Pacific Ocean
SSW of Iwo Jima**

After two days of furious weather, the storm ended almost as abruptly as it began. The winds diminished and the skies brightened. The once powerful waves shrank to ripples. It was hard to believe there had ever been a storm.

As the ocean calmed, the entire task force came to life again. New flags replaced those ripped by the winds and rain. Planes were reloaded with bombs, torpedoes and missiles. Ammunition was hauled back to ready-service compartments. Gun crews manned their battle stations. TF 58.2 was preparing for the real enemy. Iwo Jima was less than eighty miles away.

At 05:30 the air wing met in the ready room to identify targets on Iwo and discuss strategy. The atmosphere was filled with tension and anticipation. Joe Taylor walked to a large map of Iwo Jima. He pointed to the southeast side of the island and said, "This is where the heavy concentrations of pillboxes and antiaircraft guns are located. Recon photos show that they're dug in very deep. The airfield is about twenty miles north of the beach and is also heavily protected."

"The plan is," he said, as he continued to point to the southeast part of the island, "to clear out any units of the Jap fleet. If they're anywhere, they should be somewhere between the East Boat Basin, here, and Tachiwa Point, here. Next, we'll hit the heavy defenses along the beach. Ordinance men are fitting our missiles with high explosive heads. They think they'll work well on beach defenses. Once you've taken care of these two things, if you have any ammunition left, go after the guns implanted in Suribachi."

"Do we know how many planes are there?" Zimler asked.

"We're not sure, but you can be certain there are some—probably Zeros and Zekes."

"Don't be concerned about Jap planes unless they attack you. The attack group from the *Wasp* will come in right after you. They're scheduled to attack the airfield. Any other questions?"

Silence.

On the bridge of the *Franklin*, Shoemaker, Day and Taylor watched the planes in Able Attack Group come up from the hangar deck. The first to come up were the fighters, commanded by Joe Crowley. Next were the Avengers and Helldivers, commanded by Bill Zimler.

At 06:46 aircrews began launching planes. Sleek Hellcats zoomed into the air first, followed by bombers and torpedo bombers. The strike group formed and headed northeast for Iwo Jima. After they were airborne for twenty-five minutes, Joe Crowley's excited voice erupted through the intercom. "Zeros! Zekes at two o'clock high! They're coming in fast. Hellcat squadron commence attack."

Zimler looked to his right. "See 'em, Dino?"

"Aye sir. There's about two dozen."

"Bald Eagle to bomber squadron. Our job's on Iwo. Let the fighters handle this unless we're attacked."

"Roger."

The Hellcats, flying about six thousand yards ahead of the Avengers, streaked down toward the Japanese Zeros and Zekes.

"They're in perfect position," Zimler said. "Four thousand feet above them."

Dogfights erupted all over the western horizon.

Voices flashed through the intercom.

"Hit 'em hard! Blast right through the bastards!"

"Scratch one!"

"I'll get the one on the right!"

"I splashed one!"

"I splashed another one!"

"Pull up and over! There's one on your tail!"

"God! I'm on fire!"

Zimler saw a damaged Hellcat bank sharply to its right and spiral crazily toward the ocean.

"I see a parachute," Dino said.

"Bald Eagle to Emerald Base! Pilot abandoning fighter. Longitude 142 degrees, latitude 28 degrees, distance approximately sixty-five miles East Southeast of Iwo Jima."

"Roger, Bald Eagle. Read you loud and clear," came the response from *Franklin*.

The Avengers and Helldivers droned on. Iwo Jima came up through the haze in the distance.

Zimler looked at his chart. He identified Mount Suribachi, his first landmark. "Dino, use your glasses. Search that beach area from Suribachi to Tachiwa Pont. If the Jap Navy is anywhere, they'd be there somewhere."

Antonelli scanned the area.

"See anything?"

"I looked it over good, sir. I don't see a ship anywhere."

"Bald Eagle to bomber squadron. Anyone see any ships along the coast?"

A negative report came back from the bombers in the squadron.

"Okay, we attack the antiaircraft targets along the beach," Zimler ordered.

On the horizon, Hellcats and Zeros were locked in a furious running battle.

"How are the fighters doing, Dino?"

"I've counted seven Japs down to two of ours, sir. There goes number eight. It looks like they've had enough, sir. They're turning and running."

"Well, there's only one place they can go—unless they want to land in the ocean, Dino. As Joe Louis says, 'they can run but they can't hide.'"

"Bald Eagle to Emerald Base. Request change of target."

Joe Taylor's gruff voice came over the wire. "What's up, Bald Eagle?"

"The Jap planes are running," Zimler said, excitement filling his every word. "They're turning back to Iwo, Joe. When they land we can be right on their backs. Request permission to divert our attack."

"Roger. Go after the retreating planes. Strafe the antiaircraft positions next. Use your missiles, Bill. Let's see how many we can take out. After you've finished this sweep, go back and rough up their installations on Suribachi. Use any missiles and bombs you have left."

Zimler relayed the new attack plan to his pilots. When he finished he said, "All right, let's hit 'em hard! Let's blast 'em with everything we've got!"

Zimler's Avengers went into their dives. Helldivers followed right behind.

"Come in at fifteen hundred feet."

Red and yellow bursts of antiaircraft fire began to fill the sky.

An Avenger behind Zimler suffered a direct hit and exploded into a ball of fire.

"They got Durham, sir," Dino shouted.

"Any 'chutes?" Zimler demanded.

"I don't see any, sir."

When the airstrip flashed into view there were at least twelve Zeros and Zekes parked there, and nearly twice that many circling to land.

"This is crazy, Dino. They're flying into a trap."

"Aye, sir. They're not quite as smart as they used to be."

"Bald Eagle to squadron. Remember, use missiles first! Take out as many as you can. Then we'll come around again and get those that are trying to land," Zimler ordered.

On the first pass, most of the planes on the runways were wasted. The powerful Tiny Tims blasted the Zeros and Zekes into small pieces.

"This is like shooting ducks in a barrel!" Dino shouted.

"Bald Eagle to squadron. Let's make a long, deep circle. Let the rest of them land. They'll be easy targets on the ground."

Zimler radioed Crowley and the Hellcats who were circling like a group of angry hornets about a mile away. "Bald Eagle to Gray Fox! Bald Eagle to Gray Fox!"

"Roger, Bald Eagle," Crowley answered.

"We can take care of everything on the ground," Zimler said. "You provide us cover. Maybe there are some of those bastards somewhere else. Maybe they've got another airstrip—even a carrier somewhere. Send some of your fighters north along the coast to check. Tell them to be damned careful not to get ambushed."

"Roger, Bald Eagle. Read you loud and clear."

"Dino, did you keep a count? How many did we get?"

"I think we got nine, sir. The Japs are moving planes that land off the runway into the trees."

"Keep track of where they're trying to hide them." Zimler shouted. "Bald Eagle to squadron! Let's go back and get the rest."

The Avengers and Helldivers turned and positioned for another sweep.

Zimler could see excited Japanese ground crews rushing to hide their planes.

"Dino."

"Aye, sir."

" How many can you count?"

"I count twelve, sir. Nine that just landed and three that we missed."

"Bald Eagle to squadron. It looks like there are twelve down there. Let's get them all on this run. If we get all of them, we go after the antiaircraft defenses."

The Avengers and Helldivers hurtled back toward the airfield. Zimler drew a Zeke into his sight and pressed his firing button. The Avenger jerked violently as the missile released and blazed toward the Zeke.

"Wow!" Dino shouted. "A direct hit! That's great shooting, sir."

By the time the remaining bombers in Able Squadron made their passes, twelve more wrecked aircraft were burning furiously on the ground below.

"Dino, did we get 'em all?"

"Yes, sir. There's nothing down there that's not burning."

"Bald Eagle to squadron. Go after the antiaircraft defenses along the beach. Hit 'em hard! Then we'll go back and strafe hell out of them. If we've got any ammo left we'll go after the guns in Suribachi. Don't take any ammo back."

The Avengers circled and came back toward the beach at an altitude of sixteen hundred feet.

"Bald Eagle to squadron! Let's go down to about seven hundred feet to get bigger targets!" Zimler thundered.

Antiaircraft fire streamed up. Red and orange bursts filled the sky.

An Avenger in the second wave burst into flames.

"They just got one of ours, sir," Dino said.

"Any parachutes?"

"One, sir. Looks like he's going to land in the water."

"Radio his position."

"Aye, sir."

Zimler's section was now over target. Their missiles blazed down toward the beach defenses. Four direct hits. Three very near misses.

Zimler pulled up and circled away from the beach so he could see the devastation. Many of the pillboxes were on fire and there were some secondary explosions.

"Did we lose anybody else, Dino?"

"I saw two more, sir. Lieutenant Gruenfelder for sure and one more I couldn't identify."

"Let's strafe hell out of them now!" Zimler shouted.

Japanese ground fire had dropped off markedly. Flying even lower this time, the Avengers opened fire with all wing guns. Sand and rubble on the beach churned up furiously, as one plane followed another in the concentrated attack. When the strafing ended, Zimler regrouped his squadron.

"Bald Eagle to squadron. Identify losses. Repeat. Identify losses."

Each section leader checked in. Four planes were lost, Durham, Gruenfelder, Webber and Lewis and their gunners. Zimler shook his head. He felt bad, but death had to be expected, especially in combat as intense as this.

"Bald Eagle to squadron. Good show! Let's head home."

With that, the Avengers climbed to an altitude of eighteen hundred feet and formed up with the Hellcats. They started South Southeast toward the Task Group.

"Aircraft at ten o'clock. About fifteen miles to starboard!" Dino yelled.

Zimler raised a pair of binoculars and looked intently to his right. After studying for a few moments, he said, "They're friendly, Dino. It's the attack group from the *Wasp*."

Relieved at Zimler's words, Dino called out, "That's good, sir, especially since everybody is about out of ammo. I almost feel a little sorry for those poor bastards on Iwo. They're going to get it again."

"Too bad," Zimler said. "They brought it on themselves."

When they sighted the *Franklin,* the Hellcats peeled off and headed in. Zimler's Avengers remained in formation until the fighters landed and the flight deck was clear, then they assumed their landing positions and made their approaches. Zimler was last to land. The entire squadron landed without incident.

As Zimler pulled himself out of his cockpit, he could see Beckley standing on the edge of the flight deck. As soon as he was on deck, Beckley walked over to meet him.

"How'd it go, sir?"

"It went very well, Beck. We got at least twenty-nine planes, most on the ground. Hellcats got eight in the air. By our count, we lost four Avengers and two Hellcats. Two parachutes were sighted—one from an Avenger and one from a Hellcat. The rest of the crews were probably lost." Zimler paused and looked back toward Iwo. "The Japs seem to have some heavy guns up on the side of that mountain. I think some of the planes we lost got caught in a crossfire."

"That's too bad."

"Yeah. It really is—but for me, it's a lot different than a head-on crash off the coast of San Diego. This is the real war. You have to expect deaths like this. These men died valorously. It's those deaths by accidents that are so damned hard to take."

"What's left out there, sir?"

"The antiaircraft defenses, especially on Suribachi. They were heavy," Zimler said. "When we left, a squadron from the *Wasp* was on its way to target them."

"And Air Strike Baker is all revved up and ready to go at 14:00," Beckley said. "Maybe there won't be much left when you go back in tomorrow."

"Hope not. We sure pounded hell out of them today. I was really proud of the squadron. They flew like veterans, precise, methodical and cool under fire. There wasn't a single glitch."

Beckley glanced at the huge number thirteen on the bridge. Zimler smiled at him. "The action we just went through makes us have different thoughts about bad luck or being jinxed, doesn't it? There were thirteen Zeros burning after we made our last pass. Looks like they were ones that were jinxed."

Beckley chuckled. "Yeah, you can say that again, sir. Maybe we did let that superstitious stuff get into our heads too much."

"Maybe so. Stay in touch, Beck," Zimler said as he walked toward the bridge to make his report.

Beckley was relieved by Zimler's attitude. He was right. Death is a part of war. This time death came from a fight, not from fate. We're sticking it to the bastards now, so no more thoughts about bad luck or disasters. It was the only way to feel under the circumstances.

John saw Beckley making his way across the flight deck. He hurried over to meet him.

"Word is that we pounded hell out of 'em. What did Commander Zimler have to say?" John asked.

"He said we kicked their ass and things went very smoothly," Beckley replied. "He was very proud of his squadron. He said it felt pretty good to be in some real action again."

"And how does it feel to you, Beck?"

"I'd almost forgot how it felt to have things go so well, even though we suffered a few casualties," Beckley said. "I hope Air Strike Baker has even better luck this afternoon. Maybe no deaths or injuries."

"Luck! So much of this goddamned war seems to hinge upon luck," John said with sudden irritation. "One of these days the Japs are going to get through to us. I'm not going to depend on luck. When they get here, we're going to be ready."

"Sounds like you're feeling good about your crew," Beckley said.

"I've got a gun crew now; a damned good one, Beck. When the Japs come, we're going to throw every fucking thing in the book at them—everything!"

They walked down the ladder to the hangar deck. For some reason, what they'd just talked about made John think of Sandy. He remembered talking with her the last night they were together about coming under fire. For a moment the memory brought joy and hope. Then the hard reality of what happened in the last two months snapped him back to reality.

"What's wrong, John?" Beckley asked.

"What do you mean?"

"Something just got to you. I can see it in your face," Beckley said. "Is it about your girl?"

"I don't think she's my girl anymore, Beck," John stammered. "I mean, I haven't heard one word from her. Not one damn letter." He shook his head. "I didn't even get a 'Dear John' letter."

"Now, John," Beckley replied, "don't sour on the whole barrel just because you've tasted a bad apple or two."

"Yeah. And don't sit under the apple tree with anyone else but me. I wonder who she's sitting with right now?"

"You've got to let her go, John," Beckley said. " Maybe you should stop thinking about her. Maybe you're wasting a lot of time dreaming about some broad who jilted you even before you got to know her."

John couldn't reply.

"What about the guys who died this morning?" Beckley asked, "They'll never have a chance at love again. Hell, we're lucky! We're alive! At least we can hope for a life after this crazy war is over."

What Beckley said sobered John. "Yeah, Beck, you're right. When you're alive, there's always a chance. I guess I just started to feel sorry for myself."

"Let's try to think about what's good in life, John," Beckley said. "The word now should be 'everything's going be okay.'"

"Funny, I said the same thing to Sandy," John replied.

John left Beckley and walked across the hangar deck to one of the port sponsons. The crisp sea air made him feel better. From there he could see the *Franklin's* bow cut through the deep blue waters of the Pacific. It churned up a beautiful frilly white spray. These waters seemed serene and peaceful, yet the threat of death hovered under them—and all around them.

As he gazed at the ocean, the destroyer *Twiggs* came alongside to refuel and deliver mail. Mail call. It used to be fun, he thought. Now it's just a reminder of a shitty situation. He walked back up to the flight deck and headed for his gun pit. When he got there the crew was laughing and horsing around.

"Knock that shit off!" John shouted, "Knock it off! Be alert, goddamned it. This is no time to screw around. Just remember, one of these days the Japs will come. We'd damn well better be ready." He began to inspect the breach of one of the quads. Then he realized he was being ill-tempered. Hell these guys didn't have anything to do with Sandy not writing to him.

"Sorry guys," he said. "Something else was bugging me. But goddamn it, stay alert. The Japs can slip in here any time." Even after his apology, the disturbing thoughts of Sandy haunted him. "Fuck, it isn't worth it," he muttered as he pulled a lose piece of string from his shirt. "Every time I find a girl I can be close to something happens, and I wind up feeling like a goddamned asshole. Not one single word from her. Not one damned word…."

"Lowe!" John shouted.

Lowe came out from behind the Mark 14 gun sight.

"Yeah, John?"

"You better get somebody to use some steel wool in the breach of this gun. There's a rough spot here. I can feel it. It could cause this gun to jam."

"Aye, John," Lowe said. He looked over at Seaman First Class Carl Arnold, one of the new transfers. "Arnold!" he said sternly.

Arnold pulled himself up on the gun platform.

"You heard the gunner, get to it," Lowe said.

John watched as Arnold carefully rubbed steel wool over the rough spot. After nearly a half an hour of diligent work, he turned to John and said, "Smooth as a baby's bottom now, Gunner. Sorry I didn't see it before. It'll never happen again."

"Roger," John said.

A boatswain pipe's shrill shriek pierced the air. "Attention. Attention all hands. Mail Call will be held at 14:00."

In a few minutes a mailman appeared at the edge of the flight deck.

"Third Division," he said. He pulled out a bundle of packets of envelopes and began to toss them to the mail-hungry men in the gun pit.

"Arnold."

"Barker."

"Dixon."

"Feinstein."

"Garcia."

"Jardin."

"Kwatkowski."

"Lowe."

"Oxler."

John's spirits lifted when he heard his name. He watched as the packet of mail moved through the air to him. It seemed as though it was coming in slow motion. John caught the packet with one hand and began to thumb through the letters. The first was from his mother. He recognized her handwriting immediately. The next from his sister, but the third was in a feminine hand he didn't recognize. He looked at it closely and could scarcely believe what he saw. It was from Sandy. And the next two were from her as well. He couldn't believe it. Three letters! He took out his knife and slit open the letter with the earliest postmark. The envelope was dated May 24, 1944.

"Four days after we shipped out," he said half aloud. When he took out the letter there was a picture. His hand shook ever so slightly as he took the picture gently from between the still folded pages and stared at it. She was more beautiful than he remembered. He read hungrily:

> *Dearest John,*
>
> *It's only been four days since you left and it seems like years. I miss you so very much. You have been on my mind constantly, you and my father who was injured at the shipyards at Hunter's Point. A wayward crane struck him in the back of the neck while he was there for an inspection. My mother called me and asked me to come home as soon as possible and I am writing this letter on the train as we're going through central California. I had to get packed to leave in a hurry—that's the reason this letter is so late.*
>
> *John, I don't know if you still feel the way you did in San Diego. I dearly hope that you do. I still feel all the love I felt over those three wonderful nights—and more. I don't know if "love at first sight" is something that happens very often, but it certainly happened to me. Every day since you left I've awakened thinking about you, wondering how you*

are and where you are. I close my eyes and see your face and ask God to keep you safe.

Please be careful. I'll be waiting to hear from you and waiting for you to come back. I miss you very much—and I love you now and forever.
Sandy

P.S. Next day. I'm back in Berkley now. I got in last night. My dad's going to be okay. He suffered a concussion and a fractured shoulder and is still in the hospital—but the doctors say he is healing rapidly. I delayed mailing this until I got home so I could include the enclosed picture. I hope you like it. Will you send me a picture of you?

Love,
Sandy

Elation and happiness swept through his body. "Like it. I love it!" he mumbled. "This is almost too good to be true."

Ski looked at him like he was crazy. "Whaddya say?"

John handed the photo of Sandy to Ski. "I said I got a letter from my girl. Got a letter from Sandy, Ski."

"No shit? Let me see!" Ski exclaimed. He took the picture and looked it over carefully. "This is hard to believe. She's a knockout. You lucky bastard. Why can't something like this happen to me?"

"Well, Ski, some guys' got it—some guys haven't," John said with a happy grin. "Maybe someday when I've got a little time, I'll teach you my technique." Then he walked to an isolated corner of the gun pit and read Sandy's two other letters. They were filled with more expressions of her love. He thought about all the time he'd wasted—all that useless mistrust and anger. What a goddamn fool he'd been not to trust her.

That night, John wrote a letter to Sandy.

My dearest Sandy,
I waited and waited for a letter from you! I almost thought you'd forgotten me, or you were afraid to write because you didn't want the worry of what would happen to me because I told you we were going into combat. I knew you were worried about your brother—and I thought worry about me would be too much. It was wonderful to hear from you! I showed your picture to Ski, the guy I was with when I found you at the USO. He had trouble believing you wrote me but was nearly as happy as I was.

Sandy, I love you too. And I believe in "love at first sight." Why shouldn't I? It happened to me, too. I can't wait to see you again. I hope and pray it's soon. In the meantime, I'm going to pull out your picture (Thanks! It's beautiful!) and look at you as often as I can.

I'm coming back to you, Sandy. I promise! With all my love,
John

The next morning after he mailed the letter, wonderful thoughts of Sandy returned. Now they were even more sensual and captivating. Hope surged through him. Hope for love. Hope for the future. Hope for getting out and going back to her. Hope for a life with a girl he loved. Then as the day went on, doubt cut into him like a knife. It had been nearly two months since she wrote those letters. Did she still mean what she wrote? Would she be waiting for him? Was the love she wrote about real, or would it be just another bunch of shattered expectations and dreams that turned to nightmares?

7 July, 1944
Iwo Jima, Bonin Islands
North Philippine Sea

The next morning dawned crystal clear; not a cloud in the sky. As the sun moved slowly over the horizon, its radiance turned the whitecaps into dancing golden droplets. They glistened and fell back into the sea. It was perfect weather for flight operations. At 06:30, a strike force of eighty-six fighters and fifty-five bombers stormed off the decks of *Franklin*, *Wasp* and *Saratoga* and headed West Northwest to attack other enemy installations on Iwo Jima. *Franklin's* Air Group was assigned the northernmost airfield. They found sixteen Zeros and seven Zekes parked, but as yet unmanned. Multiple low-level strafing runs destroyed ten Zeros and two Zekes. Two Zeros and three Zekes managed to take off. Joe Crowley's Hellcat pilots, who were eager to clear the skies of all Japanese air power, quickly shot them down. Air Strike Baker came right after them and attacked the guns on Suribachi with bombs and missiles.

Commander Zimler would lead Air Strike Charley in the third attack of the day.

From his station on the bridge, Beckley watched Zimler pull himself into the cockpit of his Avenger.

While Zimler waited for his catapult hookup, he looked over and saw Beckley watching. He signaled him thumbs up and Beckley responded with a similar gesture.

In a few minutes the catapult powered Air Strike Charley into the bright early afternoon sky and just minutes later they were in attack formation.

"Bald Eagle to squadron," Zimler said over the intercom. "Hit the guns on Suribachi hard. Commander Taylor wants them taken completely out if possible. Try to get Tiny Tims into them. If we have any ammo left, we'll go after what's left on the beach. Do you read me?"

"Roger! Loud and clear."

"And keep your eyes peeled for Zeros," Zimler cautioned. "Taylor thinks we knocked out most of the planes they had here, but you never know."

Mount Suribachi loomed in the distance. In a few minutes, Charlie Squadron began its attack.

Zimler dove for the heavy cave-encased guns in the huge mountain.

"Dino."

"Aye, sir."

"Check the damage as we make this first pass. I want to get everything we can and know what we're getting."

"Aye, sir."

"Those guns look pretty beat up from here, sir. Some of them are still burning from being whacked this morning."

"Bald Eagle to Gray Fox."

Joe Crowley's voice responded.

"What do you think, Joe?"

"It doesn't look like there's much life there," Crowley replied.

"I think we'll make another run on them," Zimler said.

"Good idea. They look pretty beat up, but you never know," Crowley replied.

"Once more for good measure, Joe. You can work the beach."

Crowley and his F6Fs banked and dove on the beach installations while Zimler's Avengers attacked the gun emplacements on Suribachi.

Dino watched the Avengers blast the caves again, firing one missile after another into the already smoking battlements.

When their pass was over, Zimler called back to Antonelli, "Dino, how does it look?"

"Beat to shit, sir." Dino answered. "Those guns are wrecked. Everything's smoking and burning. I don't think they'll ever use those suckers again."

"Roger. Air Strike Charlie form up," Zimler said. "We're heading home."

As the attack group climbed away from the island, an excited voice blared through the intercom.

"Red Ranger to Bald Eagle! Red Ranger to Bald Eagle!" "Two vessels. To starboard at ten o'clock. They look like Japanese destroyers, Commander."

Zimler looked to his right. The ships came dimly into view.

"Identify them. Are they Japs? If they are, let's kick their ass."

"Red Ranger to squadron. They're Japs all right. Japanese destroyers—*Futatsu* Class. Old and not very fast."

"Let's get 'em."

Franklin's Air Group turned northeast and zeroed in on the two destroyers, who had apparently spotted them and were frantically zigzagging.

"Bald Eagle to Air Strike! Attack! Avengers and Helldivers first with missiles, then bombs. Fighters with anything you guys have left. Take aim. Don't miss. We want these bastards!" Zimler ordered.

Red and white flashes from the destroyer's antiaircraft guns streamed up. White puffs of fire filled the air. Zimler's Avengers roared down through them. Their first attack scored of fire filled the air. Zimler's Avengers roared down through them. Their first attack scored hits amidships on both ships.

"Hit 'em again with everything you've got left!" Zimler shouted.

After the second attack, the destroyers were burning furiously.

The bombers came back to inspect the damage while the Hellcats circled and watched. They were positioned to go after the burning destroyers, but it wasn't necessary. Huge explosions ripped through the crippled ships and they began to sink.

"Scratch two destroyers!" Zimler shouted, the excitement of conquest in his voice. "Dino! Do you see any more around?"

"No, sir."

"Air Strike Charlie from Bald Eagle. Anyone see any more?"

All responses were negative.

Zimler radioed the *Franklin*. "Bald Eagle to Emerald Base."

"Come in Bald Eagle."

"We ripped Iwo up pretty good. Most of the guns on Suribachi are out of commission. On the way back we ran into two Jap destroyers—old—*Futatsu* Class. We sank them, too. We're headed home."

Joe Taylor's voice echoed over the air. "Bald Eagle, Joe Taylor here. You got two destroyers?"

"Yep. That we did."

"Are they certain kills?"

"You'd better believe it. We all watched them sink. Right now they're at the bottom of the deep blue sea."

"Great show, Bald Eagle! Come on home. Over and out."

Beckley watched as the Air Group landed without incident. "Things are going well, Captain," he said to Shoemaker. "It's sure great to get over that rash of accidents and injuries."

"Yes, and the crew is shaping up. They'd better be careful. They might make me say they're the best crew I've ever served with," Shoemaker replied as a tiny smile crossed his face.

CHAPTER FOURTEEN

18 July, 1944
The Invasion of Tinian
North Philippine Sea

For the next seven days TF 58.2 attacked airfields on Tinian and Guam. Japanese resistance was much heavier than expected. D4Y Judys and G4M Bettys, daily counterattacked the Task Group with bombs and torpedoes. Judys sank two destroyers in the task group's screen with torpedoes, and Bettys badly damaged the heavy cruiser *Boston* with three direct hits. Although the Task Group's antiaircraft defenses and combat air patrols exacted a heavy toll in enemy planes, the danger increased dramatically.

After the *Boston* was swarmed over and damaged, Task Group 58.2 called for reinforcements. Mitscher ordered TF 58.1, under the command of Admiral Jocko Clark, to divert from their attacks on Ulithi and join the attacks on Tinian and Guam. Clark's Task Group, which included the carriers *Hornet, Wasp, Brennington* and *Belleau Wood* and the battleships *Indiana* and *Massachusetts* rendezvoused with TF 58.2 on the afternoon of 20 July. The increased firepower from the combined air squadrons was too much for the Japanese air defenses. After five days of continuous combat, Japanese resistance was virtually wiped out. American pilots and aircraft now completely controlled the skies over the Marianas. In the last twenty-four-hour period, there wasn't a single Japanese plane sighted anywhere in the area. The invasion of Tinian could now begin.

The loss of over thirty-four hundred soldiers and marines in the rugged fighting to conquer Saipan caused Mitscher, along with Admirals Davison and Brogan, to devise a new strategy to provide air cover for men fighting on the ground. From dawn to dusk fighters and bombers would circle eight to ten miles from the fighting. This allowed immediate air strikes to assist ground troops where and when needed.

Battle-toughened marines from the First Marine Division were poised to attack the devastated beaches on Tinian. *Franklin,* along with the carriers *Hornet, Wasp* and *Yorktown* and the light carriers *Princeton* and *Independence,* was repositioned to provide direct support to the invasion forces.

At 07:20 twelve Hellcats and fourteen Avengers from *Franklin*, all armed with missiles, flew in tight orbits eight miles southeast of the lengthy beach on Tinian's east coast. Zimler again commanded the Avengers and Crowley the fighters.

"Dino," Zimler said through the intercom. "Be alert. I think we just about wiped out all their air cover—but how the hell do we ever know?"

"Aye, sir."

"Gee, what a beautiful day," Zimler said as they flew deliberately in their tight circular formation. "They have days like this in Wyoming?"

"Aye, sir, prettier than this."

"And what do you hear from your parents?"

"Got a letter just the other day. Everyone's fine. My kid brother's the star of the football team. My mom says the girls are calling him all the time. They drive her crazy, she says—it'd be nice to have that kind of problem."

"What would you do with it, Dino?" Zimler asked through a huge smile.

"I think I could find something, sir."

"Yes, I bet you could. I bet you could...."

"Yes, sir. I bet I could."

Zimler laughed aloud at Antonelli's response. Although he was only six years older, he had come to feel like a father to this spirited, confident young man.

At 09:00, Admiral Conolly's battleships and cruisers completed their four-day bombardment of Tinian's beach fortifications. The meticulously planned bombardment was so precise and devastating it left the beach virtually defenseless. The veteran marines, conquerors of Saipan, moved toward the battered beach in LCIs. They met no resistance. Once on the beach, they stormed inland. There the situation changed.

At 10:05 a call came up from Captain R.F. Whitehead, Commander of Support Aircraft Operations, on Conolly's flagship *Rocky Mount*: "Attention Aircraft Support Squadron. The marines are pinned down by tank and mortar fire approximately twelve miles inland. They need air support immediately."

"We'll take this one, Commander," Zimler replied. "*Franklin* squadron, let's go!" Zimler did a wingover. His Avenger dove toward the embattled marines. The rest of the squadron followed.

"Dino. Be ready to strafe as we fly past. Let's throw everything we've got at them."

"Aye, sir."

In a few minutes the bogged down marines came into view. Behind them, on the crest of a small hill, a row of at least twenty-five Japanese medium tanks loomed. The Japs also had heavy artillery pieces and mortars cleverly hidden in dense vegetation. They were blasting away at the marine positions below.

"Avengers, attack! Go after the tanks first. They've got antiaircraft guns. Get 'em all. Then we'll go after the artillery and mortars."

The Jap tanks were positioned next to each other, probably to more effectively bombard the marines below. Effective against ground troops, this formation left the tanks vulnerable to air attack on both flanks.

Zimler maneuvered and began his attack on the tank column's right flank. He came in low and fired a volley of missiles. They scored direct hits on the first tank in line. The impact tore the turret off, and the undersized tank exploded like a tin can hit by a truck. He flew straight down the line and dropped a five-hundred-pound bomb on a tank in the middle of the column. At this altitude it was almost impossible to miss.

"Scratch another one!" Antonelli shouted.

The rest of the Avengers followed Zimler's lead. By the end of the first pass fifteen tanks were twisted, burning wrecks.

The tanks that escaped damage broke out and retreated northward.

"Bomber squadron. Everybody pick one. Don't let one of the bastards get away!"

Only one did. The Avengers left twenty-four tanks battered and burning.

Meantime, Joe Crowley's Hellcats attacked the artillery and mortars with missiles and machine gun fire. At the end of the attack there wasn't a single gun or mortar left undamaged—most were twisted wrecks—their crews either dead or fleeing.

"Cease the attack."

As soon as the Avengers and Hellcats stopped firing the marines roared in to mop up, waving and signaling thumbs up as they went.

"Bald Eagle to Support Aircraft Command."

"Come in, Bald Eagle."

"We took them out—all of them. The marines are mopping up now."

"We know, Bald Eagle. They kept us posted. They asked me to give you this message: 'Tell the Navy fly-boys thanks. They did a hell of a job. Next to us, they're the best goddamned fighters we've ever seen. It's a piece of cake now. We'll have this place cleared out in a week.'" Seven days later, Tinian was declared secure.

7 August, 1944
80 Miles SSW of Guam
North Philippine Sea

Guam, an American possession for forty years and the largest and most important island in the Marianas, was next. To be certain that there were no hitches in this very special invasion, Admiral Halsey and Admiral McCain airlifted the Seventy-Seventh Infantry Division from Ohau to assist the First and Third Marine Divisions in the assault. This delayed the invasion for five days, but the delay allowed Admiral Conolly to plan another devastating bombardment.

Squadrons of B-24s called in from Manus, loaded with two-thousand-pound bombs, blasted the former American possession twice daily with pinpoint accuracy. Thousands of pounds of devastating explosives rained down on the Japanese defenders. Admiral Lee's Battle Line, that included the battleships *Washington*, *North Carolina*, *Iowa*, *New Jersey* and *California,* and a huge compliment of heavy and light cruisers, pounded the beaches from dawn to dusk. Mitscher's Fast Carrier Forces, that included the *Franklin, Wasp, Yorktown, Hornet* and *Essex,* flew over five thousand sorties each day for the five-day period. Thousands of pounds of missiles and bombs cascaded onto beaches and fortified points all over the island.

Despite this pounding, the invasion and conquest of Guam was not easy. The Japanese, aware of American pride in this invasion, resisted furiously. They doggedly fought for every foot of the island, almost as though it was part of the Japanese homeland. On 28 August, nearly three weeks after the island was invaded, Guam was declared secure. Now the major islands in the Marianas and vast stretches of the northeastern Philippine Sea were solidly under American control.

Guam reassumed its function as a forward American base. Seabees from the Third and Sixth Naval Construction Battalions, working around the clock, repaired existing airfields and built new ones. Tons of materials and supplies poured ashore from transports and supply planes. Guam was being readied to be a pivotal base for the future invasion of Japan.

With its mission completed at Guam, TF 58.2 left and headed back to Saipan. The Task Group's stock of bombs was almost depleted and it was dangerously low on 20- and 40-millimeter ammunition. After nearly a month of continuous action, Spruance's decision that it was time for a rest was happily received.

CHAPTER FIFTEEN

5 September, 1944
Northeast Philippine Sea
Attack Okinawa

After six days of rest in Saipan, TF 58.2 sailed Southwest to participate in the bombardment of Yap in the Caroline Islands.

On the bridge of the *Franklin* Shoemaker reread a message he had just been handed by the chief radioman. "Were taking a flag aboard," he said to Beckley, Day and Taylor. "Admiral Ralph Davison will be here this afternoon at 14:30. The bombardment of Yap has been canceled."

"Cancelled, sir? I thought Yap was a high priority," Day said.

"It is, but we've been redirected to a new, higher priority—the invasion of the Philippines," Shoemaker replied.

"So the time has come for the big one," Taylor said. "General MacArthur must be happy about this."

"Yeah, I'll bet he is. The message says we rendezvous with *Enterprise* tomorrow," Shoemaker said. "Admiral Mitscher's in flag. We're bulking up the fleet for this invasion."

"When will we know where we're headed, sir?" Beckley asked.

"Admiral Davison will have that information when he comes aboard, Chief."

"Dave," Shoemaker said, "see that the Admiral's cabin is tidied up. Be sure arrangements are made for his staff. Arrange a meeting of department heads in the wardroom at 17:00. He handed Day the message. "And Dave, make sure the Admiral's bridge is shipshape."

At 14:30 Admiral Ralph Davison, one of Nimitz's top strategists, and his staff were piped aboard. He and his staff were immediately escorted to their quarters. At 15:00 Shoemaker met with Admiral Davison in his cabin. He and Davison spent nearly an hour discussing the new battle plans and accelerated timetable for the invasion of the Philippines. When the meeting ended, Davison said, "Captain, there is an important matter that I need to discuss with you."

"With me, sir?"

"Yes."

"Can you tell me what it's about, sir? Is it the problem we had with the crew?"

"No, it's not," Davison said hesitantly.

"Is it something related to my command of the *Franklin*?"

"Not at all, Captain. We consider you one of the best commanders in the fleet. Let's discuss it later when we have more time."

"Aye, sir."

"Can we meet here after dinner?"

"Certainly, Captain. Shall we say 19:30 in my cabin?"

"Yes, Admiral. Wow, you have my curiosity up, sir," Shoemaker said as he and Davison walked down the passageway to the meeting with *Franklin's* department heads.

This was the first time in *Franklin's* history an Admiral had flown his flag from her masts. Division Commanders and their assistants were clustered together in the wardroom, some sitting on fold-out chairs. Everyone seemed a little uncomfortable with Davison's presence.

"All rise."

"As you were."

"Gentlemen," Shoemaker began, "I have the great pleasure of introducing Admiral Ralph Davison who brought his flag to the *Franklin* today. On behalf of the officers and men of the *Franklin,* I'd like to welcome you aboard, sir."

Applause.

"Admiral Davison is here to explain the accelerated timetable and tactical changes for the invasion and recapture of the Philippines. Please pay close attention to these changes. They will define our participation in the invasion and our pre-invasion actions. He has just outlined these tactical changes to me and I want to caution each of you that there are some important new things coming."

"Admiral Davison."

"Good afternoon, gentlemen. As many of you are aware, within the last hour *Franklin* has changed course. We are now headed into actions that will result in the recapture of the Philippines. As many of you may also know, we needed the island of Ulithi as a steppingstone in *Operation Victorious*. Ulithi was declared secure last week. The Seabees are now outfitting and supplying it as an operational base. Admiral Halsey and General MacArthur have decided to bypass an attack on Mindanao Island. The first direct land attack on the Philippines will be on the island of Leyte. We expect this to be a major engagement and we expect the Japanese put up a fierce defense. We're confident, however, that we now have the strength to prevail. Soon we will avenge those brave Americans who died on Corregidor and on the Bataan death march. In the process we'll free sixteen million Filipinos and hundreds of Americans from horrible Japanese prison camps."

He paused and looked over the group.

"We're now assembling a major task force. It will include at least twenty-five carriers. *Enterprise* and *San Jacinto* will join us in the morning. When we make this hookup, we become a part of Admiral Bill Halsey's Third Fleet. Admiral Spruance has been rotated to Training Command as has been previously planned. Due to an illness suffered by Admiral McCain, Admiral Marc Mitscher will remain as Commander in Chief of Air Operations. Three days from today, October fourteenth, we rendezvous with the *Essex, Hornet* and *Lexington*, and with the light carriers *Bella Wood, Princeton* and *Cowpens*. Eight battleships and seventeen cruisers will screen them. This forms our Northern Fleet. Another task force is being formed southeast of the Philippines with ships from the Seventh Fleet under the command of Admiral Thomas Kinkaid. This becomes our Southern Fleet. It will support the Philippine invasion forces and is under the direct command of General MacArthur."

After a sip of water he continued. "Our great victory in the Philippine Sea was a major blow to the Japanese Navy. They have become weaker—and with each passing day, we've become stronger. When our task groups combine, they will form the largest fleet in naval history." He paused. "Are there any questions so far?"

"You say the invasion starts with Leyte, Admiral. Isn't that one of the lesser islands in the Philippines?" Shoemaker asked.

"Yes, it is. MacArthur chose Leyte. He argued that it would be a huge tactical surprise. He thinks the Japs will expect us to invade a more significant island like Luzon."

"And we'll all be in Admiral Halsey's Third Fleet, sir?"

"That's correct. One of our major responsibilities is destruction of Japanese land-based aircraft on the Philippines. To accomplish this objective we must sail into Philippine coastal waters. Our carriers will be within easy flight distance of enemy airfields and their land-based fighters and bombers. General Billy Mitchell contends that this is a carrier's most dangerous tactic. We're going to test that theory. We're going after every airfield and Jap plane we can locate. I don't care how close in we have to go to get them. We're going to destroy Japanese air power in the Philippines."

Davison paused and picked up a pointer. "However, first things first," he said. "As soon as we complete our rendezvous with Admiral Halsey and Task Force 38 is formed, we attack Okinawa. This is a major Japanese staging area. Ships are being loaded with men, tanks, guns, ammunition and planes there that are vital to their defense of the Philippines."

"That's getting very close to Japan, sir," Taylor said. "What defenses do you think we'll find there?"

"It's so close the Japanese consider Okinawa a part of their homeland," Davison replied. "Right now we're not completely sure what we'll find."

Davison nodded to an aide who produced a large map of the island. "We know there are about seventy-five transports presently anchored in Nakagusuku Wan," he said as he pointed to the map. "That's the large bay located on the island's southeast coast. We're not sure what naval units they have there. For now we have to assume their carriers are elsewhere."

He paused. "Naha is the island's principal city," he continued, still using the map and pointer. "It's about seven miles directly east of the bay. During the next seventy-two hours we'll blast Okinawa with all the air power we have. We need to put this important supply base out of commission."

"What about the Nip's air force?" Taylor asked.

"There we may have a big advantage. Intelligence tells us that that most of the aircraft assigned to defend this area have been redirected to bases in the Philippines. This might explain the absence of aircraft carriers."

"Is there any way to find out if they were diverted, sir?" Day inquired.

"Whether they were or not is immaterial. We attack anyhow. Nimitz and Halsey want us to take out everything in that bay. When we've finished, they want us to pound hell out of Naha. We're sending a message to Tojo that says, 'the United States Navy is knocking on your damned back door with a great big stick!'"

Davison looked around the room. "The pace of the war is intensifying, gentlemen," he said as he put the pointer down on the podium. "It's intensifying dramatically. We *must* be successful in these operations. If we are, the timetable for the war's end will advance four months. If we fail it could go the other way—it could add another year, possibly two to the war."

Jim Crowley squirmed in his chair. "Any idea what their fleet strength is, sir?" he asked.

"It could be large. That's where the First Japanese Fleet went after we kicked their butts in the Philippine Sea. Our reconnaissance didn't spot any major warships there, but you can be sure they're operating somewhere in the area."

"Wouldn't they be stupid to attack a fleet this size, sir?" Crowley persisted.

Davison rubbed his hand across his cheek to the back of his neck. "That might seem stupid to us, Commander, but you never know about the Japs," he replied. "We think they're still be looking for that one big-battle showdown. They got beat up twice, but we think there's a good chance they'll try it again. That's the best answer I can give you. Are there any further questions?"

Joe Taylor stood and said, "The Okinawa attack is something our pilots are familiar with. I'm sure we'll do a good job there, but what about the air operations in the Philippines? It sounds like we might be outnumbered when we strike that close to the land-based planes the Japs have down there."

"Yes, that's a risk, Commander, but it's a risk we have to take," Davison replied. "We think we'll surprise them in the beginning. We don't think they're expecting close-in attacks on ground installations from carrier-based planes. It's a tactic we've never used before."

"I don't know whether that's enough to surprise them, Admiral," Taylor responded. "I've found almost nothing surprises those little bastards."

"Well, we don't think they'll be expecting this kind of attack, Commander. We think we can catch them off guard. Who knows, maybe we can get some of their planes right on the ground."

"I sure hope you're right, Admiral," Bill Zimler said. "But with all due respect, sir, the Japanese airmen I'm used to are as alert as hell."

"Well, Commander, there may be other factors involved," Davison said.

"I'm not sure I understand, sir," Zimler said.

"Well, we know they're short on fuel now. Because of this, they can't put large numbers of planes up at one time. Intelligence tells us they've restricted what they're calling 'unnecessary patrols.' This is one of the reasons we think we can surprise them—at least in the beginning." Davison paused to light a cigarette. "We're also changing our air tactics," he said. "They're scheduled to be much more numerous and intense. The tactical plan is to divide our strike groups into even smaller units—four to six bombers—six to ten fighters, then attack every airfield we can find—as soon as we're in position—from the first day we get into range. This will also add to the element of surprise. We want to cripple their land-based air power.

This tactic provides us with the strength to handle their naval units, if they show up to oppose the landings. Any other questions?"

Silence.

Shoemaker rose to conclude the meeting. "Thank you, Admiral, for your detailed answers and explanations. I'm sure I speak for the officers and men of the *Franklin* when I say that we understand the gravity and the opportunity of the coming action."

He paused and looked at his staff intently, then continued, "I want to emphasize what Admiral Davison just said. The Japanese Navy's strongest fleets are somewhere in the area. These forces include the *Musashi* and *Yamato* and at least twelve carriers. As Admiral Davison said, they're probably looking for that 'knockout battle' again. Despite the size and strength of our fleet, they still have the naval power to pull this off. We need to intensify our state of readiness. Things are going to be a hell of a lot tougher than they've been up to now. We've been hitting 'em hard but we're going have to hit even harder. Tomorrow we'll hit a part of their empire they once boasted was untouchable. Intelligence thinks desperation is setting in. I'm talking about *intense* desperation. Desperate people take desperate chances. We have to expect and be prepared for anything and everything. So let's institute a condition of extreme readiness."

The master-at-arms read the standard security statement.

"All rise."

Promptly at 19:30 Shoemaker asked the marine guard stationed at the door to Admiral Davison's cabin to tell Davison that he was there. In less than a minute Davison appeared and invited him in. When they were seated, Davison, a mild-mannered, somewhat shy man, looked beyond Shoemaker. "I don't know where to begin this," he said hesitantly.

"If what you are going to say relates to the accidents we've had on the *Franklin*," Shoemaker ventured, "I can assure you Admiral, they were *truly* accidents and the circumstances that contributed to them have, as much as possible, been rectified."

Davison chuckled. "This has nothing to do with the accidents. Granted there have been more on *Franklin* than is the case with most ships, but we understand a commander cannot be held responsible for the accidental."

"Well, you said earlier it wasn't the problems with the crew, and if it isn't the accidents, I don't know what it can be, sir."

"Captain, you're an outstanding skipper with a sterling service record," Davison said.

Shoemaker was puzzled. "I don't understand, Admiral. I've got a problem because I've been an effective battle commander, sir?"

"I didn't say what I had to discuss was a problem, Jim," Davison said, calling him by name for the first time.

"What could it be then?"

"The Navy needs a commander for all naval air bases in the newly liberated area. It's a high-profile command and an excellent career opportunity. Admirals King and Nimitz want a top-flight officer to take this command. You're one of three officers being considered."

Shoemaker became very concerned. "A desk job? Oh, no, sir! A desk job's not for me, sir. I'm a battle commander."

"It's a desk job, Captain," Davison said, "but it's a *very* important desk job. To be chosen by Admirals King and Nimitz is a very high honor."

"I'm sure it is, Admiral, but it's not for me. I'd go crazy at a desk job, sir."

Davison smiled. "That's what the other two candidates said, too. We need a man with your qualifications, Jim. One with an excellent service record and successful flight and battle experience."

"Admiral, with all due respect, sir, I don't think I'm your man," Shoemaker said. He paused, unsure of what to say next. Then he said, "Admiral, are you sure it's not something I did, a screw-up or something? You're making this sound like a promotion, sir, but I'm not sure it is."

Davison laughed. "If you're selected, Jim, the future will show that it was the biggest promotion of your career."

"Right now, to me, sir, it sounds like a promotion to hell. I'm the commander of a fleet carrier. I'd go nuts in a desk job. Shoemaker paused and thought a moment. "Maybe something like that after the war's over, sir," he said hesitantly.

"Well, Captain, I'm just here to tell you about this opportunity. You haven't been chosen yet, and there are three candidates."

"If possible, Admiral, I'd rather not be considered. Can you understand why I am so reluctant, sir?"

"Of course, I can," Davison said.

"Could you explain that to the selection board, sir?"

"I'll see what I can do, Captain."

"Thank you, sir. I'd appreciate it a lot."

8 October, 1944
200 Miles North of the Mariana Islands
Sea of Japan

The next morning dawned with only light cirrus in the east. A ten-knot wind blew in over the port bow. There was visibility for at least thirty miles.

On the bridge, Beckley and Shoemaker focused their binoculars to the southeast.

"There they are, Captain, just coming up over the horizon," Beckley said.

Shoemaker lowered his glasses and said, "Dave, we've sighted them. Adjust our course so we'll be easier to meet. Chief, get positive identification."

Beckley studied the tiny ships just appearing on the horizon. "They're sure not Japanese," he said with a tint of humor in his voice. It's the *Enterprise* and the light carriers *Princeton* and *San Jacinto*, sir. The screen includes the old battleships *West Virginia, California* and *Tennessee,* eleven cruisers and about fifteen destroyers," Beckley said.

"Maybe we shouldn't call them 'old' anymore," Shoemaker observed. "After all, they were completely restored after they were damaged in Pearl Harbor. They're equipped with our most up-to-date armaments which include new Mark VIII fire-control radar."

"Right, sir, I guess they're not old anymore. That equipment is top of the line," Beckley said, still studying the task force through his binoculars.

"Even some of the newer battleships haven't been retrofitted with Mark VIII fire-control yet," Shoemaker added.

At 09:25, the two task forces joined and deployed with Admiral Mitscher as Commander in Chief.

The next day, approximately two hundred and seventy miles West Northwest of the Marianas, they made rendezvous with the major part of "Bull" Halsey's Third Fleet. This task force included Halsey's flagship, the battleship *New Jersey,* along with the *Iowa, Washington, Alabama, South Dakota* and *North Carolina.* Twelve *Essex* Class fleet carriers that included *Essex, Enterprise, Intrepid, Lexington* and *Hornet* were a central part of the huge fleet. Eight *Independence* Class light carriers surrounded them. Nine "Jeep" carriers and countless cruisers and destroyers were in the outer screen. This formed Admiral Nimitz's Northern Fleet. It was designated TF 38 with Bill Halsey as Commander in Chief.

From his station in Able 1 gun pit, John focused his binoculars on this huge task force and watched it form around him into a massive fleet. He marveled at the momentous scene. There were powerful warships moving in from every direction; sleek new battleships with modern, graceful lines, all tossing spray and churning heavy wakes, their sixteen-inch guns glittering in the sun; beautiful 'old' battleships rebuilt from near destruction, now ready to seek their revenge. Massive new carriers launched and recovered aircraft. Sleek cruisers, bristling with devastating firepower, steamed at the edge of the inner screen. Then scores of destroyers darted in and out of the huge fleet in search of enemy submarines.

John heard his name called. He lowered his glasses. Beckley came down the ladder into the gun pit.

"Did you ever dream you'd see a sight like this?" Beckley asked.

"Not in a million years, Beck," John replied. "Boy, have things changed in the last three years. Can you believe this? The biggest show of naval power in history, going on right out there before our eyes."

"Maybe if the Jap generals that started this goddamned war could see what's happening now, they'd never have started it," Beckley said. "Yamamoto must be turning over in his grave."

John surveyed the massive armada. "The size of this fleet is hard to believe," he said. "Remember the old days when two carriers and eight or ten destroyers were all we could muster?"

"Yeah, I do. Let's take a good, long look. We may never see a sight like this again," Beckley said.

John watched the huge panorama of ships a few moments longer. "Let's hope this is the beginning of the end of it all. I've got a girl that I want to go home to and the sooner the better."

Beckley turned his gaze back to the mighty flotilla. "That sure looks like a step in that direction," he said.

10 October, 1944
80 Miles East of Okinawa
Target: Hakagusuku Wan

At 06:30 the next morning, the important business of TF 38 began. Air Strike Able, consisting of one hundred and sixty fighters, bombers and torpedo bombers thundered into the clear morning sky from the decks of the carriers in the huge fleet. Flying weather was perfect. There wasn't a cloud anywhere. Deck loads of Hellcats, Corsairs, Avengers and Helldivers moved swiftly into formations and headed toward Hakagusuku Wan, now only eighty miles away. As soon as they were airborne aviation aircrews on the hangar decks began the hurried process of readying aircraft that would make the next attack.

Zimler's squadron was in the second tier of bombers in Air Strike Able. His Avenger was near the center of the formation.

"Dino."

"Sir."

"Scan the whole horizon carefully. I'm not buying that scuttlebutt that the Japs sent all their aircraft to the Philippines. It'd be fine if they did, but keep a very close watch."

"Aye, sir."

The huge air strike group roared on, like a powerful force of nature—terrible and unstoppable—driven by its great strength and capacity for destruction. Hakagusuku Wan loomed in the distance. The bright blue waters of the huge bay were dotted with scores of tankers, freighters and troop transports. As the strike group flew closer, antiaircraft fire flurried up from a group of destroyers in the channel between the small islands of Kutaka and Tsugen.

"Destroyers! *Asashio* Class. Get them first!" Commander Noreck, the combined Air Strike leader, shouted.

The first wave of Hellcats flashed down on the destroyers like giant birds of prey, with all guns blazing. Antiaircraft fire intensified. Three Hellcats, at the point of the attack, were hit and exploded in midair. Two more at the edges of the formation trailed smoke, burst into flames and careened crazily into the waters below.

"Stay the course," Crowley said. "Hit 'em with missiles!"

When the Hellcat's distance decreased to two thousand yards, Crowley's fighters fired their Tiny Tims. Two destroyers suffered direct hits and burst into flames. As soon as the fighters pulled up, bombers streaked toward the destroyers. Then they dropped a hail of bombs that exploded in deadly patterns around the remaining undamaged ships. Five more destroyers suffered hits and began to smoke. Despite their damage, they began to zigzag furiously.

"Second wave!"

The next wave of fighters swarmed over the smoking destroyers. They threw up an even heavier barrage of fire. Two more Hellcats exploded in midair. A third trailed smoke and plunged toward the water below.

"Torpedo attack!"

"Here we go, Dino. Hang on to your hat!" Zimler shouted. He put his Avenger into a steep dive. His engine whined. His speed increased dramatically. He headed for one of the remaining destroyers that had started to flee to the North.

"Let's get this bastard," Zimler said. He centered his crosshairs on the zigzagging destroyer. His Avenger shuddered as a torpedo released and streaked toward its target.

"You got her, sir! A direct hit," Dino shouted as Zimler streaked away. "Good shooting, sir."

" She's starting to break up in the middle," Zimler shouted as he brought his Avenger to a stable altitude. "Just like shooting moose in Wyoming!" he shouted.

"Yes, sir!" Antonelli said with a big grin.

More powerful torpedoes streaked toward their targets. When they impacted they triggered massive explosions.

"Lieutenant Miller got another one! Hit her amidships," Dino shouted. "Whammo! Maybe we got two dead ducks."

By the time Zimler circled to rejoin the formation, the last two badly damaged destroyers were steaming northeast with as much speed as they could muster. When he was back in formation, he asked, "Dino, how many planes do you think we lost?"

"I counted about nine, sir, but none from our squadron. At least, I don't think so."

Commander Noreck's voice said over the intercom. "Cease the attack. We've got bigger fish to fry. Prepare to attack the shipping."

As Air Strike Able approached the huge bay, five old Japanese biplanes started to take off from an airfield at bay's edge.

"Vals!" someone shouted. "Let's get 'em!"

Ten Hellcats from the first wave peeled off and streaked down on the old biplanes. They blazed away with their 50-caliber wing guns. The Hellcats shot the Vals out of the air almost as soon as they left the ground.

"Great! They didn't have a chance, Dino," Zimler said. "Now it looks like we've got that whole Japanese supply armada sitting in Hakagusuku Wan with nothing to defend it."

Air Strike Able began to pound the defenseless ships. The attack went on for over two hours. It turned into a shooting gallery! When their bombs and ammunition were depleted, Air Strike Able flew triumphantly back to the Task Group. On the way they spotted Air Strike Baker headed to take up the destruction where they left off.

"Calling Squadron Commander Air Strike Able. Come in, Squadron Commander Air Strike Able!"

"Roger. This is Commander Noreck."

"How did it go?"

"We sank or damaged at least seven Nip destroyers. When we ran out of ammo, there were twenty-six cargo ships burning."

"Wow! You had a field day. Did you leave any for us?" Noreck asked.

"There's plenty left there. Have a ball. I don't think there's any air or sea defense there now."

"Maybe we won't have to come back tomorrow," Noreck speculated.

"That depends on how good you guys are," Zimler replied.

#

From his battle station in Able 1 gun pit, John focused his binoculars northwest. He spotted aircraft on the horizon. "Aircraft on the horizon at eleven o'clock," he said. He studied the planes carefully. "They're ours. It's Air Strike Able." *Franklin* changed course in preparation to land the approaching planes.

Soon the mass of fighters and bombers moved into landing formations, brightly highlighted by the mid-Pacific sun. Hellcats and Avengers from the *Franklin* began their descent. Suddenly, an out-of-control plane from another squadron careened down toward the *Franklin* and her landing Hellcats.

John watched as shocked pilots pulled their planes into steep climbs to avoid the out-of-control Hellcat. For one Hellcat it was too late. The errant fighter smashed into its wing.

John focused his glasses on the collision. "That's Commander Crowley's plane!" he shouted.

Both planes were suspended in midair by the collision—then each went into an uncontrolled spin. A parachute blossomed.

"Commander Crowley just bailed out," John said.

The wreckage from the two planes spiraled down to the ocean and exploded.

A third pilot avoided the collision and tried to land, but he misjudged his altitude and distance. His Hellcat smashed into the edge of *Franklin's* flight deck and careened away. It went out of control and crashed into the ocean less than a hundred feet off of *Franklin's* port quarter. Three planes destroyed and two pilots killed in less time than it took to recite a simple poem! John's stomach churned and he felt dizzy. Then he saw a rescue boat speed out to pick up Commander Crowley. That helped him fight off his nausea.

On the bridge, Beckley heard a frantic call come in. He recognized Commander Zimler's voice.

"Bald Eagle to *Franklin*. All planes in the Air Group will hold their positions."

Beckley saw Taylor grab the microphone. "Bill, Joe Taylor here. This is incredible. What the hell happened?"

"I don't know," Zimler replied. "It was a crazy accident—all over in a few seconds. Is the flight deck damaged? Can we land?"

"I think you can. It doesn't look like there was much damage. I'll have a report in a minute."

"Roger, we'll reposition for landing."

When Zimler, in the last Avenger, landed Beckley met him at the edge of the flight deck.

"What a terrible accident, sir. I saw it happen," he said.

"I know," Zimler replied, distressed and saddened. "It was very bad luck. All within a few seconds and a few inches."

The next morning at 07:47 another air strike zoomed up to attack Nakagusuku Wan again. Deck loads of fighters, bombers and torpedo bombers streaked into the cloudless Pacific sky from the decks of carriers in TF 38. Their orders were to complete the destruction of any shipping still afloat. Joe Taylor, the designated flight coordinator for Air Strike Able, was still upset and angry about the accident. He waited until the huge air strike reached a cruising altitude and then said, "Get me the Air Strike's Commander."

Commander Phil Talbott answered the call.

"Execute the plan," Taylor ordered. "Let's get everything. Transports first, then anything you can find that floats. Let's teach the bastards a lesson!"

"Aye, sir, we'll do our best."

Air Strike Able went after the remaining ships in the harbor, then attacked two coves in the southern half of the island. They shot up everything there. The final tally: twenty-three cargo vessels, eleven escort ships and numerous small craft, including ten barges destroyed or damaged and burning.

After Air Strike Able landed, Air Strike Baker took off. Bill Zimler's squadron was a part of this group. Their orders: find and destroy all military targets in Naha, the island's capitol city. Naha, a town of less than fifty thousand people, located at the southern tip of the island, had a deep harbor that was often used by units of the Japanese fleet. The air strike reached Naha without incident. None of the Japanese fleet was there; there wasn't an enemy fighter in the sky anywhere. Hellcats, Helldivers and Avengers in Air Strike Baker, one hundred and sixty planes strong, descended on the helpless town like angry hornets. They strafed and bombed everything they thought might be a military target and some that weren't. After an hour and a half of savage bombardment, Naha was a blazing inferno. Loading docks, machine shops, harbor facilities, trucks, autos and even fishing craft caught in the harbor were blown to pieces.

Air Strike Baker returned to the task force and landed without incident.

Later that afternoon, after all aircraft were recovered, TF 38 turned South Southwest on course 195° toward the Japanese fortress of Formosa, steaming in Condition I, on zigzag course 6. Twilight was approaching but overall visibility was still good. A huge squall developed over the cruisers *Santa Fe* and *Cleveland* and several of the supporting destroyers on the northwest edge of the screen. The clouds became so dense and high they hid them from the rest of the Task Group.

A squadron of Japanese planes appeared on *Franklin's* radar screens. An urgent warning roared through the *Franklin's* loudspeaker system:

"Bogeys! Bogeys at nine o'clock! Range twelve miles."

The klaxon blared. The siren wailed.

"General Quarters! General Quarters!"

"All hands prepare for immediate action!"

Hidden by the high storm clouds, at least thirty bombers, Judys and Bettys, with Zeros and Zekes as escorts, had slipped past the outer screen and were readying to attack the carriers in the Task Group.

John Oxler's gunners, already at their stations, were in Condition of Readiness I.

"I can't see them. They must be coming out of that squall," John said as the *Franklin* turned into the wind to launch fighter aircraft. The Japanese planes, already in position to attack, were far ahead of the scrambling Task Group's aircrews.

"Sneaky bastards!" John shouted. "Where the hell did they come from?" He looked over at Lowe. Lowe's body was tense, his face white and strained. John gave him thumbs up. Lowe responded with a nod. John glanced to his right. Ski signaled thumbs up then defiantly flipped his middle finger in the direction of the Jap planes. "Fuck you, you sons-of-bitches!" he shouted. "Come on! We'll shoot your ass off!"

John looked at the loaders. "Your guys ready?" he asked.

"Roger, Gunner," came the replies.

"Bogeys! Bogeys!" Ski shouted. "I see 'em now! At nine o'clock—coming in through that cloud cover."

Ships from all over the fleet opened fire. *Franklin's* starboard 40s and 20s lashed out violently. They filled the airways with hot tracer and armor-piercing projectiles.

The Japanese bombers flew determinedly on. Two Judys dove directly at *Franklin*. They penetrated the hail of fire and hurled toward the vulnerable carrier.

Franklin took evasive action. She turned sharply away from the plummeting planes. The first Judy crashed into the water and exploded a hundred yards off her starboard beam— the second plowed into the ocean and exploded, less than fifty yards from her stern.

John watched what happened in amazement. "Chief!" he shouted to Sullivan, who had just jumped into his sponson. "Did you see what those bastards are doing? They aren't dropping their bombs. Bastards are trying to *crash their planes* into us! Am I nuts? How can that be?" John's face filled with contorted disbelief. "Am I nuts, Chief?" he asked again. "Were those bastards *aiming* their planes at us?"

"I think they were," Sullivan said. " I heard they were starting to use attacks like this. I think the Navy's calling them 'kamikaze' attacks."

"Kamikaze? What the hell does that mean?"

"How the hell do I know?" Sullivan replied.

John shook his head. "I don't understand this, Chief. Lord, I can't believe anybody would be nuts enough to crash into a ship!"

A Betty with a full bomb load streaked down on a collision course with the *Franklin*. It hurled right toward John's gun pit. The only protection the gun crew now had was the rapid fire and accuracy of their 40-mm guns.

"Get that son-of-a-bitch!" John shouted.

The gun crew brought the bomber under intense fire. Clip after clip of tracers and high-demolition shells blazed into the air. The Betty streaked on, despite the hail of gunfire. It fired back with its wing cannons. Thirteen-millimeter armor-piercing shells tore through Able Sponson's light metal side and ripped up the deck as they came.

Belasco was hit in the chest. A second shell ripped through his helmet. It knocked him from the gun platform to the sponson's deck. Blood spattered everywhere.

"Second loader! Take his place," John screamed. "Keep firing! Keep firing!"

Tracers and high-demolition projectiles streaked up at the Betty. One scored a hit on its starboard engine. It blasted the Betty off course. It raced past the *Franklin* and began to climb. John could see the pilot and gunner looking down. He shook his fist at them defiantly. "You son-of-a-bitch!" he shouted. Angry tears rolled down his cheeks. "You dirty sons-of-bitches!"

He rushed to Belasco's side. "Corpsman! Corpsman!" he shouted as he put his hands and arms under Belasco's head. Belasco's eyes were glassy. Blood gushed from a huge wound in his chest and poured down his cheeks from under his helmet. His face was covered with blood. John's stomach roiled. He felt sick but he was too angry to throw up. He pulled Belasco close to him for a moment, but he knew there was no hope. Nobody could survive direct hits like this. Belasco was dead. "Smiling" Andre Belasco would never smile again.

Corpsmen rushed down the sponson's ladder. One felt for a pulse then shook his head. He pulled a white-cross marked body bag from a pouch. The corpsmen compressed Belasco's body into it and hurried it away on a stretcher. The last corpsman to leave scattered towels on the deck to soak up the blood. Then he climbed out of the sponson, too.

"That son-of-a-bitch is climbing for another run at us!" Ski screamed.

"Good! Let the bastard come back!" John shouted. "This time we'll blow the son-of-a-bitch out of the goddamned sky!"

John glanced around the gun pit. The deck was filthy with blood and littered with 40-mm shell casings. He was frightened, sweaty and dirty. His clothes were spattered with blood. None of this mattered. The only thing that mattered was to annihilate the son-of-a-bitch who just killed Belasco.

The Betty stormed back toward *Franklin* at collision speed.

"Hit that bastard before it comes into range!" John shouted.

A fiery determination possessed John's gun crew. Their movements were quick and precise. Sweat poured down their faces and through their shirts. They dropped clip after clip of 40-mm shells into their gun-breaches. Round after round of death-dealing shells blazed from their smoking barrels. The deafening, rapid-fire blasts voiced their anger. They ripped into the Betty's engine and fuselage. Pieces of metal tore away. Fire flashed around the cockpit. The Betty exploded in a huge cloud of orange and yellow flames. Burning parts flew in all directions. As the wreckage drifted down, the men in Able 1 gun crew let out a triumphant shout. "We got that bastard!" they screamed. "We got the son-of-a-bitch that killed Belasco!"

The heated action went on. Hellcats thundered off decks of every carrier in the Task Group. They tore into the Japanese planes. Furious dogfights broke out all over the nearly dark sky. A Zeke avoided the rushing fighters and zoomed down toward *Franklin* at high speed. Every antiaircraft gun on *Franklin's* starboard side, lashed out at it. A mass of antiaircraft fire erupted around the careening Zeke. The Zeke ignored the deluge of fire. It continued to dive toward *Franklin's* flight deck.

On the bridge Shoemaker saw the Zeke coming. "Hard left rudder!" he screamed.

Beckley spun the helm furiously, but the maneuver was not enough. The Zeke crashed onto *Franklin's* flight deck, and ripped across it. The cockpit cover and the pilot's head tore lose—they caromed crazily down the deck together! The Zeke crashed into Sponson 35 and hung, tail up, on the rim. Men manning the two sets of 40-mm quads scattered like cockroaches. The Zeke tottered on the rim. It erupted into flames. Blazing aviation gasoline poured into the sponson. After what seemed like forever it dropped tail first into the ocean below. Its still-attached bombs exploded in a mass of fire and flames.

Above the Task Group, Hellcats scrambled after the Japanese planes. They caught them and overwhelmed them. They shot down eleven. The tide of battle turned. The remaining attackers headed back to the northwest at high speed, with Hellcats right on their tails. The fighters destroyed a Zeke and two Zeros. Then they were forced to break off the chase because of darkness.

The suicide collision did only limited damage. The Zeke's nose and fuselage absorbed most of the impact so damage to the flight deck was light. It was a very close call, but it could have been a disaster!

The 40-mm mounts in the sponson were charred and inoperative. There was loss of life. Nine men in the gun pits were killed and twelve severely burned. The *Franklin* now had the dubious distinction of being the first ship to be hit by a Japanese suicide attack.

12 October, 1944
North Philippine Sea
Target: Formosa

With the Japanese kamikaze attack thwarted, TF 38, with the battleship *New Jersey* as group leader, steamed at high speed toward the Japanese stronghold of Formosa. That night, in turbulent weather and heavy seas, John went to the ship's library. He was pressed to write Belasco's parents. As tears filled his eyes he wrote:

> *Dear Mr. and Mrs. Belasco,*
> *My name is John Oxler. Your son Andre was in my gun crew on the Franklin. I write this letter to tell you that he was killed by Japanese machine gun fire this afternoon. I was with your son when he died. He died at his battle station, a hero's death.*

Tears slipped down his cheek and stained the paper. His hand shook from the sadness that filled him. He blotted the stains with his handkerchief and continued.

> *Your son was the happiest guy in our gun crew. Everybody liked him. He was always smiling and ready for a joke or two. If I live a hundred years, Mr. and Mrs. Belasco, I'll never forget Andre. I'm so very sorry and sad. We'll all miss him a lot. This is about all I can say.*
> *Sincerely,*
> *John Oxler, Gunner's Mate Second Class*

The ugly weather continued through the rest of the night and into the next morning. By noon TF 38 had forged through the storm front, but dense cloudiness caused the attack on Formosa to be postponed. *Franklin* used the afternoon to repair her damage and take on fuel from the fleet tanker *Escambia*.

By the next day, TF 38 was within one hundred miles of Formosa. The storm was over and the sea was calm. With dawn came a clear, bright sky and excellent flying weather. At 06:10, one hundred and fifty-nine planes hurtled into the air from the decks of TF 38 carriers. They eased into formation and prepared to launch their first attack of the day on the formidable island fortress. The harbors of Takao and Toshein were their targets.

Hellcats, Avengers and Helldivers from *Franklin* led the attack that lasted the better part of the morning. A *Hiku* Class destroyer was destroyed by missile fire. Harbor facilities and warehouses were badly damaged and left burning. Twelve Zeros were trapped on the ground. All but one was destroyed. There were no planes lost in the attack. But one question haunted everyone. Where were the Japanese carrier planes?

16 October, 1944
Philippine Islands
Attack Luzon and Leyte

TF 38 steamed South Southeast to attack Japanese airfields in the Philippines. On the way, Admiral Halsey divided the huge fleet into four separate Task Groups. He deployed them on a broad front around the northern and eastern perimeter of Luzon and Leyte. Admiral John McCain's Group—TF 38.1—was North of Luzon. Admiral Frederick Sherman's Group—TF 38.2—East of Luzon, Admiral Gerald Bogan's Group—TF 38.3—Southeast of Manila Bay and Admiral Ralph Davison's Group, with *Franklin* as group leader, as TF 38.4—steamed Southeast of the Island of Samar.

The task force's combined air strike capability of over twelve hundred planes was temporarily divided into small squadrons for these attacks. On the *Franklin*, Joe Taylor began the morning briefing with details of the new battle plan. A yeoman distributed mimeographed sketches of the new formations and detailed information on the airfields that were to be hit by their first strike.

"Look these over carefully," he said, waving a packet in the air with his right hand. "Squadron size will be nine planes—five fighters and four bombers. As soon as you are airborne and formed, proceed to your designated target. In the event you are not able to hit the primary target, you've got an alternate. Understand that this alternate may already be under attack by another squadron. Blend in and do as much damage as you can."

At 06:10 the first mini-squadron, commanded by Zimler, took off. Nine planes—four Avengers and five Hellcats made up Able Squadron. It quickly moved into formation and headed southwest to make the first attack of the day.

On the bridge, Beckley watched Zimler's squadron move toward dense clouds on the western horizon. "I wish it wasn't so cloudy," Shoemaker said. "This is the most important mission so far. I'd feel better if it was clear and we had better visibility."

"Well, with due respect, sir, the clouds make it harder for the Japs to see us, too," Beckley replied.

"Perhaps," Shoemaker said, "but it also provides a place where their aircraft can hide."

"Where do we attack today, sir?" Beckley asked.

"Zimler's squadron will attack the airfield at Legaspi. It's about fifty minutes from here," Shoemaker said.

Beckley lifted his glasses and gazed into the distance at Zimler's mini-squadron. "Why are the squadrons so small?" he asked.

"By using smaller squadrons we can attack more airfields," Shoemaker said. "We're going to try to knock out as many of their land-based aircraft as we can, as quick as we can."

"How many airfields do you think they have, sir?"

"I don't have an exact count, but there're a ton of them out there. We want at least two sorties a day by each squadron."

"That's a lot of flying, sir. Isn't it going to make it tough on the air crews?"

"Yes, but it has to be done this way. It's an order from Admiral Mitscher. He wants to hit as many as we can as quick and hard as we can. We're even going in close to shore to cut down on turn-around time."

"Begging the Captain's pardon, sir, but in all the time I've been in the Navy, I've never heard of a carrier making an attack so close to shore before," Beckley said.

"Neither have I, Chief. I guess that's because we've never tried it before. Admiral Davison just outlined the strategy yesterday. He thinks we'll take the Japs by surprise—that they'd never expect a close-in attack from carrier-based planes."

"They might surprise us, sir. Won't our heavy surface ships be behind us?"

"Not all of them. The cruisers and destroyers will go in with us, and we're doubling the number of fighters in the combat air patrols. Those fighters on deck are now part of our CAP. They'll be in the air over us in the next few minutes.

"Do you think this'll work?" Beckley asked with a hint of skepticism in his voice.

"I hope so, Chief, but who knows? There are a lot Jap land-based planes over there."

"When do we go in, Captain?"

"As soon as we finish with the *Twiggs*," Shoemaker replied. "She's just coming alongside to refuel and give us a mail drop."

In the *Franklin's* gun pits, all hands were in Condition I. Helmets strapped in place. Life jackets taut. Lookouts doubled and in a state of heightened awareness. The men in Able 1 gun crew were quiet and alert. Belasco's death was still on everyone's mind. It made them doubly cautious and vigilant.

John focused his binoculars on the southwestern horizon.

"If they're going to attack they have to come from there," he said.

"Goddamn, I hate this waiting," Ski said as he trained his binoculars southwest. "You look and look and don't see a damned thing."

"Be thankful for that," John said. "I'd rather see nothing all day than a mess of Jap planes."

"Yeah, you're right, Gunner," Ski replied. "But it's still boring as hell."

"Attention all hands!" boomed the loudspeaker system. "Mail will be delivered on stations at 09:30."

"Great!" John said to Ski. "I really could use a letter from Sandy today. When I get one, it always makes everything seem a little better."

"One letter," Ski said. "You usually get three or four. I haven't had any mail in almost three weeks."

"Well, let's hope you get some today," John said, as he continued to scan the southwest horizon.

A light drizzle started to fall. The wind picked up. Whitecaps appeared all over the ocean and the *Franklin* began to pitch and roll.

"Goddamn," Bonin said. "All we need now is a storm."

The ship's mailman appeared at the edge of the flight deck. He started rattling off names and tossing packets of letters.

A rubber-bound packet of letters zipped down as John's name was called. He caught it and hungrily thumbed through it.

"Three letters from Sandy and two from my mom and sister," he said to Ski.

"Damn, John, you're so lucky," Ski said. "All I ever get are letters from my folks. I wonder if one of these days I'm going to find a girl like Sandy."

"I wish you luck, Buddy, but I think when God made Sandy, He broke the mold."

John eagerly ripped open Sandy's letters and began to read them. The first two were filled with news about home and expressions of her love. As he read the third, a deep frown wrinkled his brow.

"What's wrong?" Ski asked.

"Sandy's brother is missing in action," John replied.

"Oh no!" Ski said. "How long has he been missing?"

"Her letter says they hadn't heard from him for nine weeks. It was written three weeks ago. She and her family are worried to death."

"Are they trying to trace him?"

"Yeah. The Red Cross said they'd do everything they could to locate him."

"Damn, that's a bummer, John," Ski said.

"It makes you feel so helpless," John said. "I just wish there was something I could do."

The increased vibrations of *Franklin's* engines interrupted their conversation.

"We're changing course," John said as he watched the bow begin to come about. Looks like we're going in closer to shore."

"For what?" Ski asked. "Can't our planes find us here?"

"I don't know," John said, "but that's what's happening. Something's up. Stow the mail, guys! Let's be alert!"

On the bridge, Shoemaker, Taylor and Beckley waited to hear from the first mini-squadron of the day.

Bill Zimler's voice finally came in over the microphone. "Bald Eagle to Emerald Base."

"Come in Bald Eagle," Joe Taylor replied.

"We've got you sighted. When you said you'd be close to shore you meant it, Joe," Zimler said. "You're only about thirty-five miles east of Manila."

"That's right. How'd it go, Bald Eagle?"

"Looks like Admiral Mitscher was right. We surprised them. We got twelve confirmed kills, all on the ground."

"Good Show. You're cleared to land, Bald Eagle."

"Roger and out."

During the next two days the combined Task Groups sent a stream of fighters and bombers to attack the Japanese airfields. Mitscher's strategy worked. Although Japanese resistance stiffened during the second and third day, the pilots and planes they put up in defense of their airfields were no match for the more experienced, better trained and equipped Americans. By the end of the third day a total of two hundred and thirty Japanese planes were destroyed, either in the air or on the ground. The task force lost forty-two planes and thirty-five pilots. *Franklin's* losses were six planes and four pilots, but the liberation of the Philippines could now begin.

CHAPTER SIXTEEN

18 October, 1944
The Battle of Leyte Gulf,
Philippine Sea

The Seventh Fleet with Admiral Thomas Kinkaid as Commander in Chief would spearhead the invasion of Leyte. General MacArthur, who had long insisted that the Philippines were a more suitable base than Formosa for the final assault on Japan, was the operation's Supreme Commander. Seven hundred and thirty ships were in Kinkaid's Seventh Fleet. Admiral Jesse Oldendorf, in command of the Battleship Line, was charged with the pre-invasion bombardment.

The *Santa Fe*, *Columbia*, *Denver* and *Boise,* along with a contingent of four heavy cruisers, the *San Francisco*, *Baltimore* and *Pittsburgh* and the *Shropshire* from the Royal Australian Navy, "borrowed" from the Third Fleet by the Seventh Fleet to assist in this bombardment and invasion, steamed toward Leyte Gulf at high speed.

On October 19, at 11:10, they rendezvoused with the Seventh Fleet, joining the cruisers *Louisville* and *Salt Lake City* in the screen around Admiral Oldendorf's battleships.

Oldendorf had a simple attack plan—steam boldly into Leyte Gulf and bombard the beaches pinpointed as landing areas.

20 October, 1944
Leyte Gulf,
Philippine Sea

As the sun rose, it spread a golden haze over the quiet waters of Leyte Gulf. The weather was peaceful and calm. At 07:00 the idyllic silence was shattered by a furious naval bombardment. Thousands of pounds of high-impact shells from Oldendorf's battleships and heavy and light cruisers tore up the beaches at the two attack points in San Pedro Bay. There was no enemy resistance; no fighter or bomber retaliations; no return fire from enemy pillboxes or bunkers. The attack points were undefended. A lone Japanese patrol plane approached from the northwest to take a look. Hellcats from *Franklin's* Air Strike Group that were charged with attacks on beach defenses, shot it down.

The *Santa Fe* was positioned to bombard the northern landing site on the western edge of San Pedro Bay. Her five- and six-inch guns pounded everything they could find on the beach. When they were close enough, her 20-mm and 40-mm guns opened fire. Within two hours everything within three miles of the beach was burning.

At 10:25 Kinkaid's command came: "Halt the bombardment. Land the landing forces! Seize the beaches and move inland!" Just a dozen simple words, but words upon which the success of America's war effort in the Pacific might hinge.

As the invasion began, President Roosevelt broadcast a message to the Philippine people. It was picked up by *Franklin* and forwarded to the ships in the Seventh Fleet. With his unmistakable New England intonation Roosevelt said:

> "This occasion is the beginning of General MacArthur's return to Philippine soil. He, along with our airmen, soldiers, sailors and marines, renews our pledge to our brothers and sisters there. With the help of Almighty God and our comrades-in-arms in the Philippines—we will drive out the invader—we will destroy his power to wage war and we will restore a world of dignity and freedom to those courageous islands—a world of confidence, honesty and peace...."

Even as the President was speaking, Tom watched hundreds of LCIs and the new larger mechanized landing craft, LCMs, filled with marines from the First and Third Divisions and infantrymen from the Army's Seventh and Ninety-Sixth Infantry Divisions, churn toward the beach.

The landings were comparatively easy. There was still no opposition. Even the waters in the bay cooperated—no surf, no mines or underwater obstructions.

"This is hard to believe," Tom said. "There's no resistance at all." As he spoke, a message came in. Tom rushed it to Captain Fitz.

"Sir, this just came across," he said when he stepped onto the bridge. "Naval Intelligence decoded a message from Admiral Toyoda, Commander in Chief of the Japanese Fleet. Admiral Kinkaid forwarded it to all ship commanders by semaphore."

Fitz read the message and frowned. "Toyoda says the Philippines must be held at all costs," Fitz said. "He urges every man to offer his soul and fight to the end."

"Well, they didn't put up much of a fight here, sir," Tom said. "It's only 17:30 and most of the troops and nearly all of the supplies and munitions are ashore."

"Yeah, I know, and they're moving inland," Fitz replied. "But it's just too easy. They're waiting for us out there somewhere. You can bet on that sailor."

#

Aboard the battleship *New Jersey*, Admiral Bill Halsey's flagship, he and his executive officer, Admiral Richard Phillips, waited for news on the progress of the Leyte invasion.

At 09:32 a radioman rushed onto the bridge. "Message from the submarine *Darter*, sir," he said, partially out of breath. "Just came in over the wire."

Halsey hurriedly read the message, then said, "The *Darter's* located a large Japanese fleet seventy-five miles east of Mindoro Island in the Sibuyan Sea. There are eight battleships and twelve or thirteen cruisers. *Musashi* and *Yamato* are there, but there were no carriers."

"It's a big fleet," Phillips said with excitement in his voice.

"Get this information and location out to the Seventh Fleet immediately," Halsey ordered, "and get Mitscher and Burke over here right away! Tell them it's a matter of great urgency."

"Aye, Admiral," Phillips replied.

An hour later, Halsey got a second message. He read it and said, "Another fleet. A large Japanese task force was just sighted in the Sulu Sea, near the Island of Negros. They're steaming northeast—four more battleships, five heavy cruisers, three light cruisers and approximately twenty cans and patrol craft."

"Any carriers?" Phillips asked

"No. Not a damned one." Halsey thought a minute. "What the hell's going on?" he asked. "A mass of Jap ships like this and no air cover? I don't understand it."

"Maybe they think they've got enough cover from land-based planes," Phillips said.

"I don't see how that could be, Rich. We've destroyed over three hundred in the last two weeks. Surface fleets without air cover like this are extremely vulnerable."

"You're right, Admiral," Phillips replied. "That's sure not the way this war's being fought. The Japs must have something else up their sleeves."

"Yes, but what?"

Halsey and Phillips were leaning over a chart of the Philippines when Mitscher and Burke arrived.

"Come in. Come here," Halsey said as they walked onto the bridge. He pointed to an area on the chart. "We've located two large Jap fleets. One is southeast of Mindoro, steaming toward Leyte. This force includes the *Musashi* and *Yamato*. We received this at 09:32. Then about forty-five minutes later we got a message from the *Franklin's* Search and Strike Group. They found another large fleet near Negros headed northeast toward the Mindoro Strait. What do you make of it?"

Mitscher studied the chart then looked at Burke. "I don't know about Arleigh, but it looks like they're going to try to put a pincer around the Seventh Fleet and the transports supplying the troops on Leyte."

Halsey looked at Burke.

"I agree," Burke said.

"There's one thing missing from your assumption, gentlemen," Halsey said. "Carriers. Do you think the Japs are going to attack the Seventh Fleet with land-based aircraft as their only cover?"

"If they do, I wonder where they'd get them, Admiral?" Mitscher replied. "We've been knocking hell out of their land-based planes. By now the kill count is over three hundred and fifty."

"That's what I said to Rich, Marc. They need air support to make *any* plan work. So where the hell are the carriers?"

"My guess, Admiral," said Burke slowly, "is that there's another Japanese fleet out there somewhere. I'd guess the carriers are in it."

"Where the hell could they be? The action's here—right around the Philippines."

"Maybe they're up here," Burke said as he pointed to an area in the North Philippine Sea on the map. "Maybe they'll try to use them as a decoy—to draw us away from Leyte. If a tactic like this worked, it'd leave the Seventh Fleet at their mercy—out-manned, out-gunned, with limited air cover."

"Yeah," Halsey said. "That would strand our troops on Leyte, too. That's exactly what the sons-of-bitches are trying to do—I'd bet money on it!"

"I agree with that," Mitscher said. "This is a classic Japanese plan, full of deception, diversion and trickery. Those bastards are trying to isolate the troops on Leyte."

"Yeah, and in the process, they'll try to destroy the Seventh Fleet," Halsey said. He turned to an aide. "Alert Admiral Kinkaid. Tell him those fleets are coming at him. Tell him we're going to attack the larger fleet in the Sibuyan Sea."

"Do you men agree?"

Mitscher and Burke both nodded.

"I agree completely, Admiral," Mitscher said, "But what they're trying to do depends a lot on timing. If one fleet is delayed, it screws up their whole plan."

"Yes, exactly. That's why I think we should go after the bigger Central Fleet. Their plan won't work unless they join up," Halsey said. "And this gives us a shot at the *Yamato* and *Musashi*."

23 October, 1944
Attack the Musashi
Eastern Sibuyan Sea

When Mitscher and Burke returned to the *Enterprise* they set the stage for the attack. By noon on the twenty-third of October, Mitscher had repositioned his Fast Carrier Forces. He was preparing an air-sea engagement that could mean the success or failure of the invasion of the Philippines and the war in the Pacific. Admiral John McCain's force was deployed on the eastern perimeter of Leyte, Fredrick Sherman's group was to the northeast, and Admiral Gerald Bogan's force was in the middle, southeast of Manila Bay. Admiral Ralph Davison's group, with the *Franklin* as group leader, was about sixty miles southeast of the Island of Samar.

As soon as it was light, the cloudy Pacific sky filled with American planes. Two hundred and eighty-five planes in Air Strike Able were launched from the decks of the carriers *Franklin*, *Enterprise, Lexington*, *Intrepid*, *Cabot* and *Essex*. Once they were airborne, they circled and quickly assumed strike positions. Then headed toward the Sibuyan Sea.

Franklin's Air Strike Group consisted of eighteen Hellcats armed with missiles fitted with armor-piercing heads, sixteen Helldivers loaded with five-hundred-pound bombs and twenty Avengers armed with Mark XIII torpedoes. Because of *Franklin's* location, it had a more direct course and a shorter distance to travel. Her Air Strike Group droned on for about an hour at an altitude of fourteen thousand feet. They encountered a heavy haze and flew through it. When they emerged, they sighted the Japanese fleet about twelve miles away. The huge armada was divided into two groups separated by about eight miles of ocean. In the middle of each group were three battleships—a super battleship between two conventional men-of-war. The sleek lines of the huge *Musashi* were easily identified at the center of the first group. The equally powerful lines of the *Yamato* were at the center of the second group. Twelve heavy and light cruisers and at least twenty destroyers surrounded both groups.

As soon as the air strike came into view, the Japanese spotted them and opened fire with their sixteen- and eighteen-inch guns. Huge bursts of red and yellow flames filled the air. Death-dealing explosions erupted around the Air Strike. Blasts from the conventional battleships and cruisers were powerful, but those from the eighteen-inch guns of the *Musashi* and *Yamato* were much bigger and a lot more violent.

The Air Strike flew on at maximum speed. Concussion from the antiaircraft barrage tossed planes around like lifeboats in a storm. A Hellcat at the point of the formation exploded into fragmented pieces. In less than a minute another was blasted out of the sky.

Joe Crowley in command of the fighter squadron screamed, "Go higher! Go higher! Get the fuck up higher!" He yanked back on his stick. His engine screamed and he zoomed almost straight up. His head hurt and his arms trembled from the strain. Tears welled up in his eyes from the loss of two of his best friends. He felt sick at his stomach and angry as hell. "Level off at twenty-four thousand feet!" he shouted to the rest of the Attack Group that followed right on his tail. This quick maneuver confused the Japanese gunners. For a few moments, they continued their barrage at fourteen thousand feet. By the time they adjusted the trajectory of their fire, the Hellcats were in position to attack. They zoomed down through the heavy antiaircraft fire, countering it with a stream of 50-caliber machine gun fire of their own.

"Pour it on the bastards!" Crowley screamed. "Make 'em keep their fucking heads down."

As the Hellcats closed, the rest of the Japanese armada started to zigzag furiously. They fought back with heavier antiaircraft fire. The sky was now black with Japanese flack.

"Zero in on *Musashi*!"

The Hellcats zeroed in. Red-yellow fire trailed from Tiny Tims as they streaked toward their target. Two of the powerful missiles scored direct hits. When hit, the *Musashi* shuddered momentarily but continued to zigzag at high speed. Sparks flew from the armor plating around her deck guns as the Hellcats blasted away with everything they had.

Another fighter exploded and caromed toward the ocean. A parachute opened and floated gently downward.

"Dino, radio his position," Zimler said as he watched the chute blossom.

"I hope there's a sub down there somewhere," Dino said as he called the *Franklin* and reported the flyer's position.

"This is the most intense antiaircraft fire I've ever seen," Zimler said. "Those bastards are using every gun they've got."

"I guess that's what you have to do when you don't have air cover, sir," Dino replied. "You throw up everything—even the kitchen sink!"

The fighters completed their attack. Helldivers armed with five-hundred-pound-bombs screamed down on the huge ship. They scored at least four hits but *Musashi* continued to zigzag at high speed.

While the SB2C's attack occupied the Japanese, the much more vulnerable torpedo-armed Avengers were sneaking in, using the horizon as cover. "Torpedo squadron!" shouted Zimler. "Let's see if we can get that big bastard!" He put his squadron into a steep dive. A heavy curtain of antiaircraft fire filled the air ahead. They plunged into it. Zimler's plane bumped and shuddered from the concussion of the huge shells. He pulled out of the dive at two hundred feet and flew straight for the battleship, which was still about two miles away. The air filled with even more concentrated antiaircraft fire. Zimler prayed silently, "Lord, please keep the squadron together and steady on target."

Fiery smoking bursts exploded around him. He ignored them. Getting through to the *Musashi* was the only thing that mattered. Shrapnel ripped into his left wing and fuselage. It dug into the Avenger's armor plating with a dull thud.

The squadron pressed on at maximum speed. Shrapnel ripped into their fuselages and wings. Seconds became hours, then days. Zimler could feel his heart pounding furiously. His throat was dry and he was having trouble swallowing. The *Musashi* looked ugly, menacing, almost like it wasn't real. For a moment he felt joy—this was something he'd dreamed of— in the next moment, he was horrified. "What the hell am I doing here? This is insane!" he mumbled. Suddenly he was right in the middle of another mass of awesome fiery puffs. More heavy flack ripped into his Avenger causing it to shudder violently. He felt a burning pain in his forehead, but ignored it. The action was too intense, the adrenaline flow too strong.

About eight hundred yards from his target he dropped his torpedo and pulled up into a steep climb. The Avenger's engine screamed as it responded to Zimler's demands. When he was able to right his plane, Zimler glanced backward. His torpedo had just slammed into the *Musashi* and exploded amidships. He looked for the rest of the Avengers. They were closing right on target. He could see the wakes of four more torpedoes as they streaked toward the giant ship.

"Dino!" he shouted. "We got a direct hit! There are four more torpedoes headed right toward that big son-of-a-bitch. Dino! We got a direct hit."

"Dino. Dino!"

Zimler squirmed around in his cockpit and looked back. The Plexiglas cover on Dino's cockpit was shattered. He was slumped over. Only the upper part of his helmet was visible.

"Oh, God! Oh, God, no!" Zimler shouted. "Bald Eagle to Emerald Base! Bald Eagle to Emerald Base! Come in, goddamn it!"

"Roger, Bald Eagle. Emerald Base here."

"I'm coming home. I've got a wounded gunner. I think he's badly wounded—and I'm a little shot up, too."

"Where are you wounded, Bald Eagle?"

"On the forehead, above my left eye."

"Can you make it home?"

"This plane's pretty shot up, but I think I can."

"Open your cockpit canopy a little so there'll be fresh air. Then take the heavy gauze pad out of your first aid kit and press it to the wound. This should stop the bleeding."

"Roger, I found the gauze pad. I'll get it under my helmet to keep it in place."

"There's a pressure point at your temple, Bald Eagle. If the pad doesn't stop the bleeding, press your finger against it. That should stop it."

"Roger. Request permission for immediate landing when I get there."

"Just get here and come in. We'll have corpsmen waiting."

The weight of the world descended on Zimler. He felt despondent, helpless and alone. He pushed the Avenger toward the *Franklin* as fast as it could go. He prayed silently as tears came into his eyes, "God, please let Dino be alive. Please, dear God. Let him be alive."

The flight back seemed to take forever. Finally, he sighted the *Franklin* in a cloudy gray haze about twenty-five miles away.

"Bald Eagle to Emerald Base! I've sighted you. I'm about twenty-five miles northwest of you. I'm on my way in."

Zimler's Avenger was trailing smoke. The aileron on his right wing flapped back and forth, making control of the plane difficult. He turned awkwardly into a landing pattern and began his descent.

"You're cleared to land, Bald Eagle. Don't forget to protect your head with your hands when you hit the deck. Those leather helmets can't take much of an impact."

"Roger, are the Medics there?"

"We're waiting with all the help we've got."

Zimler's Avenger bounced violently from side to side as it descended. Its wings dipped clumsily up and down. When it hit the flight deck, its right wheel collapsed. The Avenger's nose hammered into the deck and it tipped tail-up. The prop churned into the wooden deck. It caromed recklessly down the flight deck until it came to a noisy halt less than ten yards from John's gun sponson.

When the men in Able Sponson saw the Avenger churning toward them, everyone scattered. Crashing planes could douse men trapped in sponsons with flaming gasoline. John took cover behind the Mark 14 sight's steel mount. A few seconds passed. He peeked around the mount. The Avenger was stopped. It was smoking heavily but wasn't leaking gasoline. He vaulted up the ladder to the flight deck in three giant steps and rushed to the nose-down plane. He saw Zimler struggling to open his cockpit canopy. John grabbed the jammed canopy and ripped it back.

Zimler suddenly realized help was at hand. "Forget me! Forget me!" he screamed. "Goddamn it! Help my gunner!"

John pulled himself up on the wing. He looked into the shattered canopy of the tail-gunner's cockpit. He saw a man's body awkwardly twisted, bleeding from a giant wound. Shrapnel had ripped open his throat. He reached in and tilted the gunner's head back. His face was stone cold and his eyes glassy. John knew he was dead.

Zimler, by this time, had pulled himself out of his cockpit. His head was bleeding despite the gauze pad. Blood covered the collar of his flight jacket. He stumbled down to the deck, and began to stagger toward the rear of the plane.

John stood directly in his way.

Zimler tried to push him aside. "Get out of the way, goddamn it!" he screamed. "I have to get to my gunner. Get out of my way, sailor! Goddamn you. Get out of my way. I have to help my gunner…."

John wrapped his arms around him.

"Take your hands off me. I need to get to my gunner," Zimler groaned, almost collapsing in John's arms.

By this time four corpsmen arrived. Two rushed up the wing to the rear cockpit.

John continued to restrain Zimler, now more to hold him up than back.

With all the energy he had left, Zimler tried to push himself free, but John held him tight. "I think your gunner's dead, sir," he said gently.

"Oh, God, no! Dino can't be dead…."

Zimler pulled his head around John's shoulder and shouted as loud as his frail voice would allow. "Corpsman…Corpsman…."

The nearest corpsman dropped to the deck and helped John steady Zimler.

Zimler looked at the corpsman. His face was filled with anguish. "Corpsman…my gunner…."

"Your gunner's dead, sir."

Zimler's face went white and he collapsed in John's arms.

By this time four men with a stretcher and air crewmen with fire extinguishers surrounded the plane. They placed the stretcher at John's feet and he gently helped lower Zimler into it. A corpsman removed the bloody pad and eased a larger gauze compress over Zimler's head wound.

"This man's lost a lot of blood. Let's get him to sickbay immediately," a Corpsman said. They rushed Zimler across the flight deck and down a ladder. Then Antonelli's body was lifted from the cockpit and wrapped in a blanket. Corpsmen placed it on a stretcher and moved it below decks to the ship's morgue. Within a few minutes a mobile crane lifted the battered Avenger and took it out to the port corner of the flight deck. There the mangled plane was dropped into the ocean.

Hellcats, Avengers and Helldivers laden with bombs, missiles and torpedoes came up from the hangar deck. *Franklin*'s catapult hurled them into the sky. Air Strike Baker, with a second load of destruction and death, was on its way to the battle in the Sibuyan Sea.

Over the next two days, over twenty-three hundred sorties were launched against the *Musashi* from the decks of the Fast Carrier Forces. They hit her again and again. At least thirty bombs and ten torpedoes found their mark. Finally, at the end of the second day, the huge battleship, that only a few days before seemed invincible, rolled over and slowly sank into the Pacific.

On the *Franklin*, Shoemaker, Taylor, Jurika and Beckley stood anxiously on the bridge, headphones on, awaiting word of the results of the second attack.

"Have you ever heard of a ship taking this kind of pounding?" Shoemaker asked.

"No, I haven't, Captain," Taylor replied. "This is the fifth time we've hit her in two days."

At 16:55 a message came up from the radio room.

Beckley took the message and handed it to Shoemaker. After he read it, he said, "The *Musashi* went down at 16:05! We sank a heavy cruiser, too."

Taylor threw his headphones into the air. "We did it, sir!" he shouted. "We sank the *Musashi*!"

"It's a milestone," Shoemaker said. "This is the first battleship ever sunk entirely by aircraft. But before we get too excited let's remember *Yamato* was hit by at least four five-hundred-pound bombs and they didn't even faze her."

"Does it say what happened to the rest of the Jap fleet?" Beckley asked.

"Yeah. They're retreating southwest. Fuel's a problem, so we can't chase them. The air strike is coming home."

By the time the last plane in Air Strike Charlie landed, dusk had settled around the ship. Although the *Musashi* was at the bottom of the Sibuyan Sea and the Japanese battle plan was disrupted, the cost of these victories had been great. *Musashi's* guns downed eight of *Franklin's* fighters and seven bombers and their crews. Most were presumed killed in action. Two pilots were picked up by the submarine *Albacore*. An Avenger pilot and his gunner were reported to be safe in the hands of friendly Filipinos.

Four of the crewmen in the badly shot-up planes that made it back to *Franklin* were either dead or died before morning. They would be buried after sundown. Dino Antonelli was one of the four.

At 19:00 Beckley headed down to the sickbay. He promised Commander Zimler earlier that he would go to Antonelli's burial with him. When he stepped through the hatch, Zimler was sitting there waiting. His head was heavily bandaged and he was still very pale, but he looked much better than he had when Beckley saw him earlier that morning.

When Zimler saw Beckley a faint smile crossed his face. He was suffering great anguish and Beckley knew it.

"Hello, sir," Beckley greeted. "How you feeling?"

"I've felt better, Beck."

Beckley put his hand on Zimler's shoulder and said, "It's about time for the burial, sir."

Zimler nodded and pulled himself slowly out of his chair. "I'm still a little weak," he said as he reached for his coat.

Beckley grabbed the coat and helped Zimler into it. "I'll be with you all the way, sir," he said.

The two men made their way aft to the fantail. When they arrived there were already small groups of officers and enlisted men waiting to pay their respects to their dead comrades.

Beckley led Zimler to a life-jacket canister and helped him sit down on it. Then he sat down next to him, just in case. From where they were sitting they could see four stretchers. The unmistakable outlines of four human bodies covered by American flags were outlined in the shadows of a muted deck light.

In a few minutes Father Edward Harkin, the Catholic chaplain, the master-at-arms and the Honor Guard arrived. After a few simple preparations, the burial began.

"We are gathered here tonight," the priest said, "to honor four of our comrades who have paid the highest price possible in the defense of their country: Lieutenant Arthur O'Neill, Lieutenant Junior Grade Thomas Ellis, Gunner's Mate Third Class Dino Antonelli and Aviation Ordinance Man Third Class Avery Wilson. Tonight we also honor those brave men in the air crews who didn't return from their combat missions."

He paused and took a long breath, then continued, "Were this another time and another place, all these brave men would be surrounded by the love of their families and their friends. Tonight we must replace that love with a love of our own. We must love these men because they were our comrades-in-arms and our shipmates, but also because they made the greatest sacrifice that could ever be made—they gave their lives in our defense—and in the defense of our country."

He looked into the dark, distant night sky. "Some of us might wonder," he said softly, "why they had to die. Why them, not me, we ask? The answer for us all is *it was their time*. As is written in Ecclesiastes 3-1:8:

> *To every thing there is a season, and a time to every purpose under heaven.*
> *A time to be born, and a time to die;*
> *A time to plant and a time to pluck what is planted.*
> *A time to weep, and a time to laugh; a time to mourn, and a time to dance;*
> *A time to kill, and a time to heal; a time to break down and a time to build up;*
> *A time to get, and a time to lose; a time to keep, and a time to cast away;*
> *A time to rend, and a time to sew; a time to keep silence, and a time to speak;*
> *A time to love, and a time to hate; a time of war, and a time of peace.*

He paused again. There was only the sound of the wind and the waves. "This was their time to die," he said. "For us who remain, this continues to be our time for war. But this is also our time to mourn. It is our time to weep and our time to heal. Our Lord Jesus said, 'Greater love hath no man than this; that a man lay down his life for his friends.' This is indeed true. Greater love hath no man than he who dies for another. The brave men we mourn tonight have given us proof of this—with the ultimate sacrifice of life itself."

He raised his hand and blessed the remains of each man there. "Well done, O good and faithful servants," he said. "Enter thou now into the Kingdom of Heaven."

Then he stepped aside and the master-at-arms faced the Honor Guard.

"Honor Guard. Tennn hut!"

"Ready."

"Aim."

"Fire!"

The sound of rifle fire, repeated three times, reverberated through the dark October night. Six seamen quickly surrounded the flag-draped stretchers. One by one they lifted them and braced them on the railing of the fantail. When each man's name was called they raised the back of a stretcher. Dino Antonelli's name was called last. The dread sound of a canvas-wrapped body sliding down a coarse canvas stretcher filled the air. Then the sickening weighted splash. Then silence.

Beckley heard Zimler gasp. He was emotion-bound, too. He had taken on some of Zimler's anguish and sorrow.

"I'll never be able to hunt moose with him in Wyoming," Zimler said sadly.

Beckley tried to think of something to help him, but he knew of no message that could ease this kind of pain.

24 October, 1944
Leyte Gulf
The Battle of Surigao Strait

The Japanese Southern Fleet, which included three battleships of the *Fuso* Class, seven cruisers and a dozen destroyers, continued on through the Mindanao Sea toward Surigao Strait and Leyte Gulf. At 13:25 search planes from the *Franklin* and *Enterprise* sighted them and radioed their location to the Seventh Fleet.

On the battleship *California*, Admiral Kinkaid and his staff, along with Admiral Jesse Oldendorf who commanded the Seventh Fleet's Battleship Line, discussed what was unfolding. They suspected the Japanese Southern Fleet was steaming toward Surigao Strait to attack the ships and landing forces in Leyte Gulf.

"The Japanese strategy is getting clearer," Kinkaid said to the men surrounding him. "They're trying to link up with their Central Fleet. They wanted to put a big pincer around us, but I think Marc Mitscher's air attacks fouled up that part of their plan. Now we get word from search planes that their Southern Fleet is still coming at us at full speed. What the hell do you make of it, Jesse?"

"It makes me think somebody's pretty crazy, Admiral," Oldendorf replied. "It's hard to believe they'd try to get through Surigao Strait and penetrate Leyte Gulf without the ships in their Central Fleet."

At that moment a radioman came onto the bridge. "This message just came in from Fleet Headquarters, sir," he said, handing Kinkaid the message.

Kinkaid read the message hurriedly. When he finished he said, "This is a decoded top-secret message from Admiral Toyoda in Tokyo. It confirms what we just said. Admiral Nishimura, who commands the Japanese Southern Fleet, intended to join up with their Central Fleet commanded by Admiral Kurita. This message is an order from Toyoda to both fleets. Apparently Toyoda didn't know when he sent this that his Central Fleet was pretty badly chewed up by Mitscher's aircraft."

Kinkaid read the rest of the message aloud: "The enemy has penetrated over one

THE BATTLE OF LEYTE GULF

hundred twenty miles into the Island of Leyte. We must hold Leyte at all cost. Attack immediately. Destroy the American Fleet in Leyte Gulf. Strand MacArthur's invasion forces. Annihilate them as we did at Bataan." He put the message down. "It's signed by Soemu Toyoda, Commander in Chief, Japanese Navy," he said.

"So it looks like Toyoda didn't know what happened in the Sibuyan Sea—that there wouldn't be a link up," Oldendorf said.

"Maybe he didn't when he sent this," Kinkaid replied. "He's in Japan, but Nishimura sure as hell knew about it. He was less than a hundred fifty miles away. Hell, he could almost hear our bombs explode on the *Musashi* at that distance."

Oldendorf looked perplexed. "What do you think about attacking us with a force that's now clearly smaller and inferior to ours?" he asked.

"I don't understand it," Kinkaid said. "But you know the Japanese. They never question a superior's orders. Maybe Nishimura thinks he has a chance to surprise us, especially if he can slip in under the cover of darkness."

"That seems more like blindness than darkness, Admiral," Oldendorf replied.

"Well, if they don't turn around, let's knock hell out of them," Kinkaid said. "As the old Mississippi gamblers would say, 'never, ever give a sucker a second chance.'"

Kinkaid and Oldendorf quickly structured a plan for the defense of Leyte Gulf. They would send a squadron of PT boats south to patrol the entrance from Surigao Strait. The PT boats would locate the Japanese Southern Fleet when it arrived and send an alert. If Nishimuras's force steamed through the strait, they would attack it with torpedoes, followed by a second torpedo attack by twelve destroyers located northeast of the PT boats. Next an attack by the light and heavy cruisers and, finally, the battleships would anchor the attack with fire from the Battleship Line. Within an hour, units from the Seventh Fleet and those "borrowed" from Halsey's Third Fleet assumed their positions. Once in place they became silent. The PT boats lay-to on station so as not to leave a wake.

The sea in the strait was smooth and glassy. It was just a few minutes before midnight. A quarter moon had set and heavy clouds moved in from the northwest. The night became ink black and deathly still. It was what the PT boats wanted. They waited quietly. The rest of the Seventh Fleet silently stood by to spring their trap—confident that their plan gave them a huge tactical advantage. PT boats would intercept, harass and expose; destroyers would deliver additional torpedo attacks; and a battle line of superior strength and firepower would cap it all off.

#

The Japanese Southern Fleet, in a single-file column led by destroyers, pressed on toward the trap at high speed.

Suddenly, detection gear on PT 158 picked up the sound of enemy engines and propellers. The Japanese formation was now entering Leyte Gulf. Commander Raymond White wired a message to Admiral Oldendorf.

As soon as Oldendorf got the message he said, "Message from PT 158. The enemy fleet has entered Leyte Gulf. The torpedo attack will begin in fifteen minutes."

On the *Santa Fe*, at general quarters, Tom Rashinski squinted at the developing night-clad battle scene through binoculars. Carl Corini was standing next to him doing exactly the same thing.

The PT boats began their attack. They flashed by the unsuspecting Japanese in groups of threes, firing torpedo after torpedo. Japanese searchlights cut through the night, trying desperately to locate them.

"Looks like we caught 'em off guard," Tom said. "Their fucking searchlights are going in every direction."

Two torpedoes hit home. A Japanese patrol craft burst into flames. Searchlights from Japanese destroyers finally found the PT boats. They came under heavy fire. Four were hit and sunk, but they'd done their job. Under cover of a smoke screen, they moved swiftly out of range.

#

Undaunted by the PT boat attack, Nishimura's fleet steamed northwest for over an hour. The heavy clouds moved to the southeast and the night became lighter. The silhouettes of the Japanese force stood out clearly. They were still in single-file, steaming directly toward the American invasion beaches. Aboard the *Santa Fe*, radar clearly identified the order of the Japanese fleet. Seven destroyers led, followed by six light and heavy cruisers, then four battleships. They were protected by two more cruisers and an additional nine destroyers and four patrol craft.

"The destroyers are getting ready to attack," Tom said, the excitement of battle now apparent in his voice. "Looks like they are going to attack their left and right flanks."

At 02:30 the destroyers, steaming at flank speed, began their left-flank attack, firing torpedoes at ranges from twenty-two hundred to thirty-three hundred yards. They scored two direct hits on a *Fuso* Class battleship that steamed second in the column. There was an explosion amidships! The huge warship fell out of line and began to burn.

Meanwhile the right-flank attack led by the destroyer *McDermut* targeted the *Yamagumo* Class destroyer that led the huge Japanese flotilla. She was struck amidships by two of *McDermut's* torpedoes. She blew up and began to sink. *McDermut* then attacked the second destroyer in line and scored a direct hit. It knocked off her bow. The destroyer *Remey* torpedoed a third. There was a huge explosion amidships. Raging fires consumed the ship.

The left force now attacked what was clearly identified as the new battleship *Yamashiro*. They got a torpedo into her but this failed to slow her down.

A message over the wire from the McDermut: "We're out of torpedoes!"

"Destroyers retire." Oldendorf replied. "Cruisers attack!"

Nishimura continued to steam northwest, ignoring the ships that had been knocked out or damaged and unaware of the massive forces deployed to stop him.

On the bridge of the *Santa Fe*, Captain Fitz shouted a course change and ordered flank speed. *Santa Fe's* engines surged. The ship knifed through the dark waters of Leyte Gulf. Behind her came the *Boise*, *Columbia* and *Denver*. When in range they attacked with their heavy guns. Behind them several heavy cruisers opened fire. Ten minutes later the battleships began their bombardment. Salvos of fourteen-inch armor-piercing projectiles from *California, West Virginia, Tennessee, Mississippi* and *Maryland* blazed away at the Japanese warships. The arched line of white-hot shells from the American fleet seemed endless. It lit the sky like a continuous stream of Roman candles.

The Japanese gamely returned the fire. The *Yamashiro* directed her fire back to the Battleship Line. Japanese cruisers returned the fire of American cruisers.

Fitz maneuvered *Santa Fe* in and out at high speed, giving his gunners excellent shots and leaving the Japanese with little to shoot back at. "Pass the word to the gun crews," he ordered. "Keep hammering that first cruiser aft of the battlewagons. Tell them to hammer hell out of her! She'll go down!"

A salvo from the *Santa Fe*'s six-inch guns scored two direct hits on the cruiser's forward gun turret. A second salvo from *San Francisco* blasted the turret from its mount and a third salvo from *Santa Fe* made a direct hit on the bridge, almost demolishing it. The Japanese cruiser's speed slowed to a crawl.

"She won't last long now," Fitz said. "We've hit her everywhere. Call for a torpedo attack!"

The destroyer *Albert W. Grant* flashed by the *Santa Fe* at high speed. She launched three torpedoes at the now mortally wounded cruiser. Two found their mark. There were two huge explosions! The once sleek Japanese warship listed sharply to starboard, halted there briefly, then rolled over and disappeared slowly into the water.

Oldendorf now ordered the Task Group to steam sharply Southwest. This bold maneuver narrowed the range between his fleet and the now badly battered Japanese warships. At this reduced range, fire from the battleships was more precise and accurate. The battleship *Yamashiro* and a heavy cruiser suffered a series of direct hits. Flames shot from their midsections. Secondary explosions amidships lit the night sky like fireworks.

Nishimura turned his fleet toward the entrance to Leyte Gulf.

"Close fast on them!" Oldendorf commanded from the *California.*

In less than twenty minutes, the destroyer *Newcomb* overtook the *Yamashiro.* She fired two torpedoes at close range. Both were direct hits. The *Yamashiro* exploded and started to burn. The flames were so bright that her entire superstructure stood out in the darkness. Her list increased to thirty degrees. She hung there precipitously for what seemed a long time. Then she rolled over and sank rapidly, taking all but a few members of her crew down with her. The remaining ships, some badly damaged, retreated toward Surigao Strait.

Dawn was starting to break. In the half-light, this move was easily detected.

"Polish off the cripples!" Oldendorf commanded.

Five cruisers, including *Santa Fe,* went after the fleeing Japanese at flank speed. At 05:10 they caught up with a badly damaged cruiser and destroyer. Both were sunk by gunfire and torpedo attacks.

At 05:39 the battle was over. The cost to the Imperial Japanese Navy: twelve ships. Fifteen were able to escape.

On the *Santa Fe*, tired men filtered topside for a breath of cool air and a look at what happened. Tom joined them at the port railing. Through his binoculars he could make out clusters of Filipinos on the heavily vegetated shoreline, waiting for the small groups of Japanese survivors who were swimming ashore.

"I wouldn't want to be those Japs when they get there," he said to a fireman standing next to him. "Those poor bastards are going to run into a bunch of knives, rocks and clubs."

The fireman, his clothes spotted with oil and grease from his efforts around the *Santa Fe*'s engines, didn't seem to give a damn. "Fuck the Japs," he said. "Tonight I'm just happy to be alive—just glad to breathe fresh air, have a deck under my feet and think about what the hell we'll have for breakfast."

No one on deck could disagree with that.

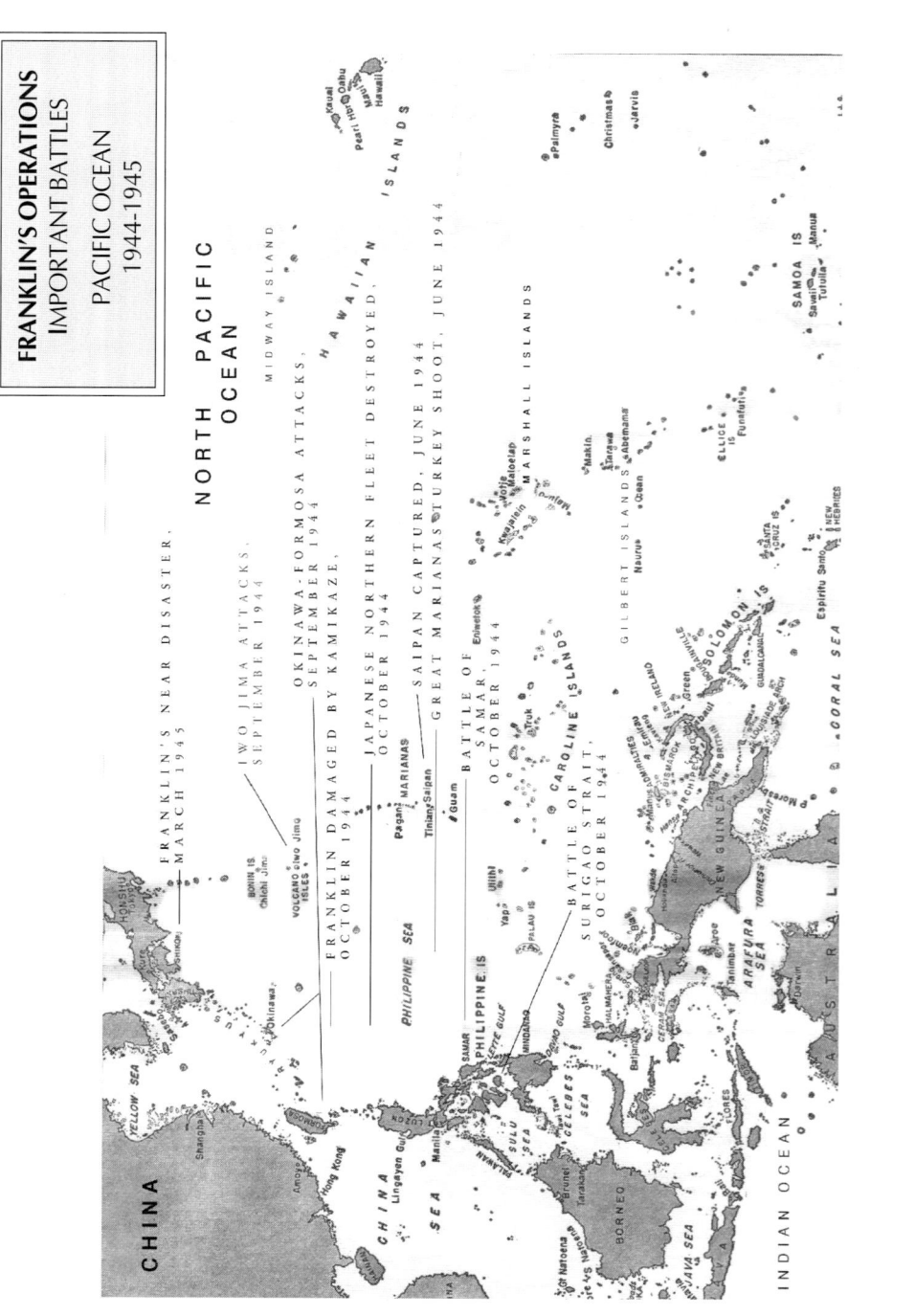

Task Force 58 raid on Japan, 40-mm anti-aircraft guns.

The *Franklin* is launched on October 14th, 1943.

Young sailors just out of "Boot Camp".

Pilots of Air Group Thirteen relax in the *Franklin's* ready room...
tomorrow will be a busy day...

Franklin's cramped crew's quarters.

Franklin's library.

Franklin's Avengers fly in formation.

Japanese cruiser is sunk in the battle of Midway.

A Japanese bomb explodes on the
flight deck of an Essex class carrier.

The *USS Lexington* sinks in the battle of the Coral Sea.

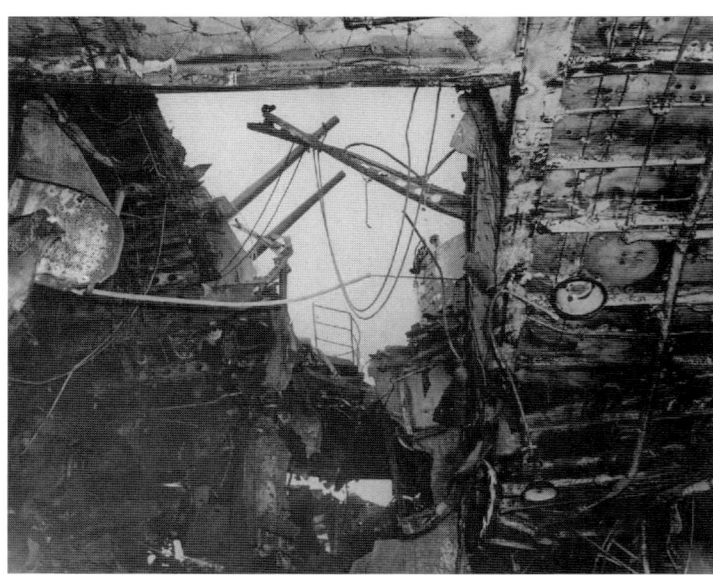

Damage to *Franklin's* flight and hangar decks from a kamikaze attack in the Philippine Sea in late October, 1944.

US Navy Combat Aircraft of the Pacific War

Chance-Vought F4U Corsair

Designed by Beisel and Sikorsky, the F4U is regarded by many as one of the greatest conbat aircraft in history, and was in production for a longer period of time than any US fighter other than the F4 Phantom. As conceived it was intended to mount the most powerful engine, and biggest propeller, of an fighter in existence, and the prototype was the first US combat aircraft to exceed 400mph.

Grumman F6F Hellcat

The Hellcat was the main shipboard fighter of the US Navy for the last two years of the Pacific War. During the Gilbert and Marshall Operations, the raid on Truk, in the Battle of the Philippine Sea and at Leyte Gulf, the entire fighter complement of the Fast Carrier Force consisted of F6Fs - at Philippine Sea Task Force 58 fielded some 450 fighters, all of them being F6F-3s, and at Leyte Gulf, as Task Force 38, the Carrier Force was equipped with nearly 550 fighters, all of them Hellcats. This illustrates the astounding degree of standardisation achieved in the American frontline forces, something made possible only by the vast output of US industry (this standardisation in its turn aiding efficiency in production).

Curtiss SB2C Helldiver

The Helldiver was ordered into large-scale production in 1940, the prototype making its first flight on 18 December of that year. SB2Cs went into action for the first time on 11 November 1943 in a heavy raid on the Japanese bastion of Rabaul, flying from the new *Essex* Class carrier *Bunker Hill*.

US Navy Combat Aircraft of the Pacific War

Grumman TBF / Eastern TBM - the Avenger

The Avenger was Grumman's first torpedo aircraft and its design had much in common with that of the Company's fighters, as its chunky and robust appearance testifies. The design and engineering team W.T. Schwenfler developed the aircraft very quickly - the order for two prototypes was placed on 8 April 1940 and the first Avengers went into service just two years later. The 'plane first saw action on 4 June 1942 against the Japanese carrier striking force at the Battle of Midway - only six Avengers were involved, operating from Midway Island. They were forced to attack against overwhelming odds, and of the six five were shot down, the surviving plane returning to Midway severely damaged and with its gunner dead. Nonetheless, the survival of this aircraft demonstrated the design's great toughness, and it was immediately apparent that the plane's battle-worthiness justified its production in great numbers.

Lochkeed P-38 Lightning

This very unconventional aircraft was the first US Army Air Corps fighter to achieve speeds of 400mph. It was somewhat inferior in maneuverability to its rivals the P-47 Thunderbolt and P-51 Mustang, as well as to its Axis opponents. It was nonetheless surprisingly handy for an aircraft of its size. Its twin-engined configuration enabled an unusually heavy gun armament to be concentrated in an ideal position in the nose, and this, combined with the P-38's speed and range, made it a very effective fighter.

Martin 162 PBM Mariner

Origin: Glenn L. Martin Company
Type: Flying Boat - Maritime Patrol / Anti-submarine / Rescue
Crew (typical): Nine
Dimensions: Span 42' 10" (13.05 metres) - Length 33' 7" (10.2 metres) - Height 13' 1" (3.99 metres)
Weights (PBM-1): • Empty 26,600 lb (12,060 kg) • Loaded (clean) 41,139 lb (18,657 kg)

Japanese Combat Aircraft of the Pacific War

Mitsubishi A6M Zero

This fighter - by far the most famous of all Japanese aircraft - dominated the first six months of the aerial war in the Pacific, and continued in service until the end of hostilities. The Zero - allied code-name "Zeke" - was remarkable in being the first carrier fighter to outperform its land-based equivalents. It had been designed by Mitsubishi to meet the severe demands of the 1937 Imperial Navy specification for a shipborne fighter - demands which included a speed of 500 km/h (311 mph) and a (heavy for the time) armament of two cannon and two machine-guns. The result was a small, lightly-built aircraft with outstanding maneuverability. The first production version received a more powerful engine than the prototype and was designated the "A6M2". As it was first produced in 1940 - the Japanese year 5,700 - it became popularly known as the "Zero-Sen" ("Type 00 Fighter"). Two squadrons with 15 planes were sent to China in July 1940 for trials under operational conditions, and quickly eliminated all opposition. The effectiveness of the Zero was emphatically reported to Washington by General Chennault, commanding officer of the Flying Tigers, but the report appears to have gone unnoticed.

A6M Reisen, Mitsubishi 'Zeke'

The A6M came as a shock to the allied in 1941 - this despite earlier reports of its appearance to China. For the first time, a carrier fighter had been built that outperformed landplanes. The A6M was fast, extremely maneuverable, and had and impressive endurance. But this performance had been achieved by the light construction of the aircraft, and this was the undoing of the type when more powerful allied fighters appeared. Development was unable to keep up with the exigencies of the time, and most of the 10964 built had to fight an increasingly superior opposition.

Japanese Combat Aircraft of the Pacific War

Nakajima B5N - "Kate"

The Nakajima B5N - Allied reporting-name "Kate" - was the sole shipborne torpedo-bomber of the Japanese Navy at the start of the Pacific War. It was by then quite old, having been designed to meet a specification of 1935, and was already judged to be obsolescent. However, when first put into production it had been a very advanced aircraft, and in war it out-performed any Allied carrier-based torpedo-plane until the arrival of the Grumman Avenger in mid-1942. In particular, it was greatly superior to the Douglas TBD Devastator - the shipboard torpedo-plane of the US Fleet at the crucial battles of Coral Sea and Midway. B5Ns played the main role in sinking the carrier Lexington at Coral Sea, Yorktown at Midway, and Hornet at the Battle of Santa Cruz in October 1942. Along with the destruction of the carrier Wasp by a Japanese submarine during the Guadalcanal campaign these were the major blows to the American carrier forces in the early stages of the War. These exploits supplemented the Kate's success in the surprise attack on Pearl Harbor, December 7 1941, in which 40 B5N2s armed with torpedoes - and 103 B5N1s armed with bombs - crippled the US Battle Fleet.

Mitsubishi G4M "Betty"

The G4M- Allied reporting-name "Betty" - was the main heavy bomber of the Japanese Navy during World War II. It was remarkable for its long range, but this was achieved by depriving the aircraft of armour while providing it with huge fuel tanks in the wings. Since the tanks were not self-sealing the Betty was extremely vulnerable, tending to go up in flames whenever hit. This led to its receiving the derisive nicknames "the One-Shot Lighter" and " the Flying Cigar." Despite its range and speed, it was therefore - not surprisingly - unpopular with its crews. It's single outstanding success was achieved at the start of the Pacific War when, on 10 December 1941, only three days after Pearl Harbor, G3M Nell's and G4Ms of the 22nd Air Flotilla sank two British capital ships - the new battleship Prince of Wales and the old battlecruiser Repulse - off the coast of Malayain the action known as "The Battle of the Gulf of Siam." These were the first capital ships ever to be sunk while at sea and free to manoeuvre. (In fact, only three other dreadnoughts were ever sunk by air attack under such conditions - the Japanese giants Yamato and Musashi by American carrier aircraft, and the italina Roma by land-based German aircraft using guided bombs).

Japanese Dive Bombers - the D3A and D4Y "Judy"

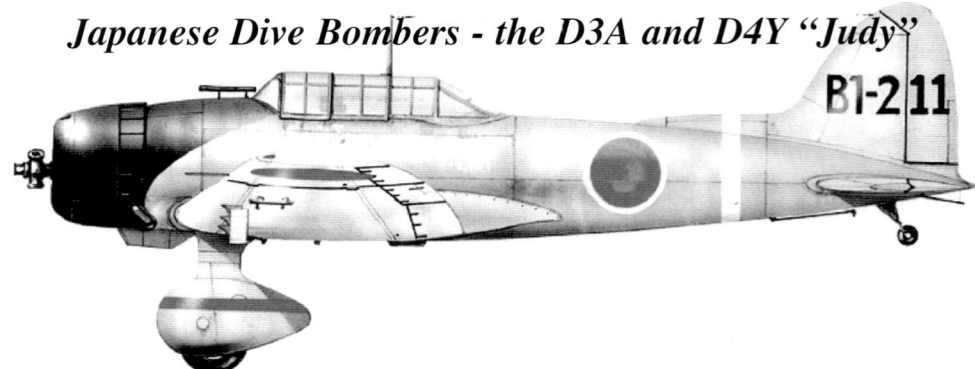

The Aichi D3A - Allied reporting-name "Val" - was the standard Japanese carrier-based dive-bomber during the opening stages of the Pacific War, participating with great success in the Pearl Harbor attack and in the great carrier battles of 1942.

The Yokosuka D4Y Suisei ("Comet") - Allied reporting-name "Judy" - was the D3A's replacement, and by late 1944 relatively few Vals were left in service.

A Corsair fires missiles into Japanese positions on Tinian in the Marianas.

Anti aircraft fire from *Franklin's* screen.

Franklin's deck crews arming a deckload of Hellcats with Tiny Tim Missiles.

A wounded gunner is lifted from the cockpit of a TBF.

An Avenger crashes nose down into *Franklin's* flight deck.

He died at his battle station.

After prayers by shipmates, the body of a seaman killed in action October 13th, is committed to the deep.

Flack bursts dot the sky, as a third suicide plane, over *Franklin*, drops its bomb.
It missed by feet then the "Zeke" crashed into the *Belleau Wood's* fantail.

Fires and explosions devastate the *Franklin*.
Santa Fe steams in to help.

USS Santa Fe (CL60)

USS Pittsburgh (CA-72)

USS Hunt (DD-674)

USS Tingey (DD-539)

USS Hickox (DD-673)

USS Marshall (DD-676)

USS Miller (DD-535)

Santa Fe moves in as flames move closer to men trapped on the flight deck. (Note the collapsed elevator.)

Flaming rivers of gasoline pour over the hangar deck, trapping men aft.

Fires rage and bombs explode.
Franklin is less than fifty miles from Japan.

Santa Fe ties up to *Franklin's* starboard side.

Wounded are evacuated to *Santa Fe*.
(Note the gangplank extended between the two ships.)

The fight goes on; fire fighting parties work into flames;
men handle lines to *Santa Fe*.

Father Joseph O'Callahan, chaplain courageous, administers Extreme Unction to a wounded man on the flight deck.

Santa Fe's fire fighters train their hoses on *Franklin's* blazing flight deck.

Franklin's list increases to 15°.
Santa Fe's mast can be seen in the background.

Wounded man is rescued by *Santa Fe*.

Santa Fe steams away from Franklin.

Franklin's survivors and wounded aboard the *Santa Fe*.
(Note her anti aircraft guns trained into the air as alerts continue.)

The cruiser *Pittsburgh* tows the *Franklin* out of the Sea of Japan.

The heavily damaged *Franklin* heads home for repairs.

Franklin's diminished crew stands at quarters while entering New York harbor.

Franklin's entire flight deck is removed in the biggest repair job in naval history.

Admiral Nimitz signs the documents of Japan's surrender.

Father Joseph O'Callahan is presented the Medal of Honor by President Harry Truman in a special ceremony at the White House.

Lieutenant Don Gary receives his
Medal of Honor from the President at the same ceremony.

CHAPTER SEVENTEEN

22 October, 1944
Aboard the *USS New Jersey*
East Luzon Strait, Philippine Sea

Bill Halsey paced back and forth in the wardroom of the *New Jersey* awaiting the arrival of Admirals Mitscher and Burke and their staffs. He was haunted by the perplexing question: "Where are the Japanese carriers?" In nearly three weeks of combat with the Japanese Central and Southern Fleets, there had not been a single carrier contact.

When Mitscher and Burke arrived they were immediately escorted to the wardroom. After they exchanged greetings and were handed a cup of coffee, Halsey stepped next to a large map of the area.

"Three weeks of fighting through this whole goddamned area and not a single carrier contact," he said as he pointed to the map. "Not a single plane of any kind from a Jap carrier. I still can't believe Ozawa sent those two fleets into combat without air cover."

"It *is* hard to believe, Admiral," Mitscher said, "especially sending in his Southern Fleet into Leyte Gulf alone after we blasted hell out of his Central Fleet. But I don't care how crazy this all sounds, there's one thing for sure—there have to be Jap carriers around here somewhere."

"Yeah, but where? What're they doing? What's Ozawa doing?" Halsey asked. "Is he saving his carriers for posterity or something? Hell, if he didn't commit carriers in the last two weeks, when he *really* needed them, then when, where and how…?"

Halsey was interrupted by a chief radioman. "Message from the *Franklin's* Search and Strike Force, sir. I thought you would want to see it right away."

"Thanks Chief," Halsey said. He read the message then said, "The Japanese Central Fleet has been sighted northwest of Mindoro Island. They appear to be trying to regroup with units from their Southern Fleet. Five battleships including *Yamato* are there. But there are still no carriers."

He scratched his head. "Now how the hell do you figure that?" he asked. "We just kicked their asses and they're coming back again, and without any air cover? Goddamn, Ozawa has got to stay out of that sake bottle."

Burke studied the huge map. "I think I see one thing for sure," he said. "They're still trying to set us up for that one decisive battle."

"How so?"

"To me, it looks like Ozawa is now trying to separate Admiral Kinkaid's fleet from ours. The only way he could do this is to position a fleet northeast of us—up here somewhere."

Burke pointed to an area about three hundred miles northeast of the tip of Luzon. "I'll bet that's where we'll find the carriers."

Halsey and Mitscher slowly nodded their assent.

"The question is," Burke continued, now more urgently, "if there is a fleet up there, what the hell is its purpose? Is it a decoy? If it is, it sure would be a big temptation. A fleet like that could tempt us to pull us away from the Seventh Fleet and the troops on Leyte."

"You're right," Halsey said. "If the Jap's Central Fleet comes back toward the Philippine Sea, say through San Bernardino Strait, and we're way up north somewhere chasing their carriers, they could go right after the Seventh Fleet. Without our air power to back him up, Kinkaid would be in a hell of a mess, outnumbered and out-gunned—a sitting duck. If Ozawa can cut off the Seventh Fleet and destroy it, the troops on Leyte are stranded and defenseless."

"Yeah," Burke replied. "Then they could come after us with *both* their Central and Northern Fleets. Whammo! We're in a great big pincer."

"Sneaky," Mitscher said. "Another goddamned way to try to divide and destroy us. We better hold tight where we are. If we find a Jap fleet up there and the Japanese Central Fleet turns back toward the Philippine Sea, we'll really have to watch our ass."

As soon as Mitscher and Burke were back aboard *Enterprise*, search planes from *Franklin* and *Enterprise* flew northeast at maximum speed to try to find the 'phantom' Japanese Northern Fleet.

24 October, 1944
Aboard the USS New Jersey
80 Miles ENE of Samar

On the bridge of the *New Jersey*, Bill Halsey and his staff analyzed a message from the submarine *Harder*:

> *Japanese Central Fleet sighted last night headed ENE through Mindoro Strait. Position 13 degrees North, 141 degrees East. Tried to maintain visual contact but lost them in the dark. Will attempt to relocate.*

"Looks like they're coming back," Halsey said after he read the message. "Those bastards just don't seem to know when they've had enough."

"Contact Mitscher and tell him I want search planes to find those sons-of-bitches. Tell them to look day and night if they have to," Halsey said, his face grim and filled with concern. "I have to know if they're headed for the San Bernardino Strait."

Within minutes after Mitscher received Halsey's message, search planes from *Franklin* and *Enterprise* were in the air headed for Mindoro. By nightfall they had been all over the Sibuyan Sea—all the way east to Sorsogan. They found nothing. That night specially equipped search planes went over the area again with the same results.

"Damn," Halsey said the next morning when he received the reports from some of the air search groups. "Where the hell can they be? Do you think they might have turned back?"

"Might have," Phillips replied. "The Japanese are sneaky that way."

At 06:32 a report came in from *Franklin*'s night search group:

> *Sighted large Japanese Fleet 14°N, 125°E. Approximately 250 miles ENE of Cape Enango, Luzon. Nine carriers, six battleships, twelve cruisers, fourteen destroyers and eleven tankers, all headed NNE at approximately 15 knots.*
> R.J. Foxx, Lt. Commander, Franklin Search Group

"We found the carriers!" Halsey said waving the message vigorously. "Get Mitscher on the wire."

"Aye, sir."

"Marc, we found the carriers," Halsey said into the microphone when Mitscher's voice came in. "They're northeast of us just like Arleigh said."

"Remember, Admiral, Arleigh also said it might be a Japanese trap," Mitscher replied, his voice filled with caution. "They might be trying to pull us away from the Seventh Fleet."

"I know! I know!" Halsey said. "What a tough choice! Logic tells me we should stay here and protect the invasion forces and the Seventh Fleet—but goddamn—that Japanese carrier fleet is just north of us! If we can hammer them, we can destroy much of their carrier capability."

"Do we have anything South to protect our flank?" Mitscher asked.

Halsey turned to Phillips. "What's down there, Rich?" he asked.

"Just the 'Jeep' carriers in Taffy Group," Phillips replied. "They're providing air support to the troops on Leyte. They're protected by seven destroyers."

"Goddamn, just those little escort carriers? Are we really that thin down there?" Halsey asked in exasperation.

"Yes, Admiral, I'm afraid we are."

"Any word on the Jap Central Fleet?"

"Not a word," Phillips said. "We've looked everywhere, Admiral. They seemed to have dropped off the face of the earth."

"Do you think they turned back? Maybe they're *not* trying to steam back and isolate us."

"How can anybody be sure, Admiral?"

"Did you hear what Rich said, Marc?" Halsey asked, redirecting his conversation back to Mitscher.

"Aye, sir. Sounds pretty risky, especially if we're that thin down there," Mitscher replied.

"We can't miss this opportunity, Marc," Halsey said. "Risky or not we have to take the chance. If we can get those carriers, we severely damage their whole war effort."

He paused for a moment. "I'm going after that Jap fleet," he declared.

"Despite the risk to those CVEs, the Seventh Fleet and the troops on Leyte, Admiral?" Mitscher asked, caution again in his tone.

"Yes, despite the risk," Halsey replied. There was a pause. Then he said, "It's a big risk, Marc, but we have to take it. This is too big an opportunity to pass up!"

The huge Third Fleet turned and steamed North Northeast in search of the Japanese carrier fleet.

25 October, 1944
120 Miles NE of Cape Engano
Philippine Sea

Before dawn the next morning, search planes from *Franklin* and *Enterprise* scoured the waters of the North Philippine Sea searching for the Japanese Northern Fleet. They located it at 06:15, steaming east about two hundred and twenty miles away.

"Well, we know where they are now," Lieutenant Commander Robert Castleman said as he reported the position of the Japanese fleet to Halsey. "It's a big fleet and all the carriers are here!"

At dawn, dense, heavy clouds shrouded the northern sky. The huge American Third Fleet cut through thick, hazy fog at flank speed. This kind of weather was what Halsey and Mitscher hoped for. If the weather front extended far enough north, maybe the Japanese could be caught off guard.

Air Strike Able, which included one hundred twenty fighter planes, ninety-five bombers and one hundred and fifty-five torpedo planes zoomed into the dense haze. They formed into attack squadrons and headed toward the last reported position of the Japanese fleet. They reached their target just before 08:10. After the initial surprise, the Japanese warships began to maneuver frantically. They put up heavy antiaircraft fire.

Commander David McCampbell, Air Group Commander, realizing that the Air Group had a brief, initial advantage, screamed, "Attack! Attack! It's pay back time! Let's kick their ass!"

Joe Crowley, the *Franklin's* Air Strike Commander, flew his squadron into the heavy antiaircraft blasts. His plane shuddered and vibrated with each fiery explosion. He squeezed the stick and kept his eyes glued on the Japanese fleet below.

"I'm zeroed in on a *Chiyoda* Class carrier!" he shouted.

"I'm right behind you!" his wingman, Lieutenant "Wattie" Neff, called out.

Crowley squeezed the trigger. His Hellcat shuddered as his Tiny Tims released. They streaked down toward the carrier. Two struck amidships and ripped a huge hole in the carrier's port side. Neff's missiles followed. They careened toward the Jap carrier and tore into the flight deck just behind the island. A huge explosion followed. It knocked three Zeros off the flight deck into the ocean.

"Good shooting! Let's hammer this bastard," Crowley said.

Three more missiles struck the carrier's starboard side. The Hellcats finished their attack and pulled away. The Japanese carrier was burning furiously. Several secondary explosions filled the air.

"We've got this one on the ropes!" Crowley shouted. "Let's sink her!"

Lieutenant Commander Albert Emig, who commanded the Helldivers and Avengers shouted, "Helldivers attack! Avengers follow with torpedoes!"

Franklin's Helldivers powered into a dive-bombing attack. Several direct hits caved in the flight deck. Avengers found torpedoes unnecessary. The huge carrier listed to starboard, held there for a few minutes, then slowly capsized and sank.

"We've got her!" Crowley shouted. "Let's get another one! Helldivers! Avengers! Get that *Zuikaku* Class carrier."

Franklin's Helldivers dove toward the huge carrier. They clustered seven five-hundred-pound high-demolition bombs on the Jap carrier's flight deck. Six were direct hits. Secondary explosions began to impair the carrier. Massive flames and heavy smoke enveloped her.

"We can get her, too!" Crowley shouted. "Hit her harder! Torpedo attack!"

Franklin's Avengers honed in on the burning carrier. Five torpedoes hit the water and raced toward the damaged ship. Three made direct hits. New fires flamed through her flight deck. More explosions filled with fire and flying debris rocked her. Smoke bellowed out of her hangar deck. Gasoline fires covered the flight deck. She began to list so heavily to port that planes parked on her flight deck slid into the ocean. Two more torpedoes sealed her fate. She listed heavily then she rolled over and sank.

Japanese Zeros from the undamaged carriers counterattacked. Vicious dogfights erupted all over the rain-laden sky. Avengers from *Essex* fired three torpedoes into a battleship. She burst into flames and fell out of formation.

"We're kicking their ass!" Emig shouted triumphantly.

"Keep hitting them," McCampbell said.

Helldivers from *Lexington*, armed with missiles and bombs, blasted a heavy cruiser. She began to burn and lost speed. A light cruiser and a destroyer suffered multiple direct hits by missiles and five-hundred-pound bombs. The cruiser absorbed these blows. She continued on course at reduced speed. The destroyer wasn't so lucky. She was rocked by a huge explosion and broke in two. She sank rapidly, taking down most of her crew. After over an hour of furious combat, Air Strike Able was forced to disengage because of lack of ammunition and fuel. Twenty-seven Zeros and nine Hellcats went down in the ferocious dogfights.

26 October, 1944
110 Miles East of Sumar
South Philippine Sea

While Halsey's Third Fleet attacked in the North Philippine Sea, the Japanese Central Fleet, strengthened by the ships that remained from the Southern Fleet, slipped undetected through San Bernardino Strait and headed southwest toward Leyte. The battleship *Yamato* was at the point of the massive battle group.

On *Fanshaw Bay*, Admiral Clifton "Ziggy" Sprague's flagship, and one of six CVEs in Taffy Group 3, a radarman spotted a large surface force about twenty-five miles northwest on his screen. Less than a minute later, the excited voice of a Hellcat pilot on anti-submarine patrol came across the wire:

> *Attention Taffy Group 3. This is Lieutenant Robert Jensen, Saint Lo Air Search Group. A large fleet of battleships, cruisers and destroyers is firing on me. Position 11 degrees North, 127 degrees East. Range about twenty-five miles. I'm taking evasive action. Will maintain surveillance.*

With Halsey's Third Fleet locked in battle over four hundred miles away, only these thin-skinned CVEs and seven destroyers protecting them stood between this huge enemy fleet and the invasion forces on Leyte.

At 09:45 the unmistakable outlines of Japanese battleships and cruisers were sighted by lookouts. "Enemy battleships and cruisers! Lots of 'em at ten o'clock!"

The huge Japanese armada opened fire. Their powerful guns hurled sixteen- and eighteen-inch projectiles at Taffy's fragile carriers. Massive phosphorescent splashes erupted in the water around the CVEs and their escort destroyers.

Sprague sent a message requesting immediate help:

> *Mayday! Mayday! Attention Third and Seventh Fleets: Taffy Group 3 under attack by major Japanese force. Battleships, cruisers, destroyers: Position 11°N, 127° E. Request immediate assistance.*

#

On the New Jersey, a radioman picked up Taffy Group's frantic call and rushed it up to Halsey. "Get Sprague on the wire," Halsey said after he reviewed the message. "Get him right away!" he barked.

"Aye, sir."

After a few minutes, Sprague's voice crackled over the loudspeaker on the bridge.

"Ziggy!" What the hell's going on down there?" Halsey asked.

"We've got the whole Jap Second Fleet on our necks, Admiral. Even the *Yamato's* here. They're blasting hell out of us."

"Jesus Christ! So that's where they are," Halsey exclaimed. "Can you put down a smoke screen?"

"Our destroyers are putting one down now, Admiral, but I don't know whether it'll help. There's a lot of wind," Sprague replied.

"What about aircraft?" Halsey asked.

"We're attacking with every plane we have, Admiral, but our pilots are trained to provide support to ground troops in amphibious operations. They're not trained or equipped to fight a battle with a big Jap fleet like this."

"Are they doing any good?"

"They're attacking with machine gun fire and anti-personnel bombs—but not doing much damage—just harassing them."

"I hate to say this, Ziggy, but we're too far away to help you. Is there any way you can hold them off?"

"I doubt it. They're still coming, firing round after round of armor-piercing shells at us."

"Halsey shook his head and wiped his brow with a handkerchief. "Goddamn, Ziggy, I think we've put you in a hell of a spot. I'll see what we can do here."

Halsey turned to Richard Phillips. "Rich," he said, "have we got *any* units near there that can help?"

"I'm afraid not, sir," Phillips replied. "We don't have a thing anywhere near there. From what Ziggy said, they need help right now. We could never get anything down there in time, sir."

"Get Ziggy back on the wire."

Sprague's voice again crackled over the airwaves.

"What's happening now, Ziggy?"

"A sudden storm just blew in. It's giving us a break. It's temporarily hiding us from them. Before it came, their fire was increasing and getting very accurate. I've formed my carriers into a rough circle about two thousand yards in diameter, Admiral. We're ready to fight to the very end, sir."

"What are your destroyers doing?"

Our lead destroyer, the *Johnston*, is attacking them right now, Admiral. She just launched four torpedoes at a heavy cruiser. Two of them made direct hits! They slowed the bastard down and she's dropped out of the action."

"You mean a destroyer attacked that Jap fleet single-handed?" Halsey asked.

"Aye, sir! She did. Now she's retreating under cover of a smoke screen."

"Who's the skipper of that ship?"

"Commander Ernest Evans, sir, a fighting Cherokee Indian. He's got more guts than anybody I ever saw!"

"I'm going to give him a medal."

"You might not be able to, sir. They just got hit by a couple of sixteen-inch shells. It looked like a puppy hit by a big truck! They're sinking right now!"

"What about the other destroyers?"

"They're all fighting hard, sir. The *Hoel* and *Heermann* are firing torpedoes. They're trying to divert the Japs away from us and inflict as much damage as they can."

There was a static-filled pause. "The *Heermann* is attacking the *Yamato*, sir! She's firing torpedoes at her! It's causing *Yamato* to reverse course!"

"A guy in a destroyer attacking a super battleship?" Halsey asked, his voice filled with admiration. "Who's that skipper?"

"Commander Arthur Hathaway, sir."

"He'll get a citation, too."

"The *Kalinin Bay's* under heavy attack. It looks like she's going to go down." There was a long pause filled with static. Then Sprague's voice came back again. "I can't understand what's happening now, sir. A pilot in Saint Lo's Air Search Group just said the Japs look like they're withdrawing."

"Withdrawing?"

"That's what he reported, Admiral."

There was another long static-filled pause. Then Sprague's voice crackled back. "I can't believe it, sir. They *are* withdrawing! That whole goddamned Jap fleet is retiring northwest!"

"Are you sure?"

"Aye, Admiral, they are. I guess we hissed and clawed and scratched at them until they turned around and steamed away," Sprague said.

"What are your losses?"

"We lost two CVEs, and three destroyers, Admiral."

"Well, I don't know how you guys did it, but you kept the Seventh Fleet and the troops on Leyte out of harm's way," Halsey said.

When Halsey signed off he looked around at the men on the bridge. "What great courage those men displayed," he said. "It's hard to believe six "Jeep" carriers and seven destroyers challenged that whole goddamned Jap fleet! Their tenacity and bravery saved a lot of lives and ships. Some could have been ours." He called for the yeoman on watch. "Get me a sheet of paper, please."

When he got the paper, he scribbled a message and instructed that it be sent to every unit in the fleet.

> *Attention all units of the Third Fleet: The conduct and bravery of the officers and men of the Taffy Group, who today fought against overwhelming odds from which survival was not expected, command our greatest respect and admiration. The fortitude and determination with which they fought, against an enormously superior enemy force, deserves the highest possible commendation. The officers and men of Taffy Group, who fought with such valor, courage and efficiency, bestow a great honor on the Third Fleet. Their actions are a tribute to the fighting skills of the entire Navy. They have made us all proud to be Americans.*
> *Bill Halsey.*

26 October, 1944
With the Third Fleet
North Philippine Sea

When Air Strike Able returned to the task force, Air Strike Baker was already in the air, headed toward the Japanese fleet. The air attacks continued throughout the day and into the next. By the middle of the second day, Japanese air defenses were in disarray. They still had a few fighter planes, but they sat uselessly on carrier decks. Most of the carriers in the Jap fleet were either sunk or so badly damaged they couldn't conduct flight operations.

Early that afternoon another *Kongo* Class battleship was sunk by torpedo attacks and three cruisers were heavily damaged. The number of destroyers either sunk or heavily damaged had risen to eight.

When the surface units, still steaming at flank speed, caught up to the action, the *Santa Fe* and the cruisers *Denver, Pittsburgh, Columbia* and *Portland* went after the three disabled carriers. They were burning, but still afloat.

Captain Fitz took the *Santa Fe* in close. Her 6-inch guns rained salvo after salvo of armor-piercing shells into the disabled *Zuikaku* Class carrier. The *Pittsburgh* and *Columbia* hammered the *Chiyoda* Class carrier until she capsized and sank. The *Denver* and *Portland* attacked the crippled *Itoka* class light carrier. At 16:30, after suffering an hour and forty-five minute bombardment, the last of the battered carriers disappeared into the gray waters of the Pacific.

Halsey's Third Fleet had vanquished the Japanese Northern Fleet. During the two and a half days of heavy fighting, they'd inflicted serious losses—two battleships, six carriers, two heavy and four light cruisers and nine destroyers. Sixty-six planes were shot down. The Japanese were now left with only three light carriers, all badly damaged and not operational. They were frantically steaming away from the battle scene, emitting bursts of smoke and fire as they retreated. By late evening all the ships in this once mighty Japanese fleet had turned tail and retreated toward Okinawa. The second great battle of the Philippine Sea was over.

From Admiral Kinkaid's inspiring victory at Leyte Gulf to Halsey and Mitscher's equally brilliant victory north of Cape Engano, the Japanese had been badly mauled and decidedly beaten. The intrepid American Navy had done it again. It topped its earlier victories in these same waters. And the indomitable courage and resolve of the sailors manning the "Jeep" carriers in Taffy Group made these victories even more remarkable and glory-filled.

But the heroic efforts of the officers and men who engaged in these historic struggles were physically and mentally exhausting. As the Third Fleet steamed back toward the Philippines, hundreds of brave young sailors, who had just fought and won this last epic battle, found places to rest and sleep anywhere they could.

On the bridge of the *Franklin*, Beckley looked out over the flight deck. Brilliant afternoon sunshine radiated from silent five-inch guns. 40- and 20-mm guns were capped and quiet. Hellcats, Helldivers and Avengers sat motionless on the flight deck. Tired sailors, sleeping in any halfway comfortable place, exemplified the tremendous effort and strain required for their magnificent triumph.

"They may not realize it, sir," Beckley said to Shoemaker, "but I think these brave young sailors just won the greatest naval victory in our country's history."

"I think you're right, Chief," Shoemaker replied.

29 October, 1944
Steaming SW toward Luzon Strait
Philippine Islands

The day dawned bright and clear. The slow moving storm that aided the Third Fleet's attack on the Japanese Northern Fleet was gone and the ocean was calm and mirror-like.

On the bridge of the *Franklin*, a course change came in from Admiral Halsey. Beckley took the message and handed it to Shoemaker. He read it quickly and said, "We change course to 310 degrees and steam Southwest to a position north of Luzon. Halsey thinks the Japanese are ready to commit land-based bombers and fighters to the defense of the Philippines."

"Seems too nice to fight a war today, sir," Beckley said as he looked out at the clear skies and deep blue ocean, "but it sounds like we're pulling out all the stops."

"That and maybe more," Shoemaker replied. "Halsey wants us to attack enemy airfields in Luzon and around Manila. The message says we should prepare for intense air attacks that include the possibilities of kamikazes." Shoemaker frowned and rubbed his hand across the back of his neck. "I know everybody in the Air Wing is pretty tired," he said to Joe Taylor, "but we'd better double the CAP. Those goddamned kamikaze attacks are causing problems all over the fleet. We have to be doubly alert."

"Aye, sir," Taylor replied.

Franklin's antiaircraft defenses were put in Condition of Readiness I. Combat Air Patrols were doubled. At 09:03 *Franklin's* radar located a group of fifty bogeys flying toward them from bases in the Philippines. The alert blared through the loudspeakers: "Bogeys! Bogeys! Pilots, man your planes! All hands prepare to defend against hostile aircraft!"

John watched Hellcats scream off *Franklin's* flight deck until a full squadron of thirty-five sleek, white-bellied fighters flew in formation above him. They joined with Hellcats and Corsairs from *Lexington* and *Belleau Wood* and sped southwest. They attacked the Zeros, Bettys and Judys when they were about fifty miles out.

John followed their path with binoculars. "Looks like there's a hell of a dogfight going on out there," he said.

Ski focused his glasses on the action. "We've got at least twice as many fighters as the Japs. We should whip their ass easy."

"It's not just the numbers," John replied. "It's skill and experience, better planes and aircrews. Look at what's happening. I've seen six Jap planes splashed already."

"Wow, look at that Hellcat at eleven o'clock!" Ski shouted. "It's making a head-on dive at that Zero just above the water."

"He's got him! That bastard's going down!" John yelled. "They're kicking the crap out of them."

"The Jap planes are disengaging," Ski shouted with glee. "They're running back to Luzon!"

What John and Ski didn't see were two G4M's Bettys that somehow evaded the fighters. As the fighters headed back to their carriers, the Bettys slipped in behind them to avoid radar detection. When they got close enough, they stormed toward the *Franklin*.

"Bandit! Bandit! Off the starboard beam," John shouted.

John's gun crew opened fire. Every gun on the *Franklin's* starboard side followed. Intense fire from the gunners in the rest of the Task Group darkened the sky.

"Get that son-of-a-bitch!" John shouted as the lead Betty zoomed into the heavy antiaircraft barrage.

The Betty somehow slipped through. It dropped a five-hundred-pound bomb that hit *Franklin's* flight deck and exploded between the Number 2 five-inch turret and the bridge. The thick glass windshield on the closed bridge shattered. Razor sharp pieces of glass and shrapnel flew in every direction. Quartermaster First Class Joe Larocci standing the wheel watch was killed instantly. Radioman First Class Stan Manning was killed, too. Lieutenant Commander Jacques Green, the ship's Engineering Officer, and Lieutenant Commander John Kelley, Communications Officer, suffered deep head and chest wounds. Miraculously, Shoemaker, who had just left his command chair and stepped behind a bulkhead to view the activities of the antiaircraft guns on the port side, was not hit. But the concussion from the explosions knocked him violently against the bulkhead. He suffered abrasions to his face but was otherwise unhurt.

After the bomb struck the *Franklin*, the Mitsubishi G4M, intent on doing more damage, climbed sharply and circled back to make another attack.

"This might be a Kamikaze attack!" John shouted.

John's gun crew zeroed in on the Betty. The noise was deafening as the 40-mms blazed away.

"Get on that son-of-a-bitch!" John yelled to Ski who was manning the Mark 14 gun sight. "Ski you're shooting too low!" he screamed.

"I'm having trouble with this goddamn gun sight, Gunner!"

John rushed over and took the sight. He made a quick adjustment and zeroed back in on the Betty. His tracers streamed out toward the speeding plane. They were on target now. Projectiles from his 40's dug into the Betty's cowling and tore into the fuselage near the wing. The wing ripped off, but the bomber's momentum hurled it toward the *Franklin*.

John zeroed in on the area behind the wing. "We have to hit the gas tanks!" he shouted. "That's the only thing that'll stop that bastard now!" His shells tore into the Betty's fuselage. The Betty jerked out of control. There was a massive explosion. It disintegrated in midair.

"Great shooting, John!" Ski screamed. "That son-of-a-bitch was less than two hundred yards away."

John looked at the fiery wreckage as it drifted slowly toward the ocean. "I don't see any signs of a body. That pilot was blown to pieces."

"Serves the bastard right," Ski said.

The first bomber circled and honed in on the *Franklin* again. A mass of antiaircraft fire from every gun in the Task Group converged on the Betty. It was hit and thrown off course. It crashed into the ocean, exploding harmlessly five hundred feet from *Franklin's* port bow.

Despite the damage to the ship, John was elated. "You guys did a great job," he said. "You blasted that bastard right out of the sky."

Within a few minutes, *Franklin* resumed air operations. She steamed Northwest on a zigzag course at high speed. On the bridge, Shoemaker asked for a damage report.

"There was damage to the bridge and the Number 2 turret but almost no other damage," Day reported. "Three men were killed and four were wounded, but we're operational. Except for the damage to the bridge and gun turret, our capacities are not impaired, sir."

That afternoon the destroyer *Albert W. Grant* came alongside to refuel and deliver mail. At 15:00 *Franklin*'s crew had their first mail call in over two weeks. When John's name was called he was tossed a whole packet of letters. He quickly thumbed through the rubber-bound packet. Two were from his mother and sister, one from his dad, and six from Sandy.

He looked over at Lowe and waved the packet. Lowe, who was working with a packet of his own, smiled. "You're a lucky bastard, John Oxler. Mine are all from my family."

Off watch that night, John found a remote chair in the ship's library. Music from the Armed Forces Radio Network played softly in the background. By a strange coincidence, just as he sat down he was greeted by the melodic strains of *Some Enchanted Evening*. The song brought back memories of that wonderful night in San Diego. Feelings of love and happiness filled his body. "Dear God," he prayed aloud, "please help me get through this war." He began to read Sandy's letters, slowly, one by one. After he'd read all six he went back to the last one in the stack. This letter had touched him deeply. It was dated October 3, 1944.

> *Dearest John,*
> *It seems so long since the last time I saw you, or even talked to you. I told my mom about this and missing you so very much. She reminded me that "absence makes the heart grow fonder" but that didn't help much. I miss you so very much and each day I seem to grow to love you more. I carry one of the pictures you sent me in a special place in my purse. I take it with me everywhere. I had a copy enlarged and framed—it's on my dresser, so now I can look at you every morning as I get dressed.*
>
> *I'm so worried about you, Darling. Nearly every day there are reports in the paper about American carriers in battle—they are almost never referred to by name but I just know your ship is in the thick of the fighting. Please take care of yourself, John and come home to me. I dream of that wonderful time when I will be with you again.*
>
> *Speaking of dreams—I had a strange one the other night. I was with you in a small chapel somewhere. We were getting married. I was wearing my mother's wedding dress and you were in your dress blues. We were standing at this small, plain altar. You knew the priest that was marrying us (isn't that strange)?. In the middle of the ceremony, planes flew right overhead. They drowned out what the priest was saying. Everyone in the*

church got frightened and rushed for the door. Then I woke up and there were real planes, right over our house! I guess they came from the air station in Alameda. I felt wonderful and sad—at the same time. Wonderful because I was with you and sad that our wedding was interrupted. The days seem so long and I live from one of your letters to the next. When will we be together again? I guess only God knows this. I pray each night that He will keep you safe and send you back to me soon. Dearest, be safe. Be careful.
Love and bunches and bunches of kisses,
Sandy

After reading it the second time, John put Sandy's letter carefully back in its envelope. A warm glow spread through his body. For a while he forgot the war. There were only feelings of love, peace and joy. He had a girl who really loved him. Somehow her love would help him get through this goddamned mess. That night he slept with Sandy's letters tucked under his pillow, clutching them tightly in his hand.

30 October, 1944
120 Miles NNW of Luzon
Philippine Sea

The clear, bright weather continued. The ocean was calm and the morning was cloudless. At 08:00 a strike force of twelve Hellcats and fifteen Helldivers went airborne to attack the airfield on Lippa.

At 10:00 the destroyer *Bagley* pulled alongside *Franklin* to deliver Fleet Command mail and refuel. Just as the fueling started, a message came in from the commander of the Fleet Tanker Force:

May Day! May Day! Under attack by at least thirty Zeros and Bettys. Position 23 degrees North, 150 degrees West. Two Oilers hit and burning. Request immediate aid!
R.J. Hakinson, Captain, USN.

"They're attacking our tanker fleet!" Shoemaker shouted.

"They're only about thirty-five miles away from us, sir," Beckley said.

"We'll go to their aid!" Shoemaker roared. "Cast off the *Bagley*! Sound General Quarters!"

The ship's klaxon blared. The siren wailed. "General Quarters! General Quarters! Pilots, man your planes! Pilots, man your planes!"

"All hands, man your battle stations!"

Men rushed to their battle stations from all parts of the ship. Activity on the flight deck was frantic. Within minutes *Franklin* launched thirty Hellcats and Avengers to aid the stricken tankers. As soon as they were out of sight, the Task Group was attacked by kamikazes. Five Zekes and three Judys, using the attack on the tankers as a decoy, streaked recklessly toward them.

"Bogeys! To starboard—two o'clock high!" the forward lookout shouted.

Every gun in the Task Group trained on the attacking planes and blazed away. The sky darkened with the heavy barrage.

John's gun crews zeroed in on the first Zeke. A trail of tracers blasted toward the Zeke. They found it. Tracer after tracer dug into its fuselage. Flames burst from the Zeke's engine. Still the fighter-bomber screamed on.

A very near miss from a five-inch shell forced the Zeke from its course. Partly out of control and streaming smoke, the Zeke flew wildly toward *Franklin's* flight deck at an altitude of about seventy-five feet. It crashed into the flight deck and careened violently across it, just missing the ship's island. Its momentum carried it into the sea. It exploded a hundred yards off *Franklin's* starboard beam.

A Judy carrying a torpedo emerged out of the sun on the eastern horizon.

"Torpedo attack!"

John's 40-mm's zeroed in on the attacking Yokosuka D4Y, but the Judy was flying so low it was difficult to hit. Round after round of 20-mm and 40-mm shells streamed out toward the Judy. It continued its run.

From the bridge, Shoemaker saw the wake of the torpedo headed straight for the *Franklin*.

"All engines back full!" he screamed. "Hard right rudder!"

The *Franklin* slowed and veered hard to port. The torpedo passed under her bow. It missed by less than ten feet.

Another Judy, its gasoline-filled belly tank glistening in the sunlight, honed in on the *Franklin*.

"Here comes another one." John screamed. "Get it!" Get that bastard!"

Every gun on ship fired furiously. The Judy kept coming.

"Don't let that son-of-a-bitch get through!" John shouted. The Judy flashed through the heavy curtain of fire and crashed the *Franklin's* flight deck inboard of the five-inch guns. There was a huge explosion. The forward elevator, jolted up by the blast, was ripped from its moorings. It crashed back into its opening in an outlandish, tilted position. Gasoline fires engulfed the deck and spread down to the hangar deck. Flames blazed amidships between frames 90 and 160. Belly tanks filled with gasoline on planes being readied for the next sweep began to explode. The intense heat triggered bombs and missiles. Fires swept down into decks 2 and 3 below.

A Zeke sliced through the *Franklin's* antiaircraft screen.

"Get it! How in the hell do they keep coming?" John screamed.

The Zeke's pilot waited until the last second then dropped a five-hundred-pound bomb. It exploded less than twenty feet from *Franklin's* bow. Flack dug into the sponson. A shell fragment bore into the handle of the Mark 14 sight.

"Goddamn! That was close!" Ski shouted.

The Jap pilot circled and zeroed in on the *Belleau Wood's* fantail. He crashed his plane into it.

"Be alert!" John shouted. "There's still three left out there!"

Two Judys tried to crash the *Enterprise*. Heavy antiaircraft fire knocked them off course. They plunged into the sea. One hit less than fifty yards from *Enterprise's* bow.

"There's one more out there. It looks like it's coming at us," John said.

The Zeke turned and began to zero in on the wounded *Franklin*.

Joe Crowley, who was returning from the mission to Lippa, entered the landing area as the Zeke started toward the *Franklin*.

John recognized Crowley's Hellcat. "That's Commander Crowley!" he shouted. "Goddamn I hope he can get that son-of-a-bitch."

Crowley did a wing over and headed straight toward the Zeke, his 50-caliber wing guns blazing. Round after round of armor-piercing shells tore into the Zeke. It burst into flames and exploded in midair. Crowley dipped his wings and banked away to land on *Enterprise*.

Fire-fighting crews attacked the raging gasoline fires on *Franklin's* flight and hangar decks. Frantically, they sprayed barrel after barrel of fire-suppressing foam over the flames. Slowly the fires subsided, and finally they stopped.

"Get me a damage and fire control report," Shoemaker said.

"The fires on the flight deck were put out at 11:30," Day said as soon as he had the report. "The hangar deck fires were extinguished at 12:25 and the galley deck fires were out at 13:55."

"What about the decks below?" Shoemaker asked, stress wrinkling his brow.

"We're suppressing smoldering fires on decks 2 and 3 right now."

The *Franklin* was badly damaged. There was a jagged hole in her flight deck. Deck planks were bulged and battered. Both elevators were blown from their mounts, the second blasted by *Franklin's* own bombs. It leaned eerily on its side, at an odd angle from the horizontal. Sunlight streamed through ugly holes in the hangar deck bulkheads ripped open by errant Tiny Tim missiles.

That afternoon the *Franklin* was declared unfit for action and ordered to withdraw from the combat area. *Belleau Wood* also suffered extensive damage. Both were instructed to steam South Southeast to Ulithi to have their damage assessed.

CHAPTER EIGHTEEN

31 October, 1944
Steaming toward Ulithi Atoll
An Assessment of Damage

At 08:00 the next day, Admiral Burke, with a team of engineers, came aboard to inspect *Franklin's* damage. Shoemaker met him at the quarterdeck with a salute.

"Welcome aboard, Admiral."

Burke returned the salute. "Captain Shoemaker, after I finish this inspection, I need a few minutes of your time," he said.

"Certainly, Admiral," Shoemaker concurred uneasily.

After a tour of the battle damage with his chief engineer Burke said, "It looks like there's too much damage to repair here."

"I don't think she can be repaired in Ulithi either," his engineer responded. "I think she might have to go stateside to a navy yard to get this damage fixed."

Burke nodded. "Okay, but let's see what they say in Ulithi first. If she has to go stateside we'll send her to Bremerton, with a stop at Alameda to unload ammunition."

Burke looked at Shoemaker. "Captain Shoemaker, can we meet in your cabin now?"

Once seated in Shoemaker's cabin, Burke said slowly, "Last week Admiral Davison talked to you about a command opportunity related to naval air bases in the liberated area. We've come to a conclusion that you may not like."

Shoemaker's heart sank. "I think I know what you're going to say, Admiral," he said sadly.

"This isn't easy for me, Captain. Goddamn, it seems like chiefs of staff always get these kinds of crappy jobs. I hate 'em."

"Before I tell you what was decided, Captain," he continued as he shifted uncomfortably in his chair, "I'd like you to remember that one of Admiral Nimitz's finest characteristics is that he cares a great deal about *all* the men in his command, even those that are in rear areas." He paused and shifted his body weight again. "We've chosen you to fill the command vacancy Admiral Davison discussed with you last week. Admiral Davison told us what your feelings about a desk job were and I understand them completely, but believe me, this is a very significant promotion for you."

"Request the Admiral's permission to speak freely, sir," Shoemaker said.

"Of course, permission granted."

"Admiral, I'm honored by being considered for this promotion, but I have unfinished business as the commanding officer of the *Franklin*, sir," Shoemaker said. "We just got this ship and crew into shape. We've worked very hard at it. With a few more adjustments in personnel, *Franklin* can become one of the top carriers in the Navy. I can't leave all that, sir."

"That's the very reason we've selected you, Captain," Burke said. "You've done a great job with the Franklin and in every command you've ever had. We feel you're exactly the man for this job."

"But, sir, that's the very reason I should stay…"

"I'm sorry, Captain," Burke said, with a solemn look on his face. "We're going reassign you as soon as we reach Ulithi."

"I guess I kind of expected this, Admiral. Is there *anything* I can do to stay with my ship, sir?"

"I'm afraid not. You're the right man for this new job. You've demonstrated a topnotch ability to command. You've got an excellent strategic mind, a fine way with your officers and men, and by training, you're a pilot. You're the right man for the job."

Shoemaker took a deep breath and looked down at the deck. He seemed resigned. "Well, I guess there's nothing more I can say, sir," he said softly.

Burke stood and offered his hand. "Congratulations, Captain," he said with a sad smile.

That afternoon there was scuttlebutt that the *Franklin* might be headed stateside. When Lowe told John, he couldn't believe his ears.

"No kidding?"

Lowe nodded.

"Really?"

"That's what I heard."

John rushed down to the armory and found Chief Sullivan. "Chief," he said, "Lowe tells me we're headed stateside. Is that true?"

"I think it's true, but there's no official word yet," Sullivan said. "We're going to get our damage inspected again by engineers in Ulithi. They may decide the damage can be repaired there or in Pearl Harbor."

"What do you think the stateside chances are, Chief?" John asked.

"I think they're pretty good, but don't hold your breath. You know how the Navy works sometimes."

**3 November, 1944
Ulithi Atoll,
Caroline Islands**

After taking a harbor pilot aboard, the Franklin entered the lagoon at Ulithi and steamed slowly, at various courses and speeds, to accommodate the requirements of the lagoon. After a short while she moored in Berth Number 11. As soon as the last line was secure, an inspection party headed by Admiral George Murray, Commander, Naval Air Force, Pacific Fleet, boarded for an official assessment of the battle damage. About two hours later the inspection party left the ship.

By 13:30 that afternoon rumors filtered through the *Franklin* like a dense fog. The findings of the inspection party concurred with the initial inspection. *Franklin's* damage couldn't be repaired in Ulithi or Pearl Harbor. They were headed stateside.

When John heard this he rushed down to the armory. "What's the real word, Chief? Are we headed stateside?"

Sullivan's smile broke into a grin. "John," he said, "I'm going to make you a happy man. What you heard was right. We're headed for Pearl Harbor, then to Alameda to off-load our ammunition. After that we go up to Bremerton for repairs."

"Alameda. That's great!" John said. "I'd like to see Sandy. Do you suppose I can get off when we dock? Just for one evening, Chief?"

"I'll do a lot better than that, John. The word is that the whole crew's going to get a twenty-day leave with seven days travel time. You can begin yours when we dock in Alameda if you'd like. No point in going all the way back from Bremerton."

"Are you sure that's okay, Chief?" John asked.

"Sure it is," Sullivan replied. "It's nothing special. Anyone who lives in the area or has kin or friends there can have it."

"Then, yes, I'll do it that way," John said. As he walked away he whispered Sandy's name. It was hard to believe he was going to be with her for twenty-seven days.

CHAPTER NINETEEN

7 November, 1944
Ulithi Atoll,
A Change of Command

The *Franklin,* moored in Berth Number 14, strained against the six manila lines and four cables that secured her. A thirty-five-knot wind blew in from the north. The sky was heavily overcast and there were sprinkles of rain. At 10:00 Joe Shoemaker met with Captain Leslie Gehres who, along with several new staff members and his ever-present marine orderly, Corporal Walter Klinkiewicz, had come aboard earlier that morning. They were there to transfer command of the *Franklin* as per Commander Carrier Division Directive #1403.

The very brief transfer ceremony was held on the hangar deck with all hands standing at quarters. The master-at-arms read the directive changing command. Then, in the time-honored custom of the Navy, the husky, six-foot, four-inch Gehres uttered the simple traditional words: "Captain Shoemaker, I relieve you, sir."

"I stand relieved," Shoemaker replied.

They exchanged salutes and shook hands.

"Take good care of my ship, Captain," Shoemaker said. "We've solved all but a few minor problems. It's becoming a great ship with a great crew."

"Aye, Captain," Gehres said. "I'll do that very thing, sir."

Shoemaker turned and walked over to Dave Day, Joe Taylor and Ben Moore. "I'm going to miss you guys," he said sadly as he shook hands with each of them.

Then he walked over to Beckley. "I'm going to miss you, Chief. I enjoyed our talks. I learned a lot from you."

"Thank you, sir," Beckley replied. "I learned more from you. We're all going to miss you, too. It was an honor to serve with you, sir."

Shoemaker walked to the quarterdeck, saluted the OD and walked down the gangway into the mist and rain. Leslie Gehres, the *Franklin*'s new skipper, was now in command.

The *Franklin* was buzzing with speculation about the new skipper, and the kind of officer he would be.

Beckley hurried down a ladder from the hangar deck and headed for the officer's wardroom. Commander Zimler had requested a meeting with him earlier that morning. When Beckley arrived, Zimler was the only one there.

"Good morning, Beck. I wanted to talk to you, before I left the ship," Zimler said. "My transfer orders came through yesterday. I'm going to be reassigned to a hospital in Pearl Harbor for further evaluation. I've had some headaches and ringing in my ears. The ship's doctors don't understand them. They think they're just from battle stress, but they're not sure. Once the tests are over, I'm going home on a thirty-day medical leave. I wondered if you'd want me to stop in Pratt with a message for Mary and your family."

"Yes, sir, I'd appreciate that very much. When do you leave, sir?"

"Tomorrow morning. I fly to Pearl for the evaluations. Then I'll catch a plane that's headed stateside."

"Think you'll be back?" Beckley asked.

"I hope so, Beck. I've put in a request to return, just as soon as *Franklin* and I are okay. I'll probably pick you guys up in Bremerton. If something should happen to these plans, I'll try to contact you."

"This is a sad moment for me, sir," Beckley said. "Two sad times in one day. I was sorry to see Captain Shoemaker leave this morning."

"Yes, I was too," Zimler replied. "He was a good skipper."

Beckley saw Zimler's face grow serious. He looked like he was a little choked up. "I want to thank you for your friendship, Chief," Zimler said. "I'll never forget the way you helped me over the last few weeks."

Beckley nodded, feeling tearful himself. "It was an honor, sir." He changed the subject, trying to cover the sadness he felt. "We've got a new Skipper, sir," he said. "Do you know anything about him?"

"Just the information we got this morning. The word is he's a tough commander—a man that will stand for no nonsense—but a straight shooter."

"Annapolis grad?"

"I don't think so, Beck." Zimler replied. "I heard he came up through the ranks. He was an enlisted man in World War I. He worked his way up to warrant officer. Then he became an ensign and went right up the line. He's from a poor family in the Midwest. He educated himself by reading a lot."

"Really?" Beckley asked with a curious look on his face.

"Sounds like somebody else I know," Zimler said with a smile. "I also heard he never spares himself and never demands anything of his men that he isn't willing to do himself."

"Well, maybe there's some hope for me," Beckley said, now smiling for the first time since he met with Zimler.

"I'm sure there is, Beck."

"I hope you can come back aboard, sir."

"I'm going to do everything I can," Zimler said.

Beckley extended his hand and shook Zimler's firmly. He realized this might be the last time he'd ever see his friend and Zimler's face showed he felt the same way.

"This makes me sad, sir," Beckley said.

"Me too, Beck," Zimler replied.

The next day at noon, pursuant to Third Fleet Dispatch #070204, the remaining pilots and airmen in Air Wing Thirteen, along with their planes, were reassigned to the *Lexington, Enterprise* and *Hancock*. At 14:00, a large contingent of officers and men, which included Admiral Harold Zanatell and Captains Earl Simms and Ralph Jameson, came aboard for transportation back to the mainland.

A CHANGE OF COMMAND

At 16:00 *Franklin*, along with *Belleau Wood* and the destroyers *Lansdowne, Lardner* and *Woodworth* as Task Unit 30.9.7, got underway. At 16:39 all antiaircraft and fire control stations were manned, and at 16:40 *Franklin,* as Task Unit Leader, increased speed to twenty knots enroute to Pearl Harbor. At 17:00 all ships were darkened and put in Condition of Readiness III.

Later that evening as the *Franklin* steamed steadily toward Pearl Harbor, Captain Gehres was in the middle of an informal meeting with the members of his staff in the ship's wardroom. When contrasted with Shoemaker, Gehres seemed more informal and totally at ease. There was something about him, his huge, powerful frame, his sun-and-wind-leathered face…something that exuded a strength and confidence that seemed to say this was the way it would be and the *only* way it would be. His tough-as-nails manner made it clear that he was a disciplinarian—one who would not tolerate even the slightest breach of regulations—and that he had the strength and confidence to expect and enforce this.

"Captain Shoemaker's last report indicated that while the discipline problems were serious in the beginning, they have almost all been rectified," Gehres said. "I'm very gratified by this. *Franklin* had an early reputation of being unruly and undisciplined. I'm glad that's changed."

He paused and lit a cigarette. "We will have dedication and devotion to duty, responsibility and accountability on this vessel. I want to make this very clear. *There is no other way*. We will not tolerate any action that does not fully conform to naval regulations and traditions." Gehres paused and looked about the room. "Are there questions or comments?" he asked.

Silence.

"Well then, this meeting's over," he said.

"All rise."

As Gehres walked through the door, Joe Taylor followed him. "Excuse me, Captain," he said. "There's a situation that Captain Shoemaker probably didn't talk to you about because there was so little time this morning. I'd like to discuss it with you when you have time, sir."

"Well, Commander, there's no time like the present. Let's drop by the wardroom and get a cup of coffee."

When they were seated in the wardroom, Taylor said. "Captain, there's a seaman by the name of Bundson on board who's somehow been able to get around nearly everything you just discussed."

"Oh, a bad apple, huh?" Gehres queried sternly. "Goddamn, there's always one or two on every ship."

"Yes, sir. I'm told he's slippery as a snake, Captain," Taylor said. "He only steals money—which is almost impossible to trace—then loans it on a two-now for four-back basis. In one way or another, he's taken advantage of a lot of men in the crew."

Gehres eyes turned steel gray. "Are you telling me this man steals from his shipmates and gets away with it?"

"That's right, sir," Taylor said. "He's in trouble a lot—drunkenness, profanity, scurrilous behavior." Taylor paused. "We had a lot of men like that to begin with, Captain. Captain Shoemaker transferred nearly two hundred before we left San Diego in May. I guess Bundson's one Captain Shoemaker missed." Taylor paused and rubbed his chin thoughtfully. "With all due respect, sir," he said. "Captain Shoemaker had so many more things to correct, he didn't have much time to find a man like Bundson."

"He sounds like a real bad apple," Gehres said.

"Yes, sir. I think he's a born loser. Trouble seems to follow him around...."

"It always does with guys like that," Gehres said.

"Yeah. I think they walk around expecting something to happen to them—kind of like they're *ill-fated* or something," Taylor ventured.

"Well, ill-fated or not, Commander, I won't tolerate this kind of crap on my ship." Gehres rubbed the knuckles on his huge fist. "Get the word to him that I said he has *one* chance to shape up and *one chance only*. If he screws up, I'll put him so far back in the brig it'll take a pack of hound dogs a year to find him."

"Aye, sir," Taylor replied.

Later that night, in a safe, quiet ocean, John and Ski headed topside to stand the twenty-to-twenty-four wheel watch, relieving quartermasters at the ship's helm.

About halfway up the first ladder, Ski stopped abruptly.

"What's the hell's the matter with you?" John asked almost bumping into him.

Ski checked the back pocket of his dungarees. "I just wanted to be sure I had my wallet," he said. "Word's out. Watch your wallet—the rat has come out of his hole."

"What the hell are you talking about?"

"Guy in the First Division lost his wallet with fifty bucks in it last night. Left it on his bunk to go down the passageway for a drink of water. When he got back it was gone—like it just flew away in the wind."

"You mean somebody stole it?"

"Yeah. That's exactly what I mean. And that wind's name is Bundson—I'll lay you a hundred bucks to one on it."

John looked closely at Ski. "I can't believe it," he said. "You mean that after all we've been through that bastard is still heisting from his shipmates?"

"That son-of-a-bitch would steal from his mother. You know that."

"Yeah, but it'll catch up to him, you just mark my words."

11 November, 1944
Enroute Eniwetok to Pearl Harbor
Territory of Hawaii

Task Unit 30.9.7 with *Franklin* as Task Unit Commander, the *Belleau Wood*, and their three escorting destroyers steamed East Northeast making twenty knots in zigzag Plan 6. Now out of the war zone, Gehres began to prepare the officers and men of the *Franklin*

A CHANGE OF COMMAND

for future combat. Although there was general quarters both morning and evening, the crew was allowed long periods of rest during the day. What was coming was a short interlude for repairs. Then the long days when there wasn't a good night's sleep, a decent meal or even a shower would begin again. Gehres' experience as an enlisted man taught him that this routine was the best form of recovery and a way to bring his crew even closer together.

On the bridge Gehres got a message from Carrier Division Command on Eniwetok. "We're to prepare for a mock attack," he announced. "Air Wing Seven, composed of rookies just out of basic flight training, will attack. Spruance wants us to show these guys a little of what the real war is all about."

"Isn't this going to be a joke after what this crew's just been through?" Beckley asked.

"Sometimes everybody has to take their turn at being a babysitter, Chief," Gehres said with a grin.

Gehres focused his binoculars on the northeastern horizon. "Get me Joe Taylor," he said.

When Taylor arrived, Gehres explained the directive from Eniwetok. "I guess he wants to give them a little seasoning," he concluded. "Let's give them a good show. They'll be towing sleeves. Rip the sleeves up but don't hit anything else—you know, just scare 'em a little."

"Aye, Captain, I understand," Taylor said with a huge smile on his face.

At 13:30 the Avengers and Helldivers, piloted by the new pilots, appeared on the horizon.

In John's gun crew there was very little emotion or enthusiasm.

"All right," John said. "Let's be on our toes. Captain wants some good tight shots. Be accurate. Get the sleeves but don't hit the aircraft. He wants to give them a little taste of the war. Do you guys understand?"

"Awww come on, John," Ski complained. "Why do you want us to make a big deal out of this? This is a walk in the park."

"Maybe it is," John said, "but these are the Captain's orders. He wants some good tight shooting and we're going to give it to him."

"Yeah, John, but this is a pain in the ass," Ski persisted.

"Not to the Captain it isn't. Make like it's a real battle, Ski," John said with a smile. "Maybe you'll get a medal out of it or something."

"Yeah, and maybe somebody will find the eighth wonder of the world, too," he echoed with sarcasm.

In a few minutes the Avengers and Helldivers were in range and began their attack. Honed by recent combat experience, John's gun crew was outstanding. His gunners methodically ripped up sleeve after sleeve. It was easy—kind of like shooting the owls in a shooting gallery—everything they shot at went down.

Thirty minutes into the attack a huge explosion ripped the port side of the *Franklin*. Startled, John rushed up the ladder to the flight deck. An ammunition ready-service compartment filled with 20-mm ammunition had exploded and was burning furiously.

"How the hell could this happen?" John mumbled. He shook his head in disbelief. "Those planes couldn't have caused this."

On the bridge Gehres shouted, "Find out what the hell that was!"

Klinkiewicz, his orderly, was off in a flash.

"What the hell *was that*, Joe?" Gehres asked, his voice filled with concern.

"I don't know, Captain. I'm sure as hell going to find out," Taylor replied.

Franklin's fire-fighting units rushed to the compartment and extinguished the flames. Later that afternoon investigators found a small handmade still, capable of distilling limited quantities of alcohol, in the wreckage. In the furor of the drill, the heating unit was activated. It started the fire that caused the explosion.

When Klinkiewicz reported this, Gehres was outraged. "Two able seamen killed and six badly burned because some son-of-a-bitch was making hooch! Find the bastard who did this," he demanded. "I'm going to personally hang him from the yardarm by his balls!"

Gehres launched a sweeping investigation.

2 November, 1944
Eniwetok Atoll
Marshall Islands

At 08:00 the Task Unit steamed into Eniwetok harbor and dropped anchor at Anchorage M 413. *Franklin* did not remain in Eniwetok long. At 10:00 supplies and passengers were taken aboard and the twelve Japanese prisoners picked up in Ulithi were put ashore. At 12:30 the Fleet Oiler, the *USS Chickopee,* came alongside and replenished *Franklin*'s fuel supply. At 14:00 the destroyer *Lardner* came alongside to deliver mail, and shortly thereafter, the Task Unit got underway enroute to Pearl Harbor, steaming at a speed of eighteen knots in Condition of Readiness III. About two hours after the Task Unit left Eniwetok, it ran into stormy weather. Rain fell and the ocean became unsettled and rough. Rough seas or not, Gehres' investigation of the explosion continued—now with increased urgency. The whole crew was determined to find the guilty party. They almost felt implicated to some degree.

At 19:45 John and Ski left their compartment and went topside to stand the twenty-to-twenty four-hour wheel watch. As they walked across the dark hangar deck headed for the ladder to the bridge, a figure carrying something wrapped in a towel flashed across their path. John thought he recognized the figure.

Instinctively, John called out his name, "Bundson."

"Fuck off bastard!" It was Bundson's unmistakable voice. He hurried toward the *Franklin's* bow, clutching whatever was wrapped in the towel closer to his chest.

"What do you think he's got in that towel?" Ski asked, his voice filled with suspicion.

"God only knows," John replied. "It sure looks like it's something important to him."

"I'll bet you a hundred to one it's a jug of hooch," Ski said. "With the heat on right now, he's probably headed to forecastle to pitch it over the side."

The bridge was in a darkened condition. They started their watch. John was at the helm and Ski was sitting in the stand-by seat. A full half-hour passed with almost nothing said.

Lieutenant Fausone, the Officer of the Deck, barked a command, "Helmsman. Come to course 065 degrees."

"Aye, sir. Course 065," John replied and quickly brought the *Franklin* to the new course.

More time passed.

"Boy it's black as ink out there. You can't see five feet ahead of you," John said.

"Yeah. It's scary, too," Ski replied.

Another hour went by. Ski took his turn at the helm. "Damn," he said absently. "What a boring way to pass a watch."

Just as he finished his sentence, the excited voice of the forward starboard lookout exploded through the intercom. "Mayday! Mayday! There's a man in convulsions on the forecastle."

"Get the Captain," Lieutenant Fausone ordered.

In a matter of minutes Gehres was on the bridge. "What happened?" he demanded.

"The starboard lookout reported a man on the forecastle in convulsions, sir," Fausone replied.

"Send the master-at-arms up there to find out what the hell it's all about," Gehres ordered.

John and Ski looked at each other.

"Do you suppose…?" Ski whispered, his voice trailing off into an unfinished question.

"I don't know, but I'll bet it is," John whispered back.

A half an hour later the master-at-arms returned to the bridge carrying a nearly empty jug.

John looked at Ski. Ski raised his eyebrows but didn't say a word.

"What the hell happened, Chief?" Gehres asked.

"I found this next to a seaman in convulsions, Captain. His name's Bundson. The medics are up there with him now." He handed Gehres the jug. "Homemade 'hooch' laced with torpedo juice, sir."

"That goddamned torpedo juice is poisonous," Gehres declared.

"Yes, sir. There's a crazy notion if it's filtered through a loaf of bread, you can drink it."

"I know. That crazy notion's killed a lot of sailors, Chief," Gehres said, shaking his head sadly.

"From the way he looked, sir, I think it might kill one more."

"Is that him I hear screaming?"

"Aye, sir, it is."

"Well, I guess I know who blew up the ready-service locker," Gehres said as he left the bridge.

On the way back to their bunks, John and Ski could hear Bundson's horrible screams.

"God, he must be suffering," John said. "Fuck-up or not, I feel sorry for him."

Ski shuddered. "Jesus Christ, John, this gives me the chills," he said.

"Me too. It's so goddamned creepy. I wonder if that poor bastard really *was* jinxed."

Next morning, word of Bundson's death was all over the ship.

About noon Beckley appeared at the edge of the flight deck just above John's guns.

When John saw him he gave him a wave and climbed up. "What's up, Beck?" he asked.

"Captain tells me you were on watch when Bundson drank that torpedo juice-laced hooch last night," Beckley said.

"Yeah, Ski and I both were."

"Did you know him?"

"Yeah. A little bit," John replied. "We were talking about him a few days ago. He was a weird guy—like he was always living in a nightmare."

"Yeah," Beckley said. "You're just sure something will happen to a guy like that."

"Things like that really get to me," John said.

"Hell, they get to everybody," Beckley replied, looking past John to the number thirteen on the island. "It's too bad, but that guy sounds like he was destined to go out the way he did."

After chow that evening, John found a chair in a quiet corner in the library and settled into it. He took Sandy's last letter out and reread part of it. The wonderful feelings that she wrote about in her dream touched his heart and filled him with passion. He wanted to feel those beautiful feelings again:

> *My Darling,*
> *I had a beautiful dream about us a few nights ago. I had a debate with my modesty concerning whether I should tell you about it—and I guess my feelings won the debate. So here goes…in the dream you were here with me. We were alone somewhere that felt very safe. You were holding me in your arms and then began to kiss me, gently at first, then more passionately. And I responded with even greater passion. You slowly began to unbutton my blouse, then began to undress me. In the next scene in the dream we were both in bed making wonderful, passionate love. The whole experience was gentle and very sexual, and it seemed to be so perfectly right. It was so vivid and real that when I awoke, I actually expected you to be laying there beside me….*

John put Sandy's letter down and closed his eyes. Joy and passion permeated his whole body. Sandy loved him. And he loved her. He reached for paper and pen and began to answer her letter. He wrote page after page, working with each word to make sure he got it right. He told her how he missed her and loved her, how he dreamed of taking her in his arms, how wonderful it would be to be with her and how hard he worked to control the passion he felt for her. He ended his letter by saying he longed for her more than he'd ever longed for anything in his life.

After he addressed the envelope, he took a deep breath and relaxed deeper into his chair. Then, for the first time, he heard the music on the Armed Forces Radio. It was Tommy Dorsey's band and the unmistakable voice of Frank Sinatra on a recording made for servicemen on a "V" record:

I'll be seeing you...
In all the old familiar places
That my yearning hear embraces
All day through...

A recurring fantasy about Sandy drifted into his mind. He realized it was much like the one Sandy wrote about in her dream. He was holding her close. He reached down and unbuttoned the collar of her blouse...then he slowly unbuttoned each button. She was wearing a white satin bra. He unhooked it and it fell to the floor. He touched her breasts...her nipples firmed to his touch. He could feel his passion mount. His heart pounded and his hand trembled as he gently pulled her blouse out of the waistband of her skirt. He eased her panties down...she stood there nude. He took her in his arms and pulled her close...he felt her naked body tremble with desire....

John stopped himself with a jolt. He was very passionate and breathing heavily. His heart was racing. The letter trembled in his hand. He put Sandy's letter back in its envelope, dropped his letter in the outgoing mail slot and walked out of the library. The crisp sea air blew into his face. This was one way he'd found to handle his sexual feelings. When he got to the fantail, he leaned on the ship's railing. Fresh air currents cascaded over him. His passion slowly subsided. He stared at the phosphorous glow of the *Franklin's* giant wake and began to dream about his future with Sandy. They'd have a beautiful house with tall trees, lots of flowers and a white picket fence. Sandy would probably prefer it to be near the ocean. They'd have children—two boys and a girl or two girls and a boy. Daughters that looked like her and sons who would love their mother as much as he did. Maybe they'd take a vacation to New York or Florida or Hawaii before they started their family—a heavy blast of wind shook him out of his reverie. In less than two weeks he'd be with Sandy. Then he hoped some of these beautiful thoughts would become reality.

**21 November, 1944
Pearl Harbor,
Territory of Hawaii**

At 08:45 the *Franklin* steamed into the Hawaiian Channel and moved toward the docks at Ford Island. At 09:00 Commander Philip Martin, chief harbor pilot, came aboard. A few minutes later two tugboats reported. At 09:50 *Franklin* moored to Pier Fox 2 with five manila lines and four wire hawsers. The day was beautiful, not a cloud in the sky. A warm tropical sun spread its radiance over the *Franklin*, making her damage somehow seem less extensive.

Beckley stood on the bridge and looked out over the tropical vegetation that hid most of the Navy's installations on Ford Island. Despite the beautiful scene, he was concerned about Commander Zimler. He looked at the note from Zimler that came in the mail delivery two days ago. It said that Zimler had been transferred to Tripler Hospital in Honolulu. He was taking further tests but felt he'd be released soon. Zimler asked him to call when the *Franklin* got to Pearl Harbor.

He put the note back into his shirt pocket, then heard someone call his name. It was John shouting up from the flight deck.

"Hey, Beck, You going ashore?"

"Yeah, I was thinking about it. I want to try to get in touch with Commander Zimler. He may still be in the hospital here."

"How do you know that?"

"I got a letter from him. I wanted to call him, but that goddamn phone line down there is so long…."

"No problem, Beck. I got a secret phone three blocks from here—almost nobody knows about it—it's kind of hidden."

"Really? Hell, if that's the case I'll be right down."

As they walked along the dock, Beckley asked, "How'd you find out about it, you know, the phone?"

"A chaplain told me about it last time we were here. I used it a couple of times. I couldn't believe it! There was never anybody around!"

When they reached the phone there was no one waiting.

"This is hard to believe," Beckley said.

"You go first, Beck, I'll probably want to talk longer than you do."

Beckley called the hospital. After he hung up, he said, "Nobody could tell me anything except that he was discharged two days ago. I sure hope he's okay."

He turned and walked slowly toward the dock. "Thanks, John," he said as he left. "See you back aboard."

As soon as Beckley was gone, John got on the phone. He toyed with the cord nervously as the Honolulu operator waited for an answer from San Francisco.

"San Francisco."

"Operator, we're calling Berkeley, California."

"One moment please."

"Berkeley."

"Berkeley operator, this is Honolulu, Hawaii. Would you please ring Alpine 3644."

John heard the phone ringing.

"Hello? Hello?"

"Sandy!" John said, his voice filled with affection.

The operator interrupted him. "Deposit one dollar and twenty-five cents for the first three minutes, please."

John poured five quarters into the phone.

"Go ahead, please."

"John, Darling. Where are you?"

"I can't tell you that…but I can tell you that I'll be back there in less than a week."

"Really!" Sandy screamed.

"Yes, Honey, *really*."

"That's wonderful. John, are you okay?"

"Yeah, Honey, I am, but our ship's not. We suffered some damage. That's why we're coming home."

"John, Darling, are you sure you're okay?"

"I'm fine, Honey. I didn't even get a scratch."

Two sailors, in oil-stained dungarees, walked up and stood right behind John—waiting to use the phone.

"I really miss you, Sandy. I can't wait to see you!"

"Me, too, Honey," Sandy said.

"Sandy, I can't talk much longer," John said. "There're a couple of guys here waiting to use this phone. I love you very much and I've missed you like crazy. I'll see you soon!"

"Oh, John, I love and miss you, too," Sandy said. "This is the best news I've ever had. I'll be waiting for you!"

"Goodbye, Honey. I love you."

John replaced the receiver in its cradle and walked back to the ship. Passion mixed with joy and happiness flooded through him. *Sandy's waiting. She's waiting in Berkeley. That's proof that she loves me as much as I love her, he said to himself.*

When he got down to his compartment Ski was lying in his bunk.

"Hey, Ski," John said. "I just talked to Sandy. She said she's waiting for me."

"It sounds like somebody's in love," Ski replied as he swung his legs over the edge of his bunk and sat upright. "When are you going to pop the question?"

There was a long silence. "You think you're doing a 'number' on me, don't you, Ski?"

"Who me, Gunner? I'd never do a thing like that."

"Not much, you wouldn't, you prick," John said with a smile. "In this case you may be right. I've thought about it for weeks. Wondered back and forth whether I should ask her. After I talked to her today, I decided. I'm going to ask her as soon as I get to Alameda."

Ski's face grew serious. "Ouuuu, that's a big step, John. Are you sure? After all, you were only with her a little while."

"Stow it, Mate. I don't want to hear any more of that," John said. "I've made up my mind. I'm going to ask her."

By 06:45 the next morning, the repairs *Franklin* needed in Pearl Harbor were completed. Gehres prepared to get underway. Two tugboats reported for duty off the port side and Commander Harry Hannus, harbor pilot, came aboard. At 07:05 all lines were cast off and *Franklin,* in Task Unit 19.12.8, with the destroyer *Fraizer* acting as screen, got underway. At 07:36 Gehres released the tugboats and the harbor pilot left the ship. At 07:51 *Franklin* passed through the anti-submarine nets and went to torpedo defense. In Condition of Readiness III, she steamed toward Alameda Naval Air Station, Alameda, California.

ALAMEDA NAVAL AIR STATION

CHAPTER TWENTY

Monday, 27 November, 1944
Alameda Naval Air Station
Alameda, California

When dawn broke and the sun began to rise, the rugged coastal mountains of northern California were visibly outlined in gold in the distance. A zesty breeze was blowing. The *Franklin's* prow cut through the choppy waters outside of San Francisco Bay with ease. She soon reached Mile Rock Light and steamed under the Golden Gate Bridge. At 09:43 she passed Alcatraz Island and headed east to Alameda.

John, wearing his dress blues, was ready—waiting to begin his leave. He, along with Beckley and Sullivan and the rest of his gun crew, had been up since sunrise, watching the golden panorama unfold. The closer they got to the coast the more anxious John became. "What time are we going ashore, Chief?" he asked.

Sullivan turned and said, "You should be on the dock by early afternoon."

At 11:18 *Franklin* docked at Berth 7, Alameda Naval Air Station, port side to the dock, with six manila lines and four wire hawsers.

As soon as the ship was secure, John walked over the fire-charred flight deck toward the *Franklin's* port side.

"I'd like to see if she found out when we're getting in," he shouted back to Beckley.

When he reached the port side and looked down, Sandy was standing there wearing a coat and sunglasses. She was carefully scanning the endless line of sailors who had gathered along the edge of the flight deck.

He rushed down the ladder to a 40-mm sponson.

"Sandy! Sandy!" he shouted. He waved his arms. After what seemed an eternity, he caught her attention.

"John!" she shouted with relief and joy.

"Wait there, Sandy. I'll be there as soon as I can get ashore."

At 13:00 passengers picked up in Pearl Harbor departed. As soon as all passengers were ashore, the OD said, "Okay, General Leave Section, you can go down now."

John was waiting behind a group of officers. They started down the gangplank, and John fell in behind them. When his feet hit the dock, he started running toward Sandy. When he reached her, she threw herself into his arms.

"Darling," she said, her voice filled with emotion. "My Darling John! I've been dreaming of this moment."

John kissed her.

"Oh, John," she said, "I've missed you so much!"

John hugged her tighter. "I love you so very much," he said. He kissed her again. Passion surged through him. He wanted to smother her with kisses. He knew Sandy felt his passion and desire. He pulled away and looked into her eyes.

She blushed and put her head on his chest. They remained there in silence, each feeling the joy and passion of the other's presence. Then Sandy pulled away. She kissed her index finger and placed it on his lips. "Come on, Darling," she said, "I want you to meet my mom and dad."

They hurried toward the Hearn's 1941 Dodge Town Sedan. When they were inside Sandy started fumbling in her purse for the car keys.

John put his hand over the purse and stopped her digging.

"What?" she asked.

He hesitated for a moment, then said, "Honey, I was going to wait for a romantic moment tonight to ask you this, but now that I'm with you I just don't want to wait that long."

A knowing smile crossed Sandy's face.

John's voice filled with emotion. "I've thought about this over and over for weeks. It's hard to know exactly how to ask, so I'll just ask." He took a deep breath and exhaled. "Will you marry me?"

Sandy beamed and put her arms around his neck. "Oh, yes, John! Yes, I will."

John put his arms around her and kissed her. "I guess I'm the happiest guy in the world right now."

"And I'm the happiest girl," Sandy replied as tears of happiness rolled down her cheeks.

Do you always cry when you're happy?" John asked with a smile.

"Sometimes," Sandy said, dabbing at her nose with a handkerchief. "But I've never been *this* happy before."

As soon as they were on their way, John looked over at Sandy. "Did you locate Robert?"

"Oh, my Lord, with all the excitement, I forgot for a minute. Yes. He's alive. He was wounded near Saint Vith in Belgium, but he's going to be okay."

"Where's he now?"

"In a military hospital in England."

"Thank God he's safe," John said. "Where was he wounded?"

"In the chest. The bullet missed his vital organs. They've operated on him twice. He said in his last letter he'll be almost as good as new." She paused and glanced at John. "He thinks he will be sent home after the first of the year."

"I wish it was sooner," John said. "I wish he could be here for our wedding."

"Oh, I do, too."

"By the way, Honey, how'd you find out our arrival time?" John asked as Sandy slowed the car and pulled into her driveway.

"Dad told me. He said I should keep it to myself, and I did. I didn't tell a soul," she said.

When they got out of the car John could see Sandy's mother waiting behind the screen door. Before they reached the top of the porch she came out. "You must be John," she said as she walked toward him, her hand extended.

"Yes, Ma'am, I am."

"Oh, forget the 'Ma'am,' call me Louise."

"Yes, Ma'am," John replied, smiling sheepishly at his mistake.

"Please, don't be nervous, John," Louise said, "Sandra's told us how you two met and fell in love. Come in, make yourself at home, and tell me all about yourself."

"Before I do, I'd like to tell you how happy I am to hear that your son is okay."

"Yes, Robert's alive, thank God," Louise said as she placed her hand over her heart. "It was a nightmare, but it's all over now."

John smiled and touched her arm. "I hope you see him real soon."

John, Sandy and Louise spent much of the afternoon talking. John told them about his mother, father and sister, and his early life in Pueblo.

About 5:30 the noise of a door opening interrupted their conversation. It was Sandy's father.

"Mark, John's here. Come and meet him," Louise called.

Mark walked into the living room and extended his hand. John took it and shook it firmly.

"It's a pleasure to know you, John."

"Thank you, Mr. Hearn."

"Mister is what they called my father, John. Just call me Mark."

"Yes, sir."

Mark took off his coat and sat down in his favorite chair. Before he could say anything more, Louise said, "They're going to be married, Mark."

"Oh?" Mark replied. He looked startled by Louise's announcement. "When did you decide this, Sandra?"

"This morning, Dad."

"You sure about this, John? It's a big step for a long time."

"Yes, sir, I'm sure. I love Sandy very much."

"And how about you, Sandra? Have you thought about it carefully?"

"Yes, I have Dad. I love John, too, and I want to marry him."

"But you've only just met. You don't even know each other."

"We spent time together in San Diego, Dad," Sandy replied.

"Yeah, but how much time?" Mark asked.

There was silence. From the look on Sandy's face, she hadn't anticipated her father's opposition. John hadn't either.

"Only a few hours, sir," John said, " but they were the most wonderful few hours I've ever spent in my life."

"It was the same for me, Dad," Sandy said. "The moment I met John I somehow knew down deep someday we'd get married."

"Okay, you're in love," Mark said. "You're both still very young. Spend some time together. Wait a year or so. At least wait until the war's over and you both can get used to a relationship without strain."

"Dad, be reasonable. Who knows when the war will end?" Sandra asked.

"Well I guess nobody does," Mark replied. Then he looked at John.

John looked back at him, preparing himself for another difficult question.

"What do you intend to do after the war, John?" Mark asked. "How will you support a wife and maybe a family?"

"I'm going to go to college and become an electrical engineer, sir," John replied. "I'll work very hard to support Sandy. Even harder if we have children."

"You're not going to stay in the Navy? You're a veteran seaman, decorated in battle. Why not?"

"The Navy's tough on married people," John replied. "I know guys who are away from their wives and families for months, sometime years at a time, sir. They really suffer and I'm sure their wives suffer more."

"Yeah, that's true," Mark said. "I run into them all the time at Hunter's Point."

"I want my life with Sandy to be the best and happiest possible," John said.

Mark became silent.

Sandy studied her father. "Dad, I almost never do anything against your wishes. I want your blessing in the worst way, but I want to marry John, and we don't want to wait until he comes back."

"God forbid, Sandra, but what if he doesn't come back?"

"Then I will have had the most wonderful marriage in the world, even if it only lasts a few weeks."

Mark turned and walked up the stairs to his bedroom.

"You know your dad, Sandra," Louise said after the bedroom door closed. "He has a tendency to put everything new off for a while. He'll come around, Honey. Marriage is a very serious thing. He just wants to be sure that you've both thought about how serious this decision is."

"Yes, I'm sure you're right, Mom," Sandra said, tears welling up in her eyes. "But we're not children, and times are different now. When you and dad got married, it was okay to take your time."

"I understand, Honey," Louise said, as she put her arms around her daughter. "The war somehow seems to make waiting impossible. Let's have dinner. If it's necessary, I'll talk to him after we're finished."

After dinner Louise asked Mark if they could talk, and the two disappeared into his study. After what seemed to John like forever, they returned.

"Sandy, Why don't you call Father O'Malley?" Louise suggested with a nod toward the phone.

Sandy looked at her father hesitantly. Mark gave her a quick nod, and she hurried across the room to the phone.

After a few rings, Father O'Malley's very Irish brogue came on the line. Sandy explained why she was calling. Father O'Malley made an appointment to see her and John the next afternoon at four o'clock.

After the call was finished, Mark asked John to join him in the living room. "I'd like to spend a little more time to get to know you better," he explained.

Sandy and her mother were caught off guard by Mark's request—then they looked at each other and said nothing.

Mark, a handsome man in his late forties, directed John to a large overstuffed chair and took one just like it opposite him. "Please tell me more about yourself, John," he said when they were seated.

John talked briefly about his early life, then they shifted to his war experiences.

John told Mark about being aboard the *Lexington* when she was torpedoed and sunk, and of the very close call he'd had on the *Vincennes*. Then he told him about the recent attacks on the *Franklin*.

"Kamikazes are tough to deal with," John said. "Even when you hit them and they're aflame, they still come blazing down at you. They don't stop unless they explode."

"Kamikazes? Are they what the papers say they are? That's hard to believe. Do the Japs really dive their planes into ships?" Mark asked.

"Yes, sir," John replied. "Those pilots don't think anything about using themselves as human bombs."

"But that's *so* hard to believe," Mark insisted.

"I couldn't believe it either until I *saw* it with my own eyes," John said. "But they do just that. They use their planes as bombs—dive 'em right into a ship."

Mark shook his head in amazement, struggling to understand what John just said.

"When the first kamikaze hit our flight deck," John said, "the cockpit's canopy and the pilot's head flew off—the head bounced half way down the flight deck. It was so ugly I almost threw up."

Mark shuddered. "Unbelievable. Unbelievable that they can sacrifice their lives like that!"

"Sometimes maybe dying isn't the worst that can happen," John replied. "Two men in our division were blinded that day—one by a gasoline explosion and the other when flying metal destroyed both his eyes and a big part of his face."

"God, John," Mark said, "what you've been through takes a lot of courage—a *lot* of courage. I don't know…I'm not sure if I've got that kind of courage." He paused and took a long breath. "I don't know," he continued in a soft voice, "whether I could stand there and fight back when some Jap was shooting at me, or bombing me, or aiming his plane at me. When I read about the kamikaze, I gave that a lot thought. I just don't know if I could…."

"You could do it, sir," John said. "There's no time to think about courage. All you think about is it's your life or theirs."

"Yeah, I know, but I'm still not sure if I could do it. I guess I'll never know. I admire your courage tremendously, John. It's young men like you that make our whole nation proud. I'm going to be delighted to have you as my son-in-law."

It was now 9:30. The two men had talked for nearly three hours.

"Why don't you call your parents and tell them your good news, John," Mark said as they came into the living room. The phone's right over there. Tell them we'd like to have them stay with us if they can come to the wedding."

"Thank you very much, sir. I'll sure do that," John said beaming.

He called his mother and broke the news. At first she voiced some of the same concerns Mark had. Was John sure of what he was doing? Was he sure he was old enough? Was Sandy the right girl? John assured his mother that everything was wonderful. Then he put Sandy on the phone. "Here's Sandy, Mom. She'll tell you all about us."

Sandy talked to John's mother, then to his sister Elena. He could tell by listening to Sandy's half of the conversation that everything was going fine. When they were finished, Sandy handed the phone back to him.

"John. John?"

"Yeah, Mom, I'm here."

"Oh, John, she sounds delightful! She's so sweet and down to earth. She seems to be very much in love with you. I'm so happy for you."

"Thanks, Mom," John said.

"Do you have a date for the wedding?"

"We're seeing the priest about that tomorrow. We hope this Sunday. Will you all try to come?"

"I'm not sure about your father—he's pretty tied up at the ammunition plant, but Elena and I'll do our best to be there."

"If you can come, Mom, the Hearns asked me to tell you that they would like you to stay with them."

"Thank them for us, and let us know the date of the wedding as soon as you can, John."

"I will, Mom." John said. "Give my love to Dad and Elena. I love you."

"I will, Honey. We love you, too. I'll call Union Pacific about reservations as soon as I hang up."

John looked at Sandy and her parents and said, "Well, I think it's about time I go back to the base. I want to thank you for dinner and everything. It was wonderful to meet you both. I can't remember when I've been so happy."

John felt fully accepted now. No one said anything further, but everyone in the room realized he was.

Sandy drove back to the base. On the way, alternating between the clutch and the brake, her skirt inched up high on her thighs.

John looked over at her long, slender legs. He couldn't help himself. He wanted to know every inch of her beautiful body.

Sandy unexpectedly caught his gaze. It was dark but John was sure he saw her blush. He sheepishly turned his eyes to the floorboard.

She reached over and put her hand on his arm. "I understand. I feel that way, too, Darling, but we have to wait," she said gently. "It won't be that long."

When they arrived at the main gate, John leaned over and kissed Sandy passionately.

She returned his passion. In a few minutes, they were both breathing heavily.

"You better go now, John," she cautioned, "before we go much farther. Besides I think the SPs at the gate are watching us."

John turned and looked. "They sure are. Those idiots are taking everything in—I hope they're enjoying themselves," he said as he slid out of the seat and looked back at Sandy through the half-opened door. "I'll see you tomorrow. I love you, Honey."

"I love you, too, John," Sandy said, shaking her head to clear away the excitement she still felt. "I'll be here right at nine."

At nine the next morning John was waiting when Sandy drove up to the main gate. When she saw John, she waved vigorously through the window, stopped and jumped out of the car.

"John," she said as she ran toward him wearing a form-fitting white suit and high heels. "I didn't even think to ask you yesterday if you wanted to drive."

John looked teasingly at her and smiled. "You're doing a good job, Honey. I think I'd rather sit in the passenger seat and look at your legs."

Sandy pounded him gently on the chest.

"You men!" she said feigning exasperation. "All you think of is sex."

"Aren't you thinking about it, too?"

"Well, yesss…but you're not supposed to know that." Sandy became serious. "John," she said nervously, "I need to tell you something…and I guess this is as good a time as any. I made a mistake once a couple of years ago, and I've regretted it ever since. I'm not a virgin, John. I was very young and…."

John put his hand over Sandy's lips.

"I don't want to hear about it, Honey," he said softly. "For every mistake you've made, I've made a hundred. Let's leave it at that."

Sandy put her arms around his neck and hugged him. "Oh, thank you, Darling," she said. "I've been worried about telling you that since the first night we met."

"What do you say we go to Berkeley?" John said, changing the subject. "We've got a lot of things to do today."

When they arrived in downtown Berkeley, their first stop was Hamond's Jewelry Store.

When they walked through the door, Ray Hamond greeted Sandy with a huge hug.

"Hi, Sandy," he said. "I haven't seen you in awhile. You sure have grown into a beautiful young lady." He released her, then looked curiously at John.

"Mr. Hamond, this is John Oxler," Sandy said. "We want to buy wedding rings. We're going to be married."

Hamond extended his hand to John. "Congratulations," he said. "You're getting a wonderful girl. I've known her all her life."

Hamond led them to the wedding ring case. He patiently displayed one ring after another. Finally, after nearly an hour of intense comparisons and questions about different prices, John and Sandy selected an engagement ring and two wedding bands.

Mr. Hamond put the rings back into their boxes and into a bag and handed them to John.

Before they left, Sandy gave Hamond a little kiss on the cheek.

"You sure look wonderful without your braces, Honey. All grown up and beautiful," he said. "I wish you all the happiness in the world."

Their next stop was home. Sandy wanted to wear her mother's wedding dress. Mrs. Lenney, the local seamstress, was coming to make the necessary alterations.

When they arrived, the seamstress was already there. Sandy disappeared into a bedroom with her. John was left with nothing to do until the meeting with Father O'Malley at four that afternoon.

He picked up the morning copy of the *Berkeley Gazette*. There in huge bold print was the headline:

Japanese Desperation!
Kamikaze Attacks Increase.

Washington, D.C. November 28, 1944 (AP). The Navy Department reported the Japanese have intensified the use of "kamikaze" bombing attacks in the Philippine Operational Area.

The report indicated that the decisive victories scored by the Third and Seventh American Fleets in the Second Battle of the Philippine Sea were the primary reasons for the acceleration. When these fleets recently withdrew for repairs and rest, the kamikaze problem magnified.

According to the communiqué work on airfields in Leyte was another problem. Completion of Tacloban Field, earlier designated by the Army Air Force as a major air base, has been disappointingly slow, due mainly to bad weather and the nature of the boggy soil that surrounds it. These circumstances resulted in temporary Japanese control of the skies in large areas over the Philippines.

The intense use of the kamikaze has given them a surprising tactical advantage. Because of their recent heavy losses in both ships and aircraft, the Japanese have resorted to random attacks on all ships, from capital ships such as carriers, down to the smallest destroyer escorts.

To maximize the effects of their "human bombs" they're utilizing anything that will fly, even old slow fixed-wheel biplanes.

Many of the Japanese pilots who are flying to their death in the kamikazes are very young; some of them in their early and middle teens.

> Sources indicated that General Douglas MacArthur has requested the immediate return of Admiral "Bull" Halsey's Third Fleet to counter the kamikaze attacks.

John remembered that he was in the middle of action there less than two months ago, but now that seemed like a distant, terrible nightmare. The article troubled him. The *meaning* of the war had changed for him now. A deep need to get the war over surged through him. *I'll have a wife soon and some day some kids. I sure as hell don't want them to live under the dictatorial foot of some goddamned Jap emperor, he said to himself.*

Sandy came out of the bedroom with Mrs. Lenny, who had carefully re-measured the wedding dress. "I'll have it back for you late tomorrow afternoon," she said as Sandy walked her to the door.

The moment she was gone, John took Sandy into his arms. "Now," he said, "there are two more things we have left to do."

"Two things?"

"Yeah. We have to see Father O'Malley about our wedding date, and we have to get engaged."

Sandy started to laugh.

John took the engagement ring out of the box and slipped it on her finger. "Will you marry me, Sandy Hearn?" he asked with a broad smile.

Sandy smiled and gave him a long kiss. "That I will, John Oxler," she whispered.

"Good, that's settled," John said, still smiling. "Now let's go get our wedding date from Father O'Malley."

They arrived at the rectory fifteen minutes early. Mrs. Samora, the parish housekeeper, seated them in the study. In a few minutes Father O'Malley appeared and greeted them warmly.

"Father, this is John Oxler," Sandra said. "He's the man I'm going to marry."

"Are you a Catholic, John?" O'Malley asked as he sat down.

"Yes, Father, I am."

"And what are the wedding plans?"

Sandy outlined the wedding plans and finished by saying, "We'd like to have the wedding as soon as possible, Father—Saturday, the second of December or Sunday, the third."

Father O'Malley rubbed his chin thoughtfully. Then he said, "I'm afraid that's impossible, Sandra. We're booked with weddings for both of those days, and you know the Church requires a reasonable amount of time for reflection on the Sacrament of Matrimony."

"But, Father," Sandra said, her voice filled with disappointment, "we've only got twenty days. We'd like to be married for as many of those days as possible."

The old priest looked at her over his spectacles. "I understand your sense of urgency," he said. "But even if I waived the waiting period, there isn't an open date until Sunday, December tenth. I know this is disappointing, but maybe it's a good thing. Marriage is for a whole lifetime, and this will give you both time to consider that aspect of the Sacrament."

John and Sandy left the rectory and walked back to the car. They were both dejected. December tenth seemed like years away.

"It's so long to wait," Sandra said. "And there's nothing we can do about it. I know Father O'Malley. Once he says something…."

"I just got an idea," John interrupted. "Why don't we get married in my parish?"

"John, that's ridiculous. Your parish is over twelve hundred miles from here."

"No it isn't, Honey. My parish is right over at Alameda Naval Air Station. Let's see if we can get a chaplain there to marry us sooner."

Sandy's face lit up. "Do you suppose we can?"

"It doesn't hurt to try. Besides, I'll bet Navy chaplains are easier to deal with than priests in parishes," John said, gaining confidence as he talked. "Let's see if I can do it!"

The next morning John called the chaplain's office and asked to speak to a priest.

After a few minutes a deep male voice answered, "Father O'Callahan."

John gulped. Another Irish Catholic priest. "Father, I wonder if I could talk with you concerning a very important problem regarding a marriage?" John asked tentatively.

"What's the problem, sailor?"

Desperate now, John explained his whole predicament. Then he stopped and waited—expecting the worst.

"He wants you to wait ten days—half of a twenty-day leave?" O'Callahan asked.

"Yes, sir," John replied, now fearing the worst.

The priest chuckled. "Irish Catholic priests," he said. "We can often be set in our ways. Why don't we see what a U.S. Navy Chaplain can do for you?"

"Gee, Father, do you think you can help us?"

"What time can you and your fiancée come in?"

"We can be there at eleven."

"No, better make it twelve o'clock. Come to the main entrance of the base chaplain's office."

He paused, "Do you know where it is?"

"I can find it, sir. Thank you very much."

At noon the next day, Sandy and John walked into the vestibule of the base chaplain's office.

A yeoman greeted them. "Yes," he said, "Father O'Callahan's expecting you. He asked me to tell you he'd be here shortly." He escorted them into a study and pointed to two chairs.

The minute he was gone Sandy whispered, "What do you think?"

John shrugged his shoulders and whispered back, "We'll know pretty soon."

A few minutes later, Father O'Callahan walked into the room and sat down opposite John and Sandy.

John stood and introduced Sandy and himself.

O'Callahan took off his glasses and squinted. Then he returned them to his nose. He pointed his index finger at John and said, "Your face is familiar, sailor. Have we met?"

John had recognized O'Callahan the minute he walked through the door.

"Yes, Father. Well, sort of…" John stammered. "I was the sailor that nearly knocked your glasses off in Pearl Harbor. I was looking for a telephone, sir."

Father O'Callahan laughed. "Oh, yeah, I remember now. You sure were in a hurry," he said. "Is this the young lady you were rushing to call?"

"Yes, Father, it is." John replied.

"Well, I can't say I blame you," O'Callahan replied with a smile.

Sandy blushed, then they all laughed.

"So the problem is that your parish priest can't marry you for ten days?"

"Yes, Father," Sandy replied. "I know ten days is not a long time, but…."

"Not a long time? In these days, it could be lifetime," O'Callahan said. "How about Saturday at eleven?"

"You mean this *coming* Saturday, Father?" Sandy asked.

"Of course," he replied. "Eleven o'clock—sharp."

John and Sandy were speechless.

O'Callahan detailed the documents required for the wedding. John's situation was easy. He was of age and his dog tags and the records he carried could be used for his religious requirements. Sandy, still several months away from her twenty-first birthday, would need written permission from her parents. She would also need her birth certificate and the certificates of her first communion and confirmation.

"Do I need permission from my parish priest?" Sandy asked, twisting nervously in her chair.

"Hmmm…maybe you better let me handle that one," O'Callahan said with a trace of a smile. "What's Father O'Malley's number? As far as I'm concerned this can be considered a wartime emergency."

Sandy gave him the number. Both she and John looked at him gratefully. They knew this handsome, athletic-looking priest was stretching a long way to help them solve their problem.

Then O'Callahan asked, "Did *Franklin* suffer damage, John?"

"Yes, sir, she did. Two kamikazes crashed us. They started some gasoline fires. Our ordinance exploded and knocked out both of our elevators. There was damage to the flight deck and some to the hangar deck. I guess we were lucky though," he concluded slowly. "It could have been a lot worse."

"Was there loss of life?"

John looked tentatively at Sandy. Then he said, "We lost a hundred men."

"That's very sad," O'Callahan said. "I served two and a half years in the Atlantic on the *Ranger*. She didn't make any headlines, because we never took a hit, but we dodged German torpedoes from the arctic to the equator. We had a very near miss in the invasion of North Africa."

"If you don't mind my asking, sir, why'd you leave Pearl Harbor?"

"I asked for a transfer. I want to go back to sea again," O'Callahan replied. "I'd like to get somewhere near the Philippines. My sister Alice is a Maryknoll nun there," O'Callahan replied. He paused and a sad smile crossed his face. "Funny, her religious name is Sister Rose Marie, and has been for some time, but I'm so used to Alice…."

He stared out toward the Pacific for a long moment. "The Japanese put her in prison, and we haven't heard from her for nearly three years," he explained. "As children we were very close. I think of things we did together as kids all the time, things like playing jacks and hopscotch and singing in the choir…."

"Having a sister in a Japanese prison camp must be awful, Father," Sandy said.

"It is. It's a very heavy burden."

"You put in for sea duty, sir?" John asked.

"Yeah. I'm here waiting for an assignment now." He walked with John and Sandy to the door. "Get back to me as soon as you can with the papers. Tomorrow if possible."

"We will, Father," John said. "Thanks again. We're very grateful."

As soon as John and Sandy got back to her house, John called his mother. "The wedding is scheduled for Saturday at eleven o'clock, Mom. We just made the arrangements. You'll have to leave tomorrow to make it."

"We're coming, Honey," his mother replied. "We're all packed. Elena and I can't wait to see you and to meet Sandy."

"What time does your train get in? We'll meet you at the depot."

"It's Union Pacific. It gets there at three-forty-five on Friday."

"We'll be there."

"Well, that takes care of that," John said as he hung the phone up, "and tomorrow's payday. I'm going to call Chief Sullivan and ask him if he will pick up my money. Maybe I can get permission to take you aboard the ship. Would you like that?"

"Oh, yes, I would!" Sandy replied.

Later that afternoon Chief Sullivan called back. "You're all squared away," he said. "You can come aboard any time after eleven. Don't forget to warn Sandy about our damage. Otherwise, it might be a shock when she sees it."

30 November, 1944
Alameda Naval Air Station
Boarding the Franklin

The next morning John met Sandy at the main gate and drove from there to the dock. From the dock, the *Franklin* loomed huge, powerful and deceptively indestructible. Almost none of the damage could be seen from the ship's port side.

As they walked toward the gangway John cautioned Sandy, "You might see some damage, Honey."

"I know. You told Father O'Callahan about it yesterday," Sandy said as she looked the entire length of the ship. "I can't see much of it from here."

"Yeah, you can't. Most of it was to the bridge and flight deck," John explained.

They reached the gangway and started the steep climb. As they climbed, John said, "Be prepared, Honey. You're going to get a lot of attention. These guys almost never see a woman aboard, especially on a ship that's suffered battle damage. Sullivan and Beckley had to pull some strings to set this up." When they reached the quarterdeck, John saluted the Officer of the Deck, a young ensign he'd never seen before.

"Gunner's Mate Second Class John Oxler and guest requesting permission to come aboard, sir."

"Permission granted, Gunner. We've been expecting you." The OD looked at Sandy. "Congratulations," he said as he walked around the small podium on the quarterdeck and took Sandy's hand. "Welcome aboard, Miss Hearn."

Then he turned to John. "You're very fortunate, sailor. She's a beautiful young lady."

"Aye, sir."

By this time Beckley, Sullivan, Ski and Lowe and the rest of John's gun crew came up from below and walked toward the quarterdeck. John saw them coming and escorted Sandy to meet them. He flipped them all an informal salute and thanked Sullivan and Beckley for their help. Then he introduced Sandy to the group, one at a time, beginning with Beckley and Sullivan. Each man came forward and politely shook hands with her.

Lowe seemed especially enthusiastic. "I'm so happy for you and John," he said with a broad smile.

Jardin was standing next in line.

"This is Seaman Second Class James Jardin," John said. "He's the youngest guy in our gun crew."

"How old are you?" Sandy asked as she shook his hand.

"I was eighteen on September twentieth, ma'am."

"How long have you been in the Navy?"

"Seven months, ma'am. I volunteered when I was seventeen and a half," Jardin said, his face turning a bright red. "You sure are beautiful, ma'am. Even my girlfriend back home isn't as pretty as you."

It was Sandy's turn to blush. "Well, thank you very much," she said.

Sandy and John reached Kwatkowski. He was grinning broadly. "You don't know this, Sandy, but I've already seen you," he said. "I was with John the first night he saw you in San Diego. I had to drag the big lug out of the USO and back to duty." Ski laughed. "He almost bit my head off for it."

"Oh, yes, I remember you. You were with him the night we met, too."

"Yes," Ski replied. "Since then he's told me a lot about you. I want you to know that I can sure tell when he gets a letter from you at mail call, he...."

"Okay, wise guy," John interrupted. "Now that you've told her all of my secrets, I've got a job for you."

Ski frowned. "A job, John? Now?" he asked.

"No, Saturday," John replied.

"Saturday?"

"Yeah, Saturday. I want you to be our best man."

Ski laughed with relief. "For a minute, I thought I was in deep trouble," he said, "and now I'll have the pleasure of you finally admitting that I'm the best man!" Ski became serious. "It's an honor, John. Thanks for asking me."

The guys in the gun crew gave a little cheer.

Sandy beamed. She reached into her purse and took out a packet of hand written wedding invitations and presented one to each man.

When Sandy handed out the last invitation, Sullivan came down the line with an envelope in his hand. "Your last month's pay," he said to John with a smile. "They allowed me to sign for it. Hope they'll be that reasonable again sometime when I *really* need money."

John laughed. "Thanks, Chief. What's this?" he asked pulling a folded page from the envelope.

"Read it."

John read aloud. "Promotion list."

"That's right," Sullivan said. "Look under 'O'. You'll find your name there. Congratulations! Gunner's Mate First Class John Oxler."

John looked down the list of names. He found his promotion. "God! What a great week this has been," he said.

Beckley stepped up to offer his congratulations.

"What do you think, Beck?" John asked with a smile.

"I'm not sure about those other two stripes," Beckley said with a grin. "But this is a combat promotion. I know you earned this one, John."

Small talk, combined with friendly ribbing, went on for nearly half an hour. Everyone in the gun crew was joking and laughing. The camaraderie between John and his gun crew was obvious, and John's friendship and respect for Beckley and Sullivan and their affection for him touched Sandy deeply.

"They seem to be making our happiness their own," she whispered to John.

Then she said, "John, I've never seen 40-mm guns up close. I'm curious about what they look like. Could I see your 40-mm guns?" she asked.

John looked at Sullivan. "Is that okay, Chief?"

"Sure it is," Sullivan replied. "I'll go up with you."

As John, Sandy and Sullivan walked toward the forward ladder to the flight deck, Sandy became aware that everyone she passed was looking at her. "John, they're staring...."

John leaned toward her and said, "I told you they would, Honey. Sailors stare at beautiful women, especially when they've been at sea for five or six months."

Sandy blushed and shook her head.

As they climbed the ladder to the flight deck, Sandy said, "I understand now why you told me that I should wear slacks."

When they reached the top, the shocking damage suffered by the *Franklin* stopped Sandy in her tracks. The flame-scared bridge loomed ahead, shattered windows, smoke and fire-charred paint and the badly battered steel bulkhead. The gun turret, next to the bridge, was ripped from its moorings. Its five-inch barrel pointed awkwardly down to the battered flight deck. The planks in the deck were hideously burned and scarred.

"God, John. I can't believe the damage," Sandy said, seeming horrified.

"I told you there was damage, Honey."

"But I never dreamed it would look like this. Where were you when this all happened?"

John pointed to the starboard side of the ship. "Over in the gun pit forward of the island."

"What happened to that gun, John?" Sandy asked, her fear apparent in her voice.

"It took the kamikaze's first hit. Then the plane ricocheted and exploded again against the island and bridge."

Sandy looked at the ship's awkwardly tilted elevators and at the charred planks and holes in the flight deck. "It looks like the fires spread all over," she said. She shook her head violently. "This is dreadful. I don't want to be anywhere near it. Let's go! It's too scary for me."

They rode home in silence. When they were in the Hearn living room, Sandy said, "I wish I hadn't seen that damage, John."

"I wish you hadn't seen it either, Honey. We were just trying to show you what our guns looked like."

"John, you could have been killed!"

"Well, I wasn't, Honey. Lord, I sure wish we'd thought before we took you up there," John said, his voice filled with sadness and concern. "It was a mental lapse. I guess Sullivan and I got so used to seeing the damage…."

He could see Sandy was shaken. She seemed overcome by the affects of what she'd seen. "Honey, I'm sorry. I…We didn't think…I shouldn't have taken you up there," he said.

"It wasn't your fault," Sandy said. "I asked to see those guns."

"Yes, but we should have thought of the damage up there," John said sadly. "I sure wish there was some way I could change what happened."

"It was shocking! It didn't hit me until I saw the damage," Sandy said. "Men were out there shooting and bombing each other. Some were killed, others hideously burned and wounded." She paused. "What if something like that happened to you?"

John realized the war now had become very real to Sandy. He didn't know what to say, but he had to reassure her. "Don't worry, Honey, nothing's ever going to happen to me," he said with as much confidence as he could muster.

"When you said that in San Diego, I asked you how you could be sure, remember?"

"Yeah, I remember, Honey, " John said. "I'm even more sure now."

"Even after being that close to death?"

"Yes. Remember I told you that love saves men's lives? There's nothing the Japs could do to keep me from coming back to you. Nothing's going to happen to me. I just *know* it."

"But, John, how can you be so sure?"

"Because I have you and your love, Honey."

"What about the hundred men who were killed? Didn't any of them have wives and sweethearts who loved them?" Sandy persisted.

John couldn't answer. I should have known, he thought. I should have thought more about Sandy's request to see the 40s. But deep down John knew Sandy's fears were real. "Sandy, I need to go for a walk for a while," he said. "I have to be alone. I have to think about what just happened."

John left the house and walked until he found University Boulevard, then turned and walked toward the bay. When he got there, he sat on the seawall and leaned back against a post. He began to go over the events of the morning again. He said a silent prayer asking God to help him do the right thing. The warm late afternoon sun and gentle sounds of the water made him drowsy. He dozed for awhile. He was startled awake in the middle of a hideous dream….Belasco's bloody face appeared to him, so real that he could almost touch his lifeless eyes and death-contorted mouth. The dream told him what he had to do. He had no right to ask Sandy to go through with the wedding. He loved her too much to put her through the agonizing life of a wife who was never sure if her husband would come home in one piece or in a coffin.

He was relieved. He walked briskly back; the conflicting thoughts were gone. When he got there it was almost dark.

Sandy met him at the door. "Where were you, Honey? Mom and I were beginning to worry…."

"Where is your mom?" John asked, intending to tell her he was sorry.

"She and dad went to a movie. They thought we needed some time to ourselves," Sandy replied as she fidgeted with her engagement ring.

"Sandy," John said. "I agree with you. I think we should wait…."

Sandy put her fingers over his mouth so he couldn't finish what he was saying. Then she put her arms around his neck. "While you were gone I had a long talk with Mom about what I saw this morning. I told her how much it frightened me."

John nodded. He was now prepared to hear the worst. "You decided we should wait," he said, looking into her eyes. "Honey, I understand. I'm sorry I pushed so hard…."

"No, I didn't decide to wait," Sandy interrupted, with a tiny smile beginning to appear across her face. "I decided we should get married now, just as we planned."

John was shocked. "Really?"

"Yes, really," Sandy said happily. "John, I love you very much. I want to be your wife forever, but if something should happen and forever is just twenty days, then they'll be the happiest twenty days I'll ever have lived. I said that to Dad the other day and now I really understand what it means."

John fought back tears. "I don't know what to say, Honey," he said, "except that I love you more than I ever thought possible."

"I believe in you, Darling. I believe you'll come back," Sandy said. "If it's God's will that you don't, then I'll try to live without you; but no matter what happens, I'll never stop loving you."

John took Sandy in his arms and held her close.

"I love you so much," he said. He gave her a tender, love-filled kiss.

Sandy responded passionately. She pressed her body against his. Her tongue touched his lips, then moved provocatively into his mouth.

This startled him. He responded by holding her even tighter. Sandy let out a deep sigh and began rubbing the back of his neck.

John moved his hand over her breasts. Sandy's breathing became heavy. She pulled herself even closer. Sensuous feelings flooded his body. He pressed himself firmly against her and looked into her eyes. Her eyes were filled with unconditional desire. "I want you so much," she whispered.

John lowered her to the thick carpet on the living room floor, kissing her as he lowered her. He knelt beside her and began to undo the buttons on her blouse. Suddenly he became aware of where they were—of the room, the lights, the carpet. He pressed the last button between his thumb and index finger but couldn't undo it. Instead, he lay down beside her, and in a whisper said, "Honey, we can't. Not this way…not now. You're too wonderful, and I love you too much. My love and my vows to you are for a lifetime…" He gently kissed her on the cheek. "It's only a few days. Let's wait till were married."

By this time Sandy's eyes were wide open. She shook her head to clear her passion. "Yes, you're right, John." She took a deep breath, released it and sat up. "It was my fault, Darling," she said as she began to button her blouse. "I don't know what came over me. I guess I felt I needed to be more than just close to you."

"I think we both felt the same way," John said. He helped her up and they sat down on the couch. He turned down the lights, and took her in his arms. "Sandy," he said, "everything's going to be wonderful. Just you wait and see."

Sandy kissed him. "Promise?" she asked with a smile, as tears of happiness rolled down her cheeks.

"I promise, Honey," he replied.

They held each other until they fell asleep.

When John woke up, Sandy was still sleeping. He covered her with her coat, quietly left the house and caught a bus back to the base.

Friday, the first of December was overcast and gloomy. It was drizzling, and there was a hint of winter in the air.

John waited for Sandy at the main gate with his pea coat buttoned up as far as it would go. When she drove up, she was waving through the windshield and smiling. She parked at the curb, got out and ran over to John.

"Hi!" she said tentatively.

"How do you feel, Honey?" John asked.

"I'm fine. I'm sorry about yesterday, John," she said.

"No, it was my fault. I should have known...."

"What do you have to do today, Darling?" Sandy asked, interrupting him.

"Not much," John replied. "What do *you* have to do?"

"Well, I've got a bunch of girl things to do," Sandy said. "Get my hair done and a manicure. Go to the florist. Meet with the photographer. Pick up a few more invitations. Buy some things for our honeymoon. I thought I'd come by and get you. We can do what you need first. Then I can drop you at my house. I could pick you up there about three to meet your mother and sister."

John was relieved. Sandy was her old self. "That's a plan," he said. "But I don't need anything. I'm all squared away. My shoes are shined, my dress blues are pressed, I've got the rings, and I'll be meeting my best man at nine o'clock tomorrow morning."

"Oh, okay. I'll just drop you at my house. Then I can go on my way." When they pulled up to her house, Sandy said, "I'll be back right at three. Gee, I hope your mom and sister like me."

John kissed Sandy lightly on the cheek and got out of the car. "They'll love you," he said.

CHAPTER TWENTY-ONE

2 December, 1944
Alameda Naval Air Station
A Wedding

John's wedding day dawned bright and beautiful. He was up at reveille. He looked out the window. The storm had passed, and there wasn't a cloud in the sky. The warm California sunshine had started to dissipate the touch of winter. He could see some of the base's hearty flowers beginning to open. As he walked toward the head swinging his shaving kit, he had vague feelings of apprehension. "I had a good night's sleep," he muttered, "but still I'm kinda nervous."

Ski was waiting when John came down the steps.

"You all set?" Ski asked.

"As set as I'll ever be. I'm glad I only have to do this once."

When they reached the chapel it was beginning to fill, mostly with Sandy's relatives and friends. John's mother and sister were seated in the first row on the left-hand side of the church. Soon Beckley, Sullivan and all the guys in John's gun crew entered the chapel. When John saw them, he moved quickly toward the door and greeted them.

"Am I glad to see you guys," he said as he walked past an usher. "I'll seat them," he said to the usher. "Come on, guys. I want you to meet my mom and sister."

He seated them in the second row right behind Helen and Elena. As soon as they were all seated, he taped his mother gently on the shoulder.

When she looked around, he whispered, "I want you to meet some of my friends from the ship, Mom."

Both she and Elena turned. Each man introduced himself in tones just above a whisper.

By 10:55 the chapel was filled and the organist began playing *Some Enchanted Evening. At* exactly eleven o'clock, she moved deftly into the wedding march.

Everyone turned toward the rear of the chapel. Standing there ready to walk down the aisle were Sandy and Mark. As Sandy walked slowly down the aisle on her father's arm murmurs of admiration greeted her. Sandy was a radiant, lovely bride.

John, with Ski, was waiting at the small steps that lead up to the sanctuary. When John saw Sandy he almost burst with pride and happiness.

"Boy, is she beautiful," Ski whispered.

"She's also wonderful, Ski," John whispered back.

When she reached John, she took his arm and they stepped carefully up the two steps into the sanctuary. Ski and Margaret Ann Hizer, Sandy's maid of honor, followed.

Father O'Callahan smiled and nodded to them. Then he blessed them and turned to begin the Mass:

"In nomine Patris, et Filii, et Spiritus Sancti...."
"Amen," replied the acolytes in unison.
"Introibo ad altare Dei...."

The wedding Mass had begun. John recalled the meaning of the Latin prayers—he had served Mass as a boy. "I will go unto the altar of God," John translated mentally...."

"Judica me Deus et discerne causam meam de gente non sancta...." O'Callahan continued....

"Judge me, O God, and distinguish my cause from the nation that is not holy...." he translated...then his mind began to drift away from the Latin prayers. The chapel was overcrowded...it had become warm and stuffy. Father O'Callahan's voice brought him back at the Gloria...*"Gloria in excelsis Deo et in terra pax hominibus bonae voluntatis...."*

John fidgeted on the kneeler and looked over at Sandy. She was intently following O'Callahan's every word.

The time for the Gospel arrived. O'Callahan read the Gospel message, then turned and addressed the congregation.

"Dearly Beloved," he began. "We are gathered here today to unite John and Sandra in the Sacrament of Holy Matrimony. We administer this Sacred Rite to this wonderful young couple in a time that is filled with conflict and danger—in a time when great sacrifices are often required of both partners in a marriage. This is a time, as never before, when courage, honesty, fidelity, understanding and trust must be the foundations upon which this Sacrament is based.

He paused and looked over the congregation. "John and Sandra typify these wonderful values. John, a veteran seaman with five battle stars, has survived great adversity. One ship he served on was torpedoed and sunk, another nearly sunk by Japanese naval gunfire and a recent kamikaze attack badly damaged the carrier he was aboard.

"In Sandra, we have a young lady with beauty, faith and courage—with the faith, courage and devotion to trust that God will keep John safe from whatever future perils might confront him. It is young people like John and Sandra that make us feel secure—confident on the battlefield, safe at home, and assured of our ultimate victory. They are the foundations upon which our great democracy is built and I think the future will show they are molding the most historic time in the history of our beloved country. Today's wedding should be a tribute to the love, devotion and courage of all of these young men and women. As we unite John and Sandra in the Sacrament of Holy Matrimony, we honor them, and all young men and women like them."

O'Callahan paused. Then he said, "Please come forward. Take Sandra's hand, John." He read the sacred words that consecrated the marriage. When he finished, he turned to Ski. "Do you have the rings?"

Ski fumbled with them for a moment, then handed them to John.

"Do you John, take Sandra as your lawful wife," O'Callahan asked, "to have and to hold, for richer of poorer, in sickness and in health, until death do you part?"

A WEDDING

"I do."

"Do you, Sandra, take John for your loving husband, to have and to hold, for richer or poorer, in sickness and health, until death do you part?"

"I do," Sandy replied in a voice just above a whisper.

"Now, through the authority vested in me by Our Holy Mother the Church, I pronounce you man and wife."

John just stood there staring.

Father O'Callahan smiled and said, "You can now kiss your bride, John."

"Oh," he said, shaking his head slightly. He turned to Sandy who was smiling and waiting for his kiss.

"You're the most beautiful bride in the world," John said. Then he kissed her and gently hugged her.

The Mass ended. O'Callahan turned to the congregation and extended a blessing, "The Mass is ended. Go in peace."

The organist began to play the wedding march again, this time with such zest that the small chapel fairly resonated.

John turned and Sandy took his arm. Together they stepped from the altar and walked toward the door.

Everybody in the congregation was smiling and clapping.

John especially noticed Lowe. He was standing at the edge of the pew with both arms in the air, grinning.

When John and Sandy passed him, he said, "Hey, this is great. Congratulations!"

In a few minutes people surrounded them, wishing them well. Father O'Callahan made his way through the busy gathering and congratulated them.

"I'll be at the reception," he said. "It's at the NCO Club, right?"

"Yes, Father," Sandy said. "We'll be so happy to have you. It starts at two o'clock. We'll be expecting you."

"I've got something to show you, John," O'Callahan called back over his shoulder.

"Something to show me," he said softly to Sandy. "I wonder what he's got to show me?"

John and Sandy arrived at the NCO Club just a little after two o'clock. Most of the guests had arrived, and the festivities were beginning. Beckley, Sullivan, Lowe and the rest of John's gun crew were in the bar waiting. When they saw the wedding party, they began to applaud again.

Father O'Callahan arrived just before they cut the wedding cake. He watched, smiling, as Sandy shoved an oversized piece into John's mouth.

When this ceremony was over, O'Callahan motioned to John, and John stepped over to join him. "I said had something I wanted to show you, John," he said with a smile. He reached into his inner breast pocket. "What do you think of this?" he asked as he produced an envelope and handed it to John.

John looked puzzled. He removed the folded sheet and opened it. It was a dispatch from the Fleet Chaplain, Captain John Moore. John read it slowly, then finished it on a high note, "You are hereby detached from Chaplain's duties, Naval Air Station, Alameda, California. Proceed immediately and without delay. Report for duty to L.E. Gehres, Commanding Officer, *USS Franklin, CV 13*."

"Hey, Father! Were going to be shipmates," John said, delight in his voice. "Hey Beck! Hey you guys! Come here. Father O'Callahan's going to be our new chaplain."

They all gathered around O'Callahan and congratulated him.

"Welcome aboard, sir," Beckley said. "It'll be an honor to have you on the *Franklin*."

O'Callahan laughed. "It's sure a happy coincidence, Chief." He shook hands with Beckley and then Sullivan. "I fell in love with the *Franklin* the first time you guys brought her into Pearl."

"When are you coming aboard, sir?" Beckley asked.

"My gear's all packed. It's right over there near the door. I'm going aboard right after I leave here."

"That's great, Father," Sullivan said. "Maybe we can all go back together."

"Sounds good to me, Chief," O'Callahan replied. He paused and looked carefully at Beckley. "Chief, I've got a heavy case of books with my gear," he said. "Do you think your guys can help me get it aboard?"

"Sure, Father, we'll be happy to get it aboard," Beckley replied.

"Tell the lads to be very careful with it."

"Why, Father? Books don't break," Beckley said.

"These books might break," O'Callahan replied with a wink.

About five-thirty, the party thinned out to just John and Sandy and their relatives. Sandy's friends and classmates had left about four-thirty. Father O'Callahan, with his new shipmates lugging his heavy box of books, left shortly thereafter. While Helen and Louise repacked the wedding presents, Elena tidied up by stacking the cups, glasses and plates and emptying the ashtrays.

John took Sandy's hand and guided her onto the terrace. The winter sun was just sinking below the horizon. It turned San Francisco Bay into a sea of gold. John put his arm around Sandy's waist and they stood there, watching the beautiful scene in silence. Then he drew her close and kissed her. "You'd better change, Honey," he said rubbing his nose against hers. "I'd like to get our trip underway."

Sandy put her arms around his neck and hugged him. "So would I," she said.

When Sandy emerged from the club's dressing room, she had changed into a beautiful powder blue suit and a matching pillbox hat. Under her jacket, she wore a stylish white blouse that buttoned daintily up to a beautiful sapphire necklace.

John was speechless. "You're so beautiful, Honey," he finally said.

There were more hugs, and kisses and tears of happiness when they started to leave.

John extended his hand to his new father-in-law. "I don't know how to thank you," he said.

Mark took his hand and turned the handshake into a hug. "No thanks are necessary, John. Drive carefully."

As they drove southwest toward Oakland harbor, John said, "Your parents are wonderful, Honey. I never dreamed they'd get us a honeymoon suite at the Alta Mira Hotel."

Sandy reached over and caressed John's cheek. "Yes, they really are," she said.

When they arrived at the Golden Gate Bridge, John gave a little cheer. "Hey! We're almost there," he said as he paid the toll and started over the massive bridge to Sausalito.

They arrived at the Alta Mira. The doorman opened the car door and said, "You must be Mr. and Mrs. Oxler. Congratulations and welcome."

At the registration desk, it was the same.

"Mr. and Mrs. John Oxler," the registration clerk said.

This startled John—someone calling them Mr. and Mrs. Oxler. He and Sandy were *really* married. The realization surprised and delighted him. He looked at Sandy. She seemed to be having much the same experience.

"Welcome. You'll be in Suite 38," the clerk said. "It has a bay view and a romantic terrace. I think you'll like it."

Their suite was elegant. It was richly decorated in shades of gray and gold, with a beautiful fireplace and French doors that opened onto a terrace. From there, they had a spectacular view of the bay with San Francisco in the background. A bottle of champagne chilled on the coffee table. John tipped the bellboy, and he left. Then he sat on the couch and stretched his legs on the coffee table. "Boy, is this great! Would you like a glass of champagne, Honey?" he called to Sandy, who was looking over the bedroom.

"Please," she called back. "I'll be out in a minute."

When she came out, she'd taken off her suit jacket and shoes. She walked over to John and he handed her a glass of champagne. He lifted his glass, "To you, Mrs. Oxler. To the beautiful Mrs. Oxler."

Sandy beamed and raised her glass. "To you, my Darling, I love you with all my heart."

They had a sip of champagne. Then John took her glass and with his, carefully put them on the table. He took Sandy in his arms and kissed her. At first it was a gently kiss; then as the kiss lengthened, they became more passionate. John moved his hand to Sandy's breasts and she pressed her hand down firmly on his. John began to unbutton her blouse, all the while looking into her eyes. He saw pure trust, so he continued. He unbuttoned each button until her entire blouse was open, exposing a beautiful white satin bra. The blouse dropped to the floor. John leaned to kiss the delicate skin above Sandy's bra. He wanted her now, but he wanted to take time to adore everything about her, too. He kissed her neck and unfastened her bra. It fell to the floor. The beauty of her breasts startled him. He unbuttoned her skirt, and Sandy wiggled out of it. It dropped to the floor. She was standing there in her hose and panties.

John picked her up and kissed her. He carried her to the bedroom. Sandy took her hose and panties off. John took off his clothes and dropped them in a heap at the side of the bed.

He lay down beside her and drew her to him. Sandy's eyes were sparkling, as he had never seen them sparkle before. "Sandy, I love you," he said. "You can't imagine how many times I've dreamed of this moment."

"So have I, Darling," Sandy said.

John kissed her lips, then her neck, and slowly worked up to her ear. He blew his breath into it. Sandy responded by running her fingers over his face and through his hair. Their breathing became heavy. He felt her hand slide down his chest. He felt it tremble and withdraw. He took her hand in his and together their hands moved to his groin. She groaned slightly as she touched him. "I love you, John," she whispered. "I'm nervous, Darling, but I trust and want you."

Their lovemaking began in earnest. They moved in unison, both in the most passionate embrace of their lives. All the love they felt for each other cascaded into unrestrained ecstasy. Then exhausted, they fell asleep in each other's arms.

The next morning John awoke early. He rolled over and looked at Sandy. The sheet covering her had worked down exposing her breasts. He felt a surge of passion. He reached over to nudge her awake. At the last moment he stopped. She was sleeping so peacefully. She must still be exhausted from the wedding. He slipped out of bed and quietly put on his shorts and trousers. He placed his hand on the half-empty bottle of champagne. The ice around it had melted, but it was still cool. He poured himself a glass and stepped out on the terrace. The beautiful panorama of San Francisco Bay greeted him. In the distance, he could see an *Essex* Class carrier steaming toward him. Could it be the *Franklin*? He watched it for a while and realized it was. He stuck his head back into the bedroom. Sandy was awake and had slipped into her robe.

"Honey, come out here," John said.

"Why, John?"

"The *Franklin's* coming."

John stepped back into the bedroom. "Here, let me get you a glass of champagne. We can drink a toast to Beckley, Sullivan and the guys as she goes by."

Sandy took the glass of champagne and they stepped back onto the terrace. They sipped champagne and watched the *Franklin* steam toward them. When the carrier got close, John stood and started to wave. Seamen on the flight deck waved back.

"John, they're waving back! Do you know those men?"

"No, I don't think so, they're too far away to recognize."

"Then why are they waving back?"

"Sailors almost always wave back when they're waved at, Honey."

John continued to wave. Sandy watched him with amused interest. At that moment he looked like a big overgrown boy. She loved seeing this side of him. The *Franklin* steamed past them. She moved slowly under the Golden Gate Bridge and faded out of sight. They watched until she did.

Sandy pressed her body gently against the outside of John's thigh. "Let's go back to bed, Darling," she said with a smile.

CHAPTER TWENTY-TWO

8 December, 1944
With the Third Fleet
Ulithi Lagoon, Caroline Islands

The Pacific sun rose above the eastern horizon as the PBM carrying Fleet Admiral Ernest King settled gracefully into the water in Ulithi Atoll. Admiral King had come to Ulithi to be a liaison for the Joint Chiefs of Staff and Admiral Nimitz. The purpose of his trip was to define and expand the future goals for *Operation Victorious*. A meeting was scheduled at 09:00 in the wardroom of the *USS Enterprise*.

At 07:30 he was piped aboard and welcomed by Admirals Bill Halsey, Ray Spruance and Tom Kinkaid. After they exchanged salutes and pleasantries, King said, "Okay, now who's here?"

"Just about everybody, sir," Admiral Halsey said. "Mitscher, Burke, McCain, Davison, Lee, Turner, Conolly, 'Jocko' Clark."

"And," Admiral Kinkaid said, " Oldendorf, Wilkenson, Cunningham, Brogan, Berkey and Barbey."

"Did Admiral Ingram make it in from Europe?" King asked.

"Yes sir," Spruance replied.

"That's great. We expect intensified Japanese submarine activities the farther North we go. Admiral Ingram is an expert on anti-submarine warfare. He kicked the crap out of the Kraut subs in the Atlantic. We'll sure need him here."

King looked at his watch. "Meeting time still at 09:00 hours?

"That's right, Admiral."

"Could you show me to my quarters? It was a long flight, and I'd like to get a shower and rest for about forty-five minutes."

"Right away, sir."

Exactly at 09:00 King walked into the smoke-filled conference room. "Wow. This air is tough on non-smokers. Chief," he said to the master-at-arms, "would you open up a few of those port holes and get a couple of fans in here?"

When the fans were running and the smoke had begun to clear, King addressed the assembled Admirals of the Pacific Fleet.

"Gentlemen," he said, "I'm here on behalf of the Joint Chiefs of Staff and Admiral Nimitz. In this connection I'd like to tell you that Admiral Nimitz sends you his best regards. He was upset that he was not able to be here himself. He's got a very severe cold—one so bad that he was confined to the hospital in Pearl Harbor when I left Wednesday.

"This morning," he said with a smile, "I'm delighted to tell you that we have completed the final phases of our strategy for the conquest of the Japanese Empire. We're here to discuss our next steps in *Operation Victorious*. These steps will lead us to our final victory. That's the happy part of my message, gentlemen. The sad part of the message is it's estimated it will take an additional twenty-four months, or more, to get an unconditional surrender." He paused and looked slowly about the wardroom.

There was silence.

"Now, concerning the progress of *Victorious*," he continued. "You all know that General MacArthur's Sixth Army under General Walt Krueger is marching on Manila. The campaign to free the Philippines and liberate Allied prisoners is now in full swing. As soon as the First Cavalry Division flushes the Japanese out of Bataan and Corregidor, Krueger will attack Mindoro, Negros and Mindanao and complete the liberation. Admiral Kinkaid's Seventh Fleet will provide sea and air cover for this operation."

King stopped and acknowledged Kinkaid. Then he continued, "Admiral Nimitz and the Joint Chiefs of Staff thought these islands could be 'leapfrogged,' but General MacArthur convinced them they should be recaptured. He wants the Japs out of every square foot of the Philippines. Regarding areas north of the Philippines, the timetable which appears on this chart will generally apply."

An aide placed a large hard-back outline labeled *Operation Victorious* on a tripod beside him. He pointed to the caption and said, "As you can see, this represents implementation of *Victorious* from December 1944 through November 1946—a period of just less than two years. This is the amount of time the JCS estimate will be needed for the invasion and conquest of the Japanese Empire."

He pointed to the Island of Iwo Jima. "The first step in this final phase of the plan is to attack and conquer Iwo Jima. As you can see, this is planned for the third week of January, 1945. The Air Corps needs Iwo as a halfway base for Superforts if emergency landings are necessary on their flights to or from Japan. It will also be used as a base for fighters protecting them. I'm sorry to report the Japanese know this attack is coming. Despite very heavy sea and air attacks, they're turning Iwo into a fortress."

He looked over the gathering of powerful naval commanders. "In hindsight, if we had attacked Iwo right after we took Tinian, it would have been easier. We know from aerial photos that they're now digging connecting tunnels to the caves in Mount Suribachi, installing concrete mortar and machine gun emplacements and adding tons of heavy artillery to their defenses. As some of you already know, nothing we've been able to throw at them has been able to stop them, so now it's a lot tougher."

"The next step in this phase of *Victorious* is the invasion of Okinawa," he said after he had a sip of water. "As you can see on the chart, this advances us to within eighty miles of the Japanese mainland. This operation is scheduled around the first of April, next year.

"Our third target is the invasion of Kyushu," he said as he pointed to Kyushu on the *Victorious* chart. "Here. The southernmost island in Japan. The approximate date for this attack is between October fifteenth and November fifteenth next year. Then comes Shikoku, an island less than a hundred miles from Osaka and just a little over one hundred and fifty miles from Tokyo. This is scheduled for early in 1946."

King pointed to Honshu, the primary island in the Japanese Archipelago. "Finally comes the attack and conquest of Honshu and the capture of the cities of Osaka, Kyoto and

Tokyo. It's scheduled to begin sometime between July and November of 1946." He paused and put the pointer back on the podium. "Only God knows how *accurate* these projections are—or how long they'll take—or what we'll *finally* have to do to implement them," he said. "We know for certain the Japanese will fight like hell for every inch of their homeland and the fighting will be frantic—especially when we get to Honshu. Both the Army and the Marines are estimating that Honshu's capture will take in excess of three million men and you all know what that might mean in terms of American casualties."

"Well, that's the plan in a nutshell," he concluded. "Are there any questions?"

Admiral Conolly raised his hand. "Any possibility the schedule can be shortened, Admiral?"

"Barring a miracle, probably not. I know another two years of war is not something any of us look forward to. But at best, it will take this long, maybe a lot longer. The closer we get to Tokyo, the more desperate the Japs become. All you have to do is look at their increased use of the kamikaze to see that."

Admiral Charles Ingram raised his hand. "I've been in the European Theater until just a few weeks ago, Admiral. This whole business of the 'kamikaze' is baffling to me. It's hard to believe that we're fighting people who will crash planes into enemy ships. What the hell *is* all this kamikaze stuff?" he asked.

King nodded toward Commander Arthur Yoshimura, his Intelligence Officer and his expert on Japanese strategies. "Yosh," he said, "could you explain the kamikaze to us? Considering the amount of damage we're suffering from these attacks, maybe some of the rest of us would like to hear more about them, too."

Yoshimura joined King at the podium. "The word kamikaze means 'heavenly wind,' he began. "It comes from a famous event in Japanese history. A huge Chinese invasion force, sailing to invade Japan in the sixteenth century, was blown away in a typhoon. It saved Japan. The Japanese believe the gods sent this heavenly wind."

"But what does this have to do with what they're doing now?" Ingram asked.

"They're looking for another miracle, Admiral," Yoshimura explained. "They're desperate. Their air force is impaired. We've crippled their Navy. They have to protect their homeland, no matter what it takes."

"With human bombs? That's crazy!"

"Yes, sir, to us, but that doesn't stop them from using them. They'll do anything to try to quell their fear and desperation. They'll use anything and everything they can. They're even using teenagers as pilots. Some as young as fourteen years old."

Silence greeted this fact. Then from the back of the room, someone said. "That's my youngest son's age."

"I know it's hard to believe, but the kamikaze is their way of retaliating for the defeats they've suffered recently. It's a tactic devised to try to destroy our Navy, especially our carrier forces." He paused for a sip of water. "From messages we've decoded recently,"
he continued, "we also know that our B-29's are causing heavy damage in Japanese cities, and there's great fear and anxiety in Japan."

"So thousands of Japanese boys in their early teens are called to a duty that is certain to end their lives?" Ingram asked.

"That's right, sir. It sounds crazy but that's exactly what's happening. The Japanese tiger is fighting for its life."

"Yosh," Ingram said, still perplexed. "Your ancestors were Japanese. Is it in their blood? Would you do it?"

"Hell no, sir," Yoshimura replied. "Do you think I'm crazy?"

His reply brought a wave of laughter.

"It's still goddamned hard to believe," Ingram said.

"Not when you're being attacked by them," Admiral "Jocko" Clark replied with a huge grin.

This brought more laughter.

Admiral King moved back behind the podium. "We've been on a kamikaze alert ever since these attacks began early last month. We've expanded the alert again and again. No one ever dreamed when these attacks began that they would be so widespread and intense."

Yoshimura raised his hand and was acknowledged. "There's a practical side, too, Admiral. These tactics allow the Japanese to use obsolete aircraft, even biplanes like the old Val. Their pilots need very little training to fly the kamikaze. Even if one is killed, his plane's momentum often carries it into the target."

About that time a chief radioman came into the conference room. "Admiral, sir, I'm sorry to interrupt," he apologized, "but we just received a message for Admiral Kinkaid from General MacArthur. I thought I'd better let you know, sir."

King nodded him toward Kinkaid.

The radioman made his way around the table and handed Kinkaid the message. He read it, then said, "The Japanese are entrenched in the tunnels and caves on Corregidor. General MacArthur's invasion is stalled there. He can't get to them with air bombardment. The only way he can attack those caves is by sea. He wants two or three cruisers to get in close and fire directly into their mouths."

Kinkaid turned to Admiral Conolly. "The Philippines are the General's grand obsession," he said. "He wants them back and he wants them back now! What ships in the Third Fleet are near enough to Corregidor to get there quickly?"

"If I were picking," replied Conolly, "I'd pick *Santa Fe*, *Columbia* and *Denver*, Admiral. They're very near, and I think they're three of the best we've got. Captain Fitz on the *Santa Fe* can maneuver a cruiser around a dime and give you five cents in change. The other skippers are great, too."

He turned to Bill Halsey. "Bill, do you mind if I borrow them again?"

Halsey smiled impishly. "We're right down there ready to help you and the General any way we can, Admiral."

This brought laughter and some scattered applause.

Kinkaid ignored it and said, "Thanks. Can we expedite this?"

"I'll attend to it personally. I'll be back with the Third Fleet the day after tomorrow,

Tom. I don't want to put it on the wire because our position there could be exposed. We're trying hard to keep our movements a surprise right now, but I'll do it the minute I get back."

11 December, 1944
With Task Force 38, Third Fleet
80 Miles NNW of Manila

The *Santa Fe*, as part of a huge Task Group composed of nearly all of the ships in Halsey's Third Fleet, was steaming southwest toward the South China Sea on a secret seek-and-destroy mission. This bold, skillfully engineered incursion was designed to destroy any Japanese sea power that remained and to demonstrate to the Japanese that the American Navy could now take its firepower anywhere, at anytime, without fear. At 07:00 Halsey, who had just returned from Ulithi, was on the bridge of the *New Jersey*.

His first order of business was to notify the light cruisers. "Rich," he said to his Exec, "would you have this message sent right away. Send it by semaphore," he added, "I don't want to take the chance of exposing our position."

Captain Fitz was in conn on the *Santa Fe* when Tom Rashinski rushed onto the bridge with Halsey's message.

"Message from Admiral Halsey, sir," he said. "We just got it."

Fitz took the message and read it aloud, "The cruisers *Santa Fe*, *Columbia* and *Denver* were recommended by Admiral Conolly to assist General Douglas MacArthur in the conquest of Corregidor. Detach from TF 38 and proceed at maximum speed to Manila Bay. MacArthur wants some bulls-eye shooting to root the Japs out of caves there. He says this is the only way it can be done. So let's show the General our seamanship and marksmanship. Get in close, and blast their ass. I have every confidence in you."

"Okay," Fitz said. "Let's get with it."

The *Santa Fe*, *Columbia* and *Denver* pulled away from the huge fleet and steamed at high speed toward Manila.

When Tom returned to his station he was glowing. "We were especially selected by Admiral Conolly to assist General MacArthur," he said to Carl Corini. "This is something we can tell our kids about."

"Hell, yesss," said the ever-pessimistic Corini, "That is if we live long enough to have kids. Don't kid yourself, mate, this war ain't over yet. There's still plenty of fighting left. Don't make it sound like some goddamn waltz through the tulips."

"Who's making it a waltz through the tulips?"

"You are. What makes you think you'll live long enough to have kids?"

"What makes you think I won't?"

"The Japs—the war—the kamikaze for openers, mate."

"Aww, screw you, Corini, you're a pain in the ass. You always look at the bleak side of things." He turned away from Corini and began to scan the horizon with his binoculars. In his heart he had to admit Corini made a good point. A very good point.

13 December
Manila Bay
Philippine Islands

As the three cruisers approached the entrance to Manila Bay, the island fortress of Corregidor appeared through the early morning haze.

Fitz squinted at the rocky fortress through binoculars. "It's going to be tricky. We'll have to maneuver in that small channel. The chart says it's less than three miles wide. It looks like there's a lot of crap in there too, all the way from shoals to sunken wrecks. Get Captain Hertz and Captain Peters on the wire," he said to Tom.

"Aye, sir."

Tom listened intently as the three commanders worked out a strategy. Fitz and the *Santa Fe* would go into the channel first and establish a "path," then *Columbia* would follow with *Denver* standing by to protect against possible hostile fire from Corregidor. As soon as *Santa Fe* completed her bombardment, *Columbia* would take her place, with *Denver* next in line and with *Santa Fe* standing guard. Finally *Denver* would complete the shelling.

Fitz maneuvered the *Santa Fe* deftly through the shoals and partially sunken wrecks. When they were within a thousand yards of the beach, he got a message from the gun turrets:

"Coming on target, sir."

"Bearing 185."

"Range 1003 yards."

"Commence firing," Fitz ordered. "Fire at will! Drill right into the mouths of those caves. Strafe anything that moves."

"Aye sir."

As soon as the first salvo exploded against the solid, rock-faced north edge of the island, Fitz got a message from an American infantry unit on the recently occupied island of Caballo, located in the channel nearby.

"You're very close, *Santa Fe*," the voice on the radio said. "Let us direct your fire— you'll get 'em in there then."

They wired new coordinates. *Santa Fe*'s gunners quickly adjusted their fire control.

"New coordinates in place, sir."

"Request permission to resume firing."

"Fire at will."

From the bridge, Tom watched the bombardment through binoculars.

"We're getting some direct hits now," he said to Corini. "I can see the shells explode inside the tunnels."

"Have you heard how deep those fuckin' tunnels are?" Corini asked.

"I don't give a damn how deep they are, we're putting them right in the holes," Tom replied.

The *Santa Fe's* five- and six-inch guns fired one salvo after another until her guns began to overheat. She moved out to let her guns cool and *Columbia* steamed in and took her place. With the firing coordinates established, *Columbia's* accuracy was as good as *Santa Fe's*.

The shelling went on most of the day. When it stopped, the mouths to the caves were heavily damaged and smoke was billowing out of them.

"How much good do you think we did?" Fitz asked Ed Wassern.

"Hard to tell, Captain, but MacArthur sure as hell can't complain about our marksmanship," Wassern replied.

A radioman came on to the bridge. "Message from Commander in Chief Pacific Fleet, sir."

"CinCPac?"

"Yes sir. Admiral Nimitz himself."

Fitz read the message, then said, "Nimitz wants us to defer to Subic Bay and stand by until they can evaluate the damage we caused. He says MacArthur might want more bombardments."

"Anything else?" Wassern asked.

"Yeah. MacArthur congratulated us for our excellent seamanship and marksmanship," Fitz said phlegmatically. "We'll know by morning whether we have to go back in." He paused. "Nimitz sent us congratulations, too," he added. "He said our marksmanship was excellent; that it was a tribute to the whole fleet."

Wassern nodded. "That's nice to hear, even if they don't know how much damage we caused," he said.

Helmsman," Fitz commanded. "Come to course 310 degrees."

"Aye, sir."

The three cruisers turned Northwest and headed for Subic Bay. The bright winter sun was beginning to sink behind the Pacific horizon when the entrance to the bay came into view.

"I'd like try to work in some liberty for the crew," Fitz said, "but I don't think it's possible. We can't take the chance of having half of the crew ashore and get an order to go back in."

Tom was distressed when he heard the Captain's words. He was deeply hoping he could get ashore. He thought about last time *Santa Fe* was in Subic Bay shortly after the war began. It was then that he met Angela. The bittersweet memories of his one night with her came flooding back to him. He realized her beauty still haunted him. He was this close….

The Captain's voice brought his thoughts back to the bridge. "Damn, Ed," he lamented to his Exec, "we put on a hell of a show for MacArthur and we've been at sea for a lot of months, but there just won't be time."

"Yeah, it's too bad, Captain," Wassern concurred. "Come to think of it, there're some pretty nice little towns around here; Subic, San Nicholas, Oranti. I don't know what they look like now, but when I pulled liberty here a few years ago they were very friendly and some of the women were gorgeous."

Tom smiled sadly. "Yes, sir, they sure were," he said. He picked up his binoculars, walked to the edge of the bridge and focused them on the area where Oranti was located. His thoughts carried him back to the small bar at the edge of that haunting little town. It was there that he met her…he was sitting at the end of the bar having a beer. He'd been at sea, and it was the first drink he'd had in some time. He was enjoying the warm feelings the beer sent through his body when the bar doors opened and there she was—so beautiful she almost took his breath away. She had the slender figure of a Philippine woman and the classic face of a Western beauty. It was like he was having a dream. How in the hell did a woman this beautiful get to this shitty part of the world, he'd wondered.

She sat down at the other end of the bar, and as she did, she'd looked at him and smiled. He stared at her, so perplexed he didn't realize he was staring.

She ordered a drink and began to toy with the ice cubes in her glass.

His whole body filled with passion and excitement. He could remember his heart beating rapidly; how he'd ached to have her look his way again. Just one more time….

Then she looked toward him again and whispered something to the barkeep. The barkeep nodded and looked at him. Then he walked the length of the bar and said, "Sailor, the lady wonders if she could join you down here."

Tom couldn't believe what he heard. "Me?" he asked in shock.

"Yes, *you*," the bartender replied, as he looked curiously around the otherwise vacant bar.

"What does she want?" he'd asked.

"I'm not sure," the barkeep replied.

"Is she a prostitute?"

"I don't think so, sir. She looks like a dignified woman to me."

"Okay, but what does she want?"

"I really don't know sir," the barkeep said. "But things here are very bad. There are no jobs in Oranti. No money for food or clothing."

He'd looked at the beautiful woman again. Her eyes were focused on the drink in front of her. "All right, tell her it's okay."

The barkeep walked back to the woman and whispered to her. She'd picked up her drink and walked hesitantly to where Tom was sitting.

"You're an American," she said in English without an accent. "Welcome. Very few Americans come to Oranti."

Now Tom was even more mystified. "You speak English like an American," he said in a tone that reflected how puzzled he was.

"Yes," she said as she moved onto the stool beside him. "My father was an American, my mother Filipino. I learned to speak both languages."

Tom looked at her long, shiny dark hair and her beautiful olive skin. She had the darkest brown eyes he had ever seen.

"My name is Angela," she said, extending her hand.

Tom took her hand. "I'm Tom," he said, feeling the warmth and delicate texture of her palm.

She smiled and revealed beautiful white teeth. "You're on a ship, somewhere near?" she asked.

"Yeah," Tom replied.

"You live here?" Tom asked.

"Yes. For many years."

"You married?" Tom asked, hoping the answer was no.

"I was," she said sadly. "My husband died of malaria a year ago."

"Oh, I'm sorry," Tom said. "Would you like another drink?"

"No," she said. "This one is enough."

"The barkeep said there is great poverty here," Tom ventured.

"Yes," she replied, "and it will be worse when the Japanese come. They've invaded the north part of our island and are moving south rapidly."

"Yes, I know," Tom had replied. "And it doesn't look like there's much that can stop them."

She'd smiled a distant smile. "It's all so frightening for me," she said, her voice reflecting her fear.

There was a long pause. Then she said, "I don't know how to say this. I'm very frightened and embarrassed. I need money for food. Would you like to be with me, Tom?"

"Be with you?" he'd asked.

"Yes," she replied. "Be with me in bed." She paused. "Tom, there's no economy here," she said sadly. "There's no money. There are no jobs. The Japanese will be here in a few weeks and I fear there will be even greater poverty. I have a three-year-old daughter and a grandmother who's very old. I must do what I can to help and protect them."

Tom didn't know how to respond to what she said. Moments passed.

"I'm sorry," she said, slowly standing, "I didn't mean to make you uncomfortable."

"No. Don't leave. Please don't leave," Tom said. He put his hand lightly on her arm to restrain her. "You're so beautiful, I just didn't know what to say."

Angela sat back down.

He thought a minute, then took out his wallet and said, "Here's twenty dollars. Will that help you?"

He remembered her eyes widening. "Twenty American dollars. That'll help very much. I don't know how to thank you," she'd said.

"You don't have to," Tom replied.

She looked down at the floor, then she said, "Maybe I can invite you to my house for a bowl of soup. It's all I have...."

The blare of the ship's loudspeakers interrupted his thoughts and jerked him back to the present.

"Attention all hands! Prepare to enter Subic Bay!"

Tom moved to another area of the bridge. He again trained his binoculars on the shoreline and resumed his thoughts....

They'd walked to Angela's house in silence. When they arrived, she'd unlocked the door and they went inside…he looked the place over carefully. There was an empty child's bed, a chest and some old toys in an adjoining room. He peeked into the kitchen. It was empty. He was surprised it was so clean and well kept.

"You don't have to be so cautious," he remembered her saying as he looked around. "There's no one else here."

"I didn't mean to offend you," Tom tried to explain. "It's a foreign country and…."

"You don't have to explain. I understand."

"Where's your daughter?"

"She's with my Grandmother. She stays with her most of the time. I miss her very much."

He remembered a beautiful old oak table…he sat down at it and looked at Angela again…she was even more beautiful than she was in the bar. His body flooded with warmth and passion…he was feeling sensations he'd never felt before.

Angela took off her coat. She was wearing a black, form-fitting dress with an intricate metal belt inlayed with polished turquoise stones. She slipped off her shoes. "Would you like the soup?" she asked.

"I'm not very hungry right now," he answered.

Angela studied him for a moment. Then she put her arms around his neck.

He drew her close. "Can I kiss you?"

"Yes," she'd said. Their lips met, hesitantly at first, then with passion and yearning.

Then she broke the embrace and said, "You're warm and generous. I can't tell you how thankful I am for what you gave me."

Tom kissed her again. His affection and passion increased. He'd never had feelings like this with any woman before. "Are you sure this is okay?" he asked.

"Yes, I want you to make love to me, Tom," she'd whispered. He unbuttoned her dress and she helped him pull it over her head. He remembered his fingers shook as he removed her bra. Her breasts were firm and inviting. He kissed her again. Then he carried her to the bed in the next room.

He took off the rest of her clothes and then took off his uniform. They lay there for a few moments completely nude, just looking at each other. Then Tom put his arms around her and pulled her close to him. He kissed her, gently at first, then with passion and desire.

She responded by touching her tongue to his lips. "I want you very much, Tom," she whispered.

Tom pushed his tongue deep inside her mouth. He could hear her breathing heavily as he ran his hands over her breasts. Passion consumed them. He was filled with rapture by her body as they became one. Her breathing became heavy. Her body stiffened. She ran her fingers wildly through his hair. He was transported by the ecstasy he felt. They lay there locked in a passionate embrace, both still breathing heavily.

Angela pressed her face into his chest. "I feel safe with you here, Tom," she whispered.

Tom's feelings of warmth and tenderness increased. Angela put her arms around his neck and pulled him to her. She kissed him. It was a tender kiss filled with affection and wanting. They became as one again, lost in affection and desire. It was as though there was nothing else…anywhere in the world.

He lay quietly next to her for a long while. Then he fell asleep. When he woke up it was past midnight. He was AWOL. He'd looked at Angela lying beside him, still asleep. A wave of emotion washed through him. It was more than passion now. He'd come to truly care about this beautiful, exciting woman. He had thoughts of saying the hell with it, of just staying with her. He'd argued back and forth with himself. Finally he realized he had to go back. He reached into his wallet and took out nearly all the money he had. The he shook Angela gently and pressed the money into her hand. "Here my beautiful lady. I have to go."

She sat up. "I can't take this," she said.

"Please, take it," he'd said. "I can get more money. You need it here more than I do."

Angela took the money. She put her arms around his neck and kissed him. She held him close for a long while. When she released him, there were tears in her eyes.

It was too much. Tom kissed her again. Then, as he put on his uniform, he heard Angela crying softly into her pillow. He remembered rushing out the door and running all the way to the bus stop. When he was on the bus back to Subic, he'd tried to think of an excuse for the Duty Officer, but all he was able to think about were the wonderful memories of the last few hours with Angela….

When the bus chugged up to the bus stop in Subic it was 02:10. He was an hour and ten minutes over leave. He'd rushed to the dock and up the gangway to the quarterdeck. When he saw the officer who was on duty, he felt a little relief. It was Ensign Lowell, a supply officer and a pretty good guy.

"You're over leave, Signalman," Lowell said. "An hour and ten minutes over."

"Do you have an excuse, sailor?"

"No, sir."

Lowell seemed exasperated. He thought for a few seconds, then said, "Okay. At least you're not drunk. Go below. I'll forget this, but it's only because you're not all ginned up."

Tom remembered going below and climbing into his bunk. He was exhausted but he couldn't get to sleep. He remembered the agony he felt knowing that he might never see Angela again….

The roar of Santa Fe's anchor chain tumbling into Subic Bay startled Tom. The anchor chain's noise brought his longing thoughts to a close. Darkness now obliterated the bay and coastline. He went below, still filled with sadness and longing.

The next morning word came that MacArthur was satisfied with the bombardment. The *Santa Fe, Columbia and Denver* hoisted their anchors and steamed out of Subic Bay. Tom was on the bridge when they left. He focused his binoculars in the direction of Oranti again. A feeling of hopelessness hung heavy around his heart.

CHAPTER TWENTY-THREE

18 December, 1944
Berkeley, California
The *Franklin* Jinx

The weather turned wet and miserable. At dawn the fog was so thick it was hard to see through. At nine o'clock John and Sandy left the small, quaint apartment they'd rented to go into town. The fog still hugged the streets. A cold, thin drizzle was falling.

Sandy went into Patterson's Drug Store to pick up some toiletries while John waited for her in the car.

When Sandy came out, she was waving a copy of a magazine. "John," she said as she squeezed into the car, "there's an article on the *Franklin* in *Time* Magazine." She handed him the magazine.

"What does it say?" John asked as he took the magazine.

"I only glanced at it," Sandy said, but I think it's about what happened to the *Franklin* that caused all the damage."

Sandy's forehead wrinkled quizzically. "The caption says the *Franklin's* jinxed," she said. "What *is* this about a jinx, John?"

"Aww, it's nothing, Honey, just a bunch of foolish gossip—it probably started out because her number is CV 13. You know how superstitious some people are."

"Do you believe it?" she asked cautiously.

"Hell no, Honey. It's just empty talk. There's nothing to it."

"Does *anybody* believe it?" she pressed.

"Awww, I don't know. Maybe Beckley does, but he's from Kansas. There's a lot of superstitious people out there in Kansas."

When they got back to their apartment, John leafed through the magazine and found the article. Time Magazine, Dateline December 11, 1944**:**

WORLD BATTLEFRONTS
Jinxed Warrior?

The huge aircraft carrier *USS Franklin*, (CV 13) limped into Puget Sound and entered dry dock the victim of massive explosions caused by kamikaze strikes and the explosion of her own bombs and missiles. The damage occurred when Task Force 38, under the command of Admiral William "Bull" Halsey was launching air assaults north of Luzon in the Philippine Sea. *Franklin* was crashed by two Japanese kamikazes. The first kamikaze hit the after part of *Franklin's* flight deck and careened off but the second crashed into the bridge. Explosions and gasoline fires swept across the flight deck and spread to the hangar deck. While the first deck load of *Franklin's* planes had taken off, there were more planes on the hangar deck armed and awaiting their turn to be elevated to the flight deck.

Bombs on these planes, triggered by the gasoline fires, exploded. Missiles swooshed through the air and tore through the ship's sides. Livid fiery explosions erupted in the heavy smoke and flames. The forward elevator, that weighed thirty-two tons, was jolted up by the blasts—its plungers blown from their sockets. Explosions hurled the aft elevator into the air. It then smashed back into its well and landed at a ninety-degree angle from the horizon. Flaming aviation gasoline flowed through the hangar deck into the decks below **creating roaring fires.**

Heroic efforts by *Franklin*'s crew extinguished the fires. The carrier was badly damaged. There were a hundred fatalities. One hundred and seven men were injured.

Recent information released by the Navy Department reveals a "continuing series of mishaps and accidents" on the *Franklin* that included the midair collision of two of her Hellcats off the coast of California in May of this year.

What is the reality of the charge that the *Franklin* is jinxed? Captain Leslie Gehres, the *Franklin's* new skipper, said in a personal interview conducted on the badly damaged ship, that there was no truth to the rumor. "I'm going on record, as the skipper of this ship," he said, "that this is nonsense. The *Franklin* is not any more unlucky than any other ship in the fleet. Yes, we've had some accidents and the bad luck of a hangar deck filled with planes armed with bombs and missiles when the kamikazes hit us, but it's my job to assure you and prove to the rest of the country that there is no jinx. The *Franklin* is not jinxed. We'll prove it—take my word for that."

John read the article. When he finished, Sandy asked, "Is that how it happened?"

"Yeah, pretty much. But it was a freak accident—a bunch of crazy things—that happened one right after the other. They probably couldn't happen again in a million years."

"But how did the planes get to the ship in the first place?"

"I...I don't know," John replied. "I've thought about that a lot. They just seemed to come from nowhere. Our lookouts and gun crews were alert and our radar was working. Its hard to explain, but, damn it, *it was all a freak accident*. It could never happen again."

He looked at Sandy who was still frowning. She was not completely convinced.

Later that night, the subject came up again. They had just slipped into bed, when Sandy said, "John, that article still worries me…and your explanation of what happened didn't do much for me either. Could it be true? Could your ship be jinxed?"

"Honey, don't worry about that jinx stuff," John pleaded. "Freak accidents happen sometimes. Captain Gehres will put a stop to all that stuff…just you mark my words." Then he put his arms around her and pulled her close. He gently kissed her hair and her neck. Then he kissed her. They held each other close. Sandy finally fell asleep. But John couldn't sleep. He lay awake recreating those terrible minutes before the kamikazes broke through. He thought about them over and over. "How the hell *did* they get through?"

The next morning he awoke at six and looked over at the calendar. It was the nineteenth of December. He'd started using the extra days of his travel-time. He found it hard to believe that his leave had gone by so fast. It seemed like he'd just got here, and now, in a few days, he'd have to go back. He looked at Sandy. She was still asleep. He thought about how wonderful each day with her had been. How happy he was to get to really know her and how he loved everything he found. He adored the way she smiled, the way she giggled when he tickled her feet, the loving way she sometimes looked at him. He loved everything about her. In his mind, he tried to push away the day he had to go back.

He got up and put on the coffee. He puzzled over the article in *Time* again. Sandy got up and came into the kitchen. "Morning, Honey," she said, stretching her arms to come awake. "We have to go shopping. I haven't done any Christmas shopping yet"

"Okay," John said. "I need to pick up some things, too." On the way downtown, John turned on the radio. The airwaves were filled with Christmas music. Bing Crosby was singing one of his newest hits, *White Christmas:*

I'm dreaming of a white Christmas, Just like the ones I used to know….

"Not in Berkeley," John said.

"What?" Sandy asked.

"I said not in Berkeley, not a white Christmas here. Maybe in Colorado there will be. It snows a lot on Christmas in Colorado."

They turned into the downtown area. Christmas decorations were everywhere. Windows in shops were filled with red, green and gold ornaments. Restaurants had glittering trees. The barbershop and library were decked out in their best Christmas finery and even the streetlights had their tinsel and bows. As they got out of the car, they were greeted by the sound of more Christmas music drifting out of stores. As they walked along Shattuck Avenue, John became aware that there were war posters everywhere: A stern-looking Uncle Sam pointing straight ahead with the caption: *I Want You.* A beautiful young woman in a Navy uniform urged: OK! *Enlist In The Waves.* A handsome naval aviator in the cockpit of a plane proclaiming: *You buy 'em, we'll fly 'em*! *Buy Defense Bonds.* When they walked past the Navy recruiting station there was a mural of three muscular sailors firing a five-inch naval rifle: *Fire Back! Join the Navy*, it urged. The war was really never very far away.

"Where are you going?" John asked.

"I have some things I have to pick up for you."

"Surprise things?" John asked.

"Yes, surprise things."

"What are they?" John asked.

"I can't tell you, silly," Sandy said with a smile. "They wouldn't be a surprise then."

"I've got a couple of things that I have to pick up for you, too, Honey," John said.

"Surprises?" Sandy asked.

"Yes."

"What are they?"

John just smiled and shook his head. "I'll meet you back here in about an hour," he said.

Sandy nodded. They walked in the same direction.

"Are you following me?" Sandy asked.

"No, not really. I'm going this way."

They walked to the end of the block. Then they both turned into Hamond's Jewelry Store, giggling as they went.

Mr. Hamond saw them come in and waved. "You coming to pick up your surprise gifts at the same time?" he asked smiling.

John and Sandy shared his humor. The three laughed together.

"Yes. I guess we are—would you please wrap them so they will still be a surprise?" Sandy asked.

"They're already wrapped and in separate packages," the jeweler said as he produced the gifts. "I've put your names on the cards on them. They won't get mixed up. Congratulations again. You make a beautiful couple."

When they reached the door of their apartment, John said, "Honey, I've got an urge to carry you across the threshold again."

"John," Sandy protested gently. "I've got these packages and my scarf and purse."

John took the packages and her purse and scarf out of her arms and set them on the doorstep. Then he picked her up and carried her into their tiny apartment. When he put her down, she put her arms around him and kissed him.

"What a wonderful thing to think of, Honey, " she said. "I hope you'll always be this romantic."

"With you, Honey, that'll be very easy."

"Even when I get old?"

"Yes. You'll always be beautiful to me."

John built a fire in the little fireplace. Sandy began to prepare dinner. She poured a glass of wine for herself and one for John. He studied the wine bottle. "Cabernet Sauvignon—from the Mondavi Vineyards in the Napa Valley. I didn't know they made wine in the Napa Valley. I didn't even know they made wine in California, for that matter," he said.

"Yes, they do," Sandy replied, "California wines are starting to get well known. Some people say the grapes they grow up in the Napa and Sonoma valleys are even better than those they grow in France."

"Mondavi. Is that an Italian name?" he asked.

"I'm sure it is." Sandy replied.

John laughed. "I learn something new every day—the only Italian wine I knew about in Pueblo was called 'Dago Red'. The Italians made their own and stored it in barrels out in a wine cellar." He took another sip. "This is really smooth. Some of that homemade stuff was powerful. It'd make your hair stand on end."

John watched Sandy move about the kitchen. She was beautiful. Everything she did, even little things in the kitchen, touched his heart.

After dinner they sat on the sofa, watched the fire and listened to Christmas carols. It seemed like every station they tuned to was playing them. It was only six days until Christmas Eve. The thought that in three days he had to go back crossed his mind—with this came the certainty of being in harm's way. He tightened his arm around Sandy. "Honey," he said, "I know I have to leave in a few days, and it's going to be very hard for both of us."

"That article about *Franklin's* jinx makes it even harder," Sandy said.

"It's been on your mind, hasn't it," John said.

"Yes, I'm sorry, but it comes back sometimes. I've tried to put it out of my mind but it still creeps back."

"I know. Sometimes feelings like that hit me, too," John said. "But one thing is certain for me, Sandy. I'm going to come back to you. I just know that. Your love will help me through. I believe this with all my heart, Honey."

"John, where will we live when you come home?" Sandy asked, apparently relieved by what John said. "I'd like a nice house somewhere with a yard filled with lots of flowers and trees and maybe a white picket fence."

"Where would you like to live, Honey?" John asked.

"Oh, somewhere in the Bay Area, maybe with a view of the ocean."

"What about Colorado?"

"There's no ocean in Colorado."

"We've got great mountains, Honey," John said with the hint of a smile. "Bigger and taller than any around here."

"If we live in the Bay area we can have a boat," Sandy replied, realizing John was teasing.

"Maybe by then I'll have had all the sailing I want for a lifetime," John said, his smile widening.

"John…" Sandy protested.

"We'll live wherever you want, Honey," John said. "I just want you to be happy. That's the most important thing for me."

Sandy put her arms around him and hugged him. "Thank you, John," she said. She put her head on her husband's shoulder and tightened her embrace. "I feel so safe when you're near me, Darling."

They held each other for a long while in quiet, absorbed in each other's presence. Then Sandy asked, "John, have you ever been to Lake Tahoe?"

"No, I haven't, Honey."

"It's beautiful up there," Sandy said. "The lake is gorgeous and the trees are wonderful. Some are fifty and sixty feet tall."

"That sounds like the mountains and trees in Colorado."

"I love it there," Sandy said. "If we live somewhere here, we could spend vacations there. That would give you a taste of home."

"It sure would, Honey."

They became quiet again. Then Sandy sighed and asked, "John, how many children do you want?"

"I don't know, Honey. I really haven't given that too much thought."

"I'd like two, a boy and a girl," Sandy said.

"Maybe three," John said. "Two boys and a girl or two girls and a boy. If it's two girls, I'd want them to look just like you."

Sandy ran her fingers through his hair, then let her hand drop gently to his cheek. "John," she asked, "what would you think if I was pregnant now?"

John was startled by her question.

"Are you?" he asked.

"No. At least I don't think so."

"Wouldn't it be better if we waited until the war ended, Honey? A family is a big responsibility. What about your studies?"

"Oh, I could handle both," Sandy replied. "I think it'd be wonderful to have a son or daughter waiting with me, when you got home."

"Yeah, but what if something should happen to me?"

"John, you just told me *nothing* could happen to you," Sandy replied. "Wouldn't a son or daughter's love make that even more certain?"

"Gee, I haven't really thought about that, Honey," John said, still a little dismayed. "Yes, I think it would." He paused, then said, "Something about this makes me think you might be pregnant now."

"Well, I don't think so, but how can we be sure I'm not. What if I am?"

"Oh, if that's the case, I think it would be the most wonderful thing that ever happened to me, Honey," John said.

Sandy's eyes sparkled. "I'm so happy you said that, Darling," she said as she moved closer to him. "I just had to know it was okay if I was."

Sandy put her head on John's chest and cuddled close to him. "I'll always love you, Darling," she said. "No matter how far away you are, I'll be with you in spirit every moment."

John took her into his arms and kissed her. Then he said, "And I promise I'll come back, Honey, no matter how tough it gets."

The fire flickered. Sandy put her arm around John's shoulder and snuggled even closer. Their bodies seemed to be as one, filled with the love, joy and rapture of the moment.

John kissed Sandy to seal the promises they'd just made. Then they fell asleep in each other's arms.

By the next morning the weather had changed. A storm blew in overnight and it was cloudy with a light drizzle falling. Sandy was up early. John got up and peeked around the bedroom doorway. She was sitting on the sofa in her robe thumbing through a magazine.

"Hi, Honey," John called.

Sandy looked up. "Oh darn, I was going to surprise you. I was going to serve you breakfast in bed."

"Really? I never had breakfast in bed before. You better watch out. You'll spoil me."

"I want this to be a memory that you take with you. Then every morning at breakfast you'll think about me."

John walked over and took Sandy in his arms. "I'll think of you all the time, not just at breakfast."

Sandy served breakfast on a silver tray they'd received as a wedding gift, then sat down beside him and had her own.

After breakfast, Sandy said, "John, I have to go over to the university library. There are some books I have to pick up for a term paper."

"Can I come with you?" John asked.

"Of course, Darling, that's why I mentioned it."

After she checked out her books, the two decided to take a walk through the campus. As they walked along, Sandy pointed to a massive marble bell tower just a few hundred yards away. "That's the Campanile," she said as the densely forested campus spread out before them. The pungent scent of eucalyptus trees filled the humid air.

"I love to walk here," Sandy said. "I have wonderful memories from childhood. Dad used to bring Robert and me here on Saturdays. They walked quietly, hand in hand, toward the Campanile, absorbing each other's presence as they went. When they reached the massive tower, Sandy said, "Let's go up."

The view from the top floor was breathtaking. They could see the entire campus and the hazy outline of San Francisco with the Golden Gate Bridge in the background.

John put his arms around Sandy. "I'll take the memory of this scene with me. It'll always remind me of how much I love you, Honey," he said.

"Me, too," she replied gently touching his cheek.

The huge bell in the tower tolled. It was three o'clock.

They descended from the tower and drove silently toward their apartment. Sandy turned on the radio and Bing Crosby's voice sang:

> *Now is the hour when we must say goodbye*
> *Soon you'll be sailing, far across the sea...*
> *While you're away, O please remember me*
> *When you return you'll find me waiting here....*

"Where has it gone, John?" Sandy asked in a voice just above a whisper. "It seems you just got here, and the day after tomorrow you have to go back." She paused and took a long breath, then she put her head oh John's shoulder.

John's sorrow increased. Where *had* the time gone? What would he do without her…his wife…the most wonderful woman he had ever met…the woman he loved more than anyone in the world?

When they got to their apartment, Sandy opened a window and turned on the radio. John fixed a fire and opened a bottle of wine. They sat on the sofa in front of the fire, sipping wine and holding hands.

The sounds of the Tommy Dorsey band and the voice of Frank Sinatra singing *I'm Confessing That I Love You* gently filtered through the room. Darkness fell. John threw more wood on the fire. The flames flickered and the fire began to crackle. John walked to the bedroom and came back with one of his gifts. He slipped behind the sofa and put his hands over Sandy's eyes.

"Surprise," he said. "I'd like to open one of our gifts tonight."

"Oh, John, what a wonderful thought," Sandy said as he placed his present in her lap. "I'll get one of mine."

She returned. John turned his back to her so her gift would be a surprise, too.

Before they started to unwrap their presents, John said, "Let's have a toast. To us, forever and ever."

"Yes," Sandy replied, as she clinked her glass to John's. "For all eternity, my Darling."

John opened his present. It was a sterling silver Saint Christopher's medal. He was deeply moved. "I don't know what to say, Honey," he said. "This is the most precious present anyone ever gave me."

"Saint Christopher protects the traveler, John. I'm sure he has a special blessing for men who go to war. That's the blessing I ask of him for you—that he will keep you safe."

John took Sandy into his arms. "Thank you from the bottom of my heart, Honey," he said. "Both for Saint Christopher's protection and for telling me last night how much you loved me."

"Of course I do, Darling, and you're coming back is the most important thing in my life."

John smiled and kissed her.

Sandy opened her present. It was a beautiful chain with a miniature golden hour glass attached."

"It beautiful," she said.

"I want it to remind you that I'll always love you, and that the time *will* come when I'll come home to you," John said.

They sat back on the couch together and sipped their wine. Sandy put her head against John's chest and fell asleep. John picked her up and carried her to bed. Sandy was asleep again in minutes, but John's sleep was troubled. He tossed and turned. Just after midnight, he awoke with a start. He realized he *had* to come back, no matter what happened. His wonderful dream with Sandy would die if he didn't.

The next morning when he awoke, John reached over to find Sandy, but she was already up. He heard her moving about in the kitchen. He looked at the clock. It was 7:30. He'd overslept. He wandered into the kitchen. Sandy was in her robe busily making a pot of coffee. He sat down at the kitchen table.

"Gee." he said, "I must have been really tired last night."

Sandy blew him a kiss, then went on with her coffee making.

John watched his wife. Her movements caused the sash on her robe to loosen revealing the cleavage of her breasts. She looked up and saw John staring at her. She hesitated a moment, then walked around the table and cradled his head to her breasts. John was startled. He could hear her heart beating through her robe.

After a few seconds she moved his head gently away from her and kissed him. Then, in the same motion, she slipped into his lap and pulled the sash open. John put his arms around her. He picked her up, and carried her the few steps to the bedroom. They sank into the unmade bed, their bodies trembling with anticipation. Then they made love with the tenderness and yearning of two people deeply in love.

That afternoon, they went to Sandy's parent's house for an early Christmas celebration.

Louise was overjoyed when they came through the door. "Hi, you two. Come in. John, put your presents on the sofa until we get the tree decorated."

"Mmmm, Mom, I smell turkey and dressing. It smells wonderful in here," Sandy said. She gave her mother a hug.

Sandy and Louise began decorating the tree. When John offered to help, Louise said, "Three people bustling around a tree are one too many. You can read this morning's paper." She tossed him a copy of the *Berkeley Gazette.*

Grateful to be excused from tree trimming, John began to leaf through the paper. On the second page there was a column entitled:

The War At A Glance
Corregidor Shelled

Leyte, Philippine Islands (AP): General Douglas MacArthur's Headquarters announced yesterday that the bombardment of the island fortress of Corregidor the stronghold the Japanese forced him to abandon in March 1942 was in progress. In addition to relentless attacks by B-24 Bombers from their new airfields in Leyte, MacArthur's Headquarters announced a daring and highly successful attack on the mouths of Corregidor's many tunnels by cruisers from Admiral "Bull" Halsey's Third Fleet. According to the communiqué, the attack by the cruisers *Santa*

Fe, *Columbia* and *Denver* was delivered with "deadly efficiency and accuracy," as an added phase of the pre-invasion bombardment.

Iwo Jima Bombed

Pearl Harbor (AP): Iwo Jima, the most bombarded Japanese base in the Pacific was attacked repeatedly in December. B-29 bombers from the Seventh Bomber Group based in the Marianas are now attacking this Japanese fortress on a daily schedule. According to Major General Willis Hale the B-29s dropped over 1200 tons on bombs on Iwo during the first three weeks of December.

Sea bombardment accompanied the air attacks. Three heavy cruisers from Admiral "Bull" Halsey's Third Fleet bombarded the island six times in the same period. According to General Willis, the islands of Chi Chi and Haha Jima were also heavily attacked to prevent reinforcements from reaching Iwo. General Hale declined to disclose whether Iwo Jima will be the next Japanese stronghold to be attacked but this is widely expected because of the concentrated air and naval bombardments.

John walked into the living room with the paper still in hand. "Look, Honey, this article mentions the *Santa Fe*," he said. "I've got a good buddy from home on the *Santa Fe*. From this it looks like General MacArthur asked for the cruiser attack because the *Santa Fe*, *Columbia* and *Denver* are in the Third Fleet, not the Seventh. At one time or another they've all been a part of our screen."

Sandy got up from her kneeling position at the base of the tree and read the article.

"God," she said. "Sometimes the war is very close to home."

At that moment Mark came through the front door. "Merry Christmas, everybody," he called out. "It's starting to drizzle, and this storm looks like it may be around for awhile. I'll build a fire and we can get cozy." He looked around the room. "We need some Christmas music," he said. He turned on the radio. There was Christmas music on nearly every station. He picked one playing *Silent Night*.

Evening came. Sandy turned on the lights on the tree. Sitting in a semicircle around the tree with the crackle of burning logs and Christmas music drifting through the room, they opened the rest of their presents. Sandy got John a beautiful silver identification bracelet with a gold anchor centered just below his name, rank and serial number. John gave Sandy a heavy braided gold necklace. Mark and Louise bought each other matching sweaters. There were gifts from John's family and, best of all, there were two large boxes of his mother's special Christmas fudge and cookies. The war, for awhile, was far away.

About 7:30 Louise announced, "Christmas dinner is ready."

When they were seated around the dining room table, Mark said grace. When he finished the prayer, there was silence. He turned to Sandy and said, "Your mother showed me the article in *Time Magazine* about the *Franklin*."

Fear registered on Sandy's face.

John and Mark exchanged glances. John knew Sandy was frightened and he desperately hoped Mark wouldn't say anything that would frighten her more.

"I think it's a bunch of hogwash, Honey," Mark said.

"*Do you, Dad?*" Sandy asked, relief in her voice.

"Absolutely. There's no such thing as a jinx," he said with even greater conviction. "The *Franklin's* no more jinxed than any other ship in the Navy."

"You *really* mean that, Dad?" Sandy asked.

"Of course I do, Honey. We talked about it at Hunters Point today. It's just superstition," he said. "Don't you give that kind of nonsense a second thought."

Sandy breathed a sigh of relief. "That's exactly what John told me. I'm glad to hear it from you, too. I've tried to put it out of my mind, but it's bothered me off and on ever since I read it."

John smiled and touched Sandy's cheek. "See, I told you so."

After dinner, when John and Mark were alone, John said, "Thanks a lot, Mark. What you told Sandy helped her and me, too. She got pretty upset by that rumor and she needed more reassurance. So did I, for that matter."

Mark put his hand on John's shoulder. "Don't worry, Sandy's a strong young woman. She'll be okay, " he said. "Just be careful with it yourself."

John nodded, slowly taking in what Mark said.

"I read in the paper that the Japanese have increased their kamikaze attacks," Mark said, changing the subject.

"Yeah, that doesn't surprise me," John replied. "We're hitting them closer to Japan now—they could get even worse, too."

"Those goddamned things are so dangerous," Mark said. "I sure wish we could find a quick, effective way to handle them. The article said they sank four destroyers and damaged a light cruiser."

"Which cruiser?" John asked.

Mark picked up the paper and pointed to the article. "The cruiser was the *Spokane,*" he replied.

John let out a sigh of relief. "Gee, I'm glad it wasn't the *Santa Fe*. I've got a good friend on her."

"There's a rumor that the Fifth Fleet is assembling at Ulithi for an attack on Okinawa. Does that sound right, John?" Mark asked.

"Yeah, it does. That's where I think we're headed."

"I can keep track of your ship, now. I just got a top-secret clearance. I can find out, in three or four days, about the location of any ship in the Pacific. Now we can at least know where you are and how you're doing."

Sandy and Louise came into the living room. Louise, Mark and John began to make small talk but Sandy said very little.

Finally Louise asked, "Are you okay, Honey? You're awfully quiet."

"I know, Mom. I just need some time alone with John now. I hope you'll understand." She got up to leave. Mark put his arms around her and Louise caressed her hair. "Of course we understand, Honey," they both assured her.

They turned to John and hugged him. "Be careful. Be safe," Mark said. "We'll remember you in our prayers."

"We'll miss you very much, " Louise added.

As they went through the door, Louise said, "I'll see you two in the morning."

When they got back to their apartment, John built a fire and they undressed and went to bed. They watched the fire's flickering shadows from their bedroom. For several minutes neither spoke. Then Sandy whispered, "I wish there was some way to keep you with me. I wish we could always be this close."

"So do I, Honey," John said. "I wish it from the bottom of my heart."

He took her into his arms and kissed her. "I'm going to miss you like crazy," he said.

"Me, too," Sandy responded, as she snuggled closer and put her head on his chest. John could smell her perfume and feel her heartbeat. She pressed against him. Passion and unrestrained desire consumed them. They made love with the fervor of two people facing a time of great uncertainty, loneliness and, above all, danger.

22 December, 1944
The Final Day
Return to the Franklin

The storm passed and the area was bathed in radiant sunshine. The sun's warm rays streaming through the bedroom window awakened John. He turned over and shook Sandy gently. "Time to get up, Honey," he said.

Sandy shook herself awake. "I was hoping this morning wouldn't come," she said. "Maybe we could go back to sleep and the whole thing will go away."

John smiled and kissed her. "No such luck," he said as he got out of bed and headed for the shower.

While Sandy was getting dressed, John carefully packed his sea bag and shaving kit. "Ready, Honey?" John asked.

"I need just a couple more minutes."

They had a lingering last look at their apartment. Then they drove the few blocks to her parents' home. Louise was waiting when they got there. She put her arms around Sandy and hugged her, then she hugged John and said, "Ouuu, I'm going to miss you."

"Me, too, Mom," John said.

"Our prayers go with you, John," Louise said, trying to hide her sadness.

"Thanks, Mom."

The ride to the depot seemed longer than John remembered. Everyone was very quiet, preoccupied with their own thoughts. When they arrived, the train was just pulling in. When it came to a stop John hoisted his sea bag up on his shoulder and put it in the luggage compartment. He came back down the steps and found Sandy crying. He took her in his arms and kissed her. "Don't cry, Honey," he said, as he caressed her. "I'll be home before you know it."

"I know, but this morning those fears came back, John," Sandy said "The war, the killing, the kamikaze…."

He kissed the tip of her nose. "Don't worry, Honey. Remember what I promised you. The Japs haven't made a kamikaze that could keep me from coming back to you."

He turned to Louise and hugged her. "Thanks, Mom," he said. "Having you here makes this a lot easier."

He took Sandy in his arms and gave her long, sensitive kiss. "So long for a while, Honey," he said. "I'll write you as often as I can."

"I'll write you every day. I love you, John."

"Me, too, Honey, with all my heart."

John moved slowly away, then climbed aboard the train. At the top of the steps he turned and blew them both kisses. Then he handed his travel orders to the conductor who was standing nearby. When the conductor looked at John's uniform, he said, "You're a Gunner First Class. I'll get you in a sleeping compartment."

John followed the conductor toward the sleeping compartment. The deepest sadness he had ever felt spread through his body. When they reached the compartment, John tipped the conductor two dollars and thanked him for the accommodation.

"Thank you. Thank you, sir," he said. "We got a lot of men from the *Franklin* on board. I hope you have a good trip."

John tossed his bag up onto a luggage rack and fell into a seat. There was other luggage on the rack, so he knew that he already had bunkmates. He looked out the window to see if he could get one final glimpse of Sandy, but she was gone. The train jerked a couple of times, then moved slowly forward. His sadness deepened.

A tall, muscular Chief Steward's Mate came into the compartment carrying a towel on his shoulder. "How you doing, Gunner?" he asked in a deep, melodious voice. His smile revealed white teeth that highlighted his handsome face and black skin. He instantly reminded John of Belasco.

"Alphonso Frasure," he said, extending his hand. "My friends just call me 'Fonz.'"

"John Oxler," John said as he shook hands.

John noticed a bandage on Fonz's right forearm. "What happened?" he asked.

"I took some shrapnel when the *Lexington* was crashed by a kamikaze—got a little tendon damage."

"I read about the attack in the paper the other day," John said. "I was on the old *Lexington* when she went down in the Coral Sea."

"The first '*Lady Lex*,'" Fonz said with a touch of sadness in his voice. "I saw her many times over the years. I always thought she was one of the most beautiful ships afloat."

"When did *Lexington* get hit?"

"Over five weeks ago, but you know the Navy Department, they're slow as hell about releasing that kind of news."

"You lost some men…?"

"Yes, we did, over fifty. Most were officers. We were serving breakfast and the damned thing crashed the officers' mess and galley." He paused a moment. "I was lucky to only get this," he continued, raising his arm. "Fifteen men in my division were killed. The only other consolation was that the ship wasn't badly damaged. I got a twenty-day leave out of it and a transfer to the *Franklin*." He let out a long sigh. "Well, that's the Navy," he chuckled. "I was happy on the *Lex*."

The compartment door opened again. A thin-faced, slender Lieutenant Junior Grade carrying a heavy bag squeezed in. He struggled to get it up onto the luggage rack; he stumbled back and forth with it as the car swayed.

"Need some help, Lieutenant?" Fonz asked. He reached over and helped him shove the bag onto the rack.

"Thanks," replied the Lieutenant. "Damn thing's packed with everything I own." He hung his coat up. Then he took off his tie and settled into the seat next to Fonz. "Wow!" he said. "Have I got a hangover. My wife and I drank champagne last night. That stuff always leaves me with a headache. I almost missed this goddamn train." He extended his hand. "My name's Don Gary."

"Alphonso Frasure, sir."

"I'm John Oxler, sir."

"Forget the 'sir' stuff. Call me Don."

He looked closely at John. "Didn't we get off the *Franklin* in Alameda together?"

"I think so," John replied. "I think I was right behind you."

"That was sure a pretty girl you met," Gary said, with appreciation in his voice.

"She's my wife now," John replied.

"Congratulations. You're a very lucky sailor."

"Chief Frasure is just coming aboard," John said as he nodded to Frasure.

"Just transferred?"

"Yes, sir, I was aboard the *Lexington*."

"She took a kamikaze…."

"Yes, sir."

"I hate those goddamn things," Gary said. "Everything you throw up at them sometimes isn't enough."

"Yeah," John said. "Even when you kill the pilot and the damn plane's on fire, its momentum still carries it into you."

"Were you aboard when the *Franklin* was crashed, Gunner?" Fonz asked.

"Yeah, it came in right over our gun pit," John replied. "There wasn't a damned thing we could do about it."

"It's the helplessness that pisses you off," Gary said. "You want to reach up and tear the bastards apart with your bare hands."

Fonz chuckled. "You got that right, sir. That's *exactly* the way you feel," he said.

The three lapsed into talk about their combat experiences. Being forced to talk took John's mind off his thoughts of leaving Sandy. By the time the conductor came through the car to announce dinner, John was feeling better. Fonz was an open, friendly guy and the lieutenant was an enlisted man's officer—unpretentious, down-to-earth and humorously self-effacing at times. He liked them both.

After dinner they came back to the compartment and talked until lights-out was signaled. Talking to Fonz and Lieutenant Gary had helped him a lot. He was even looking forward to seeing his buddies on the *Franklin* now. He thought of Beckley, Sullivan, Ski, Lowe, Feinstein, Bonin, Garcia, Colson, Jardin—his whole gun crew. Father O'Callahan would be there, too. The thought of seeing O'Callahan made him feel even better. Then his thoughts drifted back to Sandy and the wonderful vows they'd made. One thing he was sure of this time—she'd be waiting for him when he got home. He fell asleep with this thought. During the night his longing for Sandy returned. Twice he awoke with a start and the painful realization that she was not beside him.

CHAPTER TWENTY-FOUR

23 December, 1944
Dry Dock # 5
Bremerton, Washington

The *Franklin* rested on keel blocks in dry dock Number 5, Puget Sound Navy Yard. Her battle damage had been almost completely repaired. New steel reinforcing beams were installed under the flight deck, and a layer of steel was placed, in many areas, over these heavy steel beams. A complete new wooden flight deck had replaced the burned, battle-scared planks. Additional sheets of steel plating were integrated into the hangar deck with great attention paid to water tightness. This would prevent gasoline fires, caused by draining aviation gasoline, from ravaging the *Franklin's* lower decks again. The bulkheads on the hangar deck were completely restored and painted, and the bridge looked like it had never been touched. *Franklin* was starting to look brand new again.

New barrels were installed in all of her 20-mm and 40-mm guns. The latest modifications to the Mark 14 gun sights would be installed within the next week, and her radar was being upgraded with the latest high frequency detection technology. *Franklin* was now an even more potent weapon of war than she was before she was damaged.

When John, Fonz and Lieutenant Gary reported aboard, the Officer of the Deck handed John a message. He opened it and read it. "It's a note from Father O'Callahan, the ship's new chaplain," he said.

"We got a new chaplain?" Gary asked as they started across the hangar deck toward one of the ladders that went below.

"Yeah," John replied. "He's the chaplain that married us in Alameda."

"What's he like?" Gary asked.

"He's a great guy," John replied as they went down the ladder and turned toward their separate compartments. "Sometime I'll tell you guys the story of how I met him and what he did to help us get married."

"That sounds like a good story, Gunner," Fonz said over his shoulder. "I'd like to hear it."

"Me, too," Gary said heading for officers' country.

"Maybe we could have a cup of joe soon," John called back in a loud voice. "I'll tell you about it then."

John puzzled over O'Callahan's message. "I wonder what he wants," he said half aloud.

John made his way to the chaplain's office. When he arrived he asked the yeoman for Father O'Callahan.

The yeoman disappeared through a doorway and in a few moments O'Callahan came out. "John, Sandy told me you were an acolyte when you were young," he said. "I need someone to serve Mass. Would you do that for me?"

"Gee, Father, I don't know. I haven't served Mass since I was fourteen," John replied, not completely comfortable with the request. "I…I don't know if I'd remember how. I might make a bunch of mistakes and embarrass you."

"They say once you've done it, you never forget it," O'Callahan said. "Mistakes wouldn't embarrass me. Everyone would know you haven't served in a long time."

John deliberated a moment. "Oh, I'll give it a try, Father," he said.

"It's agreed then. We might as well start tomorrow. It's Sunday and the next day's Christmas, so you'll have two days in a row to try it out."

John hesitated.

"I need an acolyte for Christmas and Sunday Mass, John," O'Callahan said. "I had to work without one last Sunday."

"Okay, Father, if I'm going to do it, I might as well jump right in."

"Thanks, John, I appreciate this," O'Callahan said as he put his hand on John's shoulder and led him to the door. "I wonder why it's always so hard to find men to do this kind of thing…." he added, his voice trailing off into conjecture.

When they reached the door, O'Callahan said, "When you write to Sandra, please give her my best."

"Yes, Father I will," John said, then he stopped. "Father, can I talk to you for a minute? Sometimes a fear comes over me that I'll never see Sandy again. It hurts me right here," he said, pointing to his solar plexus.

"What do you mean you might not see her again, John?"

"You know, Father, that something might happen to me. I promised Sandy I'd come home to her and I truly meant it at the time, but it's hard to control this now. What if I should be killed or something?"

"Have you ever thought of turning to God for help?" O'Callahan asked.

"What do you mean?" John asked.

"God is your Source and Protector, John," O'Callahan said. "He is the Source of all things to all of us. He is your Protector. He is the Source of your love for Sandy and her love for you."

"Yeah, Father, but how does that help me with the heartache and fear of not seeing her again?"

"Turn to God and feel His unlimited love. When your heartache and fear are greatest, let God fill the void."

"But Father, I've tried praying. I've said the Our Father and the Hail Mary lots of times and they didn't work."

"I'm not talking about that kind of prayer," O'Callahan said. "I'm talking about just being quiet and letting your mind and body find the Great Source of love that God has for you."

"I don't understand that," John said. "You mean I can actually feel God's love or his protection around me?"

"Yes, that is exactly what I mean," O'Callahan replied.

"I sorry, Father, I don't think I know how to do that," John said, shaking his head.

"Try it. It works for me," O'Callahan replied. "When I get scared or lonely, I say a short prayer, 'God is my Great Source of love and protection.' Sometimes at night when I worry about my sister, Alice, or my mother, I say this prayer. Then I let God's love and protection surround and fill my body. It always helps me."

"Yeah, but you're a priest," John said. "You know how to do those kinds of things."

"You try it. You'll see it works. God's love and protection are like sunshine, John. They're available to all of us, priest or not."

"Even for the Japs?"

"Yes, even for the Japs if they'd look for Him. But that's a matter of philosophy I don't want to go into right now." He paused and rubbed his chin. "Don't be concerned about the Japs, John," he said slowly. "Just look at your own situation. God will protect you and love you—all you need do is ask."

"God is my Great Source of love and protection," John mumbled. He thought for a moment, then he asked, "Do you *really* think it'll work for me, Father?"

"I'm sure it will, John. Just give it a try."

John pondered the thought, then said, "Maybe I'm starting to understand what you mean, Father. I'll try it."

On the bridge, Gehres and Beckley leaned over the railing and watched the ocean gushing into the cavernous dry dock below.

"In about thirty minutes we should float off the keel blocks," Gehres said. "We'll complete the repairs in Pier 3 D in Seattle."

"Aye, sir," Beckley replied.

Gehres turned to Joe Taylor who had recently been promoted to his Executive Officer. "We should be out of here around noon, Joe," he said. "Is everything getting shipshape?"

"Everything's going great, Captain," Taylor replied. "We'll soon be the most modern, best-equipped carrier in the fleet."

At 12:05 Captain Carl Christensen, the harbor pilot, reported aboard and the *Franklin* backed out of dry dock and headed for Pier 3D in Seattle. When she arrived, she moored starboard side to the pier, with five manila lines and three wire hawsers.

That afternoon, Sullivan gave John the responsibility for retrofitting the ship's Mark 14 sights. "You've got them all, John," he said.

"Aye, Chief," John replied, "it sounds complicated. Is there somebody we can call in if we hit a snag?"

"Yeah. The manufacturer's got an expert right in Seattle. He can be here on twelve hour's notice."

At 14:00 John mustered his gun crew in Able Sponson. "We've got a very important job," he said. "Chief Sullivan's assigned us the job of retrofitting the Mark 14 sights. It's a very big responsibility. I'm going to need seven men. The following men will be in this detail: "Kwatkowski, Lowe, Arnold, Bonin, Garcia, Colson, Feinstein. The rest of you guys will work on the 40's. I want them glistening by the time we go to sea."

"Hell, John," Jardin protested. "Why do I get the shitty detail?"

"What do you mean shitty detail?"

"You guys get to work on gun sights and we have to play grease monkeys to the 40's."

"One job's no more important than the other," John said. "You've been on the other end of a Jap machine gun shell, Jardin. You know damned well how important these guns are. I picked these guys because of their experience."

"What the hell, I'm as experienced as most of them are," Jardin said.

"Well, right now you're going to be an experienced grease monkey. If nobody objects, I'll make you my number one alternate."

"I object, John," Jardin said, his voice now filled with anger.

"I just told you, you're going to work on the guns. That's an order and it's final," John said in an even tone. "You're still the number one alternate. Any questions or other comments?"

Silence.

"Okay, that's settled," he said. "Now let's talk about tomorrow. It's Sunday and the next day is Christmas Day. I let Father O'Callahan talk me into serving Catholic Mass, so you Catholics better be there, and not for any kidding around. I need your *moral support*. That goes for Christmas Day, too. We'll begin the sight modifications next Tuesday morning. We can hook up for breakfast. Then after muster, we can go our separate ways. In the meantime, we've got two days off, so let's go below. I'm tired. I traveled nearly all day yesterday and didn't sleep very well last night. I need a little rest."

As the gun crew started to disperse, John asked Ski and Lowe to stay. When everybody was gone, he said, "I'm getting concerned about Jardin. He seemed edgy as hell today."

"Yeah, I've noticed it, too," Lowe said. "He's been jumpy ever since he got back from leave."

"He was squirrelly before that, too," Ski said. "He keeps a record of our accidents in a notebook in his locker."

"Really?" John asked. "Why didn't I know about this?"

"I didn't think anything about it until just this minute," Ski replied.

"Didn't it seem kind of weird?" John asked.

"It didn't then, but it sure as hell does now," Ski replied.

"Why?" Lowe asked. "He's been in combat."

"Yeah, I know, but it was his *first* combat," John replied. "Going in the second time can be scary. I know it was scary as hell for me."

"You mean you're not afraid of it anymore?" Ski asked.

"Afraid of what?" John replied, hoping in some way to avoid Ski's question.

"Combat, Gunner, combat," Ski said, in a tone that revealed his frustration.

John looked at Ski. "Hell, yes, I'm afraid of it," he said sharply. "I'd be a goddamned fool if I wasn't." He paused. "Aren't you?"

"Hell yes," Ski replied.

"Knock that bullshit off, Ski," Lowe said. "Don't be an asshole. Everybody's afraid of combat. I don't care how many times you've been in it," Lowe said. "Jardin might have another problem, too. He just came back from a long leave. You think more about living and dying after you've been with your girl friend and family for a long time."

"Boy, you can *really* say that again," John said. "Anyway, let's keep an eye on Jardin. I don't want him to do anything crazy."

24 December, 1944
Pier 3D, Seattle
Catholic Mass

The church flag fluttered on the forward trucks below the Stars and Stripes. On the bow end of the hangar deck, two seamen completed preparations for Catholic Mass. The altar was a mess table covered with a white cloth. It sat on top of a canvas tarp that covered the grease and fire-stained deck. The tarp permitted an acolyte to kneel. Everyone else was allowed to sit or stand.

John met O'Callahan in his office. Together they walked toward the ladder to the flight deck.

"Are you nervous?" O'Callahan asked.

"A little, Father," John replied.

"Don't be," O'Callahan said. "If you forget something, I can remind you with a little signal. Everybody will understand."

"Did you try what I suggested last night?"

"Yeah, Father, I did. It's hard to believe, but it helped me quite a bit."

"Good," O'Callahan said as they arrived at the altar.

O'Callahan's "congregation" had gathered. Sullivan and Ski were there, as were Lowe, Garcia, Jardin, Arnold, and Bonin. Even non-Catholics, Beckley, Barker, Feinstein and Colson were sitting in the front row. John was surprised to see Fonz and Lieutenant Gary there, too.

O'Callahan looked over the gathering, then said with a smile, "I'm pleased to see all of you men at Mass. I think John Oxler 'serving' for me is one of the reasons. I'm sure he's happy to have you here, too."

John looked back at his shipmates. He was very glad they were there.

He gave them a wave, then signaled a special welcome to Gary and Fonz. He noticed as he did this that many of the men looked strangely at Fonz.

O'Callahan faced the altar and began the Mass.

"*Introibo ad altare Dei*: I will go unto the altar of God."

"*Ad Deum qui laetificate juventutem meam*: To God who giveth joy to my youth," John responded, reading awkwardly from the card.

"*Judica me Deus, et dicerne causam meam de gente non sancta: ab homine iniquo et doloso erue me*: Judge me O God, and distinguish my cause from the nation that is not holy: deliver me from the unjust and deceitful man...."

John struggled with the Latin words. He hadn't uttered them in a long time, but the meaning of the prayers was still there, and after his talk with Father O'Callahan the day before yesterday, he seemed to have a greater understanding of them.

The Mass went on. The time of the Gospel arrived.

O'Callahan read the Gospel. Then he faced the congregation and spoke of the meaning of the Christmas season and his abiding hope that that there would soon be "peace on earth and good will among all men." When he ended the sermon, he said, "Let this Mass be a blessing to everyone here and all the men in the military services of the United States where ever they might be at this very moment."

"*Gloria in excelsis Deo*: Glory to god in the highest..."

John again struggled with the response, but it wasn't as tough as he thought it would be. The Latin was awkward, but he was beginning to feel more comfortable.

When the Mass ended, Sullivan, Beckley, Fonz and Gary and the other guys in his gun crew gathered around John and offered their congratulations.

Bonin was especially impressed. "I used to serve Mass, John," he said in a low voice. "When Father O'Callahan put out the word for a server last Sunday, I almost responded."

"Well, why didn't you?" John asked.

"I was 'chicken' but maybe I can help you tomorrow."

"Yeah, that'd be great, George," John replied. "Why don't you tell Father. I think that'll make him very happy."

Fonz and Gary waited until the men in John's gun crew finished their congratulations. Then they stepped toward John.

"Hi, you guys. I haven't seen you since the train ride," John said. He shook hands with Gary. Then he made a special effort to show everyone that Fonz was his friend. He put his hand on Fonz's shoulder and said in a loud voice, "How you been, Buddy? It's great to see you."

Fonz smiled. "I know what you're trying to do, Gunner," he said in a voice just above a whisper. "The Navy pretty much keeps us separate. Thanks a lot."

"There's nothing separate between you and me, Fonz. I'm happy as hell to see you and Don," John said.

"Let me invite you guys down to the Warrant Officer's wardroom for coffee and rolls," Fonz said. "You'll get my very special coffee...."

When they were seated in the wardroom, Fonz served coffee and rolls. "This is the same coffee we serve the Captain," he said with a wink.

"So what's been happening?" John asked.

Commander Downes, the new damage control officer, slapped my unit with a big job the day after we got back," Gary said. "We have to inspect ever ventilator trunk and duct on this ship."

"Every duct and trunk on the ship!" Fonz exclaimed. "Mannn, that's a lot of work."

"It sure as hell is," Gary replied. "But he wants to be sure they're all clean, tight and shipshape."

"How far did you get?" John asked.

"Oh, only about eight percent so far," Gary said. "Gee, I thought I knew this ship before I got this detail, but after I finish this job, I'm going to know it like the back of my hand."

"What's with you, Fonz?" Gary asked.

"Oh, the same old stuff. Keeping the officers fed and happy. John, you told us you'd tell us about the way you met the chaplain, remember?" Fonz said.

"Oh, yeah, I did," John said. He told them the story. When he finished both Fonz and Gary were smiling and shaking their heads.

"That's quite a story," Gary said. "Sounds like the Padre is a sailor's priest."

"You can say that again, Lieutenant," Fonz added.

Late that afternoon John went down on the pier to call Sandy. He was relieved to find the area quiet and no one around the phone. He slipped a nickel in to the circular slot and after a couple of rings he got the operator. She went through the chain of operators and got connected to Berkeley. Sandy answered the phone.

"Hi, Honey," John said, delight in his voice.

"John. I was hoping it was you. How are you?"

"I'm fine, Honey. I really miss you, Sandy. It's only been a couple of days and it already seems like a year."

"Yes," Sandy replied, "for me, too. I had trouble getting to sleep because I was thinking about you so much."

"Yeah. What I miss most is being able to be close to you. I dream about being with you, kissing you and holding you again."

There was a pause. Then Sandy said, "Yes. Me, too, Darling, I reach over and you're not there. How long are we going to be apart?" Sandy asked sadly.

"I don't know, Honey, but every hour seems like ten to me and it seems they get longer as days go on."

Sadness crept into Sandy's voice. "They seem that long for me, too…"

"Guess what," John interrupted, trying to move to a happier subject. "I served Mass for Father O'Callahan this morning."

Sandy's voice perked up. "You did?"

"Yeah. He told me you mentioned I was an acolyte as a boy."

"Yes, I did, at the wedding reception. Well, tell me, how did it go?"

"After I got used to it, it was fine. I have to admit I was a little uncomfortable about what the guys would think, but even the non-Catholics congratulated me afterward."

"That's wonderful, John. I feel good about you're being close to Father O'Callahan. He's such a wonderful priest."

"He's more than that, Honey. He's a wonderful officer, too. He's only been on the *Franklin* a few weeks and from what I hear, everybody thinks he's great."

"As a chaplain?" Sandy asked.

"Both as a chaplain and as a man," John replied. "Lowe told me yesterday a lot of the officers call him 'Padre' and even some of the Protestants contact him when they have a problem." John paused. He was tempted to tell Sandy about the prayer O'Callahan had given him yesterday, but decided not to. She'd worry; besides, he promised her that nothing could happen to him. He'd vowed this. He'd keep that promise whether the prayer worked or not.

"John. John?" Sandy's voice pulled him away from his thought.

"I'm sorry, Honey," he said. "Something Father O'Callahan said yesterday came into my thoughts for a moment."

"I wondered what happened. I thought maybe we got cut off," Sandy said. "What did Father say, John?"

"Oh, just that God would protect us from harm if we asked him to," John said.

"Of course, that's so very true, Honey," Sandy replied matter-of-factly. "I ask God to care for you and protect you every night."

"Thanks, Honey. That's another reason why I love you so," John said, delighted he hadn't mentioned his discussion with O'Callahan. "Well, I think my time's about up," he said with a sigh. "I love you and I miss you a bunch. I'll call you every chance I get until we leave."

"I love you and miss you, too, John," Sandy said. "Please take care of yourself, Darling."

"I will, Honey. Good-bye." As John put the receiver back on the hook, he felt a wave of fear and loneliness seep through him.

26 December, 1944
Pier 3D, Seattle
Preparations for Combat Continue

The day after Christmas dawned clear and beautiful. Although it was cold, the sun was shining and there wasn't a cloud in the sky. After morning muster, John and his retrofit detail began the task of upgrading the *Franklin's* Mark 14 sights. John's crew patiently dismantled, retrofitted and reassembled the first sight. It took the entire morning. By the end of the day they had completed the second and were halfway through the third. The retrofitting was difficult and exhausting, but John was grateful for it. It occupied his mind completely. It was at night, when his other activities ceased, that his thoughts turned to Sandy and the wonderful moments they'd shared while they were together. He dreamed of the day he'd go home and hold her in his arms—always the same dream—always the same result. Sandy was thousands of miles away—not anywhere close to him.

The retrofitting took six full days. Finally, on the morning of the seventh, John reported to Sullivan. "We're finally finished, Chief," he said with pride in his voice. "The guy's did a good, thorough job. The *Franklin* now has the best, most accurate gun sights in the Navy—not much can get past those babies now."

2 January, 1945
Pier 3D
Franklin Readies for Sea

The lengthy process of re-supplying *Franklin* for duty in enemy waters began the day after New Year's. Heaps of provisions of all kinds, enough to last for at least ten weeks at sea, were waiting on the dock. Two gangways were in place, one amidships and another near the ship's stern. An endless chain of men stood by—waiting to haul the provisions up to the hangar deck. Case after case of medical supplies were stacked there, next to gallon after gallon of cooking oil. Scores of extra airplane engines were there, waiting to be hoisted aboard along with extra wings and countless crates of extra parts. There had to be enough diversity to be certain that planes could be efficiently repaired, no matter what damage they suffered in combat. Each item and every crate would be carefully catalogued, then stored below in a way that they could be quickly located and retrieved. Canister after canister of 20-mm and 40-mm ammunition, loaded on pallets, were also there, ready to be hoisted by crane up to the hangar deck.

The men in John's gun crew, along with work details from the rest of the Gunnery Division, were standing by.

John silently counted his men. Somebody was missing. "Lowe, Ski, who's missing?"

Lowe looked around. "It's Jardin," he said. "He went to sickbay this morning after muster. I guess they kept him there."

"What's the matter with him?" John asked.

"He said he had bad cramps in his stomach."

"You sure he was sick?" John asked. "We've got all this damned ammo to handle."

"I don't think he was screwing off, John," Lowe said. "He looked pretty sick to me. He was all doubled up with his arms crossed over his stomach."

"How's he been acting?" John asked.

"He seems upset. Keeps looking through that notebook of his," Ski replied.

"You guys know what's bothering him?"

"He hasn't said anything to me," Ski said.

"Did you ask him?"

"No. I figured he'd tell me if he wanted to."

"I think we need to find out. If he's still in sickbay tonight, I'll go down after chow and see how he's doing," John said as the crane on the dock lowered the first pallet of ammunition to the hangar deck. As soon as it got there, ammunition-handling details crowded around. Each man grabbed a canister and put it on a conveyor that moved it to the magazine hoists. Then the canisters were lowered to the magazines four decks below.

"Goddamn, I hate this work," Ski said as the morning wore on. "It's so damned boring it makes everybody touchy and pissed off."

"It's a pain in the ass, but it's a part of the job," John said.

"I wish somebody else had this part of it," Ski said as he struggled with a heavy 40-mm canister.

"Maybe you should hire your own personal roustabout," Lowe said with a grin.

"Hey, that's a good idea," Ski replied. "How about it, John?"

"What would you be doing if you had one?" John asked.

"I'd be in Seattle chasing pussy. There're some beautiful women out there," Ski said with a smile.

"Is that all you think of, Ski?" Feinstein asked.

"Is there anything else?"

"See what I mean? You got your brains between your legs," Feinstein said.

"Fuck you, Feinstein. You keep your goddamned opinions to yourself," Ski snapped, his smile gone.

"Knock it off, you two," John said.

"I don't have to take that kind of crap from a jerk from New York," Ski retorted.

Feinstein made a move in Ski's direction. John stood directly in his path and restrained him. "You looking for brig time, Feinstein?" John asked. "Remember, it's a capital offense to strike a superior officer."

"He's not going to call me a jerk!" Feinstein shouted, struggling to get out of John's grasp.

"Let him come, John," Ski said, his fists clenched and ready. "I'll whip his ass."

"Belay this bullshit," John said, still restraining Feinstein. "You guys want to fight each other when there are thousands of Japs out there to fight? That's crazy. Knock it off!"

Feinstein backed away from John's grasp and Ski dropped his guard.

"You guys have to work together and what's more important, you have to fight together," John said.

"Well, I don't have to take that kind of bullshit from him," Ski said.

"No, you don't, Ski, and you don't have to sling it back, either." John replied. "I want you guys to bury the hatchet. Right now—and not in each others skulls."

John looked at Ski. "Shake hands with him, Ski," John said.

"Bullshit, he can shake hands with me."

"You two can shake hands with each other. Come on, you guys were always friendly," John said.

When the two shook hands, Feinstein said, "I'm sorry, Ski, it's this goddamned, shitty job. Makes me a little crazy."

"Yeah, I didn't mean what I said either," Ski replied.

The dreary ammunition handling now continued in silence.

Finally, John said, "Ski, you've got liberty tonight. Are you going ashore?"

"Yeah, Ski replied. Why don't you come with me and drink some beer?"

"I'm afraid I'd cramp your style, Ski," John said with a laugh.

"Boy, since you got married, you're not much fun anymore," Ski said. "I remember when the only thing you wanted to do was go ashore."

"If I had a beautiful wife like John's, Ski, I'd stay out of bars and pick-up joints, too," Garcia chimed in.

"Thanks, Ramon," John said. "Okay, you guys, let's knock off the bullshit and move ammunition."

They worked for another hour, then John wiped the sweat off his brow with the back of his glove and said, "We all need a break. Let's take fifteen minutes. The 'smoking lamp' is lit. Smoke back on the fantail. Be damned careful with matches and be sure you put your butts in those cans filled with water. This ammunition would cause one hell of an explosion."

John walked back to the fantail with Ski and Lowe. When they got there Ski lit a cigarette, then looked down at the truckloads of ammunition on the dock waiting to be hoisted aboard. "How long do you think this is going to take, John?" he asked.

"Sullivan says about seven days if everybody works hard," John replied.

"Shit," Lowe said. "It feels like seven months."

"I know, but the quicker we get loaded," John replied, "the quicker we can get out of here and get this goddamned war over."

"I can't remember ever taking on this much stuff," Lowe said.

"The magazines were empty," John said. "Remember, we have to replace everything we unloaded in Alameda."

"Well, it's still a pain in the ass, John."

The tedious ammunition handling went on all day. By 17:30 everyone was tired and ready for chow.

Right after chow, John waved to Ski, Lowe and some of the rest of the gun crew as they headed ashore. Then he went down to sickbay to see Jardin. When he arrived, Jardin was asleep. "He's in my gun crew," he said to the corpsman on watch. "What's wrong with him?"

"I don't know, Gunner," the corpsman replied. "The chart says he's suffering from 'general anxiety with extensive physical symptoms.' We're going to hold him overnight, just to be sure it's not something more serious."

"Can I talk to him?"

"Sure. He'll be a little woozy. We gave him something to sleep."

John sat on the edge of Jardin's bunk and shook him gently. "Jardin, wake up."

Jardin came awake with a start. "Oh, it's you, Gunner," he said, appearing disoriented.

"What's wrong, Buddy?" John asked.

"What do you mean, Gunner?"

"You've been nervous and edgy as hell lately. I want to know what's bothering you."

Jardin looked down at the deck and said nothing.

"Come on," John said. "You can talk to me about it. Maybe I can help you."

"I had a bad time at home," Jardin finally said.

"What happened?"

"Everything. My girl dumped me for another guy. I got mad at her and slapped her around. When my folks found out about it, they were pissed off. I got drunk and left town without saying good-bye, and I've been miserable ever since."

"Something like that happened to me," John said. "It can be tough as hell to get over."

"I've got a feeling I'm not going to get over it, Gunner," Jardin said. "I got a feeling I'm not going to come back this time."

"So that's why you're so edgy?"

"Yeah, I think the ship's jinxed and I am, too."

"Why?" John asked.

"It's that article in *Time* Magazine and all the bullshit that happened back home," Jardin said, his eyes focused down on the deck again. "I think something's going to happen to me. I've been trying to fight this off, Gunner, honest, but it just seems to be getting worse."

"Maybe you ought to talk to a chaplain," John said. "We got two good chaplains aboard."

"What's the new Catholic chaplain like?"

"He's a great guy. I've talked to him. He helped me a lot."

"You've talked to him?"

"Yes."

"Let me think about it, Gunner," Jardin said, slowly looking up. "I'm kind of ashamed to have to go to a chaplain."

"There's nothing to be ashamed of," John replied. "I did it and I felt a lot better."

"Honest?"

"Yeah, honest."

John turned to leave. "If you want to talk to him, I'll arrange it," he said. "I'm available, too, if it gets too tough."

"Thanks, Gunner," Jardin said, tears coming into his eyes. "Please don't tell any of the rest of the guys, will you?"

John nodded. He left the sickbay and walked through the passageway to the ladder. He realized Jardin had a hell of a problem and it could get worse when combat came. If he broke down in an attack, it could put a lot of other guys in danger. He'd have to be put someplace where a breakdown wouldn't cause a disaster. As he went back to his compartment an idea came to him. As soon as Jardin was released he'd assign Jardin to the loading detail in the ammunition ready-service locker. It was cramped, stark and somber there, with only a single light protected by a metal grille, but he'd at least have the protection of some steel bulkheads and any hostile action would be out of sight. "As soon as he's released and back on duty…," he muttered.

The next morning after chow, Jardin reported back from sickbay. When John saw him he called him aside.

"I'm going to assign you to the loading detail in the ammunition ready-service locker," John said.

Jardin looked distressed. "Why, Gunner? What the hell's wrong now?"

"Nothing. I think you'll do a good job back there."

"Yeah, but isn't it dangerous in there?" Jardin asked nervously.

"Not half as dangerous as it is outside. You've got a couple of inches of steel all around you there," John reassured him.

"Yeah, but what if we get a direct hit?"

"If we get a direct hit, we're all going to go," John said. "At least in there you won't be able to see all the action."

"You're doing this because of what we talked about last night, aren't you?"

"Yeah, I'll be honest with you, I am."

Jardin nodded slowly and looked down at the deck.

"Thanks, Gunner," he said.

The tedious loading went on for six full days. Finally, after what seemed forever, the *Franklin's* magazines were fully loaded. A last task was loading the other things necessary for an effective antiaircraft defense. Extra barrels were hauled aboard and crate after crate of spare parts for the five-inch and the 20- and 40-mm guns were hoisted up, painstakingly identified and stored below.

John, along with Ski or Lowe, checked and re-checked what had been done at the end of each day. John wanted everything done perfectly. It had to be right. This would help him get home to Sandy….

17 January, 1945
Air Group Five Assembles
A Marine Fighter Squadron

Wednesday morning brought bright, sunny weather with just a few scattered cirrus clouds on the eastern horizon. From the bridge, Gehres, Taylor and Beckley watched the loading activities.

"How long do you think it's still going to take, Joe?" Gehres asked Taylor.

"I think about two more days will do it, Captain. We should be out of here by late morning on Wednesday. Then we can load our bombs and missiles and get underway."

"We're taking that Marine fighter squadron aboard later this morning," Gehres said.

"Yes, sir, the 452nd Marine Fighter Squadron," Taylor replied.

"Marine squadron?" Beckley asked. "Why are we getting a Marine squadron, Captain?"

"I don't know, Chief. They were just assigned to us but I'm glad to have them. The 452nd is a veteran outfit. A lot of the pilots are from Greg Boyington's old 'Black Sheep' Squadron."

"Really. Is Boyington with them?"

"No, Boyington was captured by the Japs."

"I didn't know that," Beckley said, shaking his head. "That's incredible. When was he captured?"

"Just about a year ago now," Gehres replied.

"Funny, I didn't hear about it. Was he shot down?" Beckley asked.

"Yeah, he went down in the waters around Rabaul. A bunch of Jap Zeros jumped him and his wingman, George Ashmun. A Jap sub picked Boyington up but Ashmun didn't make it."

"How did you know that, sir?"

"Ashmun was an old friend," Gehres replied. "I knew him for years. That's why I'm so close to the matter, but there really wasn't much about it in the paper."

"I sure don't remember reading about it," Beckley said. "But you know how it is when you're being transferred around. You miss a lot of things."

"Well, I think the Navy Department and the Marines wanted to keep it quiet, too. When one of your ace pilots is shot down, you don't go around shouting about it...and they didn't know Boyington was alive for several months."

There was a long pause, then Beckley said, "Well, sir, I'm glad we got experienced pilots. We'll need all the experience we can get, if we're going where I think we're going."

"Well, I can't say for sure where we're going, Chief, but I know they'll complement our own pilots and maybe even stir up some healthy competition."

At 11:05, pursuant to a letter from the Commander of Fleet Air—West Coast, dated 14 January 1945, the 452nd Marine Fighter Squadron joined *Franklin's* newly formed Carrier Air Group Five. Sixty-two officers and one hundred and eleven enlisted men tromped up the gangway to the hangar deck with all their gear. Captain Gehres, Joe Taylor and Steve Jurika welcomed them aboard. After a simple greeting by Gehres, a special detail of noncoms began the painstaking job of assigning each officer and enlisted man his billet. After the assignments were completed, they directed the marines to their quarters.

At 12:30 the giant dock cranes hoisted the first of the squadron's still-wrapped, gull-winged F4U Corsairs aboard. They were lowered, two at a time, onto the forward and after elevators. Then air crewmen moved them down to the hangar deck and reattached them to *Franklin's* onboard cranes. The powerful cranes carried them to a staging area for unwrapping and final assembly. Because this process required great care and precision, it slowed loading down considerably and delayed *Franklin's* departure by two full days. Since John's work was finished, he now had time to catch up on his letters to Sandy. He was grateful for the time off. The ship's library, with sentimental music from the Armed Services Network playing in the background, provided him a place to think and write. He wrote:

January 21, 1945

My dearest Sandy,
Well, it looks like we are about ready to go to sea. My work was finished yesterday, so I've got some time off. When I told Ski and Lowe I was going to the library to write to you, they asked me to give you their best—everybody here thinks the world of you—they ask about you all the time.

Going back to sea this time is one of the roughest things I've ever had to do in my whole life. I miss you very much, and the thought of not seeing you for a long time makes me feel terrible. It's not that I'm afraid or worried—it's just that I love you so much and want to be with you more than anything I've ever wanted in my whole life. When I think about it, maybe what we have do is go back out there and get it all over with. Then I can come back and we can be together forever.

I'll write you often and call you when I can. I don't know when I'll see you again but I want you to know that I love you with all my heart and miss you like crazy. Please pray for us.

You loving husband,
John

When he finished his letter John relaxed for a while. It had been a long, tough three weeks. He wondered how the war was going. He picked up a copy of *Time* Magazine and found the section entitled *World Battlefronts:*

IWO JIMA BOMBARDED.

(AP): January 9, 1945. Scores of battleships and heavy cruisers from Bull Halsey's Third Fleet poured thousands of shells into the fortifications on Iwo Jima, Pacific Fleet Command reported yesterday. According to this source, carriers hit the island with over ten thousand tons of bombs and hundreds of missiles. The bombardment extended from Mount Suribachi on the southern tip of the island to the East Boat Basin. The attacks are believed to signal the beginning of the invasion of this tiny, strategic pear shaped island. During the past two weeks, Iwo underwent the most prolonged sea and air bombardment in naval history.

According to Admiral William "Bull" Halsey, the Japanese have made a fortress of Iwo Jima. "We've fired over sixteen thousand rounds into the fortifications on that hunk of rock, all the way from five-inch to sixteen-inch shells," he said. "I'm sorry to say we didn't seem to hurt it much. It's hard to believe that a piece of rock two and a half miles wide by four miles long could stand this kind of pounding. You'd think it would sink into the ocean by now."

Iwo Jima is believed necessary to the bombardment of Japanese cities. It will provide B-29 Superforts a "half-way base" for emergency landings on their bombing missions from the Marianas.

MANILA UNDER SIEGE

Luzon, Philippine Islands (AP): From temporary headquarters on the outskirts of Manila, General MacArthur announced the First Cavalry Division had broken into the capitol city's suburbs and liberated over five thousand Allied prisoners and internees. According to the communiqué, heavy house to house fighting continues.

In a broadcast to the people of the Philippines, MacArthur declared that the Commonwealth of the Philippines had been permanently reestablished: "My country has kept the faith," he announced. "Your Capital City, although cruelly punished, will regain its rightful place as the citadel of democracy in the East."

According to the report, the fighting was ravishing the city. It seemed to be suffering greater damage than was done to Cologne, Hamburg or London.

PARATROOPERS DROP ON CORREGIDOR

Bataan, Philippine Islands (AP): General Walter Krueger's headquarters reported today the city of Mariveles had been liberated by amphibious attack and the last of the fourteen thousand Japanese on Bataan had been killed or captured. The island fortress of Corregidor was under siege from sea and air. A regiment of paratroopers has been dropped on the island and a beachhead established. The drop was supported by destroyer units from the Fifth Fleet, which moved within twelve hundred yards of the beach. With fire control provided from shore, the destroyers concentrated their attacks on pillboxes and fired directly into the mouths of caves filled with Japanese marines. According to the communiqué, the recapture of the island fortress was imminent.

John read the articles twice. *The pace of the war is speeding up and we're winning it, he said to himself. Maybe what I just wrote to Sandy about going out and getting it over with is going to happen. Maybe this will really be the last time I'm away from her.*

The next morning at 08:00 *Franklin* left Pier 3D. In heavy fog, she steamed to Sinclair Inlet, an isolated area in the waters of Puget Sound, to take on bombs and missiles. At 08:34 she dropped anchor and at 10:10 Ammunition Lighters YF-813 and YF-132 tied up to the starboard side. Within a few minutes, conveyors began to move the ship's aviation ordinance aboard. Aviation ordinancemen loaded five-hundred and one-thousand-pound bombs and scores of Tiny Tim missiles onto padded rigs. Slowly, one at a time, they were stored below. The very slow and dangerous process took four full days.

25 January, 1945
Sinclair Inlet
***Franklin* Heads Back to War**

Thursday dawned cloudy and cool. A stiff twenty-knot wind blew in from over the cold waters of the Sound and snaked through the ship. At 06:15 *Franklin* began taking on the rest of her aviation gasoline, and in less than half an hour all final preparations for getting underway were finished.

At 10:53, with Beckley at the helm and Gehres in conn, and Joe Taylor and Steve Jurika on the bridge, the *Franklin* left Sinclair Inlet. She steamed, at various courses and speeds, through the waters of the Straits of Juan de Fuca, with Canada on her starboard side and Washington to port, toward the sweeping waters of the Pacific Ocean.

When they reached Tatoosh Light, Gehres opened the envelope containing the secret instructions for *Franklin's* return to combat.

"Chief," he said. "Come to course 230 degrees."

"Aye, sir." Beckley responded.

The *Franklin* headed West Southwest away from the Washington coast into the waters of the Northern Pacific.

"We're headed for Pearl Harbor, then on to Ulithi and the Fifth Fleet," Gehres said. "We'll be part of the forces that attack Okinawa and the Japanese mainland."

"That figures, sir," Taylor said. "We've just about taken Iwo, so Okinawa seems like the next target."

"Yeah, and when we get to Okinawa, the Japanese mainland is less than a hundred miles away," Gehres replied.

Gehres turned to Jurika. "Steve," he said, "I want to begin antiaircraft drills as soon as we hook up with the *Wilkes;* she'll be our escort. We'll begin drilling the air wing first thing in the morning."

Franklin surged into open waters. At 13:15 they sighted the *Wilkes* and Task Unit 06.12.1 formed.

On the bridge Gehres, Taylor and Jurika watched the *Wilkes* come abeam. When she was directly abeam, Gehres ordered, "Sound General Quarters."

The ship's klaxon bonged. The siren shrieked. "General Quarters! General Quarters! All hands man your battle stations!"

Men rushed away from their lathes, dropped their work in the wardrooms and galleys, ran from the laundry and sheet metal room—all headed to their battle stations.

"Signal *Wilkes* to release target balloons," Gehres ordered.

John's gun crew was topside immediately. In seconds they were on station scanning the horizon for targets.

When *Wilkes* released the first cluster of balloons all the guns on *Franklin's* starboard side drew them into their sights. One balloon after another was blasted into bits by *Franklin's* 20- and 40-mm guns. After firing over two thousand rounds, the command came to cease-fire.

John was pleased. "Good show," he said to Ski and Lowe. Then he congratulated the rest of the gun crew. "Great job, guys. Feinstein, Colson, Bonin, Garcia. All you guys. I never saw you move so fast and smooth. You must've been eating Wheaties or something."

This brought laughter. Pride and confidence spread over their faces.

John stuck his head into the ready-service locker. "That was a great job," he said, looking directly at Jardin. "I'm proud of you guys."

Jardin nodded and gave John a little wave, but John saw fear in his eyes. He recognized that even this drill was tough for Jardin to take.

On the bridge, Gehres scanned the horizon. "Everything seems to be working well," he said.

"Yes, sir," Taylor replied. "*Franklin's* now a better ship than she's ever been."

"Joe, what's your feeling about the crew now?" Gehres asked.

"The offenses are way, way down and relatively routine. I think we finally have ourselves a crew, Captain."

"That's what I gathered from the reports, too," Gehres said. "It can't come at a better time. I think there's going to be some rough going out there. We'll be fighting very close to the Jap mainland and they can do a lot of damage from there."

"Aye, sir—but I think now we got a crew that can handle it."

Later that afternoon, Beckley and Sullivan walked down the hangar deck to the fantail. There were marines milling around everywhere; looking into corners, climbing into gun pits, taking photographs from the fantail and crowding the 'gedunk' bar.

"I'm not going to say this too loud," Beckley said, "but all these goddamned 'gyrenes' make me nervous."

Sullivan smiled and nodded. "It's like taking on a bunch of attack dogs. You never know when one's going to turn on you."

Beckley laughed. "Marines and sailors—we don't mix very well—unless we're fighting someone else," he said.

"Well, that's the reason they came aboard—I hope," Sullivan concluded.

That night, after taps, John lay in his bunk, anxious about the war and longing for Sandy. He used the prayer Father O'Callahan had given him. He slowly relaxed and finally drifted into a light sleep and began to dream...He was in the middle of a beautiful yard filled with flowers and trees and a velvety green lawn. It was surrounded by a white picket fence. Behind him stood a white house with large bay windows and a porch with two brightly-colored lawn chairs on it. There were two children playing in the yard…a boy about five and a beautiful little girl about three. John looked closely at the little girl. She was the very likeness of Sandy. He looked at the little boy. He could see his image in the boy's face. His heart filled with joy. He looked back to the porch and Sandy was standing there smiling and waving. He raised his hand and called to her. She waved back and ran toward him. He held out his arms to receive her. When she was about to come into his arms, the ship's siren began to wail….

"General Quarters! General Quarters! All hands man your battle stations."

John dropped to the deck and hastily wriggled into his clothes. Ski was next to him doing the same thing. They strapped on their life jackets and helmets.

"Son-of-a-bitch," Ski groused. "I hate these fucking night drills."

"How do you know it's a drill?" John asked as they rushed up the ladders to the flight deck.

"Because they didn't announce that it *wasn't* a drill," Ski replied, amid the clatter of thousands of footsteps on the rungs of steel ladders.

"That doesn't always make it certain," John said, still feeling the warm glow from his dream.

When they reached Able Sponson, Lowe and Garcia were already there, pulling off gun caps and breach covers. Within minutes everyone in John's gun crew was on station.

John looked out at the horizon. There wasn't a cloud in the sky. The bright moonlight created a shimmering path across the ocean to the *Franklin's* starboard side.

"This is a drill," Ski said. "There's no fucking Japs this close to the United States."

"That's what they said at Pearl Harbor," John replied. "You be alert. Even if it's a drill, we need to be ready."

John scanned the horizon through binoculars. He and his gun crew waited in silence. The winter wind gusted through the sponson. It was cold and irritating. Minutes ticked on….

"Goddamn, this fucking wind bites right through you," Garcia said. "When this war's over I'm going right back to sunny California and never leave it again."

"Where you from in California?" Bonin asked.

"Beautiful Laguna Beach," Garcia replied. "I'm going back and have a big plate of my mom's homemade tamales. Mannn, can she cook…I'd give two week's pay for one of them right now."

"Well, when this goddamn thing is over," Bonin replied, "I'm going back to Minnesota and sleep for two weeks—and nobody better bother me."

"Minnesota? It's colder than piss up there," Garcia said.

"Yeah but it's home, cold or not," Bonin said.

"It'd be too fucking cold for me," Garcia replied.

They fell into silence. The only sound was the wind as it rushed through the sponson and over the flight deck.

"Man, I miss my mom," Garcia said, breaking the silence. "I miss my old man and the rest of my family, too, but I really miss my mom."

"I miss my dad," Bonin said. "I never realized how much I'd miss him. When I go home I'm going to take him fishing—just him and me."

"Fishing? Do they have good fishing in Minnesota?" Garcia asked.

"Hell yes, some of the best! But that's not the only reason why I'll take him fishing."

"What're the other reasons?"

"I was pretty wild when I was younger," Bonin answered after he thought a few moments. "My dad busted his butt to straighten me out and I didn't appreciate it."

"So you're going to try to make that right with him?" Garcia asked.

"Yeah, I am. I know now what he meant about my drinking and fucking around. He's my best friend and I didn't realize it."

"So what are you going to say?"

I'm going to tell him he was right. Then I'm going to take him fishing and try to square everything up."

"Okay, be alert you two," John interrupted. "Save that chatter for another time."

"We can talk and be alert at the same time, Gunner," Bonin said.

"Yeah, maybe you can and maybe not," Ski said.

"I wonder when this goddamned drill's going to end?" Colson asked.

"It'll end when it ends," Lowe replied. "Be alert."

Finally the command came: "All hands secure from General Quarters."

"See, John, they never did announce that it wasn't a drill," Ski said.

"So you're going to blame me for the way the Navy works?" John replied with a smile.

"Naww, Gunner. I just like to remind you when you're wrong."

"Okay, Ski, I'm reminded. Now let's go back down and hit the rack."

As John went down to his compartment the wonderful, warm glow his dream had created returned. He'd seen Sandy again. And he'd seen his children. He hoped his dream meant that he was going to survive—to live to have it all become a reality….

The *Franklin* and *Wilkes* both darkened and in Condition of Readiness III, making eighteen knots on course 245° steamed on through the choppy waters of the Pacific toward Pearl Harbor.

26 January, 1945
155 Miles SW of Seattle
Air Drills Begin

Beckley was at the helm early. He and Gehres, along with Joe Taylor, Steve Jurika and the new Air Officer, Commander Henry Hale, watched the sun come up through a layer of thin cirrus clouds. He looked westward. There wasn't a cloud in the sky. A fifteen-knot wind made the weather perfect for flying.

"Commander Hale," Gehres said, "I want the Air Group exercised every day—twice a day if possible, and every evening, too. I want night flying exercises. We have to improve our night flying skills. We've got a new group of pilots—all battle-tested veterans—but even veterans need to keep a fighting edge. I want an Air Group that's coordinated right down to the last man—synchronized—clock-like—let's work them hard and steady until they're flawless."

"Aye, sir," Hale replied. "It'll take time but we'll get it done."

"We've got over two weeks for these drills. That sure as hell should be enough time."

"Aye, Captain, it should. We start today. Air Strike Able should be taking off in about twenty minutes."

At 06:18 *Franklin* began launching fighters. Sixteen sleek F4U Corsairs, flown by newly boarded Marine pilots, streaked into the sky. John watched the sleek Corsairs climb into formation. The huge white stars on their fuselages glistened in the sun. Their engines, adorned with jagged shark's teeth, made them appear doubly ferocious. Their tails, striped in marine red and blue, added a final distinction.

"That's a sharp outfit," John said as he watched the Corsairs form into squadrons. "Look at those planes, nose art, tail art, white stars...."

"I hope they can fly as sharp as they look," Ski replied.

As soon as the Corsairs were airborne a squadron of *Franklin's* own Helldivers and Avengers, with Bill Zimler in command, thundered off the flight deck. They gained altitude and assumed positions. Zimler called for the execution of Operational Plan 1-45, a plan that consisted of a series of mock attacks on the ship. With engines screaming, the Corsairs attacked first. When they completed their run, Zimler's planes went in. They continued the attacks until 10:55 then, as scheduled, they landed without incident.

Soon after Air Strike Baker catapulted into the air. They executed the same plan and landed again without incident.

Then specially equipped Hellcat night-fighters were launched for combat air patrol drills and they, too, landed without incident.

Gehres and Hale watched as the arresting-cable jerked the last night fighter to a stop. "That was smooth, Henry. Tomorrow we execute Plan 1-55. It's a hell of a lot tougher than today's plan. If all goes well, then we'll give everybody Sunday off."

27 January, 1945
Plan 1-97-Z
Exercise "Moose Trap"

At dawn the next day, Gehres, Taylor, Jurika and Hale were on the bridge preparing for *Moose Trap*, a training exercise devised by Pacific Fleet Command for defense against kamikazes. This drill was scheduled for the first time. A squadron of *Franklin's* Corsairs, Hellcats and Avengers would go out beyond the horizon. They would then fly back on any course they chose, simulating a "kamikaze attack"—riding down the nulls in the ship's radar and attacking her at different angles and altitudes.

"The plan calls for some of the kamikazes to attack in twos and threes," Hale explained. "One will come in high and drill a lot of fire. The second will attack low over the water, right at the side of the ship. The third might dive straight down into the flight deck."

"This should test our air defenses," Gehres said as the first of the Corsairs took off. "It'll take them about fifteen minutes to get up and ready. He focused his binoculars on the Air Group and watched them maneuver into positions, then he ordered: "Sound General Quarters."

The klaxon sounded. The siren shrieked.

"General Quarters! General Quarters! All hands man your battle stations!"

John and Ski were standing in the chow line waiting for breakfast when the alarm came. They scrambled up the ladders to their guns.

"Goddamn, they could have at least waited until after breakfast," Ski griped as he slipped into the harness of the Mark 14 sight.

"Green canisters!" John shouted, signaling that they would be firing blanks. The 40-mms were loaded with a four-shell clip. The first three planes appeared on the edge of the horizon. John studied their movements through binoculars. "It looks like they'll attack us head-on," he said.

They did. The "kamikazes" headed, at full throttle, directly for *Franklin's* starboard side. When they were in range, *Franklin's* batteries opened fire, tracking their accuracy through gun-cameras installed in their gun sights.

In Able Sponson, John watched two Corsairs zoom toward the ship. They flew in low and headed directly toward the flight deck over the bow. He realized this might be a vulnerable place for *Franklin*. Most of her 40-mm and 20-mm didn't turn far enough into the flight deck to protect her from a head on attack over her bow. There was just one set of 40-mm guns mounted on the bow and one set of 40-mms above the bridge. The *Franklin's* five-inch guns were the main line of defense in this kind of attack. They were very powerful but slow compared to the speed of 40- and 20-mms....

The two Corsairs raced boldly in over the bow. As John suspected, the 20s and 40s on both the starboard and port sides couldn't track them in all the way. The 40-mms on the bow and behind the bridge took them under fire and the five-inch guns opened up—but their response seemed a little late for the fast-moving Corsairs.

The raids continued for three hours with attacks from Corsairs and then *Franklin's* own Helldivers and Avengers.

Finally, an order to cease-fire came over the loudspeakers.

John and his men were exhausted. They'd fired over twelve hundred rounds. Brass shell casings were a foot deep on the deck in the sponson.

"I'm sure the film will show our fire was accurate," John said, as his crew pitched the casings over the side and policed the area.

As they all went down the ladder to the mess hall, John said to Ski, "I'll bet we got at least three planes."

"Hell, maybe a couple more than that," Ski said, as his foot hit the deck at the bottom of the ladder. "I'd guess it was five, maybe even six."

They walked down the last passageway. John noticed that Jardin was walking by himself, well behind the rest of the gun crew. He fell out of line and waited for him. When Jardin was beside him, John asked, "How's it going, Jim?"

"It's pretty rough, Gunner," Jardin replied. "I still can't shake the thought that I'm not going to make it."

"Want to talk to the chaplain?" John asked.

"Not yet, but I've been thinking about it. These close-up drills drive me crazy."

"I don't know what to say about that," John said. "I thought we could help by assigning you to an area where the noise wouldn't be a problem."

"I know, Gunner, but it didn't help. I'm as nervous as ever."

"Well, keep working on it, Jim. You'll be okay."

"I hope so," Jardin said.

"Don't forget, if you want to talk, let me know. I'll get you with Father O'Callahan right away."

That afternoon Air Wing Five returned to more traditional drills. They practiced dive-bombing and strafing the ship. The drills went smoothly the rest of the day. At 16:55 *Franklin* recovered all aircraft safely and without incident. Later that night Hellcat night-fighters took off on combat air patrols and at 21:33 all landed safely.

The intense air activity continued morning, afternoon and night for over two weeks without a mishap. By this time, Gehres was convinced that he had an air wing that was honed and combat ready.

13 February, 1945
Pearl Harbor
Territory of Hawaii

Late Wednesday afternoon the forward lookout on the port side of *Franklin's* flight deck sighted the island of Molokai about thirty-five miles away. In Condition of Readiness III, *Franklin*, in company with the destroyer *Wilkes*, steamed South Southwest at a speed of eighteen knots to Pearl Harbor. As they approached the Hawaiian Channel, *Franklin* detached *Wilkes* and made preparations for entering port. At 20:37 *Franklin* moored port side to Berth Fox 11, Ford Island, with six manila lines and four wire hawsers.

The next morning John got permission from the OD to go down on the dock. He was going to talk to Sandy for the first time in nearly three weeks. To top this off, it was Valentine's Day. He walked down the gangway. The scent of tropical flowers filled the air. Gentle trade winds blew in from the ocean, and the sunshine was radiant. Before he reached the bottom of the gangway, he heard someone call his name.

He looked back. Beckley and Sullivan were standing at the top waving.

"Where you going?" Sullivan asked.

"I'm going to call my wife," John replied.

"There's a long line," Sullivan said, pointing to the line of men waiting to use the pay phone on the dock.

John walked back up to them. "I know where there's a secret phone," he said in almost a whisper.

"A secret phone?" Sullivan asked.

"Yeah. Beck knows about it. We both used it the last time we were here."

Sullivan looked at Beckley. "A secret phone?"

"Yeah, there is. Down between those warehouses."

"No shit? If there's a secret phone in Pearl Harbor, I have to see it," Sullivan said. "Mind if I come along, John? I'd like to call my family, but I didn't want to wait in that line."

"I think I'll go, too," Beckley said. "I'd like to make a call."

On the way John told Sullivan how he'd found the phone. When they walked by the spot where he almost ran over O'Callahan, John said, "Right here. This is where I almost ran over him."

When they reached the phone, there was no one around.

"I'll be damned," Sullivan said. "It's hard to believe. A phone without a line of sailors."

"You guys go first," John said.

After Beckley and Sullivan finished their calls, they started back to the dock.

"Hey you guys, stand by a minute. Say hello to Sandy," John said. "I think she'd feel great if she knew you guys were right here beside me."

Sullivan and Beckley stepped back to the phone.

"Hi, Honey," John said, when Sandy answered the phone. "Happy Valentine's Day. I love you."

"John. I was hoping it was you," Sandy said. "It's been nearly three weeks. How are you, Darling?"

"I'm fine. Guess who's standing next to me?"

"Who?"

"Beckley and Sullivan."

"Can I say hello to them?"

"Sure, Honey, that's why they're waiting."

"How's the prettiest girl in California?" Beckley asked when he took the phone.

Beckley and Sandy talked a few moments, then Sullivan said, "Come on, it's my turn."

"I think you're prettier than the prettiest girl in California," Sullivan said.

They began to talk; then there was a pause.

"Oh! You don't have to worry about that, Sandy," Sullivan said. "We'll take care of John, and he'll take care of us. That's the way it works out here. Besides, the worst part of the war is over. We're knocking on Tojo's doorstep with the most powerful fleet in the world. Nothing's going to happen to a powerful fleet like ours."

There was another pause, as Sandy said something to Sullivan.

"Don't you worry. We'll all be fine, Sandy," Sullivan replied. "Well, I'll get off the line—we just waited to say hello…."

Beckley took the receiver back "…and to tell you that we think about you. I'll get your husband back on the line."

Beckley handed John the phone and, with a little half-salute, he and Sullivan began to walk back toward the ship.

"You see, Honey, I'm not out here alone," John said.

"They're so great, John. Tell them I love them for what they just told me. I feel a lot better now."

"I will, Honey."

"You've been on my mind constantly since you left, Darling."

"I think about you day and night, too, Honey," John said.

"Can you tell me how your trip was?"

"We had a good trip, Honey. There wasn't a single glitch, and we had some exercises that could've caused one."

"What kind of exercises?"

"Oh, mock attacks by our own planes."

"That sounds dangerous."

"We didn't have *any* problems with them," John assured her. "Honey, it's wonderful here," he said moving away from talk that might get worrisome. "Orchids grow right out in the open, right in people's backyards. The weather's always beautiful and warm, and the trade winds are balmy and gentle."

"John, it sounds so beautiful. I'd love to see it all. Maybe someday…."

"Not maybe, Honey. When the war's over we're going to spend at least a month here together. I promise you this."

"Oh, John, that would be wonderful." There was a pause. Then Sandy said, "'When the war's over'—I just love those words…."

The operator's voice interrupted them. "Sorry, sir. Your three minutes are up. To continue this conversation for another two minutes, please deposit seventy-five cents."

John stuck in three more quarters. "The war can't go on forever, Honey," he said. "Like Chief Sullivan just said, we're winning it. Scuttlebutt says it'll be over in two years at most. Then we can be together for good. No more being away from each other ever again."

There was a pause filled with static.

"I sure miss you, Sandy," John said through the static, "especially because today's Valentine's Day. But there will be many other Valentine's Days after the war's over—and we can be together on all of them."

"Oh, I hope so," Sandy replied. "I didn't realize being apart could be so miserable."

"Well, Honey, we've probably got only a few seconds left. I'll try to call you every day until we leave."

"Is there *anything* you can tell me about where you're going?"

"No, Sandy. Nobody knows. It's top-secret. But I'm pretty sure it'll be the area we talked about before I left."

Sandy was silent.

"Are you okay?" John asked.

"Yeah, but I still worry...."

"Don't worry, Honey. We'll be okay. I'll call you tomorrow afternoon."

"About the same time?"

"No. We'll be loading ammunition tomorrow. Probably very late in the afternoon," John said. "Good-bye, Honey. I love you."

John caught Beckley and Sullivan just as they started up the gangway. "Gee, thanks a lot. You both made Sandy feel a lot better. She worries, but she always feels better when she talks to you guys."

John left Beckley and Sullivan and walked slowly toward the ladder to the flight deck. Maybe waiting was worse than being away, he thought. He'd hoped it wouldn't be this tough for Sandy. For a second the old fear that she might not wait flashed through his mind. He shoved it aside. *Don't be a damned fool, he said to himself. Of course she'll wait. She loves me. She's my wife, one of the most honest people I've ever met*. He visualized Sandy being here with him, spending time in this wonderful climate, on these romantic islands. He'd come back. They'd come here...He loved the thought...."

17 February, 1945
Pearl Harbor
On to the Combat Area

On the bridge Gehres, Taylor, Jurika and Beckley watched Oil Barge YO-71 come alongside. *Franklin* began taking on fuel oil. The work of restocking provisions, fuel and ammunition continued. Conveyors moved heavy supplies of 20-mm and 40-mm ammunition up to the hangar deck to replace the blanks fired in the "kamikaze" drills. As soon as the canisters reached them, John and his gunners moved them below and stowed them in the ship's magazines. Supplies of all kinds were hauled aboard and were stowed in their places below decks. *Franklin* was loading up, preparing to go back into the war.

"The trip from Seattle was smooth," Gehres said as he watched the activity on the flight deck.

"Yeah, it was, Captain," Joe Taylor said, "and we didn't have any problems with those "kamikaze" drills."

"Those marine pilots are reckless but they're skilled," Gehres replied." They came in awful damn close before they pulled up. You can sure see some of 'Pappy' Boyington's intensity there."

"Yeah," Beckley said. "They made me a little nervous, but I think they were just showing off a tad."

"Well, all that crap about being jinxed has settled down," Gehres ventured.

"Yes, sir," Taylor replied. "You must bring us good luck. Before you came aboard we had some kind of an accident almost every day."

"It's no wonder those rumors got started," Gehres replied.

Beckley looked out on the huge number thirteen on the flight deck. "I was sure getting convinced there was *something* going on, sir."

Gehres laughed. "Horse feathers, Chief. You know damn well there's no such thing as a jinx."

"Aye, Captain, I guess you're right," Beckley replied as he watched one crate of food after another come up from the dock.

Fueling and taking on ammunition and supplies went on most of the day. By 16:30 *Franklin* had taken on over five hundred and fifty thousand gallons of fuel oil and all the supplies and ammunition she required. She would be completely fueled by early evening, and ready to go to sea in the morning.

Late that afternoon, right after he finished his call to Sandy, John became troubled and dejected. As he walked back to the *Franklin*, he realized that telling her he wouldn't be calling her for awhile had frightened and troubled her, but there was nothing he could do to help her. He couldn't tell her when he was leaving, or where he was going, or when he was coming back. He knew she'd worry. It disheartened him to think of what she'd have to go through, and there was nothing he could say to help her—even if he called her again right now….

When he got back to the *Franklin* he went to the library and wrote Sandy a long letter. He told her how much he loved her and how sorry he was that he would have to be out of touch. He poured out his heart and soul. He told her how much he missed her, how she was always in his thoughts and how he yearned to get back to her and spend the rest of his life loving her. This was all he could do. The only consolation he had was he could mail his letter from Pearl Harbor. It would get to her sooner that way.

He went down on the dock and dropped his letter into a mailbox. After he got back he walked across the hangar deck toward his compartment and as he did, he ran into Beckley and Sullivan coming up from chief's quarters.

"Hey, where you guys going?" he asked.

"We're going into Honolulu to drink a few beers," Beckley replied. "Might be awhile before we get the chance again."

"Want to come along, John?" Sullivan asked.

"Would you mind? I'm kind of down—maybe a couple of beers will do me some good."

"Hell, get your dress blues on and come with us," Sullivan said.

When the bus reached Gecko's Place, a small bar that catered to sailors, just across the street from the Royal Hawaiian Hotel, they got out. Before they went in, John bought a piece of fresh pineapple for each of them from a sidewalk stand. "This stuff is great," he said, his spirits uplifted somewhat by the taste of the delicious fruit. "You can't find pineapple like this in Colorado."

When they were seated, they all ordered beer.

"Thanks for letting me come," John said. "I was really down when I stumbled into you guys. I'll buy the first round."

"Why were you down?" Beckley asked.

"Because I realized after I talked to Sandy how much she'd worry and what I was about to put her through."

"Yeah," Beckley said. "We all feel that way. I guess that's one of the reasons I'm here, too."

"The worst part of it is you can't say anything to help them," Sullivan said. "Nothing."

"Yeah, that's what got to me, too," John said. "You can't say a goddamned word—you feel so helpless. I did write her a long letter, though. I mailed it just before I ran into you guys."

The drinks arrived. They drank in silence for a while. The beer relaxed John and boosted his spirits a little more. "When the war ends, maybe the three of us can get together here again and *really* have a celebration," he said.

"Yeah. I like that idea, John," Sullivan said, as he ordered a second round. "Let's make a vow. Let's drink to it." He raised his glass. "To the end of the war and getting together back here to *really* celebrate."

"I'll drink to that," Beckley said with a smile.

"So will I," John added, raising his glass.

One beer followed another. They talked about the things they wanted to do when the war ended. Beckley said he might leave the Navy and go to college. Sullivan said he loved the Navy and was going to stay in. John talked about becoming an engineer and having a family.

They got a little tipsy. They rambled on, drank beer and enjoyed each other's company. For a short while they stopped thinking about loved ones and their fears about the war. Their thoughts were far removed from the danger they'd face when they reached the treacherous waters ahead of them.

Finally it was 22:00. "We better get back to the ship," Beckley said. As they walked toward the bus stop, John said, "Thanks a lot, guys. Sometimes I wonder what I'd do if I didn't have your friendship."

CHAPTER TWENTY-FIVE

18 February, 1945
Rejoining the Fifth Fleet
Caroline Islands

The next morning Fleet Oiler YOL-131 moored along the port side and delivered the last of the aviation gasoline, and at 07:16 *Franklin* received Lieutenant Alvin Little, harbor pilot, aboard. Two tugs arrived and were standing by, churning water.

"We're about ready," Gehres said.

"Division heads report they're all okay," Beckley said.

"Single up all lines!" came the call over the loudspeaker. "Cast off the bow line! Cast off the stern line! Now cast off all lines!"

"All engines back one third," Gehres commanded.

Franklin's powerful engines made her decks tremble as she moved slowly back from the pier. The waiting tugboats came alongside and turned her around, and at 08:53 she was underway. At 09:56 the harbor pilot was released and *Franklin* steamed through the Hawaiian Channel to the Pacific. When she reached open waters, she joined the carriers *Hornet, Intrepid* and *Bataan*, the cruisers *Guam, Pittsburgh* and *Athelina* and nine destroyers that included the *Wilkes, Fletcher, Hubbard, Walker* and *Zellars*. Together they formed Task Group 58.1.3.

Hornet with Admiral Joseph "Jocko" Clark in flag, was Task Group Guide. *Franklin* and *Intrepid* flanked her at distances of twenty-five hundred yards and *Bataan* was in arrears at thirty-one hundred yards. They assumed a course of 259° and a speed of eighteen knots and, in zigzag Plan 6, steamed toward Ulithi Atoll.

At 10:30 Gehres received a message from *Hornet*. He read the message, smiled and said, "It's from Admiral 'Jocko' Clark. He welcomes us back to the Fifth Fleet. He says from where they are, we look brand new—that Bremerton must have agreed with us—that he's happy to have us in his command again."

"You served under Admiral Clark, sir?" Beckley asked.

"Yes, in the Solomons. Since then there's been a lot of water under the bridge for both of us, but it's always great to reconnect with an old friend, especially one like 'Jocko.'"

"Admiral Clark's got a great reputation," Beckley said, "both as a gentleman and as a warrior."

"That Cherokee Indian Admiral is one of the finest men in the Navy," Gehres said.

"They say he's one hell of a fighter, too," Taylor chimed in. "The word about him is that he asks or gives no quarter. I'm glad we're on his side."

"He *is* a hell of a warrior," Gehres replied. "I was with him in action around Guadalcanal and Salvo Island. He proved that to us there all the time." Gehres turned to the chief signalman. "Chief, send this message back to Admiral Clark. I'll dictate:

Dear Admiral,

Thank you for your heart-warming message. The officers and men of the Franklin are proud and honored to serve in your command. I do indeed remember those tough days gone by. Let's hope what's coming up is easier than it was. It should be. We've got a lot more firepower than we had then. Thank you again for your warm welcome."

He paused as though he would say more, then said, "Sign it Les Gehres, Captain, *USS Franklin*."

About fifteen minutes later, a message came from Clark:

To: Captain Leslie Gehres
From: Admiral Joseph J Clark
It should to be easier Les, but don't count on it.
Jocko Clark

20 February, 1945
270 Miles SW of Pearl Harbor
Collision

It was a perfect day for flying. A few cirrostratus clouds nestled on the eastern horizon in an otherwise clear sky. A ten-knot wind that blew toward the Task Group from the northwest raised tiny whitecaps on the blue ocean surface. Task Group 58.1 again prepared to defend against "kamikaze" in a *Moose Trap* exercise. Planes from the *Hornet* and *Franklin* would fly as "kamikaze." Fighters from the *Intrepid* and *Bataan* would provide the air defense. All ships would fire blanks and record their hits and misses through gun cameras as *Franklin* had earlier.

At 8:22 thirty F4U Corsairs, manned by Marine pilots, were elevated to the flight deck and positioned behind the catapult for take-off. As soon as they were airborne they joined thirty-six Hellcats from *Hornet*. They divided into groups of twos and threes and flew toward the horizon at almost all points on the compass. When they were out of sight, Hellcats and Corsairs from *Intrepid* and *Bataan* catapulted into the sky and assumed defensive positions about ten miles away from the Task Group.

Beckley and Commander Zimler, who would fly later in the day, watched the developing scene from positions on the fantail.

"The whole sky is busy," Zimler said as he moved his binoculars in an arc around the horizon. "Looks like an easy place to have an accident."

"I hope not," replied Beckley. "Since we left Bremerton things have been smooth. I sure as hell wouldn't like that jinx stuff to surface again."

"Captain Gehres wouldn't either," Zimler replied. "He gave us a talk before we left. He came down heavy on people who circulated rumors about bad luck or jinxes."

"Wasn't that directed at the newspaper reporters who were there?" Beckley asked.

"Yeah, pretty much," Zimler said. "But he put the word out for everybody, especially the officers."

"What'd he say, sir?"

"He said he'd have none of those rumors on the *Franklin*; that he didn't believe one damned thing about jinxes or bad luck."

"Yeah, I *know* that's how he feels," Beckley said. "He told me that on the bridge before we left the other day."

Beckley watched the planes take positions on the horizon. Zimler had come back aboard just before they left Bremerton and this was his first chance to visit with him. He seemed to be very in control. "How are you feeling now, sir?" he asked.

"I'm as good as new, Beck," Zimler replied as he focused his binoculars toward the horizon. "My headaches are gone. There's no more ringing in my ears. The doctors at Bremerton Naval Hospital said I was fit for flight duty."

"And how do *you* feel about what the Captain said about jinxes, sir?"

"Aww...I don't know. I guess he's right," Zimler replied. "I think I'm almost over my jitters. We had our problems—maybe more than most ships—but I had some time to think about it in the hospital and back home."

"You think there's nothing to it?"

"Well, I'm not sure, but we've been through too much to worry about it, Beck. If we're jinxed—we're jinxed. What can we do about it? Besides, it's been very smooth the last few weeks."

"Aye, sir, that it has," Beckley replied.

On the horizon the "kamikaze" turned and surged toward the Task Group at top speed. The Hellcats and Corsairs in defensive positions countered the attack. Frantic dogfights erupted in the skies above the Task Group. Some of the "kamikaze" broke through the fighter screen and hurled toward the carriers. The destroyers and cruisers in the outer screen opened fire. Then every gun on the *Franklin* and every carrier in the Task Group began to blaze away. Still the "kamikazes" sped on.

In Able Sponson, the activities of John's gun crew became frantic. John had instructed his men to view these drills as an actual attack. They blazed away at the attacking Corsairs. The noise from the blanks was deafening. Shell casings flew out of the 40s.

The bold-as-brass Marine pilots zoomed by.

Shell casings, a foot deep, cluttered the deck. "We've got a minute now," John said as a pause in the action developed. "Throw those shell casings over the side."

Everyone in the crew scrambled after the casings. "Get 'em off fast!" John shouted. "Then get back to your stations. They'll be back at us in a flash."

The Corsairs turned and streaked back.

"Commence firing! Commence firing!" John shouted, as they hurled toward them.

As the 40-mms began to fire, John heard shouts coming from the ready-service locker.

He turned to see what the commotion was. As he did, Jardin rushed out of the locker. He shoved Lowe violently in the back and stormed toward the ladder.

John rushed over and stood in his way.

The slender seaman tried to get around him, but John planted his feet directly in his path. He wrapped his arms around Jardin and restrained him. "What the hell are you doing, Jardin?" he shouted.

"Lemme go! I can't take this any more, Gunner!" Jardin shouted back.

John released him. "You get back to your post, Jardin. Now."

"I can't stand it there any more, Gunner. I've gotta get away from all this shit."

John looked into Jardin's eyes. "You get your ass back to your post, or I'm going to have to kick your ass back there, sailor."

Jardin glared up at John.

"Goddamn it! I said go! Get the fuck back there," John shouted with anger in his voice now. "Come on, those planes are coming back! Go!"

Jardin dropped his eyes and moved back into the ready-service locker.

"Resume firing!"

Ammunition flowed. Guns blazed away at the oncoming attackers. Still they came. The *Franklin*'s Marine pilots were fearless—they headed directly toward her side. At the very last second, they'd pull up—sending waves of booming engine noise over the flight deck. The ear-splitting noise was deafening and unnerving.

As soon as they sped away, John went back to the ready-service locker.

"Where's Jardin?" he asked.

"He slipped out in the middle of that last attack, Gunner," Dixon said. "We were too busy to say anything."

"Where the hell'd he go?"

"He headed up the ladder to the flight deck."

John called Ski and Lowe. "Take over," he said. "I think the attacks are finished, but I can't be sure. I'm going up to try to find that kook."

John made his way down the starboard side of the flight deck. He couldn't locate Jardin anywhere. He circled around the fantail and walked up the port side. Suddenly he saw Jardin standing on the edge of a life jacket storage locker just below the flight deck. He was staring at the ocean below.

"Jardin! Don't move! I'll be right there," he yelled, trying hard to make his voice heard above the wind and flight deck noise. "Jardin! Don't do anything stupid! Come on, Buddy, step back from that edge," John shouted when he was near enough to be heard.

Jardin looked over his shoulder at John. "Leave me alone, Gunner. I've had it. I can't take any more of this crazy fucking bullshit."

"Step back, Jim," John said. "Let's talk about it."

There was a long pause. Jardin seemed to be thinking about what John said. He started to move back. Then, as though possessed he took a step forward, and jumped.

John tried to grab him, but he was too late. He looked over the side. Jardin was still alive. He was caught in some rigging below a sponson off the hangar deck. John watched him for a moment. He was struggling to get free, but the more he struggled the more enmeshed he became.

John hailed a fire-fighting crew and they rushed down to the sponson. The fire fighters produced a rope and lowered him toward Jardin.

"I know what you're going through, Jim," John said when he was just above him. "I know it's tougher than a bitch!"

"It's those noises," Jardin said, hysteria in his voice. "I get so scared, I don't know what I'm doing."

"Grab hold of my waist," John ordered when he was near enough. "I'm taking you back up. We'll have a talk with the chaplain."

"No! I don't want to see a chaplain."

"Come on, he helped me. He'll help you."

"You *really* think he'll do any good, Gunner?" Jardin asked.

"Wrap your arms around my waist and we'll see."

After they were hoisted into the sponson, John took Jardin directly to O'Callahan's office. His yeoman passed the word for him. In a few minutes O'Callahan came in, wearing complete battle dress.

When John explained what happened, O'Callahan asked them to join him in his small, private conference area.

When seated, John gave him a full account of recent events. Then Jardin told his story. When he finished, O'Callahan asked, "So you're afraid you're going to be killed, Jim?"

"Yeah, Father, I am," Jardin replied, looking down into the deck.

"Well, I want to tell you something, son. *You're not alone in that.* Everybody on this ship's got that fear. I've got it. John's got it. I can't name a man that hasn't."

Jardin looked at John. "You afraid, Gunner?"

"Hell yes! I wouldn't be human if I wasn't."

"Let's face it, Jim. We all face the possibility of being killed," O'Callahan said. "Sure you could get it, but I could, too. So could John or anyone else in your gun crew—or on this ship for that matter."

"But Father, this time I think *I'm* the one that gets it. I can't shake the feeling that we're going to get blasted and I'm going to get killed," Jardin said, still looking down at the deck.

"Sure, and you might, sailor," O'Callahan said. "Any of us might. But I want you to understand one thing. When your time comes, *it comes*. The time of death is not in our hands, Jim—*it's in God's hands.*"

"Yeah, but what if I wasn't here on this damn ship? What if I was home, away from all this?"

"People die in their sleep, sailor," O'Callahan said. "I don't care where you are. You could be home in bed or hiding behind a steel wall. If it's your time—*it'll happen* no matter where you are or where you hide."

Jardin thought for awhile, then took a deep breath and raised his eyes from the deck. He looked at John, then back to O'Callahan. "So it's in God's hands, not mine," he said slowly.

"That's right, son."

"That makes it sound different, Father."

"He looked back to the deck and was silent again. "John said you gave him a special prayer, Father. Can you give me one, too?"

"Sure. I'll give you the same prayer I gave John. When your fears mount and seem to be getting out of hand, say 'God is my Great Source and my Protector.' Feel down deep inside yourself what this really means."

"I don't think that little prayer will help me, Father."

"Yes it will, Jim," John said. "Try it—you'll see."

"If it's my time, it's my time," Jardin said slowly. "Maybe that's a better prayer, Father."

"It might be, Jim. As long as you remember it's God's call, not yours," O'Callahan said. "But there's something else you have to remember, too, Jim. If it's *not* your time, it's *not your time*. You have to keep that in mind, too, son."

Jardin sat motionless for a long while. Then he said, "Thanks, Father. I think what you said helps me."

He turned to John. "Thanks a lot, Gunner." He looked back down at the deck. "Am I going on report?"

"Next time, sailor," John said. "I don't think you could help yourself this time."

On the fantail, Beckley and Zimler watched the Hellcats, Helldivers and Corsairs regroup to return to their carriers. The drills were over. They'd come off without a single hitch.

"Wow! Was that ever a show," Beckley exclaimed. "If you'd let yourself go for a minute, you'd swear it was the real thing."

"Yeah. I hope it goes this well when the kamikaze are flown by real Jap pilots," Zimler said as he turned to walk across the hangar deck.

There was a sudden violent collision. Two Corsairs, flown by Marine pilots from *Franklin*, smashed into each other in mid-air. A violent explosion! A huge fireball engulfed both planes. Fatally damaged, they hung there for a few seconds, then plummeted into the ocean. There was no sign of life.

"Good God! What the hell happened?" Zimler asked, his voice filled with the grim feelings only a pilot could have about a mid-air collision.

Beckley shook his head. "I don't know, sir. They were all alone. There wasn't another plane within a mile. It all happened in a matter of seconds."

That night there was another crash. One of *Franklin's* night fighters, flown by Ensign George Stanley, crashed into the water off the ship's port quarter while in a landing approach. The destroyer *Hubbard* rescued Stanley, but his gunner, Joe Cobb, was killed by the impact. The next day a Corsair accidentally dropped its belly tank while landing. It burst into flames on *Franklin's* flight deck. At almost the same time, another Corsair crashed off the port bow.

The pilot, Second Lieutenant Robert Guetzole, was badly injured. Jitters about a jinx began to surface again.

**26 February, 1945
Ulithi Atoll,
Caroline Islands**

Task Group 58.1.3 entered the waters surrounding the Caroline Islands. There were American and British warships everywhere—converging on Ulithi from all points on the compass. Battleships, carriers, cruisers, flotillas of destroyers, ammunition ships, LCIs, LCMs and LSTs and all kinds of other attack vessels cut through the water toward the tiny volcanic atoll.

When *Franklin* steamed through Mugai Channel into Ulithi lagoon, there were at least twenty carriers at anchor. The captains of other ships in the Fifth Fleet knew that *Franklin* had been damaged in the Philippine Sea. They had their crews on deck standing at attention and rendering honors. Messages flashed by semaphore: *Welcome back to the fighting forces! Welcome back to the Fifth Fleet! You look great, Big Ben!*

John, with Sullivan and the rest of the gun crew, watched the panorama unfold. When they steamed past the cruisers, John saw the *Santa Fe*.

"There's the *Santa Fe,*" he said. "I hope I can see my buddy, Tom, this time."

A few minutes later a signalman came up to the edge of the flight deck.

"Are you John Oxler?"

John nodded.

"I got a message for you. It's from Tom Rashinski."

John read the message aloud: "Can you meet me at the beer station tonight about 19:00?"

He looked at Sullivan who laughed and nodded. "He's way ahead of you," he said.

On the bridge the harbor pilot, Commander William Doak, was at the conn with Beckley at the helm, and Gehres, Taylor and Jurika standing by. As the *Franklin* steamed toward Berth 21, she passed one huge warship after another. There was an armada of fleet carriers weighing at anchor: *Enterprise, Yorktown, Essex, Wasp, Lexington, Hancock, Independence, Monterey,* the *Bon Homme Richard* and *Saratoga*. Powerful battleships were anchored next in line: the *Iowa, Wisconsin, Missouri, New York, North Carolina, Alabama, Washington* and *New Jersey*. Mighty heavy cruisers came into view next: *Pittsburgh, Baltimore, Indianapolis, San Francisco, Dallas, Salt Lake City, Birmingham....*

"It's awesome. That's the only way to describe it," Gehres said as they went by.

"It sure is," Joe Taylor replied. "To me, this looks like the biggest fleet ever assembled. The Fifth Fleet is probably ten times as big as *all* the ships in the prewar Navy."

When *Franklin* arrived at her anchorage she dropped her starboard anchor into twenty-four fathoms of crystal clear water, so clear the anchor could be seen on the sandy bottom of the atoll.

"Joe," Gehres said as he looked over the crowded lagoon, "we're taking Admirals Davison and Bogan aboard this afternoon. Better make sure the Admiral's quarters are shipshape."

"Aye, sir."

At 13:20 Rear Admiral Davison came aboard. Rear Admiral Gerald Bogan, who would be an advisor to Davison because of his extensive carrier tactical skills, was with him. Later that afternoon a Fleet Oiler came along the starboard side to deliver fuel and aviation gasoline. *Franklin* started to receive provisions. Almost as soon as they were hoisted aboard breakout details stowed them below. Extra crates of ammunition for all of *Franklin*'s guns and planes were hauled up next. Work details from the Gunnery Division moved them down into the magazines. *Franklin* was getting prepared for a major carrier strike.

Late the next afternoon John caught one of *Franklin*'s motor whaleboats and went ashore. As soon as he arrived he spotted Tom leaning on the fender of a Jeep reading a paper. They greeted each other warmly and started to walk to the beer station.

"I got a letter from Jo Ann," Tom said. She told me you got married—was it the girl we talked about on Eniwetok?"

"Yes," John said. "I got three letters from her all at once about two weeks after I saw you."

"But you didn't think she'd write?"

"I know. I didn't think she would, but she did. It turned into the most wonderful thing that's ever happened to me." Then he told Tom what happened. "I couldn't believe it when Father O'Callahan walked into that study," John said, shaking his head. "Sandy said I looked embarrassed, but when he remembered what happened, he laughed about it. He turned out to be one the finest men I've ever met." He paused. "Now he's one of our chaplains on the *Franklin*."

"What a story!" Tom said. "It's hard to believe."

"That's exactly the way it happened."

A lull developed in their conversation. John broke the silence. "While I was in Berkeley, I read about you guys shelling Corregidor," he said, searching for something else to talk about. "Is it true that MacArthur asked for the *Santa Fe*?"

"Yeah, it is. I took the message to the Captain myself," Tom replied.

"I've never seen Corregidor," John said. "I was near Subic Bay once when I was on the *Vincennes*, but we never went down to Manila."

"Subic Bay brought back some memories," Tom said.

"What kind of memories?"

"Memories of a beautiful woman I met near there."

"Where?"

"Oranti. A little town south of Subic Bay."

"What happened?"

"Well, it didn't work out for me like it did for you," Tom said.

"Why?"

"Well, for openers, we only had part of one night together, but it was the happiest night I ever had in my life."

"What was she like?" John asked.

"She was gorgeous."

"You going to try to see her again when this mess is all over?"

"Maybe, if I get a chance, I'll go back."

"You think you can find her?"

"I hope so, but I think she's too beautiful and too smart to stay in Oranti."

Tom paused for a moment, seemingly lost in his memory; then he changed the subject. "Did you hear Corregidor was captured?"

"No, I didn't. When?"

"A couple of days ago. It's right here in our *Daily Information Guide*. It took a paratrooper drop and a shore-to-shore amphibious operation to get it."

"Corregidor was tough," Tom said as he handed the paper to John. "They had to rout those bastards out in cave-to-cave fighting. They used flame-throwers that fire around corners to get to them."

"Those Japs must have fought like hell—they suffered over five thousand casualties," John said. He looked at the article again, then handed it back to Tom. "It's good news. It's another step on the road that leads back home."

Their conversation turned to other matters, to family and friends and things that happened, both happy and sad, that were a part of their growing up. Finally, after talking for over three hours, the motor whaleboat from *Franklin* pulled up to the dock.

"Well, Buddy, it looks like I have to go," John said.

"If the war keeps going like it has, maybe the next time we get together we'll be in our 'civies' back in Colorado," Tom replied.

"Yeah," John said as he turned to leave, "at least somewhere in the States." He climbed into the whaleboat. "I sure hope you can find your girl, Buddy."

"Me, too," Tom said.

3 March, 1945
Ulithi Atoll
Caroline Islands

The winter sun rose through a dark cluster of cumulus clouds. A strong wind blew in from the north. It ripped at *Franklin's* flags and strained the cables that lashed Hellcats and Corsairs to the flight deck. At 06:10 *Franklin's* official orders from Admiral Spruance came in over secret wire. Gehres read the orders then said, "We'll come together as Task Force 58.2. *Franklin* will be the Task Group Leader. Our mission is to raid airfields on the Japanese mainland. We'll attack Kyushu, Shikoku, and western Honshu. Our goal is to eliminate aircraft of all kinds, especially those that can be used as kamikazes. When the Marines invade Okinawa, most of the Jap's aircraft defenses will come from these areas. Spruance wants us to try to destroy planes on the ground—especially if they're being refitted for kamikaze attacks."

Gehres handed the message to Joe Taylor. "We're scheduled to ship out tomorrow, Joe. Can we be ready by then?"

"We'll make it easy, Captain," Taylor said. "We're about eighty-percent ready now. All supplies are aboard, we're fully loaded with missiles and bombs, and the rest of the ammunition is being loaded this morning. We'll be completely fueled by 14:30."

"Good," Gehres replied. "I'd like to get back into the action." He paused and watched the Oiler Antacosta come back along the starboard side. "How about you, Chief?" he asked Beckley.

"What do you mean, sir?"

"You eager to get back at 'em?"

"Do you want the truth, sir?"

"Sure."

"I guess I'm not eager to tangle with the Japs on their own doorstep, sir," Beckley said. "Everyone says they're going to be fanatic there. I'd rather be fighting them where they aren't so crazy."

"Well, maybe that's right, but I'll kick their ass wherever they are, fanatic or not."

"I guess I can't argue with that, sir," Beckley replied. "Anyhow, there's always a chance their craziness has been over estimated...."

"Not a chance in a million, Chief," Gehres interrupted.

Why do you say that, sir?" Beckley asked.

"I just feel it in my gut, Chief," Gehres replied.

Beckley nodded thoughtfully. *Captain's probably right, he said solemnly to himself.*

Two ammunition lighters crowded up to the port side and began sending up canisters of 40-mm shells. At 16:42 all of *Franklin's* ammunition was aboard and stowed in the magazines below. At 17:37 Franklin finished loading aviation gasoline. *Franklin* was now ready to lead the first carrier strike on the Japanese mainland.

CHAPTER TWENTY-SIX

4 March, 1945
Task Force 58.2 Forms
Enroute to the Sea of Japan

The next morning at 07:00 the *Franklin* got underway. As soon as she was underway, the carriers *Hancock*, *Bataan* and *San Jacinto* fell into line behind her. Then the battleships *Washington*, *North Carolina* and *Iowa* steamed in, and the heavy cruisers *Baltimore* and *Pittsburgh* followed. The light cruisers *Santa Fe* and *Denver* came next, and nine destroyers included the *Miller*, *Wilkes*, *Owen*, *Tingley*, *Hunt*, *Walker*, *Hickox*, *Marshall* and *Zellars* completed the Task Group.

They steamed through Mugai Channel. When they reached open waters they deployed as Task Group 58.2, with *Franklin* as Task Group Leader. Task Group 58.2 headed North Northwest at a speed of eighteen knots, zigzagging on Plan 6 toward the Sea of Japan.

On *Franklin* at 07:40 the ship's loudspeakers crackled into life:

"Set condition of Readiness I."

"Set torpedo defense."

"All gun crews man your battle stations. Maintain maximum degree of readiness!"

There was a pause, then another command: "Prepare to fire on drone aircraft!"

Lookouts scanned the horizon. Gun crews were on high alert at their battle stations. At 08:10 the destroyers *Miller* and *Owen* released drone aircraft from their positions on the outer edge of the screen. As soon as the drones came into range, John's guns opened fire. They blasted the first drone into tiny pieces. The attack went on for nearly two hours. When the attack was over John's gunners had shot down four of the drones.

"Secure from gunnery alert."

"Maintain Condition of Readiness I."

At 13:10 when the Task Group reached a point ninety miles north of Ulithi, *Franklin* sent up a powerful combat air patrol. Sixteen F4U Corsairs, with their Marine pilots, catapulted into the cloudless Pacific sky. They swiftly joined twenty Hellcats from *Hancock* and *Bataan*. After they grouped they formed small squadrons of four and fanned out to points beyond the edges of the outer screen searching for enemy aircraft.

At 18:45 all planes returned and landed without incident. No enemy aircraft were detected.

At 18:55 Combat Air Patrol Baker consisting of Corsairs and Hellcats from *Franklin* and *Hancock,* equipped with special night radar, were jettisoned into the dark, wintry sky. At 23:35 they returned and landed without incident. Again no enemy aircraft were detected.

8 March, 1945
Latitude 19° N. Longitude 137° E
Northwest Pacific Ocean

The sun rose through a few thin cirrus clouds. The blue-gray ocean was covered with frilly whitecaps stirred up by a cold twenty-knot wind. Visibility was excellent. At 06:16 the Task Group changed course to 340° and steamed steadily Northwest toward the Sea of Japan.

It was Sunday. The church flag flew from the forward truck. On the forecastle Father O'Callahan readied to say Mass. Because the hangar deck was now crowded with aircraft, his church was the forecastle—his sanctuary the open Pacific sky. A cold winter wind whipped the white cover on his mess-table altar. A canvas backdrop, strained by the twenty-knot wind, acted as his only windbreak.

O'Callahan faced the altar and began the Mass.

"*Introibo ad altare Dei.*"

John and Bonin read the Latin response in unison.

The wind whistled through the forecastle.

Soon it was time for the Gospel. Father O'Callahan turned from the altar and faced his shipmates who were sitting cross-legged on the deck and on the links of the huge anchor chain.

"We gather here today in a time of great crisis and danger," he said. "We sail into waters that for centuries have belonged to the Japanese. Soon we will be attacking cities and airfields in the very heart of Japan. We know the Japanese will retaliate. There may be bloodshed. Some of us *may,* and I emphasize the word *may*, suffer from their retaliations. Who among us will suffer and when this might happen is not for us to know. Only the Mind of God has these answers."

He paused. His chasuble flapped in the wind.

"I see among us today men who embrace the Protestant and Jewish faiths—Commanders Taylor and Jurika, Commander Zimler, Gunner Lowe, and Seamen First Class Barker and Feinstein just to name a few of you. While our ways and traditions of worship may differ, there is one fundamental fact that is the same for all of us. That fact is we are all sons of a loving God."

"There is a further magnificent truth that is a part of our religions," he continued, an atmosphere of confidence exuding from his words. "That truth is that there is life on earth and there is *Eternal Life* after life on earth. When men face the danger of death, they come face to face with God and with the mystery of this Eternal Life."

He paused. The wind surged against the canvas backdrop.

"Each of us has been granted a certain time on this earth," he continued. "For some of us the time is longer than for others. It is important to remember if we are among those who are chosen to leave, that there is Life beyond this life on earth—a life of unimaginable joy, wonder and bliss. This is a Universal Truth. Today is a time to renew our faith in this Truth. Death is only feared when we forget it."

O'Callahan paused again. There was quiet. The only sounds were the wind and the muffled echo of *Franklin's* massive hull resonating through the cold waters of the northern Pacific.

"Let us now say a prayer of affirmation," he said. "Let us affirm that there is life and there is Life after life. Let us be firm in the belief that the grace and goodness of a loving Creator will care for us in the days ahead, no matter what happens. This, my fellow shipmates, is the message of this Mass. Trust this message. Go with courage. Go with strength. Know that wherever you go, God is always there. Know that whatever happens, God is always with you. May this thought bless you today, tomorrow, every day of your lives."

O'Callahan turned back to the altar and continued the Mass. *"Pater Noster, qui es in coelis*: Our Father, who art in heaven…."

John's response was halting, but this didn't bother him. What Father O'Callahan said had brought tears to his eyes. He looked to his right where his friends were kneeling; Ski, Beckley, Sullivan, Lowe, Frasure, Gary. They all looked like they were touched by his words, too.

The Mass ended. O'Callahan gave the final blessing. It was lost in the roar of *Franklin's* powerful catapult as it jettisoned off the first combat air patrol of the day. Twenty-two F4U Corsairs powered into the sky—they climbed and joined *Hancock*'s CAP. Together they flew out to scour the area beyond the Task Group's perimeter again, searching every corner of the sky for enemy aircraft.

On the outer edge of the screen destroyers zigzagged in and out, their sonar-pings seeking submerged objects of any kind. The Task Group had entered an area of great submarine danger. If an enemy submarine penetrated its screen, it could cause disaster. The threat of destruction was everywhere now—in the air, on the ocean's surface and in its depths. Every man in the Task Group knew where he was, and of the immeasurable danger he faced in the waters ahead.

"All hands man your battle stations!"

"Set Condition of Readiness I."

Gunners rushed to their guns. Torpedo defenses were manned and ready. Thoughts of loved ones diminished. Personal issues were put aside. There was one common purpose—to spot the enemy before being spotted—to attack the enemy before they could attack.

On the bridge, with Beckley at the helm, Gehres, Taylor and Jurika alternately scanned the horizon through binoculars.

"We're going into the lair of the tiger," Gehres said. "A Japanese tiger's out there somewhere, waiting to pounce on us."

"Yeah, sir," Jurika replied. "The waiting is what's tough. We'll be hitting them with a close-up attack on their homeland for the first time. This is going to bring out their greatest fears…."

"And their greatest wrath, " Gehres said as he continued to search the horizon. "It has to be hard for them to believe that the hour of death for their empire is coming. They don't know when, or how, but I think they know it's coming. The big problem for us is we're fighting people who have no concern for life. They live by the Japanese warrior's code called 'Boshido'—it means victory or death. They'll try anything to stop us."

Joe Taylor thought about what Gehres said and slowly nodded his head in agreement. "Yes," he said, "and in their history, their empire has never been invaded. This should make them even more desperate."

At the top of *Franklin's* island the radar antenna scanned the horizon in a continuous 360° circle. In the radar room eyes strained, looking for blips on green-hued radar screens that signaled enemy intrusions. Lookouts in key locations strained to find anything that radar missed.

At 11:55 *Franklin* maneuvered into position to land Able CAP. All planes landed without incident. At 12:05 CAP Baker took off. Veteran Marine pilots in their Corsairs and seasoned Naval aviators in their Hellcats flew out to sweep the area around the Task Group again—looking for only one thing—enemy planes. At 16:32 all planes in Baker CAP landed safely. No enemy planes were sighted.

Later that afternoon the winter sun sank slowly behind a cover of heavy cumulus clouds. Every so often, it pierced through and projected an eerie golden radiance on the dark, cold ocean. Night fell. An occasional star peeked through the cloud-shrouded darkness.

In John's gun sponson there was quiet. The usual talk and bantering that took place in drills was absent. The only sound was the wail of a twenty-five-knot wind that snaked in over *Franklin's* bow from the southwest and seemed to signal a change in the weather.

"We have to be alert tonight," John said as he scanned the horizon through binoculars. "The closer we get, the more alert we've got to be."

"We're still on the outer edge of their range, John," Lowe said. "It'd be tough to hit us from here."

"As far as I'm concerned, we're in range now and every mile we travel brings us closer."

"Goddamned, it's cold," Ski said with a shiver.

"Get one of those blankets and wrap it around you," John said.

Ski grabbed a blanket from a stack near the ready-service locker and wrapped it around his shoulders. "Staring at that empty horizon is hard on the eyes," he said as he raised his binoculars again.

"Look a little above it. It's easier on the eyes that way," John said.

The sound of footsteps echoed down from the flight deck behind them. John looked up and saw Father O'Callahan and Lieutenant Gary at the edge of the deck.

"How's it going, John?" O'Callahan asked.

"Everything's okay, Father," John replied.

O'Callahan and Gary climbed down into the sponson.

"What's going on, Father?" John asked.

"We're making the rounds of the gun pits," O'Callahan replied. "Captain Gehres asked Lieutenant Gary to guide me."

"Yeah," Ski said. "It's easy to get lost on this ship now, Father—even for someone who knows his way around. We're so blacked out and battened down."

"Everyone was happy to see the Padre," Gary said. "I'll tell you one thing. There are no atheists in these gun pits tonight."

"They'd be nuts if they were," John said as he focused his binoculars back on the horizon. "You just getting started with your rounds, Father?"

"No, this is our last stop. We started on the port side."

"How's everybody holding up?"

"They all looked like they're ready," Gary replied.

There was a long pause. The only sound was the wind and the moan of the ocean as the *Franklin*'s prow knifed through it.

"It's quiet out there," O'Callahan said.

"Yeah. It's so darn quiet it's scary," John replied.

He scanned for a few more moments, then lowered his binoculars and said, "Anybody here want to talk to the Chaplain? This is a good time if you do."

The men in the gun crew turned briefly from their stations and acknowledged Gary and O'Callahan. Then there was silence.

"Jardin?" John called.

Jardin's head appeared in the hatch in the ready-service locker. "Hi, Padre," he said. "I saw Father O'Callahan this afternoon, Gunner."

"Anyone else?"

Silence.

"I guess not, Father."

"Okay," O'Callahan said. "Remember, if any of you men need me I'm available twenty-four hours every day."

A chorus of muffled thanks came from the crew. O'Callahan and Gary left the sponson.

12 March, 1945
70 Miles SSE of Shikoku
Empire of Japan

The weather turned foul. The early morning sky was heavily overcast. The wind's intensity increased. It spun the blades of the wind gauge like a roaring propeller.

On the bridge, Beckley heard Gehres talking with Commander Hale.

"We don't have the best flying conditions," Gehres said to Hale as he looked out over the bridge.

"We're going after them anyhow, Captain," Hale replied. "We'll strike Ripongi airfield south of Takashima."

"Are you all set?"

"Aye, sir, we're ready to go. Our final briefing is in fifteen minutes. We're hoping to surprise them and get as many planes as possible before they can take off."

"Our launch point is about fifty-five miles southeast of Shikoku," Gehres said. "We'll be there in about a half an hour."

"Aye, sir, I know," Hale replied. "And it'll take somewhere between thirty-five and forty-five minutes from the time of launch to get to the target."

"That's an important part of the Japanese archipelago," Gehres cautioned. "It'll probably be heavily defended."

"Aye, sir, everyone's aware of that."

Bill Zimler concluded his briefing in the ready room. Target, course, speed, position and communication procedures had been fully discussed. "Stay in tight formations," he said. "Maintain radio silence. Be alert. Who knows what we'll run into from here to the coast."

"Pilots, man your planes!"

Adrenaline flowed. Determined Marine and Naval aviators crowded through the ready room doors and raced up to the flight deck.

Franklin came about into a thirty-five-knot wind that blew directly over the flight deck.

"Launch planes!"

Twenty-two Corsairs and twenty-five Helldivers streaked into the cloudy morning sky. Once airborne they were joined by sixty-seven Hellcats and Helldivers from *Hancock* and *Bataan*. Air Strike Able formed. One hundred and eleven planes headed Northwest on course 310° toward Ripongi airfield.

After flying a few minutes Zimler's new gunner, Gunners Mate Third Class Pete Barrett, spotted the attack group from Jocko Clark's TF 58.1.

"Those planes look like the air strike from *Hornet*, sir," he said over the intercom.

"Yeah," Zimler replied, glancing to his left. "Looks like they're headed southwest—probably to Kyushu."

Air Strike Able droned on in silence for about twenty-five minutes. Suddenly, the coastal area of southern Japan became visible through the clouds.

The vegetation surprised Zimler. "It's much greener than I expected," he muttered.

In a few minutes the air strike was in an approach pattern to target. The airfield was a gold mine! It was lined with at least seventy planes, mostly old, fixed-wheeled Vals and Tonys and even a few older bi-planes.

"It looks like a fucking kamikaze nest!" one of the lead pilots shouted.

"Yeah, it sure looks like they're refitting those planes for kamikaze attacks," Zimler shouted through the intercom. "Keep your eyes peeled for enemy fighters."

"Pete," he said to his gunner, "what do you see?"

"Not a thing. Nothing but clouds and sky, sir."

"Keep a close watch, Gunner. You'd expect fighters at an airfield this size."

"Maybe they're short of fighters now, sir."

"Maybe. But I'm not going to bet on it, so stay alert."

When the air strike reached a good position to attack, Zimler looked around again. There were still no Japanese fighters.

"I think we surprised them, sir," Barrett said.

"Yeah. Maybe they never dreamed they'd see this many enemy planes over a Japanese airfield."

Antiaircraft fire erupted from defenses around the airfield. It was heavy and concentrated. "Let's get the guns first!" Zimler said. "Helldivers! Missile attack!"

Forty-five Helldivers dove away from the formation and attacked the antiaircraft installations with missiles. They honed in on the pillboxes. Their missiles streaked down toward their targets. In a few minutes wrecked pillboxes and burning, mangled antiaircraft guns surrounded the entire airfield. The attack was devastating.

As soon as the initial sweep cleared, Hellcats and Corsairs attacked the parked planes. Some were now trying to take off. Like a swarm of hungry mosquitoes, wave after wave of Hellcats and Corsairs descended on them and blasted them to pieces. When they finished over sixty planes were destroyed and the rest were badly damaged.

"None of those bastards are ever going to crash an American ship," Zimler said, satisfied with the job the attack group had done. "Let's get back to the Task Group."

Air Strike Able turned and headed back. The trip was without incident. Every plane landed safely. Two planes suffered minor damage.

That afternoon planes from *Franklin* and *Hancock,* and *Hornet* and *Intrepid* from Jocko Clark's Task Group, hit the Japanese again. One hundred and thirty-six bombers and fighters hit the airfields around Kochi, Wakayama and Matsuyama. Japanese resistance was now much stiffer. Three Hellcats and their pilots from TF58.1 were lost and four of *Franklin's* Corsairs suffered damage so severe they had to be jettisoned, but their Marine pilots escaped with only limited injuries. The air strike destroyed another sixty planes.

That night a huge storm moved in from the southwest. On the bridge of the *Franklin* Gehres asked for a radar-fix.

"We'll be in it in about an hour, Captain," came the reply from radar. "It's pretty ugly and it's moving right toward us. We could be in the middle of it for a couple of days."

"Is it a typhoon?" Gehres asked.

"No, but it's sure a huge storm. It extends over a hundred miles in a northeast to southwest direction. Winds are estimated to be eighty to ninety miles per hour. Clouds are thirty thousand to thirty-five thousand feet high."

"What do we have southeast of us?"

"Weather's pretty good there, but you'll have to go about a hundred and twenty-five miles to avoid this storm."

"Rig for foul weather," Gehres ordered. Then he said to the Officer of the Deck, "Lieutenant Lisot, see if Admiral Davison can meet with me for a few minutes and ask Commander Jurika to come to the bridge."

The OD informed Jurika, then went to the flag-bridge and came back with Admiral Davison and two members of his staff.

"Admiral, we've got a huge storm bearing down on us," Gehres said with Jurika standing by. "I'd like to get out of its path by going southeast. It'll take about a hundred and twenty miles to avoid it."

"I sure hate to leave the point of attack," Davison said after thinking about the situation for a minute. "How about attacking over it?"

Hale, who had just joined them, said, "It's too high, Admiral,"

"What would it take to stay here and try to fly around it?"

"It extends too far north and south. We can't send our pilots that far along the front and then come back again on the other side. It leaves them without enough fuel to get back."

"What'd you think about the Japs getting around the front and attacking us?"

"They'd have the same problem, Admiral," Hale replied.

"Okay, notify the task force to steam South Southeast. Even with this move we have to be very alert. When this storm is over they'll be coming after us. The surprise is over. The Japs now know there's a major fleet out here."

"Notify all the ships in the Task Group. Come to course 105 degrees," Gehres said.

Task Group 58.2 changed course and headed Southeast at a speed of twenty knots. Even while they were changing course, the ocean became very rough. Winds of over sixty-five knots surged down the flight deck. *Franklin* began to pitch and roll violently. Three Corsairs, hurriedly and improperly lashed down, ripped off the deck and crashed into the angry ocean.

"All hands exercise extreme caution!"

"All hands stay away from outer railings!"

"Use guidelines to get about the ship!"

That evening, after the 16:00 to 20:00 watch, with the *Franklin* directly in the middle of the violent storm, John struggled along the hangar deck bulkhead to the ship's library. Walking was difficult. Early that morning, while the ocean was still relatively quiet, the destroyer *Owen* came alongside to refuel and deliver the first mail they'd received since they left Ulithi. John received two letters from Sandy and one from his mother, but he couldn't take time to read them until he got off watch.

He burst into the library and sat down. Music from the Armed Forces' radio network created a strange contrast with the howling winds and rain that pounded *Franklin's* flight deck and bulkheads. He read Sandy's first letter:

> *My dearest John,*
>
> *I miss you so very much. My Darling, it's been only a short while but it seems like forever since we've been together. I think about you every day and dream about you nearly every night. Last night after you called, I dreamed that we were in Hawaii together. It was a really good dream, Honey—the weather was beautiful and we were very happy. I pray each day that this dream will come true and we'll soon be together again.*
>
> *I'm so happy that you are serving Mass for Father O'Callahan. Somehow this makes me feel that you have a special protection. This might*

seem strange but it's the feeling I get—it helps me every day—especially since, by the time you get this letter, you might be in enemy waters. All this frightens me, John. I pray and trust in God that you'll be safe.

  Mom and dad are both home tonight. They asked me to give you their love and to tell you that each night they remember you, and all of your shipmates, in their prayers.

  I pray for all of you, too, and for Beckley and Sullivan, Ski and Lowe and all the rest of your gun crew. Beckley and Sullivan were so wonderful to me when I talked to them. What Chief Sullivan said really helped me. Please tell them both that I send them my love.

  I dream of the time when you are out of danger and safely back with me. I miss you so very much, John. I love you so very much. May God bless you and keep you safe.

Your loving wife,
Sandy

John put the letter down and closed his eyes. Vivid images of Sandy's face, her beautiful eyes, her soft brown hair, came into his mind. He yearned to take her in his arms, to make love to her again. Although he'd only been gone a few weeks, the days he'd spent with his new wife seemed a distant memory. A deep sadness filled him. He wondered when he would get back to her, when the war would end. The howling wind interrupted his reverie and he made his way back to his compartment. At least they'd be safe tonight, he thought. No Jap planes could fly through this kind of storm.

16 March, 1945
170 Miles ESE of Shikoku
Task Force 58 Forms

By morning most of the storm had moved into the northern Pacific. The ocean was calmer but the weather remained overcast and cold.

At 06:30 Admiral Davison, on the bridge with Gehres and Beckley, got a message from Jocko Clark in TF 58.1. "It looks like Admiral Clark moved southeast because of the storm, too," he said.

"Yes, sir," Gehres replied as he scanned the horizon through binoculars. "I can see them northwest of us."

"The message says Nimitz is doubling the size of the fleet, Les," Davison said. "We're scheduled to rendezvous with TF 58.3 and TF 58.4 within the hour. We'll be operating with seventeen carriers."

Gehres looked southeast through his binoculars. "Yeah. They're out there now, Admiral. They're about an hour away."

"The combined fleet will be designated TF 58," Davison said. "Our revised mission is to attack the supply ports of Kagoshima and Nagasaki. Some of the remaining Jap fleet is reported to be there. Spruance wants us to destroy any enemy vessels we find, then attack harbor facilities, transports and barracks. Tomorrow we go after aircraft, hangars and assembly points at Kochi, Takamatsu and Osaka."

"We'll be a huge fleet," Taylor said. "Seventeen carriers. That was unheard of three years ago."

"We sure will, sir," Beckley added. "At Midway, we thought we had a big fleet when we had three."

"Well, seventeen carriers will make it a lot easier," Davison said. "But it's still going to be a tough, dangerous operation."

"Yes, it will be, Admiral," Gehres replied. "Midway was one thing and the Sea of Japan is another. We're not a surprise for the Japs anymore and, unlike Midway, they have the big, unsinkable island-airfields now."

Down on the flight deck, *Franklin* launched her first CAP in two days. Eight Corsairs catapulted into the cloudy sky. They headed Northwest, to search the area between the Task Group and the Japanese mainland. When they were about forty miles out, they spotted a group of G4M bombers headed their way.

Marine Lieutenant Charles Crittenden, CAP leader, rushed a call to the *Franklin*. "We've got six Bettys out here flying toward the Task Group!" Crittenden shouted.

"Bettys! Are you sure?" Hale asked.

"Yes, sir."

"How the hell can that be? They're at least a hundred and seventy miles from shore—they'll never get back."

"Yes sir," replied Crittenden. "Begging the Commander's pardon, sir, but maybe they didn't intend to go back. This looks like a one-way trip."

It took Hale a few seconds to understand what Crittenden was saying. "Kamikazes! Way the hell out here? Engage 'em! Stall 'em! We'll scramble a squadron and send it out immediately."

In less than ten minutes a squadron of seventeen Marine Corsairs headed west toward the CAP. When they arrived there were still five Bettys in the air, fighting hard to get to the Task Group. They were now only about thirty miles away. The additional Corsairs made the difference. They stalled the bombers' attempts to get through by recklessly diving in front of them. As soon as they were diverted the Corsairs blasted them out of the sky.

On the open bridge, Davison said, "Captain, that could have been a disaster!" He shook his head. "We fell into a trap, Les. We thought the Japs are like us. I'm as much to blame for this as everyone else. This sure shows how far those bastards will go to get a shot at us."

"Well, we're not taking any chances on the trip back," Gehres replied. "We've tripled the CAP. We'll remain in Condition of Readiness I—morning, noon and night—twenty-four hours a day."

At 12:35, with scores of fighters from TF 58 now flying multiple patrols, the huge combined fleet turned West Northwest toward the Japanese mainland. The bulk of the storm had passed, but radar reported dense clouds and unsettled weather all the way back to the coast.

17 March, 1945
Back in the Sea of Japan
85 Miles East of Shikoku

The next morning TF 58 had steamed to within eighty-five miles of the Japanese coast and right into the teeth of Japanese aircraft defenses.

At dawn, Gehres got a report from Jocko Clark. After he read it Gehres said, "Chief, ask Admiral Davison to come up to the bridge."

When Davison arrived, Gehres said, "Admiral Clark's Group was attacked by three Judys last night. They somehow avoided her radar. One tried to make a vertical attack on *Intrepid* but missed. Our night fighters caught them and shot two down. The last one got away."

"They say where it went?" Davison asked.

"The report said it looked like it was retreating back toward the Japanese mainland," Gehres replied. "But how the hell can we know for sure?"

"Sneaky! They'll slip in on you any way they can," Davison said.

"Yeah," Gehres replied. "We have to stay doubly alert."

TF 58 steamed steadily Northwest at twenty knots in Condition of Readiness I. Radar units from all over the huge fleet, which now stretched fifty miles from edge to edge, reported bogeys at distances of up to a hundred miles from the Japanese coast. Combat air patrols tried to track them down, but they had only limited success. Usually the Japanese were gone when the fighters got to where they were reported.

At 06:55 *Franklin* turned into the frigid March wind and launched her first attack group of the day. Twenty-three Corsairs, armed with missiles fitted with armor-piercing heads, took off and headed northwest to attack Japanese naval units at Kagoshima.

At 08:10 a squadron of Helldivers was propelled aloft to attack two airfields south of Nagasaki. Just over fifteen hundred yards from *Franklin*, *Hancock* was launching Helldivers and torpedo-armed Avengers and astern *San Jacinto* was doing the same thing.

There was the same kind of intense air activity throughout the huge fleet. Carrier planes from TF 58.3 and TF 58.4 were attacking airfields and shipping up the coast all the way to Tokyo.

The attacks continued all morning; Hellcats, Corsairs, Helldivers and Avengers thundered into the sky and returned after blasting targets on the Japanese mainland.

Just after 11:30 the Japanese retaliated. Twenty-four Judys and Bettys were detected by radar—but not until they were within sight of the Task Group 58.1. Air patrols from *Franklin*, *Wasp*, *Hornet* and *Intrepid* drove them off after shooting down eleven.

The rest of the day was one long series of alarms—one after another—made more threatening by the dense clouds that shrouded the entire fleet. Reports of bogeys came in from all over. Radar reported a large number of single planes trying to slip through the fleet's heavy defenses.

At dusk, on the bridge of the *Franklin*, Gehres, Taylor, Hale and Beckley watched the last plane from the last strike group land safely.

"What were our losses?" Gehres asked his Air Officer.

"We lost four planes, Captain," Hale replied. "Not bad for all that combat."

"Yeah, and we've been lucky as hell with bogeys, too," Gehres said. "There were a bunch around, but none even came close to us." He thought for a moment. "We've been lucky," he said, "but we have to remember that luck follows vigilance. We're hitting the Japs hard—right on their doorstep—and they'll do almost anything to try to blunt our attacks. We have to stay constantly alert."

He raised his binoculars and searched the horizon again. "Pass the word. Exercise *extreme* caution."

That night the entire fleet was shrouded in darkness. The only signs of life were the occasional dim silhouettes of ships against the dark horizon. Radar screens scanned every point on the compass. Lookouts scanned the horizon; their eyes and ears strained by the darkness and quiet—each man trying to detect any sign of change; a flicker of light, an unusual movement, a strange noise. Fire control units were equipped and ready. Guns were loaded, ready to fire. Alertness and undivided vigilance filled every man's thoughts.

CHAPTER TWENTY-SEVEN

19 March, 1945
55 Miles ESE of Shikoku
Tragedy Strikes

As dawn broke *Franklin* had steamed into an attack position fifty-five miles East Southeast of Shikoku. Although it was lighter in the east, there was no sun—the heavy clouds persisted. The ocean was rough and cold. A twenty-five-knot wind blew in from the west.

On the bridge, Gehres gazed into the dense cloud cover. "I hate these goddamned clouds," he said. "There could be anything sneaking around in them. I wish we had some clear skies and sunny weather."

"Aye, sir," Joe Taylor agreed as he scanned the horizon. "This is tough visibility. It's like this all over the fleet."

"We got a report from *Hancock* a few minutes ago, Captain," Jurika said. "Their lookouts thought they'd spotted single-engine aircraft."

"Did they say it was Japanese?"

"They couldn't tell for sure, Captain, but they said it looked like a Judy."

Gehres grabbed the phone and contacted the combat information center. "CIC says there are no bogeys on their radar screens," he said, "but I don't want to take any chances. Alert all lookouts and gun control stations to be extra alert—especially in those low lying clouds ahead."

"Aye, sir."

At 06:35 *Franklin* turned into the wind and readied to launch her first attack group of the day. Twenty-three Corsairs, armed with Tiny Tim missiles with armor-piercing heads, were staged behind the catapult preparing to join fighters from *Hancock* and *San Jacinto* for an attack on remnants of the Japanese Navy believed to be at Kagoshima and Nagasaki.

Father O'Callahan, Commander Taylor and Chief Beckley were on the fantail finishing burial services for Aircraft Machinist Mate Third Class Jessie Ortiz who was killed when he stumbled into a whirling propeller the previous afternoon.

When the service ended they headed, through a cold, whipping wind, topside to the flight deck. There they huddled next to Lieutenant Commander Fred "Red" Harris, the flight deck officer who was in charge of deck operations. The elevators were up and in place, and he was signaling pilots to "rev up engines!" Air Strike Able was beginning to be launched.

They watched the operation for a few minutes. Then Beckley said, "I'd like to see Commander Zimler before Air Strike Baker comes up." He headed down to the gallery deck.

O'Callahan left, too. He made his way through the frigid gusts to the edge of the flight deck and pushed forward to John's gun sponson. Over the roar of wind and engines he called down to the gun crew, "How you guys doing?"

"We're okay, Father," John called back.

"Wind's colder than heck," O'Callahan shouted.

"It sure is, Father," John yelled back.

"Do you see anything out there, John?"

"Nothing, Father. Just a lot of clouds."

"Keep up the watch," O'Callahan said as headed for the forecastle.

Beckley made his way across the hangar deck toward the gallery deck. On the way he threaded through cart after cart of Tiny Tim missiles waiting to be loaded onto aircraft. He climbed the ladder to the gallery deck, walked to the ready room and stuck his head around the edge of the door. Zimler was leaning on the table, in full flight gear, waiting for his briefing to begin. When he saw Beckley he waved and walked to the door.

"How's it going, sir?" Beckley asked. "I watched you come in yesterday. How was the strike?"

"It was okay. They're all tough now. At least we didn't lose anybody yesterday."

"Well, I just wanted to wish you the best, sir," Beckley said. "I know you're busy, so I'll shove off. Good luck and safe hunting today."

"Thanks, Beck," Zimler replied. "I'll see you later."

Beckley left the gallery deck and went back toward the bridge. On his way he looked toward the starboard guns and spotted John. He walked up to the sponson and shouted, "John! How are you?"

John waved to him and shouted back, "We're okay here, Beck!"

Beckley returned to the island just as another Corsair roared off. He began to climb the ladder to the bridge and, as he did, he looked at his watch. It was 07:07. When he reached the stair-head a terrific explosion jolted the ship! The concussion threw him violently against the bulkhead! He fell to his knees, stunned and nearly unconscious.

"Bomb! Bomb!" he heard someone scream. There was a frantic clatter of footsteps on the ladders beside him. Everything began to spin. He sank to the deck behind the ladder and lost consciousness.

From his position in the gun sponson, John spotted the Judy streaking out of the heavy clouds, less than two hundred yards from *Franklin's* bow.

"Bogey! Bogey!" he'd screamed as he pointed frantically to the speeding plane. His warning was muffled by heavy fire from the 40s in the bow and atop the bridge and from *Franklin's* five-inch guns. The Judy streaked through the heavy flack and flashed over the bow. It dropped two five-hundred-pound bombs. The first hit forward on the flight deck, penetrated it and disappeared. The second hit the deck with a glancing blow and ricocheted into the Corsairs waiting to take off. It struck a Corsair's propeller. There was a huge explosion. Planes blasted into the air—engines racing—propellers whirling! They crashed back into the flight deck and cut into other Corsairs! A thousand-pound bomb exploded. Gas tanks filled to capacity with high-octane aviation gasoline flashed into flames. A huge cloud of dense, fetid smoke and fire mushroomed into the air and obscured his view. It didn't hide the threat of sudden death. That was very real—death by fire—by explosion—by collision—and by disintegration.

From the forecastle, O'Callahan watched as the unbelievable scene unfolded. On the hangar deck pilots waited in their cockpits and crewmen under their planes' wings. The first bomb cut through the reinforced flight deck as though it was a piece of balsa wood. A huge explosion shook the hangar deck. The blast blew the forward elevator two feet into the air! Flames spread toward the Helldivers waiting to be lifted topside, engines running, all armed with missiles. O'Callahan reacted quickly. He rushed to a hatch that opened onto the hangar deck. The moment he opened it there was a third explosion. A huge wall of fire blazed into the Helldivers and they started to explode! He slammed the hatch shut and tried to bolt it. Concussion from another blast ripped it open! It knocked him down. Pieces of shrapnel, airplane wings and human body parts flew through the open hatch. Bombs were exploding in the gasoline fires. There was another huge explosion! Then another! A shroud of flames and heavy smoke filled the hangar deck amidships and blazed out of both sides of the ship. It moved up to the flight deck, then onto the bridge.

O'Callahan pulled himself up to an unsteady standing position. His first thought was to give the men on the ship a general absolution. "*Ego vos absolvo*," he said, then quickly headed below decks. There were men dying. He'd be needed there. On the way down he stopped by his compartment. He grabbed his life preserver and, more importantly, the sacred oils for the Sacrament of Extreme Unction. He tightened the strap on his helmet. He needed it both for protection and identification. Men could recognize him from the white-cross painted on the front of it. He searched through the passageways until he stumbled into the junior officer's bunkroom, a large open compartment that had started to fill with burned and wounded sailors and marines. The Protestant chaplain, Reverend Grimes Gatlin, was already there, beginning to minister to the wounded.

"Where're the doctors?" O'Callahan asked as he surveyed the battered bodies of the wounded and dying.

"There aren't any here. Maybe there are none alive," Gatlin replied. "We've got Bob Mason and three of his men though. Mason's a warrant pharmacist."

O'Callahan nodded. He scanned the room and saw two of the four men working on a wounded sailor, using only a first aid kit that contained sulfa powder, burn jelly and morphine. Sadness mixed with horror gripped him. The smell of burnt flesh filled the room. It was sickening. Chills ran up his spine. His stomach roiled. He fought the urge to throw up. He said a prayer. He asked God to guide him in his efforts to stem the suffering of these young men. He knelt beside a badly burned seaman and rested his hand on the young boy's forehead. It was charred and dripping body fluid.

"Are you a Catholic, son?"

The seaman nodded, unable to speak.

O'Callahan spoke the ancient words of the Sacrament of Extreme Unction: "*Dominus Noster Jesus Christus vos Absoldat*: may our Lord Jesus Christ forgive you." The young seaman died moments after O'Callahan uttered the prayers.

Explosion after explosion shook the compartment. The lights went out. The makeshift hospital was now illuminated only by battery-driven battle lamps.

He went to another boy who had a gaping wound in his chest. Blood streamed out, despite a makeshift bandage. As he bent over him a series of explosions above them rocked the room.

"Father, are those the Tiny Tims?" the wounded sailor asked.

"I think its the 20-mm and 40-mm stuff, son."

"They're too loud for that, Father."

"Here. I'll give you something to relax you and relieve some of the pain," O'Callahan said. He gave the seaman an injection of morphine, and, as he did he asked, "Are you a Catholic, son?"

The seaman shook his head.

O'Callahan helped him say the *Lord's Prayer*. He went on to the next boy.

On the opposite side of the room, Gatlin was doing the same thing. They moved from boy to boy, praying with them and consoling them. It was important to avoid adding panic to their enormous suffering. When they had been to every young man in the room, O'Callahan said, "Gats, I think I'll go topside now—there are probably a lot more wounded up there."

"Okay, Joe," Gatlin replied, "I'll stay with the boys down here. We can't leave them alone. I'm afraid they'll panic. I'm praying for just one thing now—the courage to do my job and keep these youngsters calm."

O'Callahan nodded. He took one last look at the body-laden room. "I still can't believe this," he said. "My God, what a tragedy!"

Beckley lifted himself to his knees. He shook himself back to consciousness. Still woozy, he pulled himself to his feet by using the bulkhead as a brace. He looked at his watch. 07:21. He had only been out a few minutes. He strained at the ladder railings and slowly climbed toward the bridge. Two more violent explosions jolted the ship! They nearly knocked him off his feet again. When he reached the bridge he found Gehres and Jurika bent over, coughing and gasping for air. Lieutenant Cappen, the OD, struggled with the helm, strenuously trying to breathe. Jesse Thorne, the Quartermaster he was going to relieve, lay face down in a pool of blood. Shocked, Beckley rushed to Thorne's side and turned him over. His eyes were glassy. A piece of metal was stuck in his neck. Thorne was dead. He groped through the dense smoke to the Captain who was choking and furiously fighting for air. Beckley pulled out his handkerchief and handed it to Gehres.

"Here, sir. Breathe through this!"

He moved to Jurika who was now standing erect, leaning against the bridge railing. He pulled at his back pocket trying to get his handkerchief out. "Those handkerchiefs have to be wet, sir," Beckley said. He stumbled through the smoke toward the ship's drinking fountain. He nearly tripped over Corporal Klinkiewicz, the Captain's aide. Klinkiewicz was lying on the deck, his breathing obstructed by the increasing smoke and soot. "Loan me your helmet," Beckley said to the struggling marine.

TRAGEDY STRIKES

Klinkiewicz pulled off his helmet and handed it to him. Beckley filled it with water from the cooler and stumbled back. The smoke was now so dense the bridge was as black as night. He found Thorne's body and searched for a handkerchief. He found one and wet it down. It helped him breathe. He struggled to the Captain and Navigator.

Captain Gehres was now on his feet, and though still coughing and gasping heavily, seemed ready to resume command.

"Here, sir, wet that handkerchief down in this water," Beckley said offering Gehres the helmet.

"Thanks, Chief. This'll help."

Gehres turned to Jurika. "Here, Steve, use this water and then give it to the OD and the corporal."

Then he asked, "What the hell happened?"

"I don't know, sir," Beckley replied. "I got knocked out by the first blast. I just got to the bridge a couple of minutes ago. I...."

"We took two bombs on the flight deck, Captain," Jurika said.

"Did you see the plane?"

"No. I just saw a shadow flash by—but I did see the bombs. Two five-hundred-pounders. The first went right through the flight deck!"

"Where'd the second hit? Gehres asked, still coughing.

"Somewhere aft among planes still waiting to take off, I'd guess," Jurika gasped. "One of the five-inch gun crews started firing at the plane just before the bombs hit the deck but I don't think they hit it."

Beckley, along with Gehres and Jurika, staggered over to the bridge railing and looked out on the flight deck. One gas tank after another was exploding! Dirty, sooty flames streaked across the flight deck. Bombs detonated! Sheets of acidic smoke billowed up from the hangar deck. There was a huge explosion! Then another! The second was worse than the first! The concussion knocked them back from the railing. "I can't believe this is happening!" Beckley said. "These dammed explosions are soul-shaking!"

One huge blast after another shuddered and rocked the ship.

"When we get past one, we get wracked by another," Gehres said, his voice very weak and hoarse. A missile swooshed up the flight deck toward the bridge. Beckley, along with everyone else on the bridge, dropped to his knees. The missile screamed by. It missed by inches and exploded in the ocean two hundred yards to starboard.

"Damn, that was close! Why don't you go down on the forecastle where there's less danger?" Gehres asked Klinkiewicz.

"Begging the Captain's pardon, sir, the Captain's Orderly will remain at his post." the young marine replied.

Despite the fire and danger, Beckley couldn't help but smile and shake his head.

An explosion blew an aircraft engine thirty feet into the air! It dropped back into the fiery mass below. Gasoline spilled over the ship's side and flamed on the water! More heavy fire and billowing smoke raced up from the hangar deck! This blazing mass combined with smoke from the fires on the flight deck. It converged on the bridge.

"This smoke is so thick, it's more like night than day," Gehres said, coughing and choking again.

"Maybe if we changed course, sir...." Beckley replied.

"Yeah that might do it. Try the helm, Chief. Come right to 315 degrees."

"Aye, sir, right to 315 degrees."

Franklin moved to the new course. The strong, icy wind quickly cleared most of the smoke off the bridge and forward quarter.

"Goddamned wind is cold, but at least now we can breathe and see what's happening," Gehres said.

Another massive gasoline explosion sent a giant sheet of flame streaking up the flight deck toward the starboard gun pits! Beckley watched the giant fireball burst toward John's 40-mm sponson. "Look out!" he screamed.

"Tell 'em to get the hell out of those gun pits!" Gehres shouted.

In Able sponson, John saw the huge mass of fire careening toward him. Instinctively he dove through an open hatch to a catwalk. Then Bonin, Colson and Garcia rushed in after him—and Barker and Jardin stumbled in after them.

"Where're the rest of the guys?" John shouted. "Where's Ski? Where's Lowe? Where's Feinstein, Arnold and Hazelton?"

John moved back toward the fire and smoke-filled hatch.

"You can't go out there, John!" Garcia screamed. "It's suicide!"

Garcia and Colson restrained him.

"Don't be a dammed fool, John," Garcia shouted. "That fire will burn you to a crisp!"

"Did any one else make it?" John asked, still struggling toward the hatch.

"I think I saw Arnold and Hazelton duck into the ready-service locker," Jardin said.

"Jesus! I hope that damned thing doesn't explode! Was Sullivan out there?"

"I don't know, John. We just tried to stay alive," Bonin said, struggling for breath.

John felt helpless. There was nothing he could do. Coughing and struggling for air, he said, "Let's see...if we can get...to the forecastle."

They started toward the forecastle, stumbling and groping as they went. There was a huge explosion behind them! Everyone stopped.

"Was that the ready-service locker?" Jardin asked, fear resonating in his voice.

"God, I hope not," John said.

"Sure sounded like it was, Gunner," Jardin replied, his voice filled with fear.

John looked back at Jardin. "Don't worry about it, sailor. We're going to be okay," he said, coughing and choking as he spoke.

"Yeah, I guess we will. At least we made it this far, Gunner," Jardin replied weakly.

"Okay," John said hoarsely. " Let's keep going. Let's go on!"

Dense smoke clogged the passageway. Occasionally it parted. When it did, they could glimpse the enormous damage on the hangar and gallery decks. Fires were raging everywhere.

The gallery deck was filled with white-hot flames. Planes on the hangar deck were ripped apart by exploding bombs and gasoline. Debris flew into the air with each new explosion! Some of it showered down on the catwalk.

"Keep going!" John shouted. "Kick that burning crap off the deck!"

"What the hell's the use!" Garcia screamed. "It just gets blasted back by the next explosion!"

"Kick it off and keep going, goddamn it!" John shouted. "We'll make it!"

"Yeah, if we don't burn to death we will," Garcia replied.

Tanks of aviation gasoline located on *Franklin's* port side erupted and burst into flames! The burning liquid flowed into the ocean like lava from a volcano. The hangar deck was a mass of twisted, white-hot metal. A Tiny Tim went off and smashed into the starboard bulkhead. It ripped the *Franklin's* side like it was made of cardboard. Another fired straight up and impacted the underside of the flight deck. It blew open a jagged hole! Fire and thick smoke filled it immediately.

"This air is so goddamned hot and smoky, I can't breathe," Colson said, coughing and struggling for breath.

"Stay low to the deck," John shouted.

"I can't see!" Jardin yelled.

"Stay close to me and save your breath, Jardin," John called back. "Keep going! We'll make it. We're getting there."

"You sure, Gunner?" Jardin asked, his voice barely audible.

"Save your breath and move. Stay low to the deck. We'll make it, goddamn it!"

They crawled along, coughing and choking. Smoke nearly blinded them. Fire singed their hair and clothing! They snuffed it out by thrashing it with their hands. They struggled on. After what seemed forever, they stumbled through the hatch to the forecastle. The fire had spared this area. The air was clear. They gasped fresh, clean air into their smoke-clogged lungs.

Back on the bridge, Beckley watched as Joe Taylor hauled himself over the railing from an escape ladder on the starboard side.

"God," he gasped, as he dropped down on deck. "I'm glad you guys aren't hurt."

"It's good to see you, sir," Beckley said. "I'm glad you're okay."

"How did you get here, Joe?" Gehres asked, as he put his arm on Taylor's shoulder and looked at him carefully.

"I crawled on my hands and knees through one goddamned catwalk after another. I finally stumbled into a sponson that led me to that escape ladder."

Gehres shook his head and said, "Your face is dirty as hell, Joe!"

"Yeah, I'll bet it is, sir. What's the condition of the ship, Captain?"

"We're still making twenty knots," Gehres said. "We still have all our boilers and inter-ship communications, and we're still steering from the bridge, but we've taken a hell of a pounding and God only knows when it'll stop. I don't know how long this ship can hold together."

As he spoke Admiral Davison and his aide, Captain David Russell, climbed onto the bridge using the same emergency escape ladder Joe Taylor used a few minutes earlier. As soon as he got his feet on deck, Davison said, "Les, I have to consider this ship out of commission. I hate to leave at a time like this, but I've got responsibility for the rest of the Task Group."

"I'll see if I can get a destroyer in here so we can transfer your flag, sir," Gehres said. "Joe, signal the nearest destroyer to come alongside."

Taylor found the one signalman left on the bridge and the message went out by semaphore.

The *USS Miller* was steaming about a thousand yards from *Franklin's* starboard beam. She answered *Franklin's* call.

As she steamed toward *Franklin's* starboard side, Davison followed her through binoculars. A huge explosion on the flight deck knocked the binoculars out of his hand! Another one followed. Flames licked up at the bridge! Davison turned to Gehres. "Les, this ship is a wreck! You should abandon her."

Gehres thought for a few seconds, then replied, "I think we can save her, Admiral! I'd like to try…."

Davison shook his head. "I don't think you can, Les,"

"I'd like to try, Admiral."

"Les, I think she's going to sink," Davison retorted. "Those fires are out of control. This is too much damage to overcome!"

"Hell, we're still afloat, Admiral," Gehres said curtly.

Davison smiled, shook his head and nodded his consent.

The *Miller* closed to *Franklin's* side. Lines were thrown between the two ships and a breeches-bouy was rigged. As Davison, Bogan and their staffs left the ship, Davison yelled back to Gehres, "I wish you the best, Les. I hope I'm wrong! Adios! Good luck!"

Miller steamed away. Gehres turned to Taylor and Jurika and asked, "What do you men think we should do? Should we abandon ship?"

"I don't think so, Captain." Jurika replied. "I sure wouldn't. I think we can pull her through."

Taylor listened carefully to what Jurika said. He nodded his head. "I agree with Steve, Captain," he said. "I think it's possible if we all work as hard as we can."

"I'm glad you both agree," Gehres said. He thought a moment. "We're going to save her!" he said, determination resonating in his voice. "Steve, call in the *Santa Fe* to pick up our wounded." He turned to Taylor. "Joe, if we're going to save this ship we have to get her under tow and get the hell out of here. I know it sounds almost impossible, but I have to put that responsibility on your shoulders."

"Aye, sir," Taylor replied. "I'll do my best, Captain."

"And, Joe," Gehres said, "make sure the magazines are flooded."

"Aye, sir," Taylor replied.

TRAGEDY STRIKES

Taylor called and got the Gunner's Mate in charge of the magazine aft.

"Gunner, we need to flood both main magazines."

There was a pause as the Gunner replied.

Taylor relayed his message to Gehres. "They can flood the magazine aft, Captain, but the passageways to the forward magazine are blocked."

"Try to reach somebody in the forward magazine, somehow," Gehres said. "Give him the word to flood."

"Aye, sir. I'll do my best!" Taylor tried to contact the forward magazine. The phone just rang and rang. Then he headed down through the mass of hanging cables and wreckage and reached the forecastle. When he got there, he spotted John.

"Gunner," he said as he approached, "I need your help. I have to be sure we flooded the forward magazine. I'm pretty sure of the magazine aft. I spoke directly to the gunner there, but I'm not sure about the forward magazine. I couldn't contact anyone. Take a couple of men and go down there. See if it's flooded. We have to be sure."

"Aye, sir," John replied, despite the fear that his life could be snuffed out in a flash if the magazine exploded.

"I need two volunteers," he said.

Jardin stepped forward. "I'm the first one, Gunner," he said.

John was taken aback for a moment. "Okay, Jim," he said, perplexed by Jardin's sudden offer.

"Now, I need one more."

No one moved.

"Okay, Garcia, you're my second volunteer."

Garcia still didn't move.

"Come on, Garcia," John said. "You heard the Commander's order. Front and center."

Garcia stepped reluctantly forward. The three rushed down the ladder to the hatch that led to the main magazine three decks below. When they reached the first deck, it looked a lot like it did when John was there two days earlier, but when they turned to go down the ladder to the second deck, smoke and flames from a gasoline fire shot up at them. John stopped in his tracks. He could feel the heat from the flames on his cheeks and forehead. Fear seized him. His hand trembled and his heart pounded wildly.

"It's blazing down there, John!" Garcia shouted as he looked at the deck below.

"I can see it," John said, surprised by the steady tone of his voice. "I think we can get through."

"Bullshit, John," Garcia replied. "I'm not going down there!"

Thoughts of Sandy flashed through his mind. He had to get back to her, but Garcia was right. They could get killed or burned to death. He thought of Sandy again. He pressed his Saint Christopher medal between his thumb and index finger and quickly prayed, "God is my Source and Protector. Please God, protect me now…"

"Let's go! We have to reach that magazine," he said, his stomach still churning with fear.

"Christ, John, that's crazy!" Garcia screamed. "We could burn to death!"

"Belay that crap!" John snapped. "I don't want to hear another word of it. We have to flood that magazine. If this fire gets to it, this whole goddamned ship's going to explode and we'll explode with it! Let's go!" He rushed down the ladder. The fires licked out at him. He shielded his face with his right arm and forged ahead. Flames singed his hair and his uncovered ear. He kept going. He could hear footsteps behind him…this was a good sign…they were coming….

When they reached the bottom of the ladder on the magazine deck, the red warning light on the magazine was flashing. This signaled the magazine wasn't flooded.

Garcia hesitated on the last step.

"Christ, John, that thing's hot!" he shouted. "It's not flooded. It could explode any minute! Let's get the hell out of here!"

"Where the hell can we go?" John shouted back. "If it explodes we've had it—wherever we are—here or back on the forecastle."

Garcia didn't move.

"God Damn it, Ramon! Don't you understand? If the ammunition in that magazine blows, this whole ship gets blasted apart and so do we!"

John rushed to the giant wheel-valve that manually opened the flooding system.

Garcia still wavered.

Jardin pushed past Garcia and ran to John's side. "I'll help you, Gunner!" he shouted.

They began to wrestle with the wheel-valve.

"Come on Garcia! Get off your ass, goddamn it, give us a hand!"

"Come on you son-of-a-bitch!" John shouted again as they struggled with the giant wheel. "We have to open this thing! The heat's made it tighter than hell. Come on, goddamn it! Help us turn this valve! Then we'll get the hell out of here!"

Garcia hesitated, then he charged to their side.

They wrestled with the wheel. It squeaked and moved slightly.

"It's going to come!" John shouted. "Everybody together. Push!"

The giant wheel squeaked. Then it started to move—very slowly at first—then a little more easily. Finally it slipped loose and released! John spun the wheel rapidly until it was open.

Jardin watched the gauges beside the valve. "They're signaling 'flooding,' Gunner," he shouted.

John put his ear to the bulkhead. "I hear a lot of water gushing. Okay. Let's get the hell out of here!"

They rushed back to the fire-threatened ladders. John looked up. The flames continued, but luckily they weren't spreading. "Cover your face and eyes, guys," he ordered. "Now! Let's get the hell out of here!"

They rushed up the ladders that led to the forecastle taking two and three steps at a time.

Taylor was waiting when they got there.

"Were they flooded, Gunner?" he asked.

"Not when we got there, Commander," John said, gasping for breath, "We opened the valve by hand and the gauges registered 'flooding.' I listened and heard water gushing, so I'm sure they are now."

"Good job, Gunner," Taylor said. He looked at them. "That took a lot of courage, men. I'm proud of you!"

John felt a warm sense of pride at Commander Taylor's words. He turned to Jardin and Garcia. "I'm proud of you guys, too!"

Jardin and Garcia both nodded.

"What the hell came over you, Jim?" John asked. "I thought you'd be the last guy to volunteer."

"Father O'Callahan was right, Gunner," Jardin said. "When it's your time, it's your time. When I dodged that fireball this morning and fought through all that burning crap on the catwalk, I knew I could make it all the way." He paused. "I guess I'm ready for anything now, Gunner."

On the bridge Beckley, Gehres and Jurika watched helplessly as explosion after explosion devastated the *Franklin's* midsection. A huge gasoline explosion erupted aft of the bridge just over the engine room. Almost immediately a frantic call came up. It was Commander Greene who was in charge of the engine and boiler rooms. "That last explosion about did us in, Captain," he said, gasping for breath. "It's getting hotter and hotter down here, and there's heavy smoke, too. Nobody can breathe."

"What's the condition of the boilers and engines?" Gehres asked.

"Two fire rooms are out of commission. The third is too hot to occupy. The temperature there is over two hundred degrees. Explosions are ripping the steam lines. That last one blew a whole bunch of them apart."

"How long can you hold out?"

"Not much longer, sir. We can't sustain pressure. My men are collapsing from heat. They're suffocating! I hate to do this but I have to request permission to leave our stations, sir."

Gehres was silent for a moment, then he said, "Permission granted. Set the engines to eight knots, if you can. Then get the hell out of there!"

Gehres turned to Beckley. "Can you find out if Commander Taylor got the magazines flooded, Chief?"

Beckley grabbed the phone. It was dead. "I can't, sir. We've lost our communications, too," he said, "and we're listing more to starboard."

The *Franklin's* list was alarming. When contrasted to the level of the horizon, it was strikingly obvious. It could be felt under foot as well. More and more the ship's starboard side was tilting toward the ocean.

#

On the *Santa Fe* Captain Fitz watched the explosions decimate the *Franklin*. His binoculars had been trained on her from the time the first explosions began.

On the after-bridge Tom Rashinski was also glued to his binoculars. He was watching his best friend's ship being ripped apart by her own bombs and missiles. "Dear God, I hope he's okay," he prayed as one explosion after another rocked the *Franklin.* "Dear God, please keep him safe."

At 09:20 Tom picked up a semaphore message flashed from *Franklin*. He rushed it to the bridge. "Message from *Franklin,* Captain."

Fitz took the message and read it rapidly. "They want us to go alongside to help with their wounded," he said. "Come right to course 90 degrees. Sound the general alarm. All fire-fighting units man their battle stations. Rig to take on wounded," he commanded.

The *Santa Fe* swung into a tight arc and headed for the *Franklin*.

"Helmsman!"

"Aye, sir!"

"Stay right with me, sailor. I want to get very close to her. We have to get lines over."

"Aye, sir. I'm with you, Captain."

At 09:31 Fitz had positioned *Santa Fe* less than thirty yards off *Franklin's* starboard bow.

"Rashinski!"

"Aye, sir."

"Get a message over to them. Ask them if their magazines are flooded."

Tom flashed out the message.

#

Gehres read the message. He knew why Fitz was concerned. The cruiser *Birmingham* was nearly blown apart by a magazine explosion when she tried to help the sinking carrier *Princeton* in the Philippine Sea. "Signal him that we've ordered them flooded, but tell him we can't be completely sure because we've lost all our communications," he ordered.

#

When he read Gehres's reply, Fitz said, "Okay, to hell with it! We'll take the chance. They've got wounded. Flooded or not, we're going in!"

Santa Fe edged in closer. "Fire a messenger line across!" Fitz shouted. In a few minutes two high lines were rigged and *Santa Fe* started taking wounded men off the blazing *Franklin* on trolleys.

"Watch *Franklin's* list carefully, Ed," Fitz said to his Exec. "She's drifting. We might have to move fast in case she starts to capsize."

The transfer of wounded went frantically on. On the bridge Fitz was having trouble keeping *Santa Fe* in line alongside *Franklin. Franklin* was beginning to drift and was listing even more dangerously to starboard.

The explosions on *Franklin* continued, each one filled with more flaming debris and wreckage than the last. A lot of this rubble landed on the *Santa Fe*, cluttering her decks and starting fires.

After assessing the situation briefly, Fitz decided he had to move away. "*Franklin's* drift had become too erratic," he said. "Ed, I'm concerned that wounded men will be lost in the water if those lines snap."

Wessern nodded. He was concerned about the fire dangers, too. "Captain, we need to clear the decks of that fiery clutter and damned fast, sir!"

"Abandon the operation," Fitz ordered.

The *Santa Fe* cast off all lines, turned and began to steam away.

#

Beckley struggled with the helm. It had stopped responding. "I think we just lost steering control, Captain."

Loss of steering was just the beginning. In a few minutes *Franklin* lost all power. She slowed, then went dead in the water.

"We're drifting, Captain," Beckley said.

"Yeah," Gehres replied, "right toward the Japanese coast. Shikoku is less than fifty miles away."

The explosions on both the hangar and flight decks continued. At 10:03 the worst blast of the morning occurred when fire detonated a five-inch ready-service magazine. The huge explosion shook *Franklin* from stem to stern. Whole aircraft engines with propellers attached were hurled into the air! Debris of all descriptions, including pieces of human bodies, flew up with them! Then everything dropped back onto the burning deck like hail hitting a roof.

"This ship feels like a rat shaken by an angry cat," Jurika said.

19 March, 1945
10:31 Hours
Franklin's Flight Deck

O'Callahan stopped for a moment on the edge of the flight deck. He looked aft toward the fantail. Nearly the whole deck was on fire. Of the thousand feet of flight deck, over eight hundred feet were in flames. Fires raged. Smoke spread across the deck planks like an evil fog. He looked at the dead lying just about everywhere. He couldn't even count them, let alone pray for them. There was a groan behind him. A young boy, scarcely eighteen, called to him. Tears rolled from the boy's blue eyes down his blistered, blackened face. His teeth chattered uncontrollably, both from shock and the chilling wind.

O'Callahan took his hand. "Are you a Catholic, son?"

The marine nodded.

He bent close to him, held his head and crossed his forehead with holy oil. The last breath rattled out of the dying boy's lungs as he said the absolution.

Wounded sailors and marines on the edge of the flight deck watched the *Santa Fe* steam away. No one said a word, but their eyes reflected the trauma of the past few hours and the despair of what her leaving might bring.

"Is *Santa Fe* leaving for good, Padre?" a severely wounded young marine asked, his voice filled with fear.

"I'm not sure, son," O'Callahan replied. "It looks like she just might be going out to turn around."

"God, I hope so, Padre," he gasped. He didn't say anything more. His voice reflected his terror.

What chance does he have? O'Callahan wondered. A hopeless cripple, weak from loss of blood and stunned by combat shock. He gently placed his hand on the young man's charred forehead. "Don't worry son, we're going to try to get you off safely, whether she comes back or not."

"Honest, Father?" he gasped.

"We'll do our best, son."

The young marine struggled convulsively for breath. He died as O'Callahan began to utter the absolution.

The putrid odor of burning flesh filled the air. O'Callahan took a breath and with it inhaled the stench of hundreds of burning men. Rancid smoke burned his eyes. He choked as he took it into his lungs. It was harder to breathe up here. He moved briefly out of the smoke's path to get fresher air. Mournful groans of injured and burned sailors and marines resonated through the heavy smoke. "Oh my God, what more can I do?" he prayed. "What greater prayer can I offer for these men?"

He moved back to the next boy and spoke to him. He could see his words weren't registering. The young sailor's eyes weren't focused. His jaw sagged. He had a huge wound in his chest. O'Callahan took no chances. He gave him absolution immediately—Catholic or not. When he finished he released the young marine's head. His dead eyes stared vacantly, seeing nothing.

Ignoring the heavy smoke made worse by the frigid blasts of wind, O'Callahan went from one man to another, speaking words of hope if they were alive and blessing them if they weren't.

He knelt beside a wounded sailor and quickly gave him the last rites. As he did a missile blasted off and zoomed right over his head. He felt the heat from it as it buzzed by. A war photographer's camera flashed, capturing the scene. O'Callahan ignored the blazing missile and the camera's flash. "This man's badly wounded!" he shouted to the photographer. "Forget the damned pictures! Help me get his bleeding stopped!" The photographer rushed to his side. Together they fashioned a makeshift tourniquet.

From the bridge Beckley watched the horrific scene on the flight deck. He saw O'Callahan move among the wounded and burned. "Look at Father O'Callahan. He seems to be everywhere, giving Extreme Unction, encouraging the wounded—praying with them."

"Yeah, Chief," Gehres said, "and look at the detached way he goes about it. He just moves from one wounded man to another, his head bowed like he's in constant prayer."

"He doesn't seem concerned about the fires and explosions, or the danger of freaky missiles blasting off," Beckley added as he looked down through a pair of binoculars at the bespectacled priest.

"He's an inspiration to us all," Gehres said.

Beckley focused his binoculars out toward the *Santa Fe*. He saw her beginning to come about. "*Santa Fe* might be coming back, Captain," he said as he pointed out toward the maneuvering cruiser.

19 March, 1945
11:43 Hours
Santa Fe Returns

On the *Santa Fe*, Captain Fitz had not forgotten *Franklin's* wounded. He steered *Santa Fe* in a large arc. "Get the decks cleared, on the double! I'm going to have another run at her!"

Deck crews hurriedly cleared the smoldering debris. Fitz turned back toward *Franklin's* starboard side.

"All ahead flank speed!" he shouted.

The *Santa Fe's* engines whined. Her bow lifted high in the water from the surge of extra power. Spray flew as she cut through the ocean toward the *Franklin's* flame-ridden starboard quarter. Her speed increased dramatically as she went.

"I'm going to crash through that wreckage and get to her starboard side," Fitz said. "I'm going to try to tie up next to her. We can get her wounded off faster by using gangplanks and lines!"

At a speed of over thirty-five knots, *Santa Fe* ripped into *Franklin's* debris. She tore through the horizontal radio mast and wrenched sharply through the mass of tangled steel cables. She crashed through the projecting 40-mm gun platforms and outboard catwalks. Steel screeched against steel. Sparks flew. Cables strained and snapped. The impact sheared off some of her main deck and tore into two of her five-inch guns, but her speed carried her through the obstructions and entanglements! She jolted against the *Franklin's* hull.

"Full speed astern!" Fitz shouted.

The *Santa Fe* was now parallel aside *Franklin*. Fitz held her in place by the force of Santa Fe's engines using her forward gun turrets as fenders against the Franklin's overhanging decks.

"Get lines on her!" Fitz shouted.

Santa Fe was quickly tied to the burning carrier. Gangplanks were shoved in place.

"Ahoy, *Franklin*!" Fitz shouted over his loudspeaker. "Send over your wounded. They can walk over now!"

#

On the *Franklin's* bridge Gehres and Jurika watched the dangerous drama play out.

"He came in fast, sir. He brought her in at flank speed," Jurika observed, seeming astonished by Fitz's actions.

"He had to come that fast," Gehres said. "She'd get snarled in our wreckage if he didn't." Gehres looked down at the *Santa Fe*. "That's the greatest piece of seamanship I've ever seen," he said, his voice filled with admiration.

The locked-together ships provided easier access to safety. Volunteers carried men across in stretchers. Corpsmen aided the weak and immobile. Badly burned men stumbled over. Buddies helped buddies. But the possibility of destruction from fire or explosion presented constant threats, and both ships were now sitting ducks—easy targets for Japanese planes—their only protection provided by the gallant cruisers and destroyers in their screen that steamed in a tight circle around them.

#

Tom watched from the bridge as the *Santa Fe*'s fire fighters entered the fight with all of their hoses gushing. They poured tons of water into the flames on *Franklin*'s hangar deck, fighting fires that fire fighters on *Franklin* couldn't reach. As he watched the valiant efforts, a feeling of relief spread through him. Maybe the blazing carrier had a chance. He looked up at *Franklin*'s forecastle. He thought he saw John Oxler among the men working there. He focused his binoculars. It *was* John. "John!" he shouted. "John Oxler!" There was no response. He shouted again. There was still no response. He grabbed a signal flag and waved it back and forth, all the while shouting John's name.

At last, John noticed him and waved back.

"Are you okay, John?" he shouted.

"Yes," came John's noise-muffled reply.

"What the hell happened?"

"We took two Jap bombs in the wrong places!"

"If she starts to go down get the hell off of her quick!"

"I will! Tom! If I don't make it back, tell my folks you saw me. Ask them to call my wife. Tell them I love them!"

Tom nodded vigorously and flipped him a salute. "I've got it," he shouted.

Santa Fe's fire fighters surged forward; they climbed aboard the *Franklin*, dragging their hoses with them. They poured tons of water into the fight. The *Franklin*'s hangar deck fires began to recede. They moved courageously into the flames. They fought the fires for the entire time *Santa Fe* was aside *Franklin*.

After an hour and a half, *Franklin*'s wounded were across. Air Wing related personnel and men not necessary to fire fighting came across next. There were still men trapped on the flight deck and fantail—isolated and stranded by the huge fires. They were jumping overboard into the debris-cluttered ocean. They had no place else to go.

"Fish those men out!" Fitz shouted.

"Rashinski!"

"Yes, sir."

"Signal the *Miller*, *Owen* and *Tingley* to come in and help with the rescue, and

TRAGEDY STRIKES

Rashinski, go down to the galley and tell the bakers to send over all the bread we have on hand. Send over all the rescue-breathers we've got left, too. On the double, sailor!"

Tom rushed down and delivered Fitz's orders. The tasks were quickly completed.

"Disengage from the *Franklin*," Fitz said. "All engines ahead one-third." The *Santa Fe* pulled away from the *Franklin* into the open Pacific.

\#

Gehres and Beckley watched the *Santa Fe* steam away. "Chief," Gehres said, "get me the signalman on watch."

When the signalman stepped onto the bridge, Gehres said, "Send this message to Captain Fitz:

"The officers and men of the Franklin are deeply grateful for your courageous help in circumstances so adverse and calamitous they are difficult to believe. Your efforts were far beyond the call of duty—the most valorous actions by a ship and its crew I have ever seen. God bless you all."

\#

On the *Hornet* Admiral Jocko Clark followed the entire scene through binoculars. "What an incredible job! That whole ship's company should be decorated," he said as he watched *Santa Fe* steam back into position in the Task Group. "See if you can get Les Gehres on the wire," he said to the radioman on watch.

In a few minutes a voice came up through the intercom from the radio room. "Admiral, we can't reach them by either radio or teletype. Their power must be gone, sir."

"Get me a signalman."

In a few seconds a signalman was on the bridge. "Can you reach *Franklin* from here?"

"I think so, Admiral. I'll ask a ship at the edge of the screen to relay it if I can't, sir."

"Okay, take this down and get it to the *Franklin*:

Les, I guess I called it. It looks like it's worse over there than it was at Guadalcanal. We're providing you cover. We've suspended all attacks on the mainland. We're going to fly all of our fighters above you and on your perimeter. They'll be up twenty-four hours a day until your fires are out and you're safely underway. I think the Japs need a trophy victory. They'll be coming after you with everything they've got. They're not going to get the Franklin. We're going to stop them, partner. Right at the pass. I've put out the word: Nobody gets through to Franklin. Nobody! The whole fleet is pulling for you. If I know you, you'll pull her through.

"Sign it Jocko Clark," he added.

"Aye, aye, sir."

Just as the signalman left to flash out the message, a radioman climbed onto the bridge. "Message from Admiral Nimitz, sir," he said.

Clark took the message and read it rapidly aloud. "Admiral Nimitz says the Japanese need a revenge victory. He wants to save the *Franklin* no matter the cost," he said. He smiled wryly. "We're way ahead of him on this one," he said.

As Admiral Clark spoke the first of thirty-three Hellcats roared off *Hornet*. Their mission—to protect the *Franklin* no matter the cost.

19 March, 1945
12:15 Hours
Enlisted Men's Mess Hall

On the *Franklin* in the enlisted men's mess, three hundred men were trapped by the first big explosion. They were eating breakfast when it struck. The blast blocked every exit. Huge fires erupted on the decks above them. The mess hall had become a virtual oven. Smoke fouled an atmosphere already vitally short of oxygen. All the elements for panic were there. There was grave peril and the great torture of not knowing what would happen. Self-help was impossible. Fear dominated the compartment. It gripped one man after another. Voices that began as whispers ended in hysterical shrieks.

Don Gary, who had been eating with the enlisted men, realized he had to squelch the possibility that men would panic. He climbed atop a mess table and said, "Quiet, men! We're trapped here, but it's only for a while. Don't lose your heads and don't squander your energy. We haven't got much oxygen, so don't waste it. Breathe quietly. Get down on the deck and say a silent prayer. Now!"

Men sank to their knees at his command. The silent prayer brought some stability. Then Gary spoke again. "There's a way out of this somewhere. It might be down several decks and by way of a lot of junctions, but there has to be a way to get out of here."

Joe Fuelling, one of the ship's doctors, rose in support of Gary. "Lieutenant Gary's right, men," he said. "Don't lose your heads. He knows this ship like a surgeon knows anatomy. If anyone can find a way out, he can. Trust me. I know this is true."

Gary acknowledged Fuelling's remarks with a nod. "Stay calm. I'll find a way out," he said, "and I'll come back here and get you. I mean this. *I'll find a way out. I'll come back and get you!*"

Then he stepped down and moved away through a smoke-filled passage. When he was gone, Fuelling asked for prayers again, this time not only for themselves, but also for Gary. They prayed that he would find a safe way out of the stifling trap that held them captive.

19 March 1945
12:27 Hours
Franklin's Bridge

On the bridge, Gehres, Beckley and Jurika watched as a radioman attempted to restore a voice-activated phone. Somehow he connected with the ship's steering-aft compartment.

"Captain, I'm in contact with steering-aft," he said.

Gehres grabbed the phone. "This is the Captain. Who's on the line?" he asked.

There was a pause, then Gehres said to Beckley, "Chief, it's Seaman First Class Larry Holobrook."

"Yes, sir," Beckley replied. "He's one of my men."

Gehres shoved the phone at Beckley. "Here. See what the situation is down there," he ordered.

"Holobrook, this is Chief Beckley. What's happening there?"

"Five of us are trapped here, Chief. John Davis, Bill Hamlet, Joe Gudbrandsen, Norman Mayer and me. It's hot as hell and the water's rising, but we're ready, if needed, to steer the ship."

Beckley turned to Gehres. "They're down there ready to steer, Captain," he said.

"Let's give it a try," Gehres said.

"What's the course, sir?"

"Ask them to come to course 160 degrees."

"Aye, sir. Try to come to course 160 degrees."

"You're going to have to guide us, Chief," Holobrook said. "It's pitch dark here, too."

"They're in the dark, Captain," Beckley said. "I'll have to guide them. Give me an easy right rudder, Holobrook. Okay? A little harder to the right."

Franklin slowly moved in the direction of the course change. When she was on course, Beckley said, "You're there! Steady as you go, right there."

Gehres was elated. He took the phone back from Beckley. "You men are doing an important job," he said. "Maybe the most important job on the ship right now. Stay at your post and don't worry. We'll get you all out. I know it's hard to believe, but I promise you, we'll get you out."

"They're standing by down there," Gehres said as he put the phone down. "That takes a hell of a lot of courage. I'm going to get those men out, even if I have to cut through to them myself!"

Franklin's ordinance continued to explode. Five-hundred-pound bombs detonated all along the middle of the flight deck. Some dropped into the hangar deck and exploded there. This triggered Tiny Tims; some streaked to starboard ripping out bulkheads; some swished to port tearing gaping holes; some blazed straight up through the flight deck—some tumbled end over end! It was an awesome spectacle. The eerie, screaming sound of missiles in flight was a terrifying experience. Each time one went off the fire-fighting crews hit the deck. After every explosion they got up and resumed fighting the raging fires. They stood by their hoses, in spite of what sometimes appeared to be certain death.

A signalman came onto the bridge. "Message from Admiral Clark, sir," he said.

Gehres grabbed the message and read it. Despite the chaos he smiled and handed it to Jurika.

"Jocko Clark's putting up a Combat Air Patrol of over one hundred and twenty-five fighters," he said. "With this kind of air cover we might have a chance."

19 March, 1945
13:30 Hours
Rigging for Tow

On the forecastle, Joe Taylor read a message flashed over by the *USS Pittsburgh*. "*Pittsburgh* is going to tow us," he said. "They'll be sending over a messenger to haul in an eight-inch hawser and a two-inch cable. They want us to signal with three flashes or flags when we're ready to start."

Taylor reacted swiftly. "Clear the deck for rigging a tow!" he shouted. He rushed to the starboard side of the forecastle. "Unshackle and drop this anchor. If you can't get it loose, cut it off with that emergency cutting outfit. Move!"

Men jumped into action! Somehow they knew from the tone of Taylor's voice that there was a chance they might survive.

"We're taking the hawser and cable from *Pittsburgh* through that bulls-eye," Taylor shouted. "The winches are out, so we have to heave them in by hand."

Then he turned to John. "Gunner, get these men ready to haul those towlines in!"

"Aye, sir," John replied. He quickly lined up the eighty able-bodied men on the forecastle. Just as he finished he spotted the *Hornet's* CAP. "There's the air patrol from the *Hornet*, sir."

Taylor nodded. "I hope they can buy us enough time to tow this ship out of here."

A squadron of Judys and Bettys escorted by Zeros broke through the clouds on the western horizon. *Hornet's* Hellcats streaked after them. A wild dogfight erupted! Fighters from the *Belleau Wood* and *Hancock* joined the fray. An enemy Judy broke free of the Hellcats and slashed toward the *Franklin*. Everyone on *Franklin's* forecastle scattered for cover, aware that the helpless carrier had no antiaircraft defense—that they were sitting ducks.

John took cover behind the barrel of the capstan. The Judy's shells ripped into the deck boards on the forecastle and whined off the side of the capstan. Every ship in the tight screen around *Franklin* brought the Judy under fire. The intense antiaircraft barrage caused it to veer off course. Its first bomb exploded short, off target by less than fifty yards.

John could see the pilot and gunner as the Judy flashed by. He shook his fist at them. "You bastards! You sons-of-bitches!" he screamed.

The Judy turned and flew back.

"Goddamn it," he said angrily, "if something could just happen to stop that son-of-a-bitch. Anything, Lord!"

As though his angry prayer was heard, six Hellcats from Jocko Clark's CAP streaked toward the speeding Judy. They overtook it and opened fire. The lead pilot's wing cannons tore at the cover of the Judy's cockpit. It ripped off! The trailing Hellcats filled the sky around it with 20-mm armor-piercing shells. After what seemed an eternity, the Judy exploded in a mass of flames. Its wreckage slithered down into the ocean. It was within a hundred yards of *Franklin's* starboard side.

"Yes! Goddamn it! Yes, you rotten son-of-a-bitch!" John shouted. Everyone on the forecastle let out a loud cheer of relief. Then they rushed back to prepare to receive the towlines.

Pittsburgh fired a line over and the process of hauling the heavy hawser and steel cable through nearly a quarter mile of ocean by hand began. Men on the towline strained to pull in the heavy hawser and cable. They wouldn't budge.

Joe Taylor drove them. "Heave ho! Heave ho!" he shouted. But strive as they might, they couldn't get them to move. "Gunner, see if you can get us some more men," Taylor said nodding his head toward John.

John rushed off the forecastle and headed aft. When he reached the officer's wardroom, he ran into Fonz.

"Fonz. Am I glad to see you! We need some men on the forecastle. We're trying to haul in a hawser and we can't budge it."

"I'll help you with that, Gunner," Fonz said. "I'll get you all the extra help you need."

Within a few minutes Fonz came through the hatch on the forecastle. With him were at least fifty stewards from the officer's mess. Despite the cold, they ripped off their shirts and took up positions on the towline. Black sailors lined up shoulder to shoulder with whites. They tugged, strained and sweated. They gasped, cussed and pulled some more. The added strength didn't seem to help. No matter how hard they all pulled and strained, the hawser and cable wouldn't move.

Then something amazing happened. Fonz moved into the line. In his deep melodious voice he began to chant, "Heaveee Ho! Heaveee Ho!" His voice was filled with inspiration and determination. Quickly, the black stewards took up the chant. They started an impromptu kind of chanting, making up the words as they went along.

"We pullin' with all of our might!"

"Heaveee Ho! Heaveee Ho!"

"This line ain't gonna be tight!"

"Heaveee Ho! Heaveee Ho!"

"I gotta get home to my wife!"

"Heaveee Ho! Heaveee Ho!"

"She's the light of my life!"

"Heaveee Ho! Heaveee Ho!"

The response was electric! The rhythmic chants spawned new courage and strength. White sailors began chanting with blacks. Officers dropped what they were doing and moved into the line. The chants took on an energy of their own—a rhythmic spiritual energy—arising out of the ruins of a battered, burning ship.

"This line ain't gonna be tight!"

"Heavee Ho! Heaveee Ho!"

Suddenly the heavy line began to move! It tightened, then slackened, then tightened. The chanting and refrains continued. They gained strength with every chorus. The hawser came in more rapidly. Soon it appeared out of the water and was threaded through the bullseye. Then the two-inch cable was threaded through. After a couple of jerky attempts, they were both shackled to deck stoppers. *Franklin* was ready to be towed!

"Gunner, signal the *Pittsburgh* that *Franklin* is ready," Taylor said.

John sent the signal out—three flashes from a battery-powered light.

In a few minutes the hawser and cable stiffened and lifted. *Pittsburgh's* bow jerked up in the water as she began to slowly tow the heavier *Franklin*.

A loud cheer went up from the men on the forecastle. Black sailors hugged white—white sailors hugged black—two even danced a funny kind of jig.

Franklin put a tremendous strain on the *Pittsburgh*. She was over forty thousand tons. *Pittsburgh* was less than half that size. Despite this difference, *Pittsburgh* slowly increased her speed. Soon *Franklin* was moving at two knots and starting to inch out of harm's way.

Joe Taylor called out to John. "Gunner, see if you can get those 40-mm's up behind the bridge to work! They look like they missed most of the starboard damage."

"Yes, sir," John said, delighted to do something to fight back. "Bonin, Colson and Garcia! Front and center," he ordered. "Barker! Jardin! Fall in."

Then he asked for volunteers. "I've got five men. I need some more."

Bob Diamond, a Staff Sergeant in the Marine Corps, volunteered, as did Wilfred Williams, a Yeoman Third Class. Charles Ginsberg, a Seaman First Class who worked in the ship's store, stepped forward. So did Wells Wilson, a Seaman Second Class.

"This is enough to get started with, Commander," John said. "Okay. Let's go." They headed for the ladder to the flight deck.

19 March, 1945
13:05 Hours
Struggling in the Ducts

Don Gary struggled from smoky passageway to smoky passageway. Despite his knowledge of the *Franklin's* lower decks he couldn't find a way out. He coughed and struggled through the darkness. Finally he found a passageway that he felt was a possibility. He groped through the dark, smoke-filled passageway. It led nowhere. It dead-ended in a bomb-storage compartment. Then his memory flashed! The bomb-storage compartment had an opening in it to a ventilator trunk. Maybe he could get through there. He found the grate that covered the opening. He tore it loose and peered inside. There was nothing but darkness. He shoved his body into the aperture, knowing he faced a tremendous challenge. He had to find an undamaged series of ducts that would carry him to safety. His even greater challenge was to find a way to go forward nearly six hundred feet and up three decks to do it. He knew explosions had damaged many of the ducts—that a wrong choice might lead him into greater danger. Fear that the weakened ducts might give way stopped him. He thought about turning back. Then he remembered the men trapped in the mess hall and what he'd promised. He took a deep breath and forged ahead through the darkness.

19 March, 1945
13:35 Hours
40-mm Quad Repaired

From the bridge, Beckley spotted Oxler's group moving across the body-strewn edge of the flight deck toward the bridge.

"Looks like they've got a gun crew together," he said. "They'll probably try to get one of the 40-mm quads working again."

"That's great. I hope they can," Gehres said.

Klinkiewicz watched John's crew make its way across the tip of the flight deck. "Request the Captain's permission to join that gun crew, sir." he said.

"Do you know what to *do* on a 40-mm gun?" Gehres asked.

"Begging the Captain's pardon, sir, a marine can do anything," he replied.

"Permission granted," Gehres replied shaking his head.

Klinkiewicz headed down the ladder to the flight deck to join John's gun crew.

As John and his men fought their way through the frigid wind and mangled bodies toward the 40-mms, he looked over Able Sponson. It was a shambles, smashed by *Santa Fe*'s rescue thrust. His 40-mm guns were battered—and blistered by the intense flames. The ready-service locker was now just a jagged cavity filled with smoldering ashes and blackened, scorched bodies. The sight horrified him. Bodies of gunners burned to a crisp littered the locker's deck. John thought of Ski, Sullivan, Lowe, Arnold and Hazelton. He hadn't seen or heard from any of them since the big blast. A chill ran up his spine. He touched his Saint Christopher's medal, said a silent prayer for their safety and pressed on, trying hard to deny the blackened bodies below were once human.

They reached the ladder that led up to the gun tub and climbed in. The gun tub was full of debris. John looked at the 40-mm quad. It was blackened and filled with soot, but he felt the guns could be made to work. "We'll have to aim them manually," he said, "at least until we get some of our electrical power back. Garcia, take the pointer's seat. Colson, take the trainer's seat."

When they were in place, John said, "Okay, give 'em a try." The 40-mm's moved fluidly both horizontally and vertically.

About that time Klinkiewicz climbed into the gun pit with three more marines he'd recruited on the way from the bridge.

"We want to be part of your gun crew, Gunner," he declared.

"Okay, you're in," John said. "Let's get these guns ready to fire!" Let's begin by getting them cleaned up. There are some rags in that rag-storage bin. Let's start with those."

Everybody pitched in and went to work. Despite the cold and the soot, the guns were soon cleared. They began to look a little like they did before the attack. John was heartened by the cooperation he saw among his new crew. The fact that they were both marines and sailors didn't even come up. A team spirit, born in adversity, seemed to emerge through these men. They had survived and they were determined that their ship would survive, too.

CHAPTER TWENTY-EIGHT

19 March, 1945
14:20 Hours
A Ray of Hope

Franklin's list increased to thirteen degrees. All communications within the ship and all general announcing systems were out. Signal flags were ripped and tattered. The intercom, radio and telex were dead. The radio antenna on the main mast was missing. The radar antenna had been broken. It hung by its wires like a wounded swan, threatening to crash down over the navigational bridge at any moment. The flight deck from the forward elevator all the way back to the fantail was fire-scarred and filled with gaping holes. The steel structure underneath it was a mass of blistered metal.

On the hangar deck things were even worse. Massive I-beams and girders were twisted and tortuously bent. They looked like huge, distorted pretzels. Steel cables hung awkwardly from the overhead. Steel mesh, steel netting, steel catwalks and steel equipment, badly mangled and knotted, littered the deck. Heat-warped aircraft engines, shattered propellers and human body parts were everywhere. But there was a ray of hope. *Pittsburgh* was now towing *Franklin* at nearly two-and-a-half knots.

Because of *Franklin's* steering problem, she suddenly drifted so far out of line that she was being towed at almost a right angle.

Gehres saw what was happening. "We have to try to swing South."

Beckley got Holobrook. "Holobrook, can you swing us twenty degrees to the right?"

"We'll try," Holobrook said.

Under Beckley's guidance, *Franklin* slowly moved back into position. The tow proceeded.

"We need an evaluation of what happened below, Chief," Gehres said. "Get a new quartermaster to take the helm, and you and Commander Jurika go down and investigate."

Beckley and Jurika made their way to the forecastle. When they got there Beckley spotted John, Colson, Garcia, Bonin, Barker and Jardin.

He waved and rushed toward them. "God, I'm glad to see you guys!" he shouted. He gave each of them a warm hug. "What have you heard from Sullivan?" he asked.

"Nothing," John said. "We're also missing some of the other guys. We haven't heard from Ski, Lowe, Feinstein, Dixon or Hazelton. Last time we saw any of them was just before the big explosion that took out our starboard guns this morning."

"Commander Jurika and I are going to try to get some answers. Do you want to come along?" Beckley asked.

"I don't think we can, Beck. We've got those 40-mm guns atop the bridge working— we're just down here to get a few more men for our gun crew."

"Okay," Beckley said. "I saw you guys working on them earlier. It'll be great to have a gun operating again. I'll see you later, John. It's wonderful to know you're okay!"

"For us too, Beck," John replied, smiling for the first time in many hours.

Beckley and Jurika went aft through officers' country and got their first look at the hangar deck. "What a nightmare," Jurika said. "Look at all the bodies! They're everywhere—in the passageways, on ladders, on the gallery deck—lying right where they were killed."

One man was hanging from a catwalk by one arm. Another was draped over the bottom edge of a watertight door. Still another was trapped in a mass of electrical wiring. The hangar and gallery deck were engulfed in clouds of white-hot smoke and flames. Here and there, like coals of special brilliance, airplane engines glowed so intensely they hurt their eyes.

"No one can be alive there," Jurika said as he shielded his face from the flames. "No one could live there for even a second!"

Beckley looked at the entryway to the gallery deck. It was warped and blistered. Everything else was battered, too. Bombs and missiles had torn holes in the deck and bulkheads; huge holes with jagged edges that were horrible to behold because no human hand had designed them.

There was a constant crackle of flames. A blast would come, compounded by a whine, a hiss and a shriek—followed by another blast; another rocket exploding.

Beckley thought of Commander Zimler whom he last saw less than six hours earlier. His hope that Zimler had somehow made it out alive was dim. At some level he knew his friend was gone, burned to death by the white-hot fires. He pushed his sad thoughts of Zimler out of his mind. There would have to be another time for grief. He had to go on.

Forward on the hangar deck, there was some order. Fire fighters had been on duty here since the first blasts, and fire fighters from *Santa Fe* had been a big help. Hoses were plied on the fires that remained. There was progress here.

Jurika and Beckley watched them for a moment, then Jurika said, "Let's get up on the flight deck, Chief."

When they reached the flight deck they found another disaster. Although most of the fires were now isolated, the deck was a ghastly mess—a shambles of burned, warped, broken wood and mangled steel. Bodies, rubble and wreckage were scattered everywhere. Ugly holes had been chopped in the deck to poke hoses through in a futile attempt to quell the flames raging on the hangar deck below.

Beckley looked up at the battered bridge. The huge number thirteen was so blistered and blackened by the flames it could scarcely be distinguished. He stared at it intently. It seemed to echo back a mocking message: Jinx! Jinx! The sight depressed him. He looked away and moved on. He made his way through the charred bodies and smoldering debris to the starboard 20-mm gun pit. It was another horrible scene, filled with the corpses of men who manned these guns only a few hours earlier. Beckley climbed down into the wreckage and looked among the hideously burned bodies and water-soaked ashes. He spotted an identification bracelet and worked it free. He rubbed the soot-covered bracelet until he uncovered a gold anchor—then he made out a name. It read: Peter J. Sullivan, CPO. He stood there, silently staring at the charred remains of one of his best friends. A deep sadness nearly overwhelmed him. He felt tearful, but pushed his tears aside. Here, too, there had to be another time for grief.

He looked toward John's 40s. The scene was the same. The ammunition ready-service locker was filled with still-smoking ashes and burned bodies. There was no life there. He'd seen enough. He rejoined Jurika who was watching him from the flight deck.

"Find someone you know, Chief?" Jurika asked.

"Yes, sir," Beckley replied, his voice filled with great sadness. "Chief Gunner Sullivan."

Jurika shook his head sadly.

"I'm sorry, Chief. Sullivan was a good man."

"Yes, sir," Beckley said. Tears blinded him. He rubbed them from his eyes. "He was a very good man and a good friend...a very good friend, sir."

They went back to the bridge. Jurika gave Gehres a report. When he finished, Gehres said, "It's not very pretty, is it Commander?"

"No, sir. It's not pretty at all."

There was a pause. Nobody said a word. Nobody wanted to talk.

After awhile, Gehres broke the silence. "I asked Commander Greene to investigate the condition of the engine and fire rooms," he said. "He got back to me a few minutes ago. He said that as soon as the space is cool enough to let men get in, one of the engines could probably be coaxed back into action."

"Really? Did he say when it might be, sir?" Jurika asked.

"He hoped sometime tonight."

"I'll keep my fingers crossed, sir."

19 March, 1945
14:45 Hours
A Tiny Light

Don Gary groped his way through the darkness, trying to find cooler ducts. The going was slow and exhausting. It seemed like days since he'd left the mess hall. He forged into ducts that were damaged or destroyed and led nowhere. Each time he failed, he tried another way. When that way led him forward and up, he mentally fixed the passage clearly in his mind. Explosions rocked the ship. He doggedly went on. Finally he turned into a duct and saw a tiny light. It was seeing heaven! He pushed his way toward it and kicked the grate out. He let himself down. He was standing in officers' country near the warrant officers' wardroom. He walked into the wardroom. It was filled with wounded. Chaplain Gatlin and Sam Sherman, one of *Franklin's* doctors, were kneeling among them.

"Ahoy!" Gary said.

They both turned around, startled by his voice.

"I've got nearly three hundred men trapped in the enlisted men's mess. I've just found a way through the ducts to get them out."

"Through the ducts?" Sherman asked.

"Yeah," replied Gary.

"That's over six hundred feet aft and down four decks," Sherman said. "God, that's hard to believe!"

"Yeah. I guess it is. Either of you got a flashlight or battle lantern?" Gary asked. "I have to be sure I can find my way back."

Sherman shook his head.

Then Gatlin said, "Wait, I've got a candle."

"That's better than nothing," Gary said.

Gatlin walked to a small bag on the wardroom table and pulled a candle and a votive glass out. "Father O'Callahan gave me these this morning," he said. "He thought they might help me with Catholic boys in prayer." He handed Gary the votive glass and candle. "If you see him, don't tell him where you got them. I wouldn't want him to know I forgot to use them."

"You don't have to worry about that, Chaplain," Gary said. "There's nobody in those ducts but me."

Gary walked back down the passageway to the opening. He lit the candle with his cigarette lighter and pulled himself back in. It was still very smoky and there was the threat of more explosions, but with the aid of the candle he moved much faster. Several times he took wrong turns. He fixed them in his mind and went on. In about fifteen minutes he was back in the bomb storage compartment. He made his way to the mess hall.

"I'm back," he said. "I know a way out."

There was a stunned silence. Few believed he'd ever come back. Then there was an exhausted cheer.

"Count off by fifty and form a chain," Gary ordered. "You," he said, as he pointed to the man who started the counting. "Put your hands through my belt and hang on tight. Each man grab another man's belt the same way. I'll lead you out."

Murmurs arose about being left behind.

"Don't worry," Gary said. "I'll come back and get you all!"

Re-lighting the candle, he led the first fifty swiftly through the smoke-filled ducts. Then he went back again and again. Doctor Joe Fuelling, who had been such an inspiration earlier, was in the last group to leave. As he grasped Gary's belt, he whispered, "You saved nearly three hundred lives, Don. I knew you wouldn't let us down."

19 March, 1945
15:05 Hours
Kamikaze

Despite the strength of Jocko Clark's CAP's, the Japanese continued to try to sink the *Franklin*. Sometimes they attacked with a single plane, sometimes they came as doubles or whole squadrons, but their attacks continued. At 15:50 every ship in both Task Groups began firing at a Judy that had somehow slipped through the powerful combat air patrols. It zoomed out of the clouds at high speed and flew straight toward the *Franklin's* bow, strafing with all its guns. For the first time since she was damaged, *Franklin* returned fire.

John, functioning as the spotter at the forward edge of the sponson, shouted directions and encouragement to his new crew. "Feed 'em smooth. Drop 'em straight. Get into a pattern. Way to go guys! Way to go!"

Colson and Garcia brought the Judy under fire. Tracers from the 40-mms ripped up at the plane. Bullets from the bomber's wing guns ripped into the flight deck as it dove toward the *Franklin's* bow.

"Look out!" John shouted to Bonin, who was working near him. He pushed Bonin violently. While Bonin escaped the oncoming Japanese bullets—John was left exposed. Pieces of shrapnel tore into his shoulder. The impact knocked him off his feet. He was stunned for a moment—then he pulled himself up and struggled back to his station.

Fire from the 40-mms tore into the Judy's wing. The bomber swerved violently off course! It dropped one of its bombs as it did. John watched the bomb fall. It seemed like it was in slow motion. It struck the ocean less than seventy-five feet from *Franklin's* starboard side and exploded.

The Judy headed away, circling to attack again.

John felt his shoulder. His shirt was ripped and soaked with blood.

Garcia looked down at him. "You better get that bleeding stopped, John," he said as he cranked the 40-mms toward the circling Judy.

Jardin saw what happened. He dropped the canister he was carrying and leaped into the gun tub.

"I'll help you, Gunner," he said.

He pulled an old tee shirt and a handful of rags from the rag-storage bin. "These things look ugly, but there're clean," he said. He stuffed rags under John's tattered shirt and wrapped the tee shirt around his shoulder. "That ought to stop the bleeding," he said. "I don't understand how that bastard ever got though our air cover, Gunner."

"Sometimes when a CAP is so spread out, one can sneak through," John said. He sat down on a shell canister still shocked by what just happened.

"You better get to sickbay with this, Gunner," Jardin said. "The CAP is packed in tight up there now. I think we'll be all right."

"No way! I'm staying right here until we get that bastard! I can still use my right arm and fingers."

The Judy zoomed back. Tracers from John's 40-mms streaked up to meet it. They dug into the engine and ripped back toward the wing. The Judy's cockpit cover flew off. John could see the Jap pilot and gunner. "Faster! Load faster! Aim at the bastard's wing roots! The blazing 40-mm shells dug into the fuselage and moved to the wing roots. The Judy shook violently then exploded in a massive ball of fire.

"Yes!" John shouted. "Great job, guys! You got the gas tanks!"

"That son-of-a-bitch won't ever drop another bomb!" Klinkiewicz yelled triumphantly.

"That's sure right," John echoed. "What an explosion! I've seen a lot of planes explode but never like that. That must have been a thousand-pound bomb load!"

19 March, 1945
16:10 Hours
Franklin's **Hangar Deck**

When O'Callahan's work with the wounded was finished, he joined a fire-fighting crew on the hangar deck. When he arrived, fire fighters were slowly forcing the fires back. As they retreated, O'Callahan and the fire fighters spotted six one-thousand-pound bombs that for some reason hadn't exploded, despite being armed and enveloped by flames for hours. While one crew fought through the smoke and flames toward the bombs, another crew sprayed water over them to protect them from the intense heat. Slowly they worked their way to within eight feet of the bombs and then, choking with smoke and singed by the flames, they started to wet the bombs down.

"Bounce the water on the deck before the spray hits the bombs, boys," O'Callahan shouted to the fire fighters. "There's a chance they'll explode!"

The leader of the fire-fighting crew turned to O'Callahan and shouted back, "That's right, Padre. Let's not take any *unnecessary chances*!" Despite the gravity of the situation, O'Callahan managed a laugh. "Let's not take any 'unnecessary chances,'" he repeated under his breath as he shook his head in disbelief.

After wetting the bombs down for a few minutes, they were cool enough to move.

"Okay! Let's dump 'em over the side!" O'Callahan said.

"That's right, Padre," the same fire fighter replied. "Praise the Lord and *dump* the ammunition!"

O'Callahan laughed aloud. Then he helped jettison the heavy bombs.

Violent explosions continued, but they seemed to be spaced farther and farther apart. Fires on both the hangar and flight decks were starting to come under a little control. Repair crews restored the ship's bridge steering—but major problems remained. An explosion from a five-hundred-pound bomb jarred the *Franklin* and increased her list to fifteen degrees. On the bridge, Gehres watched the inclinometer carefully. "We have to find a way to correct this list," he said. "We have to get some Handy Billies below decks to start pumping some of that water around."

"Steve," he said to Jurika. "See if you can find the Damage Control Officer."

"Aye, Captain." In a short while, Jurika returned with Commander Robert Downes.

"Commander, it looks like things are stabilizing a little," Gehres said. "Let's flood some of the empty lower compartments—see if we can get the ship back on a more even keel."

"Aye, sir."

"I've had some experience with this kind of thing," Gehres said. "I caution you—don't over correct. Don't flood too many compartments. Just take it easy, and get us fairly level."

Downes nodded.

"I don't care if we carry a few degrees of list, one way or the other," Gehres said. "*Just don't over correct*—too much or too fast and we could capsize. I don't want to waste the heroic efforts of this crew."

"Aye, sir, I understand," Downes said as he disappeared down the ladder to set up the pumping equipment.

19 March, 1945
18:07 Hours
Sickbay

John and Jim Jardin struggled down three ladders to the sickbay. It was loaded with stretchers filled with burned and wounded men, so crowded that many had been put in the passageway and in adjoining compartments. By this time the wounded had received all the help they could be given. Commander Owen, the ship's chief doctor, and Chief Pharmacy Mate Daniel Berger sipped a cup of coffee and rested for the first time in many hours.

"Looks like you took some shrapnel, sailor," Doctor Owen said as John walked in and was helped to a metal operating table. "I need to take this St. Christopher medal off," Owen said after he removed the tee shirt and blood-soaked rags. He unhooked the clasp and handed the medal to John.

"The most wonderful girl in the world gave me this medal, sir," John said. He took the medal and brushed it to his lips. "It's helped me through a lot so far. I hope it helps me with this."

"You're going to be fine," Owen said as he examined John's wound. "There's still some shrapnel in there. I'll have to get it out. I'm going to put this needle in your shoulder. It won't hurt much."

Owens jabbed the needle into John's shoulder.

John responded with a wince. "Please fix it up good, Doc," John said with a tortured smile. "I hope I'm going to see that girl soon, and I'd like to be as good as new when I do."

As he left the bridge Beckley looked at his watch. It was 18:15. It had been a long day. He was very tired, but he headed up to John's 40-mm gun pit.

"Garcia!" he shouted when he got to the top of the ladder. "Where's John?"

"He got wounded by shell fragments," Garcia called back. "He went down to sickbay."

"Is he okay?"

"I think so, Chief. He just went down a little while ago."

Beckley headed for sickbay. On the way down he met O'Callahan.

"John took shell fragments in the shoulder, Padre. I'm headed down to sickbay to see him."

"I'll go with you," O'Callahan said.

When they arrived, John was sitting on a bunk resting his left arm on a pillow. When he saw Beckley and O'Callahan he smiled and acknowledged them with a tiny wave of his right arm.

"How you doing?" Beckley asked.

"I feel okay," John said. "Doctor Owen told me it was a little bigger problem than he first thought. He wants to be sure there's no ligament damage so I'm going to check into a hospital in Pearl Harbor to have it looked at again. He thinks it'll heal good as new."

"That's good news," O'Callahan said.

"Yeah, it is," John said as he moved the fingers on his left hand back and forth.

"You've got good movement in your fingers," Beckley said. "You get some rest. You'll feel a lot better in the morning."

"Chief Berger told me I was going to sleep in officers' country tonight.

"Oh? How so?"

"He said the officers who were standing night watches turned their bunks over to enlisted men."

"I wondered where enlisted men would sleep," O'Callahan said. "Most of their quarters were wiped out by the fires."

Beckley stopped by for John just before 19:40. The two made their way down to officers' country. John gave his name to the master-at-arms, who checked his hand written list.

"You're in Compartment 36, right over there."

"How's your shoulder?" Beckley asked as they got situated.

"It feels okay."

"They give you anything for sleep?"

"Yeah," John answered, producing a small packet of pills. "They gave me these. They said to take two before I went to bed."

"You've had a long day, John," Beckley said. "Get a little rest. I'll bunk out here for a while, too. I've got to be back on watch at four o'clock tomorrow morning. I'll try not to wake you when I leave."

20 March, 1945
After Midnight
70 Miles SSW of Shikoku

When Beckley arrived on the bridge to stand the four-to-eight watch, Gehres and Jurika were there. Commander Taylor was getting some sleep in the small room just off the bridge. They had worked this way the entire night.

"How's everything going, Captain?" Beckley asked as he took the helm.

"Looks like things are shaping up a little, Chief," Gehres said. "But we still don't know how badly we're hurt."

"You think there's more damage below decks?" Beckley asked.

"There might be," Gehres said. "We don't know whether the propellers or shafts are damaged or the full extent of the destruction in the engine rooms."

Beckley looked out over the battered junk heap that just a few hours before was the flight deck. The charred, smoldering scene was illuminated by the brilliant moonlight. All that remained of the ship's number thirteen was the upper part of the number 3. The rest of it was a charred mass of ashes. "Do we have to form an inspection party, sir?" he asked turning his attention from the burned identification number to his duties on the bridge.

"Not right now," Gehres replied. "Our goal is to take care of the things we know about—to be sure what we're doing is balanced and effective."

"Aye, sir," Beckley replied.

At 04:07, Gehres got a call from the engine room on a voice-activated phone.

"Who's this on the wire?" Gehres asked. "Commander Green? This is the Captain. How is it down there, Tom?"

Beckley could tell from Gehres' conversation and tone of voice that important things were happening in the engine room.

"Get those boilers back on line and I'll buy all you guys a drink," Gehres said.

There was a pause as Greene responded.

"You do that and I'll buy you men a bottle," Gehres said. "What do you drink? Only the best scotch whiskey? You've got it, and we'll all help you drink it."

Gehres paused for Green's response.

"Lieutenant Gary's down there with you? Wonderful! Wonderful, Tom. Keep me advised," Gehres said. He put the phone back in its cradle and turned to Beckley and Jurika. "They're doing great down there," he said. "They've got the compartment temperature down below one hundred and twenty degrees. It looks like they can have one boiler back on line in about an hour and maybe one more by morning."

Gehres announcement brought jubilation. "That's great news, Captain," Jurika said. "We're getting back our own power!"

"Yeah," Commander Green said, "if all goes well and they don't find any 'gremlins,' they should have a third boiler on line by late morning."

"If that happens, it'd allow *Pittsburgh* to tow us at close to six knots," Beckley said. "Does he think they can really get all that done, sir?"

"He said they could," Gehres replied. "He said they're going to get it done and he was going to hold me to my promise to buy whiskey."

"He was that confident about it?" Jurika asked.

"He said I should get the money out," Gehres replied with a tiny smile. "That he could taste that whiskey right now." He turned to Beckley. "What a crew!" he said. "Bravest bunch of men I've ever served with."

A signalman came onto the bridge. "We just got a message from Admiral Davison, sir."

Gehres read the message aloud: "We are sending the destroyers *Bullard* and *Kidd* to your screen for added daytime protection. They should join you about 04:30. The battle cruisers *Guam* and *Alaska* should arrive about that time, too. I was wrong, you were right, Les. It looks like you can save her. We'll do everything we can to help you."

Gehres handed the message to Jurika. "This is great news," he said. "We're getting a lot of firepower around us."

At 04:20 a report from damage control came to the bridge. Gehres read it and said, "They've fired up the pumps. They're beginning to counter-flood to correct our list."

In a few minutes, *Franklin's* list began to correct slowly from starboard to port.

"Slowly," Gehres said. "One degree at a time."

"We're moving awfully fast, Captain!" Jurika shouted. "I think we're correcting too fast, sir!"

The *Franklin* moved faster.

"We're going out of control!" Gehres shouted. "Goddamn! I warned Downes!"

Franklin's list to starboard vanished. She moved past the horizontal and jolted into a list that registered seven degrees to port. Then she stabilized.

"That was piss poor," Gehres said, upset with the correction.

"Well, at least we've stopped, sir," Beckley said.

"Yeah, but we might've capsized."

"I'm sure they did the best they could down there, Captain," Jurika said.

"It was a piss poor effort, Steve," Gehres replied.

"Maybe seven degrees to port is not as bad as fifteen degrees to starboard," Beckley said.

"That's not the way I see it, Chief," Gehres replied.

He looked at the horizon and thought a minute. "I guess we'll have to live with it though. We've still got a lot of other obstacles to overcome, and it *is* a smaller list."

The *Franklin's* rough correction jarred John awake. For a few seconds, he thought the Franklin was sinking, then he realized someone was trying to correct her list. He touched his shoulder. It was sore. He moved his arm and fingers. Although movement was painful, he was able to get dressed. He went down the passageway and, as he started to go up the ladder to the hangar deck, he heard his name called. He turned and saw Fonz waving and moving toward him. When Fonz arrived he greeted John with a huge smile and put his on hand on his good shoulder.

"It's good to see you, Gunner. I heard you got wounded."

"Yeah," John replied. "In the shoulder."

"Where you headed now?" Fonz asked.

"Up to the 40-mms above the bridge," John replied. "Where you going?"

"Down into the storerooms to search for food—that is if we can get through."

"Did anything survive the fires down there?"

"We don't know. There's a hell of a lot of damage, but there has to be something to eat there somewhere."

"I hope you find something. I'm hungry. I haven't eaten anything since the day before yesterday."

"We'll find something. We'll look until we do," Fonz said. He smiled. "I'll remember where you are when chow's ready, Buddy."

"Thanks, I appreciate that, Fonz," John said. "Don't get trapped down there. I'll bet it's a mess, so be careful."

"I will, Gunner," Frasure said. "The Japs are probably going to try to finish us off when daylight comes, so you be careful, too."

When John reached the hangar deck, his stomach turned at what he saw. There was death and destruction everywhere. Piles of wreckage filled nearly every square foot of the hangar deck. The glow of embers made it look like the oven in a giant stove. The stench of burned, decomposing flesh seeped up through the smoldering ruins. John covered his nose with his hand and rushed up the ladder to the flight deck. The ugly smell of decomposing flesh was here, too. It was tempered only by a brisk wind that came in from the port quarter. The explosions and flames had devastated nearly the entire deck. The blackened wreckage of Hellcats and Corsairs, caught on deck by yesterday's conflagration, were silhouetted against the moonlit sky causing them to look weird and sinister. Smoke curled up through the wreckage. The huge holes in the deck plates, chopped by fire fighters in futile efforts to get water down to the gallery and hangar decks, made the whole scene look nightmarish.

John shuddered, then made his way through bodies and body parts to the edge of the deck. When he passed Able Sponson and his battered 40-mms, he thought about Sullivan, Ski, Lowe, Feinstein, Hazelton and Dixon again. He touched his Saint Christopher's medal, said a silent prayer, and hurried on.

He reached the gun tub and climbed in. Garcia was standing watch.

"Garcia," he said.

"Gunner, how's the shoulder?" Garcia asked. Bonin, Colson, Barker, and Jardin gathered around.

"It's still a little sore," John said. "Where are the rest of the men?"

"They're down sleeping," Garcia replied. "We split up into two watches. We had the first and they're on the second."

"Good idea," John said. "It's going to be a long day, so let them get some rest."

"We can reach them in a couple of minutes, if you want them up here, Gunner," Garcia said.

"No, let them sleep but be sure they're on station before dawn," John said. "Those Jap bastards are coming back today, just as sure as I'm standing here. We're all alone so we'll have a big job to do when they come." He walked to the edge of the gun tub and picked up a pair of binoculars. As he worked the strap over his head, he said, "These things are hard to get on with one arm."

Garcia moved to help him.

"No, I'm okay, I'll get them on, Ramon. Thanks," he said.

He focused the binoculars on the eastern horizon. Faint traces of dawn were appearing. He moved to the silhouette of the *Pittsburgh*, steaming off the port bow about eight hundred yards away. He could make out the towlines. They were taut. *We're making about four knots, he said under his breath*. He looked out at the western horizon. Dawn will be here soon, he thought. That'll bring the Japs back. That's as sure as sunrise. He looked down on the devastated flight deck. Only about a hundred feet had escaped the flames. The rest of the deck was scarred and blackened. He checked the ship's mast. The radio antenna was missing. The radar antenna was hanging by its wires. It looked like it would fall to the flight deck any minute. A sense of being completely alone filled him—it expanded into fear and hopelessness. His shoulder ached, much more than it had earlier. He thought of Sandy and his pledge to get home. He had to get back to her. He just had to…Dear God you are my Source and Protector. Protect me today….

An explosion amidships startled him! Flames mushroomed into the air on the port side of the flight deck.

"Looks like a ready-service locker blew up," John shouted.

"Yeah," Garcia responded in a loud voice. "We've had three or four explosions like that over the last few hours, John."

"Did the fire fighters get to them?"

"Yeah, they did," Garcia said. "And a couple of times destroyers spotted flames and came over and helped with their hoses. They got 'em out."

As he spoke, John focused his binoculars on the nearest destroyer in the screen. "Looks like the *Tingley* is coming in to help," John said.

As John was speaking, the destroyer was rushing to *Franklin's* side; her hoses pointed and ready. *Franklin's* fire fighters rushed up to the edge of the battered flight deck, hoses gushing as they went. Together they brought the fire under control.

"They got that one pretty quick," John said.

"They got the others quick, too," Garcia said. "It's a good thing. I'd hate to see those fires get out of control again."

"Yeah," John said. "This ship's a tinderbox now. It could go up in a minute."

20 March, 1945
At Dawn
80 Miles SE of Shikoku

The sun pushed above the horizon. John looked out over the ocean. "The screen's stronger this morning than it was yesterday," he said to Garcia. "Look out there. There are two new battle cruisers and two more destroyers."

"Yeah," Garcia replied. "And I can hear the engines from the combat air patrols. They've been circling over us like hawks all night."

John searched the sky. In the early light he could see the blue flames from the exhausts of scores of fighters, circling at every point on the compass. "It feels good to have those guys all around up there," he said.

He looked down at the bow. It was cutting through the water—not very fast—but they were slowly moving out of harm's way. Although great danger still threatened, John felt better. The sight of all the air power above him and the powerful warships that surrounded his wounded ship lifted his spirits.

Fonz's voice pierced the morning air. "Breakfast, Gunner!"

He climbed into John's gun tub. "It's a slice of bread with bacon fat!" he said triumphantly as he cut into one of the giant loaves sent over by the *Santa Fe*. "We found some canned sausage and orange juice, too. It's not like dining at the Ritz, but it's all we could come up with on short notice."

John and his men took the food and hungrily devoured it. "This is great, Fonz," John said with a mouthful of food. "It's the most welcome breakfast I ever had!"

"We'll try to have a better meal tonight," Fonz said.

"Can you leave some for the rest of our crew?" John asked as he finished a long drink from a can of orange juice.

"How much do you need, Gunner?"

"Enough for five more men."

"You've got it," Fonz said. He placed the additional rations near the edge of the gun tub then waved as he went down the ladder.

"Get all the guys up, Garcia," John said. "Let them have some breakfast." He focused his glasses toward the western horizon. "The sun's coming up and it's getting light. Those bastards might come back any time now."

An hour passed without incident. Suddenly, Garcia spotted a huge group of Japanese planes. "Bogeys! Bogeys! A big bunch of them at five o'clock!" he shouted.

John focused his glasses. "There's a lot of them all right," he said.

Garcia trained his binoculars on the Japanese planes. "Look at 'em, John. They don't look like they're coming this way."

John re-focused on the Japanese attackers. "Hell, it looks like they're flying toward the spot where we were yesterday."

"Maybe they're flying to where they *thought* we'd be," Garcia said.

"Tough shit," John replied. "We ran a trick play—a sweep around end. We're over thirty miles away from there now!"

"What a dumb mistake! How could they make a mistake like that?" Colson asked.

"Maybe they never played football," John said. "Maybe they decided a burning hulk this size couldn't be rigged with a towline. Maybe they just guessed where we'd be."

"Do you think they're that stupid?"

"Who the hell knows?"

"If they keep on that course they're going to get blasted," Colson said as he shaded his eyes with his hand. They look like they're headed right into the teeth of our CAP."

"Let them get blasted," John said curtly. "Their mistake is our gain. Just be wary if one turns and comes our way."

The Japanese fighters and bombers flew on. Hellcats and Corsairs from Jocko Clark's CAP's waited. Huge dogfights erupted! Japanese Zeros and Zekes went against Corsairs and Hellcats.

John watched the violent battle. Glaring flashes exploded in the sky! Flaming debris plummeted into the ocean!

"Who's winning, Gunner?" Klinkiewicz asked.

"It's hard to tell. They're too far away and it's a little hazy out there," John said. "But if any of those bastards get through that CAP we could be in deep shit."

The frantic battle went on—a blinding flash in the sky—a mass of flames hurtling downward. One flash after another lit up the horizon. One flaming mass after another plunged into the sea. Finally the fiery splashes ceased. The Japanese planes turned and headed back toward the mainland.

"They're turning tail and running," Klinkiewicz shouted. "We won!"

"How can you be sure of that, Corporal?" John asked.

"They broke it off, didn't they?"

"That doesn't mean a goddamn thing," John replied. "They're still out there somewhere and they know we're here somewhere. They'll try to get us again, just mark my words. We could still lose this ship."

"They'll have to get through a lot of ships and planes," Klinkiewicz said.

"There were a lot of ships and planes yesterday and one got through," John replied. "It might be even easier today with our radar gone."

"Come on, Gunner, we've got a lot more protection than we had yesterday," Klinkiewicz said.

"How do you figure that?"

"Everybody's focused on defending us today."

"Well, maybe so," John said, "but the bastards will try to slip a plane or two in and just one kamikaze hit would blast this ship right to the bottom of the ocean."

John searched the horizon. "Everybody stay alert," he said loudly. "Don't concentrate on finding squadrons. The CAP and the rest of the fleet will take care of that. Concentrate on that single son-of-a-bitch that might sneak through—that's what I'm afraid of."

"Bogey! Bogey!" Barker shouted

"Where?" John asked.

"On the horizon at eleven o'clock!"

"A Judy!" John shouted. "The same kind of son-of-a-bitch that hit us yesterday!"

The Judy, avoiding the Hellcats and Corsairs in the CAP, zoomed toward them at high speed—its machine guns blazing.

John jumped into the pointer's seat. "Let's stop that Jap bastard!" He cranked the pointer's wheel on the 40-mm rapidly with his good right arm. The Judy streaked on. All the guns from the cruisers and destroyers in the *Franklin's* screen opened fire. The sky filled with tracers and exploding steel. The Japanese bomber sped on, somehow untouched by the hail of fire, its wing guns blazing. Bullets whined as they ricocheted off the bow and ripped up chunks of the charred flight deck. John tightened his focus on the careening plane. His Navy-Marine gun crew blasted away with one clip of armor-piercing shells after another. Puffs of fiery flack peppered the Judy's course, but it zoomed on. Shells from John's 40s found the Judy and tore into its fuselage and wings. The plane jerked violently and careened over *Franklin's* battered flight deck. One of the Judy's bombs plunged down and exploded less than twenty feet from Franklin's port side.

"Keep firing! Get that son-of-a bitch!" John screamed. Smoke streamed from the engine of the attacking plane. The Jap pilot pulled the Judy into a steep climb.

John recognized what he was doing immediately. "Get that bastard! He's going to try to loop back into us and crash us!"

A hail of shells from John's gunners flashed up at the looping plane. John saw a 40-mm shell blast into the bomber's cowling. The Judy shuddered wildly as it began its back-loop. John could see the Jap pilot frantically struggling to complete the loop. More antiaircraft fire from John's 40-mms powered up and dug into the wings and engine. The Judy stalled in midair for a split second—its engine streaking flames. Then it exploded into a jagged mass of fiery debris.

At that moment six Corsairs from the CAP flashed onto the scene. They put the Judy's wreckage under 50-caliber fire and blazed away at it all the way down to the water. When it hit the ocean, the Corsairs turned and over-flew the Franklin's bow. The pilots dipped their wings in a silent salute to the courage of *Franklin's* intrepid gunners as they flew past.

On *Franklin*, John's gunners raised their arms and shook their fists defiantly. John, his right arm and clenched fist in the air, led their triumphant declaration.

On the bridge, Beckley, Gehres and Jurika watched the fiery scene.

"Who's the gunner on that 40-mm up there?" Gehres asked.

"It's Gunner First Class John Oxler," Beckley replied.

"Is he the same man that flooded the forward magazine?"

"Aye, sir, he is," Beckley replied.

"That's twice he and his gun crew saved this ship from destruction," Gehres said, as he turned his attention from the bow to the dogfights on the distant horizon. "Looks like we're driving the bastards off. We've got a hell of a CAP up there. Only one Jap plane out of at least fifty got through it."

"Yes, sir," Jurika replied, "and thanks to God and that gunner and his gun crew up there, we got that one, too."

At 11:02 Gehres received a call from the engine room. "They've got the third boiler ready to come on line and they're building power up in another one," Gehres said. Then he said into the phone, "Great, Tom. You kept your promise and earned your whiskey. You and your men did a wonderful job. The entire ship's beholden to you."

In a short time *Franklin's* speed increased to six knots.

"Looks like we're slowly getting out of here, Captain," Beckley said.

"Yeah, Chief," Gehres replied. "Now there's just one more problem. The Japanese coast is less than a hundred miles that-away and home is over thirteen thousand miles in the other."

"Despite the problem, sir," Beckley replied, "it's comforting and even a little exciting to be going along at six knots—even if we are under tow."

Gehres smiled at Beckley. "In ordinary times even a tramp steamer would scorn a six-knot speed—and the flagship of a Fast Carrier Task Force wouldn't even think of it."

"Yes, sir, but today's not very ordinary," Beckley said. "There's a big difference between sitting dead in the water and moving at even six knots."

Gehres laughed and nodded in agreement. "I guess you're right, Chief, maybe a *little* is better than nothing after all."

20 March, 1945
11:35 Hours
Steering-Aft Rescue

Gehres hadn't forgotten his promise to the men in steering-aft. He contacted them and said, "Men, we've got steering back on the bridge so your work there is finished. You did a great job. We're assembling a rescue party to get you out. Lieutenant Wasserman is organizing it. They'll be ready to start down there shortly."

Gehres put the phone down. "I don't think they believed me," he said.

"Well, they've been down there a long time, Captain," Beckley said. "Maybe they're close to losing hope."

"Go down with the rescue party, Chief," Gehres said. "I want to be sure *every* effort is made to get those men."

At 11:53 Wassermann, Beckley and a twenty-man rescue party, equipped with hammers, crowbars and an acetylene torch, headed down to the trapped men. They found a ladder that was usable on the starboard side.

"This ladder is pretty beat up and fire scarred but we have to use it," Wassermann said.

"Yeah," Beckley agreed. "It looks like it's the only way down now, sir." He looked at the ladder. "It's going to be a hell of a lot longer this way."

"Yeah, I know, Chief," Wassermann replied. "I don't care how long it takes. We have to get those guys out."

"The Captain's gung-ho about this rescue," Beckley said as they started down. "He said he'd do it himself if necessary."

"He told me the same thing. We'll get 'em. I'd be afraid to face him if we didn't."

As they made their way below decks, they passed a very weary looking crew that had been fighting fires all night. They were now washing aviation gasoline off the hangar deck.

"Keep up the good work, men," Wassermann shouted. "We're starting to get things under control."

The fire fighters waved and carried on.

The rescue detail started through the destruction with only battle lamps as a source of light. They forged into old passageways that were blocked by explosions. They twisted through new passageways that were blown through bulkheads. They stumbled through one passageway after another. It was like digging through a jungle. They moved through smoke-filled compartments, fighting through twisted cables and mangled debris. They ran into dead ends. When they did, they searched until they found a way that worked, always moving aft and down. They went carefully, knowing that making a wrong turn might put them in peril. Finally they came to the compartment above steering-aft.

"This compartment is just above them," Wassermann said.

"Yeah," Beckley replied as he knocked on the bulkhead with a hammer. "The problem is it's filled with water, too."

"Yeah, but it's the only chance we have," Wassermann reasoned. "Every other way is blocked. We'll have to pump it out. Then I think we can get to them."

"We'll need pumps," Beckley said.

"Take eight men and go back. Get at least two—more if you can."

Beckley and his detail fought their way back and got the pumps. It took them nearly an hour. Finally they returned with three gas-driven pumps.

"We found three, sir," Beckley said.

"Three ought to do it. Burn some holes in the top of that bulkhead and fire up those pumps."

They cut through the bulkhead. After a few tugs at a lanyard the pumps started. Hoses were forced into the flooded compartment. In a few seconds water started gushing out. When the compartment was almost drained, Beckley took a hammer and pounded open a jammed hatch. All but a few inches of the rest of the water spilled out.

"The rest of this water has to drain down," Beckley said. He tapped a message to the men below: *"Can you take more water?"*

In a few seconds they got a message back: *"Yes. Let it come."*

Beckley hammered the clamps that sealed the hatch separating the two compartments and pulled it open. The water drained down.

After a few minutes Holobrook's head and shoulders appeared through the hatch. "Boy are we glad to see you guys," he said.

Davis, the last man out, said, "There were times last night, when the water was rising, that I thought we were goners."

"Captain Gehres promised he'd get you out," Beckley said. "He keeps his word."

20 March, 1945
16:42 Hours
A Little More Hope

Back on the bridge Gehres received a message from Jocko Clark. He read it and said to Joe Taylor, "Admiral Clark says the Japs sent fifty planes to get us. Instead of getting us they ran into his combat air patrol—one hundred and nine fighters strong. They shot down forty-six of the bastards."

"Forty six! Wow," Taylor replied. "And we got the forty-seventh. That's a hell of a kill ratio."

"Jocko said he wants us to keep up the good fight—that he got word from Nimitz that he wants the *whole fleet* to protect us," Gehres said as he folded the message and handed it to a yeoman.

"That's great news," Taylor said. "I'll get this word out to the crew. This should really lift their spirits."

The contents of the message were circulated. There was jubilation all over the ship.

At 20:23 Gehres got a message from Tom Greene in the engine room.

"They've now got four boilers fully back on line," Gehres said. "Commander Greene says we're ready to steam faster than the *Pittsburgh* can tow us."

"Great! That's wonderful news," Taylor said.

"Signal *Pittsburgh* we're ready to cast off her towline and proceed on our own power," Gehres said. "Tell them we're very grateful for their help and protection."

"Aye, sir," Taylor replied with a grin.

"By midnight our speed could be up to twelve knots," Jurika said. "It looks like were going to make it, Captain. It looks like we've saved her!"

"It all depends on our combat air patrols, Steve. If they can keep the Japs off us tonight—then until we're out of range tomorrow, you're right."

"What do you think the possibilities of that are, Captain?" Beckley asked.

"They should be good, Chief," Gehres said. "All the combat air patrols have been beefed up. They're stronger today than they were yesterday."

"Yes, sir. But one did get through this morning."

"I know, Chief. I also know if one kamikaze crashed us in the wrong place, we'd be in deep trouble. That's all it would take."

"I think that's right, sir," Beckley said.

"But we also have to remember were getting farther and farther away," Gehres said. "If we can avoid being hit and if we can steam at an average of eleven knots an hour, we'll be at least two hundred and twenty-five miles farther away by late-morning tomorrow. If that happens, it should about put us out of range."

Beckley let out a long sigh. "That's a lot of 'ifs,' Captain, "but it sure would feel great to be out of here, sir."

At 21:45 Gehres received a current damage report from all division heads. He read it over rapidly, then said, "This is a good report. Nearly all the explosions have stopped. Fires on the flight deck are under control as far back as elevator 2. Although there are still some explosions, they're from 40-mm and 20-mm ammunition. Fires on most of the hangar deck and in the gallery deck are under control—at least for the moment—and another boiler has been brought on line."

"That's hard to believe when you consider where we were this morning, sir," Beckley said. "What this crew accomplished in just a few short hours is remarkable."

"Yes," Gehres replied. "Our crew was outstanding, and we owe a debt of gratitude to *Santa Fe* for her extraordinary help, too," Gehres replied. "We just *have* to keep those Jap planes away. It'd be a terrible shame to waste the courageous efforts of the men on both ships."

CHAPTER TWENTY-NINE

21 March, 1945
225 Miles SSE of Shikoku
Clearing the Wreckage—Burying the Dead

Just after noon *Franklin*, along with her protective screen, steamed out of the range of Japanese planes. Although skirmishes and flashes could be seen on the horizon, not a single enemy fighter or bomber got anywhere near the *Franklin*. Jocko Clark's combat air patrols had done their job.

But *Franklin* now had another gigantic task—the task of clearing her wreckage and burying her dead.

"Red" Harris was charged with assembling work details to remove as much debris as could be cleared by hand from *Franklin's* flight and hangar decks. Tons and tons of junk and twisted steel had to be ripped loose and dragged to the sides of the ship for jettisoning. Equipped with hammers, saws and cutting torches from the machine shop, which had been only lightly damaged by the fires and explosions, a detail of eighty men dug into this job with gusto. They cut, pounded, ripped, broke apart, separated—then moved, pushed, shoved and dragged the refuse and rubble to *Franklin's* side and gave it the deep six. Until a dead body impeded their path, this was a job that most of the men saw as a kind of diversion; they could pound, saw, cut and jettison, and in the process release some of the frustration and pent-up emotion of the past two days.

But much of the wreckage was too massive and imbedded to be cut apart and moved by hand. Men struggled and strained against it, but it just wouldn't move.

"Sir," a frustrated seaman said to Harris, "this goddamn stuff ain't never gonna move. We need a tow-motor or a crane or something."

"Tow-motors and cranes are all out of commission," Harris replied. "Keep trying. I'm sure you'll get it to move."

"Not this year, it ain't gonna, sir."

"Chief," Harris said to Boatswain's Mate Luke Frisbee, who was standing nearby. "Let's lend a hand and see what we can do."

Harris and Frisbee lent their weight to the belabored detail. They pushed and strained. "Heave ho! Heave ho!" Harris shouted as he grunted against a mass of twisted metal. They tried another huge pile without success. "You're right, sailor," Harris said to the seaman. "This mess ain't gonna budge."

"The second one's worse than the first," Frisbee said. "Most of this junk was bonded to the deck by the fires. It'll take something mechanized to move it, Commander."

"Well, it has to be cleared," Harris said as he removed his hat and wiped his brow with his sleeve. "What a hell of a situation," he said. He thought for a few moments, then an idea came. "Wait a minute. One of the deck crews parked four Jeeps in the forward elevator pit the night before we got slammed. Let's see if they might still run."

"My guess is that they got blasted like everything else," Frisbee said.

"Well, let's take a look-see, Chief. What the hell do we have to lose?"

They made their way to the forward elevator digging through twisted cables, wires, warped metal and gnarled body parts.

"I don't mind the junk, but goddamn, I hate these human parts," Frisbee said as they fought their way along. "They're so mutilated they make me sick to my stomach."

"I know, Chief," Harris replied as he took out his handkerchief and covered his nose. "And they smell like hell, too."

"You never know *what* or *who* you're walking over," Frisbee said as he stepped over a headless torso. "It could be the body of one of your best friends and you wouldn't even know it."

They dug their way along and finally reached the forward elevator. They looked behind it into the pit.

"Well, I'll be goddamned," Harris said, "They're not as bad as I thought they'd be." He gave the battered elevator a gentle kick. "This big bastard shielded them from much of the fire and destruction."

Frisbee looked over the rubble-laden Jeeps. "Three tires are blown out," he said. "Otherwise they seem to be in pretty fair shape."

"Let's dig all this junk off them and see if we can get them to start," Harris said. "If they do, we can use tires and parts from one to get the rest going."

"Yeah if we can get three to work, it's a home run."

"If we can just get two, they'll help a lot."

They pulled away the larger pieces of debris that had landed on the Jeeps.

"This one looks the most beat up, but two of the tires are okay." Frisbee said.

Harris pounded his fist on the Jeep's spare, then checked the spare of a second Jeep. "Eureka." he said. "We've got tires."

The two men cleared off much of the rest of the clutter. "Okay, let's give 'em a try," Frisbee said. He climbed into the first Jeep and hit the starter button. The motor turned over and over. After awhile, it coughed and started.

"Yes!" Harris said. "Try the next one."

Frisbee hauled himself into the second Jeep. It coughed and choked, then its engine started, too. The third engine started the same way.

"Three out of four," Harris said. "Yesterday and the day before were horrible, but we got lucky today!" They removed and replaced the blown-out tires. "Let's get these gems down where they can do some good."

Within twenty minutes three tattered Jeeps were winding their way through the maze of debris on the hangar deck. They provided some of the mechanical power that was needed to continue. The Jeeps tore clusters of the tangled, embedded wreckage loose and dragged them to the ship's sides for jettisoning. No three Jeeps ever built did so much good or made so many seamen happier. Because of the Jeeps a little more order returned to decks that, the day before, were chaotic infernos.

As the decks began to clear, Taylor sent word to the chaplains, the ship's doctors and all available petty officers to muster on the forecastle.

When he got the word Beckley left the bridge and started toward the forecastle. John fell in with him when he reached the flight deck. About twenty yards ahead, they spotted O'Callahan and Gatlin walking in the same direction.

"Padre! Chaplain! Wait up," John called out.

They stopped and John and Beckley jogged toward them.

"What's going on?" John asked when he and Beckley joined them.

"We don't know," Gatlin answered. "We just got word that Commander Taylor wanted us."

"It has to be some kind of tough job," Beckley said as they walked along.

"That's the only kind Execs give out," Gatlin replied.

When everybody assembled Taylor said, "Men, we now have the solemn task of burying our dead. I know it's a terrible job. But it has to be done. The Captain and I want to honor the brave men who were killed. I'm sure you all do, too."

Taylor paused. His voice became emotion-laden. "They were our shipmates and our friends. Most died doing their duty at their stations. Some died trying in any way they could to save this ship. Others died in passageways; still others in the explosions and fires. How they died and where they died is central to a greater consideration. They all died as heroes. We want their burial to reflect our deep feelings of reverence and respect for their great sacrifice. They deserve the most honored and dignified burial we can arrange."

He took a long breath and let it out. "May God bless the sacrifices of each and every one of them."

"Do either of you have anything to add?" he asked, directing his question to O'Callahan and Gatlin.

"I'm sure I speak for every man here," O'Callahan replied, "when I say that I concur with everything you just said, Commander."

Taylor looked at Gatlin.

"Certainly, Commander," Gatlin said. "Father O'Callahan and I will do everything possible to help with this."

Taylor nodded. "We need at least a ninety-man detail. "We'll divide it up between Doctors Owen, Sherman and Fuelling and Chaplains O'Callahan and Gatlin."

"Where do we get the men?" O'Callahan asked.

"Chiefs and petty officers, go back to your divisions and get all your available men," Taylor answered. He nodded toward John. "Since we're now pretty much out of harm's way, some can come from Gunnery."

John went back to the gun crew. "We're forming a special detail, he said. "I'm going to take six men. Garcia, Colson, Bonin, Barker and Jardin, fall out down here. Klinkiewicz, do you want to volunteer?"

"Aye, Gunner, I'll go," the young marine replied.

"What are we going to do, John?" Garcia asked.

"We're going to bury those guys who died in the explosions."

"Oh, God no! I can't do a job like that," Garcia said, shaking his head vehemently. "That's too fucking tough for me."

"Sure, it's a tough goddamned job for all of us, but it has to be done," John said. "We're going to do it, tough or not."

"But, Gunner, that's *worse* than tough! It's a terrible fucking job! Can't they find somebody else to do it?"

"This is an order from Commander Taylor," John replied.

"Sure, but why the hell does he always pick us?"

"Goddamn it, Garcia! It's not always us," John said, beginning to grow angry. "We're getting men from every division." He looked directly at Garcia. "No more grousing, Ramon. Let's go!"

John and his detail joined Father O'Callahan on the forecastle. Beckley was waiting with eight men from the Quartermaster's Division.

After a few brief words of gratitude from Commander Taylor, the burial details set about their gruesome task.

John and Beckley were in O'Callahan's detail.

"We'll start on the hangar deck," O'Callahan said grimly as they walked down from the forecastle.

"That's going to be the messiest place, Padre," Beckley observed.

"Yeah, I know," O'Callahan replied as they stepped onto the hangar deck. "But somebody's got to do it."

"Good God!" John said. "Look at those mangled bodies."

O'Callahan nodded. "Most of those guys were killed by early explosions. Their bodies were enmeshed by the debris of explosions that came later."

"Some of them are going to be hard to get to," John said as the detail started down the ladder to the hangar deck.

"Yesterday this deck was a jungle of twisted scrap, steel mesh, wires and cables contorted and knotted by flames and explosions," Beckley said. "Today it's a bunch of hellish entrapments filled with blistered, mutilated human bodies and body parts."

"That's sure a good assessment, Chief," O'Callahan said. "Come on men. Let's get with it."

Equipped with the rescue-breathers sent over by *Santa Fe*, and rubberized gloves found in the forward hold, they started their gruesome task. A terrible stench from blood, urine, vomit, excrement and rotting bodies filtered up at them.

"Damn! This place stinks," Bonin complained.

"Yeah. The smell's almost unbearable," Beckley said. "It even comes through the rescue-breathers."

"I'm gonna be sick," Garcia warned, trying hard not to heave. "I can't stand the smell of these fucking bodies!" Then recognizing he was standing next to the chaplain, he said, "Oops! Sorry, Padre."

O'Callahan nodded. "I usually fine people a dollar for a word like that, Garcia, but I'll wave my fine today. I agree with you, it does smell like hell."

They gathered around the first body. It was a young aviation ordinanceman whose body had been ravaged by the flames. His face was badly burned and blistered. He lay there with his eyes bulging and his mouth agape. His head was surrounded by several inches of slime. It flowed in and out of his mouth with the pitch and roll of the ship.

John's stomach turned. He felt nausea creeping over him. He fought it off. "Let's get this man first," he said. He bent over the corpse. It was nearly covered by twisted wreckage. Jardin and Colson followed.

"Bonin, Garcia. You guys pull back the trash. Jardin, Colson, let's try to pull him loose."

John pulled on one shoulder. Colson pulled the head and Jardin pulled the other arm.

"He's wedged in pretty tight," Jardin said.

"Pull harder!" John demanded.

Suddenly Jardin stumbled backward. He was holding the seaman's arm in his hands. It had pulled free from the body like the wing of an over-cooked chicken. Blood oozed out. It trickled down on his shoes and dungarees. Jardin's face registered shock, then panic. He covered his mouth with his arm and rushed to the sponson, vomiting all the way.

"That's just too much for a kid," John said.

"Maybe it's too much for any of us," O'Callahan retorted. "Get word to him to go up on the forecastle and get some air."

The horrific burials continued. After a short time men in burial details started to realize that despite the debris, dirt and hideous odor, these unrecognizable, mutilated bodies were the remains of friends and shipmates—the mortal remains of men who died in the line of duty. They began to handle the mutilated bodies with greater reverence. A man could not offer a greater sacrifice than his life. They all deserved an honorable burial.

By 11:30 John's crew had dug out twenty bodies. When the dead were freed from the mass of steel and wire that clutched them, they were gently slipped into canvas body bags that, ironically, had been stored in the forward hold and were never touched by the explosions or fires. Body parts, so badly burned that most were difficult to discern as human, were dug from the wreckage. Hands, arms, legs, feet, and two heads that were horribly charred were pulled free. They too were put in body bags. Then the white-cross marked bags were lifted, one by one, onto stretchers and carried to the quarterdeck for burial.

"We've cleaned out this area," O'Callahan finally said. "Let's move closer to the bow." As they walked up toward the bow, Barker said, "Father, I'm feeling sick again. I've thrown up twice. I'm sorry, but I can't take this anymore."

"Go up on the forecastle and join Jardin. Tell him if he's feeling better to come back—otherwise he should stay there with you."

John, along with Garcia, Bonin, Colson and Klinkiewicz carried on the grim work.

John watched Klinkiewicz for signs of strain. The young marine had carefully covered his feelings since they began their gruesome task earlier.

The detail moved to a mass of tangled cables, wires and filth in an area closer to the bow. Suddenly, Klinkiewicz stood erect and covered his mouth. Then he began to vomit. Amongst the tangled wires and cables, he'd spotted the mangled body of another Marine. "Oh Christ, no!" he gasped. "Not you, Rich! Not you, Buddy." He began to vomit and rushed to the sponson, heaving and choking all the way.

"Colson, tell him to go up on the forecastle with Jardin and Barker," O'Callahan said. He paused and wiped his forehead with a handkerchief. "This is repulsive work, especially for lads that age, but it has to be done," he said sadly.

Late that afternoon the ship's chief electrician, Lieutenant Carl Phillips, asked O'Callahan for a burial party to go below with him to the ship's main switch boxes.

"I know there are dead men down there," he explained, "because they were at their post when the ship's power sources overloaded and burst apart. They never came up."

O'Callahan formed a search detail and put John in charge. Phillips led the way down.

"Here they are," Phillips said when the detail arrived.

"They died at their posts manning these boxes," John said, gently touching the fire-scarred switch boxes.

"Yeah. They were electrocuted there," Phillips replied. "Here are two more on the deck beside them. They all remained at their posts until the end."

The bodies were slipped into bags, lifted onto stretchers and carried up to the quarterdeck to be buried. When they reached the quarterdeck, O'Callahan blessed them. Then the stretchers were solemnly tilted and the bodies slipped into the blue ocean, consigned to the care and love of a merciful God of the deep.

When O'Callahan finished their burial services, he said, "bravery and courage like this have to be recognized and remembered. I'll try to see this is done." He got each man's name, rank and serial number from Phillips. "I'll talk to Captain Gehres and Joe Taylor about decorating these men."

The work of extricating, identifying and burying the dead went on. Bodies and body parts were extracted from one pile of rubble after another. Finally, O'Callahan asked John and Beckley to search the perimeter of the flight deck—to see if there were bodies hidden in the recesses and crannies that became death traps during the explosions and ravaging fires. John and Beckley took a detail and went up. They walked slowly along the edge of the flight deck.

They peered and poked through huge piles of twisted cable, steel and wire. John inspected each pile carefully. He dug into a pile. It held the mangled and decomposing body of a young sailor, with an arm and foot torn off. They worked the corpse loose and placed it in a bag.

The detail moved on. John spotted several bodies hidden by twisted, blackened cables and junk in the next pile. He hailed a crew with a Jeep to help dig them out. The Jeep tore away at the wreckage. In a short while the grisly remains of five men, thrown together by an explosion, were uncovered. Near the bottom of the pile they found Feinstein's body. At the bottom they found Lowe.

"This is so sad," Beckley said, his voice quivering. "They must have been killed in one of the early explosions."

John shuddered. "Jesus, look at their faces!" He became nauseated and dizzy. He went down on one knee with his head in his hands, and stayed that way for several minutes. Finally, with sadness and shock in his voice, he said, "My God, less than five months ago they were at my wedding."

With the help of the men in the Jeep, the detail put the bodies in bags. Lowe and Feinstein's remains were last. John asked for special care for their bodies. They were gently placed in bags, then on stretchers. John took the forward handle of the stretcher that held Lowe's remains. Three men took up the other handles. The detail made its way slowly to the quarterdeck with the bodies. When they got there, John said to O'Callahan, "It's Lowe and Feinstein, Father, from my gun crew. Do you remember them? They were at my wedding."

O'Callahan nodded. He blessed them and said prayers for the dead. As soon as he finished the stretchers were braced against the railing and raised. Feinstein's body slipped off. Lowe's body followed. They bobbed on the ocean's surface for a few moments, then disappeared into *Franklin's* immense wake.

Greater sorrow came over John. The question of what happened to Ski haunted him. Was he lying dead somewhere like Lowe and Feinstein? Was he in the pile of charred bodies still stacked on the hangar deck waiting to be identified? Was he one of over four hundred men burned to ashes on the hangar deck by the nine-hundred-degree temperatures? He took his Saint Christopher's medal between his thumb and index finger and prayed, "Dear God, please, not Ski, too."

Despite his grief, John went on. The work of identifying and burying the dead had to be finished.

That evening John lay in his sack, exhausted but unable to sleep. He couldn't get the hideous events of the day out of his mind. Each time he started to doze off, he awoke with a start—the horrifying images of the dead men he'd seen and touched haunted him. He tried to erase them with thoughts of Sandy and home, but each time they forged back, stronger than before.

As he struggled with these ghastly images, Father O'Callahan's yeoman came down the ladder. "I've got a message from Father O'Callahan for you, Gunner. He wants you to come to the officer's wardroom after 20:30 hours. He said it concerned some books your men carried aboard for him in Alameda."

"Books?"

"That's what he said. He asked me to tell you to find Chief Beckley and bring him along, too."

John pulled himself from his bunk and found Beckley. Together they headed toward the officers' wardroom.

"After what we went through, he wants to talk about the *books* we brought aboard for him...." Beckley said as they wound their way through the smoky, fire-blistered passageways.

"That's what his yeoman said," John added.

"After today who wants to talk about books?" Beckley asked.

"Yeah. I thought it was very strange, too," John replied.

"Do you suppose today was too much for the good Padre?"

"Naaaa. Not for Father O'Callahan! He's too tough-minded to break down. It has to be something else."

They walked into the wardroom. O'Callahan greeted them and pointed to chairs. "There're a few more men coming," he said. "Then we'll open this." He pointed to the chest that Beckley last saw when Lowe, Ski and Garcia carried it aboard.

"Last time I saw that chest we were in Alameda," Beckley said.

O'Callahan's face reflected a sad smile. "Yeah, in a much happier time," he replied.

Exhausted men, clothing blackened by grime and soot, filtered in. Joe Taylor came in and sat down heavily on a chair. Steve Jurika and Commander Moore came in right after Taylor. Then Doctors Owen, Fuelling and Sherman arrived, followed by Pharmacist's Mate Daniel Berger. William McKinney came in, as did Don Gary, "Red" Harris and Chief Boatswain Frisbee....

O'Callahan looked about the room of exhausted officers and petty officers. "Men, we've all been through a terrible ordeal," he said. "During the last two days we've been subjected to more stress and trauma than the average person experiences in a lifetime. Frankly, at this moment, I don't know how any of us made it. There were times when I didn't think I could take another minute. It was the most repulsive, nerve-wracking experience in my life. Even now, when I close my eyes, I have visions of the mutilated corpses on the hangar deck. I'm sure you all see the same things, too."

There was a collective sound of agreement.

"My Irish father would take three fingers of whiskey at a time like this," O'Callahan said. "He said it helped him soothe his nerves and sleep."

O'Callahan asked Beckley to help him open the chest.

"Books?" Beckley asked as they struggled to get the chest open.

"Yeah, I brought them aboard in case of an emergency," O'Callahan replied. "Remember I told you some of them were breakable?"

"Breakable, Padre?"

"Yeah."

They lifted the lid. There amid a dozen carefully packed books were seven quarts of Seagram's Gold Label whiskey.

O'Callahan pulled one of the bottles out. "I know what you're all thinking—that it's against regulations to drink alcohol on a Navy ship. Doctor Owen and I convinced Commander Taylor that this would be for medicinal purposes."

Fonz and two Steward's Mates appeared with several trays holding slightly battered but otherwise usable mugs.

"All the glasses got broken, but these mugs weathered the storm," Fonz said as he began to distribute them. He set the first mug down in front of John Oxler. Then he leaned toward him and whispered, "You're first, Gunner. I think without you and your gun crew, this ship might not be afloat today."

John smiled. "Thanks, Buddy," he said.

Fonz went through the room distributing the mugs. O'Callahan followed behind him, pouring whiskey.

As the whiskey was poured, Doctor Owen said, " Even if you guys don't drink, have a drink or two. The whiskey will diffuse some of the burden of the last few days."

About that time Gehres walked in. Everyone stood, some looking uncomfortable about the drinks in their hands.

"Belay the standing," Gehres said. "Not tonight. Tonight I stand here and honor you, and all the other brave men who saved this ship."

He looked at Fonz who was holding a half-full bottle of whiskey. "Is any of that medicine left, Chief?"

"Aye, sir," Frasure said.

"I'll have some. I've had a hell of a day, too."

The whiskey helped push much of the tension and horror of the day aside. John felt warmth in his stomach from the first few sips. He looked around. Everyone else seemed to be reacting the same way.

Beckley took John by the arm and said, "Come on, I want you to meet the skipper."

They walked to where Gehres, Taylor and O'Callahan were standing.

"I want to introduce Gunner Oxler, Captain," he said. "He's the man whose gun crew was firing the 40-mm gun above the bridge."

"The man whose gun crew shot that last kamikaze out of the sky?"

"Yes, sir," Beckley replied.

Gehres offered his hand to John.

"You're one of the few people whose hand is bigger than mine, sir," John said with a smile as he shook hands with Gehres.

"It's a pleasure to meet you, Gunner," Gehres said. He put his hand on John's shoulder. "If it weren't for you and your crew, we might not be here drinking whiskey tonight."

"Thank you, Captain," John replied.

They all had another drink. Then Beckley smiled and said, "Begging the Captain's pardon, but I sure wish I had a camera to record this—the Captain, Executive Officer and Chaplain of a fleet carrier drinking whiskey in the officers' wardroom."

Gehres smiled. "It's for medicinal purposes, Chief," he said as he handed O'Callahan his mug for a refill.

"This sure helps us, Captain," John said. "But I wonder about the crew. Some of those young guys were really shook up today."

"They'll have some 'medical help' too, Gunner. Chief Frasure's stewards located seventeen cases of beer in the beach-party locker. I ordered it distributed to the crew. They're doing that right now."

"That's great, sir. I know the 'medicine' will be appreciated. I just hope a couple of beers are enough," John said as he took another sip of whiskey from his mug.

CHAPTER THIRTY

21 March, 1945
Slipping Out of the Sea of Japan
349 Miles SSE of Shikoku

By the next morning clear skies and a radiant sunrise greeted the battered, still smoldering *Franklin*. On the bridge Gehres received a report from damage control. "This report is uplifting," he said. He read the report aloud to Beckley, Taylor and Jurika. "All but a few stubborn fires on the gallery deck, and in some of the lower spaces aft are out. The forward five-inch battery is back in commission. The 40-mm quads above the bridge are cleaned and in a high state of readiness. Four 20-mm guns in the sponson amidships on the port side are ready for use. The radar antenna was salvaged from the forward topmast and mounted on the port side of the ship's stack. It's now wired through CIC to a receiver on the navigation-bridge and our radar is operating reliably and accurately."

"Great report, Captain," Taylor said.

"Great crew!" Gehres replied. "When a crew is under the kind of pressure our men have been under—in disaster like this—it either disintegrates or unites. This crew united. I know what some of those old reports said about *Franklin's* crewmen, but as far as I'm concerned, that all flies away in light of their actions the last few days."

Jurika agreed. "Aye, Captain," he said. "They worked hard to save this ship, their shipmates and themselves. They're the finest crew I've ever served with."

"Yeah, and it looks like we're going to make it out of here; our chances of getting home are getting better every hour," Gehres said. "We owe our men a great deal—maybe more than can ever be repaid."

Franklin was now steaming at fifteen knots. She was getting farther and farther away from the Sea of Japan and harder and harder to find. Her list had been reduced to six degrees by engineers cutting and jettisoning six batteries of burned out 20s and 40s and their mounts from the starboard side.

Messages started coming in to *Franklin's* restored radio compartment. At 07:05 Gehres got a message from Jocko Clark:

> *To Captain Gehres and the courageous crew of the USS Franklin. From Admiral J. J. Clark.*
> *Les, I knew you could do it. Congratulations to you and your courageous men. There were times during the last two days when some might have doubted Franklin's capacity to survive. For me there was never any doubt. You, and the officers and men in your valorous crew will be long remembered for overcoming some of the most difficult challenges in the history of our Navy. I congratulate and salute you, one*

and all, for this great triumph. I'm grateful that the men in TF 58.1 and I were able to play a small part in helping you overcome the enormous obstacles that you faced. The next time I see you, the drinks are on me.
    Jocko Clark, Vice Admiral, USN

Another came in from Admiral Davison:

> To Captain Les Gehres and the officers and men of the USS Franklin.
> From: Admiral Ralph Davison.
> Les, You saved her. Congratulations! I may now be on a stranger's doorstep but I claim the Franklin again with pride. Battered though she may be, she is still my child. This was one of the most valiant efforts I have ever had the privilege to observe. I salute you and your courageous crew. Great work!

Later, messages from Admirals Spruance and Mitscher came. Admiral Mitscher's message said:

> You and your historic crew cannot be too highly applauded for your historic and successful battle to save your gallant ship in spite of the difficulties, the enormities of which are appreciated. Deep regrets for your losses which we feel as our own.

Admiral Spruance's message said:

> The courage, fortitude, and ability of you and of your crew in bringing back the Franklin for future use against the enemy cannot be too highly praised. Your intrepid actions will forever be an inspiration to the entire United States Navy.

Then a wire came in from Admiral Nimitz:

>   It is evident that the deliverance of the Franklin required skill and courage of the highest degree on the part of those who participated. The officers and men who are returning on the Franklin and the officers and men of the Santa Fe who rendered such courageous assistance, have set a high standard of seamanship, valor and devotion to duty which will forever be an inspiration to the fleet. Well done to all hands.

A few minutes later, Gehres received a message from Captain Fitz. He read the message and smiled. "After all the *Santa Fe* did, Captain Fitz is congratulating *us* for our heroic work and efficiency," he said.

"Didn't he say anything about what they did?" Taylor asked.

"He said they watched from the sidelines," Gehres replied. "He congratulates *us* for 'our courage and tenacity under horrendous and adverse circumstances.' Said it was an example he'd never forget."

"What an outstanding man," Jurika said. "You mean he didn't say a word about *Santa Fe's* efforts?"

"Not a word," Gehres replied handing Jurika the message.

Jurika read it rapidly. "Well, we now know what happened to our wounded and the survivors *Santa Fe* picked up."

"What?" Taylor asked.

"*Santa Fe* transferred them to the *San Francisco*. She's proceeding, at high speed, directly to Pearl Harbor. They should be there in about five days. They've contacted the medics in Pearl and they're waiting."

Gehres called for the Chief Yeoman. "Take this message down and send it to Admiral Spruance:

Dear Admiral, thank you very much for your inspirational message of 20 March. Our entire crew is beholden to you and the protection provided by the Fifth Fleet. They were magnificent."

He paused to collect his thoughts, then continued: *"There was one ship that, in my judgment, helped us far beyond the call of duty. The courage and fortitude of Captain Harold Fitz and the crew of the USS Santa Fe must be highly commended. Santa Fe steamed through cables, steel, wire mesh and nearly every other conceivable obstacle and tied up against our starboard side, risking the great danger of explosions and fires. Many of our wounded were able to walk aboard her. Her men helped fight our fires, for much of the time right on Franklin's decks. I wired Captain Fitz that I thought his actions and those of his gallant crew were the most courageous acts I had ever seen. I respectfully repeat these words to you. It is my deep belief that he and his entire crew should be decorated."*

"Sign it, Respectfully, Leslie Gehres, Captain, USN."

"Chief," Gehres said. "Circulate these messages among the crew. I want every man to realize what we've accomplished and the part they played in it. They can carry a special pride in this heroic work for the rest of their lives."

He turned to Joe Taylor. "Joe, we went to sea with over thirty-two hundred men. We need a count on how many were killed and wounded, how many died later from burns, and how many are missing."

"That's going to be very tough to get," Taylor replied. "We were burying those bodies without the thought of counting them."

"Can you get me some kind of estimate?"

"I'll try, sir. A lot of the burials were just body parts. One man's head could have been put on the same stretcher as another man's torso."

Gehres grimaced. "That's ugly, Joe."

"It's worse than that, Captain. A lot of the stretchers were just body parts—arms, legs, hands, feet—and we haven't found all of the dead yet either."

"Let's try to get some kind of count by tomorrow afternoon."

"We may not be finished digging them all out by tomorrow, Captain."

Gehres nodded slowly and looked down at the deck. "I have to have something for the log, Joe. Just make it as accurate as possible."

"I'll begin with the living, Captain," Taylor said. "I'll get that count first. Then we can decide how we handle the dead and missing."

On the forecastle, O'Callahan was making preparations to say his first Mass since the attack. Almost all of the surviving crewmen in John's gun crew were there—Garcia, Bonin, Colson, Barker and Jardin. Beckley was there. Don Gary and Fonz were there. Doctors Joe Fuelling and George Owen were there. "Red" Harris and Daniel Berger were in attendance, as were Sam Sherman and Mark Edelstein, both of them Jewish. Joe Taylor and Steve Jurika arrived from the bridge just as the Mass began....

"Introibo ad altare Dei: I will go unto the altar of God," came the ancient yet familiar Latin prayer.

"Ad Deum qui laetificate juventutem meam. To God who giveth joy to my youth," John and Bonin responded.

The March wind wailed as it slithered through the jagged holes in the *Franklin's* hangar deck. It flapped the canvas backdrop. There was quiet—the only other sound was from *Franklin's* bow as it cut through the choppy Pacific Ocean.

The Mass continued. *Judica me, Deus, et discerne causam de gente non sancta...*

John read the response. Then he began to drift into thoughts of what happened...of Sullivan's hideous death...of finding Lowe and Feinstein and the terrible way they looked...of the possibility that Ski was dead...of the horrible deaths by fire...the slimy corpses he'd handled...the reverent but ugly burials at sea. His thoughts shifted to Sandy, the one light in the enormous darkness of the past few days. Maybe he'd see her soon. His mood lightened. He had faint memories of her perfume...the fine texture of her skin as she lay next to him, her beautiful smile, her passion and openness when they made love....

O'Callahan's voice interrupted his thoughts: *"Kyrie eleison...."*

He was back on the battered Franklin. He responded to the prayer."

The time for the Gospel came. He watched O'Callahan turn from the altar and face his dwindled congregation.

"My shipmates and brethren," O'Callahan began, "we gather here today to pray for the departed souls of our brothers-in-arms and shipmates who died during the last two horror-filled days. We also gather to give thanks for the strength and courage of those of us who are still alive—for all of you here—for the entire crew of the *Franklin*. To speak of the great sacrifice of our dead comrades is necessary and important. They died in the line of duty; they gave what is most sacred of all—their lives—so that we might live in freedom. Their souls are now with their Divine Creator, blessed by the solemn words of His Divine Son who said: 'Greater love hath no man than to give his life for another.' I'm sure they've been rewarded with a special place in Heaven."

He paused and took a deep breath.

"To speak to you, who survived, about your heroism and bravery seems banal. No words can begin to describe the countless acts of courage and sacrifice manifest everywhere on this ship. They are beyond words. They are beyond description. They are beyond praise. Admiral Nimitz said of another battle a few months ago that 'uncommon valor was a common thing.' So also was it on the *Franklin*. This is the second message of my sermon. It is a tribute to your courage and bravery. We can all be very proud of what we did—not only for ourselves—and the ship—but for each other."

He paused again. The wind calmed—as though it was honoring what he said.

"May God's blessings surround each and every one of you, now and for the rest of your lives."

The Mass ended. O'Callahan left the altar and walked among the men there. He extended personal blessings and words of praise and encouragement. When he came to John he said, "God Bless you, John. Sandy's going to be very proud of you."

John's eyes were misting as he shook O'Callahan's hand.

Elsewhere on the ship seamen in repair details were hard at work. Some had started before dawn. As the day went on, others joined them from fire-fighting details and gunnery units. Storekeepers, signalmen and yeomen pitched in. They tore wreckage away from compartments where food was known to be stored. They worked with electricians repairing circuits, and with ship fitters piecing together ducts and valves. Some of the ship's intercommunications were restored. Radio crews wired a makeshift transmitter. Radar crews worked to upgrade radar capability. Gehres ordered the ship's store, located four decks below the hangar deck and untouched by *Franklin's* tragedy, to issue each man two complete sets of clothing and shoes if needed. By 11:03 the galley was back in operation, and by midday the crew had fresh baked bread, sardines and beans for lunch. That night *Franklin's* men were served a hot meal for the first time in three days. Although the smell of death lingered, *Franklin* was beginning to show signs of rebirth.

At 19:30 an order came from Admiral Davison whose flag was now in *Hancock*. Gehres squinted at the message, then said, "We're going back to Ulithi. A repair ship and crews equipped with cranes are there. They'll help clear the heavy damage and make temporary bulkhead repairs."

Taylor nodded. "That makes sense," he said.

"Come left to 155 degrees." Gehres said.

Franklin headed South Southeast. The *Santa Fe, Miller, Marshall* and *Hunt* took positions around her. As Task Unit 1.58.1 they steamed at seventeen knots toward the Caroline Islands.

CHAPTER THIRTY-ONE

22 March, 1945
370 Miles SSE of Shikoku
A New Ship's Motto

At dawn the next morning, *Franklin's* speed was up to twenty knots. *Santa Fe*, *Miller*, *Marshall* and *Hunt* steamed beside her. The weather was perfect. There wasn't a cloud in a very blue Pacific sky.

On the bridge Gehres looked over the morning damage report furnished him by Taylor. "It's a good report, Joe. Fire rooms and engine rooms are now running at almost normal. The machine shop is operating at full capacity, and a lot of the switchboards have been fixed. Most important, you've identified nearly all of the dead."

He paused and handed back the report. "Those burials were a tough job, Joe," he said. "The thought of those bodies stacked on the hangar deck like cordwood still gives me the chills."

"Yes, sir. It was a tough, tough job. Most of it was just too much for the younger men. The doctors, officers, petty officers and the two chaplains handled a lot of the bodies."

Gehres grimaced. "In all the time I've been in the Navy, I've never been exposed to such horror, or had to ask men to do such a terrible job."

"I was down there both days," Taylor said, shaking his head sadly. "The worst part was the nauseating smell. Even with rescue-breather masks, it almost knocked us down." He paused. "We have to thank God for O'Callahan and Gatlin. Their presence lent something to the task—they brought a kind of stability to the chaos. The crosses painted on their helmets created a reverence—a respect for what had to be done. Even with this, everybody was having awful problems. I'm sure glad it's over with."

"Aye, Commander, so am I," Gehres said. "I think every man in that detail deserves a medal."

"Captain," Taylor said, "most of the men's wives and families don't know whether they are dead or alive. I'd like to try to reward the crew by setting up a radio-telephone link from Ulithi to Honolulu, then on to the mainland."

"That's a great idea, Joe. Can you make it work?"

"I talked to Commander Kreamer in communications. He thinks it will. We'd connect by radio from Ulithi to Honolulu and then by conventional telephone to the states."

"Wonderful, Joe. Great for the whole crew! Let's get right with it. Put me somewhere on that list."

Taylor went below to the CIC and located Ben Kreamer.

"Captain approves the idea—in fact he likes it. He wants to be on the list."

"Great, Joe," Kreamer said. "I'll contact Ulithi and start setting it up. Hell, I want to be on the list, too."

Word about the radio link spread through the ship like lightning.

After breakfast John spent some time below decks moving his gear. Three sleeping compartments on the port side forward had suffered water and smoke damage but were made habitable by restoration crews the day before.

He selected a bunk and a locker, stowed his gear, then went up on the flight deck looking for Beckley. When John saw Beckley he was waving his arms with the kind of fervor that signaled good news.

John hurried over to meet him. "What's up?" he asked. "Why all the excitement?"

Beckley told him about Taylor's plan to call the mainland.

"Wow! Where do I go to sign up?" John asked, his face beaming.

Beckley pointed to the bridge. "The line's forming there; it leads up to the navigator's shack."

"You coming?"

"Yeah, I'll get in as soon as I deliver this message from Commander Jurika to Father O'Callahan."

John looked over at the line. "It's getting long—you'd better hurry."

"I'll be back as soon as I can."

John got in line. It moved faster than he expected. In about twenty minutes he reached the top of the ladder. The seaman in front of him went in. John was next. When he reached the door, Commander Taylor acknowledged him immediately.

"Gunner," he said. "Come in."

John walked in and Taylor pointed to a chair.

"Who do you want to contact?" he asked. "I'm sorry—it can only be one call."

"I'd like to call my wife, sir. We've only been married four months and I'm sure she's worried about whether I'm alive or not."

John gave Taylor's yeoman Sandy's full name and telephone number.

"Thank you very much, Commander. I really appreciate this."

"No thanks necessary, Gunner," Taylor replied. "You more than earned it. You demonstrated courage and leadership—all through the crisis that we just went through. Without your help we might never have been able to rig that towline, or get that magazine flooded or those 40's working."

"Chief Frasure was responsible for what happened on the towline, sir."

"I agree. That chant was one of the most inspirational things I've ever heard and we're giving his actions meritorious consideration. But whose leadership found Frasure, Gunner? Going down into that magazine in the face of certain death was an act of extraordinary bravery…and blasting those two kamikaze before they crashed the ship…."

"That was the whole gun crew, sir."

"Of course, Gunner, but you were their leader. I think you should know that we've recommend you for the Navy Cross."

John was startled. "Me, sir?" he asked.

"Yes, you, Gunner. It's a high citation—a just reward for great courage and valor."

"I had help, sir."

"We know that. We won't forget the men who helped you."

"I...I don't know what to say, sir."

"You don't have to say anything, Gunner. Your actions have already spoken for you."

John rose and stood at attention. "Thank you, sir." he said. Then he left feeling overwhelmed. Next to his marriage to Sandy, this was the most wonderful thing that had ever happened to him.

At 17:00 Gehres asked Beckley to request that all hands muster on the forward hangar deck. When they were in ranks they were given a mimeographed sheet printed on a machine that survived the explosion. It was a message from Commander Taylor.

To the officers and men of the USS Franklin:

Due to our gasoline system being damaged, smoking regulations must be strictly enforced. You may smoke on the forecastle during the daylight hours. You may smoke in the forward messing compartment between reveille and taps. Officers may smoke in the wardroom. Never throw a lighted butt over the side.

Keep busy doing something all the time. If you aren't on a scheduled working party, work anyway. We've got the world by the tail now, so hang on.

Don't throw any usable article over the side. If you think it can be salvaged, stack it neatly on the hangar deck just forward of the Number 2 elevator on the starboard side.

Any personal effects found, such as wallets, watches, etc., should be turned in at the Executive Officer's cabin.

Captain Gehres and I want to commend each and every man in the crew for your bravery and determination during the past few days. Your valorous actions in defiance of circumstances that were disastrous and horror-filled are a tribute to your courage and determination. We both commend you and salute you. Captain Gehres said that your actions have created a new ship's motto: ***A SHIP THAT WILL NOT BE SUNK—CANNOT BE SUNK.*** *Joe Taylor, Commander, U.S.N., Executive Officer*

After the muster was over Beckley studied the Executive Officer's message. Then he looked about the battered hangar deck, still filled with huge warped I-beams and heavy debris that it would take a crane to move. He thought of Sullivan, Zimler, Lowe...and the many other men who had had died on the dirty, ugly deck. But although ugly and filthy, the *Franklin* was still alive. Full of holes, ripped, mangled, maimed, she was making her way back to Ulithi under her own power. If she was jinxed, she'd survived the jinx. If she was destined to die, she'd defied that destiny. If she was meant for disaster, she'd now dimmed the power of that curse. They'd rebuild her and she'd sail again without the plague of her identification number. Other strong men would take the place of the valiant men who were killed. The indomitable *Franklin*, battered but unbowed, had lived to fight again. For Beckley, the jinx of the number 13 was gone. It would never come back again. It had been purged by the heroic actions of the men who lost their lives, by those who lived to snatch her from the jaws of death, and by the soaring spirit of an unconquerable ship.

CHAPTER THIRTY-TWO

24 March, 1945
Ulithi Atoll
Caroline Islands

Two days later *Franklin* dismissed her destroyers and took her place steaming in column with *Santa Fe* and the carriers *Wasp* and *Enterprise*. When they arrived at Mugai channel and entered Ulithi harbor, they were living proof of Gehres's words that "a ship that will not be sunk, cannot be sunk." As *Franklin* steamed through the harbor, ships rendered honors again. For the first time since the explosions, *Franklin* tried to use her siren and whistle to return the honors. Neither worked. The fire and heat had ruined both.

"I wonder what's on the minds of the men watching us," Gehres said as *Franklin* steamed along to her anchorage. "I'll bet a lot of them are thinking, 'Oh, God. Look what we're going to be up against.'"

"Oh, they might not be looking at us that way, Captain," Taylor said. "They might be thinking 'hell, they lost a lot of men and took a lot of damage. If they can survive something like that, there's hope for us, too.'"

"Naaa...I think the Captain's right, Joe," Jurika said. "This ship's an awful mess. If I were a young sailor watching her come in, it'd give me a hell of a jolt."

Taylor nodded. "Maybe you're right. We're not a very pretty picture right now."

At 14:14 *Franklin* dropped anchor at Berth 6, Carrier Anchorage. Shortly thereafter, Lieutenant Albert Jennings, a demolition expert, was called aboard. An unexploded missile head had been found in a remote corner of the hangar deck. He and his crew were called in to disarm it.

When word of his presence went out, most of the crew displayed curious amusement.

"A demolition expert," Bonin snickered. "Hell, we could probably teach him a few things about demolitions." At 15:05 the unexploded missile head was jettisoned over the starboard side.

At 15:15 the first contingent of fifty men climbed into motor whaleboats and headed ashore to a large communications center for the radio-telephone hook up. When they arrived they were ushered into the radio room and seated on fold out chairs.

When John's turn came, he was issued a pair of earphones and directed to a small booth. As the duty radioman connected with Pearl Harbor, John looked nervously at his watch. "It's four o'clock in the morning in Berkeley," he said.

John listened patiently as telephone operators sequenced his call through Honolulu and San Francisco to Berkeley. He crossed his fingers as Sandy's phone began to ring.

Sandy answered.

"Sandy, it's John."

"John! Oh, God! It's so good to hear your voice!" Sandy said. "I've been so worried—we've all been worried to death."

"I'm okay, Honey," John replied. "I took some shrapnel in my left shoulder, but other than that I'm fine."

"We knew from Dad's reports that the *Franklin* was badly damaged. The agony of waiting to find out about you was terrible. What about your shoulder, Honey?" she asked.

"The ship's doctors want me to get it looked at again, just to be sure there's no tendon damage."

"How does it feel now, Darling?"

"It feels good. Every day it gets stronger. I have full use of my fingers and arm. I don't think they'll find much when they examine it."

"Oh, God! I'm so happy to hear your voice, John. What happened? God, what happened?"

"We got hit. We lost some men, but we saved the ship."

"Is Father O'Callahan okay?"

"He's fine. He was all over the ship, Sandy. He took some incredible chances and didn't get a scratch. God must have really been watching over him."

"How about Beckley?"

"He's fine, too. Not a scratch."

"What about Ski?"

"We don't know about Ski. He's missing. A lot of guys are missing. Not everybody's been identified."

"Sullivan?"

"He didn't make it, Honey."

"Oh, God! No!" Sandy started to cry. "I'm so sorry for him and for you, John. I know how much you respected him."

"Yeah, I respected him and cared for him," John said, his voice filled with emotion. "When Beckley told me he was dead, I didn't want to believe it."

"John, I'm going to try to meet you. Dad can find out when you'll arrive in Pearl Harbor. He said when we heard from you, he'd try to arrange for me to go over."

"If you could, it would be wonderful, Sandy."

"I'm coming—no matter what it takes."

A voice broke into their conversation. "Time's nearly up, Gunner."

"Honey, will you call my folks? Tell them I'm alive but don't mention the shrapnel wound. Mom would get too worried."

"Yes, Darling, I'll call them—I'll call them as soon as I hang up."

"I'll see you, Honey. I love you. I hope you can come," John said.

"I love you, too, John. I'm going to do everything I can to get there."

John moved out of the booth. The three minutes seemed like a couple of seconds. He walked out of the smoke-filled radio room into the clear tropical air. He hoped his father-in-law could arrange her trip. He missed her terribly—talking to her brought back the wonderful memories—he needed to see his wife, his love and his life.

John left the building and looked down to the area where the cruisers were docked. He saw the *Santa Fe* and decided to try to see Tom. He walked to the gangway and went up to the *Santa Fe*'s quarterdeck. The Officer of the Deck greeted him.

"John Oxler, Gunner's Mate First Class, sir. I'm aboard the *Franklin*. I'm looking for Signalman Thomas Rashinski. We're both from the same town in Colorado."

"Oh, sure, Gunner. I'll see if we can find him."

Ten minutes later, Tom emerged from below decks and walked hurriedly to his friend waiting on the quarterdeck.

"Hey, Buddy, it's good to see you," Tom said as he approached. "After I talked to you the other day I was worried as hell. I checked on you as soon as I could. The next day, before we got out of there, I found out you'd been wounded in the shoulder—but you were okay otherwise."

"Yeah, I caught some shell fragments," John replied.

'How does it feel now?"

"Still sore, but it'll be okay."

"Want a cup of joe?" Tom asked.

"Yeah, that'd be good."

They went below decks to the *Santa Fe*'s gedunk bar and Tom got two coffees.

When they were seated, John said, "I was on the forecastle when your skipper pulled aside us. I've never seen anything like what he did. It was amazing."

"I told you he was the best skipper in the fleet."

"I sure as hell agree with that now. We've got a lot to thank all you guys for; you saved a lot of our wounded."

"Yeah…and we fished a bunch of your guys out of the water, too. The ship was pretty crowded and messy until we finally put them all aboard the *Frisco*."

"We've still got over four hundred on our missing list," John said. "One's a guy by the name of Kwatkowski—he was the best man in my wedding." John paused. "You didn't by any chance run into him or hear his name, did you?"

Tom shook his head. "I was up on the bridge most of the day and into that night. We had wounded packed in all over the ship, even men on mattresses on the decks in the passageways. We didn't make a list—too many men—too many wounded—too few doctors and corpsmen to look after them. They just patched them up as best they could; then we transferred them."

John nodded his head slowly.

"Damn. I'm going to miss that guy," he said sadly.

"Yeah. I know what you mean. I've lost a few guys like that, too. It's tough. It's like losing a brother."

Both men became silent—each lost in his thoughts.

Then Tom said, "I was going to contact you tomorrow. We got a message this afternoon that we're going to be your escort back to Pearl Harbor. Then we go on to San Pedro for repairs and reconditioning."

"You going to get leave?" John asked.

"I hope so."

"You going back home?"

"Yeah, for three weeks, if I get four," Tom replied. "Then I'll probably go back and spent a little time with a guy by the name of Corini whose folks live in Los Angeles."

"Will you give my folks my love for me?"

"Sure thing."

"My wife might meet me in Pearl," John said. "Her dad's going to try to arrange it. They found out we got blasted, but she didn't know I was alive until about a half an hour ago when I talked to her on a radio-telephone hook up."

"No kidding. You just talked to her from here?"

"Yeah. I didn't think they could do it either, but they did. It was pretty clear, too." John paused for a few seconds. Then he said, "Boy, I really love and miss her, Tom."

"Yeah. I know what you mean. It can be tough as hell. Do you know where your ship's going?"

"I think the ship's going to a shipyard on the East Coast, probably Norfolk or Brooklyn. I'm getting off in Pearl. They want to look at my shoulder again."

"Well, this might be the last time we get together for awhile," Tom said.

"Maybe not," John replied. "If my shoulder's okay, I might be in Pueblo when you are. Sandy really wants to go back and see what it's like there."

"She might be disappointed," Tom said smiling. "No ocean, no palm trees, no university—just a smelly steel mill town."

John laughed. "She might at that, but it's home," he said. "No matter what, we'll see each other when this thing's over."

"For sure. And it seems we're getting closer to the end," Tom said. "Ship's paper says we're getting ready to invade Okinawa. After that, the next step is Japan."

He handed John a copy of the *Santa Fe's Daily Information Guide.* "Look at this," he said. We've already started."

John read the article. "It says we captured Kerama Retto. We sailed right past that little cluster of islands," he said.

"Yeah, so have we. The article says that we're going to use them as a staging point for the invasion of Okinawa."

"That ought to scare hell out of the Japs," John said.

"Aww, I don't think so. Those bastards don't scare very easy," Tom replied. "But it sure as hell sends them a message that we're serious."

"Yeah. And that were getting ready to go after it all," John said. "Okinawa, then right up the chain to Tokyo. We're in the toughest part of the war. I heard we'd need over three million men to take Japan—maybe as many as nine-hundred thousand casualties."

"Yeah. It'll be tough, but I think we have to do it. The Japs won't ever give up. It's the only way to end this goddamned war."

"Can I keep this?" John asked as he got up to leave. "We don't have a paper aboard any more. Just one old mimeograph survived. I'd like to show this to the guys."

"Sure," Tom said as they started to walk back to the quarterdeck.

John went down the gangplank to the dock. "I'll see you somewhere—either on leave or at home after the war," he called back.

"Roger! Take care of yourself," Tom shouted. "Say hello to my folks if you get home first."

When John got to the pier, he went aboard a barge loaded with a group of guys from the *Franklin* who were being returned by the *USS Hunt*.

Tom walked through the barge asking each man the same question: "Do you know anything about a Stan Kwatkowski?"

Each time he got the same answer. "Sorry, I don't, Gunner."

He came to a civilian war correspondent. "My name's John Oxler, sir," he said as he extended his hand.

"Ralph Wheeler, *Life* magazine," the correspondent answered.

"I'm trying to find a man that's missing-in-action. His name's Kwatkowski. I just wondered if you had heard anything about him?"

"No, I haven't, Gunner. I'd remember a name like that."

Wheeler looked at John. "Lose a good buddy, Gunner?"

"Yes, sir, a very good buddy."

"We took a bunch of pictures but haven't got them developed yet," Wheeler said. "We'll develop them in Pearl Harbor. You're welcome to look through them if you think they'll help you."

"Thanks a lot," John said. "If he doesn't turn up, maybe I'll take you up on that."

That evening there was a steady stream of traffic between the *Franklin* and the docks. At 18:30 a Fleet Oiler came alongside to take off aviation gasoline and a barge pulled up to transfer ammunition ashore. At 20:12 an LTC with Marine officers from Air Group Five edged in to retrieve personal effects that might have escaped damage. Forty-five minutes later another barge came alongside to retrieve the personal effects of deceased and missing men. What remained of a body, found in a hidden corner of the hangar deck that afternoon, was put aboard the barge for burial ashore.

Franklin stayed in Ulithi only long enough to do the necessary unloading and allow workmen to clear away more of the heavy wreckage.

On the 27th of March *Franklin* and *Santa Fe* departed from Ulithi. With six of her eight boilers now fully repaired, *Franklin* steamed, abeam of *Santa Fe*, at nineteen knots on course 059° enroute to Pearl Harbor.

CHAPTER THIRTY-THREE

3 April, 1945
Pearl Harbor
Was the *Franklin* Jinxed?

Franklin reached the Hawaiian Channel and steamed toward Pearl Harbor as dawn broke on the third day of April, just under four weeks from the day she left for the Sea of Japan. When dawn came, a beautiful cloudless sky and gentle winds greeted her. The rising tropical sun glistened on the undamaged part of her flight deck. Warm tropical winds drifted through the hangar deck.

The graphic dispatches received by the Commander of Naval Air Forces in the Pacific had everyone at Pearl Harbor waiting and wondering what *Franklin* would look like. After *Franklin* passed Waipio Point abeam to port, she made a huge turn. Then she headed slowly toward the pier. Gehres had ordered all hands to muster at quarters for entering port. In the past, when Franklin rendered honors of this kind, there were over three thousand men standing at attention on the flight deck. But now, mustered on the forward section of the only part of the flight deck that wasn't completely ruined, were about four hundred men. The remaining three hundred were on duty at their engineering and mooring stations. The maimed but unconquered *Franklin* had returned to Pearl Harbor.

As *Franklin* edged toward the dock a glee club of WAVES, specially selected by Admiral Nimitz's staff, began to sing *Aloha,* the traditional Hawaiian song of welcome. Lovely feminine voices lilted out clearly and melodiously. The *Franklin* edged closer. The Waves looked…they stared…amazement turned to shock…they faltered…their song of welcome drifted away. Many had tears in their eyes. So did most of the people there. Vice Admiral George Murray's eyes were misted. Admiral Nimitz was there with a large contingency of other officers. They were aghast at *Franklin's* damage. No ship had ever come in torn up like this before.

But the proud young men on the battered flight deck stood confident and erect. They'd survived the fiery destruction. They'd saved the *Franklin.* They'd brought their ship home. As *Franklin* moved into the dock, with Father O'Callahan directing them, they began to sing a dashing song:

> "Old Big Ben, she ain't what she used to be—she ain't what she used to be—just a few days ago…."

Mooring lines were tossed. *Franklin* tied up at Fox 12, port side to the dock with six manila lines and four wire hawsers. When the docking was complete, Gehres ordered liberty for the entire crew. The crew could go ashore but, for security reasons, no one could board the *Franklin*. The Navy Department had ordered that the full extent of her damage be kept secret as long as possible.

From the flight deck, John looked for Sandy in the huge crowd below. He started from one end of the dock and went slowly to the other. He looked again, this time very slowly, going from face to face. There was just a mass of unfamiliar faces. He didn't see her. "I guess she couldn't make it," he muttered. He walked down to the forecastle and edged up to the railing. He could see better from there. As he did, he heard his name called. He grabbed the railing and looked down.

Sandy was standing on the edge of the dock. She had worked her way to the front of the crowd. And Ski was standing next her, shouting his name. He was leaning on crutches and waving his arms like a man about to drown.

For a second John couldn't believe what he saw. "Sandy's here and Ski's alive!" he muttered unbelievingly. A burst of joyful energy surged through him. He waved back vigorously. "Sandy! Ski!" he shouted, his voice filled with unrestrained joy. He rushed over and grabbed Beckley. He dragged him to the rail, pointing at a sight that seemed more like heaven than anything he'd ever seen. "Sandy and Ski! They're right down there, Beck," he said.

"Yeah, I see them, now" Beckley said after looking for a few seconds. "Thank God, Ski made it. It looks like he's got a cast on his leg."

"Yeah, he has. It looks like he broke it," John said. "I'm going to go down on the dock. You coming?"

"I'll be right after you. I've got ten minutes work on the forecastle."

"We'll wait for you there."

John hurried down to the quarterdeck. A line had already formed. John fell into it. Soon after he got there, the line began to move. He got to the quarterdeck. "Permission to go ashore, sir."

"Permission granted," The OD replied.

John hurried down to the dock. Ford Island was the same, but it seemed strangely different. It dawned on him that it had only been a few weeks since he was here before, but it seemed more like a couple of lifetimes. He sorted through the huge crowd toward the place he thought Sandy and Ski were standing. Finally he spotted them. At just about the same time they saw him. John pushed through the crowd toward Sandy. She surged toward him. In a few seconds they were in each other's arms, showering each other with kisses.

"God, Honey, it's so good to see you," Sandy said as she put her head on his shoulder and hugged him.

"For me too, Honey," John whispered. "You don't know how many times I've dreamed of this day."

He kissed her again. This time it was a longing, passionate kiss—the kind that said he was deeply grateful to be alive with her in his arms. Then they just held each other**.** It was as though there was nobody else on the dock.

Finally John released Sandy and looked at Ski. "What happened to you, Buddy?" he asked.

"I got blown overboard by the concussion from that blast," Ski said. "I landed on something and broke my leg. I wasn't in the water thirty minutes when I got picked up."

"Who got you?"

"*Santa Fe*. I was lying on a mattress on her fantail the entire time she was next to the ship."

Ski paused and looked at John. "I wondered how you were doing, John, but there was no way to contact you. The decks were loaded with wounded and everybody had to wait their turn for everything. I just couldn't get word to you." Ski hugged him. "God, I was so worried," he said as tears welled up in his eyes. "I thought I might never see you again, Buddy."

John hugged him back. There were tears in his eyes, too. "I thought you were dead, Ski. I thought I left you stranded. After that fireball hit and I dived through that hatch, I wanted to go back after you, but they stopped me. God, I'm so glad to see you. I'm so happy you made it!"

Sandy stepped into John and Ski's arms. The three just stood there wrapped in a long embrace.

"Thank the Lord we're all back together," Sandy said.

"Thank God we're alive," John added.

On the bridge Gehres, Taylor, Jurika and O'Callahan watched the huge, milling crowd on the dock. O'Callahan heard his name called from flight deck. He looked down and saw Captain Sheehy, the Pearl Harbor District Chaplain.

"Joe," Sheehy called. "The OD let me on for a minute. He said no one was allowed aboard but when I told him I had a message for you he made an exception. When I came down here I didn't know whether you were still alive. Praise God, you're okay."

"Thanks, Father. I'm grateful, too."

"Joe, I've got an important appointment, so I have to rush," Sheehy said. "I came to tell you we got word from the Red Cross yesterday—your sister is alive—weak but otherwise well. She was liberated in Manila. She's enroute to your mother's home in Boston to recuperate."

O'Callahan's body flushed with joy. Alice was alive! He'd prayed and dreamed that someday he'd hear those words. "Thank God, Father!" he shouted. "And thanks for letting me know."

"Boy this ship sure took a pounding, Joe," Sheehy said as he looked around the battered flight deck. "I've never seen a ship with this much damage. I can sure understand why they're not letting anyone aboard."

"Yeah, she's battered but we're taking her home—we're going to have her repaired—then we'll go back out again."

On the forecastle, Beckley wrapped up his duties and headed down to the dock. He spotted John's head in the huge crowd and hurried toward him. When he was within ear's range he called out, "Hi Sandy! Ski! You made it!"

When he reached them, he gave Sandy a big hug. "I'm sure glad to see you, Sandy," he said.

Sandy hugged him back. "Me, too. I'm so glad you're okay."

Beckley turned to Ski, shook his hand and put his arms around him. "You sure had us worried, Ski. We thought you were dead."

"I lucked out," Ski replied. "I got blown overboard and the *Santa Fe* picked me up. Broke my leg—but I'm still here, Chief."

Ski looked at both John and Beckley. "Who else got it?" he asked with apprehension.

"Sullivan, Lowe, Feinstein, Arnold, Hazelton and Dixon," John replied. "A burial crew found Dixon's body on the hangar deck. The 20-mm gun crew just aft of us was completely wiped out."

"Yeah, that's where I found Sully," Beckley said. "He must have been working there when that blast hit."

"What happened to Lowe?" Ski asked.

"John and I found him on the edge of the flight deck. He must have been killed in an early explosion," Beckley replied.

Sadness covered Ski's face. He shook his head, slowly trying to accept what he was being told.

"How about Feinstein?"

"The same explosion."

"What about Arnold and Hazelton?" he asked, barely able to get the words out.

"They died in the ready-service locker explosion."

Beckley paused. There was silence…a long silence.

Finally Beckley spoke, "Remember what Sully said the last time we were here? That he liked the idea of meeting at Gecko's and celebrating when the war ended?"

John nodded.

"I think we should meet there tonight," Beckley said. "The war's over for him and for a lot of the other guys. Maybe this'd be a way to say good-bye."

"I think that's a good idea," John said. "Would you mind doing that, Honey?"

"Of course not," Sandy replied.

About that time Fonz and Don Gary walked up.

"John, how are you? This must be the beautiful lady you're always talking about," Fonz said, smiling and extending his hand to Sandy. "Alphonso Frasure. My friends just call me 'Fonz'. This is Lieutenant Don Gary."

Gary shook hands with Sandy and then they both acknowledged Beckley and Ski with a tiny hand signal.

Sandy saw O'Callahan walking toward them. "Father O'Callahan!" she cried out and rushed toward him.

"Sandy, it's wonderful to see you," he said as he gave her a fatherly hug. "John told me you might be here. It's great that you could come, young lady."

He looked at Frasure and Gary.

"Fonz. Lieutenant Gary."

"Hello, Padre," they replied.

Beckley explained what he and John had just discussed to the rest of them. "We're going to meet at Gecko's in Honolulu—to say a final good-bye to Sully, Lowe, Feinstein—and the rest of the guys we lost. You're all invited to meet us there. I'm sure there are people you'd like to say good-bye to as well."

"I'm in," Fonz replied.

"Me, too," Gary said.

"Father?"

"Humm...yeah. I'm in," O'Callahan replied. "There are a lot of men that I can grieve, but today there's room for joy in my life, too. I received word a little while ago that my sister, Alice, has been liberated. Except for being malnourished and weak, she's in good health and on her way to my mother's home in Boston to recuperate."

"Hallelujahhh, Padre! That's wonderful," Fonz said.

"How do we get to this place?" Gary asked.

"We catch that bus across the street," John replied. "It'll take us right to Gecko's. It's just across from the Royal Hawaiian Hotel."

It was late afternoon when they arrived. John and Beckley talked to the manager. "Yes," he said, "I understand what you want. I'll give you a place back in the corner."

He ushered them into a semi-private area at the rear of the bar. "My friends, here you'll have all the privacy you need." He lit the two candles on the table and arranged the chairs.

Everyone sat down. They left a chair at the head of the table vacant.

After they placed their order, John said, "Father, maybe you could get us started in the right direction. Would you say a few words to begin?"

O'Callahan thought for a few moments. Then he said, "We're here to honor the great sacrifices that many of our shipmates made on the nineteenth and twentieth of March. Many gave their lives so that we might be here safely today in freedom. The courage and great sacrifices of these brave men should never be forgotten. We're among the fortunate. We should be grateful and joyous that we lived. By living, we have become the custodians of the tribute that is due those brave men that died. We—indeed our entire nation and the free world—owe them a debt that can never be fully repaid. But there *is* a way we can pay a part of this debt—we can vow here today never to let their courage and bravery be forgotten."

He paused. "May God's blessings surround each and every one of them and His love be with them forever."

There was quiet for a few moments as the others contemplated what O'Callahan had just said. Then each responded with an "Amen."

Sandy, who was resting her head on John's shoulder, spoke the last Amen. Then she said, "Thank you, Dear God, for watching over the men at this table and all the others who came back." She lifted her head and kissed John gently on the cheek.

Beckley raised his glass and said, "I'd like to propose a toast: To Lieutenant

Commander William Zimler, fearless aviator, recipient of the Distinguished Flying Cross, adoring husband and father and never-to-be-forgotten friend. Wherever you are now, Commander," he continued, fighting back tears, "I want you to know we miss you."

"To Commander Zimler."

They raised and clinked their glasses.

Next John raised his glass. "To Chief Gunner Peter Joseph Sullivan," he said with great sorrow. "To an honored leader and wonderful friend. Wherever you are now, Chief, I want you to know that we'll always remember and love you."

They raised their glasses and drank a toast to Sullivan's memory.

Then Gary said, "I'd like to toast the memory of Machinist's Mate First Class Peter Kubala and Machinist's Mate Second Class Gerald Rothstein, two men that I sent down to the hangar deck to repair a fan motor that morning. I never saw you guys again. I'm really sorry to be the one who sent you down there." He raised his glass. "I hope you're in a place of peace and happiness."

They drank a toast to the memory of two men only one of them knew.

"I'd like to drink to my good friends Gunner Lowe and Seaman Feinstein," Ski said. "And to Seamen Arnold and Hazelton. I just found out about what happened to you guys a few hours ago. It's really hard to believe you're gone. If I live to be a hundred, I'll never forget you."

"To Lowe and Feinstein! To Arnold and Hazelton!"

They'd come around the table to Fonz. "I going to propose a different kind of toast," he said. He raised his glass. "To my wonderful shipmates at this table. You guys are white and I'm black, but it never made a difference to any of you. When things got tough I knew I could count on you and I tried hard to be the same for you. May God bless you and keep you safe for the rest of the war and the rest of your lives."

"I'll drink to that," John said as they joined in Fonz's toast.

O'Callahan was next. "I'd like to drink a toast to all the brave men, both sailors and marines, who died in *Franklin's* great misfortune. May they have lasting peace and everlasting joy in the hands of a Loving and Merciful Creator."

A long, empty silence followed—each alone with memories of the men they had just toasted.

After awhile Ski looked up and said, "I...I haven't heard. Did we get the bomber that hit us?"

"Oh, yeah," Beckley replied, "Captain Gehres got a report just before we left for Ulithi. There were two of them—Judys, and we got 'em both—the one that hit us and the one that was trying to crash the *Hancock*. A Corsair came down right after the Judy hit us. Shot it down just as it started to climb. The report said the plane was blasted into pieces. The Corsair was still firing at it when the wreckage hit the water."

"What about the other one?"

"Antiaircraft fire from the screen got it before it could get lined up on *Hancock*. It never got closer than a thousand yards."

"What about the rest of the task force?" Ski asked.

"The only other damage was to the *Santa Fe* and we caused it," John said. "Her decks and her five-inch guns on the port side were ripped up when she cut through all that debris to reach our starboard side."

"Yeah, I was there on her fantail," Ski said. "I watched that happen. That skipper was one courageous man. In all the confusion, I never got his name."

"Captain Harold Fitz," John said. "My friend Tom Rashinski's on the *Santa Fe*. His whole crew is convinced he's the best seaman in the fleet."

"After watching what he did, I agree," Ski said. "Let's drink a toast to Captain Fitz and the guys on the *Santa Fe*. Without them I might not be here."

"Yeah," John said. "Maybe none of us would."

"To the *Santa Fe*."

There was another period of silence.

"Well, maybe now I'm going to ask a question that might be *unanswerable*," Fonz said. "I know the Captain is against anyone talking about this, but I'd like to hear what you have to say about it, Padre."

Fonz hesitated, then after a deep breath, he asked, "Do you think the *Franklin* was jinxed, Padre?"

O'Callahan seemed startled. He thought about the question for a few moments, then said, "I guess my faith doesn't allow much room for things like a jinx, Fonz. I...."

Don Gary broke into the conversation. "With all due respect, Padre, it had to be some kind of a jinx or very bad luck."

O'Callahan grimaced and looked down at the floor.

"Padre, you yourself just called it a *mis*fortune," Gary said.

"Yes, but that might have been a poor choice of words," O'Callahan replied defensively.

"Well, let's look at what happened," Gary said. "To penetrate the flight deck like it did, that first bomb had to land in an area *five feet square*. Two feet forward or aft and it would have hit an I-beam and exploded right there. Just two feet, Padre—twenty-four inches. That's the difference between a small flight deck explosion and seven hours of horror where men died in every way imaginable—burning, electrocution, asphyxiation, hanging, even drowning."

"Are you saying that *Franklin* was destined for misfortune—like many people say the Titanic was, Lieutenant?" Sandy asked.

"Yeah, I guess I am," Gary replied. "Consider the second bomb. Commander Jurika saw it fall. It didn't come straight down. It came in nearly flat, nearly parallel with the flight deck. Bombs that fall like that usually don't explode."

"Yes, but that one did," Fonz said.

"No, it didn't, Fonz. At least it didn't explode on *impact*. It hit the flight deck and *ricocheted* into the Corsairs waiting to take off. Even then, it might not have exploded. It exploded because it collided with a propeller."

Gary paused and looked at John.

"How many times have you seen bombs ricochet like that—then skip right off the deck into the ocean, Gunner?"

"A lot more than once, Lieutenant." John replied.

O'Callahan sat very still, running his finger around the edge of his glass. "A jinx is still hard to accept, Don," he finally said.

"But Padre," Gary countered. "Let's look at the facts. A Fleet Carrier, in a full state of readiness, suffered all that damage from just *two* bombs. A destroyer can take three times that many bombs and survive."

O'Callahan didn't respond. Instead, seeming deep in thought, he continued to run his forefinger around the edge of his glass.

"It's the timing and accuracy of it all that bothers me, Padre," Gary continued, his manner and voice now almost apologetic. "That wasn't precision bombing, Padre. That Jap pilot didn't aim for that five-foot area of weakness in our flight deck. He was just hoping to get two bombs down on us *anywhere* and get out of there as fast as he could. He didn't plan the ricochet into the prop of a waiting plane either. Something other than that pilot was responsible for that. From my point of view, the *Franklin's* near destruction was *something more* than sheer bad luck. How else could you explain it, Padre?"

O'Callahan looked at Gary and slowly nodded his head. Then he said, "I guess you *can* make a case for a jinx, Don."

"The more I think of what happened, the more I can believe it *was*, Padre," Gary said.

"Well, maybe we'll never know what the real cause was or what the final consequences will be, for that matter. There was unbelievable horror out there. Moving those bodies from the hangar deck was the most repulsive thing I've ever done."

O'Callahan paused, then hesitantly went on. "Men are still having nightmares about what they saw and had to do. I know I am."

John looked at Beckley, who had been noticeably quiet during the entire discussion. "Are you, Beck?" he asked.

Beckley nodded. "Yeah, I am," he said. "Are you?"

John looked cautiously at Sandy. Then he said, "Yeah, I've had 'em, too."

"It may be impossible to understand the why or how of *Franklin's* tragedy," O'Callahan reflected. "Maybe we're trying to understand because we survived. Maybe we somehow feel a little guilty because we lived and others we were close to didn't." He paused a few seconds. "Those who died must now surely know the answer," he said. "But for us, what happened may always remain a mystery—much like the riddle of the Sphinx or the miraculous cures at Lourdes. Maybe we were never meant to have an answer."

Beckley nodded. "Yes," he said slowly. "I think it *will* always be a mystery, Padre. It reminds me of some lines from *Hamlet*. Let's see if I can remember them…

In my heart there was a kind of fighting that would not let me sleep. Methodically I lay there, worse than the bilboes. Rashly, and praised be rashness for it, let us know that our indiscretion sometimes serves us well when our deep plots do pall. That should teach us there is a divinity that shapes our ends, rough-hew them how we will....

"Yes, Chief," O'Callahan said, nodding thoughtfully, "and if I remember my Shakespeare correctly, Horatio responded, *That is most certain, lord.*"

That seemed to bring an end to the discussion. It was dusk and their talk turned to other things; to the impending invasion of Okinawa; to home and families; to how long it would take to repair the *Franklin* and to speculation about the coming invasion of Japan.

Before they realized it, the sun had disappeared behind the palm-tree-lined beaches in the western part of the island and they felt what they'd gathered for was complete. They'd discussed the *Franklin's* disaster; recalled the memories of their dead; gave them their blessings and said their grateful last farewells.

O'Callahan was the first to leave. He rose and walked around the table to John and Sandy. "I understand you're staying here to get another look at that shoulder, John," he said as he shook hands with him. "I'd like to see you again somewhere—maybe back on the *Franklin* when she's fit to sail again." He paused and smiled. "You're the best acolyte I've ever had."

Then he hugged Sandy and said, "You take care of him and yourself. Be sure you both write to me."

"We will, Father," she replied, her eyes filled with tears.

He shook hands with Ski. "Take care of that leg, sailor."

"I'll see you guys back aboard," he said to Gary and Fonz and then, after a half salute, he walked through the bar and out into the night.

Soon Fonz and Gary said their farewells and headed for the door. They turned and waved when they reached it. Then they were gone, too.

"What great guys," Ski said. "Think we'll ever seem 'em again?"

"I don't know, but I sure hope so," John replied. He paused, then said sadly, "How can you ever know? Scuttlebutt is that the *Franklin's* crew will be broken up and reassigned. It'll be a long time before she's ready for combat again and the Navy's still turning out a carrier a month—they'll all need crews."

"Yeah, and we know how that works," Ski replied. "They transfer you from one ship to another at the blink of an eye—it makes it tough to keep in touch with old friends."

"Well, *you're* going to write us, aren't you?" Sandy asked, pointing her index finger at him.

"If he doesn't, I'll personally hunt him down and choke him," John said as they got up and headed for the door.

"You don't have to worry about that, Sandy," Ski said. "No matter what, you guys got me. I'm your friend for the rest of my life."

"You'd better be," John said. He put his arm on Ski's shoulder and they walked into the balmy Hawaiian night.

"You couldn't get rid of me if you tried, Gunner," Ski said as they went.

"Let's try to get together and see the ship leave. We can make our plans after that," John said.

"Right, I'd like that," Ski called back, as he hobbled to catch a bus back to Pearl Harbor.

When he boarded the bus, John and Sandy were alone for the first time in the long, emotional day. Their feelings were a mix of both happiness and sadness—sadness because of the memories and pain the evening's conversations brought—and because they had just parted with faithful, genuine friends. Happiness because they had each other. John put his arms around Sandy and hugged her. She hugged him back. They stood there silently under the starry Hawaiian sky for a long while, finding relief from their sadness in closeness. Then John kissed Sandy, tenderly, affectionately. Sandy kissed him back with equal ardor and affection. A balmy trade wind gently ruffled the palm leaves. They walked slowly into the beautiful Hawaiian night, headed for the small apartment Sandy had rented, feeling both blessed and enchanted that they were together again.

4 April, 1945
Pearl Harbor
***USS Santa Fe* Stands Out**

The sun rose at 05:58 to start a beautiful tropical day. Birds were tweeting in the vegetation that lined the area behind the dock. The pungent aroma of tropical flowers filled the balmy, clear air. Gehres, Taylor and Jurika were on the bridge to oversee the *Franklin* taking on fuel in preparation for her voyage to the East Coast.

"There comes the Oiler, Captain," Taylor said, pointing past the wreckage of the *Arizona*.

Gehres shaded his eyes. "Yep. That's our fuel supply. Make preparations for taking on fuel," he ordered. Then he said, "Joe, *Santa Fe*'s leaving this morning. I want every man we can possibly spare to stand at quarters as she goes by."

At 09:30 nearly four hundred of *Franklin*'s crewmen were standing at quarters on what remained of the flight deck. *Santa Fe* steamed slowly by.

"Attention! Hand Salute!" Gehres commanded. The crew snapped to a salute. It was the highest possible honor Gehres could send under the circumstances.

"Front!" Gehres said. The salutes came down in unison.

"At ease," Gehres said. Then he turned and began to wave. The crew followed his lead and the crew of *Santa Fe* waved back. *Santa Fe* steamed past *Franklin*'s starboard side. She changed course to conform to harbor conditions. In a few minutes she was out of sight.

That afternoon, preparations for getting underway quickened and lasted through the next day. Yard workmen scoured *Franklin*'s hangar and flight decks with power saws, crowbars and cutting torches. They cut and bundled huge loads of twisted metal and warped I-beams. Huge cranes came alongside on the port quarter and lifted them into trucks waiting on the dock below.

These activities continued throughout the next two days. Workmen removed two battered sponsons and their 40-mm mounts from the starboard side. Two generators were taken apart and repaired. New searchlights equipped with shutters for sending semaphore were bolted in place. Large quantities of food supplies were hauled up the gangway and deposited in newly cleared spaces on the hangar deck. Fleet Oiler 85 came alongside to finish delivering fuel. Workmen in a cranny on the hanger deck discovered the remains of Aviation Ordinance Man First Class Don Marion, who was killed in action on that fatal day. His remains were transferred ashore for proper burial.

On 5 April, all preparations for getting underway were complete. *Franklin* would leave at 09:30 the next morning for the Panama Canal, with her final destination Brooklyn Navy Yard, New York City.

6 April, 1945
Departure to the Panama Canal
Going Home!

The next morning Beckley and O'Callahan stood on the forecastle as the *Franklin* readied to cast off. It was a beautiful day. The ocean was calm as far as the eye could see and a gentle, warm wind circulated through the ship.

"Were you able to get Sandy and John by phone yesterday?" O'Callahan asked.

"Yeah, Padre, I did," Beckley replied. "They said they'd be here about 09:30 and they'd bring Ski."

O'Callahan shaded his eyes with the information guide he'd been reading and looked down the dock. "I don't see any of them yet."

He handed Beckley the *Franklin's Daily Information Guide*, now being printed on a new small press brought aboard two days earlier. "The invasion of Okinawa started a few days ago," he said.

Beckley took the paper and read the article. "They sure threw a lot of manpower at the Japs. The First, Sixth and Seventh Marine Divisions and the Ninety-Sixth Infantry Division," he said. "That's a ton of combat troops."

"Yes it is, Chief. Paper says the shore bombardment was one of the biggest and longest of the war, too."

Beckley handed the paper to O'Callahan. "It says casualties on both sides were high, sir," he said. "I wonder how many men the Japs lost?"

"Probably a lot. They'll defend that island with everything they've got."

Two tugboats assigned to *Franklin* chugged next to her starboard side, ready to help her get underway.

The *Franklin's* engines, now restored to near full capacity, sent waves of power vibrating through the ship as she prepared to pull away from the dock.

"Cast off the bow line."

"Cast off the stern line."

Just as these commands came over the loudspeaker, Beckley spotted Sandy, John and Ski hurrying down the dock.

"There they are, Padre," he said pointing.

They both began to wave.

John, Sandy and Ski waved back.

When they got within shouting distance, John yelled, "Ahoy! You're about to get underway!"

"Yes," Beckley yelled back over the engine noise.

"What about the shoulder?" O'Callahan asked.

"It's going to be fine, Father. Good as new the next time I see you."

"Don't forget to write," Beckley shouted over the increasing engine noise.

"Write to both of us," O'Callahan yelled.

"We will, Father. Don't you guys forget to answer!" John shouted back.

"Good-bye, Father," Sandy called up to O'Callahan. "Be sure not to forget us!"

"We won't," O'Callahan shouted back. "God bless you Sandy. God bless you John—Ski—take care of yourselves."

"Now cast off all lines!" There was a flurry of activity and, with none of the fanfare of a few days earlier, the battered *Franklin* got underway.

Beckley and O'Callahan waved.

John, Sandy and Ski waved back

In a few minutes *Franklin* was steaming through the harbor headed toward the Pacific.

O'Callahan and Beckley watched as Sandy, John and Ski, who were still waving, faded into the distance.

"What great young people," Beckley said.

"Yes. A wonderful young couple," O'Callahan replied.

8 April, 1945
***Franklin* Steams SSE**
Final Destination: Brooklyn Navy Yard

As *Franklin* steamed Southeast toward the Panama Canal, the weather became warmer. Balmy breezes wafted through the gaping holes in the bulkheads making them seem less onerous and a little easier to endure.

After standing the four-to-eight watch, Beckley looked out over the calm waters of the Pacific. What a beautiful, peaceful day, he thought. It's hard to believe that just three weeks ago we were fighting for our lives. He walked down to the mess hall and saw Father O'Callahan having a cup of coffee. O'Callahan was reading a copy of the *Franklin's Daily Information Guide*.

"What's the news, Padre?" Beckley asked as he sat down beside him.

"We sank the *Yamato*," O'Callahan replied. "Sank her with air power. Air strikes from carriers in the Fifth Fleet and the British Pacific Fleet."

"She was the last big one," Beckley replied. "Eighteen-inch guns that could fire a projectile over twenty-five miles—I'm glad we never had to tangle with her."

"Paper says she was steaming to attack the invasion forces on Okinawa," O'Callahan said. "It took nearly four hundred and fifty bombers and torpedo planes to sink her. She finally went down after five hours of continuous bombing and torpedo attacks—took all but a handful of her crew with her."

"What's the other news?"

"There was a huge kamikaze attack on the Fifth Fleet," O'Callahan replied. "Over six hundred Jap planes—they attacked southeast of Okinawa."

Beckley's eyes widened. "Really? That's the biggest kamikaze attack I ever heard of."

"Paper says it's the largest one of the war. They crashed three carriers, *Bunker Hill, Enterprise* and *Hancock*, but it says they were only slightly damaged."

"How many kamikaze did we get?"

"They shot down over three hundred in two attacks," O'Callahan said. "The fighting on Okinawa is still heavy. After seven days of combat, marines and infantrymen just reached the three-mile waist of the island."

"Gee, that's heavy fighting. That isn't very far from shore," Beckley said.

"That's right, but listen to this," O'Callahan said as he adjusted his spectacles and read from the information guide. "For the first time, American authorities have been confronted by the sobering fact that civilians on Okinawa were throwing their bodies into the fighting in kamikaze fashion. According to Major General Roy Geiger, USMC, Commander of Amphibious Corps III, 'the capture of Okinawa will be the same as the conquest of all of the islands in the Japanese Empire. It will be fought island by island, town by town, house by house, door by door, yard by yard, man to man.'"

"Yes, it's going to be very rugged the rest of the way, Padre," Beckley said.

"Yeah, and it could be even worse than anyone thought," O'Callahan replied. "They think the Japanese war lords will use their whole population as 'human kamikaze' to defend Japan."

"What a horrible prospect," Beckley replied. "Can you imagine invasion forces confronted on beaches by tidal waves of civilians carrying knives, guns and grenades?"

"That's hard to imagine, Chief. But it looks like our only option is a full scale invasion," O'Callahan replied. "It's a terrible thought. I pray that somehow, something will happen to end the terrible killing on both sides."

Franklin steamed on. On 15 April she moored in Pier 16, Balboa, Canal Zone, alongside the *USS Topeka* and *USS Oklahoma City*. The next morning at 09:41, with canal pilot Captain Larry Ferguson at the conn and Gehres, Taylor and Jurika on station, *Franklin* came through the last lock and moored at Colon, Canal Zone, port side to Pier 9. On Sunday, 22 April, she headed North Northeast on course 042° for New York harbor. She arrived off of Gravesend Bay, New York on 26 April and two days later moved to the Brooklyn Navy Yard. She thus ended her journey of over thirteen thousand miles from the Sea of Japan.

#

While *Franklin* was being repaired her crew moved into barracks ashore and prepared to go on leave. While most of the *Franklin's* crew was on leave, the Navy Department gave the media the go-ahead to publish photographs and accounts of *Franklin's* gallant struggle. In the last week in May, *Time* magazine published a detailed narrative of her heroic efforts. During the same week an article by Ralph Wheeler of *Life* magazine featured photographs of the *Franklin's* efforts to save herself from Japanese bombs and from her own exploding bombs and missiles. Father O'Callahan, John Oxler and Don Gary's heroic actions were prominently detailed in these articles. Pictures of O'Callahan ministering to the gravely wounded sailor[1] as a missile zoomed over his head—taken by the battle photographer on *Franklin's* flight deck that near-fatal day– and photos of John Oxler's valorous gun crew defending the battered *Franklin* were also featured. The articles appeared in newspapers and magazines all over the country and in many newspapers throughout the world. The heroism of the *Franklin's* intrepid crew was thus duly acknowledged and recounted.

On 15 August, while *Franklin* was still undergoing repairs, the war came to a dramatic, climactic end. Two powerful new weapons, atomic bombs, thousands and thousands of times more powerful than humans had ever seen before, were dropped on Hiroshima and Nagasaki by B-29 Superforts flying from bases on Tinian in the Marianas. After the second bomb virtually destroyed Nagasaki, Emperor Hirohito accepted the terms of unconditional surrender demanded by the Allied Powers through an emissary in Switzerland, and on 2 September, the documents of Unconditional Surrenders were signed aboard the *USS Missouri*. The bitter, bloody war in the Pacific had finally ended.

---

[1] The wounded sailor survived. His name is Robert C. Blanchard (YM 3C). He lives in Barnegat, New Jersey.

World Battlefronts

TIME May, 28, 1945

Warrior's Ordeal

One of our ships was seriously damaged and is returning to port under her own power—Pacific Fleet Communique 305, March 21, 1945.

Last week the Navy let the rest of the story be told:

It was March 19. Fifty miles off the coast of Japan, Task Force 58 was launching an air assault against Shikoku and Kyushu when a Jap bomber dropped out of the low overcast, rocketed in over the bow of the 27,000-ton carrier *Franklin* ("Big Ben") and swept the length of her flight deck. Not until too late did antiaircraft crews get their guns on the raider. From the Jap's belly two 500-lb. bombs plummeted down.

Afterward men remembered their moments of preoccupation just before the disaster. The first of the *Franklin's* planes had taken off; on her flight deck were Hellcats, Helldivers and Corsairs, weighed down with full loads of bombs and rockets, engines thunderously turning over. On the hangar deck more armed and laden Helldivers were warming up, awaiting their turn on the elevators. Below, a crowd of enlisted men were lined up for morning chow. On the fantail a little group of men had just turned away from burying a sailor who was killed by a propeller, the day before. On the bridge men scanned the skies with glasses. It was 7 minuted past 7 in the dull dawn.

The first bomb hit near the bridge. The second smashed through the flight deck amidst the parked planes. The explosions rolled into one tremendous detonation.

"Big Ben." Ablaze & Listing
The skipper was stubborn, the ship was staunch.

The Holocaust. Commander Robert Downes, damage control officer, had just left his cabin. Concussion hurled him back through the closed door and up against the outer bulkhead. The forward elevator weighing 32 tons, popped up from the flight deck, its plungers blown from their sockets. In a control room in the towering island structure, Lieut. William Simon was flung against the overhead. He came to and managed to crawl through a door. Simon was one of three men to escape; 30 died inside. On the gallery deck men were trapped inside jammed doors and baked to death by the breath of fire which reached 900F in their sealed compartments.

Fire engulfed the planes, shot up and swept the fantail, from which men jumped or were flicked overboard. On the hangar deck, now a roaring furnace, pilots blundered into still whirling plane propellers, climbed frantically up the folded wings. Later some were found hanging like black, charred monkeys, caught in the overhead structure. The sailors who had lined up for breakfast died with empty bellies.

All the *Franklin's* volatile cargo—40,000 gallons of aviation fuel, .50 caliber, 20-mm and 40-mm ammunition, armor-piercing and incendiary bombs—began to explode. Rockets whooshed through the air. Livid white flashes tore the smoke. Gasoline gushing from open lines flowed across the decks, carrying fire four decks below, cascaded over the side and set the sea ablaze.

Captain's Decision. Smoke enveloped the bridge, but there men had at least had moments for decisions. From the screen of cruisers and destroyers spread across the sea, ships were rushing to the *Franklin's* aid. One of them was the destroyer *Miller*, which nosed in recklessly, turning her inadequate hoses on the fires. Rear Admiral Ralph E. Davison, commander of the *Franklin's* division, decided to transfer his flag and get on with the war. With Rear Admiral Gerald F. Bogan, aboard as an observer, he climbed down to the *Miller*. But the Big Ben's Captain Leslie Gehres decided that his ship might be saved.

To stay meant risking the lives of those who could still get off; to abandon her meant that many men, trapped below, would surely die. Gehres, a stubborn man, 49 years old and the only carrier skipper in the U.S. Navy who had come up through the ranks, determined to stay.

It looked bad. All inner communications were gone. Only 29 of Downes's 118-man damage-control crew were still alive. Volunteers were dazedly fighting fire. As soon as streams of water were turned away, the glowing planes again burst ablaze. The best men could do was try to hold the fire. The engine room was still working but rapidly growing too hot for the crew. Gehres ordered the engines set at eight knots and told the men to come topside.

Panic & Heroism. Above and below deck men stood transfixed with fear and scattered in panic at each new explosion. There were also many who did their jobs with quiet heroism. One of them was Lieut. (j.g.) Donald A. Gary, a veteran of 20 years in the Navy who, like his skipper, had come up from the ranks. Four times Gary went down through a ventilating shaft to lead 300 men to safety.

Bespectacled Liet. Commander Joseph Timothy O'Callahan, Jesuit priest and senior chaplain, ministered to the dying, manned fire hoses, helped jettison ammunition, even led rescue parties below.

Another strong man that afternoon was not aboard the *Franklin*. He was Captain Harold C. Fitz of the cruiser *Santa Fe*, who came alongside and asked one question: "Are your magazines flooded?" When the answer came back "yes," he brought his ship in close enough to put lines across.

The wounded and the men of the Air Group — those who were left — were being transferred when an after 5-in. magazine let go. Flame and smoke shot 7,000 feet in the air; human bodies pinwheeled through the air. Chunks of armor plate were tossed aloft like leaves; airplane engines hurtled heavenward.

The *Franklin's* untended engines failed, leaving her dead in the water and unmanageable. Fitz pulled away, circled, and with magnificent seamanship brought his ship hard up against the carrier's smoking hulk, so they could grapple and control her until they finished the job. More than the wounded scrambled over the side. In the confusion some men thought the order to abandon ship had been given; a few were too terrified to care. Tough Gehres finally told Fitz to stand clear, he wanted to keep his crew aboard.

South from Kyushu, Jap planes buzzed out of the overcast. Escorting warships deployed around the dead *Franklin*, fought them off and fought the *Franklin's* fires. It was now past noon. The *Franklin* was still belching smoke and beginning to list heavily when the cruiser *Pittsburgh* finally succeeded in taking her in tow. At two knots the convoy started crawling away from the shores of Japan, the *Franklin* yawing and staggering in her agony. Men went to work to correct her 13 degree list. Hydraulic controls from counter-flooding were out, but Downes and his men put on rescue breathers and groped their way below to the hand valves. Gradually Big Ben regained an even keel.

Trapped men were still being hauled out. At the first muster that evening only 250 fit men and 75 officers had turned up. Two days later more than 600 men and 100 officers were able to answer roll. In the chief petty officers' quarters, rescuers found a mess cook who, with half of one foot severed, in water up to his armpits, had managed to stay alive for three days.

The fires slowly burned themselves out. About 9 o'clock the first night, men were able to get into the engine room and light one boiler. As the hours went by, the other vital functions were restored — water pumps, communications, ventilation, power. By noon of March 20, four boilers were lighted and the *Pittsburgh* cast off. The crippled *Franklin* was able to make 14 knots under her own power. By the second day, still convoyed by cruisers and destroyers, which again and again had to fight off Jap planes, she was making a steady 20 knots.

Stench of Death. Men began to come out of the numbed state in which, by instinct, they had performed their heroic deeds. The implacable Gehres gave them no rest. The hangar deck, where the worst fires had raged, was a nightmare of crushed planes, ruptured bulkheads, melted debris, burned and shattered bodies. Men had died by burning, by drowning in flooded compartments, by concussion, by electrocution, by hanging, by asphyxiation. Their shipmates cut away the wreckage to get at hundreds of bodies, hauled them out and consigned them to the sea. The stench of death pervaded the passageways. Weeks later parts of men were still being discovered. From sunup to sundown, to save them from insanity, Gehres drove his crew.

On March 24, the proud and shattered ship steamed into a fleet base in the Western Pacific, rested briefly in that haven and headed for Pearl Harbor and the long voyage home.

The 704 men who had stayed with her — out of an original total complement of more than 3,000 — still manned her. Gehres would allow no one else aboard. He issued beer. An octet of Negro messmen and other talent, with a band of pots & pans, an accordion and coronet, put on a pathetic and courageous show •— "The *Franklin* Frolics." For four days they rested in Pearl Harbor, then sailed on for Panama. On April 26 — after 38 days and 13,400 miles — they dropped anchor at last in New York's Gravesend Bay.

Last week the charred hulk of the *Franklin* lay in Brooklyn Navy Yard. Whole sections of her were gone; it would be a long time before she fought again. By official count, 832 of her men were dead or missing, 270 had been wounded. In all naval history, few warships had taken such punishment; perhaps none had ever suffered so and come home.

© 1945 TIME INC.
REPRINTED BY PERMISSION

LIFE

May, 1945

© 1945 TIME INC. REPRINTED BY PERMISSION

THE CARRIER "FRANKLIN" REFUSES TO GO DOWN

A heroic crew saves her from her own and Jap bombs

At 0707 hours on March 19 some 60 miles off Japan, a Jap "Judy" streaked down out of a low cumulus cloud. Apparently the pilot had been cruising above the clouds diving periodically in the hope of coming on something. This time he found something: the middle of a carrier group from U.S. Task Force 58. Ahead of him lay a 27,000-ton carrier. Instantly he let go two bombs. They struck fore and aft directly down the center of the carrier *U.S.S. Franklin*. Men on deck pinwheeled through the air. Flame flared from the forward elevator. Fire crackled below the flight deck. Profanely the crew leaped for hoses. Seconds later the Judy was shot into the sea by a vengeful *Franklin* pilot already in the air.

The initial blasts were bad enough but the worst was yet to come. Forty-five planes were on deck, loaded with gas, bombs and rockets when the attack came. These began to blow up in a series of explosions which were not to end for five hellish hours. As they caught fire, planes discharged their rockets waist high across the deck. Meanwhile spreading flames ignited stores of oil, bombs, ammunition boxes. The flight deck turned cherry red. Men leaped or were hurled into the sea. So were planes, some of their bombs detonated, killing all the swimmers around them. In the hangar deck, tracer bullets streaked pinkishly through the smoky gloom. Bodies littered its floor. Black smoke, so thick men felt drowned rather than suffocated by it, flooded the ship. In all over 100 large bombs exploded.

Burly Captain Leslie E. Gehres refused to abandon his first carrier command. Smoke enveloped the bridge, blasts shook it. All but one communication line were severed. But until the untended boilers' fires went out, the helmsman steered his course, the navigator regularly reported her position, the quartermaster coolly logged each order and explosion as it came. The Jesuit chaplain, Lieut. Commander Joseph O'Callahan, fought fires, administered extreme unction, tossed scaring hot ammunition into the sea. Lieut. Donald Gary repeatedly descended into the ship's perilous bowels to lead out groups of the 300 men entombed there. While a chamber above them filled with water, five crew members remained in the aft steering compartment to steer the ship and relay messages. They were rescued after 18 hours.

After she was towed through the night the *Franklin's* boiler fires were rekindled and she started the 15,000-mile trip to the Brooklyn Navy Yard where she is now being refitted. Of a crew more than 2,500 she had lost 832 killed and missing, 270 wounded. But on the way back men were able to assemble an "orchestra" (ocarina, tub, slide whistle and guitar) under musician I/C Saxie Dowell, peacetime author of *Three Little Fishies*. They played songs they made up about the bombing, including one by Captain Gehres himself, entitled: "In One Day We Lived Six Long Months."

Footing becomes slippery on *Franklin's* flight deck for men waiting to take their turn manning fire hoses.

One of the explosions thtat tore the ship for hours hurled a plane engine (center) into the air. Explosions roared continuously, yet later the wearied crew could not recall hearing anything.

Five-inch gun mount blazes fiercely. Molten steel rivueted the deck and melting plane motors welded themselves to it. No other ship in modern times has survived such a holocust.

EPILOGUE

27 October, 1945
Brooklyn Navy Yard
Honors and Awards

On Navy Day, just eight weeks after the Japanese officially surrendered, thousands of visitors inspected the fully restored *Franklin* in the Brooklyn Navy Yard. The next day there was a historic ceremony. On this bright autumn morning, the *Franklin*'s crew reassembled on her new flight deck.

Many distinguished guests were in attendance. Father O'Callahan and Don Gary were there, each was wearing his Congressional Medal of Honor. They'd received their Medals of Honor from President Harry Truman in a special ceremony held in their honor at the White House a few weeks earlier. Several Senators and Members of the House of Representatives were in attendance as special emissaries of the President along with Admirals Spruance, Mitscher, and Burke who represented Admiral Nimitz and the Fifth Fleet.

Many of the relatives and friends of *Franklin*'s crew were there. Sandy, now a radiant expectant mother in the fifth month of her pregnancy, was there. Sandy's parents, Mark and Louise, and her brother Robert, home from the fighting in Europe, were present, as were John's family, Helen, Elena and James. Father O'Callahan's aging mother and his sister Alice sat next to them. Beckley's wife and family and Ski's mother and father were there. Don Gary's family was in the gathering, as were Fonz's wife and children, and many of the families of the three hundred and ninety-one men who would receive medals and Special Letters of Commendation.

Nineteen men would be awarded the Navy Cross, the Navy's highest award and twenty-two would receive the Silver Star Citation, the Navy's second highest award. One hundred and fourteen Bronze Star Citations, and two hundred and thirty-four Special Letters of Commendation would be awarded. It was a historic ceremony for a gallant ship and her crew.

Admiral Joseph "Jocko" Clark was especially chosen by President Truman and Admiral Nimitz to preside over the ceremonies. This respected Admiral would confer the awards and citations.

"It is a great honor," Clark began, "to have been selected to present these richly deserved awards and citations to the officers and men of the *USS Franklin*. He paused and looked over the gathering. "I know they are deserved," he said, "because I was there. I saw many of the acts of courage and sacrifice of this intrepid crew. I watched their monumental efforts to save their wounded ship and I can report to you and to the nation that, on those fateful days in March, the gods of heroism and valor ruled the day. Exceptional bravery was a common virtue. Cowardice and fear were outcasts—they were nowhere to be seen. While there was suffering and death that we as a nation will be eternally sorry and grateful for, there was also great heroism; acts and deeds that will be forever honored as a part of the tradition of the United States Navy."

He paused and took a sip of water. "How can we describe such acts and deeds?" he asked. "It's difficult to put them into words. If I were to describe them I would have to use words like 'heroic achievements, fearlessness under great adversity, bravery, valor, duty'—and these words would still not be enough. Today, as we pause to honor the courage of the officers and men of the *USS Franklin*, we also honor every other sailor, marine and airman who participated in the *Franklin*'s defense. This is especially a tribute to the *USS Santa Fe,* whose captain and crew risked their lives in bold and daring actions on that horror-filled day. I am pleased to announce that *Santa Fe* and her crew have been awarded the Navy Unit Citation for their heroic actions."

"The Congressional Medal of Honor," he continued after the applause faded, "is awarded by the President in the name of the Congress of the United States, for 'risk of life while engaged in an action against an enemy of the United States of America.' The deed or deeds performed must include personal bravery that involved risk to individual life. They must distinguish the recipient for 'bravery above and beyond the call of duty.' I'm honored today to introduce two members of *Franklin's* crew who were awarded this medal just four weeks ago by the President of the United States at the White House. It is my privilege to ask Lieutenant Commander Joseph T. O'Callahan and Lieutenant Junior Grade Donald Gary to come forward."

O'Callahan and Gary stood and came forward.

Clark presented each with a special written citation outlining their unique acts of bravery. Then he added his personal congratulations.

There was thunderous applause. John looked at Sandy. She was standing and applauding vigorously. He looked over to Father O'Callahan's mother and sister, sitting a few seats away. They were clapping and beaming. He thought of O'Callahan kneeling on that burning flight deck giving comfort and the last rites, while bombs exploded, missiles zoomed over his head and fires raged around him with ever-increasing fury. What great courage and compassion—what a great priest and brave man....

Clark continued. "Today we will award the Navy Cross to nineteen men in *Franklin's* crew. Next to the Medal of Honor, it is the Navy's highest citation. It is awarded for 'extraordinary heroism in the presence of great danger and great personal risk to life.'" He turned and nodded to his aide, Captain David Foder, who announced, "Will the following men please come forward:

Captain Leslie E. Gehres, Commander Joseph Taylor, Commander Stephen Jurika, Commander Henry Hale."

Then he intoned the names of Commander Thomas Greene, Doctors Sam Sherman, George William Fox,[2] Jim Fuelling, Lieutenant Fred Harris and eight other officers. Finally, Gunner's Mate First Class John R. Oxler's name was announced.

---

[2] Awarded posthumously. Dr. Fox died a hero's death at his post on *Franklin* on March 19, 1945.

When they assembled before the podium, Clark stepped down and presented the first Navy Cross Award to Les Gehres. He had a huge smile on his face when he did. "I knew you could do it, Les," he said. "Congratulations! You did a great job."

"Thank you, sir." Gehres replied.

Clark went from man to man, presenting each a Navy Cross and congratulating each with warm personal praise. When he came to John, he said, "Congratulations, Gunner. Your Captain and Executive Officer told me of your courageous actions. They asked me to tell you that this award is richly deserved."

"Thank you, sir." John was awash with pride and joy. He was proud of what Admiral Clark just said and happy because his wife and whole family were watching. The war was over, he and the woman he loved were together again, and they would soon have a child to add to their bliss.

The group turned and started back to their seats. The flight deck resonated with applause.

Sandy was standing. Tears of joy rolled down her cheeks. She turned to her mother and put her arms around her. "I'm so proud of John," she said, "and I love him more than anyone can ever know."

Admiral Clark continued the presentations. "The Silver Star Citation," he said, "can be awarded to any person in any branch of the service who is cited for gallantry in action against an enemy of the United States. In the Navy it's awarded to an individual who, while engaged in military operations involving conflict, distinguishes himself by gallantry and intrepidity in action. This morning it is a great honor to award the Silver Star to twenty-two members of the *Franklin*'s crew."

Captain Fodor again announced the names of the recipients. Chief Petty Officer Richard D. Beckley was among them.

As he watched Beckley receive the Silver Star, John's thoughts flashed back to the first time he met Beckley. He was a bewildered Seaman Second Class from a land-locked state going aboard a huge warship for the first time. He warmly remembered Beckley's welcoming remarks to him and the rest of the "boots" who had just boarded the *Lexington*...and how Beckley helped him survive her sinking. He thought of how his respect and their friendship had deepened aboard *Franklin* and smiled at his feeling that sometimes Beckley still thought of him as that "skinny-ass" seaman he met aboard the *Lex*. Next to his father, he respected Beckley more than any man he'd ever met.

The last Silver Star was awarded. There was another long round of applause. Beckley returned to his seat next to John. After he sat down, he reached over and shook John's hand.

"Congratulations, Gunner," he said.

"Gunner? You never called me *Gunner* before, Beck," John said.

"Hummm, I guess that's right," Beckley replied. Then he smiled broadly. "Seems like before I fully realized it, that skinny, scared seaman I met aboard the *Lex* slipped up on me and became a hero! Congratulations again, Gunner."

"Thanks, Beck," John said.

EPILOGUE

The ceremonies went on. "The Bronze Star is a citation awarded to an individual in any branch of the military services who has distinguished himself by heroic acts, meritorious achievement or distinguished service. Today we will honor one hundred and fourteen men with this award." Chief Petty Officer Alphonso Frasure was called. Seamen First Class Charles Bonin, Elmer Colson, Ramon Garcia and James Jardin were also called.

John watched as Frasure stepped to the podium to receive his Bronze Star. What a good man and trusted friend...the war was over now and everyone was going his separate way. This was probably the last time he'd see Frasure. He'd miss him...he'd miss him a lot....

When Jardin stepped forward to receive his citation, John felt a warm glow of pride and happiness. Less than eight months ago, Jardin was so troubled and frightened he'd been ready to drown himself...now he was about to receive the Bronze Star. A picture of that morning on the forecastle when Jardin volunteered to help flood the *Franklin*'s forward magazine flashed through his mind. What great courage! What an amazing turnabout for a kid who hadn't yet reached his nineteenth birthday....

Captain Fodor read the names of the two hundred and thirty-four men who would be awarded Special Letters of Commendation. Gunner's Mate Third Class Stanislau Kwatkowski was among them. Ski smiled and winked at John as he walked back down the aisle after receiving his Citation. John smiled back and flashed a little half salute. The one and only Ski...golly, would he miss him...he'd miss all the guys, Beckley, Frasure, Garcia, Bonin, Colson...everyone that survived...and all those that didn't, too...in a few, short, danger-filled months, he had come to feel as close to them as brothers....

"To conclude this ceremony," Clark announced, "*Franklin* earned four battle stars on the Asiatic-Pacific Service ribbon for participation in the following operations: The Marianas Operation, 1944; the Third Bonin raid, 1944; the Capture of Guam, 1944 and the Okinawa-Japan operation March, 1945."

On this beautiful October morning, the officers and men of the *USS Franklin*, "the ship that would not sink," received the greatest number of citations ever awarded one ship in the history of the United States Navy. They'd done their duty. They'd taken every blow a strange and capricious fate had thrown at them. They'd persevered and they'd overcome. They saved their ship and won their victory. Tears came into the eyes of many of these strong, proud men as the ceremony ended and they came to attention. They were sailors—in the victorious United States Navy—the greatest Navy the world had ever known.

THE *USS SANTA FE*

The damaged *Santa Fe* required extensive repair. She entered the US Naval Shipyard at San Pedro, California on the 10th of April and remained there until July 12th. After she was refitted, she sailed from San Pedro to Pearl Harbor and on twelfth of August, three days before the end of the war, she steamed with the carrier *Antietam* and the cruiser *Birmingham* to attack Wake Island. The raid was canceled when Japan surrendered, and on the 2nd of September, *Santa Fe* was ordered to Sasebo, Japan, where she assisted in the occupation of Honshu and Hokkaido. On the 10th of November she was assigned to "Magic Carpet" duty, returning troops home from Saipan, Guam and Truk, before arriving in Puget Sound in January, 1946. It was at this time that the author, while serving as Gunners Mate Third Class aboard the *USS Altamaha* (CVE18), spotted *Santa Fe* and contacted a boyhood friend, Thomas Paulovich, who had been aboard *Santa Fe* for three years. Sometime in early February, 1946, the author had the great pleasure of boarding and spending the afternoon on *Santa Fe* as Paulovich's guest. From the details learned that afternoon, over half a lifetime ago, and from a life-long love of the United States Navy, came the inspiration to write this book.

Santa Fe received thirteen battle stars for her service during World War II. For her crew's heroism during the defense and rescue of the Franklin in March of 1945, she was awarded a Navy Unit Commendation.[3] *Santa Fe* was decommissioned on the 19th of October, 1946, and attached to the Bremerton Group, United States Pacific Reserve Fleet.

---

[3] The Navy Unit Commendation was established by the Secretary of the Navy on December 18, 1944 and is awarded by the Secretary with the approval of the President. This Unit Commendation is conferred on a ship, detachment, or other unit of the Navy or Marine Corps which, subsequent to December 6, 1941, "distinguishes itself by outstanding heroism against the enemy." It is also awarded for "extremely meritorious service not involving combat but in support of military operations that were outstanding when compared to other units performing similar service."

SHIPMATE ACKNOWLEDGMENT

In this novel the reader finds the names of Richard Beckley, Peter Sullivan, Stan Kwatkowski, Al Lowe, Andre Belasco and many others. Although these are the names of characters in the novel, they were also real people—they were some of my shipmates. I am sure, however, that along with the many heroes who *actually* served on the *USS Franklin,* whose intrepid actions are depicted in the story, they treasure the memory of this great time in the history of the United States.

Finally, I would like to honor some of my shipmates on the *USS Altamaha, CVE 18*. Here is a salute to Richard Beckley, Stan Kwatkowski, Al Lowe, Andre Belasco, Bob Webber, Alvin Little, Tom Tedesco, Monte "Monk" Lewis, Robert Gruenfelder, Vernon Doak, Clarance Alley, Robert Cassole…my memory dims…. If I omitted others of you, I want you all to know that your friendship has become more and more important to me as the years have passed. Without your friendship and camaraderie, this book could never have been written. So wherever you are now, and whatever you are doing, I'd like to tell you I honor you. I hope some day, somewhere, we'll all meet again.

APPENDIX

Citations Accompanying Medal Awards

Congressional Medal of Honor Award to Lieutenant Commander Joseph T. O'Callahan, S.J., Chaplain *U.S.S. Franklin, CV 13.*

For conspicuous gallantry and intrepidity at the risk of his life above and beyond the call of duty while serving as Chaplain on board the U.S.S Franklin when the vessel was fiercely attacked by enemy Japanese aircraft during offensive operations near Kobe, Japan, on 19 March 1945. A valiant and forceful leader, calmly braving the perilous barriers of flame and twisted metal to aid his men and his ship, Lieutenant Commander O'Callahan groped his way through smoke-filled corridors to the flight deck and into the midst of violently exploding bombs, shells, rockets and other armament. With the ship rocked by incessant explosions, with debris and fragments raining down and fires raging in ever increasing fury, he ministered to the wounded and dying, comforting and encouraging men of all faiths; he organized and led fire-fighting crews into the blazing inferno on the flight deck; he directed the jettisoning of live ammunition and the flooding of the magazine; he manned a hose to cool hot, armed bombs rolling dangerously on the listing deck, continuing his efforts despite searing, suffocating smoke which forced men to fall back gasping, and imperiled others who replaced them. Serving with courage, fortitude and deep spiritual strength, Lieutenant Commander O'Callahan inspired the gallant officers and men of the Franklin to fight heroically and with profound faith in the face of almost certain death and return their stricken ship to port.

Congressional Medal of Honor Award to Lieutenant Donald A. Gary, Engineering Officer, *U.S.S. Franklin, CV 13.*

For conspicuous gallantry and intrepidity at the risk of his life above and beyond the call of duty as an Engineering Officer attached to the U.S. Franklin when that vessel was fiercely attached by enemy aircraft during operations against the Japanese Home Islands near Kobe, Japan, 19 March 1945. Stationed on the third deck when the ship was rocked by a series of violent explosions... Lieutenant Gary unhesitatingly risked his life to assist several hundred men trapped in a messing compartment filled with smoke, and with no apparent egress. As the imperiled men below decks became increasingly panic-stricken under the raging fury of incessant explosions, he confidently assured them he would find a means of effecting their release and groping through the dark, debris-filled corridors, ultimately discovered an escape way. Staunchly determined, he struggled back to the messing compartment three times despite menacing flames, flooding water and the ominous threat of sudden additional explosions, on each occasional calmly leading his men through the blanketing pall of smoke until the last one had been saved. Selfless in his concern for his ship and his fellows, he constantly rallied others about him, repeatedly organized and led fire-fighting parties into the blazing inferno on the flight deck and when fire-room 1 and 2 were found to be inoperable, entered the No. 3 fire room and directed the raising of steam in one boiler in the face of extreme difficulty and hazard. An inspiring and courageous leader, Lieutenant Gary rendered self-sacrificing service under the most perilous conditions and, by his heroic initiative, fortitude and valor, was responsible for the saving of several hundred lives. His conduct throughout reflect the highest credit upon himself and upon the United States Naval Service.

APPENDIX

Navy Cross Medal to Captain Leslie E. Gehres, Commanding Officer, *U.S.S Franklin, CV 13.*

For distinguishing himself by extraordinary heroism in operations against the enemy while serving as Commanding Officer of an aircraft carrier on 19 March 1945 when his ship was struck by enemy bombs which caused tremendous fires and explosions among a large number of fully armed and fueled planes, both on the flight deck and in the hangar. Although handicapped by severe damage to his ship's fire-fighting equipment and communications system, he displayed outstanding resourcefulness in directing the measures which eventually brought the fires under control, got power back to his ship, and enable her to be withdrawn from a position close aboard a hostile coast. His skill and courage were at all times in keeping with the highest traditions of the United States Naval Service.

Navy Cross Medal to Commander Joseph Taylor, Executive Officer, *U.S.S Franklin, CV 13.*

For distinguishing himself by extraordinary heroism in operations against the enemy while serving as Executive Officer of an aircraft carrier which was striking the Japanese home islands in the vicinity of Kobe, Japan, on 19 March 1945. When his ship was hit and severely damaged by enemy air attacks and rocked by violent explosions of her own ordinances, he supervised and directed the efforts to save the ship, controlling raging fires, flooding magazines and personally leading and participating in the jettisoning of heated live ammunition and bombs. With utmost disregard for his personal safety, he visited all sections of the badly damaged ship, leading, inspiring the crew in the gallant and successful effort to salvage the drifting and erupting carrier. In the face of further enemy attack and explosions of the carrier's own arms he took charge of the towing operations which resulted in getting his ship underway. His cool, calm determination and outstanding leadership were an inspiration to all officers and men, and contributed greatly to the ultimate saving of the ship. His conduct throughout was in keeping with the highest traditions of the United States Naval Service.

COMPOSITION OF TASK FORCE 58 DURING THE PERIOD 14 THROUGH 22 MARCH 1945

Vice Admiral Mitscher, Commander in Chief

58.1, Carrier Task Group One, COMCARIDIV 5, Rear Admiral Clark (58.1)
USS Hornet (CV 12) .... CVG 17
USS Wasp (CV 18) .... CVG 86
USS Bennington (CV 20) .... CVG 82
USS Belleau Wood (CVL 24) .... CVLG 30

58.1.2, Support Unit COMBATDIV 8, Rear Admiral Shafroth
USS Indiana (BB 58)
USS Massachusetts (BB 59)

58.1.22, COMCRIDIV 14, Rear Admiral Whiting
USS Vincennes (CL 64)
USS Vicksburg (CL 86)
USS Miami (CL 89)

58.1.3, Screen, COMDESRON 61, Captain Carter, DESDIVS 61.21,22, 25, 49 & 50

USS Shroeder (DD 501)	USS Murray (DD 576)	USS Collett (DD 730)
USS Sigspee (DD 502)	USS Dashiell (DD 659)	USS Maddox (DD 731)
USS Harrison (DD 573)	USS DeHaven (DD 727)	USS Blue (DD 744)
USS J. Rodgers (DD 574)	USS Mansfield (DD 728)	USS Brush (DD 74)
USS McKee (DD 575)	USS L. K. Swenson (DD 729)	

58.2, Carrier Task Group Two, COMCARDIV 2, Rear Admiral Davison (58.2.)
USS Franklin (CV 13) .... CVG 5
USS Hancock (CV 19) .... CVG 19
USS Bataan (CVL 29) .... CVLG 47
USS San Jacinto (CVL 30) .... CVLG 45

58.2.2, Support Unit, COMCRUDIV 10, Rear Admiral Waltse COMBATDIV 6, Rear Admiral Cooley

58.2.21, Battleships
USS North Carolina (BB 55)
USS Washington (BB 56)
58.2.22, Cruisers
USS Baltimore (CA 68)
USS Pittsburgh (CA 72)
USS Santa Fe (CLAA 60)

58.2.3, Screen, COMDESRON 52, Captain Womble, DESDIVSM 13, 104, 53, 105, 106

USS Miller (DD 535)	USS Potter (DD 538)	USS Colahan (DD 658)
USS Owen (DD 536)	USS Tingey (DD 539)	USS Hickox (DD 673)
USS The Sullivans (DD 537)	USS Weining (DD 540)	USS Hunt (DD 674)
USS Hancock (DD 675)	USS Wedderburn (DD 684)	USS Benham (DD 796)
USS Marshall (DD 676)	USS Halsey Powell (DD 686)	USS Cushing (DD 979)
USS Stockham (DD 683)	USS Uhlmann (DD 687)	

APPENDIX

U.S. NAVY DEPARTMENT
BUREAU OF NAVAL PERSONNEL
WASHINGTON 25, D.C.

MEMORANDUM

SUBJECT: AWARDS GIVEN TO PERSONNEL ABOARD THE U.S.S. FRANKLIN FOR ACTION ON 19 MARCH 1945.

Records of the Bureau indicate the below listed men have been awarded decoration for action on 19 March, 1945 while attached to the U.S.S. Franklin.

Medal of Honor

LCDR. Joseph Timothy O'Callahan
Lt. (jg) Donald A. Gary

Navy Cross

Capt. Leslie E. Gehres
CDR. Henry H. Hale
CDR. Joseph Taylor
CDR. Stephen Jurika
LCDR. George William Fox (MC Post)
LCDR. Thomas J. Greene
LCDR. William R McKinney
LCDR. Walter H. Kreamer
LCDR. Robert B. Downes
LCDR. George Stone
LCDR. Mac G. Kilpatrick
LCDR. Sam Sherman (MC)
LCDR. James J. Fuelling
Lt. William S. Ellis
Lt. Fred Harris
Lt. (jg) Lindsey E. Morgan
Gunner Thomas M. Stoops

Silver Star Medal

LCDR. David Berger
Lt. Grimes W. Gatlin
Lt. Ernest B. Rodgers
Lt. (jg) Joseph B. Tiara
Lt. (jg) Bill J. White

Lt. (jg) Stanley S. Graham
Lt. (jg) Edward H. R. Wassman
1st Lt. Walter M. Newland
Ensign Robert D. McCarary
Chief MaChief Clarence B. Reid
MaChief Walter E. Macomber
Boatswain Marion Frisbee
MaChief William E. Green
Air. TeChief Donald H. Russell
Hamel, William H., EM3rd Class
Miller, Charles E., SF 1st Class
Stone, Harold S., RT1st Class
Guderbandsen, James H. MM 1st Class
Abbott, Gilbert P., QM3rd Class
Davis, Holbrook R., QM3rd Class
Costa, Laurentino E, MM3rd Class
Mayer, Norman C., S 1st Class
Gold Star in Lieu of Second Bronze Star Medal
Lt. Melvin M. Tappen
Lt. (jg) Gordon L. Hassig
Lt. (jg) Robert M. Thayer
Chief Electrician Elmer C. Phillips
Chief Carpenter Lewis R. Eddins

Bronze Star Medal

LCDR. John D. Whitaker
LCDR. Lewis F. Davis
LCDR. DeVon M. Hzer
LCDR. James W. West, Jr.
Major John Stack

Major Herbert T. Elliott, Jr.
Lt. Bart Slattery
Lt. Charles G. Durr
Lt. Clyde H. Fellows, Jr.
Lt. Elmer L. Fox
Lt. James A. Vaughn, Jr.
Lt. Frank C. Cheney
Lt. Charles Carr
Lt. George W. Cheney, Jr.
Lt. Philip O. Geir, Jr.
Lt. John B. Barr
Lt. Edward Monsour
Lt. Charles B. Turek
Lt. Robert H. Fank
Lt. Jesse M. Albritton, Jr.
Lt. Theodore T. Huntington
Lt. Frederick S. Robertson, Jr.
Lt. George R. Watkins
Lt. (jg) John P Ryder
Lt. (jg) Robert J. Wineman
Lt. (jg) Joe Aizpuru
Lt. (jg) Everett J. Taylor
Lt. (jg) Maurice M. Brundice
Lt. (jg) William K Helzel
Lt. (jg) George B. Ritz
Lt. (jg) John B. O'Donnell
Lt. (jg) Marvin Leff
Lt. (jg) Hugh W. Close Jr.
Lt. (jg) Marvin K Bowman
Lt. (jg) Donald R. E. Barnaby
Lt. (jg) Walter Nardelli
1st Lt. John Skorich
Ensign Guy S. Marshall
Ensign William A. McClellan
Ensign Frederick S. Lightfoot
Ensign Richard E. Jortberg
Ensign C. Probst
Ensign George a Hamilton
Chief Gunner Walter S. Hatcher
Chief Torpedoman John M. Kalvin
Chief Pay clerk Alvin L. Fowler
Chief Pay Clerk John W. Shepard, Jr.
Gunner Roy G. Hale
Acting Pay Clerk Harold Leblanc
Brown, John Franklin, Y2nd Class (T) (Post)

Durrance, Benjamin Myron, CSF (AA) (Post)
Valloni, Thomas J., CEM
Valloni, Thomas J., CEM
Orendorff, Carl S., ACOM
MacAllister, William H., EM 1st Class
McCaffrey, John W., WT 1st Class
Brumfield, James I., WT 1st Class
Turner, james W., WT 1st Class
Barry, Ralph (n), WT 1st Class
Abellon, Placito, CCK
Odom, James P., MM 1st Class
Locke, Robert (n), Jr., SF 1st Class
Monkus, Frank (n) SF 1st Class
Noble, Charles M., BM 1st Class
Fowler, William J., Jr., AOM 1st Class
Nycum, Edward C., RT 1st Class
Kidwell, Irving L., Y2nd Class
Holstrom, Edward (n), MM2nd Class
Nott, William J., MM2nd Class
Wellman, Frederick E., MM2nd Class
Friedman, Herman S., SF2nd Class
Tammeaid, Miloai, BM2nd Class
Ryan, Vigil R., QM2nd Class
Gowen, Michael (n), GM2nd Class
Dickson, Brobert C., S/Sgt.
Williams, Wilfred "J.", Y3rd Class
Streich, Hans A, WT3rd Class
Chambers, Patrick A., WT3rd Class
Lindberg, John H., EM2nd Class
Finkenstedt, Charles L., SSML2nd Class
Bowman, Alex E., Y3rd Class
Browning, William L. SM3rd Class
Hart, Stephen C., SM3rd Class
Oxley, Robert W., GM#
Cartwright, John E., GM3rd Class
Reynolds, William W., AERM3rd Class
Alemida, Arthur S., AOM3rd Class
Kissell, Lynn M., AOM2nd Class
Astorian, Gerald E., S 1st Class
Jacobs, Charles W., S 1st Class
Boyd, Robert L., SM 1st Class
Guglielmo, William (n), S 1st Class
Wilson, Dorris W. S 1st Class
Oliver, Audrey L., SM 1st Class
Albrecht, William R., S2nd Class

Mozdiak, Henry J., S2nd Class
Ricks, Benjamin M., S 1st Class
Tucker, Charles B., S 1st Class
Hottinger, Eugene J., S 1st Class
Hopkins, Joseph P., S 1st Class
Kleiber, Bernard (n), WT2nd Class
Collins, Arthur L., F 1st Class
Hogge, Wilton G., F 1st Class (WT)
Smith, John F., F 1st Class
La Blanco, Joseph (n), S2nd Class
Klimkiewicz, Wallace L., Cpl.
Chase, Frank T., Jr., S2nd Class
Brown, Paul W., S2nd Class
Charnstrom, Lloyd E., Pfc.
Allen, Edward T., Pfc.
LCDR. John D. Whitaker
LCDR. Lewis F. Davis
LCDR. DeVon M. Hzer
LCDR. James W. West, Jr.

Gold Star in lieu of a Second Bronze Star Medal

Lt. Melvin M Tappen
Lieutenant (jg) Gordon L. Hassig
Lt. (jg) Robert M. Thayer
Chief Electrician Elmer C. Phillips
Chief Carpenter Lewis R. Eddins
LCDR. John D. Whitaker
LCDR. Lewis F. Davis
LCDR. DeVon M. Hzer
LCDR. James W. West, Jr

Letters of Commendation

Lake, James (n), GM3rd Class
Dudiak, Peter Paul, S 1st Class
Crowther, Thomas Dwight, GM2nd Class
Fuller, Billie (n), BM 1st Class
Cesar, John Norman, GM3rd Class
De Roche, Edward Thomas, GM3rd Class
Poff, Calvin Robert, S2nd Class

Wise, Charles Paul, S2nd Class
Brunn, Wilby Francis, S2nd Class
Steinbron, Harold Ray, FCO3rd Class
Christman, Frederick William, S2 (GM)
Darrington, Keith Olsen, S 1st Class
Burke, Russell Emmett, S 1st Class
Swann, Bert (n), BM2nd Class
Jackson, Dan (n), CK 1st Class
Brown, Charles (n), CK 1st Class
Shaw, Dudley Emanuel, StM2nd Class
Baker, William Latta, CMM
Lecus, Edward (n), MM 1st Class
Bereska, Paul (n), MM 1st Class
Meggins, Charles Curtis, MM 1st Class
Slifies, Robert Ulysses, MM2nd Class
Lepore, Frank Peter, MM3rd Class
Gobrigall, Calvin Frank, MM3rd Class
Ray, Gerald Abniwake, F2nd Class
Bolopue, Herman Carl, F 1st Class
Soltvedt, John Phillip, MM 1st Class
Stites, John Talbert, GMM 1st Class
Skean, William (n), MM2nd Class
Ramey, Glenn Thomas, MMR2
O'Neill, Ernest Frank, F 1st Class
Chasse, Richard Damasse, F 1st Class
Long, Henry Arthur, MM3rd Class
Defillipo, Michael Vincent, MoMM3rd Class
Curtis, Thomas Franklin, MMS2nd Class
Gassman, Robert Francis, F 1st Class
Kieliszak, Raymond John, F 1st Class
Lazerski, Richard Joseph, S 1st Class
Peterman, John Allen, FC2nd Class
Cusick, James J.
O'Connell, Richard Daniel, S 1st Class
Mantone, Antonio, S 1st Class
Oxley, Robert William, GM3rd Class
Caldwell, Charles Guy, BM 1st Class
Dowell, Horace Kirby, MuSm 1st Class
Kincaide, Robert Doane, Mus2nd Class
Watson, James Kenneth, Mus2nd Class
Bergman, Earl Allen, Mus2nd Class
O'Donovan, John Richard, QM2nd Class
Tarr, Bernard (n), Jr., S2nd Class
Varilen, William (n), QM 1st Class
Walsh, Eugene Thomas, QM3rd Class

Russell, Allen Clarence, S 1st Class
Day, Robert Wayne, S2nd Class
Anderson, Willie "B," StM2nd Class
Brooks, Floyd (n), StM2nd Class
Little, Major (n), StM 1st Class
Matthews, Williams R., StM2nd Class
Glossom, Sylvester (n), StM 1st Class
Bartley, Albert (n), StM 1st Class
Dickerson, Leslie J., StM 1st Class
Pearson, Ernest (n), StM2nd Class
Cobb, James (n), StM2nd Class
Grier, Edward A., StM2nd Class
Gibson, Howard (n), StM2nd Class
Gordon, Arnold E., Ck2nd Class
Rhodes, Robert Tiennie, StM2nd Class
Williams, Mack Henry, StM 1st Class
Abagon, Angel (n), CST (AA)
Gregory, William Tency, StM 1st Class
Brown, Don Graviel, StM2nd Class
Culberson, Leonz (n), StM2nd Class
Dennis, Jeff (n), StM2nd Class
Coffie, Thomas (n), StM2nd Class
Francis, Edward (n), StM2nd Class
Grant, Eugene Newton, StM2nd Class
Marks, Leon (n), StM2nd Class
Boulton, Ulysses (n), StM2nd Class
Basham, John Russell, RM3rd Class
Kusy, John Michael, Prtr3rd Class
Lawson, David Vernon, S 1st Class
Mushc, Harold Edwin, S2nd Class
McGough, William Joseph, Y3rd Class
Cox, John James, RM3rd Class
Miller, George Edward, S 1st Class
Petrill, Frank Gilbert, S2nd Class
Antall, Richard Charles, S 1st Class
Ensign Norman Arthur Eichner
Mihal, Victor Michael, RM3rd Class
Ritchie, Edward Augusta, SM 1st Class
Kassover, Martin Lewis, SM3rd Class
Prather, Donald Eugene, AMM 1st Class
Jones, James Leonard, EM3rd Class
Caldwell, William Bowles, EM3rd Class
Stork, Glenn Dean, F 1st Class
Zeller, Heinz (n), S2nd Class
Spriggs, Robert Lee, EM2nd Class

Richardson, Haron James, CEM
Dyer, Joseph Arthur, F 1st Class
Elsey, Gordon John, EM 1st Class
Freggens, Robert Alfred, F 1st Class
Dunn, Charles Rex, EM2nd Class
Sutherland, Hiram Daniel, EM3rd Class
Clingerman, Kermit Gene, S 1st Class
Hopkins, Leo Francis, RM3rd Class
Privett, William Allen, MM 1st Class
Matson, Ernest (n), SM2nd Class
Munzing, Harry Ernest, S 1st Class
Robinson, John Wallace, S2nd Class
Dodaro, Louis (n), RM3rd Class
Drolsom, James Hilo, S 1st Class
Cook, Ralph Marcell, ART 1st Class
Wook, Chester Roy, S 1st Class
Burton, Edward Arthur, S2nd Class
Burton, Vernon Luke, RM2nd Class
Greshko, Stephen (n), S 1st Class
Martin, Voley Arval, S2nd Class
Ellis, Thomas Ollie, S2nd Class
Pederson, Harry LeRoy, S 1st Class
Rafuse, John Oscar, GM3
Gehelnik, Dave George, S2nd Class
Lanley, John Steward, S2nd Class
Catt, Harold Raymond, S2nd Class
Cole, Russell Edgar, S2nd Class
Cullen, Charles Albert, S2nd Class
Willard, Henry Kellogg, II, S2nd Class
Cody, Charles Lewis, S2nd Class
Gatulis, Joseph William, GM2nd Class
Wills, Scott William, Cox
Drouin, Leo Willie, WT3rd Class
Roy, Henry Napoleon, F2nd Class
Root, Gordon Harvey, F2nd Class
Hamm, Robert Lee, WT3rd Class
Dunne, James Louis, WT3rd Class
Lt. (jg) George Kensly Leitch
Brenner, William Ernest, WT3rd Class
Wollett, Clair "C," WT3rd Class
Birch, George Bobby, WT3rd Class
Nichelson, Jack Alexander, WT 1st Class
Stewart, Robert Charles, CB
Swanson, Robert Walter, WT2nd Class
Murphy, Rex Gluck, B3rd Class

APPENDIX

Stratton, John Ross, F 1st Class
Vaughn, William Thomas, AMM 2nd Class
Larsen, Stephen Lorang, S2nd Class
Mollett, Samuel Wesley, S 1st Class
Friend, Alon Louis, S2nd Class
Handrop, Jack Corbet, S 1st Class
Hanna, Isom (n), S2nd Class
Hand, John Willard, AMM3rd Class
Bergin, Kyran Francis, AMM2nd Class
Thomas, Earl Roy, Jr., RdM 1st Class
Hampton, John Emmitt, AOM2nd Class
Corliss, Wayne Albert, S 1st Class
Graves, Earl Eugene, AMM2nd Class
Guba, Henry Arthur, Jr., S 1st Class
Sherwood, John (n), S 1st Class
Littlefield, Dewey Carl, S2nd Class
Jacobs, Harold Wilbury, S 1st Class
Marquess, Lawrence Calvert, S 1st Class
Ludlow, Myron Edward, S 1st Class
Snyder, Harold Thomas, S2nd Class
Bonine, Donald Leander, S2nd Class
Finney, Charles Fenton, Jr., S 1st Class
Glasberg, Irving (n), S 1st Class
Lt. Harry Woods ARTZ
Lt. John Vincent Heddell
Chief Electrician Arthur Hinsen Hoffner
Chief Electrician Joseph Jacobs Wolfe
Chief Machinist Edwin August Schwenkner
MaChief Albert Louis Head
MaChief George Ede, Jr.
Ensign Clyde "T" Massey
Ensign Rudolph Ernest Schmalz
Ensign William Birch Haylor
Lt. (jg) Robert Thomas Connolly
MaChief Allen Garfield Ensign
Ensign John Reilly Tucker, Jr.
Thomas, Harold Leslie, F 1st Class
Yearick, Robert Day, F 1st Class
Andrews, Robert Frederick, EM 1st Class
Dyickanowski, Andrew (n), MM2nd Class
Lt. (jg) Kenneth Paul Rockhill
Croff, donald Eugene, F 1st Class
Wayman, Ronan Edward, MM 1st Class
Cole, Frederick Thomas, F2nd Class
Knoeller, William Wrren, WT3rd Class

Barnes, Franklyn Ralph, MM3rd Class
Krause, Leonard Robert, F2nd Class
La Role, Arthur Dorsey, F 1st Class
Hutton, Stanley Richard, F2nd Class
Dressel, William Richard, F 1st Class
Luptak, Louis William, F 1st Class
Freek, George Marshall, Jr., F2nd Class
Frandle, Gerald Truman, F2nd Class
Collum, James Harold, F2nd Class
Harris, James Samuel, F2nd Class
Long, James Moore, WT3rd Class
Giles, Raymond Gerald, WT3rd Class
McRae, Donald Elliott, WT2nd Class
Leipel, Clayton Buford, WT3rd Class
Personen, Veikko William, WT3rd Class
Harris, James Houston, F2nd Class
Furrow, John Harry, F2nd Class
Webster, Hubert Cread, F2nd Class
Bryant, Mathew William, F2nd Class
Adelson, Albert (n), WT3rd Class
Hall, Stanley David, WT 1st Class
White, john Montague, WT2nd Class
Petrunyak, Emery Louis, F 1st Class
Oxford, John Marvin, F2nd Class
Roach, John Marvin, F2nd Class
Blackwell, Ralph (n), F2nd Class
Hall, Leonard Melford, WT2nd Class
Magee, Paul Leland, MM 1st Class
Ricchetti, Paul Anthony, MM2nd Class
Moses, Benjamin (n), WT2nd Class
Siebold, Donald Alfred, WT3rd Class
Weinley, Harold DeWayne, F 1st Class
St. Peters, Robert Edward, Em3rd Class
Lt Mason, Peter T. (HC)
Lt. Ross E. Wales
Lt. (jg) Harold W. Richardson
Ensign Harrison D. Mitchell
Severson, Royal Roscoe, SK1st Class
Lt. Mevern C. Wookburn
Lt. Donald J. Fitzgerald
Lt. William McGuire
Lt. Donald G. Billington
Lt. Joseph F. McMeel
Rizzi, Vito (n) SK 1st Class
Gunner Thomas M. Stoops

Lt. (jg) Joseph B. Tiara
Lt. (jg) Bill J. White
Lt. (jg) Stanley S. Graham
Lt. (jg) Edward H.R. Wassman
1st Lt. Walter M. Newland
Ensign Robert D. McCrary
Chief MaChief Clarence B. Reid
MaChief Walter E. Macomber
Boatswain Marion Frisbee
MaChief William E. Green
Air. TeChief Donald H. Russell
Hamel, William H., EM3rd Class
Miller, Charles E., SF 1st Class
Stone, Harold S., RT 1st Class
Gudbrandenson, James H., MM 1st Class
Abbott, Gilbert P., QM3rd Class
Davis, Holbrook R., Qm3rd Class
Costa, Laurention "E.", MM3rd Class
Mayer, Norman C., S 1st Class

U.S.S. FRANKLIN (CV-13)
Care of Fleet Post Office
San Francisco, California

20 April 1945

List of Men Killed in Action

ABATE, Victor Emanuel	RdM2nd Class (T), SV V-6 USNR
ADKINS, Harm Keith	S2nd Class, V-6 USNR
AJA, Joaquin	ACOM (AA) (T), U.S. Navy
ALBISTON, Roy Seth	SM 1st Class(ACM), V-6 USNR
AKINS, Thomas J.C.	S2nd Class, V-6 USNR
ALBRIGHT, Edward Chester	ART2nd Class, V-6 USNR
ALDERISIO, Frederick Alfred	ART3rd Class, V-3 USNR
ALT, Harold	AMM2nd Class, v-6 USNR
AMES, Floyd Ray	PhM2nd Class, V-6 USNR
ASHURST, Charles Isaac	StMlc, SV V-6 USNR
BACA, Marcos Roland	S2nd Class, V-6 USNR
BAGGETT, Walter, Jr.	S2nd Class, SV V-6 USNR
BAKER, Earl Raymond	AOM2nd Class, V-6 USNR
BAMBURG, Robert Leon	F2nd Class, V-6 USNR
BARR, Fred Neal	RM1st Class, U.S. Navy
BEANE, Clifford Elsworth	S2nd Class, V-6 USNR
BECK, Willie Cletis	S2nd Class, SV, V-6 USNR
BECKWITH, Raymond Oscar	SM 1st Class (SK), SV U.S. Navy
BEICHER, Billy Dean	S2nd Class, V-6 USNR
BERG, David	SM 1st Class, V-6 USNR
BINGAMAN, Mark D.	Y1st Class(T), V-6 USNR
BIRCHALL, William Henry, Jr.	F1st Class, V-6 USNR
BLAIR, Clarence J.	CM3rd Class, SV V-6 USNR
BLANKENSHIP, Warren Harding	AM1st Class, U.S. Navy
BLANTON, William George	Mus3rd Class, SV V-6 USNR
BOBO, Arthur Leo	S2nd Class, SV V-6 USNR
BOCHENEK, Morris	SK2nd Class, V-6 USNR
BOOTH, George Melvin	S2nd Class, SV V-6 USNR
BOSCO, Anthony Valentino	SM 1st Class, V-6 USNR
BOYD, Edward Joseph	F1st Class, U.S. Navy
BRETON, Edmond Ernest	S2nd Class, SV V-6 USNR
BUCKLEY, Clarence Edward	SM 1st Class, SV V-6 USNR
BUMBAUGH, Elwood Bruce	MM3rd Class(T), SV V-6 USNR
BURKHAMER, Allen Roger	S2nd Class, V-6 USNR

BURTON, Willard Herbert	SM 1st Class (AOM), V-6 USNR
BYCZKOWSKI, Edward Stanley	S2nd Class, SV V-6 USNR
CAMPIGLIA, Joseph Theodore	RM2nd Class(T), V-6 USNR
CARAWLANIS, Peter J.	RdM3rd Class(T), V-6 USNR
CARR, Christopher James	SM 1st Class (AOM), V-6 USNR
CARRARA, Joseph Jr.	SM 1st Class, SV V-6 USNR
CARTWRIGHT, William Henry	S2nd Class, V-6 USNR
CARUTHERS, Morris Edward	F2nd Class, SV V-6 USNR
CASTELLUCCI, Charles Dominick	S2nd Class, SV V-6 USNR
CENTERS, Darral Frederick	AOM3rd Class, USN
CHAMBERS, Bliss Edward	SM 1st Class, V-6 USNR
CHILCOTE, Kermit W.	S2nd Class(RdM), V-6 USNR
CHIVAS, Stanley John	RdM3rd Class, V-6 USNR
CLOUSER, Earl Warren	AM2nd Class, V-6 USNR
CODREA, Charles V.	RdM3rd Class(T), V-6 USNR
COLEMAN, Carl Edward	RdM3rd Class, V-6 USNR
COLUMBO, Valentino Corrini	S2nd Class, SV V-6 USNR
COOK, Thomas Joseph	SM 1st Class, V-6 USNR
CORBETT, Odis Leo	ACOM(PA), USN
COWARD, Radford Sano	S2nd Class, V-6 USNR
COX, Walter Ben	S2nd Class, V-6 USNR
CROSS, Donald Lester	AMMC2nd Class, V-6 USNR
DATZMAN, Rolland Paul	Y3rd Class(T), V-6 USNR
DAVIS, Arthur Linton	2nd Class(RdM), SV V-6 USNR
DE LAY, Roy Franklin	2nd Class(RdM), V-6 USNR
DEMOLEATSOS, George James	S2nd Class(RdM), V-6 USNR
DEMPSEY, Edwin John	SM 1st Class, V-6 USNR
DESMARAIS, Raymond Edgar	SM 1st Class, SV V-6 USNR
DEUEL, John Rickolt	RdM3rd Class(T), SV V-6 USNR
DI PALMA, Michael Joseph	SM 1st Class, V-6 USNR
DIZEK, Norman	SM 1st Class, SV V-6 USNR
DOINEN, Romelia John	RdM3rd Class(T), V-6 USNR
DRAKE, Albert Newton	S2nd Class, V-6 USNR
DRISSEL, Robert Leo	Y3rd Class(T), SV V-6 USNR
DUFF, Richard Herrick	CM1st Class, V-6 USNR
DURANTE, Luke John	CPhoM(T) USN
DURRANCE, Benjamin Myron	CSF(AA), USN
DYE, Benjamin Blanton	PrtrM1st Class (T), V-6 USNR
EDWARDS, Dan	S2nd Class, V-6 USNR
ELLIS, Richard Lee	PC3rd Class(T), SV V-6 USNR
ENDRESS, Melvin Harvey	S2nd Class, SV V-6 USNR
EPTING, John Robert	S2nd Class, V-6 USNR
ERICKSON, Richard B.	S2nd Class, V-6 USNR
EVANS, Edward	AMDc, V-2, USNR
FAIRCHILD, Lloyd Thomas	S2nd Class(RdM), V-6 USNR

FENECK, Patrick Francis	S2nd Class, SV V-6 USNR
FISCHER, Kenneth Christian	Y2nd Class(T), SV V-6 USNR
FISHMAN, Irving	S2nd Class, V-6 USNR
FLEENOR, James Horley	S2nd Class, V-6 USNR
FLEMING, Russell Evan	ART3rd Class, SV V-6 USNR
FLUHR, John Herbert	S2nd Class, V-6 USNR
FORBES, Billy Gene	S2nd Class, V-6 USNR
FORD, Thomas Patrick, Jr.	S2nd Class, V-6 USNR
FORSYTH, Donald Walter	Y1st Class, V-6 USNR
FOOTSKY, Thomas Andrew	S2nd Class, V-6 USNR
FOUTS, Cecil Edward	S2nd Class, USN
FOWLER, Edmund, Francis	SM 1st Class (GM), SV V-6 USNR
FRANGIAMORE, Rosario	SM 1st Class (AOM), SV V-6 USNR
FRIEND, Donald Calvin	AMM2nd Class(T), V-6 USNR
FROST, James Franklin	SM 1st Class (AOM), SV V-6 USNR
GARBER, Charles Adam	AOM3rd Class(T), V-6 USNR
GERARD, Donald	SM 1st Class, (AOM), V-6 USNR
GIBEAU, Wilfrid Joseph	S2nd Class, V-6 USNR
GIFFEN, Robert Graham	SM 1st Class, SV V-6 USNR
GILL, Ray Allen	S2nd Class, V-6 USNR
GLEASON, Clarence Ozem	S2nd Class, SV V-6 USNR
GOBLE, Alan Franklyn	AEM2nd Class, V-6 USNR
GOETZ, Jack Thornton	FCO3rd Class, SV V-6 USNR
GOLDEN, Mitchell Albert	SM 1st Class, SV V-6 USNR
GRAHAM, James Lamar	S2nd Class, SV V-6 USNR
GRATA, Paul	AOM3rd Class(T), SV V-6 USNR
GRECO, Joseph John	SM 1st Class, (AOM) SV, V-6 USNR
GREENLAW, Dalwyn Frederick	S2nd Class, SV V-6 USNR
GREGG, Robert Alton	SKV1st Class(T) V2, USNR
GREITNER, Henry George	WT3rd Class(T) V-6 USNR
GROSE, Darryle A.	RM1st Class(T) V3, USNR
GUIDROZ, Fernand Joseph	S2nd Class, V-6 USNR
GWARJANSKI, Philip Walter	AMM2nd Class, V-6 USNR
GWIN, William Joseph	SM 1st Class, V-6 USNR
HAGERSTROM, Carl Frederik	GM2nd Class (T) SV V-6 USNR
HAGGERTY, William Joseph	EM3rd Class (T) SV V-6 USNR
HALL, James William	RdM2nd Class(T) V-6 USNR
HALLMAN, Albert Lloyd, 3rd	S2nd Class, V-6 USNR
HAMES, Vernon Hugh	S2nd Class, SV V-6 USNR
HAMILTON, Troy Wallace	Cox V-6 USNR
HANEY, Louis Michael	SM 1st Class, V-6 USNR
HANLON, James Lawrence	S2nd Class V-6 USNR
HANSEN, Kenneth Marvin	RdM3rd Class(T) V-6 USNR
HANLOW, Albert Dana	BM2nd Class, V-6 USNR
HARMON, Carl Mac	Y3rd Class(T) SV V-6 USNR

HARRISON, Robert John	AOM3rd Class V-6 USNR
HART, Clyde Melvin	S2nd Class, SV V-6 USNR
HATTON, David Maurice, Jr.	S2nd Class, V-6 USNR
HAWTHORNE, Lowell Edward	SM 1st Class, V-6 USNR
HAYES, William Richard	S2nd Class, V-6 USNR
HEREFORD, Evertt Earl	SM 1st Class, USN
HERMANCE, George Nelson	F2nd Class, V-6 USNR
HERROD, Thomas Claude	S2nd Class, V-6 USNR
HILL, Franklin Horace	EM3rd Class, V-6 USNR
HILLAS, Robert	ARM1st Class(T) V-6 USNR
HINDS, Ferren Ralph	AOM1st Class(T), V-6 USNR
HOGANSON, Calvin Wayne	S2nd Class, V-6 USNR
HOFFMAN, Anthony	S2nd Class, V-6 USNR
HUDDLE, Jack Adrian	SM 1st Class, USN
HUDSON, Grady	StM2nd Class, SV V-6 USNR
HURD, George Sherwood	SM 1st Class., SV V-6 USNR
IRWIN, Duane Lester	S2nd Class, V-6 USNR
JACKSON, William Lyman	Cptnr M 1st Class USN
JAKUSKA, Henry	AOM1st Class(T), V2, USNR
JAMES, Carl Lloyd	S2nd Class SV V-6 USNR
JOHNSON, James Benjamin	Y2nd Class SV V-6 USNR
JOHNSON, James Edward	S2nd Class SV V-6 USNR
JOSLIN, Bernard William	SM 1st Class, V-6 USNR
KAI, Charles Ernest	S2nd Class SV V-6 USNR
KARR, Forrest Ernest	SM 1st Class, SV V-6 USNR
KEENER, Howard Harold	S2nd Class SV V-6 USNR
KELLEY, Richard Gordon	EM3rd Class SV V-6 USNR
KIMBALL, Philip Harold	S2nd Class, V-6 USNR
KIRK, Thomas Norman	RM2nd Class(T) SV V-6 USNR
KLING, Julian Smith	SM 1st Class, V-6 USNR
KRENSKE, James Herbert	AM3rd Class V-6 USNR
KUBALA, Robert Peter	RdM2nd Class(T), USN
KYRKLUND, Franklin G.	SM 1st Class(RdM) SV V-6 USNR
LA FOREST, Marvin Cletus	PhoM2nd Class, V-6 USNR
LAINSON, Leslie George	S2nd Class SV V-6 USNR
LAZZARO, Guy Joseph	AM3rd Class, V-6 USNR
LEAKE, Philip Rusk, Jr.	S2nd Class, V-6 USNR
LEANZA, Anthony Salvatore	F2nd Class, V-6 USNR
LEHNHOFF, Russell Harold	S2nd Class, SV V-6 USNR
LEWIS, Chester Ray	S2nd Class, V-6 USNR
LEWIS, Evan Minto	Y2nd Class, V-6 USNR
LINDSAY, Johnnie	SM 1st Class, V-6 USNR
LINEBARGER, Henry Falvey	Cox, USN
LITTLE, John Richard	S2nd Class (AMM), V-6 USNR
LOGUE, John Richard	Cox(T), USN

LOFTUS, George Robert	SM 1st Class, V-6 USNR
LONG, Charles Raymond	S2nd Class, SV V-6 USNR
LOVE, Wiley Hamilton, Jr.	S2nd Class, SV V-6 USNR
LOVITT, William Francis	ACM1st Class(T), V-6 USNR
LUCAS, Santos Domino	St3rd Class(T), V-6 USNR
LUCAS, Warren Pershing	S2nd Class, SV V-6 USNR
MARDIS, Lawrence Hugh	PhoM1st Class, V-6 USNR
MARINO, Paul Joseph	AOM1st Class(T), V-6 USNR
MARTIN, Earl James	SM 1st Class, V-6 USNR
MARTIN J.G.	S2nd Class, SV V-6 USNR
MARTIN, John Joseph	S2nd Class, SV V-6 USNR
MC CAULEY, Donald Edward	S2nd Class, V-6 USNR
MC CRACKEN, Robert Frederick	FCO3rd Class, SV V-6 USNR
MC DONALD, Eugene Dominick	MM3rd Class(T), SV V-6 USNR
MC DONALD, Havard	StM1st Class, SV V-6 USNR
MC DUFFIE, Julian Hains	S2nd Class, SV V-6 USNR
MC GLONE, Leonard, Jr.	FC2nd Class, V-6 USNR
MC KENZIE, Howard Parker	SM 1st Class, SV V-6 USNR
MC MULLEN, John Aloysius	S2nd Class, USN
MEXUS, Peter, Jr.	RdM3rd Class(T), USN
MENDOZA, Calido Gonzales, Jr.	AOM1st Class(T), V-6 USNR
MILLER, George Joseph	AOM2nd Class, V-6 USNR
MITCHELL, Fred Mortimer	MM1st Class, V-6 USNR
MIXON, James Marvin, Jr.	S2nd Class, SV V-6 USNR
MOE, Raymond Leonard	AOM2nd Class, V-2, USNR
MOODY, Garlan Carl	SM 1st Class, USN
MORAN, Joseph Robert	EM2nd Class(T), V-6 USNR
MYERS, Kenneth Johnson	S2nd Class, V-6 USNR
NESS, William Lavon	GM2nd Class(T), V-6 USNR
NEUKAN, Henry John	ACOM(AA), USN
NICHOLAS, Peter Harry	SM 1st Class(AOM), V-6 USNR
NORMAN, Joe Emory	HA1st Class, V-6 USNR
NORTH, Robert Weldon	AOM3rd Class(T), V-6 USNR
NORWOOD, Horace Joseph	Y1st Class, USN
PARKER, Boney Beauregard, Jr.	SM 1st Class, V-6 USNR
PARKER, Fred LaVore	S2nd Class, SV V-6 USNR
PARISE, Lewis James	SM 1st Class, SV V-6 USNR
PARSLEY, Johnnie Franklin	SM 1st Class(AEM), SV V-6 USNR
PATTERSON, James Francis	SC2nd Class, V-6 USNR
PENDLETON, Jack Sylvester	AM3rd Class, SV V-6 USNR
PERLMAN, Morris	RM3rd Class, SV V-6 USNR
PERRY, Phinis Jerry	Ptr3rd Class, SV V-6 USNR
PETEREX, Laddie E.	ARM3rd Class, V-6 USNR (Passenger)
PIPOLO, James Joseph	SM 1st Class(AEM), SV V-6 USNR
PLAGGERMAN, Richard Charles	RdM2nd Class, SV V-6 USNR

POLANSKY, William Sylvester	S2nd Class, SV V-6 USNR
POLLICK, Walter Edward	S2nd Class, SV V-6 USNR
POLLOCK, Paul	EM1st Class, V-6 USNR
POWELL, James Robert	QM3rd Class, V-6 USNR
PRESET, Douglas Robert	S2nd Class, V-6 USNR
PUGH, Albert Newton	S2nd Class, SV V-6 USNR
RAY, Harry Edward	AOM2nd Class, USN
READER, Charles George	SM 1st Class(AOM), SV V-6 USNR
REDMOND, James Edward	ART2nd Class, USN
REED, Willard Elliott	SM 1st Class(GM), SV V-6 USNR
REYNOLDS, Roland Leon	S2nd Class, SV V-6 USNR
SADLER, John Irving	PtrV2nd Class V-6 USNR
SALERNO, George Anthony	SM 1st Class, V-6 USNR
SANDERS, Christopher Columbus Jr.	S2nd Class, SV V-6 USNR
SANTIAGO, Gabrial Larry Jr.	S2nd Class, SV V-6 USNR
SCHMIDT, Andrew Jackson	EM2nd Class, V-6 USNR
SCHODER, George Richard	S2nd Class, V-6 USNR
SCHULTZ, Arthur Walter	S2nd Class SV V-6 USNR
SCHWEITZER, William Peter	RdM3rd Class(T) V-6 USNR
SHEA, Gerald Anthony	ART2nd Class(T), USN-I
SHEEHAN, James Jeremiah	Cox (T), SV V-6 USNR
SHIREMAN, Christian Coss	S2nd Class, SV V-6 USNR
SIMS, Omar Dee	SM 1st Class, SV V-6 USNR
SIMPSON, Donald Edward	S2nd Class, V-6 USNR
SMITH, Hughlin Hayes, Jr.	S2nd Class(RdM) V-6 USNR
SMITH, Ralph Vernon	PhM1st Class, V-6 USNR
SMITH, Thomas Gibson	S2nd Class, V-6 USNR
SNYDER, Robert Earl	F1st Class, SV V-6 USNR
SOKOLOWSKI, Raymond Henry	SM 1st Class, V-6 USNR
SOLOVICOS, Demetreos C.	S2nd Class SV V-6 USNR
SOUKUP, Robert Joseph	SM 1st Class, USN
SPAIN, Roy Nelson	S2nd Class, V-6 USNR
SPRAGUE, Chester Ray	F1st Class(EM) SV V-6 USNR
SPROWL, Ernest Clifford	AOM3rd Class(T) SV V-6 USNR
STEPHENS, Elwyn Earl	S2nd Class, SV V-6 USNR
STEPKOVITCH, Edward Michael	SM 1st Class, SV V-6 USNR
STEPPACH, Dave Henry, Jr.	PhOM3rd Class(T), V-6 USNR
STEARN, Robert Cyril	S2nd Class, V-6 USNR
STRAUB, Theodore Anthony	AOM2nd Class, V-6 USNR
STRECK, John Francis	Y1st Class(T) SV V-6 USNR
STUDENY, George Constantine	ART2nd Class V-6 USNR
SWEARINGEN, Austin Bell	S2nd Class (RdM), SV V-6 USNR
SYREK, Frank Edward	AOM3rd Class SV V-6 USNR
TAYLOR, Dwight Thoburn	EM3rd Class, SV V-6 USNR
TAYLOR, Jay A.	AOM3rd Class SV V-6 USNR

THOMPSON, Orville Wallace	F1st Class (EM), SV V-6 USNR
TOOMAIAN, Leo	F2nd Class, SV V-6 USNR
TORO, Louis Amalio	S2nd Class, V-6 USNR
TOWEY, Michael Anthony	RdM2nd Class(T) V-6 USNR
TRIVISONNO, Pasquale	SM 1st Class, V-6 USNR
TROMBINO, Joseph Frank	S2nd Class, V-6 USNR
TRZEPACZ, Edwin Stanley	AMM2nd Class, V2, USNR
TSCHIDA, Michael James	S2nd Class, V-6 USNR
VAN ETTEN, Ralph Dan	SM 1st Class, V-6 USNR
VENABLE, Charles Elmer	SM1st Class, USN
VINCENT, Earl Kay	RdM3rd Class(T), V-6 USNR
WALSH, Philip Michael	SM 1st Class, V-6, USNR
WALTON, Stanley Robert	SM 1st Class(ARM), V-6 USNR
WARNER, Howard John	S2nd Class SV V-6 USNR
WEEKS, William Michael	ARM2nd Class(T), V-6 USNR
WEIDENBACHER, George Frank	S2nd Class V-6 USNR
WHEATLEY, Howard Carl	SM 1st Class, V-6 USNR
WILKERSON, Dennis Clark	PhM1st Class, V-6 USNR
WOODARD, Howard Dale	S2nd Class(RdM) V-6 USNR
WOODARD, Lonnie Hiram	S2nd Class V-6 USNR
YAGLE, Frederick Clarence	Coxswain, V-6 USNR
YOUNG, George A. Jr.	RdM3rd Class(T), V-6 USNR
ZIMMERMAN, Dale Edgar	S2nd Class, SV V-6 USNR

List of Men Missing in Action

ACKERMAN, Gerald Reeder	SM3rd Class, U.S. Navy
ADKISON, Luther Vernon	S2nd Class, SV V-6 USNR
ALLEN, James Raymond	S2nd Class, SV V-6 USNR
AMBROSELLI, Lawrence Joseph	AMM2nd Class, V-6 USNR
ANDERSON, Guynn LeRoy	Coxswain, V-6 USNR
ANDERSON, Henry	RdM3rd Class(T), V-6 USNR
ANDERSON, John Bascombe	SM 1st Class(GM), SV V-6 USNR
ANDREWS, Robert Ellsworth	S2nd Class, V-6 USNR
ANDREWS James, Jr.	WT2nd Class, U.S. Navy
ATANASOFF, Keyro	SSMB3rd Class(T), SV V-6 USNR
ATKINSON, William Mitchell	SM 1st Class, U.S. Navy
BACHMAN, John Nicholas	AOM2nd Class, V-6 USNR
BALDWIN, Walter Clifton	RdM3rd Class, V-6 USNR
BANICKE, Werner Frank Otto	CSK(AA), V-6 USNR
BARBASH, Abraham Jacob	S2nd Class(QM), SV V-6 USNR
BARRETO, John Joseph, Jr.	SM 1st Class(AOM), SV V-6 USNR
BARRON, Joseph Anthony	SF2nd Class(T), V-6 USNR
BARTLETT, Henry Elliot	AMM2nd Class, V-2, USNR

BARTOLOTTA, Carmelo Salvatore	SM 1st Class, V-6 USNR
BARTON, Byron Wendell	SM 1st Class (FC), V-6 USNR
BELOIT, William Edwin	AM3rd Class, V-6 USNR
BERBERICH, Elwood Harvey	F2nd Class, SV V-6 USNR
BERGMAN, Marvin Warren	F2nd Class, V-6 USNR
BERKOWITZ, Philip Alfred	Coxswain, U.S. Navy
BERRINGER, Charles Edward Jr.	F1st Class, V-6 USNR
BIGUSIAK, Walter Patrick	RM1st Class(T), U.S. Navy
BLAIR, Raymond Douglas	CPrtr(PA), U.S. Navy
BLANCHARD, Ray Milton, Jr.	AM2nd Class, U.S. Navy
BLOSCH, Lester Roy	AMM1st Class, V-2 USNR
BOWEN, John Wesley	S2nd Class, V-6 USNR
BRESNAHAN, Robert Charles	SM 1st Class(FC), SV V-6 USNR
BROWN, John, Jr.	CEM(AA)(T), U.S. Navy
BROWN, John Earl	ACM2nd Class, U.S. Navy
BROWN, John Franklin	Y2nd Class(T), SV V-6 USNR
BRYANT, Earnest Vernon	S2nd Class, SV V-6 USNR
BRYANT, Everett, Jr.	RdM2nd Class(T), SV V-6 USNR
BUESCHER, Edwin Charles	EM3rd Class(T), SV V-6 USNR
BULSON, Willard Delo	S2nd Class, SV V-6 USNR
BURKE, Harold	S2nd Class, V-6 USNR
BURKET, Jackson P.	RdM3rd Class, V-6 USNR
BUSH, George Dean	S2nd Class, V-6 USNR
BUZA, George Edward	PhM2nd Class, V-6 USNR
CALLICOTT, Webber Watkins	RdM3rd Class, V-6 USNR
CAMPBELL, Peter	F1st Class(EM), V-6 USNR
CAMPORA, Robert Frank	RdM3rd Class(T), V-6 USNR
CANNON, John William	SF1st Class(T), V-6 USNR
CAPELL, Calvin Berum	S2nd Class, V-6 USNR
CAPOBINCO, Patsy	S2nd Class, SV V-6 USNR
CARSTENS, Lawrence Conrad	S2nd Class SV V-6 USNR
CASON, Clyde Muriel	S2nd Class, V-6 USNR
CHACON, Joe	SM 1st Class, V-6 USNR
CHAMPION, Mark	CMM(AA)(T), USN
CLARK, Cecil Vernon	S2nd Class, SV V-6 USNR
CLARK, Walter, Francis	SM 1st Class (AOM), SV V-6 USNR
CLARK, William Roy	S2nd Class V-6 USNR
CLARKE, Richard James	SKD3rd Class(T), SV V-6 USNR
CLIBURN, Cletus	S2nd Class, SV V-6 USNR
COBURN, Thomas Wayne	S2nd Class, SV V-6 USNR
COCHRANE, Robert	S2nd Class, V-6 USNR
COFFEY, John Thomas	AOM3rd Class(T), SV V-6 USNR
COLBERT, Wallie Richard	S2nd Class, SV V-6 USNR
COLLINS, Estil Vincent	SM 1st Class, USN
COMBS, Earl N.	RdM3rd Class(T), V-6 USNR

CONANT, James W.	RdM3rd Class(T), V-6 USNR
CONLON, James Henry	S2nd Class, V-6 USNR
CONNER, Charles Calvin	AMM1st Class, V-6 USNR
COOPRIDER, Wilford Wayne	S2nd Class, SV V-6 USNR
CORRETA, Edward	SM 1st Class, V-6 USNR
COSSON, Thomas Wesley	EM1st Class(T), USN
COURCY, Roland Raoul	S2nd Class, V-6 USNR
COX, John Leslie	SM 1st Class(AOM), V-6 USNR
COX, Wayne Louis	SM 1st Class(ARM), SV V-6 USNR
CRISWELL, Herman Norris	S2nd Class, V-6 USNR
CROOK, Grant Arthur	SM 1st Class, V-6 USNR
CROSSLEY, Graham Young	SM 1st Class(AOM), V-6 USNR
DAMICO, Ernest Eugene	AMM3rd Class, V-2, USNR
DARJANY, John	CEM(T), USN
DAVIDSON, Clarence Lacy	AM3rd Class, V-2, USNR
DAVIDSON, Everett Eugene	MM3rd Class(T), V-6 USNR
DAVIS, Roy Edgar	S2nd Class, V-6 USNR
DELAP, James Richard	PhM3rd Class(T), SV V-6 USNR
DEL SOLE, Carmine	SSMB2nd Class(T), V-6 USNR
DENDINGER, Lawrence Burgle	SSM3rd Class(T), V-6 USNR
DENNIS, William Victor	S2nd Class, SV V-6 USNR
DEVINE, Samuel Thomas	AMM2nd Class(T), V-6 USNR
DOUGHERTY, Joseph Bernard	S2nd Class, SV V-6 USNR
DUBE, George Lawrence	S2nd Class, V-6 USNR
DUNCAN, John Tedford	S2nd Class, V-6 USNR
DUNLAP, William Arthur	SKV2nd Class, SV V-6 USNR
DUPRAS, Edmund Everette	EM3rd Class(T), SV V-6 USNR
DURDEN, Joseph Henry	GM3rd Class(T), V-6 USNR
EDWARDS, John, Jr.	SM 1st Class, USN I
FAISS, Norman Eugene	AMM3rd Class, SV V-6 USNR
FALCONE, Dominic	S2nd Class, V-6 USNR
FEDENA, Otto Leovarn	S2nd Class, SV V-6 USNR
FELMER, John Andrew	S2nd Class, V-6 USNR
FERRELL, Nat	SM 1st Class, V-6 USNR
FIESEL, Peter Richard, Jr.	RM3rd Class(T), SV V-6 USNR
FIKE, William Edward	AOM2nd Class, V-6 USNR
FINEBERG, Paul Mathew	AM2nd Class, USN
FISH, William Warren	BM2nd Class(T), V-6 USNR
FLANNERY, Thomas Peter	SM 1st Class, SV V-6 USNR
FOREBIGGER, James Anthony	SM 1st Class, V-6 USNR
FOURROUX, Nathan Ignatius	GM1st Class, USN
FROEHLY, Robert Ellis	CRT(AA)(T) V-6 USNR
GADDY, Alford Cheatham	AMM2nd Class(T), V-6 USNR
GALLES, Sylvester Lewis	EM1st Class, USN
GARLAND, Bernard James	S2nd Class, V-6 USNR

GARON, Edgar Paul	F1st Class, SV V-6 USNR
GEIGER, Albert Charles	S2nd Class, V-6 USNR
GELLER, Herbert	PhM3rd Class(T), SV V-6 USNR
GIBSON, Edward Joseph	AOM1st Class, USN
GILLENBERG, Erle Jay	EM1st Class(T), V-6 USNR
GILLIS, Clothz	AOM3rd Class, USN
GILMORE, William Forker	ACMM(AA) V-6 USNR
GILSTRAP, Lorenza Dale	S2nd Class, SV V-6 USNR
GINDI, Jacob	S2nd Class, V-6 USNR
GODLESKI, Anthony Carl	WT3rd Class, SV V-6 USNR
GOLDSMITH, Elias Joseph	S2nd Class, SV V-6 USNR
GOOCH, Roger Alvin	S2nd Class, USN
GOTTLICK, Paul Edward	SM 1st Class (AOM), SV V-6 USNR
GRAVES, James Melvin	S2nd Class, SV V-6 USNR
GRAY, Kenneth Basil	AOM2nd Class V-6 USNR
GRAY, Oscar Gilen	S2nd Class, SV V-6 USNR
GRIFFIN, Raymond	SM 1st Class, V-6 USNR
GROBARICK, Robert Joseph	AMM3rd Class, V-6 USNR
GROLL, Abraham L.	SM 1st Class (AOM), V-6 USNR
HACK, Frank John	AOM3rd Class SV V-6 USNR
HALPIN, David Francis	SM 1st Class, SV V-6 USNR
HANNAH, Robert Henry	EM1st Class, V-6 USNR
HANS, Albert William	AMM2nd Class, USN
HARBIN, Edward	SM 1st Class, USN
HARPER, James Albert	S2nd Class, V-6 USNR
HARRISON, William Eldridge	EM1st Class(T), USN
HART, John Joseph	SM 1st Class, SV V-6 USNR
HARTE, Thomas	EM2nd Class, V-6 USNR
HAYES, Doddrid Ellsworth	S2nd Class, SV V-6 USNR
HENDRICHS, Evan Robert	S2nd Class (RdM) SV V-6 USNR
HENDRICKS, Theodore Paul	S2nd Class, SV V-6 USNR
HENSON, Archie Lewis	S2nd Class, USN-I
HIGHFIELD, William George	EM1st Class(T), USN
HINKLE, Rhudy Leslie	AMMI2nd Class, V-6 USNR
HITZEMAN, Harold William	AMMC3rd Class, V-6 USNR
HOFFMAN, Samuel	ACOM(PA) V-6 USNR
HOLDSWORTH, Frederick F.	AM2nd Class, USN
HORTON, LaVarne Albert, Jr.	S2nd Class, SV V-6 USNR
HUDSON, James Edward	SC1st Class, V-6 USNR
HUGHES, Willard David	F2nd Class, SV V-6 USNR
INGELIDO, Anthony George	SKV2nd Class(T), SV V-6 USNR
JACKSON, Thomas	StM1st Class, SV V-6 USNR
JACOBSON, Harold Gordon	S2nd Class, USN
JAMES, Esteen	S2nd Class, SV V-6 USNR
JOHNSON, Audley Eugene	S2nd Class, V-6 USNR

JOHNSTON, George Richard	AOM3rd Class(T) V-6 USNR
JONES, Howard George	TMV3rd Class(T), SV V-6 USNR
JOYNER, Thomas Kimbrough	S2nd Class, V-6 USNR
KARVATSKY, Joseph Thomas	HA1st Class, SV V-6 USNR
KEMPOWICZ, Joseph John	S2nd Class, V-6 USNR
KIEFEL, Ralph Walter	SM 1st Class, USN-I
KIMMICH, Walter Irving	AMM3rd Class, V-6 USNR
KNUTSON, Vernon Henry	GM3rd Class, V-6 USNR
KOPEC, Emil Vincent	ART1st Class(T), V-6 USNR
KOPEC, Frank Joseph	S2nd Class, SV V-6 USNR
KRAUSE, Leonard Robert	F2nd Class V-6 USNR
KRYNSKI, Matthew Joseph	SM 1st Class, V-6 USNR
KUHN, Glen Willard	S2nd Class, V-6 USNR
KUJAWSKI, John Stanley	AM1st Class, USNR
KUST, Valentine Frank	SM 1st Class, USN-I
KUTA, Paul Francis	SM 1st Class, V-6 USNR
LANCASTER, Dwight Julius	S2nd Class, V-6 USNR
LEACH, Vernon Luther	S2nd Class, V-6 USNR
LEAVY, Bernard Joseph	SC2nd Class(T), V-6 USNR
LEDBETTER, Tilbert Reagan	CBM(PA), U.S. Navy
LEE, James W.	CM1st Class, U.S. Navy
LEE, Robert Eugene	SM 1st Class, SV V-6 USNR
LIDDELL, Fred Alexander	SM 1st Class, V-6 USNR
LITTLE, Dock	AMM2nd Class, V-6 USNR
LOWRY, James Lee	SM 1st Class(AOM), V-6 USNR
LUCHIK, John Junior	CSK(PA), U.S. Navy
LUKOSKI, Edward Felix	AMM3rd Class, V-6 USNR
MACKENZIE, Harrison Alexander	AMM3rd Class, V-6 USNR
MAC LANE, John Edward	ACOM(AA)(T), 0-1st Class, USNR
MANGINA, Joseph Anthony	SM 1st Class, SV V-6 USNR
MANN, James Wilson	S2nd Class(RdM), V-6 USNR
MANSUR, Robert Charles	S2nd Class, V-6 USNR
MC ABEE, Felix	BM2nd Class, V-6 USNR
MC GARRY, Charles Sylvester, Jr.	SM 1st Class, SV V-6 USNR
MC GONIGAL, Robert Emmett	S2nd Class, SV V-6 USNR
MC GUIGAN, John Joseph	AOM3rd Class, SV V-6 USNR
MC WILLIAMS, Roger Donald	PhM3rd Class, U.S. Navy
MEEKS, Ellis Eugene	GM2nd Class, V-6 USNR
MERCHANT, Alfred	S2nd Class, SV V-6 USNR
MILLER, Frank Herbert, Jr.	AMM2nd Class, V-6 USNR
MILLER, Samuel Arnold	S2nd Class, SV V-6 USNR
MILNER, Raymond	GM2nd Class, SV V-6 USNR
MINTONI, Alfonso	MM2nd Class, V-6 USNR
MITTLEMAN, Morton Joel	MMS3rd Class, SV V-6 USNR
MIZELL, Marvin Randall	S2nd Class, V-6 USNR

MOHR, Joseph William	AM3rd Class, V-6 USNR
MONTAGU, John Vincent	AOM2nd Class, V-6 USNR
MOORE, James Trouton	S2nd Class, V-6 USNR
MORGAN, Granville	F1st Class, SV V-6 USNR
MORGAN, William Edward	SM 1st Class, U.S. Navy
MOSLANDER, Robert George	SM 1st Class(RM), SV V-6 USNR
MURPHY, James Paul	SM 1st Class, U.S. Navy
NAPIWOCKI, Richard Valerian	AMM1st Class, U.S. Navy
NELSON, Clifford Vincent	S2nd Class, V-6 USNR
NELSON, Donald Ellis	SM 1st Class(RM), SV V-6 USNR
NELSON, Robert Roy	SM 1st Class(RM), SV U.S. Navy
NEUDORF, Norbert Joseph	S2nd Class, SV V-6 USNR
NEWMAN, Harry Edward, Jr.	RM1st Class(T), V-6 USNR
NEWTON, Charles Porter	Cox(T), V-6 USNR
NEWTON, Eugene Paul	CMcMM(T), U.S. Navy
NICHOLAS, Harry Wilson	SM 1st Class, V-6 USNR
NINOS, John Stephen	RdM3rd Class(T), SV V-6 USNR
NUTICK, William Russell	S2nd Class, V-6 USNR
O'CONNELL, John Raphael	S2nd Class, SV, V-6 USNR
OGDEN, Norman Gray	S2nd Class(RdM), V-6 USNR
O'HARA, William John	SF3rd Class(T), V-6 USNR
OLIVER, Orville Kenneth	ACMM(AA), U.S. Navy
ORENDORFF, Chester Olvie	S2nd Class, SV V-6 USNR
ORY, Franklyn Garfield	AMM3rd Class, V-6 USNR
OTT, Herbert John	SM 1st Class, V-6 USNR
OUSLEY, Warren Howard	EM1st Class(T), V-6 USNR
OVERLIN, Donald Eugene	F2nd Class, V-6 USNR
OWEN, Elwin Asa	F1st Class(EM), SV V-6 USNR
OZBOLT, Tony Anthony	ACMM(AA)(T), C-2, USNR
PALMER, Robert Glenn	SM 1st Class, USN
PAUGH, Raymond Harry	CEM(AA)(T), USN
PAULSON, Francis Jack	AMMH2nd Class, V-6 USNR
PECK, Raymond Francis	SM 1st Class, V-6 USNR
PERPEAULT, Arthur Edmond	F2nd Class, SV V-6 USNR
PETERSON, John Martin	S2nd Class, V-6 USNR
PEWITT, William Miller	AMM2nd Class, USN
PIDANIC, Michael	SM 1st Class(AOM) SV V-6 USNR
PIEL, Samuel	CMM(AA)(T) V-6 USNR
PIKE, Clayton Alvin	SM 1st Class, SV V-6 USNR
PLYMPTON, Robert Verne	F2nd Class(MT), V-6 USNR
POMPA, Anthony Joseph	S2nd Class, V-6 USNR
PRICE, Julius Martin Jr.	SM 1st Class(QM), V-6 USNR
PROVENZANO, Rocco	SM 1st Class(AOM), SV V-6 USNR
PUTNAM, Ward Eliel	PhM2nd Class, V-6 USNR
RATZEL, Richard Ernest	AMM3rd Class, SV V-6 USNR

REED, Wilmer Lavern	SM 1st Class, USN
REEVES, John Robert	S2nd Class, V-6 USNR
ROACH, Charles Clint	SM 1st Class, V-6 USNR
ROBERTS, Willmore	SM 1st Class, SV V-6 USNR
ROBERTSON, Alexander Bruce	SK2nd Class, V-6 USNR
ROBINSON, George Howard	AOM2nd Class, V-6 USNR
ROE, George William	S2nd Class, SV V-6 USNR
ROGERS, Elden Duane	S2nd Class, V-6 USNR
ROUTSON, Albert Louis	CTMV(AA)(T), V-6 USNR
SACRAMENTO, Morris Omido	Ck2nd Class(T), V-6 USNR
SALIDA, Kenneth Lavere Jr.	S2nd Class, V-6 USNR
SANDERBECK, James William	FC3rd Class(T), V-6 USNR
SAUNDERS, Joseph Francis	SM 1st Class, V-6 USNR
SCHELLE, Arthur Edward	S2nd Class, SV V-6 USNR
SCHREIFELS, Melvin Herman	S2nd Class, V-6 USNR
SCHWARTZ, Howard Frank	SM 1st Class, V-6 USNR
SCOTT, James Vachel	S2nd Class, V-6 USNR
SEFRIED, Clifford Robert	S2nd Class, SV V-6 USNR
SEIDLER, Richard Louis	AMM3rd Class(T), SV V-6 USNR
SERPE, Joseph Ignatius	S2nd Class(SSMB), SV V-6 USNR
SHAW, John Thomas	AMM3rd Class, SV V-6 USNR
SHEALY, James Marion	EM3rd Class, SV V-6 USNR
SHEBLOSKI, Leon George Jr.	S2nd Class, SV V-6 USNR
SHEPPARD, Grady William	ACM(T), USN
SHORT, James Jacob	SM 1st Class(AOM), V-6 USNR
SHREVE, James Noel	S2nd Class, SV V-6 USNR
SIMARD, Paul Emery	SM 1st Class, V-6 USNR
SLAYTON, Robert Wesley	SM 1st Class, SV V-6 USNR
SMITH, Harold Louis	ARM3rd Class, SV V-6 USNR
SNODGRASS, Francis Allan	AMM1st Class(T), V-6 USNR
SNYDER, John William Jr.	SM 1st Class(AEM), SV V-6 USNR
SONGER, Oscar William	F1st Class(AEM), SV V-6 USNR
SPALLUTO, Peter Joseph	F1st Class, SV V-6 USNR
SPARKS, John Thomas	S2nd Class, V-6 USNR
SPEARS, Ollie O'Neal	CM3rd Class, V-6 USNR
SPECK, Shelby	SK2nd Class, V-6 USNR
SPITZKOPF, Albert Bernard	SM 1st Class, SV V-6 USNR
STALLINGS, Pete	S2nd Class, SV V-6 USNR
STEELE, Alexander LeRoy	SM 1st Class, V-6 USNR
STEELE, James Moss	SM 1st Class, V-6 USNR
STILLMAN, Roland George	S2nd Class, SV V-6 USNR
STREHLOW, Walter George	F1st Class(EM), SV V-6 USNR
SUTHERBY, William Andrew	SF1st Class(T), V-6 USNR
SWANSON, Donald William	S2nd Class, V-6 USNR
SWISKI, Leo Stanley	SM 1st Class, V-6 USNR

THOMAS, William Albert	F1st Class, SV V-6 USNR
THOORSELL, James Vernon	S2nd Class, USN
THORGERSEN, Herbert Stanley	AMM2nd Class, V-6 USNR
THORNTON, Marshall	S2nd Class, SV V-6 USNR
TRAGER, Carl Bernard	S2nd Class(GM), V-6 USNR
TERMONTE, Johnny	PR1st Class, USN
TRIANO, Frank John	S2nd Class, SV V-6 USNR
TROTTER, Ralph George	SM 1st Class, V-6 USNR
TUCKER, Herman	SSML3rd Class(T), SV V-6 USNR
TYLER, Clarence Elmon	F1st Class, SV V-6 USNR
UTTERBACK, Robert Clayton	SM 1st Class, V-6 USNR
VAMOS, Francis Joseph	RT1st Class(T), V-6 USNR
VASEY, Ruseell Edward	TMV3rd Class, V-6 USNR
VAUGHN, Lobert Washington	SM 1st Class, V-6 USNR
VOSS, Alvin Leo	SM 1st Class(GM), SV V-6 USNR
WAGGONER, Frank Junior	F2nd Class, SV V-6 USNR
WAH, Gong Wing	S2nd Class, V-6 USNR
WALL, Harry Reaves	SM 1st Class, USN
WALTERS, Henry Semdley	F2nd Class, USN
WEAD, Joseph Stephen	S2nd Class, USN
WEBB, Earl Edward	S2nd Class, SV V-6 USNR
WEBB, Murrol H.	Prtr1st Class, USN
WELCOME, George Maurice	MM3rd Class(T), USN
WELLS, James Eugene	SM 1st Class, SV V-6 USNR
WEST, Samuel Elmer	AMM3rd Class, V-6 USNR
WILLIAMS, Clyde Hugh	SF2nd Class, V-6 USNR
WILLIAMS, John Edward	SM 1st Class, V-6 USNR
WILLIAMS, Leslie Albert	AMM1st Class, V-6 USNR
WILLIAMS, Libert Chandler	GH3rd Class, V-6 USNR
WILLIAMS, William Evan	RdM3rd Class(T), SV V-6 USNR
WISE, Victor Wayne	SM 1st Class, SV V-6 USNR
WISE, Walter John	CM2nd Class, USN
WITKOWSKI, William	SM 1st Class, V-6 USNR
WRIGHT, Carroll George	SKV3rd Class(T), SV V-6 USNR
ZASSMAN, Harry	SM 1st Class, V-6 USNR
ZEUDIK, John	SM 1st Class, SV V-6 USNR
ZELINSKI, Andrew John	SM 1st Class, V-6 USNR

REFERENCES

1. *Big Ben The Flat Top, The Story of the USS Franklin,* USS Franklin Museum Association, (1990), Albert Love Publishers, Atlanta, GA.
2. *Carrier Warfare in the Pacific,* Edited by E.T. Wooldridge, (1993) Smithsonian Institute Press, Washington and London.
3. *Hellcat Aces of World War 2,* Barret Tillman, (1996), Osprey Publishing Limited, London, England.
4. *Helldiver Units of World War 2*, Barret Tillman, (1997) Osprey Publishing Limited, London, England.
5. *Incredible Victory,* Walter Lord, (1967) Harper Collins Publishers, c/o Burford Books, Inc., Short Hills, NJ.
6. *I Was A Chaplain On The Franklin*, Father Joseph T. O'Callahan, (1956/1985) Bantam Books, New York City, NY.
7. *The Franklin Comes Home*, A. A. Hoeling, (1974), Bluejacket Books, Naval Institute Press, Annapolis, MD.
8. *USS Franklin Deck and Action Logs*, US Navy Historical Society, National Archives, Washington, D.C.
9. *The Two-Ocean War*, Samuel Eliot Morrison, (1963), Little, Brown and Company, Boston, MA, Toronto, Canada.

TO HAVE YOUR LIFE HANGING BY A THREAD...

You will feel like you're immersed in a totally foreign world where values of valor, honesty and courage really mean something. **Saving Big Ben** *took me back to my time on flaming decks on the USS Franklin, CV 13. A real page-turner that anyone with a taste for heroism, valor and adventure will not be able to put down.*

Robert E. St. Peters, EM2C,
President of the *USS Franklin* Museum Association

Fiction can be truer than life. If you want to know what it felt like to have your life hanging by a thread, trying to fight a war in the Sea of Japan, while a huge aircraft carrier is sinking under your feet and rockets are zooming over your head, read Saving Big Ben. I was there and I still find it hard to believe!

Ray C. Bailey,
Gunner/Retired Naval Photographer

I watched the daring efforts to save the Franklin while manning a fire hose on the fantail of the USS Santa Fe. Saving Big Ben enables the modern reader to experience those frightening yet courage-filled times. An outstanding book. Congratulation to Peter Prato for returning those valorous memories.

Tom Paulovich, S1C,
Crew member of the *USS Santa Fe*

Medal of Honor · Navy Cross · Silver Star · Distinguished Flying Cross · Bronze Star · Navy and Marine Corp. Medal · Purple Heart

S*aving Big Ben* is the story of the aircraft carrier *USS Franklin* (CV 13), "the ship that would not be sunk." Her crew was awarded the greatest number of decorations ever conferred on a single ship in all naval history. Taken from the Deck and Action Logs (declassified by the Navy Department in the early 1960s), Prato chronicles not only wrenching *"Big Ben"* from the jaws of death but also the raw-boned determination, heroism, loyalty and love that drive men to actions far beyond their human capacities. Sail into combat with the *Franklin* and relive the Navy's great victories in Leyte Gulf, the Philippine Sea and the Sea of Japan. Witness historic figures such as General Douglas MacArthur, Admiral Chester Nimitz, Admiral Raymond Spruance, Admiral William "Bull" Halsey, Admiral Marc Mitscher and Admiral John "Slew" McCain (to name just a few) make momentous decisions in desperately uncertain battles in the war in the Pacific during a time that Winston Churchill called "our finest hour."

★ **An exceptional chronicle of our greatest generation**
★ **A powerful history of intrepid deeds and heroic actions**
★ **A touching story of young love, courage, devotion and fidelity**
★ **A splendid book for veterans and adults of all ages**

Saving Big Ben - *A wonderful gift for any season.*
Reserve your copy today!

Stress Resource Publishing Co., LLC
699 Peters Avenue, Suite A
Pleasanton, CA 94566

Toll Free Phone: 1-866-484-2330
Fax: 925-484-3112
Website: www.stressresource.com
E-Mail: prato@worldnet.att.net

You may order by mail, phone, on-line, fax, or e-mail.

Please send me ____ hardbound copies @$34.95 ea. _____
Please send me ____ paper-back copies @$24.95 ea. _____
Shipping and handling $4.00 per book _____
Less 10% Veteran discount _____
Total Order _____

❏ Check enclosed   ❏ Visa   ❏ Master Card   ❏ Discover Card
_____ Expiration date __/__
Name _____
Address _____
Phone _____ Fax _____
City State Zip _____
Signature _____

Dr. Peter J. Prato served as a Gunner's Mate 3rd Class aboard the *USS Altamaha, CVE 18.*